Along Paths Paved With Danger and Desire . . .

"I have never felt so enthusiastic about anything in my life," he whispered, and kissed Nancy Lucia's neck. "I think we should be ready to sail by the end of the season," mumbled Richard, kissing her breasts.

"That is only three months," said Nancy Lucia, stroking his hair. "Do you really think we can be ready, in so brief a time, to leave London?"

Richard had her left nipple in his mouth, and was moving his tongue around it. He made a sound, which Nancy Lucia took to mean yes . . . Richard really had no idea how difficult a task it would be to organize the American company. He had even less idea of what its ultimately strange composition was destined to be.

At this particular moment, on this particular night, as he entered his loving wife, neither he nor she thought about America at all.

THEY CARRIED THEIR DREAMS TO MEET THE CHALLENGE OF THE NEW WORLD . . . PLAYERS IN A DARING GAME OF CHANCE—CALLED AMERICA!

Joseph Csida

The Magic Ground

The Saga of the Steeles
Volume 1

PUBLISHED BY POCKET BOOKS NEW YORK

Distributed in Canada by PaperJacks Ltd., a Licensee
of the trademarks of Simon & Schuster, a division of
Gulf + Western Corporation.

This novel is a work of fiction. Names, characters, places and incidents are either the product of the author's imagination or are used fictitiously, and any resemblance to actual persons, living or dead, events or locales is entirely coincidental.

Another *Original* publication of POCKET BOOKS

POCKET BOOKS, a Simon & Schuster division of
GULF & WESTERN CORPORATION
1230 Avenue of the Americas, New York, N.Y. 10020
In Canada distributed by PaperJacks Ltd.,
330 Steelcase Road, Markham, Ontario.

ISBN: 0-671-83135-6

First Pocket Books printing April, 1981

10 9 8 7 6 5 4 3 2 1

POCKET and colophon are trademarks of Simon & Schuster.

Printed in Canada

THE MAGIC GROUND

Much has been said at this unlucky time,
To prove the treading of the stage a crime.
Mistaken zeal, in terms not so civil,
Consigns both play and players to the devil.
Yet wise men own, a play well chose may teach
Such useful moral truths as the parsons preach;
May teach the heart another's grief to know,
And melt a soul in tears of generous woe. . .
A Barnwell's fate can never fail to move,
And strike with shame and terror lawless love.
See, plunged in ruin with a virtuous wife,
The Gamester weeps, despairs and ends his life.
When Cato bleeds he spends his latest breath,
To teach the love of country strong in death.
With such examples and a thousand more,
Of godlike men who lived in times before,
The tragic Muse renewing every age,
Makes the dead heroes tread the living stage.
. . . when to social gayety inclined
Our comic Muse shall feast the cheerful mind,
Fools of all sorts and fops a brainless crew,
To raise your mirth we'll summon to your view;
Make each pert coxcomb merry with his brother,
Whilst knaves conceal'd shall grin at one another.
'Tis magic ground we tread, and at our call
Those knights appear that represent you all.

> From an epilogue written by Adam Thomson, a Scotchman of Philadelphia, and delivered by one of the finest actresses of her day, Mrs. David Douglas in Philadelphia in 1754. Mrs. Douglas and her husband, Lewis Hallam, brought the Hallam Company of Comedians, the first troupe of professional English actors, to colonial America in 1752.

BOOK ONE

* * *

**Richard, Felicia,
Farley, Mary
and the Father**

* * *

LONDON

Here malice, rapine, accident conspire,
And now a rabble rages, now a fire;
Their ambush here relentless ruffians lay,
And here the fell attorney prowls for prey;
Here falling houses thunder on your head,
And here a female atheist talks you dead.

SAMUEL JOHNSON

❧ 1 ❧

The moment drew nearer and nearer. Young Richard
Steele paced nervously back and forth, walking to the
deepest recesses of the stage behind the flats and then
back into the wings. His muslin shirt was glued to his
lean, broad-shouldered torso with sweat. The shirt itched.
He felt the need to urinate. The black cloth breeches
were too tight. He scratched his groin, wiped his wet
palms on the seat of his pants. His knees threatened to
buckle as he walked.

Sleek, raven-haired head down, he almost strode into
Polonius, or Gilbert Weston, playing the lord and high
official, Ophelia's father. Quickly he moved aside, making
a half-bow to the older actor.

"Pardon," he tried to whisper, and was shocked when
no sound emerged from his dry throat. Weston reached up
to pat the shoulder of the frightened fourteen-year-old. It
was impossible for Richard to concentrate. From the
stage he heard the sonorous voice of Claudius, the new
King of Denmark, inquire: "How long hath she been
thus?"

And Ophelia, his friend Felicia Wandrous, responded.
"I hope all will be well. We must be patient, but I cannot choose but weep to think they would lay him in the
cold ground. My brother shall know of it: and so I thank
you for your good counsel. Come, my coach! Good night,
ladies; good night, sweet ladies; good night, good night."
Felicia was confident, polished, and had amazing skill for
an actress just twenty-three.

Richard Steele's eyes had always seemed to alter their
color, not only with the change of light or the color of the

3

clothing he wore, but also with his mood and emotions. Now in the semi-gloom of backstage, as he paced restlessly, they seemed deep blue, then pale green, now again an indigo tinted gray. But most often they were a fascinating mix of two or all three shades, like a turbulent sea. The eyes, the cleft in his strong jaw and a scar from his right cheekbone to jaw line were exceptional features in his handsome oval countenance.

The agony of uncertainty sparkled now in the troubled eyes. He licked his dry lips, wiped them with the back of his hand, licked the full lips again. The time for his entrance drew nearer and nearer. Now he heard the King's next speech.

"Follow her close. Give her good watch, I pray you. O, this is the poison of deep grief. . . ."

That *long* speech.

Richard moved to the downstage of the two doors at stage right, whence he would make his entrance. Over the King's deep rich tones, he could hear the sounds of reaction from the upper gallery. To his panicked heart, it was the muttering of a distant, hostile, oncoming army. Richard clasped his sweating hands tightly, licked his dry lips once more.

"O, my dear Gertrude," intoned the King, "this like to a murdering piece, in many places, gives me superfluous death. . . ."

"Now!" screamed a voice in Richard's head. "Now! Now! Now. . . !"

And finally he remembered. He stamped his feet in place, left, right, left, right.

The Queen's voice came from onstage.

"Alack! What noise is this?"

The King commanded, "Attend!"

Richard, the messenger, stood behind the downstage door, paralyzed from head to foot.

The slender, androgynous figure of Felicia Wandrous, who had exited after her last speech, appeared beside him, patted his shoulder firmly, leaned forward, kissed his cheek, slapped him on the buttock, and pushed him forward.

"Attend! Attend!"

Over the King's shoulder, seated at the outer edge of the stage's apron, the area in front of the proscenium, he saw a periwigged, satin-coated fop opening his snuff box. This particular fop was a close friend of Jerome Wrexham,

4

the actor who was playing Laertes. To his horror, Richard found himself trying to remember the fop's name, instead of his lines. One of the scattering of a half-dozen other richly dressed, bewigged aristocrats seated on the stage threw a kiss to a lady of quality in a nearby box.

Richard raised his eyes, trying to drive his frozen mind back to the simple lines he must deliver. But now, insanely, he became fascinated with the huge circular metal fitting, hanging from the ceiling, a chandelier holding more than two dozen candles, which lit both the stage and the small auditorium. A small draft of air was coming from somewhere, causing the candles to flicker with a mystic irritation. A slight, sulphurous odor seemed to blend into the smell of tobacco smoke and unwashed bodies. Desperately he stared into the face of the King again, and beyond him, in the erratic multi-candle glow, he saw the restless, muttering patrons in the pit, and beyond them, higher and hazy in the distance, the noisy mob in the gallery.

It was a canvas painted by a madman. With sound. Ugly, unsympathetic, unfriendly sound.

Ridiculous! Beyond belief!

Four years ago at age ten, Richard Steele had snuffed his first candle on this very stage of London's prestigious Lincoln's Inn Fields Theatre. For those forty-eight months he had been the theater's most alert snuffer. At age seven, (as part of their program to educate him beyond the scant schooling of the day) his mother and their best friend, the parish priest, Father Arnold Whittaker, had begun to read Shakespeare to him the way other parents and guardians read their children bedtime tales. He himself had since read almost every tragedy, history, comedy the Bard had written, some of them two and three times. He knew a dozen major roles by heart. He had watched London's leading players perform them over and over. He studied acting.

There might have been some excuse for his incredible lapse of memory if Gilbert Weston, actor-manager of the Lincoln Inn Fields, were given to presenting Shakespeare in rewritten, often outrageously butchered form, a practice favored by most theatrical managers of the day. But this was *Hamlet* as the Bard of Avon had created it, stirring word for word, as Richard Steele had read and loved and learned it.

Yet now, standing on the stage of the theater that was a

5

second home to him, he could not remember a single word of the miserable, insignificant eleven-line speech. Not a word. Not the first syllable.

Thus, it became the King's night for repeating Shakespeare's lines.

"What is the matter?" he said, and again, "What is the matter?"

Grabbing the petrified messenger's upper arms, he pushed him backward toward the prompter's corner. Barely in time. Barely. For the upper gallery, which always reacted out of sheer unrestrained instinct, whether in approval or anger, now began to shout and scream and laugh.

"Speak up, messenger! . . . The Switzers, the Switzers . . . Where are the Switzers?"

There were roars of laughter, uninhibited, raucous laughter.

The footmen and the sailors were having a merry time.

The more restrained writers, lawyers, doctors in the pit merely muttered critically, a grumbling, unpleasant undertone.

As the King shook him, directly beneath the prompter's corner at stage left, Richard felt as much as saw the aloof and arrogant contempt of the ladies and lords, the fops and courtesans in the boxes.

Cutting through the audience sounds, the prompter's hiss struck Richard's ears.

"Save yourself, save yourself. . . ."

Fool, fool, panicked Richard for another moment. *Heartless fool, I need help. The line, the line* . . . And then he realized those were his first two words.

"Save yourself, my lord!" he gasped to the King. The King released him, and beneath the false beard, Richard could see the approving smile break on the King's face.

Full blown, as though it were carved in large letters on a slate before his eyes, he recalled the balance of his speech. But his vocal chords and his dry tongue in the drier cavern of his mouth, his cursed nerves would not cooperate.

He stammered and stuttered and squeaked and squawked his way through the eleven-line speech. It was, if nothing else, a unique performance of the messenger's role. The raucous laughter, the ribald, sometimes obscene remarks from the gallery intensified and increased with each fumbling line the tormented young Richard recited.

Halfway through the speech, a dozen or more denizens of the upper gallery began to hurl half-eaten apples, walnuts and assorted other items toward the stage. Some of the fops on the stage, led by Jerome Wrexham's friend, stood and shook their silver- or gold-headed walking sticks at the unruly galleryites. Richard suddenly remembered that the fop's name was Reginald, son of an Earl.

"Quiet, damned caitiffs!" screamed one.

His curses and the denunciations of the others were lost in the increasing wave of strident sound from the upper gallery. The pit attendees began to yell and curse, partially at the inept performance and partially in objection to the rain of debris falling on them.

The candles in the chandelier began to sputter more furiously, seemingly intent on joining the rebellion. Several collapsed and dripped hot tallow on the restless people directly below in the pit. In the flickering half-light of the theater, amid the cacophonous lunacy of sound, the counterpoint of an occasional piece of fruit or a nut hitting the stage, young Richard Steele stammered his way through his last two lines.

"Cuh—cuh—cuh—caps, hands and tongues uh—uh—applaud it to the clouds, lay—lay—lay—Laertes shall be king, Laertes king!"

Tears welled in his eyes and ran down his cheeks. He raced offstage through the downstage door at stage left. It was the wrong door, and he crashed into Laertes, about to enter. Laertes, mightily upset at having to attempt to subdue the aroused mob, spat out, "Miserable miscreant!" and strode by the weeping boy onto the stage. But Felicia Wandrous's thin, strong arms awaited him. She dragged him to a bench downstage from the entrance door, well within hearing range of the players on the stage. She sat him firmly on the bench, squatted before him, careful to pull her gossamer gown well up over her knees, off the dirty floor.

"It happens to all fine actors, Richard. It does."

She lifted his chin, wiped away the moisture on his cheeks.

"I peed in my scarlet elf pants right on the stage in my first appearance," she said earnestly.

The remark startled Richard.

"Yuh—yuh—you did?"

Felicia nodded, one ear cocked to the voices on stage.

7

She was due to make her next entrance in less than ten minutes.

"How old were you?" asked Richard, struggling to end his sniffling, wiping a hand across his cheeks.

"Six. I was Peaseblossom, you know, one of the fairies in *A Midsummer Night's Dream*. It was the third act, scene one, when Titania the Fairy Queen summons Peaseblossom, Cobweb, Moth and Mustardseed and urges them to be kind to Bottom, the weaver. Titania says, 'Nod to him, elves, and do him courtesies.' I said, 'Hail, mortal,' and wet myself, right on stage. Not just a mere dripping, mind you, but a small puddle. It evoked much laughter, I can tell you, especially from the upper gallery."

Richard smiled.

King Claudius's voice came from onstage.

Felicia rose, bent over and kissed Richard gently on the mouth.

"Do you know your next lines?"

Richard nodded, squeezed her hand.

"Thank you."

From the stage Laertes's rich voice boomed: "How now! What noise is that?"

Felicia straightened her shoulders. By some alchemy her silver-gray eyes showed a brilliant madness. She opened the door and walked onstage, ready to play the mentally troubled Ophelia, daughter of the murdered Polonius. Her brother, Laertes, began his brief tormented speech: "O heat, dry up my brains! Tears seven times salt, burn out the sense and virtue of mine eye. . . ." He ended with Shakespeare's statement that Ophelia had lost her mind over the death of her beloved father, Polonius.

"Nature is fine in love and where 'tis fine it sends some precious instance of itself after the thing it loves."

And then Richard heard Felicia's high sweet voice, haunted, sing:

"They bore him barefac'd on the bier;
Hey, non nonny, nonny, hey, nonny;
And in his grave rain'd many a tear. . . ."

And again, just before she made her exit near the end of the scene, he listened. The sweet singing voice was so full of tragedy and loss, it almost made Richard weep anew:

8

"And will 'a not come again?
And will 'a not come again?
No, no, he is dead;
Go to thy deathbed,
He will never come again.
His beard was white as snow
All flaxen was his poll,
He is gone, he is gone,
And we castaway moan:
God ha' mercy on his soul!"

She came around behind the flat and walked directly to the bench where Richard sat. Smiling, she sat down beside him.

"It's a mark of a good actor's sensitivity," she said.

Richard looked puzzled.

"The nervousness. It's part of a good player's sensitive nature. . . . What's your first line?"

Richard had to think for a moment.

"Letters . . . letters, my lord, from Hamlet."

"And . . . ?"

"These to your majesty; this to the Queen."

Felicia smiled, nodded, in a mock bass voice spoke the King's line: "Who brought them?"

Confidently, Richard replied: "Sailors, my lord, they say; I saw them not. They were given me by Claudio; he received them of him that brought them."

Felicia patted his knee.

"Now your cap and cloak."

Richard nodded, went to the wardrobe room to fetch the black cloth cloak and cap, intended to give the audience the impression this was not the same messenger who had appeared earlier.

And indeed, when Richard made his entrance in the next scene, he *was* quite a different bearer of news. There was still a tightness in his stomach, a dryness in his throat, and his sweating hands dampened the letters he handed the King and Queen. But he read his brief lines clearly and with authority. The audience, once again completely enthralled by the play, hardly noticed his appearance. There were no laughter, no obscene remarks, no shower of missiles from the upper gallery. Of course, there was no applause either, but to Richard the rapt silence was satisfying. He felt, finally, that one day he might yet become an actor.

9

Neither he nor Felicia were in the song and dance interval, nor the pantomime afterpiece which followed the Shakespearean "history," so after taking her bows at the final curtain, Felicia came up to the applauding Richard, backstage, took him by the hand, and said, "Come, we must celebrate your debut."

Right behind her was Laertes, the excellent actor Jerome Wrexham. Wrexham was a classically handsome man in his mid-twenties, with glossy, flowing blond hair, deep brown eyes, an aristocratic profile and a manner to match. He played lovers and other leading men. Backstage gossip had it that he and Felicia Wandrous were lovers. Wrexham heard Felicia's invitation to young Richard. He took the actress by the arm, and angrily turned her to face him.

"I believe we had an engagement for this evening, Felicia," he said sternly.

Felicia lifted his fingers from her arm delicately, as though they were unclean. She looked at him coolly.

"Another time, love. I'm spending the night with Richard."

Richard could only gasp.

He was so surprised, he was scarcely aware of the flame of anger and hatred that flared in Wrexham's mahogany eyes.

2

Richard and Felicia walked out into the middle of the road in front of the theater. This maneuver helped them avoid the crush of nearly a hundred shopkeepers, clerks and other middle-class men and women who shoved, pummeled and cursed each other, fighting their way in to see the song and dance interval and afterpiece of mime at the reduced admission charge for those who did not care to see the opening drama. Jerome Wrexham was to sing four new ballads in this night's concert, and he was as great a favorite with the tradesmen and their employees as with the aristocracy and the professional groups.

A full moon penetrated the perpetual coal dust mist of the city. A brisk southwest wind blew the damp stench of the Thames across the town to blend with the unpleasant bouquet of the garbage and refuse-littered alleys, lanes and courtyards. Like all Londoners of the day, Richard and Felicia were oblivious to these common conditions.

A coach pulled by two dappled horses, whipped by a postilion who seemed drunk, almost ran them down before they could leap out of the road to safety. Someone had emptied a chamber pot out of a window, and Richard's right foot landed in its contents. Angrily, he scraped the sole of the boot back and forth in the dirt. Where the narrow street turned into an alley, a large-busted woman, with a bright orange wig and painted face, whom Richard knew as Mother Magruder, bawd of a house featuring black and mulatto prostitutes, shouted a greeting to Felicia as they passed beneath her window. Felicia adjusted the long, leather-strapped bag slung over her shoulder, and waved back at the madam.

11

In the past year or two, Richard had often thought of visiting one of the less expensive brothels or lodging houses harboring prostitutes, which dotted almost every section of the city. He had been able to fight off the urge each time, when he remembered how important it was that he save his scant funds to accumulate enough to buy a small cottage in the country. At times when his discipline flagged he recalled the older actor in the Lincoln's Inn Fields company, who contracted the pox from a prostitute and ultimately went insane.

He was thinking now of Felicia's casual remark about spending the night with him, and was about to speak, when two drunken, elegantly dressed and bewigged beaux rudely crashed into them. One of them turned, and almost fell on his face as he bowed deeply to Felicia.

"Your humble shervant, milady. Do me the honor of accep—" At this point his curled silver wig fell from his head into a small pile of fly-covered vegetables. His companion recovered the wig, slapped it on his head, askew, and the two continued on their way to Mother Magruder's.

Before a butcher shop, further along, as Richard was about to speak again, Felicia put a hand on his arm.

"One moment, love," she said, and reached into her purse, removed some coins and placed them in the hand of a young boy of about seven, sleeping in the doorway of the shop.

They passed through a court on their way to the Thames embankment, when Richard began again: "Felicia, about . . . about tonight . . ."

Before he could continue, a band of ragged, drunken youths came rollicking down the road toward them, singing bawdy songs in loud, off-key voices. They passed a bottle of gin from one to another, drinking as they strode through the littered streets.

"I forgot my cudgel," Richard told Felicia, as the rowdy group came closer. It was a time in London when all gentlemen wore swords, and citizens of the poorer classes carried cutlasses, knives or cudgels to protect themselves on the streets at night.

The drunken singers made some ribald remarks as they came abreast of Richard and Felicia, but continued on their way. Now as the young actors headed into a street that curved to the Thames embankment, a deluge of food remnants pelted them before they could move close to the sides of the buildings. Meat bones, fish heads and skeletons, rotted vegetables, cracked egg shells fell to the ground. Many of the good citizens of this lane were obviously just finishing their suppers, and disposing of the remains by throwing them out the window.

Pressed to the walls of the buildings, Richard and Felicia made their way out of the court. They rounded the corner of a street leading toward the riverfront before Richard finally said, "It's Mary's birthday, Felicia."

"How nice. I'll come by for a visit tomorrow. What is she now, thirty?"

Richard nodded. "I mean, she'll be expecting me."

"Of course. How is her health?"

Richard shook his head and shrugged. "I don't know. She doesn't seem to improve."

A heavyset drunkard came around a corner and almost staggered into them. Richard caught him and steadied him. The drunk mumbled an obscenity and staggered on his way.

They walked along the Embankment now. The river smell was stronger. The moon made a path of dancing diamonds on the restless water.

Merchantmen, barges, boats and wherries rocked languidly in the moon's sparkling path. Scores of other ships along the docks flanked those in the direct glow of the moon. Their masts made a trembling, leafless forest on the rank river. Feeble lights on a number of the ships and the shouting, screaming and boisterous laughter indicated the watermen were not retiring to their bunks early this night.

Despite the breeze, Richard felt perspiration breaking out on his forehead.

"Felicia, I—I—mean, about the night, about spending the night . . ."

The moonlight sparkled in the young actress's silver-gray eyes. Once again she adjusted the leather-strapped bag she carried over her shoulder, and laughed merrily.

"Oh, Richard, how adorably innocent. I wasn't planning to seduce you"—she looked up into his worried face —"although I must admit the thought has crossed my mind more than once of late."

She curved her arm around his, squeezed it to her side.

"I just said that to irritate Wrexham, and give him a short lesson. He's become impossibly possessive of late."

They passed a narrow boothlike structure, housing one of the Charlies, the older men the municipality paid to

13

stand watch as guards, ineffectual as they were. The Charlie piped a greeting as they went by.

"Last Sunday," continued Felicia, "I spent the afternoon with some friends at Primrose Hill, and he carried on disgracefully. And last night, he came to my lodgings and found me in bed with Elizabeth, and almost went insane."

"It must be that he loves you."

"Nonsense, he doesn't love me any more than I love him. It's simply that we're particularly pleasing to each other in bed. He knows very well how opposed I am to unalterable and permanent attachments. In the beginning, he told me he felt precisely the same."

"Did you ever truly love anyone?"

"Oh, yes. Long ago, when I was about your age. But I learned that it's much more satisfactory, and much less dangerous to love everyone and not any single one."

They turned off the Embankment toward Fleet Street. Felicia's apartment was in a very narrow passageway called Middle Temple Lane, which ran between Fleet Street and the Embankment. Abruptly she changed the subject.

"Primrose Hill is so lovely at this time of the year," she said wistfully.

"I know. Father Whittaker took Mary and me out for a day at Hampstead Heath last month, and we stopped at a tavern in Primrose Hill. One day I would like to move Mary out to the country. I think the damp air of Billingsgate perpetuates her disorder. Indeed, the doctor has said as much."

"Your mother is a dear, brave woman, and God willing, she'll soon be well."

Richard was reaching into the pocket of his coat when Felicia said, "And speaking of God, how is his most inept servant and member of the not-so-loyal opposition?"

For an instant, Richard was puzzled. Then he chuckled.

"Oh, Father Whittaker, you mean. He doesn't change. He surely has more love in him for his fellows than any man I have ever seen. And it is not so much that he is inept, as that he pursues his priestly duties in strange ways. Yet for a beleaguered Catholic priest, whose minority parish embraces Billingsgate and the waterfront, he is ideal."

"I call him 'inept' lovingly," Felicia said. "His love of the theater endears him to me, exactly as his love of the

14

sea endears him to the sailors whose souls he works so hard to save."

"He surely is the finest friend Mary and I have ever had."

As they approached an oil-lamp post at a corner near Middle Temple Lane, Richard took a small box from his pocket. He stopped under the lamp and opened the lid of the box.

"I bought Mary this cameo brooch for her birthday. Do you like it?"

"It's lovely, Richard. And amazing. The profile of the head might well be Mary's very own."

Richard closed the box, put it back in his pocket. Out of a side street, off the corner on which they had stopped, there suddenly came the clumping and thumping of running feet.

"Halt there, young lovers!" boomed a thick, deep voice.

Together Richard and Felicia turned.

The rushing figures were clear in the light of the moon. Leading a twosome, huffing and puffing mightily, was an incredibly round young man. Slitted eyes glared out of his piglike, scraggly-haired head, which sat upon a huge ball of a body. Even his large thighs seemed rounded. He was no more than sixteen and had a dirty stubble of black beard. In his left hand he held a gin bottle, and in his right a short, ugly knife. The knife reflected the moonlight, as he raised it awkwardly over his head. His companion was almost two heads taller, but probably weighed less than half of what his obese mate weighed. His clothes were filthy and tattered, and in his left hand he swung a heavy stick.

"Run, Felicia," yelled Richard, grabbing her hand, and starting away from the threatening pair.

But after two short strides, Richard and Felicia drew up sharply. Like spirits come to life, two new figures materialized at the street corner ahead of them. Their retreat was effectively cut off. With the cunning London's young thieves and cutthroats often exhibited, this assault had been primitively but carefully planned.

Each of the two men Richard and Felicia now faced were of average height, but as dirty and vicious-looking as their fat and thin companions. One was redheaded with a low forehead, the other dirty blond. Both had knives in their grimy fists.

"We saw that l'il bauble you showed the lady, mate.

15

Hand it over," demanded the redhead, as he and his partner advanced toward Richard and Felicia. He slurred his words, and as he advanced, Richard could smell the gin on his breath, and in the sweaty pores of his body.

The second man was even drunker.

"You take the bauble, old cock," he mumbled, stumbling toward Felicia, "and I'll take the wench."

With the realization that they could not escape, fear had frozen Richard where he stood. His pounding heart felt as though it would burst the tightness of his chest. Then Felicia screamed. It was a loud, piercing, jubilant sound, and it sounded to Richard like a battle cry, not a wail of terror.

Out of the corner of his eye, Richard saw her take the bag from her shoulder, begin to swing it overhead by its long leather straps, as she turned and raced toward the fat man and his thin partner. The drunken blond attacker was three feet away, staggering after Felicia. Suddenly a raging fury drove the fear from Richard's heart. It was the same blind fury he had experienced two years earlier during his first fight on the docks at Billingsgate.

Two sailors had tried to rob him of the shilling he had been paid for three backbreaking days of unloading cargo. They had finally beaten and kicked him unconscious and taken his shilling (this, indeed, was how he had acquired his scarred cheek), but he had inflicted a fair amount of damage on them before passing out. He had punched and chopped and bitten and kicked and gouged, and it was almost enough, but not quite. He was too young then, and they were too strong. But since then he had learned quickly, as a matter of survival, that you fought to win, to kill if necessary.

Like a soccer player charging a loose ball and a yawning goal mouth, he raced toward the oncoming blond man. And like a soccer player, kicked. Hard and high. The toe of his boot caught the blond man squarely in the groin. As he doubled over, groaning in agony, Richard quickly backed a step, then pounced forward viciously on top of him. His right knee and lower thigh crushed the blond man's mouth and nose, as the two men went down with Richard, holding tight, on top of the blond man.

Richard knew by instinct that the redhead was charging at them with a knife raised. He tried desperately to roll over onto his back, still embracing the blond in a tight grip. If he could get the cursing, bleeding blond on top,

16

efore the knife descended . . . but no! The man's weight as too great. Richard tugged, tugged again, and they had ıst started to roll when he felt the sharp bite of the knife ı the upper part of his right buttock.

The sudden pain seemed to give him added strength. s he twisted again, fiercely, with both arms around the lond man, he succeeded in turning himself on his back, ıith the blond on top, just as the redhead struck again! lis knife stabbed directly into the center of the blond ıan's back. The man uttered a strangled, agonized gasp. ichard saw a second knife fall out of the blond man's ight hand, as the man began to collapse onto him. The ıddenly surging flow of blood from his crushed mouth ıd nose splashed on Richard, who now released his hug-ıng grip on the blond man. The redhead cursed violently: stream of breathless obscenities. With his left hand, he rabbed his dying partner's tattered coat at the collar, ying to drag him away from Richard. In the same in-ıant, Richard gripped the blond man's bloody shirt front ı both hands. The blood made the shirt slippery in Rich-ıd's grasp, but he tightened his hold, shoved the man iciously off himself, and into the legs of the redhead. He ılled out from under and reached desperately for the lond man's knife. But the redhead kicked his lower arm, ıst as he was about to grasp the knife.

Despite the numbed feeling in the left arm, Richard ıanaged to roll over on his back just as the redhead ıised his knife and dropped heavily on top of Richard ith both knees. As the knife arm descended toward his ıest, Richard reached up with both hands and caught it ıst above the wrist, caught it just as the redhead's crash-ıg knees exploded all the breath from Richard's body. or a hundredth of a second, Richard thought he was go-ıg to lose consciousness. Then sheer instinct for survival ıabled him to tighten his grip on the man's arm. Open-ıouthed, he gasped for breath. The moon fell from the ıy and melted into a formless silver blob, which swam ızily back and forth before his closed eyes.

Yet he was able to hold onto the murderous arm. He ıld and held, as the redhead jerked and tore and swung ıe arm from side to side, up, then down, then side to ıde again. All the while he was beating, awkwardly and ithout power, at Richard's face with his left fist. Still ichard held. Not only held, but eventually, as the air filled his lungs, as the moon congealed into a solid glow-

17

ing ball and went back to its place in the sky, Richar
twisted the arm so that the knife blade faced away fro
him. He twisted and slowly, slowly, dragged the han
toward his mouth, and finally, taking a deep breath I
sank his teeth into the wrist. He disregarded the stomac
turning taste of the filthy flesh and bit, hard, clamping h
teeth together until his jaws ached with the effort. Un
his teeth grated against the wrist bone. The redhead
man's cursing and grunting changed to agonized scream
He cried, screaming louder and louder. Richard could n
bite through the bone, but he tried . . . until the re
headed man's fingers finally released the knife. As Ric.
ard's hand reached the knife, the redhead tore himse
loose from Richard's grasp, clambered to his feet, an
sobbing and groaning, holding his bleeding wrist, ra
down the street, around the corner and out of sight.

Still on his back, Richard turned his head to look dov
the street, where he and Felicia had first seen the fat m.
and his tall, gaunt companion. There a strange dance w
in progress. Felicia and the thin man were circling ea
other erratically, sometimes clockwise, sometimes counte
clockwise. Felicia swung the bag by its leather thon
over her head, constantly, every so often darting in towa
the thin man and swinging it at his head. The thin m.
would duck or back away, circle again, with the stick
his right hand. Whenever he thought he saw an opport
nity, he charged hesitantly and swung the stick at Felici
She adroitly danced away from it. Richard did not pau
to watch this strange minuet for more than the time it to
him to rise to his feet. Then he was racing down the stre
toward the dancers. As he got closer he saw that the f
man lay unconscious, his face in a small heap of garba;
at the side of the street.

When the thin man saw Richard rushing toward ther
knife in hand, he turned and ran. He, too, sped aroun
a corner and disappeared. Windows along both sides
the street had opened, but no one came down to inqui
about the violent happenings. Londoners knew better.

Richard rushed to Felicia. Her cloak lay in the cent
of her gown was torn down to h
waist. Her small, firm breasts rose and fell, as her har
breathing gradually subsided. Her meticulous golde
coiffure was wrecked, and the hair hung moist and loo
below her shoulders. Sweat glistened on her hig]

18

heekboned face, her bare shoulders and bosom. Her
ilver-gray eyes shone with triumph in the moonlight.

Picking up her cloak, panting, Richard asked anxiously,
'Are you all right?"

She nodded, then said, "But you're not, poor dear."

She stared with great concern at the bruises on the
ight side of his face and his forehead, at the bleeding
ight corner of his mouth. At the mass of dark, still moist
loodstains on his waistcoat, shirt and breeches. She
noved toward him, and turned him.

"You've been cut; you're still bleeding," she said,
rying to catch her breath, looking anxiously at the large,
lark, spreading stain of blood on the seat of his breeches,
nd down the stocking of his right leg.

Now that the danger was past, and the adrenalin flow
lowed, Richard's mind and body experienced a confusing
vhirlwind of emotions and feeling. The wound in his
uttock throbbed; he had never seen a woman's bare
reasts before; he had never dreamed that Felicia could
lispose of the fat man; the cheekbone on the right side
of his face hurt and his right eye was closing; he thought,
erhaps the blond man he had fought was dead; he had
ever seen a woman's bare breasts before.

"What happened to him?" he pointed to the body of
he fat man.

Felicia held the bag up to Richard, a bulging corner
extended toward him.

"Feel that . . . a sharp and heavy rock. Mary sewed it
nto the bag's corner for me." She paused for a deep
reath. "Makes a fine weapon against caitiffs like this
ne. . . . He managed to grab me by the shoulder, tore my
;own, before I broke away and struck him right in the
emple. . . . The tall one never really had his heart in the
ight."

Richard bent over the fat man, heard him whimper
nd blubber. There was a large lump on the side of his
alloonlike head.

"He seems to be alive."

"Yes, come, we must tend to you!"

"This way," said Richard, heading back toward where
he blond man lay on his back, mouth open, sightless eyes
taring at the moon. Richard knelt beside him, felt for his
ulse. He looked up at Felicia.

"He's dead," he said in a trembling voice. "And Felicia,
know him. . . . I thought I recognized him. He was a boy

19

who used to live on the same street as we in Billingsgate."

He rose, and stared sadly at the blond man. His eyes misted.

"His father was hanged. I think they said he stole two loaves of bread. And his mother became a prostitute. He was about ten, a year younger than I."

"You're bleeding, Richard," Felicia interrupted him. "We must hurry."

⚔ 3 ⚔

They walked rapidly, half-trotting most of the short distance to Felicia's house in the narrow passageway that was Middle Temple Lane. All the while, Richard continued to experience an agonizing chaos of mental and physical sensations. The blond man (Sam, his name was) was probably just another victim of what Father Whittaker constantly decried as the rampant poverty and class prejudice, which led to gross juvenile crime. Richard had never seen a woman's bare breasts, especially bouncing as Felicia's did as they trotted along. The throbbing in his buttock persisted—how could he dress and bandage it in front of Felicia? His right eye was almost completely closed—when he closed his left one, he could hardly see at all. He wondered if all women's breasts had such large pink areas around their nipples, and if all nipples protruded as much as Felicia's did.

In less than ten minutes they arrived at the doorway to the small building in which Felicia lived. An ancient man with a large hooked nose and bald head, leading an equally ancient, weary, brown dog on a leash, approached from the opposite direction and met them at the doorway. He peered closely.

"Felicia, are you wounded?" he quavered.

"Oh, Willy, I'm so glad we met you. We're all right, but would be very grateful if you could fetch me several basins of water."

The old caretaker of the building moved closer, till he was but inches away from Felicia.

"I'm becoming almost as blind as Oscar," he said, "but

you're a mighty handsome woman, Felicia. . . . Oh, to be just eighty years younger."

Felicia laughed and with mock modesty lifted the hanging, tattered portion of her gown over one breast.

"I'll wager you pleasured many a lady, in your time, Willy. Would you fetch us the water, please . . . ? This is my dear friend, Richard Steele, and he *has* been cut. . . . Richard, this is Willy Nilly."

"I'll do it right away, love," the old man said, leading his blind dog through the doorway.

The apartment consisted of two small rooms. Despite the fact that it got little sunlight, it reflected Felicia's colorful, cheery personality. Bright scarlet curtains hung at the two windows which faced the street. The same bright scarlet linen covered the table top and two chairs near the wood and coal stove. Framed playbills of entertainments in which Felicia had appeared hung on one wall. Felicia lighted an oil lamp and led Richard into the bedroom, where she lighted another lamp on a table beside the large bed. Over the bed hung a large silhouette of two lovers in a close embrace. The cutter of the black figures had contrived the lovers so that one could not discern whether they were a male and female, two males or two females. But the passion of the embrace was unmistakable.

Richard stared at the silhouette for a moment, and Felicia said, "Edith Forrest, the vicar's daughter, who is one of my dearest friends, did that. She's quite talented.'

The bed was covered with a sunny yellow silk spread. Felicia lifted and folded the spread, and placed it carefully on a nearby chair.

"The cut in your posterior seems the most serious, Richard," she said. "Off with the breeches."

Richard's cheeks turned pink beneath the caked blood and dirt. He hesitated.

"Come, come, love. Don't dawdle." Felicia took a clean white petticoat from a rack in a closet at the side of the room. She cut the spotless garment in two and laid one half across the bed.

"Lie on your stomach," she said. There was a kick at her door. She let in Willy Nillingham, shakily carrying a large basin of clean water.

"I'll be right along with another," he said, as she took it from him.

While she was out of the bedroom, Richard had re-

22

moved his breeches, underclothes, shoes and stockings, and had mustered the will to lie face-down on the bed. The mattress was of soft cotton, filled with thistledown, quite uncommon. Even in his nervous state Richard was aware of a sensation of luxurious comfort.

In a most businesslike manner, Felicia placed the basin on the table, cut the second half of the petticoat into a number of square cloths, and began washing the three-inch slash which ran from the upper portion of Richard's right buttock almost to his waist. The water in the basin was a deeper and muddier pink than Richard's cheeks, when she finished bathing the wound. Then she cut a large fresh square out of the garment, folded it four times and applied an ointment to the pad.

"A young doctor I lived with for a while gave me this. It will prevent the gangrene from setting in, and it will hasten the healing."

"It is comforting, thank you," Richard managed to mumble. Despite his best efforts at control, there was a stirring in his groin, and he felt the beginnings of erection at Felicia's ministrations. The pink crept down the back of his neck.

"It's going to take a little doing to bind this pad so that it will stay," she said. She cut and tore the remnants of the petticoat into long strips, tried tying them over the pad, and around Richard's waist, but the lower part of the pad lay loosely on Richard's buttock.

"I'll have to come around this way."

Felicia pulled the strip around his waist, diagonally down over the pad, gently pushed it under the inside of Richard's thigh. It was impossible for her to avoid touching his genitals, as she pushed the cloth strip out on the other side of his thigh. It was necessary for her to perform this sequence three more times, and each time, Richard became more and more fiercely erect. Felicia could see by the fiery red of his cheek and neck, even beneath the layers of caked blood and dirt, that he was embarrassed. She brushed against his erection on her last pass under his thigh.

There was a mischievous twinkle in her eyes as she completed the bandaging.

"Now just stay the way you are, love, while I clean you up a bit."

With a tender touch she washed his neck, back and legs completely clean.

23

"All right, now, turn over."

"I . . . I . . . I can't, Felicia. I can—can—can't."

Just then Willy Nillingham's second kick at the door sounded. The basin of clean water he brought this time was even larger than the first. Felicia kissed him on the cheek as she took it from him.

"Thank you, dearest Willy Nilly."

"Oh, how I enyy your young friend, Felicia," the old man sighed. "Have a lovely night, now."

Laughing softly, Felicia went back into the bedroom with the second basin. She set it down on a chair, picked up the first basin of now muddy maroon water and tossed it out of a window. She wiped out the basin with one of the cloths, and refilled it so that there were equal amounts of clean water in each of the two basins.

She stood over Richard on the bed.

"All right, Richard, turn around."

"Please, Felicia, please."

She took his shoulder and tugged, till he finally spun around. He pulled one knee up, placed both hands with palms down over his genital area. But the knee and the hands were hardly sufficient to conceal the large, stiff erection.

Felicia laughed.

"My . . . I had no idea you were so well-equipped, love."

"Felicia, I'm sorry." Richard attempted to turn back on his stomach and pulled both knees up.

"That's all right. I'll leave you this basin and cloth to wash up, and I'll perform my toilette in the living room."

She draped several clean clothes over her arm, lifted the larger basin and carried it out of the room, humming happily.

Richard got out of the bed and began washing his face, and the front of his sweaty, blood- and dirt-covered body. He was mortified over the immense erection which, despite his embarrassment, throbbed with excitement and refused to subside.

He was halfway through washing, when Felicia walked into the room. She was naked and clean from head to toe. Only her golden hair still seemed tangled and matted. She stopped humming as she saw him. Richard turned away.

"My, my," she said again, admiringly. "I need my comb, love. And then I'll be right back."

In less than two minutes she was.

All of the elements of the mental and physical whirl-wind of Richard's night now became focused in one general area. He had never seen a woman *completely* naked before. The lovely large circles around the nipples of her breasts were more tan than pink. The nipples themselves protruded even more. It was remarkable that the curly-haired V, where her thighs met, was more golden than the silken, freshly combed hair of her head; her waist was un-believably small, and flowed into slender, curved hips. What would he ever do about this pulsating rod?

Felicia smiled warmly into his panicky eyes. She went to a dresser and lit the six candles in the two candelabra on its top. Richard watched her, enraptured . . . embar-rassed. It was the first time he had ever seen a *completely* naked woman from the rear. There was a fiercely growing ache in his groin. His erection throbbed and felt as though it would explode.

"Well, get into bed, love. We're not going to do it standing up."

He was in a confused agony of desire and mortification. He could not take his eyes from her. His breath came hard. She smiled at him. Her eyes flashed with amuse-ment, yet the desire in them was plain to behold.

"At least not the first time," she said, and pushed him by the chest, gently onto the bed. She blew out the oil lamp.

In the glow of the candles, Richard thought her body was the most beautiful sight he had ever seen. With trem-bling hands, he reached up toward her, and she was down beside him, her mouth on his, her body pressed against him. The feel of her heated, silky skin made him want to sing or cry.

He groaned, and his erection pulsed insanely and exploded. Ashamed, he tried to draw away from her, so that she would not be soiled with his throbbing and con-tinuing bursts, but she pulled him closer. As he groaned and groaned, the sound threatening to turn to anguished crying, she said, "It's all right, Richard. It's perfectly all right."

And now he *was* sobbing. She kissed him again and again on the cheeks, the chin, the nose, the bruised mouth. Kissed his chest, and again his lips and chin, and nose. Tenderly, tenderly.

"I'm sorry, Felicia. I'm so sorry."

The mortification he had felt on the stage of the Lincoln's Inn Fields Theatre hours earlier was as nothing to the utter shame and disappointment he felt in himself now. But Felicia consoled him until he regained full control of himself. She washed him completely with a clean cloth, washed herself and lay beside him.

She ran gentle fingertips over his chest, caressing his nipples. She kissed his throat, raised her mouth to his and slipped her tongue through his parted lips. Her hand crept down his flat stomach to his small nest and fondled his genitals, as she kissed him soulfully all the while. To his amazement he was again as erect, possibly even more so, than he had been before. And her soft smooth hand was around him, stroking him gently.

This time she straddled him, and before he realized it, he was inside her, and she was moving up and down and in a rhythmic circular pattern. As she moved, she took his head in her hands, and leaned down to kiss him hungrily on the mouth. He moved with her. The movement tugged the bandage away from his wounded buttock, and he was dimly aware that it was bleeding again. It also ached sharply. But again in less than two minutes he reached a volcanic climax. This time, he did not groan in humiliation, but in sheer disgust with himself. Felicia continued to move on top of him, but quickly he softened, shrunk and slipped out of her.

"I'm sorry, Felicia. It's no use. I'm just . . ."

Still astride him, Felicia put her hand gently over his mouth.

"You've had a very trying evening, love. You were laughed off a stage, stabbed in the buttock and set upon by a highly sexed young lady, who hasn't made love to a virginal male in some time."

She kissed him again as she got out of bed, washed herself once more. As Richard began to rise from the bed, she pushed him gently down on his back again.

Then she lay on her back beside him.

"Does your buttock pain you?" she asked.

Richard shrugged.

"Enough so you're conscious of it at any rate," she guessed.

Richard nodded.

"Turn on your side and kiss me, love."

Timidly, he did.

She placed her hand on the back of his neck, and held him thus until his kiss lost its dutiful, obedient quality,

26

and began to take on a passion. She opened her mouth, and Richard's tongue slipped in. Their tongues played with each other. Richard's right hand slid from her shoulder to her breast. The touch of the hard nipple sent hot blood coursing through his entire body. He felt himself coming to erection yet a third time. Felicia reached down with her left hand and felt the stiff, hot member. She pressed the fingers of her right hand firmly against Richard's side, signaling for him to mount her. He did, and entered her as though they had been lovers for centuries. His thrusts were full and deep and rhythmic. He felt as though he could continue making love to Felicia through the night, and into the next day, and the next night . . . perhaps for eternity.

Now Felicia moaned, and moaned again, and gasped in ecstasy. And a deep, warm glow of happiness filled Richard. Without breaking his rhythm, he leaned forward and kissed her mouth, her neck, her breasts, her hungry mouth again.

Felicia sobbed softly, muttered, "Richard, Richard, Richard . . ." as she dug her fingers into his muscular, perspiring back. And he continued to love her, until she gasped again, and held him tightly with her arms and legs. Richard felt like the emperor of the universe, and like a small boy who has been given a thousand gifts of Noel in one miraculous package. Every nerve in his body tingled; his heart danced joyously in his chest.

What he knew he would do, without question, was to continue to pleasure this exquisite creature, his friend, without stopping, till the end of time. That thought was in his mad head when Felicia uttered a small cry and caught her breath sharply, screamed softly and happily, and writhed beneath him, squirming closer against him. Sometime, maybe moments, maybe hours later, she moaned again, and cried out in ecstasy once more as Richard continued to love her. Finally he had his own third explosion, a true Vesuvius of continuing eruptions.

He collapsed, moved gently off her and lay beside her. They held hands, taking long, even, relaxed and contented breaths. There was a sudden kicking at the door. Subconsciously, Richard must have noted Laertes Wrexham's baleful glare backstage earlier that evening. It flashed through his mind that the actor was about to kick down the door. Then he heard a quavering old voice.

27

"Would you be needing some more water?"

In the warm candlelight, Felicia smiled at Richard.

"No, thank you, Mr. Nilly," shouted Richard happily. Mr. Nillingham's blind dog, Oscar, barked mildly, twice.

4

His buttock ached and his right cheek tingled, but Richard whistled as he made his way through the dark, quiet streets toward the small house at Billingsgate where he and his mother lived. He was aware that he might encounter yet another band of ruffians, or possibly even a footpad. Lightheaded with fatigue, he nevertheless felt like he could take on and defeat an army. It proved unnecessary. He encountered no one, and soon the familiar reek of fish reached his nostrils, as he turned the corner into the narrow street where he lived.

Over the door of the crumbling little house hung a twig of mountain ash. Mary Steele was a superstitious woman, and the purpose of the twig was to ward off witches and evil spirits. She preferred a horseshoe, and one had adorned the door, until it was stolen. No one had bothered to steal the twig of mountain ash. The only sound, inside or outside the house, came from the river, where occasional boisterous shouting wafted ashore on the malodorous breeze.

Mary sat in a straight-backed chair at a blue linen-covered table in the center of the kitchen, the main room of the apartment. Squinting intently in the feeble tallow light, she busily stitched away, sewing interlinings in the cuffs of a green velvet coat. Gilbert Weston, the actor-manager of the Lincoln's Inn Fields Theatre used Mary exclusively to sew the few special costumes the company required. For the most part, actors of the day played in their own contemporary clothes, although Weston occasionally bought the cast-off gowns of ladies of quality or nobility for his actresses in more elegant roles.

29

Long ago Mary had told Richard that his father had died at sea in the spring of 1704 in the second year of Queen Anne's War. She had supported them both, working as barmaid as well as seamstress. The primary goal of Richard's life was to move his mother to a cottage in the country, where the air was clean, and where she might regain her health.

On the table before her, steam rose from a bowl of snails boiled in barley water. It was a familiar sight to Richard, since Mary ate the snails three times daily on the orders of her doctor. They were said to be the most effective medicinal treatment for his mother's disorder.

Now Mary looked up as her son entered.

"Richard, you're hurt," she said in a shocked whisper. "And your clothes . . . ?" Richard came to her quickly, bent over and kissed her.

"It's of no consequence, Mary. Felicia and I encountered a group of ruffians. . . . God bless you on your birthday!" He, too, spoke quietly. He handed her the box with the cameo brooch, and kissed her again.

"Is he drunk?" he asked in a hushed tone, nodding at the man who sat opposite Mary Steele, black-gray head resting on his arms on the table, breathing deeply and evenly. Beside his right elbow there was a half-empty bottle of Madeira wine and an empty glass. Mary shook her head as Richard sat in a third chair at the table.

She spoke again, almost in a whisper: "No. Poor Father has had an unusually difficult day—or perhaps for him, just a typical one. Before dawn he was awakened by Dame Fletcher. Peter, her fourteen-year-old, was spirited aboard a ship bound for the Colonies as an indentured servant. Father got to the brigantine just before it sailed, and managed to take the boy off, though the good Lord knows how."

The green velvet coat began to slip from her lap, and she tugged it back.

"When he got back to the rectory, Mrs. Hodges was waiting for him. . . . You know the Hodgeses. They have twelve children, the youngest just a month old, and Mr. Hodges had been taken to debtor's prison. Father spent the rest of the morning getting him released. He arranged with the magistrate for Mr. Hodges to pay off the debt at the rate of a shilling a month."

Father Whittaker made a sudden sound, a short series of three snorts, then breathed evenly and quietly again.

His right arm slid slightly and Richard moved the wine bottle away from his elbow.

"When he got back to the rectory," continued Mary, "little Henry Bottoms was waiting for him. Mr. Bottoms was condemned to be hanged, and it seemed Mrs. Bottoms was carrying on as though she had lost her senses. Father rushed to the Bottomses' with the boy, and found the poor woman had indeed become unhinged. She didn't even recognize her own children, let alone Father."

The velvet coat slipped again, and this time fell to the floor. Richard retrieved it and placed it on a long work table beneath the windows at the north side of the room.

"Enough sewing for the night," he said.

"This time when he got back to the rectory, Monsignor Walsh was waiting for him."

She shook her head sadly.

"The monsignor told him that if he didn't stop drinking so heavily, he would be excommunicated one day. He said the Catholic faith had difficulty enough in Church of England London without drunken priests running about, giving the Anglicans ammunition for scandal."

Father Whittaker snorted briefly once more. Richard expressed his sympathy with a compassionate shake of his head. He kissed Mary on the cheek.

"See your birthday gift."

Mary did.

"Oh, how lovely."

She held the brooch daintily at the neckline of the plain black blouse she wore. She looked ten years older than her thirty. Her hair was a shade darker than the sand-colored background of the brooch, and was already beginning to be streaked with gray. She had the same oval-shaped face as Richard and the same straight nose, full lips and cleft chin. But there were wrinkles on her forehead, at her eyes and at each side of her mouth. Her eyes were a soft, warm brown. Her cheeks were unnaturally pink.

"It's lovely," she said again, pinning the brooch to the blouse. "Thank you, my dear. . . . But what of your debut? Did it go well? I assumed you were rather late because you would be celebrating."

Richard blushed.

"Well, yes . . ."

Mary Steele coughed, took a kerchief from her pocket and held it to her mouth. She coughed again and again and again. Richard noted with alarm that there were brownish red, dried bloodstains on the kerchief. Finally the seizure passed, and Mary drew long, deep breaths, holding her head to her chest. After breathing heavily for several moments, she ate several of the snails and the broth in which they were cooked.

The previous winter she had contracted a severe cold, and she had never recovered. The coughing spells had lasted through the spring and summer and into the fall. They seemed worse at certain times than at others, but never vanished entirely.

Awakened by the coughing, Father Whittaker raised his head. When Mary put down the wooden spoon, he reached across the table and took her hand.

"Forgive me for having fallen asleep. Are you all right ... for the moment?"

Mary smiled wanly, nodded.

Father Whittaker stared at Richard.

"And what happened to you, lad?"

The Catholic priest was a tall man, two inches over six feet, with broad shoulders on a heavy torso. At forty, his black hair was generously flecked with gray. He had the same blue-green, restless sea eyes as Richard. Now the whites were red-veined, and his chin and cheeks were dark with a stubble of beard. Richard told of his and Felicia's encounter with the band of ruffians.

Father Whittaker shook his head sadly.

"There are more children roaming in murderous bands every day," he said. "The King or the Council must do something to help the poor. This cannot go on."

He sat down at the table and poured himself a glass of wine. He ran a finger around the stiff white collar under his chin and sipped the wine.

"I wanted to attend your debut, Richard," he said finally, "but several problems arose. How fared you?"

"Not very well."

Richard told his mother and the priest about his disastrous initial appearance, and his slightly more successful second entrance.

"I don't know what I would have done without Felicia. She assured me that she still becomes nervous before a performance," he said finally, and felt himself blushing again. Father Whittaker had drunk two glasses of Madeira while Richard told his story. Now he poured a third.

"That's a fine young lady, that Felicia, and a fine actress."

Richard and his mother both knew that Father Whittaker was fully aware of Felicia's notoriously loose morals. Richard had been present one evening, backstage, when Felicia had said to the priest, "I like you, Father, and I'd like you to like me, but I know you can't approve of my views of life and love."

Father Whittaker had said, "I do like you, young lady. A man once said, 'Let him who is without sin throw the first stone.' And I throw stones at no one."

Now the priest emptied his glass.

"And of course, Felicia is absolutely right. Many of the most gifted actors experience some nervousness throughout their careers. You'll do fine, lad. Just persist."

He poured another glass of wine, lifted it to Mary.

"One more toast to the glorious day you were born, dear Mary," he smiled. He emptied the glass, rose, kissed Mary on the cheek, bade her and Richard good night, and walked wearily to the door.

"You look somewhat the worse for wear, Richard," said Mary Steele, as she put another pot of snails and barley water on the stove. "You'd best get some rest."

Richard took a *Grub Street Journal* clipping from his pocket.

"Hear this, Mary."

He read: "At Waltham Cross in Hertfordshire. Twelve mile from London, is a very pretty house to let."

He looked up and smiled at his mother, and with increasing enthusiasm read on: " 'Tis next the road, with rails and trees before it; it stands clean, and has a good prospect over the marshes to Epping Forest, and other parts of Essex. There is orchard, garden, pasture and all other necessaries for a country dwelling. . . ."

"Oh, Richard, we could never afford such a place."

"I don't know. We've got almost sixty pounds saved now, and if I can improve my acting, and persuade Mr. Weston to give me more roles . . . and perhaps Mr. Pickering would increase my wages at the Inn by a mite—but listen, listen to the rest of this."

Leaning closer to the tallow on the table, he read again: "A great many coaches and other carriages . . ."

Suddenly from somewhere close by the rear of the house came an anguished wailing. It sounded like a child's or a woman's cry of pain. Mary smiled.

"Another conquest for Farquhar!"

Richard shook his head in mock awe, and smiled too.

33

Mary Steele had named the sturdy orange striped tom-cat, who had adopted the Steeles, after the playwright, George Farquhar, whose sentimental comedies of love, *The Recruiting Officer* and *The Beaux' Stratagem*, were among her favorite plays. And Farky's frequent nocturnal sexual encounters unfailingly were heralded by the anguished wail of his mate of the night. The sound of painful ecstasy. Richard blushed, as he recalled Felicia's moans just hours earlier. He returned to the *Grub Street* advertisement.

". . . a great many coaches and other carriages go every day by the door to and from London; and to my own knowledge, the housekeepers are very civil and genteel as can reasonably be expected from country folks."

He looked up. "And it requests one inquire there for a George Storey. I believe I'll go out there at the first opportunity."

"But Richard, I would not want you to be required to travel twelve miles to London, and another dozen back home each day."

"Mr. Pickering said he might consider selling me Sally O. If I could pay for the mare out of my wages, perhaps I could afford it, and then the journey would not be too difficult."

From the stove came the bubbling sound of the boiling barley water. Richard poured a bowlful for his mother, and she sipped the hot liquid carefully.

"I'm not sure we can manage all this right now," Richard said, "but I'm most eager to have you out in the country by next spring."

A loud, persistent meowing and an aggressive scratching sounded at the door. When Richard opened it, Farquhar entered, carrying a large rat in his mouth. He walked proudly to Mary at the table, and placed the rat carefully at her feet.

"Farky's birthday gift," said Richard.

Mary patted the cat's upraised head, and said, "Thank you, Farquhar."

Presently Mary went into the small second room where she slept. Farquhar followed her and took his nightly position, curled behind her knees. Once Farky was out of the kitchen, Richard threw the dead rat out a window, undressed and lay down on his own muslin-covered, straw-filled pallet. Somewhere church bells clanged midnight. Richard sighed. He would have to rise at dawn to report at the Inn of the King's Men, near the theater, at seven. The wound in his buttock itched, as well as ached. Every inch of his body ached, for that matter. He could not remember ever having been so utterly weary. Yet he could not fall asleep.

He lay in the darkness, eyes closed, as the events of the long day and evening replayed themselves in his head. He tossed and turned on the thin mat. Finally he must have fallen asleep, for he was dreaming that he was back in Felicia's thistledown bed, and she was doing something new. Licking his face. But it was dawn, and it was Farky, not Felicia.

A feeble sun made a dusty bright path from the window across the floor of the small room. The early morning noises of the fishmongers, opening their stalls, the fish porters wheeling their carts along the roads, signaling the start of another day at Billingsgate Market, reached Richard's ears as he let Farky out to seek his breakfast.

Richard yawned and stretched and groaned. All the aches of the day before seemed to have multiplied through his restless night. Stiffly, in a stoic stupor, he dressed. Quietly he walked into Mary's room, kissed her goodbye, and set out to do his lad-of-all-work chores at the Inn of the King's Men. He did not even notice that two new bodies hung from the gibbets at the foot of the dock. Mutineers or river pirates, tried and duly convicted.

Halfway to the Inn his mind began to function. He wondered if Mr. Weston would ever give him another opportunity to act. And if so, when? In tonight's play, *Macbeth*, he was scheduled to do stagehand duty. In the scene with the witches, he would be in the superstructure over the stage, where he would roll a heavy ball of iron down a short flight of uneven steps and beat a large drum to simulate thunder. And he would blow rosin through a candle flame to create flashes of lightning. He had done this in a performance of *Macbeth* almost a year earlier, and he remembered how fervently he wished then that he might be down upon the stage, acting . . . even if as just one of the witches. And he hoped Felicia would come into the Inn for her noontime meal, as usual.

5

The sickly sun had surrendered. Yet even at this early hour of the soot-laden, foggy morning, when the debris of the merrymaking and the debating, the wining and wenching, the feasting and the social gaming of the night before had not yet been cleared away, there was an ebullient air about the Inn of the King's Men.

Richard always felt his spirits lift as he entered the large, warm kitchen, the main room of the Inn. Although his buttock burned, his face ached and his entire body felt as though he had been stomped on by a band of angry giants, this day was no exception.

It did not occur to him that part of the reason for his feelings could have been the stark contrast between the sights, sounds and smells of the portion of London city that he passed on his way to work, and the atmosphere of the Inn. That morning he had had to stare and shout down a pack of hungry mongrel dogs, who would have attacked him at the first sign of weakness of his part.

At St. Paul's Churchyard, a young boy was newly on display in the pillory. Tears streamed from the plump head, fastened into the hold between the two heavy planks. Thin lines of dried blood, running from each side of his mouth to his ears, which had been nailed to the wood, gave him the look of a macabre clown. The boy had moaned ceaselessly.

Richard was oblivious to the muddy water running in the Fleet ditch in the middle of the street, with its refuse, its bullock dung, its horse manure and occasional cat or dog corpses, but on this morning he encountered an exceptional olfactory treat. As he passed the shop of Pritch-

36

ard, the butcher, he had to skip over the rivulet of dark blood, which still snaked sluggishly from the shop into the dusty street. Pritchard had slaughtered a cow earlier that morning, and as Richard passed, the gut spinner and the tripe dresser were busily working away on their chopping blocks behind the stalls, and in open vats, freshly sawed bones were boiling, and suet was being prepared for tallow. Flies zoomed, buzzed and feasted everywhere.

When he closed the door to the kitchen of the Inn of the King's Men behind him, the last faint traces of stale tobacco smoke were already giving way to the mouthwatering mixture of smells emanating from the large stove in the far corner of the kitchen, and from the bar, which ran almost the entire length of one wall. Richard knew that the Grateful pudding was already in the oven. He could distinctly detect the aroma of the ginger and the raisins, which gave the spicy, fruity flavor to the mixture of bread, milk, flour and eggs. Primarily, however, the ebullient atmosphere derived from the vital personalities of the Pickerings.

Mrs. Bessie Pickering hummed a bright tune, as she laid the cabbage leaves, the veal slices, the suet into the cast iron pan, before she mixed the green gooseberries with the egg yolks to make Pickering's own distinctive cabbage pudding.

"Good morning, love," she sang cheerfully, so busy with her cooking that she did not notice Richard's bruised face.

Bessie was in her late thirties. She was heavy, with a large bosom and bottom, but she still moved with the grace of the tightrope dancer she had been in her youth. There was a perpetual twinkle in her gray eyes, and her blue-black hair shone with health. Her daughter, Tillie, was a sixteen-year-old, smaller version of her mother.

Tillie suddenly halted stirring the sauce she was making for the cod, which she had cleaned and panned and covered with oysters, ready for baking. Wiping her hands on her apron, she ran across the kitchen to Richard.

"Whatever happened to your face, Dickie?"

Richard winced, as always, at the nickname. Now he explained, briefly and loudly enough for Bessie and her husband Ben to hear. Ben Pickering was a tall man. He, too, was heavy, but with muscle, rather than fat. He had brownish-red hair, and green-flecked brown eyes. He had been a lofty and ground tumbler, one of the best in all of variety. He was as exuberant and jolly a soul as his wife. Not the least of the attractions of the Inn was Ben Pickering's story-telling talent. He knew and told his patrons countless tales, some true, some fictional, but all fascinating and often amusing. He never seemed to tell the same story to the same person twice.

But Richard knew that along with his irresistibly winning personality, he was also a shrewd and frugal businessman. He would not sacrifice the quality of his food or drink, but neither would he permit any excess of expensive ingredients to be used. Richard had heard him, on more than one occasion, talk quietly but firmly to Bessie or Tillie, when they used too much meat in a stew or pie, or when they were careless in their use of cream or eggs. So even as Richard filled the Pickerings in on his misadventures with the ruffians the previous evening, he hurried to begin his own chores.

Now the muscular proprietor of the Inn was ladling gobs of sherbet into the special arrack, which was fermented from the sap of toddy palms from the East Indies. Pickering prided himself as much on his arrack, French brandy and Jamaica rum punches as on his food. The arrack punch was the house's most popular libation, although Pickering, himself, Bessie and Tillie all preferred the ebullum, which was a wine Bessie made of elder and juniper berries, ginger, orange peel, citron and cinnamon.

"Must've seemed a bad night, all in all," Pickering said now, as Richard walked by him, sweeping the thick, oak-planked floor. "But don't let that shaky performance discourage you, good Richard. I saw old Colley Cibber, himself, in his early days, so trembly he couldn't manage a whisper."

"We thought your second speech excellent, Dickie," piped Tillie.

"Oh, never fear for young Richard," said Bessie, shoving the cabbage pudding into the oven with a flourish. "He'll yet be one of our finer players."

Richard knew the Pickerings had attended his debut at the theater the previous evening, and he was pleased and grateful that they would dismiss his failure so lightly.

By eleven o'clock, the Inn was ready for the new day's patrons. Richard had swept the floors, scrubbed the heavy oak tables and chairs, dusted the crossed swords, polished the coats of arms and copper platters which decorated the whitewashed walls, cleaned out and laid new wood and coals in the stone fireplace in the center of the room.

As he worked, the aches in his muscles gradually dissolved into numbness. Only his buttock still burned. He was sure the bandage had slipped. A vivid picture of Felicia tying the bandage formed in his mind, and he felt a stirring in his groin. He hoped fervently again that she would come in for lunch.

Before the day was out he planned to talk to Ben Pickering about the possibility of having a shilling or two added to the six shillings per week he presently earned, and about his desire to buy his favorite mare, Sally O, from Pickering. But he felt the brief period after the noon rush, when the family and he lunched, would be a more propitious time. Now he still had to feed and water the horses, so he went back to the stables.

The burning in his buttock had turned into an itch. He felt a great urge to scratch it, but feared he might open the wound. Before beginning to pile fresh hay into Sally O's bin, he decided to see what had happened to the bandage and the wound. He lowered his breeches, and twisted his head to look down at his right hip. The bandage had indeed slipped, but he thought he could retie the cloth strip to hold it back in place. As he was bent over, slipping the strip up through his legs, from back to front, he heard a sharp gasp behind him.

He turned toward the stable door, desperately reaching down for his breeches. Tillie stood at the door, hand over her wide open mouth, her green-gray eyes round with surprise, shock, awe!

"You're hurt, Dickie. Let me help you!" She rushed toward him.

Richard backed away from her, tugging frantically at his breeches.

"No, no, I'm fine, Tillie. It's healing well. There's no more bleeding."

The light in the stable was dim, but Richard wondered if she could see him blushing, as he could see her cheeks pinking. She put her arms around his neck, and raised her lips to his.

"Kiss me, Dickie."

Before he could, she was kissing him so hard it hurt his bruised mouth.

Desperately he tried to push her off with one hand, while he tugged to raise his breeches with the other. It suddenly flashed through his mind that Ben Pickering might walk in at any moment. He yanked at his breeches with both hands, finally succeeded in lifting them all the way up to his waist.

Tillie kissed him again, lightly this time, and laughed.

"Father says let the horses be till later. He needs you now to set some beer kegs."

Sally O and Brutus, the stallion in the neighboring stall, both unfed and unwatered, neighed a mild complaint as Richard trotted out of the stables ahead of Tillie Pickering.

At the well, as they washed before going back into the Inn, Tillie pouted.

"Why do you dislike me, Dickie?"

"I don't dislike you. I'm very fond of you. But your father . . ."

Tillie Pickering had more or less pursued Richard for the past year, but he knew that Ben and Bess Pickering did not want her romantically involved with anyone in the theater. They were fond of actors, were performers themselves, but the paradox remained. Richard had often heard them say they hoped Tillie would marry a barrister or a doctor. Indeed, she was presently being courted by a young medical student. And Richard had no intention of getting into trouble with his employer.

Soon the first of the noontime patrons arrived. It was a group consisting of Gilbert Weston, the actor-manager of Lincoln's Inn Fields, and three of the older actors in the company. Richard could have been imagining it, but he had the feeling that Weston's greeting to him, as he came to their table to take their order, was less warm and congenial than usual. The other actors greeted him in the same casual manner as was their custom. No one mentioned his stuttering debut performance.

Richard had unusual difficulty getting their orders straight. Weston had ordered the brandy punch, and Richard marked him down for the arrack punch; Weston also ordered the cabbage pudding, and Richard made a note for the Grateful pudding. When he read back all the orders, it turned out he had the others as confused as he had Weston's. No one had ordered the roast beef, and somehow, he had written down two orders of roast beef. He realized that his mind, as well as his body, was numb with fatigue. Yet Weston and the actors were tolerant enough.

The room gradually filled, and Richard managed to stagger through taking and delivering the drinks and meals without any major mishaps. An hour passed, and Felicia was not among the arrivals. Two rough-looking, flashily dressed men, strangers to Richard, came in.

As they seated themselves, they looked carefully around the room, from one table to another. One of them, with a large, beaked nose, narrow slits for eyes and a thick-lipped mouth, signaled for Richard. When he approached their table, the man asked, "Jerome Wrexham been yet?"

"Been?" asked Richard, somewhat dazed.

"Been, *been!*" 'As Wrexham, the actor, come along for 'is feed yet! 'E eats 'ere, don't 'e!"

"Yes sir, most of the time he does. But he hasn't been in yet today."

The men ordered tankards of beer and roast beef. They ate and drank ravenously, but in a distracted manner, watching the front door of the tavern all the while. They ordered their tankards refilled several times. When Richard came to the bar for the beer for the second time, Pickering whispered as he filled the tankards, "Who are those two?"

Richard shrugged. "They're asking for Jerome Wrexham."

Pickering snorted, as the foam capped the second tankard. "Must've run up a score with some gamblers. Dunners, those two are, for certain."

Wrexham always owed Pickering a considerable amount at 'the Inn, too, and Pickering had occasionally made caustic references to Bessie, in Richard's presence, about the actor's tendency to keep himself in debt. At one point, Tillie Pickering had been quite taken by Wrexham, and her father had admonished her sternly to keep away from the handsome leading man.

Now Richard took the beers back to the table of the strangers. They made slurping sounds as they drank. The one with the crooked nose burped loudly. They kept staring at the door. Every time the door opened, Richard looked in its direction, too, hoping to see Felicia. Time passed. Neither Felicia nor Wrexham came.

6

When Felicia Wandrous had walked out of the theater, arm in arm with young Richard Steele on the previous evening, Jerome Wrexham had indeed been furious. This did not affect the quality of his performance in the after-piece concert, following *Hamlet*. If anything, his ire gave an added luster to his magnetic presence, and a richer timbre to his baritone. The thunderous applause he received wiped out his anger. Felicia was a silly wench, indeed, he assured himself, to pass up an evening and night with Wrexham, for a green, calf's head of a youth. She would no doubt discover the difference soon enough and come back.

He felt in the mood for fine food and wines and liquors, and some adventuresome gambling . . . and perhaps a round of extraordinary sexual activity at Mother Magruder's. A small mob of admirers, including two male and three female prostitutes, surrounded him outside the theater, patted his back, sought to shake his hand. Happily, he fought his way to a carriage. He felt to make sure his pocket had not been picked, then told the driver to take him to Lady Gertrude's in Pall Mall.

For the first few moments of the trip he relived his triumphal performance of that evening. *Gad! They loved it!* He wondered if this might not be the right time to demand a substantial increase from Gilbert Weston. Better yet, perhaps he could work on the Duke of Cheltenham, Edmund Fox, who was a majority shareholder in the theater. He was friendly with the Duke, as he was with a number of members of the aristocracy, and more remarkable yet, he was the only person in the theatrical profession who

42

was friendly with the Lady Sarah Palfrey, who would soon marry the Duke of Cheltenham. These nuptials would bring together two of the wealthiest and most influential families in the kingdom, and Wrexham felt he should be able to use the Duke and his new Duchess to good advantage in some manner.

As the carriage clattered past Charing Cross, Wrexham saw a haggard gray-haired woman, unconscious, in the pillory. *The old baggage is probably dead,* he thought idly. Moments later he was riding through the Haymarket, and into Picadilly. He admired the fine houses there, and in Park Lane. Then in Pall Mall, short of St. James Palace, the carriage pulled up before one of the most attractive mansions of all. It was a low, simple and graceful Greco-Roman building, with a large center dome, stately columns and arched windows.

Wrexham alighted, and paid the coachman. The man stared at the coins in the moonlight, and muttered a curse at the paucity of the sum Wrexham had given him. He whipped his horse angrily, as Wrexham strode to the large, ornately carved walnut doors of the great house. Wrexham knocked sharply three times, lightly three more times, and then sharply once more. A footman opened a small, wooden panel at eye-level in the door, recognized Wrexham and let him in, with a bow. The footman was exceptionally large and muscular. Although it happened infrequently, there were occasions when patrons became difficult.

A gilded chandelier with three dozen glowing candles illuminated the regal foyer. The candle glow shone warmly on Grecian and Roman statues in niches around the circular room. The lower part of the walls was rich, polished walnut, and the upper sections, to the full height of the ceiling, were mirrored. The mirrors reflected a ring of chandeliers, all aglow with candlelight. Royal purple valances topped the mirrors. Chairs and sofas, ornately carved with lions' heads and satyrs, and small tables of finely crafted marquetry—contrasting woods laid into a background of veneer—were grouped about the area.

The footman took Wrexham's silver-headed cane and his hat, and a butler led him toward the doors to the main dining and gaming rooms. Wrexham arched his back, pushed out his chest and raised his chin as he followed the butler. This, he always felt, as he entered Lady Gertrude's elegant house, was his natural environment.

43

He looked into the mirrored wall at his right, paused and turned so that the mirror showed his head in half-profile. *Gad! You're a noble and handsome-looking gentleman, Wrexham,* he evaluated himself silently.

His father must have been an aristocrat, probably a member of the court. He was certain of that, although his mother had always shrugged off his questions concerning his male parent, and told him she could not say for sure. He told friends that his mother had been a courtesan and an actress, although he realized that she had actually been a sometime dancer, and medium-priced harlot. She disappeared with a Welsh ironmonger, when Jerome was twelve, and he had made his way on his own ever since.

And made his way quite well. Today he earned two hundred pounds per season as a leading player at Lincoln's Inn Fields. He was one of the best paid actors in London. It was a far cry from the pennies he had been paid by Clarence Dunleavy, the fifty-year-old rogue showman, who took him along with his traveling company of actors, a one-wagon banditti troupe, when Jerome was left motherless. Dunleavy liked little boys, and was gentle enough with young Jerome in bed, although he used him regularly. He also taught Jerome to read, to write and to juggle.

Lady Fingers taught him to steal chickens and eggs, occasional fruits and vegetables—and once they even stole a piglet—from the farms the Dunleavy Company passed in their travels. Lady was a sickly, emaciated young man, four years older than Jerome Wrexham. He had sad, watery, light green eyes, sunk deep in the sockets of his narrow skull and dirty, stringy black hair.

He was called Lady Fingers—no one seemed to know his real name—because of his delicate, though usually filthy, hands, with their long, slender, feminine fingers. These he used most dexterously in picking the pockets of farmers and their good women, who attended the performances of the Dunleavy troupe in the barns, in the kitchens of small public houses, or in the village squares. Lady shared part of his proceeds with Dunleavy.

Jerome and Lady became fast friends, and one night in the third year of Jerome's time with Dunleavy, when Lady was taken with a burning fever, Jerome rode six hard miles to the nearest village to fetch a doctor. It was the middle of the night and it had begun to rain by the time he found one. But Lady had expired before Jerome and the doctor got back to camp.

Dunleavy had refused to take Lady into the wagon when the rain started, since he feared the scrawny pickpocket's disorder might be contagious. Jerome spent the next three hours, in the black night with the rain beating down on him and the corpse, digging a grave for his friend. He kept losing his footing and slipping into the slimy ditch himself. Dunleavy and the other company members, hours earlier, had crowded themselves into the single wagon and slept.

It was almost dawn when Jerome, the muscles of his arms, legs and back aching, knelt beside Lady, felt through all his pockets, took the three shillings and six pence he found, and rolled the already stiffening corpse of his friend into the muddy ditch he had dug. His own legs and back were so stiff with cold and exertion, he could hardly stand erect again, but with an agonized groan, he managed to rise. Before he finished splashing the thick mud over the body, the rain stopped and the dawn's feeble sun lighted the landscape.

Jerome climbed onto the seat of the wagon. From the interior behind him came a cacophony of wheezes, groans, moans, snorting and snoring in several tones and cadences. From the hidden compartment under the seat, he took the small strong box in which Clarence Dunleavy kept his money. It was secured with a heavy lock.

He climbed back into the wagon and, carefully stepping over slumbering forms, minced his way to where Dunleavy was lying on his back, fully clothed, snoring heavily. Water dripped steadily from a leak in the roof, a foot from Dunleavy's blubbery head. Carefully Jerome reached toward the lower left waistcoat pocket where Dunleavy kept the key to the box. The waistcoat was tight against Dunleavy's ample stomach. Jerome knew that if he stuffed his fingers into the pocket to reach the key, he would waken the showman.

Instead, he reached lower and, not too carefully, unbuttoned the fly on Dunleavy's pants. He opened the flap and grasped Dunleavy's genitals roughly with his right hand. At precisely the same moment, his left darted into the waistcoat pocket and snatched out the key. Lady had taught him well the art of the diversionary tactic.

Dunleavy half woke, spluttered, blinked at Richard and reached for his own opened fly.

45

"No, no," he muttered, "not now, lad. . . . Sleepy. . . . Go sleep. . . ." and his thick lips fluttered as he began to snort and snore again.

Jerome climbed back out to the seat and opened the box. He found six one-pound notes, twenty-two guineas, and ten shillings. He pocketed these, leaped down from the wagon and sloshed his way through the mud, east into the rising sun. He knew the company itinerary would take it westward. He hoped the sun would become strong enough to dry his soaking, mud-spattered clothes.

He was tired, and his head, his heart and his entire body ached but he did not cry. He slogged doggedly through the muck and began to sing a doleful ballad, one of Lady's favorite songs. He made his way to Bristol, and there succeeded in joining a quite reputable summer company of players.

Gwendolyn Durant, the leading lady of the Company, and wife of Horace Durant, leading man and proprietor, took Jerome as her lover. She was a beautiful, voluptuous woman of thirty. She taught Wrexham much about lovemaking, and only a little about acting, since she was not too proficient a thespian herself. Gilbert Weston discovered Wrexham at Bristol one summer two years later, when Jerome was eighteen. He immediately hired the handsome young actor-singer for the Lincoln's Inn Fields Theatre.

Jerome Wrexham had been used in many ways by many people since his mother left him for life with the Welsh ironmonger. He in turn had used many others. He planned and he schemed. He worked hard. He played and loved hard. When and where necessary—and sometimes when it was not necessary, but for the simple pleasure of it—he manipulated, lied and even stole money. He gambled frequently, and was generally lucky. He learned aristocratic modes and manners by carefully studying the gentry, and making and fostering their acquaintances at every opportunity. He did whatever he had to do without compunction. During his three years with Dunleavy, he had left at least four pregnant and heartbroken young girls, whose names he no longer remembered, in villages whose names he had never learned.

By the time he came to the Lincoln's Inn Fields in London he was a capable and calculating lover, and had exercised his erotic techniques on literally scores of females (including one named Gwendolyn), ranging from ten to forty-six, and five or six men, most of them a good deal older than himself.

In short, he stopped at nothing to further his career, but in the final analysis, the reason for his success was his talent. He had a beautiful God-given voice, soprano in his earlier years, gradually changing to a moving tenor, and finally settling into a rich baritone, although he could sing notes spanning a full three octaves.

He not only sang beautifully, but he learned to use his voice in reading his dramatic sides with the highly effective musical cadence that only the finest actors of the day could manage. The voice in this period of the drama in England was the primary weapon of the actor, for the style was basically declamatory, with little use made of the body or the face.

Now, standing inside the doors of the banquet hall of Lady Gertrude's unique establishment, elegantly attired, vibrant with youth and self-confidence, Wrexham paused to treat himself to a pinch of snuff from the intricately scrolled silver box Lady Gertrude herself had given him on his twenty-fifth birthday. He surveyed the tasteful room. To Wrexham it was a feast for all the senses. Mortlake landscape tapestries hung at appropriate intervals around the room, set off strikingly by exquisite Grinling Gibbons metal and wood carvings of birds, flowers and foliage. Very few of even the finest noble houses of London contained the delicate Gibbons works. Forty-eight long, expensive candles in silver chandeliers cast an even, steady glow over the entire room.

Two dozen tables, some small enough to seat two, some four, some six or eight, and several for parties of a dozen or more, were attractively placed around the room. Each had richly embroidered damask tablecloths, and each table held one or more cut-glass vases, filled with red, yellow and white roses.

Even now, at a little before midnight, half the tables were occupied, primarily by groups, pairs or foursomes of fashionably dressed, distinguished men, the majority of middle age. They were eating, drinking and conversing with spirit. Wrexham recognized one of the members of the newly formed Whig Council in a party of six. At two of the smaller tables, aristocratic younger men dined with attractive, elaborately coiffed, richly gowned women. Wrexham nodded to one with a high, powdered wig. She

47

was a courtesan with whom he had consorted for a brief time.

He strode toward the first of a series of long, damask-covered tables along the east wall of the room. He never tired of this eccentric mini-parade he made each time before he supped at Lady Gertrude's. The colorful appearance of the perfectly prepared and displayed edibles, and the medley of tantalizing aromas gave him a sensual pleasure. Subconsciously he was attempting to reassure himself that those desperate days, when his mother had left him, would never recur. Never again did he wish to feel those gnawing pangs of hunger tearing at his stomach. Never again did he wish to be reduced to picking bones, with tattered pieces of dried meat clinging to them, out of mounds of garbage in the streets.

At the first table, steam seeped out between the lids and the sterling silver bowls, which held hot soups and broths, turtle and chicken, beef and vegetable. On the next table, there were enormous platters of roast beef, crisp and brown on the outer edges, and oozing pink at the center. This same table contained steaks ready to be broiled to order; all manner of hams, not only pig hams, but veal, mutton and beef hams, and the highly favored Westphalian ham. There were also liver and kidney and chitterlings and bacon. All the delicacies were attractively displayed, with watercress, parsley and other greenery setting off the platters.

Wrexham's mouth watered. He strolled on to the next table, which offered seafood of every variety. There were potted lamprey and potted char from the sea, and trout and salmon from the lakes and streams. They were prepared in various ways, fried or broiled, poached or marinated. And there were lobsters and clams, and the less-favored oysters. And all were available with any of a dozen or more luscious sauces.

Making mental note of the epicurean delights he would order from each of the tables, Wrexham took a kerchief from his sleeve and wiped the saliva from the edge of his lips, as he walked to the table featuring fowl. Here were not only chicken, but partridge and pheasant, and several platters of swan, all with stuffings of sausage, chestnut, raisin or mince. A fleeting recollection of the difficulty he had, plucking his first stolen chicken, while traveling with Dunleavy, flashed through his mind.

Wrexham hastened his stride as he went by the last

table, which offered puddings and trifles and many varieties of cakes and sweets. On this same table were tall and graceful sterling silver pots of coffee, tea and hot chocolate, with smaller silver pitchers of rich cream, and bowls of crystal white sugar.

Behind each of the tables stood a male chef, immaculately clad in white blouse, trousers and full white apron. Flanking the chef were men and women assistants to slice, ladle or otherwise prepare the platters ordered. All these servants, and the waiters, were dressed in deep purple and gold-trimmed livery.

As he walked by the last of the tables, where Otto, the maitre d', awaited him with an unctuous smile, Wrexham saw Lady Gertrude herself with Edmund Fox, the Duke of Cheltenham, and Frederick Kingsley at the ornate bar across the room. The Duke hailed him with raised arm, and Wrexham strode across to the group.

"My dearest Lady Gertrude," Wrexham said, as he reached for the tall, stately woman's bejeweled hand, bowed and kissed it. He had mastered a technique for making the kissing of the hand seem a prolonged and meaningful act, without really lingering longer than the average gallant.

"*Liebchen*." Lady Gertrude nodded slightly.

She spoke only German. She was said to be a close relative of England's then-reigning monarch, King George I, who spoke no English either. George, who hailed from Hanover in Germany, of course, had ascended Britain's throne when the beloved Queen Anne died in 1714. He was the closest living Protestant male relative. George I had promptly organized a council of ministers, all from the Whig party, placed Sir Robert Walpole in charge, and with the newly established British parliamentary system taking hold, and the talents of competent interpreters, managed quite well.

No one was quite sure exactly what the relationship between the King and Gertrude was, but it was close and effective enough to enable the Lady to operate the most elaborate gaming establishment in the kingdom without interference from law enforcement officials of the kingdom or local police or courts. As a matter of fact, several members of the King's Council, as well as other members of the Court and numerous police magistrates, were regular patrons.

Wrexham nodded a greeting, in turn, to the Duke and

49

to Frederick Kingsley. Frederick was Lady Gertrude's interpreter and general manager of the establishment. He seemed to Wrexham a clean and refined reincarnation of Lady Fingers. He had the same narrow, hollow-eyed, sunken-cheeked head, but his shoulder-length black hair was sleek and shiny, his green eyes darker, and they held more of the spark of life.

Lady Gertrude was in her mid-thirties, and was *almost* one of the most beautiful women Wrexham had ever seen. Her elegantly coiffed brown hair topped a fair-skinned face with fascinating soft gray eyes and a cupid's-bow mouth. Her smooth neck sloped out to creamy white shoulders and a fine, high bosom. Her waist was narrow, and her hips magnificently rounded. In her light blue silken gown, cut low, and tightly belted with a deep blue sash, she made a breathtaking picture. Except for one blemish. Her nose.

It was as though her maker had put together this most exquisite of all female creatures, and then in an absent-minded or drunken moment, placed the wrong nose in the center of that otherwise perfect face. The nose was large and bulbous. The first time he saw her, Wrexham thought the nose would not even have looked too well on Clarence Dunleavy. But now he stared into Lady Gertrude's eyes and said with great feeling: "If I may be so bold as to say so, dearest lady, you look lovelier than ever tonight."

"Dankeschoen, Liebchen." Lady Gertrude curtsied slightly.

"We were just going to drink to the Duke's upcoming wedding," said Kingsley. "Will you join us, Wrexham?"

"I would be honored to be permitted to do so," said Wrexham, and ordered a brandy laced with port.

Frederick Kingsley lifted his glass, waited while Wrexham and Lady Gertrude did likewise.

"To two of the noblest people in the Kingdom. Long life and happiness."

"Hear! Hear!" said Wrexham.

"Prosit!"

The Duke nodded his thanks and they all drank.

Across the room, to the left of the wide-open doors leading into the gaming rooms proper, the four-man band on a small platform stage began to play. They were dressed in deep purple, gold-trimmed coats and loose, knee-length breeches, with yellow silk stockings and black high-heeled shoes with golden buckles. They wore identical powdered periwigs. The leader played the spinet; the other three, respectively, a flutelike hautboy, a bassoon, and a sackbut, an undersized trombone. They played softly and unobtrusively, with little accent or rhythm, since the music was intended merely as pleasant background for both the diners and the gamblers in the adjoining room.

Fox presently invited Wrexham to join him for dinner, and Lady Gertrude and Kingsley left to greet two new members of the King's Council, who had just come into the room.

"I'm most grateful to you for asking me to the reception, Edmund," said Wrexham, when the waiter had brought them a bottle of Burgundy and their Staffordshire bowls of turtle soup.

"Could hardly do without you, my boy," said the Duke. "After all, you're one of my brightest stars, and the only actor Sarah has ever loved—or even tolerated."

Wrexham looked into Edmund Fox's shrewd gray eyes and tried to read the expression on the strong, square-jawed face. On two different occasions Wrexham had wound up in the canopied bed of Lady Sarah Palfrey, soon to be the Duchess of Cheltenham.

Lady Sarah was a plain and frustrated woman in her mid-thirties, who had had precious little romance, let alone actual sexual activity in her life, and when Wrexham made love to her in his calculatedly passionate and highly expert way, she responded like a woman possessed. He was aware that she would have liked to continue their sexual relationship, but feared too greatly for her reputation to dare it. Now Wrexham wondered whether she had ever been foolish enough to confess her escapades to the Duke. Or whether he had learned of them from a gossiping servant.

"The Lady Sarah is a truly fine woman, sir," said Wrexham now, "and I'm sure you will both be very happy."

Fox smiled enigmatically. Sarah was his cousin, and they had known each other since earliest childhood. He had never been attracted to her, though he liked her well enough. The marriage, in his mind, was purely for the purpose of merging the wealth and power of two great families. He thought Sarah was more or less in love with him, but he considered that somewhat of an unavoidable

51

nuisance. She, too, realized, of course, that the marriage was a desirable one from a practical standpoint.

Edmund Fox, himself, had always had a mistress, usually a young actress, and although he was without one at the moment, he fully intended to acquire a new paramour soon, and to continue to support the most attractive and desirable mistresses he could find. He would be, as he had always been, discreet, and he saw no reason why such relationships should interfere with his and Sarah's ability to have a successful marriage and raise a family to continue the Fox and Palfrey lines of aristocracy.

7

When the waiter brought the fish course, and opened a bottle of chilled white wine, Wrexham decided to change the subject.

"Were you at the theater this evening, by any chance, sir?"

Fox sipped his wine.

"No, I've been rather busy."

"Well, there was not a space to be had in the boxes, the pit or either of the galleries, for the afterpiece. I sang four songs, and I must say, immodest as it may seem, that they were received with thunderous applause."

Fox smiled.

"I doubt it not, Jerry. You have a magnificent voice. I believe that was the reason Gilbert Weston brought you into our company."

Wrexham beamed, as he lifted a forkful of poached salmon to his mouth. It melted quickly, and he swallowed.

"That and, if I may say so, Edmund, my strong appeal to the ladies."

He sipped his wine.

"I'm reluctant to raise the subject, but I feel I must, sir. . . ." He hesitated, and the Duke stared at him questioningly.

"I'm convinced," said Wrexham, "that Weston is presenting far too much Shakespeare, and—"

"*Are* you?"

"Yes, and what's worse, in the heavy, unedited form the plays were written. No adaptation, no modernizing for the contemporary taste . . . no . . ."

"Business has been quite good, Jerry."

The Duke finished the last of the trout, stuffed with lobster, on his plate.

"Not on Mondays, Tuesdays or Wednesdays, sir." Wrexham signaled for the waiter to pour another glass of wine. "If we presented more of the Restoration plays, the wit, the sophisticated comedy, the bawdy jollity. More Congreve . . ."

"Weston believes interest in the Restoration plays is declining. There's a new audience. . . ."

"Ridiculous! Quite ridiculous!"

Wrexham did not wait for the waiter this time. He took the wine from the silver cooler and filled his glass.

"Isn't Gilbert planning to retire at the end of this season?" he asked boldly.

Fox smiled, shook his head.

"I think not, Jerry. I believe he has several good years left in him."

"He takes some unseemly risks," charged Wrexham, as the waiter removed their Wedgwood plates and replaced them with new dishes. Wrexham was having the roast beef rare—he had requested and received two huge slices, each an inch and a half thick. The Duke had pheasant.

The waiter opened a fresh bottle of wine, a Rhenish wine this time, a specialty of the house of Lady Gertrude.

The Duke sipped his wine, began to put it down, then sipped again.

"Excellent," he said. "Risks?"

"This very evening he had a young caitiff of a candle snuffer play Hamlet."

"A candle snuffer?"

"Young Steele, that clumsy lout who's been around the past several seasons."

"He played Hamlet?"

"Well, no. We did *Hamlet,* as you know. Steele played a messenger."

Edmund Fox smiled. For a talented, and in some ways quite bright man, Wrexham could be childishly naive and stupid, transparent and vicious. He had been hinting that he would like to become manager of the Lincoln's Inn Fields company for some time, but the Duke had never given him the slightest encouragement. He admired Wrexham's voice, and dramatic talent, but he considered the young actor to be irresponsible and of poor character.

Now he said, "Weston tells me that the boy is studying

with Farley Shannon, and that he and Shannon both believe young Steele will make a fine actor one day."

"He's fourteen years old. He destroyed the play this evening." Wrexham finished his first glass of the Rhenish wine and cut a large bite of the oozing beef with his fork.

"He's a manly fourteen," said the Duke, slicing the pheasant breast. "You were a boyish eighteen, when Weston gave you your opportunity, Jerry."

"I'd been on the stage since I was twelve."

The Duke smiled again. He knew of banditti troupes and their child actors.

Wrexham finished his wine, and the waiter refilled his glass. In a single draft he nearly emptied it again.

"He couldn't remember his simple lines. And when the prompter fed him, he stammered and stuttered all over the stage."

The Duke chuckled softly. He had seen other young actors suffer stage fright.

Wrexham continued, unrelentingly.

"I thought the rubbish from the gallery would blind us. It took me my next two speeches to subdue them."

When Fox continued to eat his pheasant without comment, Wrexham said, "A good manager does not take risks of that kind. . . ."

The Duke interrupted. "Jerry, you are so valuable to the Lincoln's Inn Fields company as its most gifted singer and dramatic player that I would feel it a truly insane risk to dilute your magnificent onstage presence by burdening you with the dull additional duties of manager."

Wrexham beamed and hung his head in mock modesty.

"Thank you, sir. You overestimate my gifts. But I'm sure I could handle the management of the company and continue my superlative performances at the same time."

"We just cannot risk it, dear boy," said the Duke, and raised his glass.

"To England's premier leading man!"

Once again Wrexham failed to bring off a blush. He raised his glass and drank the toast.

Their sumptuous dinner completed, the Duke said, "Would you care to play an hour or so of loo, my boy?"

Wrexham agreed with enthusiasm. He had been running in excellent luck lately. They adjourned to the gaming room. Here the decor was designed to stimulate and excite. Bright-striped chintz in primary colors hung at the massive arched windows. The finest India paper, affixed to canvas hangings rather than pasted directly upon the walls, displayed birds and flowers of brilliant hue. More than a dozen chandeliers holding scores of glimmering candles were precisely positioned to light the playing surfaces of the three rouge et noir wheels, the hazard tables, the faro counters and the individual card tables around the room.

Fashionably dressed players clustered about each of the rouge et noir wheels and watched the dice roll at the hazard tables. Oddly enough, the faro counters were deserted, and bored operators stared blankly ahead, or idly shuffled and reshuffled their cards. At one table, two elderly gentlemen played whist, a game which had come to be considered old-fashioned and tame, suited only for parsons. At other tables, groups of gentlemen and a sparse number of elegantly gowned ladies played various card games: piquet, basset, omber and loo, or lanterloo as it was more formally titled.

Attractive youthful barmaids, some blond, some auburn-tressed, some dark-haired, but all comely and adequately bosomed, circulated constantly among the players. The young ladies all wore extremely low-cut bodices of bright yellow, and skirts of deep purple. There was a constant, tense, though not unpleasant murmur of voices mixed with the strains of music coming from the dining room. The murmur was occasionally punctuated by the yelp of a loser, or the gleeful cry of an uninhibited winner.

The Duke and Wrexham walked to a loo table, where six men were playing. The table was round, with grooves at its outer edge. The grooves before each player held a supply of counters in the form of little fishes made of mother-of-pearl. The grooves that held the counters were called "fish ponds."

"Ah! Edmund!" exclaimed a tall, gaunt man with a powdered wig, a hooked nose and sharp dark eyes. He rose from his chair.

"You know these gentlemen!" the tall man said, and Edmund Fox nodded greetings to each, then said, "Permit me to introduce my young friend, Jerome Wrexham."

Five of the six men at the table rose.

The tall, gaunt man was Reginald Twombley, an earl. Another, a short, stout, red-faced man with beady black eyes, was the Honorable Arnold P. Prigmore, a local police magistrate. A third, distinguished-looking gentleman was the newest member of the King's Council, and the two others, Shanley and Ackers, were partners in a ship-building company.

The sixth man, who was the operator, the dealer for the house, retained his seat, and shuffled the cards silently while the introductions were being made. At Twombley's invitation, the Duke and Wrexham joined the game. Each purchased twenty fish, each fish representing a guinea from the dealer. The group was playing five-card, un-limited loo.

The pool, the total amount bet in the last round, had been completely cleared. Each of the five players had won one trick, and therefore each had taken one-fifth of the fishes in the pool. Now Wrexham and the Duke each put one fish in the pool along with the five other players.

The house's operator dealt the cards. Wrexham picked up five low, unmatched cards and chose not to "stand in," not to play the round. Prigmore also decided not to stand in, which left five players. The Duke led the play by plac-ing the king of spades face-up on the table. Ackers beat him, and won the trick with an ace of spades. Ackers won three tricks in the round; his partner won another; and the Earl won the fifth by playing the pam, the knave of clubs, which was the only wild card in the game, to top Ackers' king of hearts.

The operator took the house's share out of the pool, dropped the fish into a cloth-lined chest on a small table at his side, and divided the remaining fish among the win-ners, proportionate to the number of tricks each had won. The new member of the King's Council, whose name was Landers, and the Duke, of the five players who had stood in, had not won a single trick, which meant they had been looed.

"Fourteen, sir," said the dealer to the Duke. He shuf-fled the cards dextrously, and repeated, "Fourteen, sir," this time addressing Landers. The penalty for being looed in the unlimited game was to put in double the amount of the total pool. The Duke counted out fourteen fish (dou-ble the seven in the original pool) and placed them in the center of the table. Councilman Landers did likewise. Each of the five other players now put in a single addi-tional fish. The pool, thus, now amounted to thirty-three fish, thirty-three guineas.

"Thirty-three," announced the dealer quietly, and dealt the cards.

As the game progressed, and the price of being looed became more and more prohibitive, the seven men began to play increasingly conservatively. Wrexham, who was a venturesome man in many matters, played most conservatively of all. Round after round he chose not to stand in, and therefore lost only the single fish he was required to put into each pool.

A comely red-haired barmaid visited the loo table regularly, and each time she came, Wrexham ordered a brandy laced with port. The port tended to make the combination more potent. Approximately once to every four or five drinks Wrexham ordered, the Duke requested a brandy laced with claret. The claret softened the effects of the brandy. The Earl drank white wine infrequently during the game, while Prigmore, the police magistrate, and the shipbuilding partners drank not at all. The brandy and port did not seem to affect Wrexham's play in the slightest degree.

At one point, after some forty minutes of play, there were a hundred and eighty fish in the pool. Wrexham picked up his cards, one by one, as they were dealt to him. Ace of spades, ace of clubs, king of diamonds, king of clubs, ace of hearts. Only three of the other players stood in, and Wrexham won four of the five tricks. His king of diamonds was beaten by the Duke's ace. The dealer counted off the house's percentage and pushed the rest of the fish to Wrexham. Again two of the players, Ackers and the police magistrate, Prigmore, this time had been looed and had to double the large previous pool.

Some fifteen minutes later, the group agreed to play a final round. The pool was up to three hundred and twenty-two fish. Again Wrexham looked at his cards, one by one, as they were dealt to him. Three of hearts, eight of hearts, queen of hearts, six of hearts, and . . . the *pam*, the knave of clubs, the wild card!

A flush!

In loo, a flush, even though made with the pam, won everything. The player had merely to show his hand and take the pool.

Wrexham had all he could do to keep from leaping to his feet and screaming with joy. With a great effort he restrained himself. At his left, Prigmore threw his hand onto the table, choosing not to stand in. The five remaining players between Prigmore and Wrexham stood in.

Concealing his elation, forcing himself to be calm,

Wrexham pulled the three of hearts out of his left hand and placed it face-up on the table with a sweeping, exaggerated motion. He repeated the movement and showed the eight, then the next two cards.

"Plus the pam, gentlemen!" he announced dramatically, as he lay down the knave of clubs. The dealer's face was expressionless as he counted off the house's percentage, and left the substantial balance of the mother-of-pearl tokens for Wrexham to sweep in.

The shipbuilders were somewhat irritated with Wrexhams theatrics, and rose from the table grumpily. But the Duke, the member of the Council and the police magistrate took it with good grace.

"Congratulations, Jerry," said the Duke. "A most enjoyable evening."

The Duke and the other players left, but Wrexham decided to try his luck with the dice at hazard. In the next hour he lost half of the eighteen hundred and sixty guineas he had won at loo. The redheaded barmaid who had served him all evening approached him again. He gazed at the creamy swell of her bosom, popping out of her bodice, and decided to go to Mother Magruder's. With a flourish, he gave the barmaid a one-pound note. She curtsied politely, though she felt the amount niggardly in the light of the service and free drinks she had given him, and the large amount she knew he had won. He slapped her bottom playfully as she left.

8

Mother Magruder's was not the most elegant of the two thousand brothels in London city, nor was it the lowliest. It occupied both floors of an ancient two-story building near the Lincoln's Inn Fields Theatre. All of its dozen ladies were either mulatto or full-blooded Negroes, and in this, it was unique. Mother herself was a light-skinned mulatto who weighed close to twenty-five stone and was a gargantuan bawd. She looked even heavier, since this large weight was distributed over a body which stood barely two inches over five feet tall.

She wore an orange-colored wig, which once might have been auburn, and which consisted mainly of a cascade of curls hanging down over her elephantine shoulders. The curls framed her bloated, merry face. She had small, twinkling sky-blue eyes and a buttonlike nose, surrounded by twin balloon cheeks. Her three chins rested on the cleavage of an immense bosom. When the black manservant showed Wrexham into her warmly lit sitting room, she struggled to her feet, waddled toward the actor with surprising agility, and encased him in her pneumatic arms. She pulled his head down with her pudgy hand and kissed him wetly on the cheek.

"Jerry, the Rex!" she chirped gleefully. She had a small, thin voice. She stood back, slightly out of breath, with her hands on her hips.

"And how is the most handsome actor in all the kingdom this fine night?"

Wrexham grinned at her, as she ordered the manservant to bring in a decanter of brandy and port and went back to her oversized lounge chair. She waved Wrexham

60

to a chair alongside her, and reached into a glass jar of sugar candies on a table between them. She stuffed a large pink sugar ball into her mouth, and sucked loudly.

There was no overhead lighting in Mother Magruder's house. Attractive pewter candelabra were placed strategically to give the room a comfortable, soft glow. It was not a large room, but all of the furniture was expensively made, with the emphasis on warm colors and comfort.

"And how have you been, dear Mother?" asked Wrexham, as the manservant poured his brandy and laced it with a touch of the dark port.

"You have a nose for the extraordinary, my lad," said the bawd. She raised a sausagelike index finger to her middle chin. "Let me see, it's been eight days since you visited us last, has it not?"

"More or less." Wrexham drank his brandy and port.

"Well, this morning, Henry delivered the most special young lady we have ever had in this house."

Henry Skiffington Magruder was Mother's husband. He was an actor, who worked on the stage in Jamaica, a Caucasian, no taller than his wife, but thin as a Maypole. He imported the mulatto and black prostitutes to Mother Magruder's on the irregular visits he made from Jamaica. He auditioned each of them personally before purchasing them, or making other arrangements for their employment with Mother. She considered her husband the ultimate connoisseur when it came to the quality of whores.

Wrexham poured himself another brandy and port. His expression showed his keen interest in Mother's words. Mother helped herself to another sugar ball, a yellow one this time. She pursed her lips as she sucked for a moment, then, like an obese squirrel, she tucked the ball into one of her fat cheeks. Her speech was slightly distorted by the candy.

"A nubian beauty. A dweam fwum deepest Afwica."

Impatient with the way the sugar ball interfered with her pronunciation, she crunched it noisily and swallowed.

"And mistress of the technique of love of all the ages!" she announced as dramatically as her thin voice would permit.

Wrexham smiled.

"Henry must have written that for you. Or stolen it from a play, Mother. And how many eons did it take this beauty to learn these arts?"

"She gets about without crutches." Mother laughed. She rang a small bell on the table between them, and the manservant reappeared.

"Samuel, ask Miss Clara to come down, please."

In ten minutes light footsteps sounded on the carpeted stairs from the upper floor. Until she came into the light of the room itself, Wrexham could not see the girl too clearly. She was almost as tall as Wrexham's six feet. Her skin was the color of blackberries, rich indigo-tinted ebony. The glow of the candelabra struck fascinating highlights on the left side of the face. Her nose was straight and slightly large, and she had full, moist Negroid lips of burgundy hue.

Her eyes were almost perfect circles, with black, shining pupils centered in the milky white. There was a regal contour to her skull. She had a high forehead, and her thick, black hair was tightly braided and piled in circles on top of her head like a crown.

There was something catlike about her walk as she came toward Wrexham. On her face was a smile, somehow tantalizing, yet childlike. She ran her pink tongue across her upper lip. Wrexham had visited Mother Magruder's on several scores of occasions, and a dozen or more other bordellos of lower and higher quality, but never had he had a reaction to a prostitute such as he experienced at this moment to Clara. He wondered if it could be the brandy and port.

He tore his gaze away from her face, and ran his eyes down her slender ebony throat and body. She was wearing a brilliant crimson robe of silk. A portion of her upper chest, and flashing glimpses of her smooth legs and taut thighs were revealed as she walked toward him. Her breasts held the crimson silk away from her shoulders. The erect nipples showed clearly. A black silk belt held the robe closed around the smallest waist Wrexham had ever seen on an adult. From the tiny waist, the crimson silk flowed over lush, rounded hips.

Mother Magruder smiled as she watched Wrexham's reaction to the new girl.

"Clara," she said, "this is Mr. Jerome Wrexham. The 'Rex' is for 'King of the Theater.' Mr. Wrexham is London's finest actor."

Clara stood before him now.

"And perhops, the mos' han'some, too."

She had a soft voice and spoke languidly with a Jamaican accent.

Mother waved her to a chair alongside Wrexham. She leaned back in the chair, and the robe fell away from her thighs and legs. The candle glow highlighted the glistening blackberry limbs with golden accents. Unhurriedly, Clara pulled the robe closed. Sam brought the prostitute a glass of milk, and refilled Wrexham's glass with brandy and port. Mother took another yellow sugar ball.

"I like actors." Clara sipped her milk, licked the white line from her full lips.

"I like women who look like Cleopatra," said Wrexham, lifting his glass in a toast.

Wrexham admired the rounded, undulating crimson behind as Clara preceded him up the stairs to her apartment. All the whores' apartments at Mother Magruder's were small, but furnished precisely to serve their functions, and kept spotlessly clean. Clara opened the door for Wrexham, stood aside, then followed him in and closed the door.

There was a faint odor of a light perfume in the air. Wrexham looked around at the familiar surroundings, and felt a stirring in his groin. A large bed, with a white silk spread, white silk sheets and pillows dominated the room. On each side of the bed were small tables, and on these were pewter candelabra, each holding three candles. Their light tended to diffuse the moonglow slanting in through the single window.

Directly opposite the foot of the bed were a long dressing table with a white silk pleated skirt, and a stool with a white silk cushion and a veined-marble top. A candelabrum with six candles stood on the table, and almost two dozen colored-glass bottles, vials and jars, containing powders, perfumes, lotions and ointments covered its surface.

Fastened to the table was a large mirror, directly facing the foot of the bed. The mirror had two wings, so that a person using it could get a head-on, as well as a left and right profile view. Wrexham had always enjoyed watching himself and his partner in this three-way perspective. From the distance of the bed to the mirror, it gave him the feeling of participating in an orgy . . . an orgy in which three muscularly handsome men, who looked exactly like him, were displaying their sexual prowess.

Across the room from the window there was a dresser with a large basin of clean water, and dozens of cloths on its top. Alongside the dresser was an open closet with numerous gowns and robes of various bright colors and materials. Several leather belts, leather-thong whips and two link chains hung from hooks at one end.

"Sit yourself on my bed, if you please, King Rex." Clara smiled. Wrexham did, and she knelt before him and slipped off his silver-buckled shoes, then his stockings. A bit of dried mud from Wrexham's shoes soiled her hands. She rose, walked to the basin, and washed and dried them. Wrexham stood and removed his velvet coat. As he tossed it onto a chair, she came back to him and began to unbutton his shirt. When it was opened almost down to his waist, she paused and ran smooth hands over the golden hair on his chest.

Her motions were unhurried and sensual. She slipped the shirt off his shoulders. He moved his arms to make it easier for her to remove it completely. She tossed it lightly onto the chair, and again ran her hands tantalizingly across his chest, down his rib cage to his flat stomach.

"Lovely, lovely mon," she murmured. Her breath was warm and sweet. Her fingertips met at his navel. His erection was trapped in the tightness of his breeches. She unbuttoned the fly, and knelt before him again to slide his breeches down his hard, muscular thighs. The erection snapped free, proud and rigid. She cupped his testicles in her hands.

"Lovely, lovely mon," she said again, and kissed the deep pink head of his erection.

He could stand it no more. He stepped out of his breeches, grasped her shoulders, pulled her roughly to her feet. He whipped the belt away from the robe, slid it off her shoulders and down her sinuous body, and pulled her tightly to him. He kissed her hot, open mouth. Her fingers dug fiercely into his back. He was hard and burning, against her stomach, and he grasped her buttocks and made the slightest lifting motion.

She clasped her hands together firmly behind his neck, rose on her toes and, seemingly without effort, locked her legs around his waist. Miraculously, he was inside her, fevered and ramrod stiff. She held tightly against his broad back, and kept her mouth joined to his, her tongue darting in, out, and around his. Her breasts were crushed against his upper chest.

Still holding her buttocks, he caressed them firmly, in time to her own movements as she lifted and lowered herself on his firm, swollen shaft, all the while swiveling her hips sinuously. His penetration went deep into the tight moistness of her. Her internal liquid fires burned him, and he wanted to scream, but his busy tongue would not be interrupted. His strong fingers dug hard into her wildly moving buttocks.

Out of breath, she moved her mouth away from his, and up to his ear. She nibbled at his ear, then bit hard, almost drawing blood from the fleshy lobe. She increased the tempo of her ride of passion. Their bodies were perspiring now, and her hands began to slip on his back. He moved his left hand to the cleavage between her buttocks, and his fingers played as he lifted her. With his right hand, he took her left breast. He moved his head so that he had the hard, protruding nipple of the firm breast in his mouth. He sucked hard, then bit savagely.

Clara screamed, and he bit again, and she screamed once more. He stopped biting, and tasted blood, as he continued to suck hard on the wounded breast. The pain seemed to add fuel to Clara's fires. In a frenzy, now, she clawed and scratched Wrexham's back. She tightened the grip of her strong legs around his waist till his ribs began to ache, and she slid up and down upon his seared erection at so fierce a tempo that he actually grunted each time their groins met.

Wrexham's eyes closed in ecstatic agony. He moved his head and captured her right breast in his mouth. Again he sucked hard on the extended nipple, but just as he was about to bite, Clara grabbed his hair in both her hands and pulled his head backward. At that precise split second, she stopped her wild riding, pressed her vaginal area hard against him and made continuous, unrelenting, grinding movements against him.

His temples throbbed, as though the veins might burst. At his groin there was an eruption, which seemed to send bubbling blood coursing upward through his body, into the vessels of his head. It ran downward, too. His knees weakened, and there was an ache in his calves. Clara resumed her sensuous movements and continued them as though she never intended to stop. Then suddenly, frantically, she pulled her mouth away from his. She gasped, uttered a brief moan, then kissed his cheeks, his eyes, his nose, his forehead . . . and finally found his mouth and crushed her own against it, clinging to him, quivering.

Her damp, glistening thighs slid down his, as he softened in her. She released her hold on him, and he sat heavily on the edge of the bed. He looked toward the mirror on the dressing table, and realized he had not once gazed in that direction while they were making love. He felt slightly dizzy from the brandy and port, and from his sexual exertions.

Clara went to the dressing table, took several cloths, and poured a clear liquid from one of the bottles over them. Walking back toward the bed, she dabbed one of the cloths against the beads of blood popping around the nipple of her left breast. Still patting her own breast, she tilted Wrexham's head forward, bent over and wiped the second cloth against the thin streaks of blood criss-crossing his back.

Wrexham was breathing heavily.

Clara said, "You are one fine lovermon, King Rex." She patted the new beads of blood on her breast, and at the same time wiped Wrexham's back.

"Maybe you bite too hard, but good."

Wrexham lay back on the bed, exhausted.

"You are most proficient yourself, Cleopatra. Where did you learn to make love like that?"

His first impression had been that she was probably sixteen years old, but now, having seen her naked and experienced her actions and reactions, he was quite sure she was younger, possibly twelve or thirteen.

She walked to the dressing table, rinsed the pinkened cloths and applied more medication.

"Some things my brother teach me. Some, other mons. Most, I just know. I like de lovemakin', even de hurtin'."

She came back to the bed, knelt beside it and washed Wrexham's genital area. He closed his eyes. He was suddenly very sleepy.

" 'Specially," she said, "with fine, han'some mon like Rex King."

Wrexham kept his eyes closed. The roast beef, the fish, the brandy and port were souring in his stomach. He began to breathe heavily and evenly. He did not see Clara go back to the dressing table. She poured a thick golden oil into a fine china cup, and held the cup over the flame of a candle for several moments. She put a finger in the cup to test the heat of the oil, then came back to the bed. Wrexham was on his back, arms raised over his head, legs spread and straight out in front of him. He was snoring gently.

66

Clara poured a bit of the warm oil into the palm of her left hand, and began to stroke Wrexham's limp organ slowly, gently. After a moment he stopped snoring, and sleepily opened his eyes. Clara continued to stroke him, and in less than three minutes he was erect again. His stomach rumbled, but he ignored its queasiness. Still he did not move. Clara stopped stroking him. He lay there and watched her raise the cup to her lips, and take a mouthful of the oil. She did not swallow. She climbed onto the bed, knelt between his legs, slid her hands beneath his buttocks and took him in her mouth. The warm oil ran slowly down his stiff member, as her head moved up and down, her tongue working artfully. Wrexham found the suction she created exquisitely maddening.

Leaning on his elbows, he raised his head and upper body to look over the sleek incline of her glistening blackberry back and rump into the mirror. The sight of the three magnificently rounded ebony bottoms, the beautiful columns of the six blackberry thighs with the black-haired bush at the peak of their Vs; even the pink-tinged black of the soles of the six feet, all highlighted by golden candle glow, was a work of erotic art in Wrexham's eyes. An aroma of perspiration and perfume wafted up to his nostrils.

When he saw his own chest and shoulders, the tortured ecstasy on his face, his flowing golden hair reflected three times above the shining blackberry bottom, something snapped in his dully aching head.

He saw the madness in the eyes of the three Wrexhams staring at him from the mirrors. Still leaning on his left elbow, he reached out with his right and grabbed a strong handful of the neatly braided raven crown on Clara's head. He pulled viciously, so that she was not only torn away from his glistening, glowing erection, but also spun, halfway around on her knees. She cried out, groaned, then whimpered in fear. He squirmed off his back, onto his knees, still hanging onto her crown of hair.

He released his hold on her hair, and nimbly reached forward to grab her by her waist, just above the hips, and turned her viciously so that she was now facing the mirror just as he was. And her beautiful, blackberry bottom was there before him. His organ had stiffened even more. It pulsated, and its inflammation seemed to run to his brain. He positioned himself directly behind her,

67

moved closer and drove himself into her in one savage thrust.

She gasped in tortured ecstasy, lowered her head with the pain, as he crushed her waist, pulling her to him, as he drove, harder and harder into and out of her. She looked up, eyes closed, rolling her head with his movements. He released her hips, reached forward and grabbed several strands of the now-loosened black braids of her hair and pulled on them, as a rider might on the reins of a horse.

He watched the three wild-eyed, handsome Wrexhams in the mirror, as they held the reins on these three magnificent ebony mares, and rode forward into the chase.

"Tally-ho!" he cried, releasing the rein in his right hand and raising it triumphantly. The other three Wrexhams did likewise.

He had no idea why or how this strange phrase leaped to his lips. Perhaps it was the combined effect of the alcohol and the now-steaming room. He had only heard the phrase once before in his life, during the past summer, while participating in a new sport of the aristocracy, called "riding to the hounds." It was actually a fox hunt and he had ridden in it, at the Duke's country estate.

Then, when the glorious eruption exploded in his groin, he fell forward onto the sleek black back of Clara. She lay on her stomach with him on top of her. He rolled over and away from her, and was almost instantly asleep. He began to snore, a loud, consistent, burring sound.

Clara's cheeks were wet with tears. But she did not look unhappy. She smiled indulgently at the sweating, snoring man, and went to the basin and washed herself. Then she went to the bed, and lay down beside him. She lay with her head on the pillow, while his head was down at the foot of the bed.

Just before dawn, she awoke, and decided to wake him. She brought her knees up to the head of the bed, then snuggled against his back. She reached around him with her left hand, and began to fondle his genitals. He grunted and groaned, but would not awaken. She continued to play with him. Finally he sat up, weary and grumbling. He turned her back toward him, put his left foot into the arch of her back, and kicked her out of the bed so viciously she landed three feet away on the floor.

He fell face down on the bed and was asleep immediately, again snoring loudly.

It was noon when he awoke. It felt as if an army were hammering nails into every inch of the inside of his head. His eyeballs itched. The interior of his mouth, and his tongue, felt as though they had been coated with cow dung. Cleopatra was not in the room. He washed, combed his hair, dressed and went downstairs. Mother Magruder, Cleopatra and three of the other whores were having their noonday meal. Wrexham winced as he saw the mountain of fatty pork in thick, greasy gravy and potatoes and turnips on Mother Magruder's platter.

She rose when Wrexham came in and, seeing his expression, said, "And that's my second helping, lad. A hard-working woman needs her nourishment."

As Mother walked with him into the sitting room, on the way out Wrexham turned back and said to Cleopatra, "You were quite satisfactory, Cleopatra."

The regal-looking girl's black eyes twinkled and she smiled.

"My back it is aching, but come again soon, Rex King," she said.

At the door, Wrexham took out his leather coin pouch, and looked at Mother questioningly.

"Twenty-five guineas will do it, Jerry." She held out a pudgy hand.

"Gad! I can spend a night with a West End courtesan for that!" Wrexham protested.

"Fifty is what they get, and I should charge *you* that. Clara won't be able to work for a couple of days."

"Cleopatra," said Wrexham, counting twenty-five guineas into her hand. "You can't go about charging West End prices for a whore named Clara."

She pulled his head down and kissed him wetly on the cheek.

Wrexham winced.

"Handle the head gently, please," he said.

He walked the few blocks to the Inn of the King's Men with a pained expression on his face. He grimaced at every sound he heard in the busy streets. Voices of people talking in conversational tones were irritants; the dull thumping of horses hooves, the creaking of carriage or cartwheels were agony; the barking of a dog, the shouting of a fishmonger, torture.

It was really all Felicia's fault. If she had not broken

her engagement with him for that doltish candle snuffer Steele, he would not have gone to Lady Gertrude's; he would not have eaten so much, nor drunk so much brandy and port. And he would not have caroused half the night at Mother Magruder's. He managed a grin when he thought of Cleopatra. It wasn't that she was a better lover than Felicia—Felicia was quite magnificent. It was just that she was different—less refined, more animal. Felicia would never permit some of the things he did, and others he planned to do to Cleopatra.

His fleeting moment of recollected pleasure ended abruptly when he opened the door of the Inn and saw Polly Heffelfinger and Banger Shaw. Polly was the one with the beaklike nose. Wrexham knew them well. They were dunners for Lancelot Higginbotham. And it had been nine weeks since Wrexham had lost a hundred and thirty guineas betting with the sporting promoter and bookmaker, Higginbotham, at the cockfights, and had not paid the debt.

9

Polly Heffelfinger saw Wrexham as soon as the actor opened the door.

"There 'e is! Jerry! . . . Wrexham! . . . 'Ere. Get over 'ere!" he bellowed across the room.

Wrexham did not think they would assault him right here in the Inn, nor that they had any intention of assaulting him at all. He did know that Lancelot Higginbotham liked to be paid within a fortnight, and he did know that Polly and Banger were inclined toward violence at small provocation or for a small fee. He waved at the dunners, now, and made his way around some tables, across the room, but did not go to the dunners' table, but to one adjoining it, occupied by Gilbert Weston and his fellow actors.

"I'll join you in a moment, gentlemen." He bowed to Polly, then with great animation addressed the Lincoln's Inn Fields Theatre manager.

"Gilbert, I dined last evening at Lady Gertrude's with the Duke and several members of the King's Council. Told them what a magnificent job you were doing, producing the Shakespeare series."

"Thank you, Jerry," nodded Weston.

Feeling more in control of himself now, Wrexham took one more moment to stall his meeting with the dunners.

Turning to Heffelfinger, he said, "Polly, Banger, permit me to present my colleagues."

And he made a slow, lengthy ceremony of the introduction of the actors to the dunners. Polly Heffelfinger, who had stood for the exchange, now pushed Wrexham into a chair between himself and Shaw. Richard walked by, and Wrexham grabbed him by the sleeve.

"Muh—muh—my guh—good luh, luh—lad," he stuttered loudly, "fuh—fuh—fetch these gentle—gen—gentle—gen, these noble men another drink, and buh—buh—buh—buh—bring me a fuh—fuh French—buh—buh—brandy punch!"

The dunners looked baffled. Several of the actors with Weston laughed loudly. Other patrons seemed puzzled, but then most began to titter, and soon almost everyone in the Inn was laughing. Except Weston and the Pickerings.

Weston frowned disapprovingly, said quietly, "That is hardly humorous, Wrexham."

Ben Pickering, at the bar, scowled at Wrexham. Bessie and Tillie paused in their work, shook their heads in sympathy with the blushing and embarrassed Richard. Red-faced, Richard bumped into a patron's chair on the way to the bar, then into another. Mumbling apologies, he reached the bar, where Pickering was already filling Wrexham's order.

"Ignore the fool!" Pickering said.

At his table, Wrexham was explaining to the dunners the basis for his humor: Richard's unfortunate experience of the previous evening.

Shaw interrupted him.

"It's not that 'Igginbotham don't trust you, Jerry—"

Heffelfinger cut in.

" 'E wouldn't even mind waitin' for 'is money most times. It's only that 'e 'as this chance to buy this 'ere 'orse. A real winner, the mare is. And ol' Lancelot needs every pound 'e can lay 'is hands on."

Wrexham held up his hand.

"Say no more, my friend."

With a flourish he counted out the money he owed Higginbotham and pushed it across the table to Heffelfinger.

"Would have paid it long ago, but I've been rather busy. Been spending weekends riding to the hounds with the Duke of Cheltenham and his friends, and . . ."

"What 'ounds?" asked Polly.

"New sport the gentry pursues. Just a fox hunt, in fact. . . . Then I've been rehearsing my important roles in the new Shakespeare series we are presenting, and . . ."

72

Richard came with the drinks and placed them before the three. Gilbert Weston beckoned to him from the adjoining table.

"Wrexham's just an insensitive boor, Richard," he said. "Pay him no heed."

He said this loudly enough for Wrexham to hear, but the handsome actor was so engrossed in his own conversation, he missed the insult. Weston ordered another round of drinks for himself and his group.

Heffelfinger took a dozen copies of a handbill from his pocket, handed one to Wrexham.

"Lancelot said 'e 'opes to see you at 'Ockley."

Wrexham read the handbill.

"AT THE BEAR GARDEN IN HOCKLEY IN THE HOLE, NEAR CLARKEN-WELL GREEN

"This is to give notice to all gentlemen and gamesters, that on Monday, 18th April, there will be a match fought by Four Dogs, two of Westminster against two of Eastcheap, at the Bull, for a Guinea. Five let goes out of Hand, fairest and farthest in wins all. And a Mad Bull let loose to be baited, with fireworks all over him, and Dogs after him. With other Variety of Bull Baiting and Bear Baiting: Being a general day of Sport by all the Old Gamesters.

"Beginning at three o'clock.

"The gentlemen are desired to come betimes, because the sport will be long."

Wrexham nodded and, mistaking the date, said to Heffelfinger, "That's the day after the Duke of Cheltenham's wedding, which I must attend, but tell my good friend, Lancelot, I shall surely be there."

Out of the corner of his eye, he saw Richard carefully edging his way around a number of tables, carrying a large tray with three tankards of beer, one arrack punch and one Jamaica rum punch. As Richard reached Wrexham's table, heading for Weston's, Wrexham stuck out his foot. Richard tripped. The tray slid from his right palm, and as he tried to grasp it with his left hand, the tankards spun forward. Beer and punch splashed over Gilbert Weston and the men at his table. The tankards clattered to the floor.

73

Shocked, Weston and the other actors leaped to their feet. Several muttered curses. Wrexham and his companions roared with laughter. Other patrons reacted with compassion or laughter, according to their sensibilities. Bessie and Tillie Pickering came running with cloths to wipe the soaked apparel of the victims.

Among the most compassionate of all the patrons was one newly arrived. Felicia Wandrous stood just inside the door. She had seen Richard stumble. She gasped as the tankards flew from the tray. At her side, holding her hand, stood another young lady, perhaps a year or two Felicia's junior. She had a round face, puffy from protracted weeping. Her soft eyes were red-ringed, and she still sniffled as she watched the excited scene.

"Guh—guh—god, I'm very suh—suh—s-sorry," stammered Richard. "Fuh—please—fuh—fuh—forgive me. I—I—"

He was in such a numbed, fatigued and, now, shocked state that he did not even realize he had been tripped.

With surprising calm, considering the circumstances, Gilbert Weston, his gray eyes like ice, said, "Richard, see me in my office as soon as you finish here this afternoon."

Order was restored, and the Weston party left the Inn smelling of beer, arrack and rum. Ben Pickering was frigidly silent as Richard wiped up the tables and the floor, brought the tankards back to the bar. Felicia stood beside him. She touched his arm lightly and smiled.

"Spirits are quite washable," she said. "How is your wound?"

Richard blushed more deeply, began to stammer a reply, but Felicia was speaking happily to Ben Pickering.

"Ben, this is my dear young friend, Edith Forrest. She's going to be staying with me for a while, so she'll be a regular patron. . . . This is Mr. Ben Pickering, Edie." She turned to Richard. "And this handsome young man, Richard Steele."

Edith sniffled and curtsied.

Felicia had Richard's hand, and somehow contrived to have him lead Edith Forrest and herself to a table.

"I think Edie and I will have a little of the ebullum wine, if we may, Richard."

Her silver-gray eyes twinkled, and Richard's embarrassment seemed magically to vanish. He had hoped and

74

hoped, all morning, that she would come to the Inn as usual, and now that she had, she had seen him in another oafish situation, but his whole world nevertheless seemed brighter.

Ten minutes after the departure of the Weston group, the two dunners left, and Wrexham strode over to Felicia's table. Without asking permission he seated himself.

"You're quite rude, Jerry," Felicia said. "Miss Forrest and I were having an extremely private conversation."

Wrexham smiled. "Miss Forrest is obviously in distress, and as you know, my dear Felicia, damsels in distress are a Wrexham specialty."

He took Edith Forrest's hand and kissed it.

"Your humble servant, Jerome Wrexham, at your service, my dear."

"Humble as a hangman," scoffed Felicia, and to Wrexham, "Edie's distress is nothing you can relieve."

Richard approached the table with the two glasses of wine on a tray.

"Duh—duh—don't fall over your feet again, luh—luh—lad," shouted Wrexham, backing his chair away in mock fright.

Richard wanted to hit him. The mockery was bad enough, but his impulse derived from a sharp pang of jealousy. He restrained himself, managed a feeble smile, as he set the glasses of wine carefully before the two women.

Wrexham again stuttered loudly.

"Buh—buh—buh—bring me an—an—another—fuh—fuh—French brandy puh—puh—"

Punch! finished Richard furiously, in his mind, and turned away and went back to the bar.

"Jerry, you are a mean and heartless beast," said Felicia.

"I can't abide amateurs and general incompetence."

"I can't abide *you* a good deal of the time," said Felicia, and took Edith Forrest by the hand, rose from the table and left.

Playing his games, Wrexham had felt fine, but as Felicia and her friend stormed out, his aching head, his itching eyes, his weariness overcame him again. He finished the punch Richard brought him, in one gulp.

"I'm not paying for Miss Wandrous's and her friend's drink!" he announced angrily to Richard.

In an uncharacteristically magnanimous gesture, which he considered an investment in his relationship with the dunners, he had paid their bill, but it was painful nevertheless. And he was damned if he was going to spend another shilling on a stupid wench who did not know the difference between the finest—not to mention, the most handsome—actor of the day, and a stuttering idiot of a stableboy and candle snuffer.

It goes without saying that Richard did not feel this a propitious day to bring up the question of a wage increase with Ben Pickering. From the moment the last noontime guest departed, one thought had been uppermost in his mind.

Was Gilbert Weston planning to fire him?

He excused himself from having his own noon meal with the Pickerings, completed his clean-up chores and hastened to the second-floor office of the Lincoln's Inn Fields company manager.

Weston no longer smelled of punch or beer. He had changed clothes. He looked up from the ledger in which he had been writing, as Richard stood before him at the small desk. The ice in his gray eyes had melted, and they held their usual warm expression. Weston was in his mid-forties. He was strong-featured with a square chin, prematurely graying hair and shaggy eyebrows. He pinched the tip of his straight nose, and waved Richard to a chair.

"I admire your restraint, young man," he said.

"Again, sir, please accept my most sincere apologies. I realize it was inexcusable, but . . ."

Richard stopped abruptly. Weston's words had registered belatedly.

"My restraint, sir? You admire it—my restraint!"

"Of course. It would have been completely understandable if you had struck him."

Richard stared at the older man in total bafflement.

"If—if I struck—who, sir?"

"Wrexham, of course. He is a miscreant of the first rank."

"Oh, oh—I understand he was just making sport of my stammering last night. I suppose—"

"I'm not speaking of that imbecilic exhibition."

"You're not, sir? Then—"

"The tripping, Richard! You were aware, of course, that he tripped you, were you not?"

"Wrexham—Jerome Wrexham *tripped* me? You mean when I spilled the—"

"Of course. I distinctly saw him stick his foot out as you came by. I had all I could do to restrain *myself* from striking him."

Richard shook his head.

"I can't believe it. I was tired—rather in somewhat of a daze. I had had a long and arduous evening . . . a fight . . ."

"So I gathered from your features. What did happen?"

Again Richard briefly recounted the story of the encounter of the previous evening.

Weston listened attentively and smiled as Richard finished.

"Those lads will have saved us a bit of make-up effort, if you'll play the role I would like you to this evening."

"Tonight? In *Macbeth?*"

"Rodney Boone, our second witch, is down with a fever. . . . I believe you have a lesson with Farley Shannon this afternoon?"

Richard nodded.

"Farley is totally familiar with my presentation of *Macbeth,* and you worked through all the rehearsals with us. . . ."

"Yes, of course, sir. I was in the superstructure with the rosin and the candle, and the iron ball, and under stage—"

"I'm fully aware of that, Richard. I've arranged with another lad to handle the effects. I'll run him through those several times this afternoon. If you'll ask Farley to work with you for an hour or so on the second witch's scene, I think everything will work out quite well."

Richard's eyes grew moist. He could hardly believe his good fortune. After last night, he had not been sure Gilbert Weston would ever give him another chance to act.

"Mr. Weston, sir. I cannot tell you how grateful I am for this second opportunity. After my shameful performance last night . . ."

Weston smiled.

"In my debut performance I never did remember the four lines I had to say. I simply stood petrified in center stage with two other actors, stared at them and at the

77

audience in turn for a full five minutes, then ran off stage wailing as though I was about to die. And I believed I was."

Richard rose and extended his hand. Weston took it.

"I swear, sir, that I will not disgrace you this evening."

Weston smiled again.

"Double, double, toil and trouble; fire burn and cauldron bubble . . . You'll make a fine witch, Richard."

ᏽ 10 ᏽ

All weariness was forgotten. All the small aches vanished. The anger over Wrexham's malicious prank dissipated. Pickering's mare, Sally O, who loved Richard as much as he loved her, adjusted her trot, sensing the manner in which the exuberant young actor was favoring his wounded right buttock. Thus, the four-and-a-half-mile journey northeast from London out Mile's End Road to Farley Shannon's acting school near Stratford was painless. Not merely painless, joyful! *Another chance, another chance!* Richard's thoughts kept time to the rhythm of the mare's hooves.

Gone was the stench of London town. Here the air was crisp and free of soot; the rolling countryside lush and verdant. Occasional birdsong played pleasing melody to the clippety-clop rhythm of Sally O's hoofs on the dusty road.

Richard's head was filled with the excitement and anticipation of preparing for his part as the second witch. *Macbeth* had always been his favorite of all the Shakespeare works. As he rode, he recalled vividly the delicious thrill of terror he felt, as a child of seven, when his mother and Father Whittaker read him the dramatic story of the murder of Duncan, King of Scotland, and the horrors that ensued. The vanishing witches and their unspeakable stew, Banquo's ghost, the three apparitions, the armed head, the bloody child, the child wearing the crown with the tree in his hand, these had all given him the kind of shivers youngsters have delighted in since the beginning of time.

The priest read all the male roles, and Mary the wom-

79

en's. Richard smiled, recalling Mary's atrocious reading of some of Lady Macbeth's more horrific lines. He could still see the distressed expression on her face as she read the Lady's savage denunciation of Macbeth, when he tells her he has not murdered Duncan, as he promised he would.

Mary had faltered, paled as she read: ". . . I have given suck, and know how tender 'tis to love the babe that milks me—I would, while it was smiling in my face, have pluck'd my nipple from his boneless gums, and dash'd his brains out, had I so sworn as you have done to this."

He had read the play more than a dozen times since that day. And now, as he neared Stratford, he thought of another most interesting aspect of the present *Macbeth* situation. Felicia Wandrous, despite her young years, was to play Lady Macbeth. He had marveled, as he sat through the rehearsals, at the maturity, the iron will, the callous power and finally the eerie dementia she brought to the part. Even now, in the sky-blue, green and wide-open country, with Sally O's broad chestnut back beneath him, he felt a tremor as he recalled Felicia's reading in the scene in which her waiting gentlewoman has called Lady Macbeth's doctor. In the final dress rehearsal, the doctor and the gentlewoman watched Felicia as she walked in her night dress, unseeing eyes focused on nothing, holding a taper in a slightly quivering hand.

And Felicia, probably the youngest Lady Macbeth in the theater's history, had spoken.

"Out, damned spot! out, I say! One; two. Why, then 'tis time to do't. Hell is murky. Fie, my lord, fie! A soldier, and afeard? What need we fear who knows it, when none can call our power to accompt? Yet who would have thought the old man to have so much blood in him?"

And later, again wringing her hands, lifting them to her nostrils, holding them out before her: "Here's the smell of blood still. All the perfumes of Arabia will not sweeten this little hand. Oh, oh, oh!"

She would be the sensation of all London. He loved her madly, and admired her, and he would give a professional performance in his own minor role if it killed him. With Farley Shannon's help he knew he could do it. The performance began at 6:30 and he would have less than two hours with the great coach, but he knew it would be enough. He was supremely confident.

Shannon's school was the smallest of the thatch-roofed buildings in a complex that included a fencing school, a riding academy, a dance school and tennis courts. Eight actors, seven men and one young woman, sat on a bench facing the platform stage, which filled almost half the moderate-sized room. The elderly actor stood downstage center on the platform.

On the whitewashed walls were several handbills. One announced a performance of His Majesty's Company of Comedians in a new moral masque, *Comus,* altered from Milton's masque at Ludlow Castle, to be given at the Theatre Royal in Drury Lane.

A second and more flamboyant bill detailed an opera to be offered at Batholomew Fair, called *The Creation of the World,* with the addition of *Noah's Flood. The Stag Hunt and Fox Chase Royal Circus,* with its fricassee dancing, vaulting, tightrope dancing, pyramids and ground and lofty tumbling, was heralded on a third poster. This promised several remarkable feats, including: "Young Grossman will leap from a single horse over two Garters, 12 feet high, and alight again on the saddle and play the violin in various attitudes."

The most prominent wall decoration was a Roman sword, hilt encrusted with jewels, thick blade in its gold-trimmed, rich brown leather sheath. The sword was held by brackets on the wall at stage left. Beneath it was a placard, and on this, written in an exquisite hand, the legend: "This sword is given this 4th day of September in the year 1672 by Thomas Betterton to his good friend, Farley Shannon, in recognition of his superlative portrayal of Brutus in William Shakespeare's *Julius Caesar.* Never so magnificent a performance. Never so true a friend."

Richard knew that Shannon and the legendary Betterton had alternately played Brutus and Caesar in this production. Shannon had told him countless stories about the great actor, Betterton.

Now Richard entered the theater room quietly, for Farley Shannon was nearing the end of one of his dissertations on the theater in present-day England. The audience of young players sat as if mesmerized. Shannon was seventy years old. He was a tall man, almost six feet. He held himself erect against the body-crushing ravages of illness and the years by the sheer force of his will, and his dedication to the theater.

He was suffering from a disease that the doctors of the day had not yet been able to identify, let alone cure. It consumed the muscles of the body almost imperceptibly, but persistently, day by day, leaving him debilitated virtually all his waking hours. The skin on his skull was gray, taut yet lined. The incessant pain, which ate away at him, and his stubborn refusal to succumb to it, gave a tortured look to his steel-gray eyes. He had a straight, aquiline nose and pale, almost bloodless lips. His thinning silver hair fell back from a high, bony forehead. His hands, as he gestured while speaking, were the hands of a classical pianist, but the skin was the same shade of gray as his face, and mottled with brownish liver spots. They trembled from time to time, and when they did, he would wring them, or hide them beneath folded arms.

He was dedicated and proud and invincible. His voice, once a magnificent instrument, was now hoarse, either with the muscle-wasting illness or some kind of cancer. His speech was punctuated with "unnhhs" and "errrrrs," when he found it necessary to catch his breath. But he managed these sounds with the skill of the master thespian he was. He commanded attention and achieved eloquence in spite of the lack of tonal quality of his aging vocal equipment and the demands of his shrinking lungs. And this triumph was the result of the depth of his sincerity and conviction.

Richard quietly seated himself at the end of the bench, and listened to Shannon's heartfelt words.

"You will all live to see the day, my young friends, errrh, when the theater and its people will be respected elements of the community. As I have told you on earlier occasions, we are blessed with ever-growing audiences displaying renewed interest in playwrights who are not only dramatists, but poets . . . unnhhhh . . .

"There is a great revival of interest in the works of Will Shakespeare, of Christopher Marlowe, Ben Jonson and others. Their plays have virtues, which the works of our more recent Restoration playwrights lack almost totally. . . . Errrhhhh . . . As you are aware, the plays of William Wycherly, John Vanbrugh, even the vastly talented William Congreve, witty as they are, are cynical and unheroic. Cuckoldry is a favorite theme, and trivial intrigue a hallmark.

"Audiences have come back to the realization that the sophisticated, intellectual wit of a Congreve may supply an entertaining enough evening, but contains a paucity of food for the mind, the heart, even the soul. . . . Shakespeare, Jonson and Marlowe tell their tales with a poetry and an imagery, which our Restoration dramatists never achieved. But far more important, along with that poetry, together with that imagery, unnnhhhh . . . they reveal truths of human nature; their characters are people, whether kings or clowns, whether virtuous or villainous they are people. Errrhhhh."

He paused, and sipped from a glass of red wine on a small table at his side.

"It remains for you, unnnhhhh, for each of you to portray them as real human beings, not as caricatures. The vitality is there in the poetic lines—in all of them: the comedies, the tragedies, the histories. The intellect speaks. Consider—errrrrhhh, the disenchantment, the unaccustomed humility of King Lear, the chilling manner in which Hamlet tortures himself, the doubt, the unbelief of dashing Mercutio, the disparaging, contemptuous attitudes of Iago.

He sipped the wine again and smiled at the group.

"Study our foremost players by all means, my young friends. Study them critically. Be not unduly affected by their stature. Mr. James Quin, one of our leading players, has an impressive bass voice, and standing in the center of a London stage, bedecked in brocades and ruffles and lace, rolling sonorous phrases off his tongue, supremely self-satisfied with the glory of his appearance and his sound, he may strike you as a heroic artiste. But I ask you to note the lack of communication between Quin and his audience.

"Yet when another of our premier players, Charles Macklin, plays Shylock as a tragic human being, rather than the broadly comic Jew delineated by most actors, our friend Quin denounces him as a player lacking grandeur, as forsaking the grand manner of the supreme artist.

"The time will come—and I believe it not too far distant, errrhhhh—when we will move further and further away from the old French style of utilizing the voice, and the musical cadences with which we employ it, as the sole thespian instrument. The body, every part of the body, the mind, every wicked and holy thought it holds, are part of what we are, and part of what the people in our finest plays are. The time will come, and I hope each of you will have the opportunity to contribute to speeding the day, when actors will portray people as people, just as Shakespeare and Marlowe and Jonson wrote their characters as human beings. *To that day!*"

He lifted the wine glass, and drank the rest of the wine.

"Monday," he said, "we will discuss and work on Ben Jonson's *The Alchemist*. Please study the scene in which the tobacconist, Abel Drugger, breaks the urinal."

The small group of actors nodded appreciative farewells and greeted Richard. Discussing Shannon's remarks among themselves in hushed conversations, they left the building. Richard went to the stage, making a motion to take Shannon by the arm and lead him to his favorite leather chair in the adjoining kitchen. Shannon waved him away, strode firm and erect to the room with Richard beside him. Only when he sat in the leather chair did he seem almost to collapse. His face was ashen, and pain glistened in his eyes.

"Are you all right, sir?" asked Richard.

"Would you kindly pour me some wine?"

As Richard set the wine down beside him, Shannon stared and said angrily: "Have you been brawling, son?"

Richard realized Shannon had noticed his bruised face. It was a religion with Shannon that actors should conduct themselves as gentlemen at all times. He was bitter in his denunciations of those who disgraced the profession with unbecoming conduct of any kind. He had barely tolerated Nell Gwyn's becoming the mistress of King Charles II, and that only because the actress and he and Betterton had been friends for years. Quickly, Richard again told of his encounter with the ruffians.

"Well, errrhhh . . . in that case you seem to have survived nicely. But more important, Richard, I'm happy to see from your demeanor that you have also survived a typically stormy debut."

"Were you there?"

Richard was surprised and pleased that the elderly actor had come to see his performance.

"Indeed," said Shannon, "I would not have msssed it. Every good actor I have known has had difficulty in his initial appearance. Colley Cibber played the same role of the messenger in *Hamlet* in his first performance. Must have been about your age, too, perhaps a year or two older. Betterton played Hamlet, and I, Laertes. Cibber could not remember a single one of his lines. . . . Unnnhhh. . . . After the play Betterton was so furious, he demanded that Cibber be forfeited."

His hand shook slightly as he lifted the glass to his lips, sipped and set it down.

" 'We cannot forfeit him,' said the manager. 'He's an apprentice, and isn't paid anything at all.' Betterton shouted, 'Well, pay him ten shillings, and forfeit him five!' "

Richard chuckled, taking the chair across from Shannon.

"Weston would never forfeit you, Richard. As a matter of fact, I'm certain he'll give you another opportunity in the very near future."

"Tonight!" beamed Richard. "Will you help me? . . . If I may, I'll do the accounts next week."

In exchange for his lessons, Richard kept Shannon's accounts and performed other work for him. Now he told the distinguished elderly actor of the manager's request that he play the second witch in this evening's performance of *Macbeth*.

Shannon smiled. As well as deep affection for his young student, he had great confidence in him, and he was happy to see this same confidence so strikingly displayed by his old friend, Gilbert Weston. The part of the witch, although relatively minor, was still considerably more complex than any of the several servants or messengers in the play. The fact that Weston would cast Richard in this role plainly indicated his faith, not only in Richard's potential talent, but in his resiliency, another important requisite for success in the theater.

"Let's have at it, lad!" he said enthusiastically. "Hand me that folio."

He turned to the second page of the *Macbeth* folio Richard took from his bookshelf.

"Right here," he said, "when Macbeth and Banquo come upon the witches for the first time, we are given descriptions, which give us wide latitude in determining how we will play the witches."

Richard turned to what had been marked off as Act I, Scene 3, in his own copy of the play. He followed the script, as Shannon, hardly looking at his own folio, began the speech.

"Banquo says, 'What are these, so wither'd and so wild in their attire, that look not like the inhabitants o' the earth, and yet are on't? Live you? Or are you aught that man may question?'"

He continued, and then throwing back his head, said in an altered, deeper voice of command, "'Speak, if you can,' says Macbeth. 'What are you?' And the three witches hail Macbeth, and make their strange predictions: Macbeth, Thane of Glamis, and Thane of Cawdor; Macbeth, who shall be king hereafter. . . . Lesser than Macbeth and greater; not so happy, yet much happier; thou shall get kings, though be none."

Shannon rose from his chair with an effort.

He waved a hand.

"And in a cloud they vanish!"

Richard would have created that cloud by burning rosin, and opening the trapdoor in the floor of the inner stage, center. Now some other lad would do the effects; Richard would be one of the three witches to do the vanishing. He stared raptly at Shannon, as the elderly actor went on.

"And Banquo says, 'The earth hath bubbles, as the water has, and these are of them. Whither are they vanished?' And Macbeth replied, 'Into the air, and what seemed corporal melted, as breath into the wind.'"

He sank into his chair, and breathed heavily for a moment.

"And Banquo demands to know, 'Were such things here as we do speak about, or have we eaten on the insane root that takes the reason prisoner?'"

Richard listened, enthralled.

"So we have our witches. Are they figments of Macbeth's and Banquo's imaginations? Are they the fates? Are they three hags with occult powers? How to present them?"

He took another sip of wine.

"Gilbert Weston and I have discussed this on many occasions. The tendency, the temptation is to caricature them. But this is a grievous error. Their predictions of things to come are essential elements of the plot. Indeed, those earliest prophecies, which we have just read, obliquely motivate Macbeth to murder King Duncan . . . errrhhhh. . . . Their chantings, the images they create in preparing their hell-broth are the essence of the air of mystic horror which permeates the play."

His hands trembled slightly with excitement as he turned the pages of his folio.

"Here," he said, "again there is thunder."

Richard nodded. He knew Shannon was at the place marked Act IV, Scene 1 in his copy, and turned quickly to it.

Before he began to read, Shannon said, "Every word the witches utter must be clearly understood. Hysterical tones, cackling, superfluous tremolo will not do it. The footman on the farthest bench in the upper gallery must hear each word, each syllable . . . unnnhhhh. . . . We strive for a nether-world effect, but subtly, by pitching the voice perhaps a half-octave above normal, by speaking in a measured, unreal monotone."

"I've noted Mr. Weston stressing such directions in our rehearsals."

Shannon nodded.

"Of course. Then let us try it. Here, with the preparation of the hell-broth. At how high a pitch can you sustain and project a clear monotone through a fairly long speech, Richard?"

Richard cleared his throat.

"Approximately at—" He spoke in an abnormally high voice, and it cracked.

"A bit lower."

"This seems more comfortable, and controllable." He spoke in a smooth falsetto.

"Excellent. Now, I'm all but the second witch."

Again he rose from the chair. Richard stood, too.

"A rumble of thunder," Shannon fluttered a right hand through the air, and, as the first witch, in a higher voice said monotonously, "Thrice the brinded cat hath mew'd."

Richard, the second high-pitched, measured witch, responded: "Thrice, and once the hedge-pig whin'd."

Shannon went on. "Round about the cauldron go; *in* the poison'd entrails throw. Toad, that under cold stone days and nights has thirty-one swelter'd venom sleeping got, boil thou first i' the charmed pot."

In unison, Shannon and Richard continued. "Double, double, toil and trouble; fire burn and cauldron bubble."

Richard cleared his throat and made two unsuccessful attempts before he again found his vocal pitch. Then he spoke, in the measured monotone, only occasionally glancing at his page.

"Fillet of a fenny snake, in the cauldron boil and bake; eye of newt, and toe of frog, wool of bat, and tongue of dog; adder's fork, and blind worm's sting, lizard's leg, and howlet's wing; for a charm of pow'rful trouble, like a hell-broth boil and bubble."

Again Shannon joined him in the "double, double" chorus, then read the lines of the third witch. Without beard or wig, without cloak, merely by the fixed glint of his eye, the high tone of his voice, the convincing movement of his right hand, somehow clawlike now as it reached into an imaginary sack, and dropped venomous item after item into the invisible cauldron, he sent a chill through Richard's blood.

"Scale of dragon, tooth of wolf, witches' mummy, maw and gulf of the ravin'd salt-sea shark; root of hemlock digg'd in the dark; liver of a blaspheming Jew, gall of goat, and slips of yew silver'd in the moon's eclipse.

"Nose of Turk and Tartar's lips; finger of birthstrangled babe ditch-deliver'd by a drab, make the gruel thick and slab. Add thereto a tiger's cawdron."

Enraptured, Richard forgot to come in for the chorus.

"Alert, lad, alert!" said Shannon. "You must not break the rhythm."

They spoke the chorus in unison again, and Richard continued, "Cool it with a baboon's blood; then the charm is firm and good."

In his own ears, his reading sounded quite a bit in the mode of Farley Shannon's. Shannon patted his shoulder and said, "Fine, fine, son," and Richard beamed proudly. They worked for another hour and a half. Finally they did the entire play from the beginning, with Shannon briefly filling in characters, plot and action, and setting Richard's cues, leading into each of his scenes.

"You'll have no difficulty at all, Richard," said Shannon as he accompanied the young actor to the post where he had hitched Sally O.

"I'm forever grateful, sir."

"You'll have no trouble at all, my boy," Shannon repeated, as Richard mounted Sally O.

But then, Shannon was not infallible, or psychic.

❧ 11 ❧

All the way back to the Lincoln's Inn Fields Theatre, he
spoke his lines, over and over, in the high-pitched, unreal monotone, visualizing the scenes and characters,
mentally marking his cues by mumbling them to himself.
Sally O noted that he was not favoring his right buttock
any longer. She galloped gaily in her normal stride,
slightly baffled by the sounds her favorite rider was making. Richard's adrenalin flow was so great he could
hardly wait to get onstage to open the play. He could
hardly wait to see Felicia. He knew this was going to be
the finest night of his life.

Backstage, the air of restrained excitement and affected nonchalance common to first-night performances
prevailed. Actors and actresses chatted nervously. Mrs.
Fogarty, the wardrobe mistress, stitched a loose collar on
one of the witch's cloaks. On his way to the common
dressing table, Richard passed Jerome Wrexham, hungrily eating a thick roast beef sandwich. Most players
were too nervous to eat before a performance, but Wrexham had taken a long nap after leaving the Inn and was
hungry. Wrexham seemed to be the kind of iron-nerved
actor who frequently ate and drank before shows. He
was playing Macduff, a role he had performed before, and
seemed more relaxed than any other member of the cast.
Richard felt a momentary flicker of anger, but he ignored it.

At the dressing table, Conrad Tibble, the third witch,
helped Richard don and adjust his wig and beard. Gilbert Weston, who would play Macbeth, came up behind

89

Richard, placed his hand on his shoulder and said, "How went your rehearsal with my friend, Farley?"

Richard stood. "Extremely well, sir. Thanks to him, I'm well prepared. I will not let you down."

Weston patted his shoulder, nodded. "I have every confidence, Richard."

As Weston walked away, Felicia Wandrous came up to Richard. She had made herself up to seem older than her twenty-three years, with eye shadow, pencil-line wrinkles, and a pale lip salve. She wore an ornate auburn wig, and a long, black silk gown, embroidered with silver. To Richard, she looked radiant.

"I'm so happy you're a witch, love," she said, taking his hand. "I knew Gilbert would not wait long before giving you another role."

"Thank you, Felicia," said Richard, and mustered all his courage. "May I see you tonight, after—"

She patted his cheek affectionately, then kissed him lightly.

"I can't, love." She nodded in the direction of Edith Forrest, who was seated unobtrusively on a bench nearby. There was still a forlorn look about Felicia's friend.

"Edith is staying with me for a time."

Seeing the disappointment in Richard's eyes, she said, "But soon, love."

Richard saw Wrexham rise and stop Felicia as she walked back toward Edith Forrest. Wrexham grasped Felicia's arm, and spoke loudly enough so that Richard could hear.

"I see you're still consorting with candle snuffers, Felicia."

Felicia shook off his hand, turned her back on him and walked over to Edith Forrest.

"I wish to see you tonight," Wrexham snapped as she left him.

Richard was disturbed, but determined to let nothing interfere with his performance. Within minutes, from the stage, he heard Gilbert Weston's sonorous voice in the prologue. He rose, walked to the wardrobe room, put his long black cloak over his shoulders, tied it securely and joined the first and third witches, who were already standing behind the downstage entrance door at stage left.

Weston concluded the prologue. Richard guessed

90

from the volume of the audience's applause that the house was virtually full. They were probably packed tight on the benches in the pit. Again he felt the urge to urinate, the tension in his neck and shoulders. He cleared his throat. The witches were to open the play, set the mood in a brief scene.

The first rumble of thunder sounded. The first witch opened the entrance door, and he and Richard and Conrad Tibble stalked to the center of the inner stage with the lightning, created by passing the rosin through the candle flame, flashing, and the thunder sounding a final crash.

The first witch said, "When shall we meet again? In thunder, lightning or in rain?"

And Richard, all nervousness gone, voice pitched at precisely the right level, spoke: "When the hurlyburly's done; when the battle's lost and won."

There were seven more brief lines between the three witches, and then in unison, they proclaimed: "Fair is foul, and foul is fair. Hover through the fog and filthy air."

The lad burning the rosin in the cellar space beneath the stage did his job well. Through the slightly raised trapdoor, a substantial cloud of smoke enveloped the three witches, and they exited.

The beaux sitting around the outer edges of the stage backed away from the drifting smoke. The lawyers, doctors, playwrights and other professionals in the pit applauded heartily. Among them, not quite sure one of the witches was Richard, was Father Whittaker. He wore a coat buttoned tight around his neck to conceal his clerical collar. *Macbeth* had always been one of his favorite plays. In the upper gallery a knot of sailors shouted their approval, yet could hardly be heard over the heavy hand-clapping and stomping and whistling of those all about them. Even the elegantly coiffed and gowned ladies of quality, and the gentlemen with them in the boxes, nodded their commendation.

It promised to be one of those evenings actors, from supernumeraries to leading players, live for. Although he had spoken but thirty words, including the unison exit lines, Richard knew he had read them perfectly. As had his fellow witches. The house was full of appreciative, alert, responsive people. Richard's face and hair were wet with sweat under the beard and wig, and he felt

91

perspiration forming in his armpits and crotch, but all the tension was gone. He took a position in the wings, where he could see some of the action on the stage, but he was careful not to obstruct exits and entrances.

In the third scene of the first act, he and his fellow witches went back onstage. They were discovered by Macbeth and Banquo, who wondered whether they were real or supernatural, and then they vanished again. This time, the trapdoor was fully opened and, under cover of the sizable, burning rosin cloud, they pushed each other down into the area beneath the stage, as Banquo said, "The earth has bubbles . . ."

By the time Richard got back up the stairs, to stage level, he was perspiring profusely. Between the concentration on his lines, the fiercely burning rosin, the energy expended in plunging down the stairs and climbing back up, he began to feel slightly faint. He made his way to the wardrobe room and hung up his cloak.

Mrs. Fogarty, the plump, elderly wardrobe mistress, lifted her head from the doze she'd been in.

"I beg your pardon, Elsie," said Richard, "I didn't mean to disturb you."

She smiled and waved her hand at him. She had always been fond of him. Before he left the room, her head had dropped, and she was dozing again. The witches were not scheduled to make another entrance until the fifth scene in Act III, so Richard found a favorable vantage point to watch the onstage proceedings.

In a short time, in Scene 5 of the first act, Felicia made her entrance as Lady Macbeth. She read the letter Macbeth had sent her, telling of his encounter with the witches, and of their royal prophecies. And then, when informed that Duncan, King of Scotland, was coming to visit, she played the speech that instantly revealed her ruthless lust for power. Richard remembered Shannon's preachments that the characters be played as real people. Felicia played Lady Macbeth so that one believed her capable of inciting to murder, and of perpetrating murder herself, if need be.

"The raven himself is hoarse that croaks the fatal entrance of Duncan under my battlements." She almost spat rather than spoke the words.

"Come, you spirits that tend on mortal thoughts, unsex me here, and fill me from the crown to the toe-top full of direst cruelty! Make thick my blood, stop up the ac-

cess and passage to remorse, that no compunctious visit-
ings of nature shake my fell purpose. . . ."

Richard's mouth hung open in rapt attention, as she
finished: "Come, thick night, and pall thee in the dun-
nest smoke of hell, that my keen knife see not the
wound it makes, nor heaven peep through the blanket
of the dark, to cry, 'Hold, hold!' "

Richard was breathing heavily as he watched. The
sweat had broken out on his body once more. But this
time from excitement over what he was witnessing.

Oh, how he would love to play a role opposite Felicia!
How long, how many years would it take before he could
acquire the polish, the technique? Perhaps never, he
thought uneasily. Perhaps it was purely a matter of God-
given genius.

He was heartened again soon after, however, when
Wrexham made his entrance as Macduff in the third
scene of Act II. Richard watched him as he bowed to
the Duke of Cheltenham and a small group of nobles in
a box. Wrexham was good. There was no doubt about
that. He had the look and the posture of the great actor,
but as Richard watched him play the scene in which he
discovers the murder of Duncan, he saw vividly what
Shannon had referred to in connection with James Quin.
Wrexham's voice was rich and impressive. He read his
lines with great authority and clarity, but in a declamatory manner, which failed to bring the character to life.
And which failed to communicate with the audience.
Richard thought he had more talent as a singer than
as an actor. Or perhaps, he thought, he was being unfair
in his evaluation of Wrexham, because he had come to
dislike him. In any event, he felt that if he worked hard,
he could become a better actor than Wrexham, and in
the not-too-far-distant future.

He became so engrossed in the fourth scene of Act
III, in which Banquo's ghost appears, that he almost forgot to go back to the wardrobe room in time to get his
cloak. He was slightly out of breath as he made it back
from the wardrobe room to the downstage entrance door
at stage left to join his fellow witches for their entrance.
Fortunately, the scene was the one in which Hecate
scolds the witches for daring to "trade and traffic with
Macbeth in riddles and affairs of death," while never
calling upon Hecate to "bear her part." Apart from He-

cate's speech, the only witch with lines was the first, and he had only two.

Richard was thankful this was so, for a strange thing began to happen. He felt an urge to sneeze. He wondered if it could have been the rosin dust, or the clouds of smoke. He gritted his teeth, and concentrated on Hecate's words, and the urge disappeared, only to return and disappear again. He was happy to see the scene end, but when he got backstage and tried to sneeze he could not.

A brief scene between Lennox and another Scottish nobelman ended Act III, and the three witches opened Act IV with Richard's favorite lines, the preparation of the hell-broth. As he got to the end of his first line, "Fillet of a fenny snake," the compulsion to sneeze came over him again. The effort to control it shattered his pitch, and his performance lost a little of its edge, but he played his part out quite well. The tickling in his nostrils and in the back of his throat continued, until he could bear it no longer, but he did. Hecate finished her brief compliments on the witches' stew. "Oh, well done! I commend your pains," and it was Richard's turn again.

With a superhuman effort, he restrained the sneeze once more, and said, "By the pricking of my thumbs, something wicked this way comes. Open, locks, whoever knocks."

And Gilbert Weston Macbeth strode onstage. He could read the distress in Richard's face in spite of the wig and the beard, and the dim lighting.

"How now, you secret, black and midnight hags? What is't you do?"

Witches 1 and 2 spoke, "A deed without a name."

But Richard's violent explosion of a sneeze spattered all over the words. Now that his inflamed nostrils had won the victory, they were not content to settle cheaply. Richard sneezed again and again and again. Tears came to his eyes, and his wig twisted askew, as his head jerked backward and forward with the violence of the attack.

Gilbert Weston Macbeth tried to play through the barrage of sneezes: "I conjure you, by that which you profess—"

Among the crush in the upper gallery there was a certain Hazel Cornish, a fat, fiftyish cook in the elegant

94

house of a distinguished lady and lord. On her day off, which happened to be this day, she liked to go to the theater. Before she left her room, however, she had finished half a bottle of the cooking wine, which she kept hidden in a corner of her closet. The heat of the human bodies and the smoke had now made her slightly dizzy. In this state she had watched the play with a furious concentration.

Now she shrieked in a shrill, piercing voice, "Too much pepper in the hell-broth!" Guffaws of laughter broke through the gallery and, like a deluge, poured down into the pit.

"Too much pepper!" Hazel screamed again, and many picked it up, and soon dozens in the house were shouting the silly phrase. Perhaps this was the audience's manner of seeking release from the tense, dark and dreadful atmosphere the play had created to that point. Whatever the reason, the hysteria and hilarity came at the worst possible moment.

The brief, sneeze-shattered encounter between Macbeth and the witches led directly into the appearance of the three apparitions: the armed head, the bloody child and the crowned child with the tree in his hand. The pandemonium continued through those episodes and through the appearance of the eight kings and the ghost of Banquo.

All the players, including Richard, bravely tried to ignore the commotion and the hysterical, uncontrollable audience, but to no avail. Ringing comments, some humorous, some obscene, some plain nonsensical, burst in unrelenting wave after wave from various sections of the house, mainly from the upper gallery, with the appearance of each new apparition. It was, in a word, a disaster.

The witches vanished in the rosin-smoke cloud through the trapdoor once again, right after the show of the eight kings and Banquo's ghost. Richard, weak now from the emotional ordeal and the physical exertion of the sneezing, wished that he could truly vanish from the face of the earth. The other two witches ascended the stairs to the stage level without speaking to Richard. Richard just sat on the bottom step, head in his hands, ignoring the questions of the special effects lad. The lack of sleep the previous night and the ordeal in the Inn were catching up with him. There was no need to hurry up stairs. This was the witches' last appearance in the play. And, Richard was certain, the last appearance of Richard Steele in any play. Actors were supposed to be able to control themselves. To be unhorsed by a sneeze was not only ridiculous, it was inexcusable.

The audience was not brought under control completely until Felicia's scene with her gentlewoman and the doctor in Act V, when Lady Macbeth displays her madness. After what seemed an eternity, Richard decided he might as well return to the stage level. He estimated roughly, judging by the clattering, clumping sounds of battle, that the play was just about over. He was almost right. Gilbert Weston was standing in the wings at stage right, glaring out at the stage. Beside him stood Felicia, and beside her, the wardrobe mistress, Mrs. Elsie Fogarty.

Richard could see the stage just beyond them. From the upstage, stage left entrance door, Jerome Wrexham Macduff, dressed in general's armor, strode to center stage, holding Macbeth's bodiless head by its lank hair. There were bloody strings of muscle, tissue, veins and arteries hanging from the severed neck. It was an artfully horrible prop. Wrexham's voice boomed as he spoke to Malcolm, son of the murdered Duncan.

"Hail, king! for so thou art! Behold, where stands the usurper's cursed head; the time is free. I see thee compassed with thy kingdom's pearl. . . ."

A moment later the play ended.

Wrexham Macduff, dangling the head by his side, came offstage through the entrance door before which Gilbert Weston stood. Weston spoke to him through clenched teeth.

"Wrexham, you ungodly scoundrel. You are forfeited this entire week's compensation!"

"What in heaven has possessed you, Gilbert?"

"You know damned well what possessed me. You sprinkled Steele's cloak collar with pepper."

"Don't be asinine, Gilbert. Why would I . . . ?"

Mrs. Fogerty said, " 'E did! As God is me witness, 'e did! 'E thought I was nappin', but I saw 'im wit me own two eyes."

Wrexham gave her a withering stare.

"You lie, you old hag!"

Richard stood behind the group, dazed, confused. He had heard the words, but their meaning did not register. They repeated themselves in his head: pepper on the collar? Wrexham?

The mimicry of a stuttering novice, the clownish stumble at the Inn at noon flashed through his mind again, the drinks splashing over Gilbert Weston and the others . . . Another Wrexham mischief! Cruel! Unwarrantedly vicious!

In a sudden, insane rage, he pushed past two other members of the company, slashed his way between Weston and Felicia and charged toward Wrexham, swinging his right fist wildly. Wrexham stepped aside and the blow caught him on the shoulder. Savagely, Wrexham swung the prop head by the hair, and it struck Richard on the left temple. It stunned him for a moment, but he roared into Wrexham, grabbed him in a strong headlock and wrestled him to the floor. By this time all twenty men and eleven women in the company, as well as the fops, who were dawdling backstage, had been drawn to the battle. Four of the stronger men, led by Gilbert Weston, separated the combatants.

Tears of fury and frustration welled in Richard's eyes as he fought futilely to break the strong grip of his colleagues. He stopped fighting. He felt, suddenly, as though he might collapse. He watched in utter disbelief as Felicia Wandrous put her arm around Jerome Wrexham's shoulder and walked by his side as he strode off toward his dressing quarters.

Richard was weary. Wearier than he had ever been in his young life, wearier than he thought it possible for a person to be. Weary in his heart and down to his toes.

⚜ 12 ⚜

It was raining heads. Hundreds of bodiless heads, all Wrexham's, fell from the sky around Richard, bouncing off his upraised arms and shoulders. All night long he had been riding a series of surrealistic nightmares. In this one, now, Felicia walked up to him in the storm, oblivious to the heads falling like obscene hailstones. She was laughing. No, she was coughing. She began to shake his shoulder, rather roughly. He opened his eyes and saw his mother leaning over him, left hand firmly on his shoulder, right hand vainly trying to suppress the incessant, wracking coughs.

Between coughs she managed to say, "Richard, dear— you've been shouting and crying and screaming all night long."

He sat up in bed. It was dawn.

Apparently displeased at having the peace of his night disturbed by Richard's restlessness, Farquhar glared at him resentfully. He meowed unpleasantly until Mary opened the door to let him out.

"I'm sorry I kept you awake, Mary," Richard said.

Still in a numb, exhausted daze he led her to a chair. "We've got to do something about your cough."

He put water on the stove to boil for tea, and as he washed and dressed, he told his mother of the previous evening's events. He did not mention that Felicia had sided with Wrexham.

"I must have a talk with Jerome Wrexham," he said as they finished their tea and went to ready himself for work.

Ben Pickering had heard of the backstage confrontation.

"Best be careful of Wrexham, lad," he advised Richard, as Richard went about his chores that day. "He's a treacherous and dangerous man."

Richard shook his head in angry bafflement, shrugged and kept on working.

The first of the patrons to arrive, shortly before noon, were Felicia Wandrous and Edith Forrest, who still seemed sad and nervous. Felicia was wearing a frock of blue- and white-striped dimity. Richard thought she looked beautiful, but he turned away as she walked toward a table. Busying himself with polishing one of the heraldic shields, he hoped that Tillie would decide to serve the two women. But Felicia called in a loud voice, "Richard, please come over here. We're hungry, and I wish to talk to you."

Richard saw that Ben Pickering was staring at him disapprovingly, so he put aside his cloth, wiped his hands and walked to Felicia's table.

"At your service, my ladies," he said coldly.

"Don't be a calf's head, Richard," scolded Felicia. "Wrexham is furious. . . ."

Richard interrupted, turning pink with anger.

"I'm rather furious myself, Felicia—"

"Of course you are, but you must understand—"

"I understand perfectly well. There's no need to say more."

"Dammit, Richard, there is! I had a long discussion with Jerome last night—"

"I would guess you had," Richard said with cutting sarcasm. "May I take your order?"

"The ebullum wine," said Felicia with great exasperation. "You are a blind, stubborn boy!"

As he turned to go toward the bar, Richard saw Wrexham come in. With him was a gaudily dressed man, several inches shorter than the actor. He had a round bald head, a flushed face with a black mustache, a purple-veined nose, thick lips and darting, restless pale blue eyes. He wore flashing rings on four fingers of his left hand. His scarlet coat, and the white waistcoat that covered his substantial paunch, were both soiled.

Wrexham was elegantly attired in a neat black coat and breeches. His white shirt had a flat collar of lace and linen, and his gray waistcoat had striking silvered death's head buttons. Over his right shoulder hung a black brocaded sash, holding a short sword at his waist. There were silvered buckles on his heeled shoes. Richard noted with some satisfaction that there was a bruise on his right cheekbone.

When they were seated, Wrexham waved his hand, shouted arrogantly, "Bring two brandies and port, boy!"

Richard gritted his teeth as he walked to the bar for the drinks. Pickering said, "Control yourself, lad."

As Richard took the brandies from the pewter tray and placed them before Wrexham and the paunchy man, Wrexham said dramatically, "I will not forget last night, Steele."

Richard's jaw fell open. He could not believe this. First Felicia, and now Wrexham himself! The attitude was that Wrexham, and not Richard, had been wronged.

"Nor will I," he said icily.

"For now," Wrexham sneered, "you may fetch us two portions of cabbage pudding."

He waved Richard away.

Felicia called Richard back to her table.

"What is your pleasure, my lady?"

"Oh, behave yourself, Richard! That man with Jerome is Lancelot Higginbotham!"

Beyond the table, Richard saw Gilbert Weston and two other members of the company enter, and following immediately behind them a group of six people Richard did not recognize.

"I would not care if it were King George! May I serve you?"

"We would both like the kidney pie."

Richard turned to go, but Felicia took him by the sleeve.

"Dammit, Richard, listen to me! Higginbotham employs many thugs and ruffians. Wrexham could—"

"Excuse me, my lady." Richard tugged his arm free and went to Gilbert Weston's table.

"Good morning, Richard," said Weston. He rose from the table, excused himself to his colleagues and took Richard aside.

"Richard," he said softly, "you performed very well last night. I could not have asked for anything more."

"Thank you, sir."

"But I must replace you tonight. I must ask you to go back to your functions in the superstructure and the underground. I'm terribly sorry, but I have no choice, for the moment."

"But sir, if I performed well——"

"Wrexham spoke with the Duke last night, and the Duke talked to me. We can't spare Wrexham for the time being. He threatened to leave the company unless you were removed from the cast."

Richard cursed sharply.

Weston touched his shoulder.

"Please, Richard, I beseech you. Do not let this discourage you. It is purely a temporary situation. We will find a way—"

"Thank you, sir."

Richard turned away so that Weston would not see the moisture in his eyes. He was so furious he had all he could do to keep from trembling. He took a deep breath, and gained control of himself as he walked to Bessie Pickering's counter and requested the two orders of cabbage pudding. Bessie noticed the grim look on his face.

"Are you all right, lad?"

Richard nodded, and placed the hot puddings on his pewter tray.

Wrexham was in deep discussion with Higginbotham.

"Excuse me, sir," said Richard. "You wished the cabbage pudding?"

Wrexham waved his hand, nodding impatiently.

"Yes, yes . . ."

The pleasantly pungent aroma of the steaming pudding wafted by Richard's nostrils as he lifted one of the full dishes from the tray.

"Very well, sir," he said, and placed the dish of pudding before Higginbotham.

"Ummmmm." Higginbotham drooled. "Smells fit for a king."

Richard took the second dish of pudding and dumped it squarely on Wrexham's beautifully combed, golden head.

Wrexham bellowed in shock, pain, and outrage. He leaped to his feet. Every eye in the kitchen turned toward him. Richard stepped back quickly, as Wrexham drew his sword from its scabbard and slashed wildly at Richard.

Richard used the tray as a shield, gripping it tightly in both hands. There was an ear-shattering clang as the heavy sword struck the pewter tray. Wrexham, his vi-

101

sion slightly obstructed by the pudding oozing down his head and face, wiped across his eyes with his left hand, drew back his right arm and began a second vicious swing at Richard's head. Richard knocked over a chair as he lunged to the side and ducked under the thick blade.

Wrexham came after him, drawing back his right arm again. But before he could swing, Richard banged him sharply on the side of the head with the edge of the heavy pewter tray. The blow landed an inch below his temple, and he fell heavily to the floor.

He shook his head, still gripping his sword, and tried to rise, but Richard, standing over him, brought the tray down on the top of his head with full force. It made a dull bonging sound as it struck. Richard raised the tray and struck again. And yet a third time. Then Felicia Wandrous and Pickering and Weston and several others were on him, pulling him away from the now unconscious Wrexham.

In a fury, trembling, he tore himself out of the grasp of Pickering and Weston. Even before he stormed to the door, he saw Felicia drop to her knees beside the unconscious, pudding-spattered form of Jerome Wrexham, saw Tillie and Bessie Pickering running toward the fallen actor with clean wet cloths. He raced out to the stables, saddled Sally O, and, crying tears of rage, frustration and an underlying jealousy, rode out to Farley Shannon's.

Shannon was taking a nap when Richard arrived, so Richard busied himself, copying out the parts of Ben Jonson's *The Alchemist*, which the class would be studying and performing in the coming week. His hand trembled so that he could hardly write, but after a time he was able to bring his emotions under control, and the work went well.

Shannon was not only one of the finest actors of his day, he was also a wise old gentleman with an extraordinary understanding of human nature. He smiled as Richard finished the long tale of his sneeze-interrupted performance and of the clash at the Inn.

"But you say you felt your performance until the sneezing incident was quite good?"

Richard nodded.

"And," continued Shannon, "you made a number of references—to what point I could not detect—to the exceptional performance of Miss Wandrous."

Richard realized that he had indeed brought Felicia

102

into the story unwittingly, hardly realizing he was doing so.

"Yes sir, but—" he began.

Shannon held up a hand.

"Wrexham's childish pranks cannot have any kind of lasting effect on your career, Richard. It would be well if you could summon the maturity—and you are normally quite a mature young man, unnnnnhhh—to ignore his idiocies as totally as they deserve to be ignored. But your situation is apparently complicated by a passion for the excellent Felicia—errrrhhh—and all this will merely help you become a more accomplished actor sooner. Uncontrollable sneezes and falling in love are among the dilemmas most humans must endure. And the sooner an actor experiences them—unnnnhhh—and understands them, the better is he able to utilize and interpret them."

Over three glasses of wine, he then regaled Richard with misfortunes, comic and otherwise, which befell many leading actors and actresses in his time. He told him of the pandemonium created in 1697 by Jeremy Collier's publication of *A Short View of the Immorality and Profaneness of the English Stage*.

"The best of us were fighters, Richard," he said. "Playwrights as well as actors. Will Congreve wrote an answer to Collier. It was titled 'Amendments of Mr. Collier's False and Imperfect Citations'—errrhhh! The Duchess of Marlboro was so pleased with Congreve that she set up a statue of him at her dinner table, and each evening placed a glass of wine before the statue at dinner."

He sipped of his own wine, smiled again.

"Perhaps one of these days, Richard, a noblewoman will become your patron, and place a statue of you in her bedchamber."

Richard blushed.

He left Shannon with his spirits considerably lifted, with a new determination to succeed as an actor. His heart was still heavy over Felicia's allegiance to Wrexham, but he decided he would just have to live with this situation. He unsaddled Sally O in the stable, patted her muzzle affectionately and went into the Inn.

Ben Pickering was polishing glasses at the bar.

"Mr. Pickering, I just came in to apologize for my outburst. I should never—"

Pickering reached across the bar to take his shoulder in a firm grip.

"No apologies necessary, lad. Fact of the matter is, I was proud of you."

Richard beamed.

"Oh . . . thank you, sir. I truly appreciate your attitude. And I promise you it will not happen again."

"Of course," said Pickering, "I will have to forfeit you for the cost of a new tray, and whatever charges laundering Wrexham's fine suit comes to."

Richard nodded.

"And," added Pickering, "you owe me three extra hours of work."

"Yes, sir."

As Richard started for the door, on his way to the theater, Pickering called after him.

"And Richard . . ."

Richard turned back.

"Be careful of Wrexham. He's a bad one."

At the theater, the first person Richard encountered backstage was Gilbert Weston. He had just come down from his office and was talking with a carpenter. The carpenter left, and Weston greeted Richard.

"I'm proud of you, Richard," the actor-manager said. "But please control yourself from now on, and stay away from Wrexham. I'll have you back on the boards as soon as possible, but please exert every effort to avoid any further encounters."

"Thank you, sir. I will."

Richard went up into the superstructure to check his tinderbox, his rosin and iron ball. This done and arranged, he went to the under-stage area to be certain all was in order there.

He not only avoided Wrexham, but he also avoided Felicia throughout the evening. The performance went very well, and as soon as his chores were over, Richard rushed out of the theater and made his way home through the dark and stinking streets.

Mary's cough was worse, and he sat and told her the events of the day as she ate two bowls full of the barley and snail broth. He told her some of Shannon's stories, and of Pickering's forfeiting him, and of Weston's positive reaction. He still did not mention Felicia.

"I'm sorry about losing the money, Mary," Richard said. "It will be just that much longer before we can move you to the country."

"Tom Neely of the Haymarket Theatre came this afternoon," Mary said, "and left me two cloaks to embroider. That will more than make up for your loss, dear."

Richard shook his head.

"I don't like you to work that hard. You'll be going blind one of these days."

Farquhar brushed against her skirt, marched into Mary's room, returned, brushed against her skirt again, looked up at her and, with his emerald green eyes, said plainly, "It is time to retire."

Mary kissed Richard good night and followed the cat into her room.

In spite of the many matters on his mind, Richard fell into a deep, dreamless sleep almost immediately. He was awakened by a loud, insistent banging on the door. The room was pitch black. He did not know the hour, but sensed it must be the middle of the night. The knocking continued, impatiently, as he staggered to the door.

"I hear you. I'm coming, dammit."

He opened the door, and Felicia Wandrous glared at him.

❧ 13 ❧

"I've been knocking for an eternity," said Felicia. "I thought you and Mary were both dead."

She brushed by him into the dark room. He managed to find and light two candles. Felicia seated herself at the table.

"Sit down, Richard!" she commanded.

Sulking, he took the chair opposite her.

"What time is it?" he mumbled inanely.

"Three o'clock, or four. I've just come from Jerome Wrexham's lodgings." Felicia looked irritated.

"There's no need for you to tell me about it." Richard looked shocked, then hurt.

"Idiot boy, there *is!* Every need. Wrexham is a dangerous man and perhaps not quite sane. You have humiliated him beyond his capacity of acceptance."

"What of *my* humiliation, Felicia?"

"I've spent the last five hours, using every wile—and I have several—trying to persuade Wrexham to forget the entire matter, to leave you alone, to forget you exist. I've told him I would never see you again. . . ."

"What!"

"I won't, if it means saving you from great bodily harm, perhaps even death."

Mary, holding a candle, came out of her room. Farquhar followed, looking quite disgusted. It was plain to see that he believed something should be done about people who prevented a cat from getting a good night's sleep.

Mary's face was gray; her eyes looked sickly.

"What are you saying, Felicia?"

"Oh." Felicia rose from her chair, walked quickly to the older woman. "I'm sorry we woke you."

Mary smiled wryly at Felicia's apology. Her knocking would have awakened the dead. Felicia opened the large bag with the leather thongs which she had placed on the table, and took out a small flat box.

"Happy birthday, Mary. I'm sorry I couldn't come by yesterday."

Mary and Felicia both took chairs at the table, where Mary placed the box without opening it.

"Thank you. What bodily injury? What are you saying, Felicia?"

"You don't know Jerome Wrexham very well, Mary. He is a vain, ruthless and wicked man. He does not understand Richard's anger over what he considers harmless, rather humorous mischiefs; little games of the theater. He is furious over Richard striking him backstage last night, and emptying a dish of cabbage pudding on his head and beating him unconscious today."

Mary began coughing, uncontrollably, and Felicia opened her birthday box, handing her one of the two white silk handkerchiefs. Mary continued coughing into her own blood-stained cotton kerchief, shook her head and placed the silk cloth back in the box.

"Too pretty—" she managed, between coughs.

"What of *my* humiliation?" shouted Richard. "What of the pepper . . . the stuttering!"

"Richard! Blind, darling, stupid Richard! That is *not* the point! Wrexham is not a rational man. After five hours, very active hours, the best I could get out of him was that if you apologized, he would consider taking no further action."

Mary controlled her coughing with a great effort.

"What kind of action?"

"He would not say. But the implication is plain. He consorts with many unsavory characters. I think he is a partner in several ventures with one called Lancelot Higginbotham, who has all manner of criminals in his employ. I do believe he is capable of having you severely beaten, perhaps maimed . . . yes, even killed."

Alarm showed in Mary's dull, brown eyes. She bit her pale lower lip. She reached a hand out toward Richard.

"Richard, please, for my sake. Do as—"

She began to cough again, a more prolonged, chest-tearing series of rasping, barking sounds than Richard had ever heard. She put her left hand to her breast. Tears spilled out of her eyes, running down her gray cheeks. She rested her right arm on the table, and dropped her forehead onto the arm. Her back and shoulders shook as she fought to control the coughing.

"Do—Richard—do as Felicia asks. Please—for my sake."

She began to cough again, raised the kerchief to her mouth, and when she stopped coughing, it came away stained more deeply with blood. Felicia took the handkerchief from her hand, strode to the window and tossed it out. She came back to the table, took out one of the silk kerchiefs and handed it to Mary.

"Please, Mary. Use these."

Richard could not stand his mother's agony. He stood before her, feeling her brow, patting her shoulder gently. Trying not to sound too much as though he felt trapped, he said quietly, "All right, Mary. I will."

Felicia leaped from her chair, threw her arms around Richard and kissed him enthusiastically on the mouth.

"That's my bright lover! You'll not regret it. I'm having lunch with Jerome on Monday at the Inn. I'll excuse myself from the table after we're seated, and you will take that opportunity to make the peace."

Richard blushed, then, seemingly out of a desperate need to change the subject, said, "Felicia, since tomorrow is Sunday, would you come out to Waltham Cross with Mary and me? There is a small house for sale that I would like to inspect. We have sixty pounds saved, and perhaps I could work out some arrangement for Mary to move in before the summer begins."

Mary reached across and took his hand.

"I don't know if I'll feel up to going, dear."

"You go back to bed now and rest, and we'll see how you feel tomorrow. I think even one day in the country would be good for you."

Felicia was pondering Richard's question. Then she said with great enthusiasm, "A splendid idea, Richard. I believe Waltham Cross is only a mile or two from where Edith's schoolmaster lives, and I have been wanting to talk with him."

Richard looked puzzled, since it seemed to him that Edith Forrest was a little beyond school age.

"Now neither of you dare breathe a word of this. *Promise!*"

Felicia paused. "Edith and I grew up together. . . . She's pregnant. She fell in love with this schoolmaster, but he's married, and his wife is ill, and he can't leave her."

"Poor dear," said Mary, suppressing another cough.

Felicia continued. "Her father is the village vicar, and when Edith wouldn't tell him who her lover was, he ordered her out of the house—worse, out of the village! She's going to stay with me until we can find her some employment, and perhaps a place of her own."

"Does she sew?" asked Mary. "Perhaps I can give her some of my work."

Felicia patted Mary's lap.

"Thank you, dear, but I must find her something more regular than that if possible."

"Does she know when the baby is due?" asked Mary.

"I took her to my doctor this morning. He thinks probably December, or possibly January."

The following morning, after Richard and Mary attended mass in Father Whittaker's decrepit church near the dock, Felicia and Edith picked them up in a hired coach. It was a brilliantly beautiful spring day. The contrast between the fishy stench and soot-misted air of Billingsgate, and the clean, sun-drenched loveliness of the countryside brought tears to Mary Steele's eyes. Her coughing seemed to become less severe with each mile the coach clattered across the hard dirt road. By the time they reached the edge of Tottenham, less than halfway to Hertford, a spark of vitality shone in her brown eyes.

Edith Forrest, talking shyly at first, but ever more animatedly as time passed, discussed the fine art of sewing with Mary. Edith herself made most of her own clothes. Richard, quite happy at this long, forced proximity to Felicia, talked with her about the theater, about plays Felicia had done, and plays both of them were eager to do.

"I'm certain that in a year or two you will be ready to play Romeo to my Juliet," said Felicia. "And we will play the lovers as they have never been played before."

Richard blushed, and stole a glance at his mother to see if she had heard, but she was absorbed in her conversation with Edith. Felicia laughed.

"We will have managed to have a good deal of rehearsal as lovers by that time."

She leaned over and kissed Richard. This time Mary saw the action and smiled approvingly. Richard blushed again. He took Felicia's hand, and then a sudden worried look flashed in his sea-green eyes, as he remembered Wrexham and his own promise to apologize on the morrow.

As though she were reading his mind, Felicia took his hand in hers and whispered in to his ear, "Never mind Jerome Wrexham, love. Just listen to your Felicia, and be patient, and we shall find many ways to share our love."

She bit his earlobe, and whispered, "Many ways."

After making inquiry at the church at Waltham Cross, they found George Storey at a large stone house set in the middle of several acres of lush farmland. Cattle and sheep grazed in the meadows, and they saw three bulls, at various points, securely tethered with link chains. Storey was a short squat man with a ruddy complexion and a shock of white hair. He had a large nose and shrewd amber eyes. He smoked a strong aromatic tobacco in a clay pipe.

He mounted his horse, and led them to a small cottage less than a quarter-mile from his own large farmhouse. It stood at the edge of the road, with a long walnut rail running before it. A wide-spaced parade of walnut trees marched along behind the fence. A winding dirt road led from the main road to the door of the cottage. It had a thatched roof with a fieldstone chimney, two windows on each side of the door in the front of the house, two more in each of the sides and three in the rear.

The three rooms in the house were all rather small, but immaculately clean, with freshly whitewashed walls and a walnut-beamed ceiling. The main room was the kitchen, and in the center of its north wall was a large, open fireplace with a cast-iron kettle hanging from chains over a sturdy iron grate. Coals, ready for lighting, filled the grate, and a tinderbox, straw broom and poker were at the right side of the fireplace. In the center of the room was a large walnut table with six stools. A handsomely carved walnut bowl sat in the center of the table.

The two other rooms in the cottage were also freshly whitewashed. The wooden floors were swept and washed spotlessly clean. Against the far wall of each was a straw-filled, cotton pallet. At this hour of the afternoon the sun streamed through the western windows of the kitchen and the windows of the bedroom on that side of the house.

Richard watched the sparkle in Mary's eyes brighten with each step as they strolled through the cottage, escorted by Storey. He smiled as he watched her draw in deep breaths of the clear country air, run her fingers over the smooth, walnut table, stare at the vastness of the fireplace. *God,* he prayed, *let me find the means to bring her out here.*

As they walked through the rooms, Storey said, "It's a fine latle house, and ye'll find many coaches kumin' frad city all the day."

Richard, Mary and Edith had to concentrate to understand the farmer's dialect, but Felicia recognized it immediately as Yorkshire.

"Did ye go to skiewl in Yorkshire, Mr. Storey?" she asked.

He nodded vigorously, pleased that she recognized his place of origin.

"Indeed, in North Riding, near the North York Moors. Be ye a Yorkshire girl?"

She laughed.

"No. I'm one of those shameful daughters of the stage, and I've learned several dialects. In Norfolk you would go to shewel, and my Cockney friends say, 'skule,' just like they do in Cornwall."

They managed to follow his meaning well enough as he told them that he would no longer consider letting the house. The last two tenants had discouraged him forever in this practice. The next to last had almost burned the house down, and the last had left it in such a sorry state that it took two of Storey's farm hands a week to clean it up again.

He took them outside and escorted them around the vegetable garden in the rear of the house. There marched the varied leafy stems of corn, cabbage, tomatoes, lettuce and string beans, all in neat furrows and less than a foot high this early in the spring.

To the north stood a grove of robust apple trees.

"Yonder past the marshes," Storey pointed—"lies Epping Forest. Excellent hunting."

Off to the east, on the hump of a green hill, the chimney and roof of Storey's own house were visible.

"What price are you asking?" inquired Richard.

"Three hundred pounds." Storey blew a puff of smoke windward.

"Would you take two hundred?" asked Felicia, "if a lovely, gentle lady, like Mrs. Steele, who could do a bit of sewing for your family, became your neighbor?"

111

Mary tittered in embarrassment. Storey looked toward her.

"Mrs. Steele is that," he nodded, "but I have no family. I'm a widower, and my latle ones be grown and gone."

"Would you take two hundred?" Felicia pleaded.

"I might take two fifty."

"Would you take sixty pounds in hand, and the balance in a mortgage calling for annual payments?"

Storey shook his head.

Felicia continued the good-natured bargaining, but to no avail. Storey was adamant. Finally, he did invite the group to his farmhouse for tea and bread with rich butter, and peach jam. They accepted happily, but Felicia excused herself to take the opportunity for a quick visit with Edith's schoolmaster.

Storey's kitchen was spacious and sunny. The repast was tasty and filling and a chemistry began to develop between Mary Steele and George Storey in the bright sunlight. He was possibly twenty years older than Mary's thirty, but in vibrant health. Richard and Edith went out to stroll in the immediate area of the farmhouse, while Mary and Storey remained in the kitchen, chatting amiably.

Mary noted that a button was missing from Storey's heavy wool sweater, and offered to sew another on for him. He gladly accepted, and brought her needle, thimble and thread and a replacement button. He stood beside her as she threaded the needle, and her nimble fingers made quick work of the task.

"That should hold it." Mary handed him the sweater.

He stammered slightly, said, "My thanks, latle lady."

Edith and Richard returned, and less than ten minutes later, Felicia strode into the room. They exchanged friendly farewells with Storey, and Felicia asked once more, "Are you certain you can't work out a schedule of mortgage payments, Mr. Storey?"

He looked toward Mary Steele.

"Would do if I could. But, ah—ah, I've just bought another bull, and—"

"Oh, we understand, Mr. Storey," said Mary. "We understand perfectly. It's such a lovely little house, I'm sure you'll have no trouble selling it . . . even for three hundred pounds."

Felicia looked at Mary in mock, affectionate exasperation. As they settled in the coach for the twelve-mile trip

112

back to London, she said, "You're a fierce bargainer, Mary dear. I must remember to ask you to negotiate my next agreement with Gilbert Weston."

Mary smiled, looked back as the carriage clattered off down the road.

"It was *so* lovely," she said.

Felicia, sitting beside Richard, spoke across the seat to Edith.

"Your Josiah is a very nice and sincere man. I'll tell you about my meeting with him later."

It occurred to Richard that Mary had not coughed once in the past five hours. He looked at the contentment on her face. *Somehow,* he told himself, *I've got to get the money to buy that house.* But instead of getting a raise from Pickering, his earnings would be diminished for several weeks, until he paid for the tray and the laundering of Wrexham's suit.

And his chances of getting more important and more frequent acting roles seemed to rest with Wrexham. In addition to his other chores at the theater, he frequently helped Gilbert Weston with the bookkeeping and other routine functions involved with the theater's management. He knew that his ability to earn more money in the theater was entirely dependent on how many roles he could play.

The actors in the Lincoln's Inn Fields company were paid a fixed sum for each acting day. Wrexham, for example, earned thirteen shillings, four pence for each day he acted, while lesser actors in the company earned sums ranging from six shillings to the sixteen shillings, eight pence, which Gilbert Weston himself earned over and above his salary as manager. Richard's present fee for each acting day, in addition to the ten shillings weekly he earned for his other duties, was one shilling. Felicia was the highest paid actress in the company, receiving ten shillings, five pence per day.

As the carriage rocked along, Mary began to doze. Her head dropped and fell to one side, resting on Edith's shoulder. Edith put her arm around the older woman, and Mary began to snore softly. Again, through some extrasensory perception, which seemed to exist between them, Felicia picked up Richard's thoughts. She wondered how she could help Richard and Mary buy the Storey cottage.

She had close to three hundred pounds, which she had accumulated between the inheritance left her by her fa-

113

ther and her own savings, but she knew that Richard's pride, let alone Mary's, would not permit them to accept such help. In the same way, she could ask Gilbert Weston's permission to play a benefit for herself, as leading actors and actresses of the day did each spring, but again she knew Richard would not accept money she earned in this manner. Even if she could persuade them to accept the money as a loan, she had the feeling that Edith Forrest might need financial help in the near future, even more than Mary and Richard.

The only true solution lay in Richard's growth as an actor, in his ability to play more important parts ever more frequently. She believed Richard had the talent, and she knew Gilbert Weston was most anxious to move him ahead as expeditiously as possible. Wrexham was the obstacle, and she made up her mind to remove him as an obstacle, and quickly.

She took Richard's hand and looked into his thoughtful sea-green eyes.

"You will make your peace with Jerome Wrexham tomorrow, won't you, love?"

Richard smiled feebly and nodded.

"I will indeed, Felicia, and I pray he'll reconsider his edict to Mr. Weston concerning my performing."

She kissed him on the cheek.

"Put your arm around me, Richard."

He did, and she rested her head on his shoulder and in a moment was asleep. She slept until the coach drew up, in the early evening darkness, before the Steeles' decrepit building in Billingsgate. There she kissed Richard and Mary good night, and instructed the coachman to take them to her lodgings in Middle Temple Lane, where she dropped Edith.

"I'll see you later, love," she said, and instructed the coachman to take her to a two-story house in the Strand, just four blocks from the Lincoln's Inn Fields Theatre. On the second floor of the house lived Jerome Wrexham.

14

Wrexham was even more satisfied with himself than usual. It always gave him great pleasure to socialize with the aristocracy, and the elaborate reception following the wedding of the Duke and Duchess of Cheltenham this afternoon at the Duke's country estate in Sussex had been a most distinguished and exclusive event.

He had winked up at her as he knelt before the bride, and rose to extend his good wishes. The noblewoman had blushed, obviously recalling their last liaison. The Duke had complimented him on his performance in *Macbeth*, and had told him that he had persuaded Gilbert Weston to return his forfeiture. He had met at least six noblemen, who would prove useful contacts to him in the future, and one daughter of an earl, with whom he had danced a dozen times. He was certain he could develop this flirtation into an exciting affair. And the food and brandy and port had been magnificent.

He sat now, comfortable in his loose-fitting purple silk nightshirt with nightcap to match, in a fine tufted leather chair. His legs were stretched out before him and his feet rested on a leather-covered footstool. On the Queen Anne table beside him stood an expensive, though rather gaudy, oil lamp and two bottles, one of brandy, the other of port. The lamp gave off a good strong light. As he sipped his drink, he studied the folio he held in his right hand. It was *The Tragedy of Julius Caesar*, the last of the Shakespeare plays the company was doing in its current series. They were to rehearse the play beginning at ten o'clock in the morning for the next two mornings, and present it Wednesday evening.

Wrexham had played Brutus in the tragedy a half-dozen times, and knew the part fairly well, but his lines still required brushing up. He was refreshing his memory of scene three in the fourth act, a meeting between Brutus and Cassius in Brutus's tent. In the comfortable, reclining position, he nevertheless raised his voice as though he were onstage.

". . . Did not great Julius bleed for justice's sake?"

He belched loudly.

"What villain touch'd his body, that did stab, and not for justice? What! Shall one of us, that struck the foremost man of all this world . . ."

He belched again. A firm knocking sounded at the door.

"Enter," he commanded in his Brutus stage voice.

When Felicia did, and smilingly walked toward him, he put the folio aside.

"Ah, Felicia! Back for a bit more of the delights of last night!"

Felicia bent over and kissed his cheek. She sat on the edge of another tufted leather chair, on the other side of the table.

"Jerry, you did say last night that if Richard Steele apologized, you would drop the entire matter."

Wrexham looked annoyed.

"Must we talk about that childish recreant again?"

"I want you to go farther, Jerry."

"Farther—farther than what?"

"I want you to ask Gilbert Weston to find a role for Richard in every play we do. I want you to help in every way you can."

"Felicia, your senses are surely disordered!"

"Please, Jerry. You have always been a fine and noble gentleman. Always eager to help a woman—"

"Which woman? I thought we were talking about that vicious young candle snuffer!"

"His mother is a very dear woman, Jerry. An old friend, who has aided me on many occasions, through the years. She is ill, quite ill, with a disorder of the lungs, which requires she live in the country. . . ."

Wrexham belched again.

"I'm not responsible for his mother."

"I don't want you to be, Jerry dear. Truth to tell, she would not accept help of any kind. She is a proud, hardworking woman. She and Richard have saved sixty pounds and need some two hundred more to buy a small cottage in the country."

Felicia rose from her chair to stand before Wrexham.

"I'm simply asking you to help give the young man the opportunity to earn the money they need."

She touched his cheek gently as she bent to kiss him lightly. He pulled her roughly into his lap and kissed her. His purple silk nightcap flopped down over her head. She put her arms around his neck and returned his passionate kiss, lingering till they were both quite breathless. When he lifted his head, the nightcap hung down over his face. They almost laughed, but she said, "You will, won't you, lover!"

Wrexham tossed the nightcap back over his head, untying the lace on her bodice. She shifted in his lap, twisted suddenly as though she were trying to get into a more comfortable position. It seemed the most unfortunate kind of accident, that in shifting, her knee drove sharply into his groin.

"Ooooooooohhhh!" He bent over in agony. Felicia fell to the floor, quickly got to her knees.

Again the nightcap fell over his face as he threw back his head.

"Aaaaaaagggghhh!" he groaned, clutching himself.

Felicia got to her feet, patted his head. "I'm so sorry, Jerry. I didn't mean to—I was just trying—"

Wrexham took one hand away from his crotch to wave away her apologies.

"You must get some rest, lover." She bent over and kissed him solicitously on the cheek. "We have rehearsals all morning. Then we'll have a lovely meeting at the Inn, and tomorrow night . . ."

Pain still showed in Wrexham's eyes as he grimaced and nodded goodbye to Felicia.

Richard was tense and preoccupied as he completed his chores at the Inn the following morning. It went sharply against his proud nature to apologize to Wrexham for events Wrexham himself had initiated, and yet he realized that he must, if he were to have any chance of being reinstalled as a player in the near future. The Inn's kitchen was half filled with patrons, before people from the theater began to arrive. Wrexham and Felicia were the last of the Lincoln's Inn Fields group to come in. They found a table, and Felicia caught Richard's eye, smiled at him, immediately excused herself to Wrexham and left the table.

Taking a deep breath, Richard walked to the table, stood over Wrexham and stuttered, "Sssss . . . ssss . . . ssssu . . . sir?"

"Sit down, Richard," said Wrexham heartily, waving at Felicia's vacant chair.

The unexpected cordiality confused Richard.

"Sssss . . . Ssssssssss . . . Sssss." He reddened.

Even in his own ears, he sounded like some stupid serpent.

"Sssss . . . Sssssss . . . Sssssit . . . ? Du—du—did you sssss—sssss—sssssay, ssssit, sssssir?"

Wrexham smiled and rose from his chair, extending his hand toward Richard.

"We are fellow players, Richard. Members of the same family, so to speak. Let us forget the past and be friends."

Stunned by Wrexham's suggestion, Richard merely stared dumbly into Wrexham's face. Then he pumped Wrexham's hand violently, said loudly, "That would be fine, sir."

"Call me Jerry." Wrexham resumed his seat, smiling up at Richard. "And, when you have a moment you might bring a brandy and port for me, and a glass of ebullum for Felicia."

Felicia had returned to the table by the time Richard came back with the drinks. She smiled at Richard, and Wrexham even said, "Thank you." Gilbert Weston, who had come in earlier with another group of players, now waved to Richard and took him aside.

"Do you have a lesson with Farley Shannon today, Richard?"

"No, sir. Just on Tuesdays, Wednesdays and Thursdays."

"Fine, come to the theater as soon as you can this afternoon. We'll have several roles for you in Caesar, and you'll have to get up on them quickly."

Richard had all he could do to keep from singing through the rest of the noontime period at the Inn. Felicia had obviously worked wonders with Wrexham. But it troubled him, when he permitted himself to ponder the question, how she had worked those wonders.

For a good part of the time in the Lincoln's Inn Fields production of Julius Caesar, the stage was crowded with plebians, senators, guards, attendants and soldiers of

Rome. Richard was to play a plebian, a guard or a soldier in many of the scenes. A major part of his task was to move expeditiously from the stage to the wardrobe room, to change from cloak and wig, to doublet and helmet, to carry lantern or shout one phrase or another. He had one brief, but dramatic speaking role, Strato, servant to Brutus

In the last scene of the play, Wrexham Brutus requests his servant, Strato, to hold Brutus's sword, while he commits suicide by running upon it. Richard was to hold the sword out firmly and stiffly before him while Wrexham charged upon it, so that it would appear to plunge deeply into his chest. Gilbert Weston, of course, had staged the scene so that when Wrexham charged forward, the sword would slip in the space between his upper arm and his chest. They rehearsed this scene over and over again, slowly at first, then with increasingly rapid movement, until it played at a natural tempo.

Tuesday night, after a difficult rehearsal that morning, Richard had terrifying dreams. He saw Wrexham, carried away by the high drama of the moment, plunging directly onto the sword. Or he saw his own stiff arm, moving just enough to cause Wrexham to actually impale himself on the sword. The prop weapon would not be sharp enough to penetrate Wrexham's body, but in Richard's dream it did, and he woke in a cold sweat, trying to shake the picture of the prostrate, bleeding figure of Wrexham from his mind.

Felicia, who was playing Portia, wife of Brutus, performed diplomatic miracles dividing her time at rehearsals between Wrexham and Richard. In her relatively minor role, she sailed through her important scenes with the troubled Brutus, and counseled and encouraged Richard as he worked toward perfecting the suicide scene. As in the past, Richard watched in awe as Felicia rehearsed her first scene.

Felicia Portia's concern for her husband and the depth of her understanding was plain in every eloquent word, in every gesture, and Richard was hypnotized by her.

Richard saw Farley Shannon briefly on Wednesday afternoon, and Shannon's steadying influence and advice gave him confidence that he could handle the suicide scene properly without forgetting any of his lines. It was purely a matter of discipline. Shannon felt Weston had made a wise choice in giving Richard the part, since it was not a particularly taxing one, yet one that called for dramatic finesse and hard discipline.

Then came the opening performance on Wednesday evening. The limited Shakespeare series had found great favor with the playgoers, and again the small theater, smelling of sweat and burning candles, was filled to capacity with an eager audience. Again, as on each of his previous appearances, Richard felt the tension in his neck and shoulders, the urge to urinate, the slight weakness in the knees. He tried to overcome his nervousness, standing in the wings, concentrating on the action on the stage.

Then, as he made his first entrance as one of the crowd which followed the solemn procession of Caesar and the main players, the nervousness was gone.

Again, when he came off stage, he took a position in the wings as the play proceeded. As he watched Wrexham all through Act I, and into Act II, he thought that perhaps he had underestimated the handsome leading man's talents. As Brutus, Wrexham did indeed dominate the scenes. Until, once again, Brutus's first meeting with Portia. Then Felicia's naturalness, her communication with the audience somehow diminished the power of Wrexham's exaggerated posturing and expounding.

Richard listened, watched intently, as Portia said, "Within the bond of marriage, tell me, Brutus, is it expected I should know no secrets that appertain to you? Am I yourself but, as it were, in sort of limitation, to keep with you at meals, comfort your bed, and talk to you sometimes? Dwell I but in the suburbs of your good pleasure? If it be no more, Portia is Brutus's harlot, not his wife."

Brutus gestured dramatically, both arms outstretched toward the lovely Portia.

"You are my true and honorable wife, as dear to me as are the ruddy drops that visit my sad heart."

No, Richard thought, *Shannon was right. He does not really communicate.* But then in the second scene of Act III at the Forum, Richard felt perhaps he was wrong. Wrexham was truly moving and eloquent in his impassioned speech to the people of Rome.

". . . If there be any in this assembly, any dear friend of Caesar's, to him I say, that Brutus's love to Caesar was no less than his. If then that friend demand why Brutus rose against Caesar, this is my answer. . . ."

120

He gazed down at the crowd, stared intently at Richard, who stood onstage as one of the plebians.

"Not that I loved Caesar less, but that I loved Rome more. Had you rather Caesar were living, and die all slaves, than that Caesar were dead, to live all free men? As Ceasar loved me, I weep for him; as he was fortunate, I rejoice at it; as he was valiant, I honor him; but as he was ambitious, I slew him."

He raised his chin arrogantly. His mahogany eyes swept the crowd. He lifted his arms.

"There is tears, for his love; joy, for his fortune; honor, for his valor; and death, for his ambition. . . . Who is here so vile that will not love his country?" He finished. "If any, speak; for him I have offended. I pause for a reply."

Richard shouted, along with the other plebians, "None, Brutus, none."

After striding rapidly, back and forth, between stage and wardrobe room, working in a variety of costumes and scenes, and intently studying the performances in between, Richard's moment finally came. All the battles of Act V were over. Richard, the servant Strato, two fellow servants, Brutus and his friend, Volumnius, stood in the battlefield. Volumnius and the others exited, leaving Brutus and his servant, Strato.

Wrexham Brutus, still orating, said, "I prithee, Strato, stay thou by thy lord; thou art a fellow of a good respect; thy life hath had some smatch of honor in it: hold then my sword, and turn away thy face, while I run upon it. Wilt thou, Strato?"

He handed the gleaming sword to Richard. Richard, grief stricken at the prospect of becoming the instrument of his beloved master's death, choked out the words, "Give me your hand first: fare you well, my lord."

They clasped hands firmly. Then Brutus backed away, and Strato transferred the sword to his right hand, holding it firmly, stiffly before him.

Brutus tossed back his golden maned head and extended his arms.

"Farewell, good Strato. Caesar, now be still; I killed not thee with half so good a will."

He plunged forward, into the sword, and clutched at his breast, and pulled away, and fell on his back in the dirt of the battlefield. In the flickering light of the huge overhead chandelier, Richard stared with horror at the thick deep crimson stain spreading under Wrexham's gloved hands, clutching at his chest.

My God, what has happened? He never bled before! What—

As these thoughts raced through Richard's mind, Antony, Octavius, Messala, Lucilius and a number of soldiers stormed onto the stage.

"What man is that? Strato, where is thy master?"

Discipline! Tear your eyes away from the blood, the still body. Speak!

He did.

"Free from the bondage you are in, Messala; the conquerors can but make a fire of him, for Brutus only overcame himself, and no man else hath honor by his death."

He spoke the lines with the combination of sorrow and pride with which he had rehearsed them: with authority, with no stammers, or stutters, or sneezes. Blood or no blood. He was slightly pale, but that became the scene and added to the effectiveness of his playing.

Messala said, "How died my master, Strato?"

Richard said, again with sorrow, yet firmly, "I held the sword, and he did run on it."

Messala and Octavius made brief speeches and the play ended.

The audience burst into thunderous applause. Richard felt he had earned part of the ovation. Forgotten for the moment was the bleeding Brutus.

Wrexham rose when the curtain came down. Richard had not known, and no one had considered it necessary to tell him, that after Wrexham handed the sword to Richard, he took a sponge saturated with pig's blood from his pocket, and crushed it against his chest when the sword slid through the space between his upper arm and chest.

Backstage, he patted Richard on the back and said, "Well done, lad. I would like you to be my guest at the Bear Garden at Hockley in the Hole Monday afternoon. Two fine dogs from Eastcheap and two from Westminster will bait a bull. Exciting contest. Will you come?"

Richard nodded.

"I'd like to, Jerry. Thank you."

Felicia came over, beaming, and kissed them each on the cheek, Wrexham first.

ᘓᕫ 15 ᕬᕉ

The Eastcheap bitch stopped her charge abruptly as the raging bull lowered his head, almost scraped the hard dirt with his blunted horns in his effort to gore her. In his fierce lunge, the bull had reached the end of the long rope which was tied securely to the heavy leather collar around his neck on the one end, and to the deep-sunk iron stake in the center of the arena on the other. The taut rope jerked the huge, maddened black head sharply to the side. The bloodshot eyes blazed with agony and anger. The nostrils and mouth dripped crimson mucus. The wounded bull staggered slightly, and before he could recover, Madam Mohock, the wild-eyed bulldog bitch from Eastcheap, shot off the ground, sharp-toothed mouth agape, and clamped her jaws tightly into his throat on the left side.

The bull was already bleeding heavily from severe gashes along both his flanks, his chest, his rump and his left ear, which had been torn half off. In a crazed and desperate effort, the bull tried to shake off this last of the four savage, hard-muscled dogs, which had taken turns in attacking him this afternoon. He raised himself on his hind legs, front hooves pawing frantically. He thundered back to the ground, shaking his large, black-haired head from side to side, snorting and breathing furiously. He kicked up his hind legs violently. He wheeled, and roared in the opposite direction until he was once again jarred to a halt by the rope.

He took two uncertain steps backward, then regained his footing and whipped his head from side to side. Then with lowered head, he charged in the direction from whence he'd come. Again the taut rope stopped him as though he had run into a wall of steel. His tongue, dripping thick saliva, hung from his mouth. Snorting furiously, he again lashed his head viciously from side to side trying to shake off the dog. But the sleek coal-black Madam Mohock hung on.

Just inside the rope enclosure, four bullards with stout oak cudgels moved alertly with the bull's action. Madam Mohock's owner and trainer, a tall wiry, hard-eyed man, was down on one knee, inside a corner of the enclosure. There was a mad gleam in his eyes.

"Hold on, Madam Mo; hold on, girl; hold on—" he rasped over and over.

Richard stood with Jerome Wrexham directly behind the owner, just outside the enclosure. He was sick with whiskey and excitement. He had never attended a bull baiting before. He and Wrexham had arrived early, and Lancelot Higginbotham, who was promoting the event, met them and insisted on buying them several whiskeys at the bar, which had been set up in a small shed near the arena. Richard did not like whiskey, but on this, his first outing with Wrexham, he felt it might be unmanly for him to refuse a drink.

As the crowd arrived, Higginbotham left them to their own devices, while he and his assistants busied themselves taking bets on the four dogs in the competition. Wrexham seemed to know the dogs well.

"The Eastcheap dogs," he told Richard, "are far superior to the Westminster pair. The Eastcheap bitch, Madam Mohock, is best of all, probably one of the finest bulldogs in the Kingdom."

With some trepidation, at Wrexham's persistent urging, Richard wagered a guinea on Madam Mohock. He was quite nervous about making the bet, as he was about everything else about the bull baiting. He did not like violence or bloodletting, and he loved animals, but again he felt it would be a negative reflection on his manhood if he indicated any of this to Wrexham or Higginbotham.

The crowd made him even more nervous. In his four years in the theater, he had become accustomed to seeing mixed crowds, made up of gentry and persons of the middle and the lower classes. The sixty or seventy persons who came to the Bear Garden at Hockley in the Hole this bright April afternoon were an incongruous mixture of elegantly clad and bewigged aristocrats (even

124

a fair number of noble women) and all sorts of persons from the lower and middle classes: sailors and lawyers, and footmen and butchers, and clerks and several persons who looked like highwaymen. There were a modest number of older prostitutes, heavily painted and perfumed.

He discovered that there were some distinct characteristics of this bull-baiting crowd, which were not common to the attendees at Lincoln's Inn Fields. For one thing, all of them, gentry and lower classes, seemed to be heavy drinkers. The laborers and workingmen, and sailors and footmen drank beer for the most part, while the gentry preferred whiskeys of various kinds. They also shared a penchant for heavy gambling, and they seemed to be pronounced sadists.

Before the first dog was permitted to begin his assault on the bull, many in the crowd hurled sharp stones and rocks at the huge animal, whose dark eyes already showed a desperate fury. They laughed and screamed and cursed as the animal reacted to the early torment. And when the first dog drew the initial trickle of blood from a rip in the bull's belly, there was hysterical shouting and guffaws and tittering. It was not that they were cheering for the dogs per se, although they did scream incessant encouragement to the dogs on whom they had bet. It was that they enjoyed the bloody spectacle.

One of the most excited roars went up from the crowd when the bull caught Atilla, the second Westminster dog, on his blunted horns and hurled the young tan and white animal ten feet into the air. The dog landed hard in a twisted position, and, when he tried to get to his feet, fell over immediately onto his side, whining and writhing in agony. It was plain his back was broken. The crowd roared as his trainer carried him off. Those who had bet on the dog and lost cursed him bitterly.

Now, after four drinks and a long afternoon of watching the sickening mutilation of the bull, the insane noise of the crowd seemed to Richard to be entering his head not only through his ears, but through his entire skull. It felt as though it were pounding and jangling through his whole body.

"Madam Mo . . . Madam Mo—hang on, Madam—" they screamed.

The bleeding bull, with the wiry-muscled body of the dog swinging from his throat, and the screaming crowd in

125

the background swam before Richard's eyes like a surrealistic vision. His stomach turned and he fought back
the urge to vomit. Wrexham shouted into his ear, "That's
a fine bitch, Madam Mo. A winner, Richard!"

In a blur, Richard saw the bull stagger, lean toward
the ground on the side on which Madam Mohock hung.
Sensing that the bull was falling, the dog released her
grip. She landed on the hard dirt and leaped back just
before the bull's heavy, viciously abused carcass crashed
on its side. The cacophony of the crowd increased in volume, as Madam Mohock's trainer ran to his dog and took
her in his arms. He rushed off with her, to the increasing
cheers of the crowd, and the bull rose, slowly, painfully,
first to his knees, then his feet. He wobbled for a long
moment, then lowered his head, and raced blindly toward the crowd, directly across from where Richard and
Wrexham stood. What Richard and everyone else in the
drunken throng anticipated was that the bull would reach
the end of the rope, jerk himself to a dead stop and fall
over once again from sheer exhaustion and the cumula-
tive effect of his three score wounds.

It did not happen. The taut rope stopped the bull,
jerked him back several inches, and then as he lunged
forward again, with the last of his strength and determination, the rope snapped. Bleeding head lowered, the bull
charged straight ahead into the crowd. Six men and a
woman were hurled aside. One of the men was badly
gored. The others and the woman were merely battered
and not seriously injured.

The bull roared on, beyond the crowd, into the open
meadow, head down, with the four bullards, their oak
cudgels held high, in hot pursuit. The weakened bull
did not run very far before the bullards caught up with
him. Two on each side, the brawny men battered him
savagely about the head, mouth and shoulders with the
cudgels, until the clubs were thick with blood and tissue.
The bull dropped, shuddered for several moments and lay
still.

Wrexham, eyes gleaming with excitement, led Richard
to one of Higginbotham's assistants, who had taken their
bet. The assistant paid them off. Richard found no joy in
taking the two guineas.

"Would you like another whiskey before the next
event, Richard?"

Wrexham folded his six one-pound notes and put them

into his pocket. Richard shook his head, beginning to turn pale.

"Let's get back," Wrexham said. "In this next event, they stick darts with fireworks on them into a bull. Quite spectacular."

"I've got to leave, Jerry," said Richard, "I promised Mr. Weston I would copy some parts for him this afternoon."

Before he mounted Sally O (whom he had again borrowed from Pickering), Richard walked the mare around behind a large bush. He reached the secluded spot just in time. He vomited for almost three minutes.

The eight weeks from mid-April to mid-June were the most hectic of Richard's personal and professional life to that date. After completing the brief Shakespeare series, the Lincoln's Inn Fields company presented thirty plays in the forty-five remaining days of the season. Richard played one or more minor parts and/or made supernumerary appearances in all of them. And on eighteen of those forty-five evenings, he also played in the afterpieces.

Following *The Tragedy of Julius Caesar*, the Company presented a string of lighter Restoration plays, including William Wycherly's *The Country Wife*, George Farquhar's *The Recruiting Officer*, and to cap this series, four plays by William Congreve including the sophisticated, wicked *The Way of the World*. Of this group, the only presentation that played to capacity was *The Way of the World*. Farley Shannon's appraisal of current trends and audience tastes in the theater in England seemed to Richard to be borne out by the poor attendance at the risqué comedies.

Gilbert Weston then scheduled some of the earlier classics: Ben Jonson's *Volpone* and *The Alchemist*; *The Misanthrope* by Jean Baptiste Poquelin, better known by his stage name, Molière; and Christopher Marlowe's *The Tragic History of Doctor Faustus*.

These fared far better than the comedies of the period of the restoration of the Stuarts, and the reign of the merry monarch, Charles II. But to wind up the season, Weston went back to Shakespeare. In the final ten days the company presented *The Merchant of Venice*, *Much Ado About Nothing*, *Othello*, *Richard III*, and *Romeo and Juliet*.

The day after the bull-baiting event the weekly issue

of *The Tatler,* noted for its gossip about theatrical personalities, carried an item that threatened to rupture the incredible (to Richard) relationship that seemed to be developing between him and Wrexham. The brief commentary said:

All the battles in *Macbeth* at Lincoln's Inn Fields last week were not fought upon the stage, nor with the customary armaments. Leading man Jerome Wrexham and novice Richard Steele skirmished backstage at the conclusion of the play. Wrexham scored a telling blow with the head of Macbeth. Our secret correspondent informs us that on the day following, the battle was again joined in Mr. Pickering's Inn. The weapons, we are informed, were Mr. Wrexham's broad sword versus young Steele's cabbage pudding. The pudding proved mightier than the sword. The prize for whom the warriors are said to have contested is a lovely young actress in the company, rather well known for her flamboyant amours.

Felicia was concerned that this report might destroy the peaceable relationship she had contrived to develop between Richard and Wrexham, and Richard (though secretly pleased with his first publicity as an actor) also feared it might cause Wrexham to return to his troublesome ways. Indeed, Wrexham was rather cool to both of them for several days after the *Tatler* appeared, although neither he nor anyone else in the company said anything about it.

A week later, when Congreve's *Love for Love* was presented as a benefit for Wrexham, he seemed to have forgotten completely about the *Tatler* item. He made a concentrated personal drive to have all his friends, ranging from the nobility to Lancelot Higginbotham and a goodly number of his associates, including Polly Heffelfinger and Banger Shaw, attend the play. Wrexham himself sold tickets amounting to 121 pounds, five shillings, and tickets sold at the door came to forty-three pounds, nine shillings. Weston deducted the usual forty shillings for the house's nightly expenses, so that Wrexham netted almost 125 pounds.

He also scored a triumph in the leading role in the play. Richard had never seen him perform with more skill and polish. That evening, much to their surprise, he took Richard and Felicia to dinner at Lady Gertrude's. Richard was overwhelmed by the opulence of the establishment, its gourmet foods, wines and liqueurs, and he was stunned by its gambling rooms.

Again, Richard permitted himself to be embarrassed into drinking too much, by Wrexham's enthusiastic insistence that a continuing series of toasts be drunk to his highly successful benefit. Then he succumbed to Wrexham's persuasion that he gamble at the *rouge et noir* wheels. Guided by Wrexham, he won four pounds. Felicia had left him and Wrexham immediately after dinner. Edith had not been feeling too well, and Felicia wished to get home to tend to her.

Naturally, neither spoke the wish, but both Richard and Wrexham had each been hoping to spend the night with Felicia. When she left, Wrexham quickly comforted himself with the thought that he had not visited Cleopatra in some time. While still at the *rouge et noir* wheel, he ordered another brandy and port from the comely serving girl, and insisted she bring one for Richard. Richard was quite excited at having won four pounds. The three drinks he had already had gave him a feeling of recklessness. Disappointed at Felicia's departure, he accepted the new drink, and then two more. Some time later, when he had won another pound, Wrexham suggested they go to Mother Magruder's, and he agreed.

The jostling carriage, racketing through the dark streets from Pall Mall to the noisy, stinking Strand, did nothing to settle Richard's stomach. He was also developing a headache. By the time Wrexham introduced him to the fat bawd, he was sleepy and queasy, and wished he was home in bed. Instead, in a daze, he found himself in the white silken bed of Cleopatra Magruder. The closeness of the room and the young whore's perfume made him dizzier and more queasy than when he had entered the house. He was also terrified. He protested feebly as Cleopatra undressed him.

"Oh, come now, you honsome young mon. You will like makin' de love wit' Cleopatra."

Clara had discovered quickly that the name Wrexham had bestowed upon her was good for business. In fact, she had almost forgotten her true name. But after using oils and ointments, her delicate fingers, her mouth and other parts of her anatomy for twenty-five minutes, with no response from Richard other than a pathetic series of groans and moans, she gave up in despair.

She helped him get dressed and led him downstairs, where he paid Mother Magruder a guinea. He bid Wrexham, the bawd and the whore a forlorn farewell, and wandered out into the night to find a coach to take him home. As far as Cleopatra and Mother Magruder were concerned, Wrexham more than made up for Richard's inadequacies.

Richard was confused and displeased with himself the following morning. His head ached. There was an evil taste in his mouth, and he felt ashamed of having gone to Mother Magruder's. At the same time, he was disappointed in himself for having been unable to respond to as beautiful a creature as the young black girl. Yet he felt a need to conduct himself with fidelity toward Felicia, and his remorse at betraying her had overcome his desire.

He chastised himself for gambling at Lady Gertrude's. Mary's cough was more persistent and debilitating than ever, and it was urgent he get his mother to the country as soon as possible. He knew that he should not risk losing any money. Nevertheless, he was glad he had won. He was now six pounds closer to being able to buy a house. His acting career was developing at a rate that might well enable him to purchase a house like Mr. Storey's cottage by next spring.

In the future, however, he told himself, he must be careful not to jeopardize his career by carousing. The day was a trial. On the way to Pickering's, all through his chores of early morning, through rehearsal, during his acting lessons with Farley Shannon and through the performance of *The Way of the World* that evening, he denounced himself for what he considered to be his debaucheries of the previous night.

In *The Way of the World* he had a minor but fairly important part, that of Waitwell, manservant to Mirabell, played by Wrexham. Felicia had the role of Mrs. Millamant. In the second scene of the second act, when he made his first entrance with Foible, womanservant to Lady Wishfort and Waitwell's new bride, Richard stumbled somewhat over his opening line, but he recovered well enough and read the rest of this opening speech and the balance of his part quite well. When he spoke to Lady Wishfort in the second scene of Act IV, his final appearance, he was perspiring profusely under his wig, in his armpits and groin. His palms were moist and his throat was dry as he said, "Dead or alive I'll come—and married we will be in spite of treachery; aye, and get an heir that shall defeat the last remaining glimpse of hope in my abandoned nephew. Come my buxom widow: ere long you shall substantial proofs receive, that I'm an errant knight. . . ."

Foible said in an aside, "Or errant knave."

The curtain came down on the act.

In the wings, Felicia smiled at him approvingly as he came offstage, but he swore that henceforth, he would not drink excessively or spend late hours in bawdy houses.

The theater would shut down for the summer beginning June 15, and Richard was concerned about both the loss of income, and the loss of the opportunity to keep playing before audiences. The majority of the veteran members of the company had long since made their arrangements for the summer. Gilbert Weston was going to manage a company in the increasingly popular health resort Bath, slightly south and west of London, near Bristol, almost on the border between Wiltshire and Somersetshire. Wrexham was going to Dublin to perform in the Irish metropolis and in some provincial cities. Felicia had arranged with Sidney Colby, a leading comedian and manager, to work in his newly opened summer theater at Richmond Hill.

In addition to his financial and career worries, Richard was also troubled that he had been unable to be alone with Felicia and make love to her as he had on the memorable night of his debut. He knew that she had only spent one night with Wrexham since that time, but still he was jealous and missed her terribly. In spite of Felicia's and Edith's own best efforts, they had been unable to find employment for the pregnant girl, and she was still living with Felicia.

On the Friday, one week before the final performance at Lincoln's Inn Fields, Wrexham left the theater immediately after the curtain came down on *Much Ado About Nothing* to keep an appointment with Lancelot Higginbotham. Felicia came out of her dressing room and took Richard by the hand.

"Walk home with me tonight, Richard," she said softly.

Richard's heart leaped in his chest.

The night was misty and thick with fog. They walked

carefully through the dimly lighted streets, with Richard holding his cudgel tightly but they encountered no ruffians.

"Felicia," Richard managed to say as they turned the first corner, "may I stay with you tonight. . . ? I do . . . I do love you."

Felicia squeezed his right hand in hers, lifted it and pressed it to her breast.

"I love you, too, Richard, but Edith is still living with me."

Richard hardly dared say it, but he finally did, breathlessly, "Could we not go to an Inn?"

Even in the faint starlight, and the weak glimmer of an occasional street lamp, Richard could see the twinkle in her eyes. He interpreted the twinkle as fury when she said, "No, of course not!"

"Felicia, I didn't mean to . . ."

She laughed.

"Not tonight, Richard, but Sunday is your birthday, is it not?"

He nodded.

"Well, why do we not celebrate by spending the day in Richmond Hill? I have a friend who will permit us the use of a carriage and coachman, and you will have an opportunity to meet Sidney Colby. We can see his vaudeville entertainment that evening, and . . ."

She paused.

"And there is a lovely public house close by the theater, where we can spend the night."

Richard stopped abruptly. He was so filled with joy and anticipation, he could not resist taking her in his arms. The cudgel in his right hand banged lightly against her small, modish hat, knocking it askew.

He kissed her hard on the mouth, then abruptly released her. A picture of his mother, staggering out of her bedroom, bent over with violent coughing, suddenly flashed through his mind. It had been happening every night for more than two weeks. Prolonged, tortured, blood-spitting spells of coughing.

"I'm sorry, Felicia," he said, "I really can't be away from Mary overnight. Perhaps I could rent a horse, and—"

"Mary won't be alone," said Felicia. "She and Edith have become very good friends, and Edith is going to stay the night with her. It's all arranged."

He told his mother of his and Felicia's plans for Sunday, and she smiled approvingly.

"Yes, Richard. Felicia came by to visit me yesterday. I enjoy Edith, and she and I will have a lovely time."

That night, strangely enough, Mary slept until dawn without waking once to cough.

On Sunday, Richard and Mary had just returned from Father Whittaker's waterfront hovel of a church, when Edith and Felicia arrived. They were both wearing *contouches*, the wide over-dresses that were just coming into fashion. Women had worn them for some time in the house as morning dresses, but now some of the more daring young ladies—and Felicia could be numbered among them—wore them everywhere.

Felicia's *contouche* was a soft, green silk, and hung beautifully from her shoulders, loosely down her slim body. It was fastened down the front with bows of dark green velvet ribbon. Edith wore the same kind of loose-fitting *contouche* in pink, and it helped to conceal her pregnancy. Richard hardly noticed her. He could hardly take his eyes off Felicia.

Edith had brought a birthday cake she had baked, and the four had a gay breakfast of hot chocolate and cake before Richard and Felicia departed for Richmond Hill. The early morning was overcast when they rode out of Billingsgate, but as they bounced and wobbled through Southwark on Farrington Road, the sun came out. By the time they reached the juncture of the Farrington and York Roads, the day was clear and brilliant.

Felicia moved out of Richard's arms and took a small, neatly wrapped and beribboned box from her leather-thonged purse. She handed it to Richard.

"Happy birthday, love."

She leaned forward and kissed him gently.

With fumbling fingers he opened the package. It was a small box, and in the box was a gold chain, with a gold medallion hanging from it. His hands trembled. He stared at the engraving of the masks of comedy and tragedy.

"Felicia, it's beautiful. Thank you."

Felicia touched his cheek with her fingertips. With her right hand, she turned over the medallion. Richard shifted the box, so that the light coming through the window of the clattering carriage made the engraved inscription easier to read.

"Richard, the more I give to thee," it said in exquisitely delicate script, "the more I have. Felicia."

Richard's eyes misted.

"Sweet Felicia." He leaned forward and kissed her tenderly on the lips, as she took the chain and medallion from the box and placed it around his neck. The medallion glistened against Richard's clean, white-ruffled shirt.

"My Romeo," she smiled.

"I thought it was from Romeo and Juliet."

Felicia pushed the box and its wrapping to the side, removed her hat, placing it on the seat beside her, and lay her head in Richard's lap.

There was a coquettish sparkle in her eyes as she looked up at him. She whispered, "My bounty is as boundless as the sea, my love as deep. The more I give to thee, the more I have, for both are infinite."

From outside the coachman's voice bellowed, "Move those confounded sheep off the road, you idiot!" Felicia laughed.

"That can't be the nurse."

Richard laughed, too. He was remembering the scene now. This was the point at which Juliet's nurse interrupts the lovers' meeting. He tried to recall Romeo's lines. Falteringly, he said, "O blessed night. I am afeard all this is but a dream, too sweet to be substantial."

"Good, love! Good! You've edited Mr. Shakespeare a mite, and perhaps with profit."

She paused, and sat up.

"O blessed, blessed night"—he felt the night twice blessed—"I am afeard being in the night, all this is but a dream" (he had to explain it was night because most plays at the old Globe were performed in daylight) "too *flattering* sweet to be substantial."

Richard had never been as happy in his life and never expected to be as happy again. Even Sidney Colby's regretful announcement that he could find no place for Richard in the Richmond Hill summer season did not diminish his joy. Colby also produced shows at the Bartholomew Fair in the fall, and he told Richard he might be able to use him then. Colby was a funny man, fiftyish, fat, and as jolly offstage as on. His theater was a refurbished stable, which formerly housed asses. In fact, the small theater still had a strong smell of dung, urine and hay.

Colby introduced the evening's vaudeville entertainment with a prologue, during which he stood at downstage center with his arm around the neck of a patient and friendly ass, to whom Colby fed bites of apples as he spoke. Apart from Colby's own hilarious sketches—during one of which his breeches slipped down to his ankles as he danced a jig—the main attraction on the program was a hunchback conjuror named Fitzhugh Fitzhugh. The magician was thin, with piercing jade eyes, a sharp needle nose, and a broad thin-lipped mouth in a wrinkled face. His skull was completely bald, except for long fringes of green hair which hung down both sides of his head. No one knew by what alchemy he made his hair green. He spoke with a thick Irish brogue.

He performed a number of remarkable feats. In one he stuck a bodkin—an obviously sharp, awl-like instrument, about five inches long—into his forehead. He wiped away the blood, which appeared on his forehead, until it was completely clean, and his flesh showed no wound at all. He called Richard and Felicia, who were seated on the first bench nearest the small stage, to come up to examine the bodkin, which turned out to be real enough.

Then, with the two actors standing on the stage beside him, he set a brazier full of hot glowing charcoals in front of him, lifted one of the coals to his mouth, inserted it and chewed it happily. After a number of other tricks, he gave Felicia a sturdy link of chain and a heavy lock. He held his left arm out toward her, and asked her to wrap the chain securely around the wrist. When she did, he crossed his right hand over the chainbound left, and asked her to continue wrapping the chain around both wrists. Felicia did, and Fitzhugh Fitzhugh said, "Now, me darlin', if ye will, kindly put the lock through the links of the chain and secure it. Tightly, please! Tightly!"

When the links were locked he asked both Felicia and Richard to check to see that they were as tight around his wrists as they could possibly be.

"Are they tight and secure now, me foin friends?" he asked in a rich and booming voice.

The actors nodded.

"Well, then, say it is so to this lovely group of the king's subjects, if ye please!"

Felicia announced, "The chains around Fitzhugh Fitzhugh's wrists are as tight as they can possibly be, and they are securely locked."

135

As she finished speaking, the Irish conjuror bowed, and when he raised himself to his full, hunchbacked height, the chains were no longer on his wrists. He dangled them in both hands, then swung them around his head.

The audience applauded and cheered.

Later at the public house near the theater, Richard and Felicia had a late repast with Sidney Colby and Fitzhugh Fitzhugh. While Felicia discussed the repertoire Colby was planning for the coming summer season, Richard talked with Fitzhugh about his techniques and tricks. He was amazed to learn how simple were the secrets behind most of them. It turned out that the magician also read palms. He took Felicia's hand in his left hand, and Richard's in his right, and studied the palms intently for a time, nodding somberly. A most serious expression crossed his face.

Alarmed, Richard said, "What do you see?"

Felicia smiled.

Fitzhugh Fitzhugh looked at her, and a broad grin broke out on his wrinkled face.

"I see a long, happy life together for Richard Steele and Felicia Wandrous."

He was certainly right as far as the night that followed was concerned. They made love again and again and again. It was spectacularly magnificent, and Felicia introduced Richard to new ways of loving, some of which he had heard or read about, and two of which he had never even dreamed.

Dawn washed the darkness out of the small room. Outside the window, birds twittered morning greetings to each other. Eyes closed, Felicia breathed a long, contented sigh. As he turned to kiss her throat, Richard saw a squirrel scamper along a tree bough.

"Felicia?" he whispered.

"Hmmmmmm?"

"Could we be married later, perhaps in a year or two, if . . ."

She turned toward him, eyes half-closed.

"Not likely, love, but if I married anyone it would be you."

She closed her eyes again.

"Perhaps you'll change your mind," Richard said.

But Felicia was asleep, a smug smile on her lips. Richard turned on his back, put his hands behind his head, stared at the ceiling and listened to the melodious conversation of the birds.

Finally he fell asleep. Neither he nor Felicia thought about the strangely troubled look in Fitzhugh Fitzhugh's jade green eyes, as he read their palms, until much, much later.

ex 16 xe

Ben Pickering banged the oaken bar with the mallet he used for tapping hogsheads of beer, and occasionally for subduing unruly patrons. Loudly. Once, twice, thrice.

"Quiet! Quiet, if you please," he bellowed. "The Duke wishes to speak!"

The cacophony of chattering voices, giggles, laughter and clattering cups, glasses and dishes gradually subsided. Standing at the bar, facing the crowded kitchen, was Edmund Fox, Duke of Cheltenham, in the midst of clearing his throat.

The Duke made an imposing figure. He wore a full-bottomed wig of gleaming brown hair, divided into three tight masses of curls. His black velvet coat was trimmed with tasteful gold piping and large, richly embroidered cuffs. Diamonds, cut in the new, petite Dutch fashion, decorated his gray waistcoat. His black velvet breeches emphasized his muscular thighs, as his gray silk hose accented his strong legs. He wore glistening black shoes with high wooden red heels.

He had a deep rich voice.

"In behalf of Gilbert Weston," he said, "the honorary directors of the Lincoln's Inn Fields Theatre and myself, I wish to thank each of you for your invaluable, individual contributions to making this the most successful season in the history of our playhouse. . . ."

Pewter tray in hand, Richard stood alongside a table at which Felicia, Wrexham and Catherine Clark, a buxom, red-haired, thirty-year-old member of the company, sat.

The company had just given its final performance of

the season, the third successive evening of *Romeo and Juliet*. And the Duke had taken over the Inn for the entire evening to host this celebration. It was an extremely festive occasion.

There was a fixed smile on Richard's face, although he was unhappy and troubled.

Early that morning at the Inn, Ben Pickering had asked him to join Bessie and himself in a breakfast of hot chocolate before starting his chores.

"We're sending Tillie to a summer school in Scotland. . . ." Pickering began.

"Quite an expensive one, Richard," interrupted Bessie.

"And you know how badly business falls off after the theater closes." Pickering sipped the chocolate. "So, after next week, I'm afraid, we'll not be able to use your services, lad . . . till next fall, at any rate."

"Oh, we'll have you back next fall for certain," added Bessie.

Richard smiled.

"That's all right. I understand completely."

At the theater, he suffered through the third consecutive day of *Romeo and Juliet*. For three days, he watched with some anguish the first scene in the second act, as Felicia Juliet spoke to Romeo Wrexham with deep feeling.

". . . My bounty is as boundless as the sea, my love as deep—the more I give to thee, the more I have, for both are infinite. . . ."

He was conscious of the gold medallion, lying warm against the soft hair of his chest. Unconsciously his right hand fell to the rapier in its scabbard at his waist. There was no use denying it, he was consumed with jealousy. He knew . . . he firmly believed that Felicia did not mean those words for Jerome Wrexham, that she was merely playing Juliet with the natural skill she brought to every part. Yet each night as he listened, blood rushed to his jealous head and pounded in his temples.

Nevertheless each night, when the time came for him to make his entrance as Tybalt, nephew to Capulet's wife, kin of Juliet, in Act III, he overcame his nervousness, subdued his jealousy and strode onstage, completely under control. He fought his duel with Mercutio, Romeo's friend. He drove his rapier past Romeo Wrexham, when Romeo stepped between him and Mercutio . . . and ran Mercutio through.

Shortly after, in the same act, when he fought his duel with Romeo himself and was killed, he played dying Tybalt to exciting, yet controlled, perfection. Indeed, it was due to this conviction, that in spite of personal problems, in spite of his childish jealousy of Wrexham, he was able to give a flawless performance in this particular role—it was this which enabled him to endure these unhappy days.

For he had no work in the theater for the summer. He had no job at Pickering's. Felicia was leaving in the morning for Richmond Hill, and he knew not when he would see her again. *Yet he was an actor!* Tonight, before they all left for the party at Pickering's, Gilbert Weston had told him so; Farley Shannon had come backstage, hugged him warmly and said, "I'm proud of you, Richard." The Duke had complimented him. And most important of all, Felicia had kissed him fervently on the mouth. Even more exciting than the kiss was her joyful evaluation: "You are an *actor,* lover!"

He had seen Wrexham, standing nearby, glare at them at this point, yet Wrexham came over to congratulate him, too, before they left for the Inn. Of course, the lion's share of the approbation of his colleagues, as well as of the audience, had gone to Wrexham and Felicia, and to Rodney Finch, a young actor who had played Mercutio, but Richard still felt that in the last thirty days of this season he had truly become a professional player.

An outburst of applause brought him to the realization that the Duke had completed his speech. Richard stuck the tray under his left arm, and joined in the applause. The clamorous reception continued until the Duke made his way back to the table at which Wrexham, Felicia and Catherine Clark sat. They stood, and the entire assemblage rose to its feet, as the Duke bowed, waved his arms in acknowledgment and resumed his seat.

Gradually everyone sat, excepting Wrexham, who said in an aside to Richard, "Would you ask good Pickering to give us another bottle of the Duke's favorite wine."

Then he raised his voice so that it dominated all the hubbub in the room.

"Friends! Friends! Lend me your ears, if you will. I implore you."

As the room gradually quieted, he said in the ringing tones he used in playing a highly charged dramatic scene at center stage.

"I think I speak for the entire company, when I say that all of us believe ourselves fortunate—nay, blessed—to have a nobleman, so high placed in the Court, as the royal Duke of Cheltenham, to work with us. He is a shareholder and a most influential voice, a vital force in directing the affairs of our company, and preaching the gospel of the theater to the vast numbers of the King's subjects, subjects who still scorn us, who denounce us as rogues, vagabonds and licentious knaves and whores."

Waiting at the bar, while Ben Pickering uncorked the bottle of expensive French Burgundy, Richard glanced around the room. The members of the company, to a man and woman, seemed surprised, some even stunned by Wrexham's remarks. It seemed completely out of place for him to make a speech of this kind. Gilbert Weston struggled to convert a disapproving frown into a look of concentration and attention.

Wrexham lifted his glass of brandy and port. "I suggest we drink a toast to the Duke of Cheltenham."

Everyone in the room stood, glass in hand, excepting an elderly, elegantly attired and bewigged aristocrat and his companion at a table in a corner of the kitchen. He was Sir Chauncy Gore, an intimate of the Duke's, and an administrator in the Lord Chamberlain's office. The Lord Chamberlain's office controlled the destiny of theaters in the Kingdom, issuing the patents which permitted them to present theatricals, and determining which entertainments they could offer. Sir Chauncy had one hand under the voluminous garments of Mrs. Susannah Forbish, an older, though still voluptuous, actress in the company. His other hand fumbled with the ribbons at her bodice.

"To the Duke!" intoned Wrexham.

"To the Duke!" roared the company.

"Sir Chauncy," said Mrs. Forbish, "you *are* a rake." With which she began nibbling his earlobe.

The Duke stood, bowed graciously and sat down again. *Gad,* he thought, *Wrexham is an ass!*

They drank the toast. Babbling began in the room. Wrexham, still standing, raised his hand.

"Good colleagues!" he boomed. "I have a joyous secret to share with you. I have lately learned from the most important knight in the office of the Lord Chamberlain, our good friend Sir Chauncy Gore, that the noble Duke and our patroness, the Duchess of Cheltenham . . ."

These were titters in the room. Many were aware of the new Duchess's, Lady Sarah Palfrey's, outspoken dislike of the theater and its people. Sir Chauncy, upon hearing his name, looked toward Wrexham, but paused for less than a second in his explorations.

Wrexham repeated, ". . . the noble Duke and our patroness, the Duchess of Cheltenham, will soon bless the Kingdom with an heir."

He applauded, and there was an uncertain and embarrassed scattering of applause around the room. The Duke glared at Wrexham, shocked at this incredible invasion of his privacy. He then glared toward the corner, where Sir Chauncy now fondled a large breast in his left hand, while still probing with his right hand.

Wrexham was oblivious to the lack of uniformity in his audience's response, and to the Duke's irritation. The brandy and port bottles on the table were still half full, and Wrexham did not sound intoxicated, but Richard was surprised when he continued. As Richard made his way to the table with the freshly uncorked bottle of Burgundy, Wrexham continued, louder and more sonorous than before.

"And now, friends and supporting players, I have a gift for you."

He paused, and finished the brandy and port in his glass.

"As you know, I depart on the morrow for Dublin, where by the overwhelming demand of the populace, I will appear this summer. But, what few of you know is that before I reach Liverpool, there to board a ship to cross the Irish Sea, I shall stop in Warwickshire."

He paused, and looked around the room. He seemed to lose track of his thought as he saw Sir Chauncy and Mrs. Forbish in a tight embrace, but he tore his attention away from the couple quickly, and continued.

"Why, you ask, shall I stop in Warwickshire?"

He beamed.

"The sporting gentry among you are aware, I am sure, that in Warwickshire on Coleshill Heath, there is an excellent race track. And on the morrow four exciting races are scheduled there. I have it on unimpeachable authority . . ."

He looked slowly and slyly around the room, this time going right by the amorous corner.

". . . on unimpeachable authority, if you take my

meaning, that a certain two-year-old steed, named Bard's Bastard will win the second race of the day."

Again he paused.

"I am in a position to assure you that any person who wagers a bob or two on the Bastard will be repaid three-fold. Yes, at Coleshill Heath, the odds on Bard's Bastard are three to one."

His listeners were now completely captivated by his speech, except for Sir Chauncy and Mrs. Forbish, of course.

"Now hear this, dear colleagues," boomed Wrexham dramatically. "I have brought a friend."

He waved toward a corner of the room, opposite the one in which Sir Chauncy busied himself.

"Mr. Percival Heffelfinger!" he announced. "Would you rise, please, Mr. Heffelfinger?"

Polly and one of the older actors were sitting with two of the younger actresses in the company. He rose and lifted his glass of beer.

"At your service," he shouted.

"Mr. Heffelfinger," said Wrexham, "will happily accept whatever sums you wish to wager, make a record of your name and the amount, give you a receipt and place the bets at Coleshill Heath, and . . ."

He paused, and again surveyed the room, slowly and dramatically.

"And on the day after the morrow, Mr. Heffelfinger will return here to Mr. Pickering's fine establishment to deliver to you whatever sums you have won! As you all know, it is rare that we sporting gentry receive any information of this sort prior to a horse race."

He chuckled.

"It is even more extraordinary for us to pass it on, even to a group of friends and colleagues."

He paused again.

"This," he said, raising both arms triumphantly, "is my way of saying *adieu* to you all. Take this now, with my heartiest wish that you all have a prosperous and romantic summer."

The applause and shouts of approval were genuine enough. Wrexham's fellow players knew that he would not pass on a tip of this kind unless it was a sound one. They realized, of course, that there was always a chance whatever arrangements had been made for Bard's Bastard to win could go awry, but the majority of people in the room wagered on the horse. For the next seventy-five minutes, as general merrymaking resumed, Polly Heffelfinger moved among the tables, taking money, scribbling records and receipts. He did not write well or rapidly, which made the process an even longer one.

Almost everyone in the room made a wager, including Felicia, Gilbert Weston, Ben Pickering and the Duke. The Duke, Richard noted, wagered fifty pounds. Among the few who did not place bets were Sir Chauncy Gore and Mrs. Forbish, who seemed to be indulging in a wrestling match. Richard, too, did not place a bet. He was sorely tempted, but with no immediately foreseeable and certain source of income for the long summer, he feared to risk the money. Even on what seemed to be an excellent inside tip.

The wine and the whiskey, the beer and ale flowed. At various tables, hilarious stories of the season past were recounted to gales of uproarious laughter. A small fight broke out between two homosexual players in the company. It was quickly halted and the players kissed and made up. Friends made maudlin speeches to one another about their inconsolable grief over having to part for the summer. Lovers, casual and temporary, or earnest and long term, gave increasingly open expression to their affection, and Sir Chauncy took a now-eager Mrs. Forbish to one of the upstairs rooms. Here and there, from time to time, other couples followed.

Jerome Wrexham nuzzled into Catherine Clark's smooth neck, while sliding a hand along her warm thigh beneath the table. He had obviously and willingly surrendered Felicia to the Duke. This nobleman had one arm around Felicia's shoulders, and was leaning close to her head, still almost shouting to be heard by her above the constant, high-decibel hullabaloo in the room. Richard was kept busy rushing drinks to his colleagues.

He was sweating and nervous and becoming increasingly depressed. As the celebration progressed and became ever more bawdy, he felt more and more like an outsider, a serving boy, rather than an actor. At one point the insanely disloyal thought flashed through his head that perhaps the general populace was correct: all actors were knaves and rogues, vagabonds and whores. He noted the Duke pulling Felicia closer to him and maneuvered his way around the room till he stood directly alongside Felicia's table. Wrexham and Catherine

Clark were embracing and kissing passionately. Then Richard heard the Duke speak loudly to Felicia.

"Come now, dear girl, my house in Pall Mall would make a most desirable abode for you. . . ."

Felicia twinkled mischievous silver-gray eyes at him, and sipped her ebullum.

The Duke went on, "Small though it is, it is quite elegant and . . ."

"And," chided Felicia, "you have just these two months past installed my friend, the amply endowed Moll Davidson, of the Drury Lane Theatre company, in this very same small house, have you not, dear Duke?"

Fox laughed.

"You are well informed, my dear. However, I have learned to my regret that the beauteous Moll's physical being promises delights her spirit will not fulfill. She lacks fire."

Suddenly there was a thundering noise on the stairs. Sir Chauncy, barefooted and naked from the waist down, his wig askew on his head, came clumping down the stairs, with Mrs. Forbish, totally nude, bouncing and quivering after him.

"Enough, woman, enough," he gasped.

They raced around among the tables of their colleagues, who roared with laughter, applauding and shouting obscene, humorous remarks. Sir Chauncy raced out the back door of the kitchen with Mrs. Forbish, like an overweight wood nymph, in hot pursuit. The revelers in the kitchen soon went back to their own amours and intrigues, most assuming that Mrs. Forbish would trap the knight in the stables or one of the other houses.

Richard watched the Duke, as the nobleman took a long drink of his wine. He then wiped his mouth with a silk handkerchief, put the silk back in his cuff and kissed Felicia's cheek, resuming his conversation as though there had been no interruption.

"I tire of her lack of fire," he said loudly.

He roared his pleasure over his small rhyme.

Felicia pulled away from him a bit.

"I am indeed flattered, dear my Lord, and mean no disrespect, but I have discovered of late that the flint in my tinderbox fails to spark when struck by noblemen. So I, too, should no doubt lack the fire you desire . . . indeed require."

The Duke again roared with laughter.

"You are a bold and brazen wench, Felicia." He paused, then recited, "I tire of Moll's lack of fire, yet inspire not in you the fire I desire, nay require."

Eavesdropping Richard moved a step closer to the table, reached in for an empty bottle between the Duke and Felicia. It was difficult to know if the Duke was drunk, though he had consumed his full share of a half-dozen bottles of Burgundy. Then the Duke seemed to turn suddenly serious.

"Fear you not, Felicia, that I might be so displeased as to have you dismissed from the company, contract or no contract, and possibly even sent to the whipping post?"

Felicia smiled, patted his cheek.

"You would not be so ungallant, dear my Duke. You are far too just a gentleman, and I am far too fine an actress and asset to the company."

The Duke lifted her hand to his lips and kissed it lingeringly.

Felicia rose in the middle of the kiss.

"I must depart early in the morning for Richmond, sirrah. Would you take me home?"

Richard had been enjoying the repartee with some sense of awe, but now jealousy possessed him again, until he remembered that Edith was still living with Felicia. He was wondering whether Felicia might go elsewhere with the Duke, when she walked to an adjoining table at which Gilbert Weston, Farley Shannon and two of the older actors in the company sat. She kissed each of them and bade them farewell. She waved a goodbye to a number of colleagues at nearby tables, who had noticed her imminent departure.

"Goodbye, loves; have a happy summer."

She blew kisses with both hands. She turned to Richard, put her arms around his neck and kissed him fervently on the mouth.

"And you, love, a special goodbye, and write me soon how you fare?"

The Duke waved a general adieu.

Richard, in a daze, watched Felicia precede the Duke out the door. Somehow, he did not think now that she would spend the night with the Duke.

Shortly, Wrexham and Catherine Clark retired to one of the upstairs rooms. And a half-hour after Felicia's leave-taking, Gilbert Weston and Farley Shannon rose to depart. They stopped Richard on their way out.

"I hope you will continue working with Farley throughout the summer, lad," Weston said.

Shannon put his arm around Richard.

"We've discussed next season's repertoire," he said, "and we can work on many specific parts in the upcoming plays."

Richard assured them he would be grateful to continue working with Shannon, thanked them profusely and wished Weston well at Bath. In the space of the last hour his life had brightened considerably. He worked until the last drunken revelers left the Inn, helped clean up, then said a warm goodbye to the Pickerings, and whistled his way home to Billingsgate.

It was two o'clock in the morning, and as he stood before his door, he had the strange feeling that the end-of-season celebration was continuing in his own home. From behind the door came the merry sound of a man singing a lilting, up-tempo sea chantey in a booming bass voice. And a woman, laughing softly. He opened the door to find Father Whittaker dancing a schottische with his mother, and bellowing happily on about a sailor who had been seduced by a mermaid.

17

When Richard entered, Father Whittaker danced Mary toward him, threw one arm around Richard's shoulder and hop-skipped the three of them around the kitchen, singing all the while. In a moment, Mary broke away and collapsed onto a chair at the table, gasping for breath, but laughing happily. Father Whittaker cut off his song in the middle of a high note, reached for the gallon bottle of Scotch on the table, and poured the two glasses half-full. Mary waved her hand. "Take mine, Richard, I've had enough. My brains are all a-spinning," she laughed.

Richard lifted the glass and looked at the priest quizzically.

"You bit her nose, Richard, do you remember?" He chuckled, and drank his glass empty.

"Lily Culoghen," explained Mary, smiling at the puzzled look on Richard's face. "Father married her this afternoon."

"Aye, to a handsome young farmer from Glasgow. Surely you remember the Culoghens, and Lily, Richard."

"You were scarce three, and Lily perhaps six," prompted Mary. You were eating a bit of marzipan. . . ."

The mention of the sugar candy somehow had the effect of a magical phrase. It conjured a happy scene. Richard recalled the merry singing. He could almost taste the sweetness again, feel the stickiness around his mouth and on his fingers. A vague, unfocused picture formed in his mind. He saw a pudgy, curly-haired little girl, kneeling beside him on the floor, bending over him,

148

bringing her blub-cheeked face ever closer to his mouth and his marzipan. He was sure she was attempting to take it from him. It was not until later that Mary explained that she was only trying to kiss him. All he knew was that her face and her mouth were getting closer and closer to his treasured candy, and he bit her nose.

Now, he could almost hear, once again, her short scream as she pulled away, and her anguished wailing. And he saw the grown-up exuberant revelers stop, shocked. His mother had been dancing with Father Whittaker. The picture was not clear in his mind, but it seemed to him that Father Whittaker was not wearing his clerical habit. His mother was lovely and full of vitality. She was working as a barmaid at the time, and they were living in the hovel in Clerkenwell, Richard recalled now. The episode was the earliest of his memories. Richard did remember other, happy times with Lily Culoghen, who was his playmate till he was eight. She did kiss him every so often, but he had always disliked it.

The other dancing adult couple that day he bit Lily's nose was Tom Culoghen and his wife, Elizabeth. Richard had learned, over the years, that Tom Culoghen and Arnold Whittaker had gone through their religious training at the Jesuit seminary together, but that one week before their scheduled ordination into the priesthood, Tom Culoghen had decided he could not live the life of a cleric, and had gone into police work. Today he was one of the city's most respected police magistrates.

"It was a beautiful and joyous wedding party," said Father Whittaker now.

So that was it. After he had performed the marriage ceremony, Father Whittaker had stayed for the party, where he consumed copious quantities of some of friend Tom's finest Scotch, and then accepted a gift of another gallon of the whiskey from the magistrate. He had come straight away to the Steeles' to celebrate with Mary the marriage of the daughter of their old friends.

Now they reminisced, Father Whittaker and Mary, and recalled to Richard other episodes of his childhood. Shortly, Mary retired. Remarkably, she had not coughed once the entire evening. Also quite remarkably, the priest seemed to be perfectly sober, his consumption of alcohol evidencing itself only in high spirits. When Richard told him he was concerned because he had no employment

149

for the summer, Father Whittaker said, "You might care to work on the docks, lad. Francis Bruce is always looking for extra hands to help with the loading and unloading of cargo."

Bruce owned a number of warehouses along the Thames, all the way from the London docks, just east of the Tower of London, to the East India docks some five miles further eastward, beyond Bromley. He signed Richard on immediately.

So began for Richard a humid and soul-melting summer, filled with several emotional and physical agonies and a few triumphs.

On that first morning, right after dawn, the sun was a molten hole low in the blue wall of the eastern sky. The stinking Thames lay still as a lake in the windless day. Heat waves shimmered like translucent snakes, rising from the water. Even at this early hour of such a stultifying Monday, the London docks were noisy and odorous. Smells, some identifiable, some not, mingled and lay heavy in the air: pungent spices, sweating bodies, cured tobacco leaf, fish, salted beef and pork.

Two sailors, arms about one another's shoulders, staggered along, singing loudly. They both wore sweat-drenched, filthy white shirts and slop hose, wide-kneed breeches with blue and white stripes, now so dirty the stripes seemed black and gray. A captain argued loudly with a merchant. Aboard one of the ketches a mate shouted at his crew. A warehouseman wheeled a cart loaded with cloth bolts down the plank of a sloop. Two stout Caucasians with beards examined six shackled Negro slaves on the foredeck of a brig.

Richard smiled, noting the name of the ship he was to work: the *Merry Mary*. A good omen? She sat, unmoving, in the stagnant river, one of scores of vessels of all kinds tied up at the docks. There was a tear in the triangular lateen sail on her mizzenmast. The *e*, the *a* and the *y* in her name had faded, so that the bow introduced her as *M rr   M r* . In her hold there were thirty-four hogsheads, ten tierces, twelve barrels and fifteen half-barrels of rum, and what seemed to Richard to be hundreds of bales of cotton and casks of tobacco.

"Move yer arses!" bellowed Horatio Busk. It seemed inappropriate that he did not carry a bullwhip. Yet he achieved the same effect with his gravelly, coarse curses, and an occasional gnarled fist to the side of the head of any man who did not carry his share of the load. Busk had been a common seaman from boyhood to the age of sixteen. Then he had gone to work for Francis Bruce, loading and unloading cargo. In the twenty years that had passed since then, he had become known as the most vicious and demanding taskmaster on the waterfront. But he could get a ship unloaded and its cargo stacked in a given warehouse within an incredibly brief time.

His short stocky body seemed to have been carved out of hardwood and covered tautly with hairy, tanned leather. His muscle-bound arms and legs moved in spasmodic motions, yet with enormous strength and agility. He had been known to shove the largest of the hogsheads of rum, holding some 140 gallons, several meters into a more desirable position against a warehouse wall; the 42-gallon tierces he threw around like a child's play blocks. His leathery face was wrinkled. Permanently half-closed eyelids cut off the tops and bottoms of the murky dark gray irises in his mean close-set eyes. His nose had been broken in brawls eleven times, and was merely a blob of leather-covered smashed bone and cartilage above a thin-lipped mouth. The few remaining black teeth, erratically placed in the purple-pink gums, were visible a hundred times in the course of the long day as he bellowed curses at his men. He wore his long black hair in a heavy pigtail, which lashed around wildly as he moved from ship to plank to dock and back—heaving, lifting, hurling, and commanding and cursing his men.

After the first hour, Richard's muslin shirt was plastered to his torso. His entire body ached. He moved away from the cart, onto which he and another man had lifted a hogshead of rum, and unbuttoned his shirt. He had peeled it away from his chest, when he felt a fist from behind crash against the side of his jaw, just under his ear.

The roar was almost as painful as the blow.

"Move yer bloody arse, actor! This is no fuckin' stage yer on!"

Richard dropped his shirt, raced up the plank and down into the *Merry Mary*'s pungent hold once more. By noon his glistening, well-muscled but pale torso had turned pink in the high, burning sun; the tops of his shoulders, his nose and cheekbones were more crimson than pink. He sat apart from the rest of the deeply tanned and

151

sweating men, grateful to rest in the shade for a half-hour. He fingered Felicia's medallion on the chain around his neck, and thought of her for a moment. It did not help. He chewed his cold mutton and dry bread morosely, trying to ignore his tortured back and limbs.

He also ignored the remarks of a gaunt and scraggly-bearded veteran seated beneath the extended roof of the shed a few feet from him.

"How would you like to bugger the new lad, Frankie?" cackled Scraggly Beard to a companion. Richard munched on, ignored Frankie's reply, " 'E 'as a fine arse on 'im, that I'll testify."

Richard chewed off another mouthful of mutton, wondered idly how Horatio had learned he was an actor —Father Whittaker had probably mentioned it to Bruce, and Bruce to Busk. But Richard was far too fatigued to be concerned over Busk's obvious antagonism toward theater people, or to recognize that the attitude of the dock workers was a harbinger of a hard summer.

He worked through the afternoon like a manic mechanical man, wrestling hogsheads, tierces and barrels of rum, bales of cotton and casks of tobacco. By midafternoon his skin had turned a deep crimson. He found the smell of his own armpits offensive. His breeches were glued to his aching thighs. The sweat in his crotch was causing a rash. But worst of all, the sun seemed to be boiling the blood in his veins. His temples throbbed. He was dizzy, and he began to stagger. Then, suddenly the humidity became blessed cool water and fell in a deluge from the skies. All the men, even Busk, stopped where they stood and lifted their faces to the heavens, mouths open, reveling in the shower. But only for seconds.

Clubbing the man nearest him, Busk screamed above the sound of the heavy rain, "Get that cotton in out'a the fuckin' rain." He charged from one cluster of men to another, commanding, swearing, and swinging heavy fists.

The men went back to work, laughing. Some began singing bawdy sea chanteys as they worked. Richard smiled in relief, in spite of the pain as he tore the sunburned skin of his shoulder while heaving a bale of cotton onto his back. He staggered toward the warehouse door, licking the delicious rain from his lips, as it ran down his face. The shower ended all too soon, but it had cooled the men and cleared the air enough to make the last hour of the day's work bearable.

The walk to Pickering's Inn took Richard twice as long as it would have normally. He walked slowly and stiffly, wincing most of the way, unable to determine whether the severe sunburn or the overstrained muscles were giving him more discomfort. Bessie Pickering's beef stew lifted his spirits and eased his aches considerably. Ben Pickering joined him for a moment at the table to inquire how he was faring.

"I'm loading cargo on the docks," Richard told him.

Pickering slapped him on the back.

"Fine, lad . . ." he started, and stared as Richard moaned an anguished, "Owwwwweeeee," and gingerly peeled the shirt away from the blistering skin.

"Sorry, lad. I didn't realize your burn was that bad."

He yelled to Bessie.

"Bess, bring me a jar of that mutton fat, if you please."

She did, and they both urged him to apply the fat generously whenever he was exposed to the sun for any length of time. Bessie went back behind the bar.

"Did you get your money, Richard?" Ben asked.

"What money?"

"That you won on Bard's Bastard."

"I didn't win, Mr. Pickering."

"Of course you did. We all did. Bard's Bastard won. I won six pounds, wagering two."

Richard groaned.

"I didn't bet."

"A pity, lad. A pity . . . why did you not?"

Richard shrugged.

A pity? A veritable, lunatic folly perpetrated by a spineless calf's head! His wages on the docks were to be three pounds per month, the same as that earned by an ordinary seaman, six pounds for the two months of summer. If he had had the nerve to bet two pounds, he would have made as much as he would breaking his back these next two months. Then a single thought exploded in his head. If he had bet sixty pounds, he would have won a hundred and eighty pounds, and could have bought a cottage in the country.

He pushed his bowl aside. He felt sick. He had arranged with Ben Pickering to use Sally O on the three nights each week that he would study with Farley Shannon. Tonight was the first of the nights of the summer meetings. For a moment he thought he would not go. He was too burdened with aches and blisters, raw skin and misery. But finally he forced himself up from the table, bade the Pickerings good evening and rode out to Shannon's. Sally O's hooves went *clip-pet-tee-clop, clip-pet-tee-clop* on the dirt of Mile End Road. Which Richard's critical heart translated, *you-are-a-fool, you-are-a-fool.*

Richard recognized the small carriage and the dappled mare tied up before Farley Shannon's home. It belonged to Doctor Harvey Thorndike, who was Mary's physician as well as Shannon's. Dr. Thorndike tended a number of theater people, both in the Lincoln Inn's Field and the Drury Lane companies. The doctor came down the path from the thatch-roofed house as Richard dismounted. Richard, concerned, trotted over to meet him.

"Good evening, doctor. . . . Is Mr. Shannon poorly?"

"Evening, son. Only a mite weaker than usual." He shook his head as he climbed to the seat of the carriage.

"If only it were given us by the good Lord to understand some of old age's strange disorders."

From the seat, he inquired, "How is Mary, Richard?"

"She seems somewhat improved, doctor . . . coughing quite a bit less the last several days."

Thorndike smiled and nodded his approval, flicked his dappled gray with his whip and drove off.

Feeble though he might be, Shannon had apparently heard Richard's arrival and the voices of the two men. He opened the door just before Richard reached it, put his arm around Richard's shoulder and escorted him inside. The weight of the thin arm sent a stab of pain through the shoulder, but Richard merely winced. In the lamplight of his sitting room, Shannon squinted at Richard as he waved him to a chair.

"You look soiled and disreputable, and as though you were baked in the sun this blistering day."

"That I was, sir."

Richard explained his new employment, and lifted the dirty muslin shirt from his chest and half his shoulder to show Shannon the degree of his burn and the many blisters which had burst.

"I'm sorry, Richard, but you will heal soon, and I think the work on the docks may prove a blessing. Though few people realize it, strength and endurance are valuable assets to an actor, and there's no mental effort involved—errrhhhh. . . ."

He paused a bit longer than he normally would for a breath.

"Soon the manual effort will be automatic, and you can be studying the plays as you work."

He rose painfully, walked to the bookcase and took down two copies of a folio. He handed one to Richard and resumed his seat. He took a series of long, deep breaths.

"Richard, pour us some claret."

As Richard did, Shannon said, "You realize, of course, that Gilbert has not finalized the order in which the new season's repertoire will be presented—unnnnhhhh. Thank you, lad. . . ."

He took the wine glass from Richard, sipped from it and leaned back to continue.

"One of the earliest productions, however, will be *As You Like It*. Do you know it?"

Richard put his own wine down and shrugged.

"Not nearly so well as a number of other Shakespeare plays, but I've read it."

"It is light and pleasant, far from our poet's finest, errrhhhh. You know, too, that Gilbert has not yet cast any of the productions, except possibly in the most preliminary way in his head. Unnnnhhhh. You conceivably could play William, the country lad, who is madly in love with the country lass, Audrey. Or possibly Touchstone, the clown, which would be considerably more ambitious—errrrhhhhh —but somewhere along the way, during the season, Richard, Gilbert and I would both like you to play some comedy roles."

Listening to the legendary actor and coach, Richard could almost forget his own physical miseries.

"I would be most grateful."

Shannon waved a hand at him, and continued.

"Or perhaps even the more ambitious role of Jacques, one of the three sons of Sir Rowland deBoys."

He stopped, and his hand shook slightly as he reached toward his wine. He picked up the glass in both hands and sipped.

"Let us read it together."

They did, with Shannon making observations and comments about various characters, the spirit of a scene, the way he himself had played Orlando in his youth. After an hour, Richard could see that his coach was tiring badly.

He was about to suggest they stop for the night, when Shannon himself put down his folio, rubbing his eyes stiffly and wearily.

"Would you mind, son, if we continued Wednesday? Unnnnhhhhh. You could read the play yourself in the next couple of days, and we'll resume on your next visit."

Richard got to his feet quickly.

"I'm very sorry, sir. I didn't mean to exhaust you. By all means . . . Wednesday."

At the door he said most earnestly, "I will never be able to thank you enough for what you have done, and continue to do for me, Mr. Shannon. I hope, some day, I may find some means to repay you."

Shannon patted his shoulder, quickly withdrew his hand.

"Oooops, sorry, lad. I forgot your burns." He paused. "Your accomplishments as a fine actor will be all the payment I will ever desire."

So inspirational was his brief visit with the old actor that he was able to ignore his sore muscles and blistered shoulders on the ride back to Pickering's and the walk home. Mary was asleep, but Farquhar came striding out of her bedroom to greet Richard. The cat stretched, fell over on his side, with front and back legs extended, requesting Richard to rub his stomach in greeting. Richard groaned as he bent over to do so. Satisfied, Farky strolled back into Mary's room, nimbly leaped onto her bed and snuggled in his place behind her knees.

The night was surprisingly cool, considering the kind of day it had been. Richard pondered applying Pickering's mutton fat to his shoulders and torso, but the rancid smell of it discouraged him. He decided he would use it only outdoors. He eased down gently onto his pallet and closed his eyes. But could not sleep. If he lay on his back, it felt as though someone had set the straw-filled mat afire. He tried his left side, but this was no better. He lay on his stomach, arms outstretched over his head. So tender was his chest, that even Felicia's tiny medallion seemed to be branding him through the hair.

He hoped at least that he would dream of Felicia. But hours later, when he fell asleep, he did not. He dreamed instead about Horatio Busk. When he awoke, he remembered only fragments of the dream. Busk seemed to be whipping him with a long, hard leather whip. He could feel the lashes on his shoulders, his back, his chest. He finally escaped the savage whipping by diving over the side of the dock into the garbage- and debris-littered Thames. He awoke as he hit the water. He was wet with sweat and the moisture from his blisters. The dream was unpleasant. He could not know that it was also prophetic.

18

Thanks to the mutton fat, Richard's sunburn soon healed. By the end of the week his face and torso began to tan. In a fortnight he was deep copper from his hairline to his waist. His muscles became accustomed to the daily twelve-hour grind of lifting, heaving and hauling, as he pounded his way back and forth between ship and dock with his heavy loads. The aches vanished. He followed Busk's barked, obscene orders, and did his job with increasing competence, and more and more mechanically. Most of the time, as he worked, he was thinking through the lines in the plays he was studying, the parts on which he was working with Farley Shannon thrice weekly. During the noontime hiatus, he read plays as he ate. Occasionally his mind would wander off to thoughts of Felicia, or he would fret over his mother's erratic condition. At day's end, he hastened to Pickering's for a simple supper, then either home to Mary, or out to Farley Shannon's. And he was always back at the docks by dawn the next day.

In the course of the summer, he studied six Shakespeare plays in addition to *As You Like It*, as well as plays by other writers. He rehearsed specific parts with Shannon, and became more and more confident as each week passed. He could hardly wait for the reopening of the theater in September. Twice, Shannon fell too ill to work with him, but each time the elderly actor recovered quickly and seemed none the worse for his temporary incapacity.

Richard worried about him, for not only did he consider Shannon vital to his development as an actor, but he truly loved the old man. He also worried constantly

158

about his mother. Her coughing seemed to be diminishing in severity, and occurred less frequently, but she would have attacks at unexpected times. And she felt weak and dispirited most of the time. Richard was fully aware, of course, that Billingsgate was no bouquet of roses at any time of year, and in the summer it stank beyond description. The heat melted the pitch in the seams of the old building in which they lived, and the humid air was heavy with the smell of dead and decayed fish and the rotting garbage in the streets. Yet it was essential that the casement windows be kept open so that some air, however foul, could come into the house. That summer Richard often cursed himself for not having bet the sixty pounds on the fixed horse race.

He had a strange relationship with his fellow dock workers. All of them, even Busk, had come to respect him, however grudgingly, for the way he worked. Scraggly Beard, whose name was Timothy Tipp, and his friend Frankie continued to make occasional remarks about how delighted they would be to bugger him. Richard paid them no attention. He considered this a simple-minded, obscene dockman's effort to tease.

At the end of one particular day, however, Richard had just toted a last sack of indigo into a dark corner of the warehouse, when he heard footsteps rushing up behind him. Before he could turn fully, in the dim light of the warehouse, he saw the flash of a stout cudgel descending toward him. He raised his arm, but the club grazed the right side of his head and momentarily dazed him. As he fell to his knees, a pair of strong arms wrestled him to the ground, a hard hand grabbed his hair and shoved him down on his face. As he lay flat on his stomach, he felt powerful hands grab the waist of his breeches and tear them downward. There was loud grunting as one man leaned heavily on his back, holding him to the ground. The second man got astride him, just below the waist, and giggled lewdly as he pulled Richard's breeches down below his knees.

Richard knew the ridiculous and impossible was happening. Tipp and Frankie were actually trying to bugger him. For a deceptive moment, he lay quietly, the side of his face crushed against the dirty warehouse floor, and let the fury build in his head.

"What a loverly arse," Frankie gloated as he grasped Richard's exposed buttocks. Tipp, breathing heavily, was lying across Richard's back. Sensing where Tipp's head might be, Richard twisted his torso with all the force his newborn muscles could manage, and drove his sharp right elbow viciously upward to where he calculated the nose would be. He did not hit the nose squarely, but he was close enough. Tipp screamed in pain, and holding his smashed mouth, rolled away from Richard.

The rest was not difficult. Richard continued to twist, now with his lower as well as his upper body. Frankie was not especially heavy. He was strong, but not quite as strong, or as young as Richard. Possibly more important, to abet his strength he had only his lustful desire, while Richard had an indignation, an absolutely psychotic fury that magnified his own power immeasurably.

Richard's muscular thighs whipped Frankie off him, and as he rolled away, Richard pushed himself off the floor with both arms, first to his knees, then to his feet. Tipp was looking for the cudgel with which he had struck Richard originally. Frankie cursed and charged back toward Richard, just as Richard bent over and reached down to pull up his breeches. Frankie hurtled right over his back. Now Richard rushed toward Tipp, and pounded him with both fists. Bloodied and bent over in pain, Tipp turned and ran out of the warehouse. Frankie, suddenly realizing he was contending with a man on the edge of madness, backed away, and tried to circle Richard, who stood between him and the warehouse door.

"No need to get so bloody upset, mate," he said placatingly. "Timmie and me was just 'avin' a bit of sport. Thought you might be one o' them actor blokes who likes it up the arse."

There was a raging storm in Richard's sea eyes. He trembled with wrath. Fists clenched at his side, he moved out of Frankie's path to the door.

"Get out, you filthy son of a whore," he said, between clenched teeth, "before I kill you."

Frankie raced past him and disappeared through the warehouse door. Richard was more than halfway home that evening before he stopped trembling.

Frankie and Tipp did not bother Richard again. Three days later, Richard discovered himself pitying poor Frankie, an emotion he hardly anticipated feeling toward his would-be bugger. Six burly men from His Majesty's Navy, a press gang, came to the dock to do a bit of recruiting. They chose Frankie. He was lifting a box of cured fish to his shoulder, when the six descended on him. Each of the Navy men was armed, either with spike or club, and one had a pistol. Frankie fought briefly, but in moments they subdued him and took him away.

"Bloody, fuckin' navy," growled Busk, but he did nothing. There was nothing he could do. The navy press gang, on their next excursion, might take another of his men, or for that matter decide to take Busk himself. Under ordinary circumstances they were considerate enough not to decimate any single work crew by taking more than one of its members, but if they were irritated or met with opposition, they had been known to take three or four. It was simply the manner of naval recruitment, and accepted by all.

Richard watched as His Majesty's sailors dragged Frankie off, screaming and crying. He felt sorry for him, but not for long. In a moment, even before Busk bellowed his order to get back to work, Richard headed up the plank of the sloop they were unloading, and began to think about Ventidius's opening lines for *All for Love*.

It was a Thursday, and he arrived home early. Despite the still oppressive heat and humidity, Mary sat at the table, sewing buttons on a checked waistcoat in her lap. At her feet lay a small pile of clothing, breeches, great coats and several gowns. Each summer Mary mended and refurbished the wardrobe of the Lincoln's Inn Fields and the Drury Lane companies. She smiled wearily as Richard came in.

"There's a packet for you from Felicia."

"Where!"

"Right over there on the sewing table. I put it there, when it came this morning."

Richard trotted to the table by the window, which was wide open. There were only some remnants of a blue linen cloth, and a paper with some markings Mary had made.

"I don't see it, Mary!"

"Oh, Richard. It must be there. Find it; I can't wait to hear how the dear girl is faring."

As Richard recalled there had been little enough breeze during the day, but he wondered if the packet could have blown out the window. It was unlikely, for Mary's paper, and possibly some remnants, would also have blown away. He pushed the remnants from one place to another, picked them up, put them down again, got down on his

161

knees and looked under the table. He pushed the table away from the window and looked out into the fast fading twilight. There was litter of all kinds in the street below the window, but nothing resembling an envelope.

"It's not here, Mary. Are you sure this is where you put it?"

Mary put aside the waistcoat, picked through the clothes at her feet. Ever more frantically she and Richard looked through every conceivable place in the kitchen. Suddenly Mary slapped a hand against her forehead, and ran into the bedroom. She came out, holding a large envelope.

"Forgive me, Richard. I just remembered. I was going to put it on the table, but I went into the bedroom to take off my robe. It was so hot. I must have put the envelope down on the bed, and forgot that I. . . . I'm so forgetful of late."

But Richard was not listening. He ripped open the envelope. There was a bulky manuscript of perhaps twenty pages. Then he found the letter. It was on bright yellow stationery, and smelled deliciously of Felicia's subtle perfume. He placed the manuscript on the table, took a chair and read:

Richard, my love of loves,

How dare you not write to me! Half the summer has gone and I know not whether you are dead, alive or have sailed away to the Indies. Take pen in hand immediately and say what has transpired with you and my dearest Mary.

Richard smiled as he read on.

With this epistle you will find the pages of a nonsensical playlet, entitled *The Adventures of Squire Noodle and His Man Doodle*. As is his annual custom, Colby has again taken two booths at the Bartholomew and Southwark Fairs this September. In the one he will present his puppet show, and in the other comedies and variety featuring the mad Fitzhugh. I have quite convinced him that you would make an excellent Doodle. Mayhap this will teach you to neglect your devoted Felicia!

"What does she say?" asked Mary.

"In a moment, Mary."

Richard read further.

Seriously, love Richard, Colby will use you at the Fairs, and since the performances are in the afternoons, you may still work on the Lincoln's Inn stage with me in the evening, thus acquiring additional experience and an extra guinea or two. Speaking of matters monetary, how much did you win on Bard's Bastard? I myself won twelve pounds. I do hope you increased the cottage fund to a substantial degree. Even wretches like Wrexham are useful now and again. Have you seen Edith? Is she happy with her employment at Norman's apothecary? I did tell old Mortimer Norman that if they did not treat Edith well, I would buy my Grecian washballs, lip salves and such elsewhere in the future.

"May I read it, Richard?" asked Mary.

Richard hesitated, then nodded, as he continued to read.

Here in Richmond, the summer has been pleasant enough, if somewhat dull. The players are hardly of a uniform excellence, but the audiences do not seem to mind. Colby is a true and natural comic and his pranks and jolly conversation please us all. He has taught me to dance some silly jigs, and I have been singing in the variety portions of the programs, and find I enjoy this drollery. Fitzhugh is more and more fascinating, as one gets to know him, but the other males in the company, and in the vicinity for that matter, are rather tiresome. The women even more so.

I miss Mary very much—and I should not say this, since the male head is easily turned—but I miss you very much, too. There is simply no one quite like you in Richmond. And now that I ponder it, nor in London.

Tarry not another moment. Put this paper down, and take pen in hand, and tell me how desperately you miss me and how much you love me! Tell me that you have not sailed off to the Indies, and that I shall see you very soon. And do not be reluctant to permit Mary to read this letter. I love her, too. You should know, and she indeed does know that this will always be true of

Your Felicia

Richard smiled and handed the letter to his mother. As she read, he went over to the cabinet and took out the quill pen, ink and paper. The ink had congealed with long disuse. Carefully he added a bit of water and stirred it with the point of the pen. Finally the pen wrote to his satisfaction. He discarded the paper on which he had experimented, took a fresh sheet and stared at it, while he tried to think of what he wanted to say. Oh, he knew very well, in his heart, what he wanted to say, but to put it on paper was another matter.

Father Whittaker had taught him not only to read, but also to write, and his continuous reading of the finest poets and dramatists of the day had given him a modest flair for writing. Yet he felt almost as shy about expressing his sentiments toward Felicia on paper, as he did in face to face meetings.

"Dear . . ." He paused, then added "est," then "Felicia."

"We received your lovely letter, and Mary and I both enjoyed it greatly. It goes without saying that I not only enjoyed it, but was much moved by the complimentary remarks you made about me. I do apologize for not having written you, but please believe that it is not because I have not thought of you. You are in my thoughts, and in my heart all the time. I can hardly wait for this long summer to end, and to see you again.

I have not sailed away to the Indies, although there were several days in the past months that I surely would have liked to. I have been working on the docks, and the foreman and some of my colleagues are rather disagreeable, but I do like the work. Where I would truly like to sail away to, is to Richmond to be with you. I have relived that lovely night we spent there a thousand times.

I do like the dock work, because it makes no mental demands on me at all, and while I am working, I can and do think of you, or ponder the plays on which I have continued to work with dear Farley Shannon all through the summer. I am very grateful to you for arranging with Mr. Colby for me to work at the Bartholomew and Southwark Fairs. Mary and I have often gone to the fairs, and I know I will enjoy working there. I also realize, as you say, that the experience will be useful to me, and the Lord knows every shilling we are able to add to the cottage fund, will get Mary out of this unhealthful environment that much sooner. I will read *The Adventures of Squire Noodle and His Man Doodle* this very evening, and I will take it out to Farley's with me tomorrow evening, and ask him to work with me on the Doodle role.

It seems to me more like six hundred years than six weeks that you have been away. Mary and I miss you very much. We have not seen Edith since she began working at Norman's, but I will visit there the first opportunity I have to see after her. I am sure she is fine. I hope the next three weeks before you come back to London pass quickly. I cannot wait to see you again. I miss you very much.

He paused, and stared at the paper. His heart said, *Go ahead, you dolt, say it, say it. . . .*

"What a lovely letter," said his mother, placing Felicia's epistle on the table.

Richard hardly heard her. Finally he dipped the pen in the inkwell, bit his lower lip, and added:

And I love you very much. More than I can say on this paper or in spoken words.

Yr. obedient servant,
Richard Steele

"May I read your reply, Richard?"

He folded the letter, laid it aside as he addressed an envelope.

"No need to, Mary," he said casually. "I just told her we both miss her very much, and hope we'll see her soon."

Mary smiled and picked up her sewing.

Richard realized he had made no response to Felicia's questions about Bard's Bastard. He was ashamed to say in writing that he had not had the courage to make a wager. He went to bed quite happy that night. He lay on his pallet, repeating, in a mildly delirious way in his head, Felicia's words: *I miss you. . . . There is no one like you. . . . I miss you. . . . I miss you.* Smiling and sighing, he fell asleep.

The following day Busk was more cantankerous and

difficult than usual. It seemed particularly to irritate him that Richard performed his tasks with such efficiency, with no loss of time or motion, that Busk could find no legitimate reason to curse or cuff him. Occasionally as Richard went by him, a heavy cask on his bronzed and muscular shoulder, Busk growled a desultory, "Come on, actor, move along, move along," but for the most part, he cursed and banged the slower, less conscientious members of the crew. Ignoring Busk's surly bluster, Richard went through the day, humming happily, thinking about Felicia's letter. He pictured her dancing a jig and singing a nonsense ditty. He pictured her in his arms, naked and warm and loving.

On his way to Pickering's that evening, he stopped at Norman's Apothecary in Ironmonger's Lane. He was just in time. Edith Forrest was getting ready to leave. Her midsection had rounded considerably since Richard had last seen her, but the long, loose, navy blue gown she wore concealed the bulge rather well. In good health and good spirits, she was still living at Felicia's and liked her employment quite well. Richard walked with her through the sultry, littered streets to the small building in Middle Temple Lane, then hastened back to the Inn. He ate a hurried dinner, and rode Sally O out to Shannon's, the manuscript of *Squire Noodle* in the saddle pouch.

Shannon was greatly amused by the comedy skit, in spite of the inept writing.

"As you know, Richard, at the Fairs, it's advisable to play broadly. You must make Doodle as lovable a buffoon as possible. It will be good for you. A little uninhibited buffoonery never hurt any actor."

The last two weeks before the new season at Lincoln's Inn Fields was to open seemed never-ending to Richard, filled with difficult situations as it was. One evening, returning home from Shannon's, he found Mary agonizingly ill with food poisoning. He fetched Doctor Thorndike, who gave Mary a medicinal mixture that induced vomiting, and the excruciating pains subsided, but for the next three days she felt weak, and on the fourth day, she began to cough frequently again.

Farley Shannon's debilitating disorder flared up in the last week before the opening, and Doctor Thorndike instructed him to take complete rest. Richard visited him, but only briefly, on the nights he would ordinarily have studied. He read some of the elderly actor's favorite plays to him, and heated and served him the soups the doctor had ordered him to drink to rebuild his strength.

The long, steaming summer was taking its toll. On the docks, the oldest member of Busk's gang, a man named Jeremiah Finley, had a stroke when the sun was at its highest and hottest in midafternoon, and died the following morning. Bruce had never replaced Frankie, when the Navy had recruited him, claiming to Busk that he simply could not find men willing to take the job.

On several occasions Richard overheard Busk and Bruce in heated argument. The burly, pigtailed foreman accused the warehouse owner of being a niggardly skinflint who would not pay men a sufficient wage to attract them to the work.

The day after Finley's death, two other members of the force failed to report for work. Busk learned one was stricken with food poisoning, and the other had a swelling of the glands in his neck. The report of the swelling immediately started rumors that a new epidemic of bubonic plague was raging, one to match the horrible scourge of 1665 and 1666. The septuagenarian owner of the waterfront pub, the Billowing Sail, told the sailors at his bar and tables what to expect.

"Seventy thousand died the first three months. The dead cart came around every night. The bellmen went through the streets, ringin' their bloody bells, shoutin' 'Bring out yer dead! Bring out yer dead!' an' the people did, an' they threw the stiff bodies, mostly naked and bloated, into the carts."

"Yer exaggeratin', Tom. Weren't no seventy thousand died," a pigtailed sailor objected.

The pub owner cupped a gnarled hand around his ear as he turned toward the sailor.

"Exaggeratin', is that what ye said? Ye have no idea, ye scurvy idiot. Six, seven thousand a week, a thousand every day was dyin' in agony. My cousin, Elijah, shot himself, couldn't stand the bloody pain."

He was not exaggerating, but the rumor of a plague proved untrue. A dozen or more people died that week of the plague, or of other diseases with similar symptoms. But there was no epidemic.

Busk was frustrated and furious. He came out of the Billowing Sail during the noontime period, on the day the two men failed to report for work, staggering and weaving as he crossed the bustling dock. In lieu of his noon meal, he had had a half-dozen beakers of grog. The men were seated in the shade, underneath the warehouse overhang, still sweating, their backs against the wall, desultorily chewing away at their noon repasts. Richard looked up from the page of *Squire Doodle* he was reading as he ate. Busk, rocking slightly, stood over him. Mary had had a prolonged coughing spell the previous night and Richard had not slept much. He was in an irritable mood himself.

Busk scratched the crotch of his slop hose.

"What the bloody hell are ya readin', actor? Don't ya ever do anything but read?"

"It's a play." Richard looked up briefly, then back at his page.

"What play?"

Richard looked mildly exasperated. He felt the impulse to say, "What do you care what play? You wouldn't know *Squire Noodle* from *Coriolanus*." But controlled himself, and said, *"The Adventures of Squire Noodle and His Man Doodle."*

Busk suddenly reached down past Richard's face, startling Richard.

"What's this trinket ya wear, Doodle?"

Felicia's medallion, lying in the soft black hair on Richard's bronzed chest, had caught Busk's eye. As his grimy fingers touched it, Richard slapped Busk's hand away with an angry upward movement of the back of his own right hand.

"Leave it alone, Mr. Busk. It's a gift from a friend."

Busk peered at the inscription, grasped the medallion and ripped the chain from Richard's neck.

"What's it say?" he demanded, squinting at the inscription.

Richard threw aside his manuscript, scrambled to his feet and tried to grab the medallion from Busk's right fist. Busk swung viciously with his left, and caught Richard on the ear. Richard went sprawling across the dock on his side. He felt a large splinter penetrate his thigh. He got to his feet and charged into Busk, swinging both fists, landing a hard right to Busk's jaw, and driving his left into Busk's stomach. He smelled Busk's foul breath, as the foreman opened his mouth to roar with laughter.

Busk threw his thickly muscled arms around Richard, pinioning Richard's arms to his side. Richard was helpless. Busk squeezed, harder and harder. Richard's breath exploded from his lungs. His open mouth screamed silently for air. The stench from Busk's mouth against his face nauseated him. He was sure he heard his lower ribs cracking. Then a piercing pain shot across his lower back. He squirmed desperately in Busk's bearlike embrace, and managed to twist enough to get a momentum in his right leg. Then he lifted the foot from the floor and drove his knee murderously into Busk's groin.

Busk's hold on Richard broke. He dropped to his knees, both hands clutching at his groin, his head bent forward, twisting in agony. He groaned. Richard glared down at his dirty head, with the thickly braided pigtail lying on the filthy shirt on his broad back. The pigtail resembled a hairy snake on a wet mud bed. Richard quickly stepped around behind him, and grabbed the pigtail halfway down its length, in both hands. He twisted it around his hands, held tightly and pulled viciously with all his strength.

Busk's head snapped back. Awkwardly, he twisted to his feet, howling, staggering backward as Richard moved away. Heavy arms flailing for balance, Busk tried to turn toward Richard, but Richard danced away, held the pigtail and pulled relentlessly to keep it taut. With each effort Busk made Richard veered and skittered sharply in the opposite direction, all the while tearing at the pigtail.

All the men had long since jumped up from their places under the overhang and moved around the edges of the combatants' area. Sailors aboard the ships moored nearby rushed to the rails, hooting and roaring with laughter at the odd contest on the dock. Busk alternately screamed in agony, and bellowed curses at his tormentor, as Richard adroitly moved away from him, whirling this way and that, pulling all the while. Richard was playing Busk's beefy head and muscle-bound body like a fisherman playing a darting, diving swordfish at the end of a taut line.

"Ho! The actor is a bloody dancer!" roared one man.

"Scalp the nasty son of a bitch!"

"Tear 'is fuckin' 'ead off!"

Tugging savagely toward his left, Richard spun Busk in a half-stumbling, half-trotting circle, which almost smashed him into a section of the hooting, guffawing mob. They shoved each other over and pushed to get out of the way. Richard saw that Busk, bent over with tears of fury glistening in his maddened bloodshot eyes, was just a foot from the edge of the dock. He abruptly released his grip on the pigtail, took a sudden step backward, then charged and launched himself toward Busk's now almost erect body. He soared through the air, his hard right shoulder slammed Busk high on the chest. Busk took two backward steps, toppled off the edge of the dock and did a somersault into the Thames. A tremendous splash cut off the animal-like bellow as he hit the water.

Richard stumbled to the edge of the dock and fell to one knee where Busk went over. His arms ached. He was sure his lower ribs were broken, so sharp was the pain. He looked down into the murky water where Busk sank. Two sailors on the deck of the brig alongside which Busk had disappeared whistled and cheered. Roars of approval sounded all around him as Richard staggered away from the edge of the dock, sweating, gasping, hurting. He moved slowly and deliberately, looking down at the dock floor as he walked, waving people away. He was looking for Felicia's medallion.

It was impossible, of course. He tried to remember, at least generally, the path he had followed in this strange tug-of-war, but it had been so erratic, and he had been so totally absorbed with keeping the pigtail taut, that he knew he could not accurately retrace his steps. He had walked halfway back toward the warehouse, when the meaning of some of the louder shouts from the dock's edge penetrated his consciousness.

"First time the son of a bitch has been in the water since he was born," screamed one man.

"He'll make fine fodder for the fish."

Timothy Tipp rushed up to Richard, embraced him and gave him a slobbering kiss on the cheek. As Richard knocked him away, he screamed, "Yer magnificent, actor! Ya got rid of the bloody bastard for good!"

Richard turned and pushed his way through the crowd of men at the dock's edge. He looked down. Busk was nowhere to be seen. An irregular, restless circle of ripples showed in the water where he had gone down. But as Richard watched, Busk's black head broke through the dirty, brown-green water at the outer circle of ripples. The haunted expression on his face was that of a man who has witnessed his own death. His arms flailed wildly. Water dripped down his head; his black teeth showed in the wide-open gasping mouth, spouting and spitting bile and the Thames. His desperately clutching fingers tried to grab the water's surface. He began to sink again. Richard dove off the dock, and penetrated the water a foot to the left of where Busk had gone down for the third time. He went deep. So deep into the murky water that he thought his head as well as his lungs would burst. He opened his eyes, and beat his arms like leaden wings, trying to force his way to the surface. His right hand touched a squirming bulk. In the nearly opaque murk he could not see clearly, but he knew it was Busk. He clutched Busk's shirt in his right fist, beat with a savage up and down motion with his left arm, kicking vigorously with both legs.

The dead weight of Busk's body gave him the terrifying feeling that they were not moving upward at all, that they were anchored there in the swirling, watery gloom. He felt he could not hold his breath another second. There was a roaring in his ears. He was about to let go of Busk, and make a desperate final effort to save himself, when there was sudden brilliant light. The roaring took on a totally different tone and pitch. It was the men on the ships and the dock. He opened his mouth and gulped air hungrily. He shook the thick water out of his eyes, and looked about him, still clutching the now-unconscious Busk by the shirt. He released his grip on the shirt, gripped the pigtail again, this time inches from the head, and swam toward the sloop six feet away. A sailor on the sloop lowered a rope ladder, scrambled down, and helped Richard with Busk. It seemed the sailor, as he lifted, might choke Busk with the hold around his neck. Richard, with Busk's broad bottom on his shoulder, shoved from below. A second sailor, with a dirty blond pigtail, even longer than Busk's, helped his shipmate and they finally got Busk on deck, more dead than alive.

They lay him flat on his stomach, head turned on its side, arms outstretched. The sailor with the pigtail knelt astride Busk's broad hips, and, with arms rigid, pushed hard against both sides of Busk's back, just below the ribs. The sailor raised his hands, leaned back, stiffened his arms and pushed down again. After the third effort, a small amount of water spilled from Busk's mouth. Two more hard, downward shoves and the lungs began to empty. A sizable torrent of dirty water spewed from Busk's mouth. Then another, and another.

Richard stood over the sailor and Busk, breathing heavily, his ribs, his arms and his head aching. Busk's left hand was open, but his right hand was closed in a fist. Richard bent over and pried the stubby fingers away from the palm. Then he dropped the hand in disgust. The medallion was not there. He watched another geyser of river water spurt from the cavern of Busk's mouth, heard Busk groan. Well, Busk was still alive anyway. He turned away and walked wearily down the gangplank to the dock.

The reaction to the rescue was mixed. Some of the crowd obviously considered it a heroic deed, while not a few others cursed and taunted Richard and called him several kinds of idiot for preventing Busk from drowning. He ignored them all, walked slowly, head down, across the dock, to the warehouse shed, hoping by some miracle to find the medallion, praying that Busk had not had it in his grimy fist when he went into the river. But of course he did not find it.

He saw the scattered pages of the manuscript of *Squire Doodle,* where he had dropped them. In the windless day, none of them had blown away. Several showed footprints, where men had stepped on them, but they were all there. Richard collected them, sat down with his back against the warehouse wall, and began to put them in order. Timothy Tipp stood over him again. Richard looked up. He was exhausted and hurting, especially his ribs.

"Leave me alone, Tipp," he said dully.

"Yer quite a man, actor," Tipp said emotionally. "I don't know why ye saved the murderin' bastard, but I guess none of us should want him dead."

Richard looked back down at *Squire Doodle.*

"Just leave me alone."

"I watched from the minute 'he tore the chain from yer neck. . . ."

Richard looked up into Tipp's bearded face. Tipp nodded several times.

" 'E dropped it when you kicked 'im in the balls. I picked it up real quick a'fore anybody else seen it, I guess. Thought I could sell it for a few bob. . . ."

Richard started to say, "You didn't . . ." but Tipp reached into the pocket of his filthy slop hose, and brought out Felicia's medallion. He handed it to Richard, who looked at him in speechless wonder.

"Don't look like it's worth no bloody king's ransom," Tipp mumbled, "so I thought ye ought to 'ave it back anyway."

"Thanks, Tipp," Richard said with great feeling. One

of the links was broken, but that could be repaired easily enough.

The few remaining days of the summer passed without incident. The initial meeting of the Lincoln's Inn Fields company for the new season was called for the first Monday in September, promptly at ten A.M. at the theater. The night before, Mary presented Richard with a white silk shirt she had made him. It had ruffled cuffs and a ruffled collar. She also gave Richard a black silk neck cloth. The shirt was a bit tight across the chest and shoulders because Richard's chest had expanded several inches, and his shoulders seemed broader after the summer's labor. There was still an occasional sharp, stabbing pain in his lower ribs on both sides and a bruise the size of a guinea on the jaw just below the right ear, but these discomforts did not concern him at all. He lay on his pallet with the September moon coming through his window. He could not sleep, nor did he care to. Tomorrow he would be back on the stage of the Lincoln's Inn Fields Theatre again, there among his fellow actors and actresses. There, where he belonged.

And he would see Felicia. He thought of that first night in her apartment. He relived each moment, even the embarrassing ones. He took himself back to Richmond, and his heart and mind made pictures of that time as he savored each exquisite moment there anew. He remembered the birds singing, and the squirrel skittering across the bough. He said her name over and over and over . . . Felicia, Felicia, Felicia. And finally he slept. But only for an hour, for he was up with the dawn. So eager was he to be back in the theater . . . and to see Felicia again.

❧ 19 ❧

It was not quite nine o'clock when Richard arrived at the theater. He had stopped briefly at Pickering's for a mug of coffee and to make what was for him a special, and unusual arrangement. Pickering shook his head, not knowing whether to express tolerant approval, or to protest the changing times.

"You young people are so unpredictable these days, lad. We just had a letter from Tillie. She's fallen in love with a supercargo on a ship from Salem in the Massachusetts Bay colony. Tired of her dull doctor, says she. Hope she won't begin thinkin' of marrying, young as she is."

Bessie Pickering heard him as she went by with a large pan of pudding.

"She's a year older than I were, when you made off with me," she called.

"When you trapped me, is more like it," laughed Ben.

When he arrived at the Lincoln's Inn Fields, Higgins, the custodian, opened the backstage door to Richard's knocking.

"Kin I help you, sir?"

"Good morning, Mr. Higgins," Richard greeted, and started to walk by the stooped old man, but Higgins moved to bar his way.

"What may be yer business, sir?"

Richard looked baffled for a moment, then he smiled and said, "I'm Richard Steele, Mr. Higgins. Don't you . . ."

"Richard!" The old man peered up into his face. "Richard Steele! . . . Well, I'll be double be-damned! I

174

never would have recognized ye. Go on in, Richard. There's no one here yet, but I've got the table and chairs all set on stage. Would ye care fer a nip o' gin?"

Richard smiled.

"No, thanks, Mr. Higgins. I'll just sit down and wait."

He sat in one of the chairs at the side of the long table. For several moments he simply looked out into the small, empty auditorium, absorbing the mood of the theater. He imagined he smelled the slightly sulphurous odor of burning candles in the huge overhead chandelier, and the damp sweat of the bodies packed in the pit and the gallery. His eyes scanned the seats. His mind filled them with people. He saw elegantly clad beaux and their ladies in the boxes.

Lightheaded from lack of sleep and fevered with anticipation, he rose from his chair to stride toward center stage. Then he moved downstage out to the apron, closer to the pit, and turned toward an imaginary Friar on the stage beside him.

" 'Tis torture and not mercy," he said with deep emotion. "Heaven is here where Juliet lives, and every cat and dog and little mouse, and every unworthy thing, live here in Heaven and may look on her, but Romeo may not. . . ."

Of all the plays he had studied, of all the roles he had rehearsed with Farley Shannon, that of the ill-fated lover in *Romeo and Juliet* was the one on which he had concentrated most intensely. He believed that if he worked hard, he might indeed be able to play Romeo opposite Felicia's Juliet before the new season was out.

Now he fantasized that he was hearing thunderous applause as he spoke the lines of Romeo. Then he realized, of a sudden, that the applause was real, but that it was the sound of a single pair of hands clapping. The hearty voice from the wings startled him completely out of his reverie.

"Is it Richard Steele? I cannot believe my eyes! . . ."

Gilbert Weston strode across the stage, and embraced the blushing Richard.

A year ago, Richard would have stammered and stuttered his embarrassment. This morning, he chuckled at his own foolishness.

"Just the effect of being back onstage." He smiled.

Weston laughed.

"I know . . . I know. I had dinner with Farley last

175

night, and he told me of the fine work you've done all summer."

He held Richard with both hands at arm's length and looked him over, wide-eyed, from sleek, raven head to polished black-booted toe.

"But what in heaven's sacred name have you done to yourself, lad! You've grown! . . . Taller, and broader."

He squeezed Richard's upper arms.

"And the muscles! The bronzed face!"

Crimson suffused the bronzed face.

"How old are you anyway Richard?"

"I— I'll be sixteen. . . ."

"You've the look of a man, lad. And a right handsome young man at that. Tell me what you've been doing all summer to achieve this magical transformation. Farley mentioned you were working on the docks, but there must have been something else . . . something special."

Richard glossed over the unpleasant incident of the attempted buggery, and touched lightly on the odd fight with Busk, but Weston realized that the episodes had contributed toward hardening and maturing the young man's outlook, and had taught him a new self-confidence. Even though Richard made no reference to the brutal physical aspects of the work, and the long day, Weston could see that they accounted for the new, stronger body. Richard had always been tall and somewhat muscular, even at the age of ten, when Weston had first hired him as a candle snuffer. But, looking at him now, the actor-manager was sure he had gained a full three inches in height in the past year, and the sustained dock work had given new size and form to all his muscles. And there seemed to be a new ease in his manner.

Richard was finally able to turn the conversation away from himself.

"How did the season go at Bath?" he inquired.

Weston told him about the plays, and a number of humorous incidents during the season at the resort. In the middle of one story, Mrs. Forbish arrived, then Roland Finch and Catherine Clark. It was ten o'clock, and more members of the company were trooping in. Richard looked toward the stage-right wings each time he heard the stage door open, hoping the next person would be Felicia Wandrous. Actor after actor after actress arrived, and there was much hugging and kissing, and many elaborate greetings. Almost every member of the company made some remark to Richard about how much he had changed. It was ten minutes past the hour when Felicia arrived.

At that particular moment Richard's view was blocked by Mrs. Forbish, who was regaling him with her own amorous summer adventures with a circus dwarf. They were seated on chairs near the end of the long table at stage left when he heard Felicia's cheery voice say, "Greetings, loves."

"Excuse me," he said and ceased listening as Mrs. Forbish rambled on. He simply stood there and stared as Felicia made her way across the stage, from one member of the company to another, pausing for brief hugs and pecking kisses. She was even lovelier than he remembered. She wore a *contouche* of see-through beige gauze over an underdress of tan, green-flowered grazette. The gauze and grazette garments both hung alluringly off her round shoulders, and swirled as she moved gracefully from one colleague to the next. Her golden hair had been cut short, in the fashion of the day, and she wore a beige lace cap. As she came closer, Richard saw the fresh glow in her cheeks. Her silver-gray eyes sparkled with vitality. She touched Mrs. Forbish's shoulder, and was about to bend to kiss her plump cheek, when she saw Richard. Then she stopped and stared at Richard, just as he stared at her. There was a puzzlement in her stare.

This tall, bronzed man; this man in the elegant white silk shirt with its fashionable ruffled collar, its ruffled cuffs showing at the ends of the sleeves of the snug-fitting black coat; this man with the form-fitting black breeches, and the highly polished black boots. *Could this man . . . ?* She looked up at his face and into the blue-green sea eyes. She raced toward him and threw her arms around his neck, kissing him again and again.

"It is you, is it not?"

Richard blushed, but he was beaming. Felicia turned back to her colleagues.

"It *is* Richard Steele, is it not?"

There were roars of laughter as Richard squirmed happily. Felicia said to Mrs. Forbish, "Pardon us, Susannah," and pulled Richard toward two unoccupied chairs a little distance away from the others. She held his strong, bronzed hands in hers.

"Tell me how you wrought this magic, love."

He looked deep into her bright, silver-gray eyes.

"You're more beautiful than ever, Felicia."

Their mutual exchange of admiration was interrupted by a loud, sonorous shout from across the stage.

"Hail, players, hail!"

All eyes turned toward the regal figure at stage right. His golden head was held high. Even in the dim light his shoulder-length hair gleamed. He had a carefully trimmed golden mustache, and a neat, V-shaped golden beard. Bows of ribbons of various hues, red, yellow, blue, showed bright on the right shoulder of his deep green velvet coat. The ribbons, which extended down to the elbow, were a relic of the shoulder fastening, which at the turn of the earlier century had been used to secure the sword belt. Now, in 1717, they were merely ornamental. The coat was open in front to show an elaborately embroidered cream-white waistcoat which was stretched taut by the man's paunch. Cream-white breeches fitted his thighs snugly, and were stretched tight across his hips. Silk stockings of the same deep green shade as his coat, and black silver-buckled shoes with deep green heels completed his outfit.

The Irish summer had changed Jerome Wrexham's appearance as drastically as the season on the London docks had altered Richard's.

"I think it's Jerome Wrexham," Richard said as Wrexham made his way across the stage, shaking hands heartily, kissing the company's women with enthusiasm.

"He must have added two stone!" exclaimed Felicia.

If he did weigh twenty-eight pounds more than he had at season's end, Wrexham carried it with aplomb, even a certain air of arrogance. Richard noted that his cheeks were ruddy, and his dark brown eyes were bright, as Wrexham grasped Richard's right hand in both his own.

"Young Steele! How fared you this long summer? Did you enjoy the cottage in the country?"

Richard began a reply, but realized that Wrexham's question was rhetorical . . . that he merely assumed Richard had wagered enough on Bard's Bastard to buy the cottage. Wrexham then took Felicia in his arms and hugged her to him, kissing her first on the left cheek, then the right, then on her lips.

"And dear Felicia! Did you miss me in bucolic Richmond? You should have been with me in Dublin! The Irish are true lovers of the theater. Next summer . . ."

But now Weston called for everyone to take seats

around the table. He greeted them formally, then outlined, in general terms, the plans for the new season. The company would do some seventy plays in the one hundred and ninety-two days of the season. This would not include afterpieces. He planned, said Weston, on no more than fifty or sixty evenings of afterpieces. They would open with *As You Like It* the following Monday, and rehearsals would begin on the morrow. Richard was to play William, the country lad in love with Audrey. Wrexham was to play Orlando, and Felicia, Rosalind.

Immediately after the meeting, Richard and Felicia hastened to Pickering's Inn, and found a small table in a corner of the kitchen. Felicia was eager to discuss the summer, but Richard was content to stare at her, and occasionally reach across the table and touch her hand. He tried to conceal his excitement at what he hoped the afternoon would bring. Wrexham had strolled to the Inn with Gilbert Weston, Catherine Clark and Roland Finch. Now he brought a chair over to Richard's and Felicia's table. He began to sit down, when Richard said, "Pardon, Jerome. Felicia and I have private matters to discuss. . . ."

Wrexham was startled. He looked toward Felicia in disbelief.

"Extremely private, Jerry. Please!" said Felicia.

Wrexham's face clouded. He shoved the chair angrily back toward the table, and rejoined the others. Felicia looked admiringly at Richard and reached across the table to squeeze his hand.

"I believe we've angered the elegant Jerome again, Richard, but somehow I feel it no longer matters. You appear so capable . . . so . . ."

"Did you guess, sweet Felicia?"

Felicia looked surprised.

"Guess? Guess what, love?"

"I've taken a room . . . upstairs."

Felicia's eyes widened. She smiled. Drawing in a breath, she reached across for Richard's hand and rose from her chair.

"We can have our dinner later," she whispered, and led Richard to the stairs. Pickering had given Richard the best room in the Inn. It was large, and the single window faced the garden and the stables at the rear of the Inn, rather than the crowded, filthy street. The high noon sun made the room bright. As soon as they closed

179

the door behind them, Richard took Felicia in his arms and kissed her. First with pursed, closed lips. Then his lips parted, and his tongue slipped into Felicia's sweet mouth and played with her elusive tongue. Through his tight breeches, she felt his growing hardness against her stomach. He held her so tightly, she gasped when he finally released her.

"Richard," she managed breathlessly, "I did miss you." She took a step away from him, squirmed out of the gauze *contouche,* and began to untie the ribbons at the front of the underdress.

"I could not—understand it."

She spoke in short phrases, breathing hard. "At Richmond Hill the men seemed suddenly dull—or overbearing—or both. In bed—most unexciting, mechanical."

Richard stood and watched her as she undressed. Without taking his eyes from her, his own breath coming in short gasps, he removed his coat, reached his hands behind his neck to unbutton the neck cloth, unbuttoned and removed the beautifully ruffled white silk shirt. His broad chest was heaving as he watched her place her dress on a chair. She saw the medallion on his chest.

"My bounty is as boundless as the sea," she whispered. "My love as deep. The more I give to thee . . ." His eyes feasted on the loveliness of her naked body. He moved toward her and lifted her easily in his arms. He kissed her tenderly on the forehead, the eyelids, the nose, the mouth, the neck as he carried her to the wide bed and lowered her gently upon it. Holding her soft round shoulders, he leaned down and kissed, then hungrily sucked the nipple of her right breast. She held his head against her breast, panting and squirming with pleasure.

After a long time, he moved his mouth to her left breast, and kissed and sucked its enlarged, stiff nipple. Finally, abruptly, he sat up on the edge of the bed and frantically removed his boots and stockings. Felicia lay on her back, eyes closed, breathing heavily but evenly. Her left hand rested on his thigh. He leaned over and kissed her mouth briefly, then rose abruptly and stood at the side of the bed, facing Felicia. He could hardly slide his breeches over his large, throbbing erection. But he squirmed and twisted and finally managed.

Felicia looked at him through half-closed, hungry eyes. She sat up in bed, swung her legs over the side and grasped Richard at his waist, leaning forward to take him in her mouth. She clutched his hard buttocks, pulling him toward her as she moved her head, her tongue. Richard placed his hands on her cheeks. He gasped in ecstasy, but finally, with gentle pressure, lifted her head from his pulsating, burning member. He took her shoulders, and pushed her tenderly onto her back on the bed.

He moaned, "I love you, Felicia. I love you, I love you."

He mounted her, and slid into her naturally, easily, and the fire blazed as he penetrated deeply. On the third thrust, he exploded. But this time he was not embarrassed.

He groaned with pleasure.

"It has been so long, sweet Felicia," he said, slipping out of her, easing over onto his back.

And she said, "I know, I know."

Resting on one elbow, she looked lovingly at his body: the deeply bronzed upper portion, the well-muscled ivory lower half, and the deep rose, blue-veined member in its silken black bed.

"It's like making love to two beautifully different young men at the same time," she said happily.

She caressed his shoulders, his arms, his chest and his flat stomach. Leaning forward, she slid her soft fingers down his thigh, and up again to the black nest, kissing him lightly on the mouth, the neck, the nipples of his chest as she did so. And soon enough, the large member there was no longer limp, but rigid and throbbing. On her knees, murmuring endearments, she sat astride Richard's lower thighs, now fondly holding him in her right hand, moving her hand slowly up and down his burning length. And in a moment, she moved up his lithe body, raised herself, lowered herself, backed down on him, and the stiff, searing member entered her and was enfolded deep inside her own tight moistness.

She moved forward and back, swiveling in a circular motion. There was a sudden flicker of pain in his lower ribs. He ignored it and pulled her face down to him, kissing her savagely, with both their mouths wide open, tongues darting and probing. He reached up and cupped her small, firm breasts in his hands, squeezing gently, teasing the hard nipples with his thumbs. As she rode him, he took her right breast in his mouth, sucked and kissed it passionately, then did the same to her left breast. And then, gasping for breath, he reached down and slid

181

his hands along her smooth, warm thighs to her slender waist, and down and around to her buttocks. He caressed her buttocks feverishly, arched his back so that her final thrust brought him so deeply inside her that their pelvic areas were crushed together. Her golden brown nest and his black one merged.

Felicia gave a small joyful scream, moaned and fell forward on Richard's chest. He put his arms around her glistening, silk-smooth back, and kissed her tenderly on the side of her head, her cheek, her neck.

"Sweet, sweet Felicia," he murmured.

She took his hand and kissed the palm as she rolled off him onto her back. She held the hand to her lips, her heavy breathing gradually subsiding. His own labored breathing slowed. They closed their eyes and lay spent and rapturously fulfilled. Fulfilled briefly. Spent but temporarily. They dozed, holding hands. Richard awoke to the soft touch of Felicia's lips on his cheek. They talked for a while of Richmond Hill, the docks, Richard's upcoming work at the fairs and the new season. Neither of them mentioned Wrexham, nor even thought of him.

They made love again, and once more with exciting variations, during which Richard tasted Felicia's most intimate fruits. The light at the window faded, and it was dusk.

"I'll never forget this day," said Richard fervently, though weakly.

"I'm hungry," said Felicia, springing lightly from the bed.

When they came downstairs, the kitchen was already more than half-full with evening diners. Pickering came over to the corner table where they were seated, and smiled a half-leering, half-approving smile.

"We would like two glasses of ebullum, please, Mr. Pickering," said Richard.

When he brought the wine, Pickering said, "You made the great Irish star quite angry."

Richard looked puzzled for a moment, then said, "Oh, you mean Jerome."

"Aye. He didn't even stay for his noon meal. Said he had a meeting with the Duke, and left shortly after you went upstairs."

Felicia lifted her glass.

"To all of us," she said, "and to a happy and prosperous new season!"

182

Pickering nodded his share of the toast and went back to the bar. Richard lifted his glass to his lips.

"To us, and our love."

Felicia sipped her wine. She looked thoughtful.

"I don't think Wrexham will dare do what he did last season."

"Play his foolish pranks?"

"No." Felicia shook her head. "I mean refuse to work unless you are banned. We have displayed our affection too openly before the company, and he has permitted his childish jealousy to become apparent. He would belittle himself in the eyes of all to adopt such a revenge against one as youthful as you, love."

Richard sipped his wine and looked into Felicia's eyes.

"Whatever he does, sweet Felicia, I will contend with. For I love you and I love you and I love you."

Felicia smiled, blowing him a kiss. They were halfway through a satisfying dinner of rare roast beef and potatoes, when Wrexham came into the Inn. He saw Richard and Felicia, and headed directly for their table. He stood over them.

"May I join the happy couple!"

It was difficult to determine whether his tone was sarcastic, or reluctantly cordial. Richard nodded, and Wrexham pulled over a chair and sat between them.

"Then this affair is no longer excruciatingly private?" He laughed to diminish the insolence of the question. Felicia put down her fork and wiped her lips daintily with a napkin.

"Jerry," she looked directly into his dark brown eyes. "Jerry, you are looking at a new, a serious Felicia Wandrous. In this bright fresh season I plan to concentrate on my work, to become the finest actress in the history of the English theater."

"Hear! Hear!" laughed Wrexham.

"I plan," said Felicia, "to forego frivolity. . . ."

"Spending the day in bed with a boy is hardly foregoing frivolity."

"That's none of your business, Jerome!" snapped Richard angrily.

Felicia reached across the table and put her hand on Richard's arm.

"There are times, dear Jerry, when spending a day in bed with a man—a certain man—is much more than a frivolity. . . ."

Felicia watched Wrexham closely as she spoke these last words with cool deliberation. Now she had made it plain. She loved Richard. Wrexham could react as he would. A lump formed in Richard's throat and his heart beat wildly in his breast, so moved was he by Felicia's open, unexpected declaration. He too stared at Wrexham, awaiting the reaction.

Wrexham leaned forward, his elbow on the table, his chin cupped in his right hand.

"You have changed, dear Felicia. I never expected . . ." Felicia nodded.

"I *have* changed, Jerry. I did not expect that I would either, but I have."

"I've just come from a long visit with the Duke and the Duchess of Cheltenham," said Wrexham abruptly. "There is a masquerade in the Venetian manner at Ranelagh this evening, to which I have been invited."

He paused, reached out and touched Felicia's hand. "Would you care to accompany me?"

The masquerades at Ranelagh in Chelsea were among the outstanding social events of the season. They were gay and sumptuous affairs, attended by the nobility. Any actress, virtually any woman, would sell at least part of her soul to be able to attend.

"I am most flattered," said Felicia, "and I thank you, but I must decline. Today I shall spend the evening renewing my long acquaintance with Rosalind."

Richard thought he detected a flash of anger in Wrexham's eyes. A muscle moved in his jaw, alongside the golden beard. Then Wrexham smiled at Felicia.

"You have indeed changed, my dear." Wrexham sighed and waved to Pickering at the bar. Pickering knew his preference, and in a moment brought a brandy and port to the table.

Wrexham lifted the glass.

"To the new Felicia Wandrous, and to the new Richard Steele!"

If Richard doubted the veracity of his words, Felicia, at any rate, accepted his words at face value.

"And to the dashing, and most understanding, *new* Jerome Wrexham," she said, lifting her glass to her lips.

All three drank and Wrexham changed the subject abruptly.

"Pickering told me you did not bet on Bard's Bastard, Richard. I thought you, of all people, would. It would have given you the funds to buy that cottage. . . . But fret not, lad. There will be other opportunities, though we may have to wait some time before another prearranged contest presents itself."

The conversation and the toasts at Pickering's seemed to clear the air and mark a turning point in the relationship between Wrexham, Richard and Felicia. As early as the time of the rehearsals at the theater the next morning, tensions seemed to be dissolving. The rehearsals went extraordinarily well. And the opening night performance of *As You Like It* was received enthusiastically by both the audience and the several writers who occasionally wrote theater commentary.

In particular, Richard was amazed at his own metamorphosis from insecure idolater to confident lover, and from nervous amateur to observant professional as an actor. He watched from the wings as Felicia, alluringly mischievous as Rosalind, a good part of the time "caparisoned like a man in doublet and hose," played with Wrexham's adoring Orlando in scene after scene in the idyllic Arden Forest. He watched without the slightest twinge of jealousy, for he believed Wrexham's style was more flamboyantly excessive than ever. He wished that he himself had a more important part than that of William, the country lad, but he played his small role with appropriately diffident naturalness.

In the days and weeks that followed, all Richard's and Felicia's colleagues came to recognize and accept them as lovers, devoted to each other. They were occasionally teased good-naturedly about their obvious mutual adoration, particularly after they had spent an afternoon in the room at the Inn, which ecstatic interlude they managed once or twice each week. (Edith Forrest, now past the halfway period of her pregnancy, was still sharing Felicia's apartment.)

Jerome Wrexham's new attitude was most remarkable. Of a sudden he seemed to adopt a purely friendly, totally platonic posture toward Felicia. He was as aggressively flirtatious and romantic as ever with other female members of the cast, and made no effort to keep the knowledge of his regular visits to Mother Magruder's and other brothels from anyone. But he treated Felicia in such a sisterly fashion that her female vanity occasionally pushed her into resenting his lack of romantic interest. Yet her love for Richard was so deep that she

185

laughed at herself over these infrequent eruptions of womanly conceit.

Toward Richard, Wrexham's new attitude was even more extraordinary. He launched such an intense campaign to establish a greater camaraderie with his erstwhile rival that it surprised everyone in the company, Richard and Felicia most of all.

Would Richard like to attend another bull baiting?

Wrexham's good friend, the Earl of Peckworth, foremost patron of cockfighting—had more than 500 gamecocks on his estate—would Richard like to witness the training of the noble birds?

They were going to hang an even dozen offenders at Tyburn. Wrexham found hangings a fine diversion. Would Richard join him on this rare, wholesale occasion? Two of the convicted would be women. One had murdered her husband.

There would be horse racing at Banstead Downs quite soon. Would Richard care to attend? Wrexham knew a number of the owners, and trainers and jockeys.

There were repeated invitations to join Wrexham for a repast and the gaming at Lady Gertrude's. Wrexham seemed to recognize the futility of asking Richard to visit Cleopatra or any of Mother Magruder's other ladies. The bawdy house was the one place at which he did not request the pleasure of Richard's company.

One Saturday afternoon, just before the Monday he was to begin playing at the Bartholomew Fair, Richard did go out to the estate of the Earl of Peckworth with Wrexham. He had seen a cockfighting event eight years earlier, when Father Whittaker had taken him, and he remembered feeling great excitement, although now his recollection was a mélange of disjointed impressions. He remembered blurred, brilliantly feathered birds clashing savagely in midair, beaks tearing, claws and steel-spurred legs chopping at each other; shouting, screaming men, and even some women; a brown and white cock, lying on the ground, blood spurting from its feathered neck, writhing and dying; and a brawny man, rushing into the center of the circular table, picking up the killer cock, a bird of many hues, licking its head and body feverishly as he dashed from the arena.

On this Saturday, Richard discovered that Wrexham had not been exaggerating when he told Richard the Earl owned more than five hundred cocks. Dudley Mason, the chief feeder and trainer, one of the most famous in the kingdom, met them at the gate of the gamecock compound, and took them down the long rows of pens, each constructed and placed so that no bird could see another. They were all so trained that they would go into a frenzy in their eagerness to do battle at sight of another cock.

Mason was a squat, powerful-looking, gray-haired man, with a heavy face, thick lips and a large nose. His black eyes had the same cold gleam as those of his birds as he walked them down the path between the pens. "Down here at the end of the row," he yelled enthusiastically in a deep, hoarse voice over the squawking and flapping of the cocks. "We've got the finest young fighter ye ever laid eyes on, Jerry. Fighting his first match tomorrow at Birdcage Walk. Be sure to come, and wager all ye've got."

They stopped at an enclosure, where one of Mason's helpers was whipping a mixture of wheat flour, eggs and butter into a thick paste. He nodded and bowed to them, as he spread the paste in a pan, and shoved the pan into a primitive earth oven.

Mason spooned a large chunk of dark-looking bread from another pan into a bowl on a table next to the oven, and broke the bread into smaller pieces.

"Pour a bowl full of that hot wine, Jerry," he said, "and we'll go along and feed the new champion."

Richard gazed with interest at each bird, but when they came to the last pen in the row, he stared in utter fascination. The cock was the proudest, most arrogant creature he had ever seen. As they stood before the pen, the bird glared at them. Richard had never seen such unadulterated hate and viciousness in any living eye. The cock had a tall, stiff crimson comb, and a sharp, rock-hard beak. He puffed out his round chest, with its shining feathers of green, blue, auburn and gold. He kicked backward, first with one sharp-clawed foot, then the other. The cords in his strong throat quivered beneath the feathers as he crowed and crowed and crowed. It was a sound to wake the dead.

Mason smiled, as he opened the pen, and put the dish of bread on the floor. The cock pecked him viciously on his gauntleted hand. Jerry gingerly placed the bowl of hot wine in the pen, spilling a bit, and withdrew his own hand in a flash. The bird pecked at the bread, swallowed, pecked again, moved to the wine dish, and with thin, flickering tongue slurped up large drops of the liquid.

Later, Wrexham and Richard watched as Mason and one of the younger gamecockers prepared the high-spirited bird for his debut battle on the morrow.

"This mean devil killed forty-two dunghill cocks these ten days past, just for exercise," said Mason proudly, as he carefully cut the big bird's comb off. The cock squawked furiously, twisted and squirmed, and tried to beat his wings, as the gamecocker held him, while Mason clipped the head feathers. The bird pecked at the game-cocker's cheek and got away for a moment, but Mason was after him, and caught him immediately.

"Lookin' more like a champion every minute," laughed Mason as he carefully cut away at the tail feathers. Then he sharpened the protesting cock's natural spurs. When they had the indignant fighter back in his pen, Mason took a deadly-looking pair of glittering steel, razor-sharp spurs from a small box.

" 'E'll be wearing these tomorrow!" he told Wrexham and Richard.

Sunday was cool and crisp. The cock pit at Birdcage Walk was the most exclusive in London. Members of the Court, politicians and persons of quality, women as well as men, attended the matches regularly. The arena was a large round table, possibly a meter lower than the dining table in a home. Around this table there were two rows of expensive seats, occupied exclusively by elegantly dressed members of the nobility and a smattering of other privileged citizens. A low barrier separated these two rows from three rows of wooden benches. The people crowded on the benches were decently dressed, too, since members of the lower classes were not permitted in this Birdcage Walk establishment, which was considered one of the city's three royal pits. Behind the last row of benches, dozens of men and women crowded all the standing room available. The audience was noisy and restless with anticipation. Owners and handlers of the various cocks entered in the series of contests to be staged, milled through the crowd making wagers on their birds. Several professional gamblers were taking bets at appropriate odds on whichever cocks the bettor chose.

On their way to the excellent seats which Mason had secured for them, in the first row directly behind the starting mark on one side of the round table, Richard and Wrexham encountered Lancelot Higginbotham. He apparently either did not recognize Richard, or did not remember the pudding incident at the Inn, for when Wrexham, with one arm around Richard's shoulder, said, "Lancelot, permit me to present my dear friend, Richard Steele," the garishly attired Higginbotham merely nodded a cordial, "Pleased, I'm sure, young sirrah."

Although Richard felt Wrexham was slightly drunk, Wrexham had no trouble at all placing bets on cocks he identified clearly by owners' or handlers' names in four of the twenty contests scheduled. The largest bet he placed was for five pounds, which he wagered on Mason's newest pride.

"Make a bet on the Earl's new champion, Richard," he urged, and Richard did wager a pound. In their seats, Wrexham put his left arm around Richard's shoulder, and his right hand halfway up Richard's thigh.

"It's a great pleasure to spend this fine day with you, dear boy," he said, looking into Richard's eyes.

Richard was beginning to feel uneasy

Wrexham had been drunk by the time they were seated in the carriage on their way to the fights. "The Birdcage Walk cockpit," he'd instructed the driver, running his hand down the small of Richard's back and patting his buttock, as Richard, bending over, preceded him into the carriage. As the carriage rocked through the cobbled streets, he had put his arm around Richard's shoulder.

"Richard, my lad, I've become extremely fond of you ... do you know that?"

It only took fifteen minutes to get to Birdcage Walk. Wrexham spent that time lauding, in flowery terms, Richard's remarkable development as an actor—all the while fondling his thigh.

"In another couple of years," he said, squeezing the muscular thigh, "you may become as distinguished an actor as I."

He beamed at Richard, and winked.

"And I intend to help you in every way I can, dear boy."

Now at the cockpit, he again had his hand on Richard's thigh. Richard found it difficult to believe that Wrexham had turned homosexual over the course of the summer. He did not know what to make of Wrexham's unexpected display of physical affection. Wrexham certainly seemed to be having as many heterosexual liaisons as ever, yet . . .

A sudden roar went up from the crowd as an official, standing at the edge of the pit, announced the first fight.

"Last chance to make your wagers," he bellowed, as two men, each holding a gamecock, ran to their starting positions, directly opposite each other across the round table. The quick and savage death of the snow-white bird in the first fight abruptly ended Wrexham's attentions to Richard, and Richard's concern over the matter. Wrexham and Richard and the entire mob were on their feet, screaming and shouting over the brief, violent encounter.

At the end of ninety seconds of intense and deadly battle, the rust-colored gamecock, already having pecked one of the white bird's eyes out, managed to zoom above the white cock in midair. Madly flapping his wings, he kicked frantically with both legs, and slashed his sharp gaff into the head of the white bird. The gaff had obviously sliced the brain. The snow white cock dropped like a feathered stone, fell to his side kicking, jerking and writhing in mortal agony. The rust-colored victor pounced on him, clawing, pecking furiously, but it was clear he was savaging a corpse. His owner leaped into the circle, pulled him away, licking and sucking at several minor wounds the white bird had inflicted. The owner of the dead cock picked him up by the legs, swung the limp, bleeding mass of feathers at his side and cursed disgustedly as he trudged out of the arena.

The crowd remained on its feet, roaring, some cheering, some cursing. Wrexham pounded Richard on the back.

"The rust was Connelly's bird!" he exulted.

Richard recalled that Wrexham had bet two pounds on Connelly's rust-colored cock. The next four fights kept the crowd in a frenzy. Each contest had its own unique elements of suspense, fury, courage and bloody death. Richard was surprised at the brevity of the battles. The longest, the third match, lasted three minutes and twelve seconds, and one lasted less than a minute. Then Richard saw Mason enter, holding the arrogant rainbow cock. The bird's trim head moved erratically from side to side on his wiry neck, his cold, hate-filled eyes gleaming. He sensed that he was to go into combat. The cock raised, his fierce, combless head and crowed piercingly.

His opponent was a beige and dark tan warrior, who

190

seemed smaller and less fearsome than the Earl's bird. His handler, a thin and wiry man, younger than Mason, moved into the center of the ring with him, and Mason did likewise. The two birds began to peck furiously at each other. The referee shouted, "Get ready! Back on your marks." Both men took their birds back to the starting positions. The cocks were now maniacally eager to have at one another. The referee shouted, "Pit your cocks!"

Mason and his opponent released their holds on the birds. The cocks appeared to have been catapulted into the center of the circle. They crashed into each other, beaks slashing, trimmed wings beating, gaffed legs clawing. On the dirt and sand surface of the table, into the air, down again in the dirt, back in the air, the two gamecocks were a single, indistinguishable blurred mass of wildly flapping feathers. So frenetic was the movement that it seemed a dozen wiry, snakelike feathered necks and stone-hard beaks were striking for the kill; a score of flashing, scaly steel-gaffed legs and claws seemed to seek to tear apart the foe's body.

Blood spurted from the feathered mass. The crowd screamed. Richard felt as though he were choking with excitement. In midair, the cocks were locked together. The rainbow bird's gaff was hooked deep in the side of the beige-and-tan. The beige-and-tan's beak bit and held fast in the upper right chest of the rainbow. Twisting, legs driving, clipped wings fluttering, they crashed to the ground. Desperately they rolled, fought to get to their feet. With a vicious tug of his gaffed leg, the rainbow tore feathers, flesh and muscle out of the beige-and-tan's side. As he rolled away, scrambled to his clawed feet, he left part of his chest in the beige-and-tan's beak. Bright crimson soiled the cocks' feathers, and spattered over the battleground.

Mason and his opponent started to dash into the pit after their wounded birds, but they had hardly moved when the two gamecocks staggered toward each other once more. They crashed together again. A splash of blood shot from their bedraggled bodies as they met. Their clipped wings flapped feebly, lacking the power to lift them from the surface. Their wiry necks threatened to go limp, as they continued to feint, attempting to strike blows with their beaks. The steel gaffs on their legs were useless. They could hardly lift their thin legs off the ground. Still they fought on.

191

Nine minutes had passed since the cocks met each other in the center of the circle. The sound of the crowd now had a hoarse quality. Richard felt weak. Tears glazed his eyes, as much in emotional admiration for the incredible courage of the birds, as in compassion for their agonies. The beige-and-tan suddenly pulled away from the rainbow bird and fell over on its side. The Earl's rainbow, with sudden renewed energy, skipped toward the fallen bird, flapped his wings enough to rise several inches in the air above the beige-and-tan's head. His legs scissored, and the steel gaff on his right leg slashed into the eye of the fallen foe, tore upward into his brain. The beige-and-tan shuddered convulsively for several seconds, then lay still. The rainbow cock stood over him, raised his head and crowed, a trilling paean of victory.

Mason dashed into the center circle and picked up the rainbow, cradled him in his arms and rushed out of the arena. Wrexham grabbed Richard's shoulder.

"Come on, come . . ." he yelled excitedly over the roaring crowd noise.

Richard ran with him back to the open area outside the arena, where stood dozens of wagons, each loaded with gamecock pens. Smoke-colored rain clouds had formed in the east and a sharp wind blew. Mason stood alongside one of the wagons, holding the wounded rainbow in both hands, inspecting every inch of the tattered, bloody-feathered body. As Wrexham and Richard reached him, he began to lick the bird's feathers, and as he found each of the deeper wounds, he pressed the cock's body to his mouth and sucked hard to prevent the blood from clotting. His large nose, thick lips and unshaven chin were smeared red. He spit blood onto the ground. Finally he handed the rainbow to the young helper, who had prepared the bread and assisted with the clipping at the compound the day before. The young gamecocker, with arms extended, held the bedraggled bird before Mason, just below his waist. Mason opened his breeches and urinated over the bird. The young assistant turned the rainbow carefully so that the hot urine would spray over all the wounds.

Wrexham, noting the bafflement on Richard's face, explained.

"Helps prevent poisonous infection."

Mason adjusted his breeches, took the bird from his

helper, and placed it on a bed of hay in a deep box. The helper wiped his hands on the flanks of his breeches. The rainbow attempted to crow again, but managed only a barely audible squawk. From inside the arena came a renewed explosion of mob sound. Another victor, another vanquished.

"Congratulations, Dud," said Wrexham, clapping Mason on the back.

"Will the cock live?" asked Richard.

Mason smiled, wiping his bloody face with his sleeve.

"I think so. The wounds looked worse than they were. None seemed too deep."

"Will he fight again?" asked Wrexham.

"Aye!" nodded Mason. " 'E lives to fight."

Two more of the Earl's birds were entered in the matches that afternoon, one in the ninth, and one in the thirteenth. The first killed his rival in less than one minute, and the second was defeated after a savage two-minute struggle. When Mason came back to the wagon with the dead bird after the match, his young helper told him that the arrogant rainbow cock, for whom he had such high hopes, had succumbed moments earlier.

Mason disgustedly tossed the dead bird in his hand into a large refuse basket.

"I thought the goddam dunghill imposter was a good deal sturdier and stronger willed then 'e turned out to be." He shook his head, grinned cynically at Wrexham.

"Like a lot o' bloody humans," he philosophized, "the struttin' cock crowed a far better fight than 'e fought. . . . Ye'd think after twenty-five years of handlin' the fuckers I'd recognize them as 'as more throat than heart."

Wrexham clapped him on the back.

"Not to blame yourself, old friend! He had the look of a champion, and he was as fine trained as any bird ever I saw."

"I thought he fought well," offered Richard, but Wrexham and Mason ignored him. The young gamecocker assistant grumbled, "The Haversock bird weren't hardly no fighter!"

Richard knew he was referring to the beige-and-tan opponent of the Earl's rainbow. He saw no point in debating the issue of how well the dead rainbow had fought. After all, he knew little about cockfighting. Indeed he realized he knew little enough about people, as Wrexham renewed his physical advances, once they were in the carriage again. He sat close to Richard and put his arm around him, hugging him enthusiastically.

"You're a lucky charm for me, dear boy. I won eleven pounds."

Richard nodded. He, himself, had won his one-pound bet on the rainbow, but somehow he felt sad . . . and uneasy.

"What say you we visit Lady Gertrude's?" said Wrexham enthusiastically. "We'll dine, and play a bit of hazard. Perhaps the dice will be as good to us as the gamecocks."

"I'm sorry, Jerry. I've got to meet Felicia at the Inn. She's going to work with me on *Squire Doodle*. I begin at Bartholomew Fair on the morrow."

Wrexham removed his arm from Richard's shoulder. In the dim light inside the carriage, Richard could not tell whether he was irritated at mention of Felicia.

There was a half moment of silence, then Wrexham said, jovially enough, "Oh, you can take the time out of our rehearsal in the morning to brush up on that foolish excuse for a play."

Richard shook his head.

"I'm not truly up in my role in *Venice Restored*, either. I could not well afford to miss any of the rehearsal."

Wrexham laughed.

"You are far too conscientious, Richard. A good actor can always improvise through a spot or two he hasn't learned . . . but we'll let it go, if you and Felicia will accompany me to the opening of Banstead Downs next Sunday."

Richard nodded.

"I would like that, Jerry, and I'm sure Felicia would. I'll ask her, and we'll see you in the morning."

As he got out of the carriage in front of Pickering's, Wrexham slapped him playfully on the buttock.

"Till morning, Richard," he said with a leer, "and don't spend the entire night rehearsing plays. . . ."

Richard could not understand him at all.

❧ 20 ❧

On the morning after the cockfights, Gilbert Weston took Richard aside after the first hour of rehearsal of *Venice Restored*.

"You're playing it in far too emotional a manner, lad," he said quietly. "Try to relax, be natural."

Richard nodded as Weston moved off to discuss a scene with Wrexham and Felicia. Now Richard had completely forgotten about his concern over whether Wrexham had homosexual intentions toward him. He had forgotten the cockfights, and the upcoming Sunday at Banstead Downs. He sat, cross-legged on the floor at stage right, rereading his part. He did not feel quite at ease with some of Otway's lines in the blank verse drama. He was nervous because the rehearsal was running late, and he was due at the Bartholomew Fair at three o'clock. Although he had rehearsed it a half-dozen times, he was not quite sure that he had complete command of the silly Noodle role.

Then, in the next forty minutes everything seemed to fall into place, and Richard arrived at the Bartholomew Fair with twenty minutes to spare before the first scheduled performance of *Squire Doodle*.

It was a gray day. The sky was leaden and there was dampness in the air, but the spirits of the people were high, and substantial crowds had already gathered at the fairgrounds. As Richard pushed his way through the jostling, excited mob, the colorful procession proclaiming the Fair's opening had just concluded. The town band was playing the last of its triumphal selections, heavy with pounding drums and blaring trumpets and French horns.

195

Scarlet-coated footmen, holding white wands, led the Mayor's spectacularly caparisoned, prancing, coal-black horse into the official grandstand area. The mayor himself was dressed as richly as his steed. He waved regally at the people.

The town's aldermen and councilmen, all resplendent in embroidered and bejeweled robes and gowns, followed on fine horses, flanked by more scarlet-clad footmen with wands. More than two dozen petty constables moved around the area, seeking out pickpurses, who were a growing plague at the fairs. The mayor began his speech of welcome, but Richard hurried on. He passed booth after booth: braziers, ironmongers, milliners, toymakers, and several featuring English cloth, for which the Bartholomew Fair was known throughout the kingdom.

He turned a corner and made his way through bustling crowds along streets in which rows of booths for individual trades had been set up. There was a goldsmith's row, a skinner's row, a saddler's row. Finally he came to the entertainment area. There were as many people here as in any other section of the grounds. Balladeers and minstrels moved among them, singing and playing, and collecting a coin, now and then, in their caps. Two gracefully muscular men and a shapely young woman held a fairly large group spellbound with their rope dancing. Sidney Colby's booth was one of the largest in the entertainment area. It stood in the George Inn Yard, facing the Hospital Gate.

On the platform stage, just before his entrance into the first scene, Richard felt as nervous as he had before his debut performance at Lincoln's Inn Fields. He realized his stage fright was probably due to the unfamiliar setting. But then he clenched his fists, cleared his throat and strode onstage for his first lines, and they came out clear and loud. His nervousness disappeared as magically as if Fitzhugh Fitzhugh had cast a lucky spell upon him.

The audience laughed uproariously and applauded his playing. And with each burst of laughter, each blast of clapping hands, he felt more confident. It was the first time, on a stage, that he had intentionally made people laugh. The feeling of achievement was indescribable; the expression of the people's approval a new ecstasy. At the peak of his most hilarious scene with Sidney Colby, who was playing Squire Doodle, there was a sudden commotion in the middle of the crowd. Even as he read a line,

Richard saw a constable lift a club and whack a leather-capped man across the side of the head. The constable dragged the man through the crowd, out of the booth.

Richard continued to play his part. Colby, seasoned veteran that he was, raised his voice several decibels, and Richard followed suit. In a moment they had the audience's full attention once again. The man who had been evicted was a pickpurse, Richard learned later.

Three supporting players in the small cast were actors Colby had recruited in the provinces, as young as Richard himself, and they had not had his training. Their performances were uneven, but it did not seem to matter. The audience was not nearly as discriminating as those in the patent theaters, and they were mightily pleased with the nonsensical play.

Richard stayed at the foot of the stage to watch Fitzhugh Fitzhugh's magic show in the afterpiece. There was a long break, while the audience filed out of the booth, and Richard filled the time before the second show of the day was scheduled to begin with Fitzhugh, who was teaching him to juggle. The booth was filled to capacity for the second show. Richard felt less nervous as he climbed to the stage, yet oddly enough, his performance did not seem to get the enthusiastic reaction he won in the first show. He remembered then what Farley Shannon had often told him: the nervousness was not a matter for concern; it was rather a sign that an actor was keyed up, and ready. Colby complimented him after the second show, however, so Richard felt that he could not have done too badly.

That evening a coldly unresponsive audience, and not very large at that, attended the first performance of *Venice Restored* at Lincoln's Inn. As Richard stood in the wings before the performance began, Gilbert Weston, looking out at the less than half-filled theater, commented, "The Batholomew Fair seems to have cut into our patronage. The three shillings many of the good people might spend for our pit, or the one or two shillings for the galleries, is going for a bauble from the fair, or"—he smiled at Richard—"to see Richard Steele playing Noodle."

Richard knew that the operators of the fairs, both at Bartholomew and Southwark, as well as the patent theaters, usually tried to arrange their schedules so that they did not conflict. But this particular year, for political and other reasons Richard did not understand, the theaters' new season opened concurrently with the playdates of the two big fairs.

For Richard the opportunity to work at both the fairs and the theaters in the same period provided a much valued impetus to his budding career.

On the fourth day of the Bartholomew Fair, Felicia organized a party of the Lincoln's Inn group to spend an afternoon at the fair, and to attend Richard's performance in *Squire Doodle*. Farley Shannon came in from Avon to join Felicia, Weston, Wrexham, Catherine Clark, Susannah Forbish and Mrs. Forbish's dwarf friend, Quincy. They spent a pleasurable hour touring the retail booths, viewing the stalls of prize animals—the Welsh cattle were particularly impressive—and then went to the George Inn Yard to Colby's booth. Richard was excited and a little nervous that they should have come to see him. Felicia renewed her summer acquaintance with Colby and Fitzhugh. Such an air of pleasure marked the occasion that Richard noticed nothing strange about Fitzhugh's greeting to Felicia.

The green-haired, hunchback prestidigitator hugged her as she leaned down to him alongside the stage, where he and Richard stood, then held her at arms' length, and said, with peculiar fervor and intensity,

"Dearest lass! Oi can na say how profoundly pleased oi am, and grateful to the almighty, to see ye well. . . . Ye are well, now, are ye not?"

Felicia kissed his gaunt cheek.

"Of course, I am, dear Fitz. Why should I not be?"

She turned to Richard, took his hand and lifted her lips to his cheek.

"And you, love. Be a hilarious Noodle today!"

He was. After the show, they were leaving the booth when Gilbert Weston said to Farley Shannon, "You have performed miracles with the lad, Farley. I had no idea he could play comedy so effectively, sly and broad all at once."

Before leaving the fairgrounds, the group stopped at a booth for refreshments, and Shannon again brought up Richard.

"Did you not suspect young Steele's versatility, Gilbert?"

"Not quite. I thought he was tending toward romantic

roles, possibly in time, even some of the more dramatic tragic parts, but in all candor . . ." he drank his cider, ". . . I must admit his sense of comedy, his timing rather startled me."

"Poisonous stuff!" growled Shannon, spitting a mouthful of cider to the dusty ground, spilling the rest of the cup. He turned toward Weston.

"When are you planning to do *Volpone?*"

"In six weeks. . . . Why?"

"Wrexham to play Volpone?"

Felicia sipped her cider, listened intently. She did not find it poisonous, just a touch too tart.

Weston grinned, nodded energetically.

"Wrexham, of course. Casting to nature!"

"And Mosca?"

"Finch, I'd thought. He played it quite credibly last season. . . ." He paused, stared wide-eyed at the aged, legendary actor-coach. "Are you . . . you can't be . . . you're suggesting young Steele!"

Shannon said nothing. A faint, momentary twinkle showed in his pain-dulled gray eyes. The corners of his thin, pale lips lifted in a smile. He tugged at his nose.

"It's a long, most trying role!" exclaimed Weston.

Shannon nodded.

"In six weeks . . . you think he could be ready?"

Again Shannon nodded, and this time he said, "He will be finished with the fairs in a fortnight. We could work every afternoon for the next four weeks."

"Done!" said Weston.

Felicia put her cider cup down on the booth's counter, grasped Shannon's hands, lifted her face to kiss his cheek. She turned to Weston, threw her arms around him and kissed him too.

"You are both beautiful and noble men!"

Weston told Richard of the decision that very evening. By Sunday, when he and Felicia accompanied Wrexham and Catherine Clark to the races at Banstead Downs, Felicia had convinced Richard that the difficult and demanding part marked the real turning point in his young career, and that if he worked diligently with Shannon and with her, he would give an excellent account of himself. To both Richard's and Felicia's delight, even Wrexham volunteered to help.

"I'll work with you, too, Richard," he said one evening, when he joined Richard and Felicia at Pickering's.

"In the starring role of Volpone, which I perform exceedingly well, I'll be in a position to lift you if you falter now and again. And we can do some private boning together, apart from cast rehearsals."

Felicia was amused at Wrexham's shameless vanity, but Richard was too pleased even to notice it. On the Sunday at Banstead Downs, Wrexham truly impressed Richard, Felicia and Catherine Clark with his knowledge of horse racing. He apparently had free access to the paddocks, and seemed to know every trainer and jockey at the Downs. He introduced his fellow actors to a number of them, and discussed the entries in the day's races with them like a true expert. There were six races, and Wrexham picked the winning horses in four of the six. He won sixteen pounds on the day. Catherine Clark won ten, Felicia ten, and Richard two.

Richard himself prospered financially through the first weeks of the new season, more from his work as an actor than from his timid betting at sporting events. Weston had raised his wage per acting day from one shilling to three at the end of the second week. He promised Richard another increase to six shillings per day if he performed as well in *Volpone* as was hoped and expected. Richard was also earning one shilling per day playing Noodle, so that for the two weeks of the fairs, he would earn more than a pound. With the five pounds his mother had been paid for the wardrobe alterations, the Steeles' cottage fund had now reached seventy-three pounds.

On the second day of the Southwark Fair, where *Squire Doodle and His Man Noodle* played just as successfully as at Bartholomew, Ben Pickering came to the first show.

After the performance, Richard walked out of the booth with his old employer to the Green at the lower end of Blue Maid Alley. Richard had not been at the Inn for several days, and he was concerned at the worried look on Pickering's ruddy-cheeked face. Now as the festive Southwark crowd milled around the Green, Pickering asked, "Can you come back to work next week, Richard?"

"I'm sorry, Mr. Pickering, I can't. Perhaps I should have told you. I'll be studying with Mr. Shannon every afternoon—and there are the rehearsals in the morning, and—"

Pickering reached out, nodded, and touched his fore-arm.

"That's all right, lad. I understand. I'm going to have to find someone with a bit of experience and who is reliable. I must to Scotland to see my brother."

"Is Tillie all right?" asked Richard, knowing she was staying with her uncle.

Pickering shrugged.

"She's gone, Richard. Gone to Massachusetts Bay Colony with her supercargo. We got a letter from her yesterday, and another this morning from Angus, my brother."

Richard nodded, looked troubled.

"Did she marry the man?" he asked.

"Aye. Married him and sailed all on the same day. She's somewhere on the high seas this minute. The good Lord only knows where. She says she'll write us again when she settles in the colony, but God only knows when that will be . . . if ever she lives to arrive there. Bessie is frantic."

"I'm sorry, Mr. Pickering, but I'm sure she'll be all right. Almost all the passages to the colonies are safe enough these days."

"Angus met the man a half dozen times. I'm keen to learn a deal more about my new son-in-law. Angus is not much for writing."

"Perhaps I could come in for an hour or two before rehearsals in the morning," Richard suggested.

Pickering shook his head, managed a smile.

"Never mind, Richard. I'll find someone." He patted Richard on the shoulder.

"Thanks, at any rate, lad. Your performance was excellent. Almost made me forget my worries for a moment or two."

Misfortune in several guises threatened during the week at Southwark. On the day after Pickering's visit, Sidney Colby was called away, and an older actor, Frederick Fotheringill, a friend of Colby's, replaced him for the day in the part of Squire Doodle. Though the man was an accomplished thespian, he was so unfamiliar with the part and his style was so completely different from Colby's that Richard struggled, from his very first line, to sustain the comic quality he had managed in previous performances. What made it worse was that Felicia was in the audience.

She had brought Edith Forrest to the fair. They had come early and had spent several hours visiting the booths in other areas, eating marzipan and drinking cider. Even before the play began, Edith had seemed to him to be tired and rather pale. Although she was still at least three months away from the date on which her baby was due, her abdomen was as round as a large balloon. In the middle of the play, while Richard was struggling desperately to time his comic responses to Squire Doodle's strange delivery, he heard a feminine scream in the audience. He turned quickly, and saw that Edith was bent over, clutching her midsection, and that Felicia was pleading and pushing and clearing the way to take her out of the booth.

There was nothing for Richard to do but go on with the performance. He did, and remarkably enough, seemed not only to play his role without missing a cue, but actually to match his performance to the strange Doodle's so that the comic values in his lines and actions seemed to be working well again. But just as he felt he was gaining the control he sought, another outburst in the audience interrupted the play. This was even more distracting than Edith's scream and frantic exit.

Six burly and officious constables stormed through the crowd, shoving people, shouting, clouting one here and one there if they failed to move out of the way quickly enough. The constables elbowed and clubbed and kicked their way to the stage where they arrested Richard and the new Doodle and Fitzhugh and all the other members of the small company. They paraded them roughly across the Green to their waiting wagon, and took them before a justice of the peace.

Richard was totally baffled by the arrest and the quick trial. He had always been aware of the strong and widespread opposition to the theater and its people, particularly on the part of the clergy and the religiously inclined subjects of the kingdom. But since all of his own theatrical experience had been with the Lincoln's Inn Fields Theatre, one of the two in London which operated under royal patent, neither he nor his fellow players had ever been arrested.

The justice heard the constable's case, read a statute, which provided "all common players of interludes shall be adjudged to be rogues and vagrants, subject to arrest by constables, who shall bring them before a justice of the peace, where they shall be examined, and publicly whipped or sent to the house of corrections." Fotheringill, the older actor, respectfully protested that the statute to which the justice referred had been passed during the reign of Queen Anne, and since the Queen had died in 1714, and her Hanoverian cousin, George I, had ascended to the throne, the statute had never been enforced.

The justice was furious with the old actor. He sentenced all the members of the company to a public whipping on the morrow. Fortunately Sidney Colby returned from Richmond Hill early that evening, visited the justice of the peace in private, and a half hour after his visit, Richard and all his colleagues were released. Colby apologized to his company for the inconvenience and embarrassment the arrest had caused them. He said the entire matter had been an unfortunate misunderstanding. He took them all to his favorite tavern, for a festive evening, which Richard had to decline, since he was due at the theater for a performance of *The Beaux Stratagem*.

He arrived at the theater, breathless, just as the play began. Later, when he told Gilbert Weston and Felicia what had happened, Weston said, with a resigned cynicism, "A pound or two often clear up such misunderstandings."

Felicia then assured Richard that Edith had merely had a badly upset stomach, which she, in her inexperience, mistook for labor pains. And *The Beaux Stratagem* performance went well, although the Lincoln's Inn was still playing to half-empty houses.

Weston learned that the rival patent theater, the Drury Lane had also suffered poor business during the two weeks of the fairs. But on the second day after Southwark closed, the Lincoln's Inn Fields Theatre was packed to capacity again. The play, Shakespeare's *Measure for Measure*, was one not too frequently presented. Weston had been reluctant to include it in the season's repertoire, but the Duke had insisted. Unbeknownst to Weston, it was Jerome Wrexham who was behind the movement to include it. He had made the original suggestion to the Duke, and outlined the strategy for pursuing the commercial advantage of what he predicted would be the reaction to the play.

It was one of Shakespeare's strangest works in that it was a comedy that dealt with serious moral problems.

The plot revolved around the fate of a young lover, Claudio, who has been sentenced to death for committing fornication with a teen-age maiden, Juliet. Claudio's young and beautiful sister, Isabella, a novitiate in a nunnery, pleads with deputy Angelo to spare her brother. Overcome with lustful desire for Isabella, Angelo agrees to spare Claudio's life if Isabella will give herself to him.

With this emphasis on fornication and ignoble seduction, *Measure for Measure* produced precisely the reaction Wrexham had predicted. A number of daily newspapers, weekly, biweekly and semiweekly magazines published occasional commentary on theatrical matters and critiques on plays. Four reacted immediately to the presentation of *Measure for Measure*. *The Tatler* said:

> . . . an absorbing and titillating experience. Gilbert Weston, as the Duke who masquerades as a Friar, and manipulates the citizens of his realm to see true justice done, is most persuasive. The actor-manager of Lincoln's Inn once again displays his total mastery of Shakespeare's eloquent and poetic writings. . . .
>
> Jerome Wrexham is a nigh-perfect Angelo. One knows, virtually from his first appearance, that he is not the righteous, unbending man he professes to be —what mortal man could be?—that he has not the moral fiber to resist a fair maiden's charms. Yet he makes the transition from relentlessly virtuous judge to base seducer and knave interesting and believable.
>
> The fair maiden in question is indeed fair. Her incandescent performance as the virtuous, virginal Isabella seems all the more remarkable when one ponders her offstage reputation as a young lady of many amours. . . .
>
> Young Richard Steele, who according to our backstage spy at Lincoln's Inn is Mistress Wandrous's latest good friend, plays Claudio, the youthful lover and impregnator of Juliet, with an admirable and clear-eyed forthrightness. The scene in which he expresses his fear of dying is a highlight of the evening, a surprisingly virtuoso display of the thespian art by a youth not yet eighteen years of age. . . .

The Spectator commentator wrote in a similar favorable vein. He did remark additionally and a bit unkindly upon Wrexham's paunch, and expanded his appreciation of Richard's work.

But two other publications also published long articles about the play. *The Censor*'s was written by a Reverend Willoughby Pious:

> No less than eleven hundred and thirty-six offenses against the bible are committed in this lascivious, immoral work of the devil. . . . The theater is at best a force for evil, a corrupter of our young, a distraction to the industrious, a blight on the kingdom, but in *Measure for Measure,* with its flagrant episodes of fornication, the vile purveyors of this degenerate form of entertainment reach new nadirs of blasphemy and impiety.

The London Journal published an editorial denouncing the fornication-based motivation of the play, yet strangely enough, the editorial also made a rather left-handed mention of Richard's scene expressing the death-fear:

> Shakespeare's fearsome words concerning the mysteries of the afterlife are spoken with appropriate awe-filled trepidation by a young player identified as Richard Steele. . . .
> It would behoove this young man and his colleagues to consider the strong possibility that their presentation of lewd plays may well result in their "delighted spirits bathing in fiery floods" in the eternity beyond the grave.

Two days after these commentaries appeared there was circulated throughout London town a leaflet, a reprint of the article in *The Censor* and the editorial in *The London Journal*. Above the reprints in bold flourishing type was the headline: FORNICATION AND FIERY FLOODS! The leaflet bore the notation: "Distributed by the Society of the Commonweal."

Few knew that Gilbert Weston had had the leaflet printed and distributed as part of the strategy of Jerome Wrexham and the Duke of Cheltenham. Two days after the circulation of the leaflet, *Measure for Measure* was presented for an additional week. It was an unusually long run for a play of the day, but every performance was sold out. On two days there were riots at the box office, when those who could not buy seats disputed with the ticket seller, and with speculators, who had purchased large numbers of seats and were selling them at three and four times their face value.

Three religious organizations picketed the theater. On the second day of the picketing, one of the religious groups discontinued its efforts. This group consisted of five men who had been hired by Weston to get the picketing started. When two authentic groups marched, Weston felt it was no longer necessary to go to the expense of hiring the spurious pickets.

Eager Londoners continued to ignore the picketers, and there was standing room only for every performance of the play. Weston did not have his heart in this style of showmanship. He believed that in the long run it was not good for the theater. Farley Shannon considered it totally despicable. Felicia viewed it with tolerant amusement, taking the attitude that there would always be people like Wrexham and the Duke, and multitudes who would be attracted by stories of illicit fornication.

Richard could not make up his mind quite how he felt about the question. Indeed, at this stage of his career, he did not ponder the ethics of the matter that deeply. To him the most important element of the entire *Measure for Measure* episode was the strong and favorable comment on his own performance in the relatively secondary role of Claudio.

Following *Measure for Measure*, Lincoln's Inn presented a Colley Cibber play in which all wickedness was punished, and virtue was totally triumphant. Of this, a leading writer on theatrical matters complained:

Nothing can be better meant or more ineffective. It is almost a misnomer to call these presentations comedies. They are homilies in dialogue, in which a number of pretty ladies and gentlemen discuss the fashionable topics of gaming, of duelling, of seduction, of scandal, with a sickly sensibility that shows as little hearty aversion to vice, as sincere attachment to virtue. The sting is indeed taken out of what is bad, but what is good at the same time loses its manhood and nobility.

Richard began to understand that when it came to dramatic entertainment, it was difficult, if not impossible, to please all.

⚜ 21 ⚜

Immediately after the conclusion of the Southwark Fair, along with his rehearsals and performances in all the other plays, Richard had begun to work with Farley Shannon on the dark Ben Jonson comedy, *Volpone*. The role of the scheming, brilliant and ruthless manservant to the greedy title character in the play was by far the longest and most complex he had ever attempted. The nature of the character, manipulative, devilishly ingenious, wicked —the character Jonson called "Volpone's parasite"—was totally foreign to Richard. Felicia had the important, but relatively minor role of the beautiful Celia, wife of the merchant, Corvino, who was one of the seekers after Volpone's fortune. She knew her role well, and it took little extra time for her to polish it. Whenever she and Richard had the opportunity, she too worked with Richard.

On the Saturday nine days before the scheduled opening of the play, Shannon worked with Richard for six uninterrupted hours. The old man was gray with fatigue. Richard was so intent on refining the nuances in playing Mosca, as drilled into him by Shannon, that he had not noticed that his coach was tiring. Richard stood at the center of the small stage in Shannon's theater room, and began again to play the soliloquy in which Mosca reveals the conceit and pleasure he finds in his devilish skills in trickery.

"I fear I shall begin to grow in love with my dear self, and my most prosperous parts," he said with glee in his voice and his eyes. "They do so spring and burgeon; I can feel a whimsy in my blood: I know not how, success hath made me wanton."

He took a mincing step toward stage right, continued, "I could skip out of my skin now, like a subtle snake, I am so limber. O! your parasite is a most precious thing. . . ."

Shannon sighed, closed his eyes, opened them again, clapped his hands feebly.

"Bravo, lad. You truly have it. I think we might call it a day, a week for all that. . . ."

Richard looked down at the elderly actor slumped in his chair.

"Forgive me, sir. I should have realized I was exhausting you. . . ."

Shannon waved away his apologies.

"What I see, as you play this role, is well worth my exhaustion and more. . . . I would suggest, Richard . . . unnnhhhhh . . . that, if possible, you work with other members of the cast over the weekend. Felicia . . ." he managed a weak smile, ". . . is always an inspirational tutor . . . uhnnnhhhh . . . but most of all I would like to see you work with Wrexham."

He struggled out of the chair as Richard came down from the stage to help him. He waved off Richard's assistance as he grunted his way to his feet.

"Felicia and I have been working together for some time, and we plan to work tomorrow evening with Jerry at his home."

Shannon nodded as he wearily walked to the door with Richard.

"Good, lad, good. I'll see you Monday afternoon."

Felicia and Edith Forrest came early the next morning to the Steeles' house in Billingsgate. Although Felicia and Edith were not Catholics, they went to mass at Father Whittaker's poor waterfront church with Mary and Richard. In certain sections of the city, persons attending Catholic services were subject to arrest as recusants, suspected of disloyalty to the Crown and the Church of England, but Father Whittaker's decrepit dockside church was ignored by the town's officials.

Felicia had brought a rump of beef, and after the brief services Mary prepared it and set it to roast on the spit in the fireplace, while Edith began altering the first of four dresses she had brought along. When Mary finished with the beef, she joined Edith in the sewing, while Richard

209

and Felicia moved off to a corner of the room and began rehearsing *Volpone*.

Edith and Mary were constantly distracted by the readings. They sewed almost mechanically, and spoke in quiet hushed tones when they did speak. They listened, and frequently glanced away from their tasks to watch the young players. First Felicia took Richard through those portions of the play in which Mosca had his lengthiest and most difficult scenes.

She read all the roles but Mosca. In the earliest stages of the comedy, she read Volpone's part, and coached Richard in achieving the smarmy tones and manner that Shannon had stressed and demonstrated so effectively.

He leaned toward Felicia Volpone, glanced worshipfully at her face, and, discussing Volpone's wise use of his wealth, said with unctuous pseudosincerity, "And besides, sir, you are not like the thresher that doth stand with a huge flail, and hungry—"

Felicia, following his lines in her own folio, shook her head.

". . . with a huge flail, *watching a heap of corn* . . ."

Richard nodded.

"Sorry . . . with a huge flail, watching a heap of corn, and, hungry, dares not taste the smallest grain, but feeds on mallows, and such bitter herbs; nor like the merchant, who hath filled his vaults with Romagnia, and rich Canadian wines, yet drinks the lees of Lombard's vinegar."

Felicia nodded approvingly. Edith and Mary stopped sewing momentarily and listened as Richard continued.

"You will not lie in straw, whilst moths and worms feed on your sumptuous hangings and soft beds. You know the use of riches, and dare give now from that bright heap, to me, your poor observer, or to your dwarf, or your hermaphrodite, your eunuch, or what other household trifle your pleasure allows maintenance. . . ."

They spent the entire morning on Richard's Mosca, and, after a hearty noon meal, ran through the few scenes in which Celia, the loveliest woman in Venice, wife of the merchant Corvino, was involved. Now Richard played all the other roles. The rehearsal was amusingly and briefly interrupted several times by Edith's frequent unladylike belching. Richard had been awed by her consumption, and Mary and Felicia had made warm humor of her appetite. Poor Edith took it all in good grace, although she was mightily embarrassed.

Another interruption to the rehearsals came with a loud meowing at the door. Reading as he walked, Richard went to the door and let Farquhar in. He sniffed at the dish, where Mary had put a few pieces of the roast, and walked away, toward Felicia. He rubbed against her legs, and repeated the motion until Felicia, without pausing in her own reading, reached down and stroked him. He then settled at her feet, looking from her to Richard as each read their lines.

Richard Corvino went on, describing what he mistakenly believed to be Volpone's feeble condition.

"Why this's no more than a decrepit wretch, that has no sense, no sinew; takes his meat with others' fingers: only knows to gape when you scald his gums; a voice, a shadow; and what can this man hurt you?"

Felicia Celia said in an aside to the audience, Edith and Mary, "Lord! what spirit is this hath entered him?"

Edith belched loudly, her hand to her mouth hardly softening the sharp sound. She blushed, said, "Excuse ... please excuse me."

Richard Corvino, trying to convince his wife that no one would know of her assignation with the wealthy old man, spoke with urgency and irritation, "And for the fame, that such a jig; as if I would go tell it, cry it on the Piazza! Who shall know it but he that cannot speak it, and this fellow, whose lips are in my pocket? Save yourself (if you'll proclaim it, you may) I know of no other should come to know it."

Felicia Celia continued to plead, until in the finale of the scene, her husband began to grow considerably angry.

"Heart of my father! Wilt thou persist thus? Thou seest 'tis nothing, Celia." Richard Corvino raised his hand as if to strike her. "By this hand I shall grow violent. Come, do't, I say!"

Felicia Celia, drawing away from him, trembling, yet defiant, "Sir, kill me, rather: I will take down poison, eat burning coals, do anything ..."

The September light at the window was beginning to fade. Mary put down her sewing, cut some of the roast and several potatoes and carrots, and put them into a pot half filled with water to make a stew. She hung the pot over the fire. For the first time that day, as she walked back to her chair, she began to cough violently. They all watched her anxiously. Her face turned red, and she bent over with the ache in her chest and stomach from the sudden attack.

This was what constantly worried Richard. His mother would go for several days without any trouble, then the attacks would suddenly come upon her again. Dr. Thorndike said her earlier disorder had caused some damage to her lungs, and it might take some time to clear up entirely. Finally the harsh choking suddenly ceased. She breathed deeply and heavily, tears running from her eyes. Felicia, Edith and Richard had all gathered around her, patting her helplessly. Now she looked up at them apologetically.

"I'm sorry . . . I'm all right," she gasped.

In a short time, the stew was ready and the alterations and the play-reading halted. Again Mary, Richard and Felicia were amused and awed by Edith's voracious appetite.

Richard and Felicia were due to arrive at Jerome Wrexham's apartment sometime after the evening meal. They found a hackney and started for Felicia's rooms in Middle Temple Lane to drop off Edith. The jolting ride through the cobbled streets upset Edith's stomach. As they neared Middle Temple Lane, she began to groan and hold her midsection.

She was still groaning, crouched over and holding her hands over the churning globe of her stomach, when the hackney stopped before Felicia's house. As soon as she stepped to the curb, Edith moved gingerly away from them, leaned over and vomited into the street. Felicia rushed to her and held her by the shoulders.

Tears streamed from her eyes, her nose ran and she moaned. Felicia wiped the pregnant girl's mouth with a handkerchief as she walked Edith toward the door. Old Willy Nillingham and his blind dog, Oscar, came out just as Edith and Felicia approached the door. Felicia turned back toward Richard.

"I believe I had best forego rehearsal at Jerry's, Richard. You go ahead."

Edith protested.

"No, please, Felicia. I would feel much worse if you did not go. I'll be all right. I just ate too much." There was a shamed and apologetic look on her pale face. "I just cannot seem to control my appetite these days."

"I'll look after her, Felicia," Willy Nilly said. Felicia

212

looked after them a moment, then said, "Well, all right. I'll be home soon."

Wrexham's chambers were in disarray. Wrexham, himself, was dressed only in a green silk robe, embroidered with golden crowns. As he opened the door to Richard and Felicia, they could see that all the furniture, the tables, chairs, had been moved against the walls. A small oriental rug had been bunched up and pushed to one side of the room, as though its center had been cleared for dancing, or possibly wrestling. On one of the tables were platters containing a well-picked carcass of a large fowl, some dried slices of ham and veal, and three loaves of bread, out of which large chunks had been torn. There were eight bottles, six of port wine and two of brandy. All were empty except one three-quarters-full bottle of deep red port, and a half-full bottle of amber-colored brandy.

Alongside the fowl platter lay a folio and a number of loose pages of a play script. Draped over a chair was a brilliant scarlet satin hooped gown, and on the chair's seat, a corset, its strings hanging over the edge of the seat, touching the floor. Candles on a mantel and on one of the tables gave the room an uneven glow.

Catherine Clark, fully dressed in a gown of blue and white striped dimity, stood before a wall mirror, brushing her hair. She had not yet laced up her bodice. Reflected in the mirror, Richard could see her full, white breasts.

Wrexham threw one arm around Richard, the other around Felicia. Kissing Felicia on the cheek, he then turned and kissed Richard on the cheek as he led them into the room.

"Cat and I had every intention of spending most of the afternoon rehearsing—she's always had difficulty with the role of Lady Politick Would-Be," he said, "but Quincy decided he wanted to celebrate his debut as an actor. . . ."

He chuckled at the look of bafflement on Richard's and Felicia's faces.

"He came along with Mrs. Forbish, and that gigantic basket full of libations and a feast fit for kings."

The straw basket to which he referred had been kicked under the table. As Richard looked at it, the dwarf waddled in from the bedroom, his stumpy body moving from side to side on his muscular bandied legs. He had a full head of curly black hair, keen and merry brown eyes, a large nose and full, cupid's bow mouth. His arms and hands were disproportionately large, and as strong-looking as his legs.

He finished stuffing the long tail of the attractive purple-and-white striped satin shirt into his tan leather breeches.

"Greetings, fellow players." He welcomed Felicia and Richard, waving his right arm.

"As I have already told Weston, and my friends Jerry and Cat, I will make you all proud with my performance as Nano, the dwarf. My Susannah has been coaching me, and with her continued help and yours, I shall bring new honor to the Lincoln's Inn Fields company of players."

Felicia smiled and applauded the speech, and Wrexham and Richard followed. Quincy made a small bow and beamed as Mrs. Forbish came out of the bedroom. She was also applauding.

"I heard you, lover," she said as she strode across the room to the chair where the scarlet satin dress and the corset lay. She was naked, except for a pink turban and green plume, which she had carefully worked onto her head. It was a headdress she had worn as a lady of the Turkish court several seasons earlier, and she liked to wear it with her hooped scarlet farthingale gown on occasional Sundays. The fact that the hooped farthingales had gone out of fashion temporarily troubled her not one whit. Her ample bosom and bottom quivering, she walked regally to the chair, picked up her corset and dress, and sauntered back into the bedroom.

Richard felt sure Quincy would perform well as Nano, *Volpone*'s dwarf. There was simply something about the small man's air of total self-confidence that convinced him. He had wondered what parts Quincy would be able to play when *Volpone* completed its run, and why the dwarf would leave the circus to cast his lot with a theatrical company. But Felicia had told him that Quincy was half-owner of the circus and could return to it whenever he wished.

Wrexham kicked the bunched rug into a degree of flatness across the center of the floor.

"Move some of these chairs out here, Richard," he requested, lifting one chair himself. Quincy picked up a chair with little effort, and soon the furniture was arranged, more or less in its usual place. Catherine finished putting up her hair.

214

Wrexham poured himself and Quincy a brandy. Richard, Catherine and Felicia all asked for the port.

Wrexham drank down his brandy and smacked his lips. "Quincy has the most remarkable tool." He looked fondly at the dwarf.

Quincy lowered his head modestly.

"Show 'em, Quince!" said Wrexham.

Quincy unbuttoned and tugged down his leather breeches, and there hung the largest penis Richard had ever seen on dwarf or full-grown man.

"I simply could not believe it," said Catherine Clark.

Felicia and Richard just stared, but Wrexham roared with laughter.

"A prize-winner that, eh?"

Susannah Forbish stood at the bedroom door. She wore green silk stockings and a loosely hanging corset. She looked possessively at Quincy and, turning her back, dropped to her knees at the door.

"Come and tighten my corset strings, you beautiful man," she cooed.

Quincy lifted his breeches, buttoned them and dutifully went to Mrs. Forbish, doing a rapid and efficient job of tightening her corset strings.

When Quincy, Mrs. Forbish and Catherine Clark left, Felicia asked, "Are you sober enough for some serious rehearsal, Jerry?"

Looking hurt, Wrexham walked across to the table and picked up his folio of *Volpone*. He did not even open it. Holding it in his left hand, he faced Richard and said in a ringing voice, "Good morning to the day; and next my gold! Open the shrine, that I may see my saint."

He waved at Richard with the folio.

"Speak, Richard, speak! This is where Mosca withdraws the curtain, and we and the audience discover piles of gold, plate and jewels of every description."

The gleam in Wrexham's eyes, as he looked at the same invisible hill of wealth was even more brilliant than Richard's. Felicia relaxed in a chair and watched the two of them with amused and appreciative professional interest.

Richard marveled at the intensity with which Wrexham was speaking his lines. The corners of Felicia's lovely mouth turned up in appreciation of this vivid portrayal of a man who worships gold. Wrexham seemed inspired. The words poured from his very heart.

215

"Well did wise poets, by thy glorious name, title that age which they would have the best; thou being the best of things, and far transcending all style of joy, in children, parents, friends, or any other walking dream on earth.

"Thy looks when they to Venus did ascribe, they should have given her twenty thousand Cupids; such are thy beauties and our loves! Dear saint, riches, the dumb god, that giv'st all men tongues, that canst do nought, and yet mak'st men do all things."

He paused, turned toward Felicia and back to Richard. Extending his arms, he spoke to the ceiling.

"The price of souls; even hell, with thee to boot, is made worth heaven. Thou art virtue, fame, honor, and all else. Who can get thee, he shall be noble, valiant, honest, wise. . . ."

He paused and looked at Richard. Again Richard was so enthralled with his performance that he merely stared at Wrexham in appreciation.

Wrexham said impatiently, "Well, Richard, your cue! 'Wise,' your goddam cue! If you're going to miss your cues, you're going to destroy my masterful performance. You've . . ."

"Sorry, Jerry, sorry," Richard said, embarrassed, then, as he was about to speak, Wrexham repeated his last line, "He shall be noble, valiant, honest, wise. . . ."

Richard said obsequiously, "And what he will, sir. Riches are in fortune a greater good than wisdom is in nature."

Wrexham continued his eloquent reading, now stressing the clever manner in which Volpone gains his wealth, by trading on the greed and cupidity of other men of slightly lesser fortune, who scheme to become his heirs.

Felicia was beginning to worry about Edith.

"Jerry," she interrupted an exchange between Volpone and Mosca, "would you run through your brief scenes with me before you go on? Edith was not feeling well; I would like to get home early to see after her."

Wrexham went to the table and poured himself a large glass of brandy. This time he laced it with port.

"Of course, my dear," he said, turning to the scene where Volpone is ready to take Celia to his bed.

"You do not mind, do you, Richard?" Felicia touched Richard's hand.

"Not at all, Felicia; I should have thought of suggesting it myself."

"Pour yourself a drink, Richard," said Wrexham. Richard went to the table and filled a glass with brandy. He was exhilarated and felt the brandy would stimulate him even more.

Wrexham read from the place in the text where Corvino has turned his lovely wife, Celia, over to Volpone. He lay on his couch, as though he were the deceiving, ailing Volpone, then leaped to his feet and faced Felicia Celia.

"Ay," he shouted, "in Corvino and such earth-fed minds, that never tasted the true heaven of love, assure thee, Celia, he that would sell thee, only for hope of gain, and that uncertain, would have sold his part of Paradise for ready money, had he met a merchant.

"Why art thou mazed to see me thus revived? Rather applaud thy beauty's miracle. 'Tis thy great work that hath, not now alone, but sundry times raised me, in several shapes. . . ."

He pled his case with romantic fervor and urged Celia into his bed. Now Wrexham Volpone launched his most devastatingly romantic speech.

"If thou hast wisdom, hear me, Celia. Thy baths shall be the juice of July flowers, spirit of roses and violets, the milk of unicorns, and panthers' breath gathered in bags, and mixed with Cretan wines. Our drink shall be prepared gold and amber, which we shall take until my room whirl round with the vertigo."

He stood, and gestured with outspread arms toward Felicia. Richard watched, fascinated, mildly surprised that he felt no jealousy. He sipped his brandy.

Wrexham continued, ". . . and my dwarf shall dance, my eunuch sing, my fool make up the antic, whilst we, in changed shapes, act Ovid's tales: thou like Europa now, and I like Jove. Then I like Mars, and thou like Erycine. So of the rest, till we have run through, and wearied of all the fables of the gods."

He moved forward now, took Felicia tightly by the shoulders and drew her to him.

"Then I will have thee in more modern forms, attired like some sprightly dame of France, brave Tuscan lady, or proud Spanish beauty . . ." he continued.

Richard sipped nervously at his brandy. Wrexham pulled Felicia close to him.

"And I will meet thee in many shapes, where we may

217

so transfuse our wandering souls out at our lips, and score up sums of pleasures . . ."

In his deep, rich baritone, still holding Felicia, he now sang Volpone's small song.

Felicia Celia begged pitifully, "If you have ears that will be pierced—or eyes that can be opened—a heart that may be touched—or any part that yet sounds man above you. . . . If you have touch of holy saints—or heaven—do me the grace to let me escape. If not, be bountiful and kill me!"

There was desperation in the way she looked into Wrexham Volpone's hungry eyes, building the scene to its highest emotional pitch.

Finally she fell to her knees at Wrexham's feet.

"I will kneel to you, pray for you, pay down a thousand hourly vows, sir, for your health; report, and think you virtuous—"

Wrexham Volpone grabbed her arms, lifted her roughly to her feet.

"Think me cold!" he said scornfully. "Frozen and impotent, and so report me? That I had Nestor's hernia, thou wouldst think. I do degenerate, and abuse my nation, to play with an opportunity thus long; I should have done the act and then parleyed."

He pulled her savagely to him.

"Yield," he demanded, crushing his bearded face down on hers, "or I'll force thee!"

The performance was so real, Richard had all he could do to restrain himself from rushing toward the couple and knocking Wrexham away from Felicia. He realized with a rush of shame that he was being a total amateur, that he himself, Jonsonian ego, Mosca, had set up this imminent rape. He finished the brandy in the glass, and went to the table to pour himself another, while he watched the rest of the scene.

Then Felicia said farewell, kissed them both on the cheek. Wrexham flopped in a chair, pulled his robe over his thighs and stretched out his bare legs. He expelled a long breath.

"I believe I like *Volpone* more than any play we do. I think Ben Jonson was superior to Shakespeare," he said. "Would you be kind enough to pour me a brandy and port?"

Richard brought the brandy to him. He took a long sip, paused and then emptied the glass.

"Excuse me, just a moment, lad," he said as he stood and strolled toward the bedroom door. "I'll be right back."

Richard was studying his difficult passage in the first scene of Act III when Wrexham's magnificent voice sang loudly from the bedroom door:

> "Come, my Richard, let us prove
> While we can, the sports of love,
> Time will not be ours forever,
> He, at length, our good will sever."

Richard looked up from his folio in the direction of the rich, deep tones. Wrexham stood in the bedroom doorway, naked. Even erect and tumescent, his tool was not nearly as large as Quincy's. Richard stared at him in shocked disbelief. Wrexham paused in his song for a fleeting moment to run his tongue across his lips and wink at Richard. The pink tip slid salaciously between golden mustache and beard. Then he sang again, arms extended, leaning backward, his chest and paunch rising and falling, to the very end of the song.

It was the song Volpone sings to Celia. Richard's reaction to the serenade was vastly more indignant than Celia's in the play.

22

Wrexham finished the song and strode toward Richard, arms swinging at his sides, a broad, open-mouthed smile on his face. There was a glazed, hot look in his bright mahogany eyes. Richard gritted his teeth, dropped the folio to the floor and clenched his fists. His sea eyes blazed.

"I'm not interested, Jerry!" he said coldly.

Wrexham stopped halfway to Richard and walked toward the table. He poured himself another glass of brandy.

"Brandy?" he asked, smiling at Richard.

Richard shook his head. Wrexham moved easily to the couch, across the room from Richard, and lay back on it with his head and shoulders resting on three thick maroon satin cushions. In his right hand he held his brandy glass, with his left he idly stroked his now semi-limp member.

"I gather you've never had sex with a man," he said softly.

Richard glared at him.

"Why not disrobe, lad? I'm not going to hurt you."

"Have we finished rehearsing the play for the night?" Richard stood up.

Wrexham shook his head.

"No, no, not at all, Richard. Just an interlude, a few fleeting moments of pleasurable relaxation. Are you certain you won't have a drink? You know, lad, fucking with a man is just as great a delight—often greater—than fucking a woman."

Richard struggled with the idea of leaving. He felt he should, but on the other hand, needed the work with

Wrexham on the play. He also did not wish to appear a childish prude, totally without sophistication. Expressing firm disinterest in a homosexual relationship was one thing, acting like a novitiate in a seminary another.

Wrexham spoke again. "Only calves' heads and peasants restrict their lovemaking to one gender. Your own passionate Felicia has had women lovers. . . ."

A growing rage reddened Richard's face. Wrexham's hand, moving languidly in his lap, kept drawing Richard's attention, in spite of his effort to meet Wrexham's hot stare.

"Indeed, we might all experience a most superior delight if you and Felicia and I were to spend a long night in the same bed. . . ."

Wrexham rose and walked toward the table. He finished his brandy and strode slowly toward Richard, erect again.

"But since our lovely little whore is not with us, permit me to pleasure you, lad," he said softly. He reached for the top buttons of Richard's black cotton breeches. With a suddenness that surprised not only Wrexham, but himself, Richard leaped from his chair and shoved Wrexham hard on the chest with both hands. Wrexham staggered backward across the room and crashed against the table. As he fell to his knees, the table tilted, and the carcass of the fowl dropped onto his shoulder, and to the floor in front of him. Several glasses and the wine bottle tumbled off the table. The glasses shattered, but the bottle rolled to a stop at Wrexham's right knee. Standing quickly he grasped the bottle by the neck, raised it over his head and rushed toward Richard. The chair was directly behind Richard. He knew he could not back away from the blow, so he did what Wrexham least expected. He dove at Wrexham's knees and grabbed his legs in both arms in a fierce tackle. The bottle bounced feebly against Richard's left shoulder, as Wrexham crashed over on his back.

Richard released Wrexham's knees, scrambled quickly and seated himself astride Wrexham's waist. Grabbing Wrexham's right hand, which still held the bottle, he whipped and twisted the wrist until Wrexham released his hold. Now Richard closed his left hand on Wrexham's throat and slammed down with a hard right fist toward his jaw. He missed the golden bearded jaw on the first blow, but landed a blow high on the cheekbone.

A second vicious swing caught Wrexham just to the left of the bearded chin. Richard felt him go limp as he sat on Wrexham's stomach for a while, breathing hard.

A rattling, snoring sound came from Wrexham's mouth. Saliva bubbles formed on his lips, moistened his beard and mustache. His eyelids fluttered, but his eyes remained closed. As Richard stood over him, still gasping for breath, the flesh below Wrexham's left eye began to turn a maroon-tinged purple. Richard went into the bedroom and came out with Wrexham's green robe, placing it over Wrexham who had turned over on his side, and was snoring heavily.

The late October night had turned cold, and there was a threat of rain in the air. Richard was oblivious to the weather, and the still bustling, noisy and smelly streets, as he made his way home. He seemed unable to avoid confrontations with Wrexham, no matter how hard he tried.

He knew that he could not have accepted Wrexham's advances, yet he had the nagging feeling that it would have been much more mature and sophisticated of him to laugh Wrexham out of the proposal. He wondered what Wrexham would do or say at rehearsal in the morning. The discolored eye would probably be worse, and he wondered how Wrexham would explain it.

Just before he reached his house, the rains came. He ran the rest of the way and arrived panting. Mary had already gone to sleep, but Farquhar came out of Mary's bedroom to greet him. But when the cat discovered that Richard was wet, he quickly trotted back into Mary's room. Richard lay on his pallet, listening to the heavy rain pounding on the roof, worrying. . . .

Finally he fell into a fitful sleep. Farquhar awakened him by snuggling on the pallet beside him. He reached down to stroke the cat, and discovered Farquhar, too, was wet. Vaguely baffled, he fell into a fitful sleep once more. He thought he was dreaming, when Mary came staggering out of her bedroom, shivering, her gray-brown hair hanging wetly down her shoulders, her cotton night dress soaking and clinging to her frail body. The candle in her shaking hand created a dim, moving light. But it was not a dream.

"There is a leak, right over the—the bed," she said, her teeth chattering. Mary shivered, and coughed for some time, before Richard was able to build up the coal fire in the fireplace enough to warm her.

By the light of a large candle, Richard studied his part in *Volpone,* trying not to be distracted by Mary's troubled muttering in her sleep, or his concern over what would happen at the rehearsal in a few hours. He left the house early and stopped at the home of the landlord to ask that the leak be repaired promptly. The landlord, a crotchety old sea captain, grudgingly agreed to take care of it that very day.

By twenty minutes past ten all the members of the cast, excepting Wrexham, had assembled on the theater's stage. Felicia asked Richard how the balance of his rehearsal at Wrexham's had gone. He merely shrugged, and said it had been helpful. He remembered to ask about Edith's illness, and Felicia assured him her pregnant friend was all right. She gave Richard a puzzled look, sensing that something was troubling him, but Gilbert Weston was now outlining the rehearsal schedule for the balance of the week, and the players suspended their personal discussions.

Finally he asked whether Jerome Wrexham had said anything to any of them about the possibility of being late this morning. As if in response to the question, at that moment they heard the stage door open and close, and Wrexham walked in from the stage-right wings.

The entire company stared at him in amazement. One sleeve of his black velvet coat was ripped away from the shoulder. There was mud and dirt on both the knees of his black velvet breeches. His shirt and waistcoat were torn and stained with dirt. His usually impeccably combed and brushed golden hair fell in wild tangles around his ears. His left eye was tightly closed, and the area beneath the eye was a glistening dark lump. The left side of his jaw was swollen. The swelling had the strange effect of making it appear his golden beard was false, and had been pasted on slightly askew. He had difficulty moving his jaw as he explained to Weston and his fellow players that he had been waylaid on the way to the theater.

"Bwuddy caitiffs attacking decent citizens 'n bwoard daywight now . . ." he mumbled, rubbing his tender jaw gently.

It was difficult to make out all of the words, but the gist of it seemed to be that three ruffians had shoved him into an alley, one block from his home, and beat and robbed him. Weston and his colleagues commiserated with him. Weston excused him from the rehearsal and begged him to go home and rest, and said he hoped Wrexham would feel better the next day. On the way out, Wrexham caught Richard's confused look. With his good eye he winked at Richard surreptitiously, and waved farewell to the company. Weston conducted a very brief rehearsal, concentrating mainly on Richard's Mosca scenes. As the players were leaving the theater, Weston stopped Richard and Felicia.

"I hope you'll work very hard the rest of the week, lad," he said. "You've a long piece to go."

Richard assured him he would.

It was not quite noon, and Richard and Felicia went directly to Pickering's. Felicia immediately led Richard to their favorite upstairs room. Felicia began to undress. It had been more than a week since they had had a rendezvous. Richard sat in a chair, a worried and baffled look on his tired face.

"Now, Richard Steele!" demanded Felicia, stepping out of her bright yellow, flowered dress. "What is troubling you?"

Richard looked at her and shook his head.

"I don't understand it," he said, as Felicia continued to undress. "It's the same eye!"

Clothes neatly laid out on a chair, Felicia stood before him, naked. She began to unbutton his shirt.

"I think you said 'it's the same eye.'"

Richard put his hands on her slender waist, smiled wearily up at her amused and puzzled face. He stood and took her in his arms, and kissed her long and passionately, then undressed quickly. In bed, lying on his back, arms outstretched over his head, he told her of Wrexham's attempt to seduce him, and the fight which followed. Felicia, sitting up, stroked his chest, played with the medallion she had given him. She laughed heartily, her silver-gray eyes sparkling.

"So! Jerome Wrexham is now my rival for your affections. I have long felt you were irresistible, love."

Becoming serious for a moment, she stroked his raven-black hair.

"Jerry has always liked men—sometimes, I think, even more than women. About five years ago he had a brief affair with Alfred . . . almost caused a permanent rift between Alfred and Cecil." They were the two inseparable homosexual lovers in the company.

Richard didn't seem to be listening. Idly caressing Felicia's silk-smooth thigh, he asked, "How could the ruffians who waylaid him have hit him in the same eye?"

Felicia, too, seemed to lose track of the conversation. She slid her hand down his flat stomach and fondled his genitals. He was still not erect, his mind full of the mystery of Wrexham's eye, the inexplicable wink and lack of anger. He had wondered, on a number of occasions since his backstage fight with Wrexham after the *Macbeth* performance, about Wrexham's sudden change of attitude toward him. He had never experienced quite as drastic a change in anyone.

"The bruised eye is surely a most remarkable coincidence," said Felicia, absently continuing to caress him.

"He winked at me as he walked out of the theater." Richard placed his hand on Felicia's back, gently pulling her down toward him as he began to suck her right breast. Felicia stroked his hair, watched as he became more and more erect.

"He's a changed man," she said with a tone of finality, and Wrexham's odd behavior seemed increasingly unimportant. She gently pulled Richard's head away from her breast, and bending down, took him in her hot, moist mouth. After that there was only a brief, occasional phrase of endearment or expression of ecstasy.

They made love for a little more than an hour. Richard was due at Farley Shannon's at two-thirty to work for another two or three hours on *Volpone*. They had not mentioned Wrexham again. Now as Richard buttoned his shirt and Felicia brushed her short hair, he began to think again about his encounter with Wrexham.

"Jerry said you had women lovers," he said.

Felicia turned away from the mirror and stopped brushing her hair.

"I did," she said firmly and with some defiance. "Does it matter?"

An agonized look came over Richard's face. He knew it should not matter, yet . . .

Felicia walked slowly toward him. She stood over him as he pulled on a boot.

"Do you have any recollection of the days when Mary and I met, when we became good friends?"

Richard shook his head.

225

"Of course, you wouldn't," Felicia said thoughtfully. "You were only five. . . . Did your mother ever tell you about . . . ?"

Richard looked at her in astonishment.

"You mean you and my mother . . . ?"

Felicia was irritated.

"No! Of course not, you dolt! I merely mean that I—I hated men, I—I was a bitter and confused woman. . . ."

"Woman!" exclaimed Richard. "You were only fourteen."

"Woman enough . . ." Felicia strode back to the mirror, began to apply a lip salve. She turned back toward Richard.

"I have no intention of explaining or justifying my past to you, Richard," she snapped.

She put her comb, brush and lip salve into her bag, slung the bag over her shoulder, strode to the door. There she stopped.

"I had women lovers, Richard! I also had more men lovers than I can remember! Make of it what you will!"

She walked out, and slammed the door hard behind her. By the time Richard collected his wits, pulled on his second boot and ran downstairs, Felicia was gone. Tired and confused, he went out to the stable, fed Sally O an apple he had been given by Bessie Pickering. Then he bridled and saddled the mare, and rode out to Farley Shannon's.

Gilbert Weston and Shannon sat in the small theater room. Weston was quite concerned over Richard's poor work at the morning rehearsal, and Shannon had expressed bafflement. When they mentioned their concern to Richard, he told them about the leak in the roof, his sleepless night and his almost constant worry over his mother's health.

He did not mention his confrontation with Wrexham, nor his discussion with Felicia. Even as he talked with the two older men, he realized that he was facing an important test as an actor. If he was indeed a competent professional, he should be able to *become* Mosca and leave his mother, Wrexham, Felicia and all the world behind while he was on the stage.

Now, with Weston seated in the center of the first bench in the small theater room, Shannon and Richard went up on the stage, and began to play various of Mosca's key scenes. For the first fifteen minutes, Richard was

226

nervous and uneasy. Then, in what seemed even to him a miraculous transformation, he did become Mosca. When he played the opening soliloquy of Act III, he felt he *was* the elegant rascal, nothing more, nothing less, no one else. At the end of his speech Weston applauded. Shannon beamed. They continued with the rehearsal, and by the time Weston and Richard had to leave to get back to the Lincoln's Inn Fields for the nights performance, they had gone through three-quarters of the play. Weston was more than pleased. He was totally reassured.

The evening's presentation was *The Relapse*, John Van Brugh's satire on foolish fops. Roland Finch played Wrexham's role, while an understudy took over Finch's. Richard handled his part adequately. He had lost the fine edge he had developed during the *Volpone* rehearsal, but on the other hand, he had not permitted any of his personal worries to cause him to forget lines or miss cues. He felt this was a particularly noteworthy achievement, since Felicia avoided him when he arrived at the theater, ignored him all through the play and left immediately after her own last exit.

He himself left as soon as he had read his last lines. The late October night was unusually cold, a harbinger of the severe winter to come. He walked homeward, taking long strides, head down against the chill wind blowing off the Thames.

How could he have been so stupid as to indicate even the slightest disapproval, or even to raise the question of Felicia's past sex life. . . ? The fact that she had given up all other lovers, male or female—and he was sure she had—should have been—and indeed was—most flattering to him. . . . If he did as well as he hoped in *Volpone*, his per-acting-day wage would be increased to six shillings. . . . Right after the play, he would ask Felicia, once again, to marry him.

He bumped into an old woman prostitute, who was clutching a drunken man by an arm, trying to drag him into a lodging house doorway.

"Watch where yer goin', ya bloody, blind bastard!" the woman cursed, as Richard apologized.

But then, what of his mother? Felicia's chambers, and his own miserable two rooms were too small for the three of them. . . . And what of Mary's illness . . . ? Suppose she got worse. . . . Perhaps he should wait to ask

Felicia to marry him, until he could buy a cottage in the country. . . .

He almost tripped over two boys, each less than six years of age, punching, biting and cursing, wrestling and rolling around in the filthy street. The scene reminded him of Wrexham.

Never had he experienced so weird a coincidence as that of the group of ruffians blackening Wrexham's eye and swelling his jaw in precisely the way Richard himself had earlier. And why had Wrexham not been angry with him this morning? Why the conspiratorial wink? For that matter why had Wrexham suddenly become a friend ever since *Macbeth?*

The fresh winds had almost blown away the usual fish stench of Billingsgate. As he glanced up at the twig of mountain ash over his doorway, he remembered a line from his rehearsal at Shannon's that evening.

". . . this is the creature had the art born with him," he said aloud, "toils not to learn it, but doth practice it out of most excellent nature."

Tired or not, problems or no, he felt optimistic. Then he heard Mary coughing as he opened the door. The spasm lasted for a full ten minutes. She was sniffling, as well as coughing. The wind blew drafts of chill air into the rooms, through the badly fitted casement windows. Richard stuffed cloths into the wider cracks around the frames of the windows, added fresh coals to the fire, and soon the kitchen was warm and comfortable, and Mary's coughing ceased. She heated a kettle of snail broth, and when she brought it to the table, she took a letter from her apron pocket and handed it to Richard.

"It came for you this morning. It's from Hertfordshire," she said, with eager anticipation in her voice. Richard opened it. It was written in a neat, painstaking, masculine hand. George Storey had also evidently used a word book in its preparation, since it contained no Yorkshireisms at all.

Dear master Steele,

The cottage was purchased by a Welsh gentleman and his wife just a fortnight after you and your admirable mother and friends visited here last year. The gentleman is now called to urgent business in Wales, and is desirous of selling the cottage. He and his wife have given it excellent care. Indeed he has made in it some improvements, which existed not upon your early inspection.

Mary sipped her hot broth, eyes wide and bright. Richard looked toward her, smiled and read on,

He has caused to be constructed additional fireplaces in each of the two smaller rooms, so that the house now has three. The garden has also been well cultivated and produces goodly crops of several excellent vegetables.

The gentleman has put a price of three hundred fifty pounds upon the house and land, but I believe the urgency of his return to Wales is such that he may accept the sum of three hundred. Especially if your young friend, Mistress Wandrous should exercise her powers of persuasion upon him.

I recall your excellent mother's pleaure with the cottage, and thinking your situation might be more prosperous than last year, you might wish to consider purchase. I hope to have favorable word from you with some promptness. Till such word and our meeting again, I wish you and your admirable mother and friends good health.

Yr. obedient servant,
George Storey.

Richard placed the letter on the table and went to the cabinet, taking down the strong box which contained their savings. When he returned to the table, he counted out the money.

"Seventy-six pounds, eight shillings." He shrugged. "A long way from three hundred."

Mary read the disappointment in his face and patted his hand.

"Someday, Richard," she said.

"Would you like to reply to Mr. Storey?"

Mary nodded.

"Yes, I'll tell him we would like to come out to visit him this spring, if we may."

Richard put the strong box back in the cabinet. Returning to the table, he said, "Mary, what happened to Felicia when you first met her?"

The brightness fled from Mary's eyes and a dull and troubled look replaced it.

229

"Why, Richard? Why do you ask?"

"I'm just curious. I realized today that I have only the vaguest recollection of a nervous girl coming to our house quite often for a time . . . crying . . . most unhappy. . . . She seemed desperate. . . ."

"She was. . . ."

"I seem to recall, especially—I didn't know then. . . . I think now it was a terror-stricken look in her eyes. . . ."

"She lost a child!"

"What?"

"I would rather not talk about it, Richard. It's long past . . . best forgotten."

Richard said softly, "I love her, Mary."

His mother nodded. "I know. I know. She's a fine girl. She needs loving. And she has so much love to give. . . . Did you question her, Richard? About the past?"

"After a fashion. I won't anymore." Richard shrugged.

Mary nodded. "She's put it out of her mind . . . had to . . . best not to revive such memories."

The following morning at rehearsal Richard approached Felicia.

"Felicia, I'm . . ." He began to apologize.

"There's no need to say anything, Richard," she interrupted. "I just prefer to be left alone for the present."

She turned and walked toward Gilbert Weston, who was playing Corvino, her husband, and Roland Finch, who was playing Sir Politick Would-Be.

Wrexham, his bruised eye neatly camouflaged with creams and powder and his jaw back to normal, was sitting nearby with Quincy, the dwarf, and Susannah Forbish. He noted the brief exchange between Richard and Felicia. The rehearsals began, and Richard again forced himself to dismiss his personal concerns from his mind. The totally expert manner in which Felicia played the virtuous Celia would have convinced any observer that she had nothing other than her performance on her mind, at all.

She finished the last run-through of her part a full hour before Weston ceased working with Wrexham and Richard, and she left the theater immediately. Richard rushed to Pickering's as soon as he was through rehearsing, earnestly hoping to find Felicia there. But she had not come to the Inn. He was seated disconsolately at a small table, when Wrexham came over to the table and patted him on the shoulder.

"May I join you, Richard?"

Richard nodded, and Wrexham seated himself.

"I think I owe you an apology, dear boy," he said. "I surely did not mean to force my attentions on you."

Again Richard was startled and surprised by Wrexham's attitude. He looked into Wrexham's eyes to see if he could detect a trace of sarcasm or mockery. The left eye was still half-closed, but in the right, Richard could see that Wrexham was quite sincere.

"I should not have become violent, Jerry," he said.

Bessie Pickering came over to the table. A young man Richard did not know was behind the bar, and Ben Pickering was absent.

They ordered brandies, and Wrexham ordered three large slices of roast beef and potatoes. Richard did not feel like eating. The young man at the bar brought their drinks. Bessie walked beside him.

"This is my nephew, Jamie." She introduced the lad.

When Jamie returned to the bar, and Bessie to her food counters, Wrexham raised his glass.

"Here's to Volpone and Mosca," he toasted, "and to lovers . . . of whatever sex!"

Richard managed a wan smile as he drank.

"I could not help but notice, Richard, that you and Felicia seem to have had a falling out."

Richard nodded sadly.

"Don't take it too seriously, lad. Women are moody creatures at best." Wrexham smiled.

Richard said nothing. Bessie brought Wrexham's platter, piled high with thick slices of beef, crisp and brown at the outer edges, oozing pink in the center. There was hardly room for the three roasted potatoes on the dish. Wrexham winced as he began to chew on the first large mouthful of beef.

"Jaw's still a mite tender," he explained.

"Jerry, how did those ruffians manage to hit you in the same eye, and bruise your jaw exactly as I had?" asked Richard.

Wrexham swallowed, shouted to Jamie for a bottle of port. "Ah, dear boy. I'm enchanted by your naiveté. There were no ruffians, save *you!* I awoke shortly after

231

you left Sunday night, and had all night to think about our little encounter."

He cut a large bite of roast beef with the edge of his fork, and stuffed it into his mouth.

"I realized I'd been drunk and obnoxious. I saw no reason to make our entire company aware of our disagreement. It would have embarrassed you, and certainly me. . . ."

Jamie brought the wine and poured Wrexham a glassful. Wrexham drank half the contents in one swallow.

"I want you to know, dear boy, that one day I still hope to persuade you to the advantages of opening up your horizons of lovemaking, but in a much less aggressive manner."

Richard finished his brandy, smiled at Wrexham's frankness. Wrexham chewed a half potato, swallowed and beamed at Richard.

"That was quite an excellent entrance I made, and quite a convincing performance I gave . . . of a gentleman who had just been set upon by a band of caitiffs."

Richard nodded and chuckled.

"I want us to be friends, Richard. Good friends."

Wrexham put down his fork, extended his hand toward Richard. Richard took it. Wrexham shook heartily. He finished his wine.

"As a matter of fact, I would like you to come with me to the races at Banstead Downs Friday afternoon."

"I can't, Jerry. I'm sorry, but that will be the last afternoon I'll have to rehearse with Farley Shannon."

Wrexham looked thoughtful.

"I do see what you mean, lad. My own Volpone is so dynamic, it's vital your Mosca comes as close to matching it as possible."

Richard nodded again. Wrexham leaned across the table to him, whispered, "Yet, it may be worth your foregoing that final meeting with Farley. I've got inside information about a horse, which is predestined to win the fifth race."

Richard recalled his failure to take advantage of Wrexham's tip on Bard's Bastard. Wrexham apparently read his mind.

"The same sort of arrangements have been made as were made in the case of Bard's Bastard," he whispered. "But the odds are precisely double what they were on the Bastard, six to one."

Richard shook his head. "I *must* go to Shannon's."

Wrexham shrugged. "I thought we could spend a most pleasant afternoon together, and earn a good bit of money at the same time, but . . ."

"Could you not make a wager for me?" Richard asked.

"Well, of course, if you like . . . but I wouldn't want you to bet too heavily. I'm betting fifty myself, and if I wager much more than a hundred, the bookmaker would become suspicious, probably refuse to accept the bet."

"But I *could* wager fifty?"

Wrexham nodded. Leaning closer to Richard, he whispered so his voice was barely audible over the bustle of the Inn.

"Say nothing of this to any of our colleagues . . . to anyone. If too many bets are placed, the books will realize a special arrangement has been made, and the entire situation may be altered."

Richard nodded. "I'll give you the money tomorrow," he whispered.

"I believe the horse's name will intrigue you," Wrexham said. "Androgyno's Dream!"

"It is hard to believe!" Richard grinned.

Androgyno, of course, was the name of the hermaphrodite character in *Volpone*.

When Richard arrived home that night, after a most satisfactory rehearsal with Farley Shannon, Mary showed him the letter she had written George Storey. He took the letter and promised to mail it in the morning, but he did not mail it, of course, since it would only be a couple of days before he would be able to tell Storey they would buy the cottage.

The following morning he gave Wrexham an envelope containing fifty pounds. Wrexham winked at him, and placed the envelope in the large pocket of his velvet coat.

After the morning rehearsal on Friday, Richard had his noon meal with Wrexham at the Inn. Felicia had evidently changed her noontime patterns. Richard suspected that she either went home, or went to Norman's Apothecary to meet Edith at noon. When Richard and Wrexham finished their meal, Wrexham slapped him heartily on the back.

"I'll see you in the morning, dear boy. I've asked Weston to replace me for tonight's performance. . . . I'll be

233

out late tonight celebrating with some friends at the Downs."

Richard smiled and went out to the stables to bridle and saddle Sally O. He had resisted the temptation to tell Mary, Felicia, Shannon or anyone else of his wager, but as he rode out to Shannon's he felt a great inner joy. He thought of the happiness he would see on Mary's face when he told her Saturday afternoon that they could buy the cottage at Waltham Cross.

Wrexham was late for the final run-through of the play at the theater Saturday morning. He had dark rings under his eyes, and he seemed utterly weary.

It must have been some celebration, thought Richard. Wrexham took him aside at the first opportunity.

"The horse lost, lad," he said woefully. "Came in last."

Richard paled. The coffee and bun he had had at Pickering's earlier turned sour and heavy in his stomach. His knees threatened to buckle as he walked to the prop lounge at stage left, which would be Volpone's that evening. He sat, leaned forward, elbows on knees, thumbs under his chin, fingers pressing hard against the sides of his nose, and his closed eyes. He felt dizzy.

Nearby he heard Gilbert Weston conversing with the property man, the scene painter and the carpenter. Apparently Weston was not happy with the gold-painted coins, the colored, glass jewels and the silver plate, which would be on display as Volpone's riches. Then he heard the high-pitched voice of Quincy, the dwarf.

"You are a lucky scoundrel, Jerry," the piping voice chided. "How much did you win?"

Richard knew that Quincy and Susannah Forbish had also gone to Banstead Downs yesterday. Right above him, Richard heard Wrexham's deep, rich voice.

"Lost it all in the fifth, Quince."

Richard felt Wrexham sit beside him. He straightened up as Wrexham put his right arm around Richard's shoulder. There was almost a cheery note in Wrexham's voice as he explained the fiasco, an underlying, barely perceptible note of gleeful vengeance, a gloating quality. It was as though a bright light exploded inside Richard's head. The sly, gloating quality was what Shannon had been coaching Richard to strive for in his portrayal of Mosca's moments of triumph.

"What did you say, Jerry?" Quincy asked Wrexham.

"The men who arranged for the horse to win developed an alternate scheme. Unfortunately, I failed to learn of it before the race. I could ill-afford to lose my fifty pounds, dear boy, but I regret even more losing your . . ."

Richard looked directly into Wrexham's face. He was listening intently to Wrexham's vocal modulations, his phrasing. He watched his facial expressions, and the compassionate hand, arm and body movements. Shannon had preached for years that the way an actor learned his craft was to observe people in character-revealing situations. Richard was sure that he had been duped by Wrexham, who was an incarnate combination of Mosca and Volpone. Richard realized that he himself had behaved as greedily—never mind the motivation—as Voltore, Corbaccio and Corvino, whose lust for riches had made them easy victims of the scheming Mosca and Volpone.

He felt the loss of the fifty pounds keenly, but he pushed his regrets deep into the furthermost recesses of his mind. He kept Wrexham talking, explaining, describing the fifth race at Banstead Downs. Richard was excellent all through the rehearsal.

That night, after the opening performance of *Volpone*, Farley Shannon came backstage with Edmund Fox, the Duke of Cheltenham. Shannon had witnessed the play from the box of the Duke, whose guest he had been for the evening. Fox congratulated Richard on his performance, then moved off to pay his compliments to the others. Shannon took Richard in his arms. His eyes were moist.

His voice trembled, as he said, "Richard, that was the most brilliant portrayal of Mosca I have ever seen!"

Weston came over and patted him on the shoulder. "Lad, I'm adding four shillings per day to your compensation. And there will be more to come."

Felicia waited until all the others were through. Then she came to Richard.

"You were magnificent, love," she said, taking his hand and kissing him on the cheek. "Walk home with me, so I may forgive you properly."

Wrexham, who had given a convincing performance himself, watched Felicia and Richard leave. He could not understand the happy glow that seemed to emanate from Richard Steele. The young idiot acted as though he had just won fifty pounds instead of losing it. The pleasure Wrexham derived from the successful execution of the swindle was severely diminished by the jaunty nature of Richard's exit.

23

The leaves on the trees in the country changed color, and soon the chill winds blew the branches bare. As fall sped toward winter, the Duke of Cheltenham found his Drury Lane mistress, Moll Davidson, no more to his liking than he had at the close of the previous season. His wife, Sarah, had become increasingly peevish, uncompanionable, and less and less attractive physically as her pregnancy advanced, and he decided he must seek a new mistress more actively. Then, as often seemed to happen to him, the Duke encountered an unexpected stroke of good fortune, or at least it appeared that way at first.

His agents had been watching the progress of the unlicensed theater at Goodman's Fields, only about a mile east of St. Paul's Cathedral. Their reports were that the playhouse without royal patent seemed to be doing excellent business. A young lady, Nell Faversham by name, had joined the company at Goodman's Fields. Miss Faversham, in addition to performing most attractively as a singer and dancer in the concert portions of the program, and acting competently in the dramatic "rehearsals," had virtually taken over management of the playhouse from the ailing proprietor, Harold Spifford. The Duke had long felt that it would be highly beneficial if he could control the activities at Goodman's Fields.

Using his influence at the Lord Chamberlain's office, the Duke forced the Goodman's Fields theater to close on the grounds that they were performing dramatic shows—the law provided they could give musical performances only—under the guise of rehearsals. Spifford, as the Duke suspected he might, became discouraged, and sold the playhouse to one of the Duke's agents. Although it was not publicly revealed, the Duke thus acquired ownership of the nonpatent theater. Edmund Fox himself had attended several performances at Goodman's Fields during this period. On his very first visit, he was enchanted with Nell Faversham. On stage she danced with a fluidity that was at once delicate and sensuous. She sang in a clear soprano, with just a touch of emotional vibrato. And her performance in the one-act afterpiece was more than adequate. She was a striking young woman, with long, rich carrot-colored hair, an exquisite complexion, a wide, generous mouth and straight nose. Her figure was full, and she moved with a natural grace, seeming to be in her early twenties. But the Duke did not discover her most distinctive facial feature until later that evening when he sat across from her at a table in the small tavern adjoining the playhouse. Her eyes were as bright and green as emeralds, but held considerably more warmth.

The Duke lifted his glass of burgundy.

"To a long and mutually happy relationship," he toasted.

Nell Faversham lifted her own glass. "So our humble playhouse is now under the proprietorship of a nobleman."

Edmund Fox smiled broadly.

"Theater is not an idle interest on my part, my dear. Among my ancestors was a courtier who traded his highly profitable and politically potent post as Groom of the Bedchambers of King Charles II for the far less lucrative position of Master of the Revels."

They talked of the Goodman's Fields operations briefly, and then the Duke reached across the table, took Nell's hand and told her he would like her to become his mistress.

"I am greatly flattered, my lord," she said, "but I am married."

Edmund Fox looked startled. He had had her investigated, and he *knew* she was married. Her husband was a forty-year-old poet, who was drunk a good deal of the time, and was known to beat and abuse Nell quite regularly.

"Not too happily, I understand," the Duke said now.

"Happily or no," said Nell. "I have a husband."

To Edmund Fox this was totally beyond comprehension. He saw no reason why a woman married to one man could not be mistress to another. Nell Faversham's attitude irritated him, but at the same time, he could not help but admire her stubborn loyalty.

It also bothered him for a time that this was the second actress to reject his advances in the space of a single year. True enough, both Felicia Wandrous and Nell Faversham were extraordinary women—the one as fine an actress as trod the boards, the other a voluptuous beauty, whose physical charms concealed the sharp administrative acumen of a nobleman's steward. There was a time when almost every actress was a whore, and any of them would be flattered to be kept by a courtier. London, he thought grumpily, and the whole world for that matter, seemed to be changing drastically, and for the worse. A Hanoverian German was his King; the Council of Ministers was becoming increasingly unpredictable; the Country Party, more and more of a nuisance. He found little pleasure in attending sessions at the House of Lords these days.

And he found little enough pleasure the day after his rejection by Nell Faversham, when he had dinner with Gilbert Weston at Lady Gertrude's. The Teutonic Lady and her interpreter and general manager, Frederick Kingsley, greeted Edmund Fox and Weston, and commented enthusiastically on the fine quality of the recent presentations at the theater, and particularly on the excellence of young Richard Steele's performances. While delighted to learn of Fox's acquisition of the Goodman's Fields playhouse, Weston then had to tell the Duke of the growing air of tension and unrest among the players at the theater. He explained that it stemmed from the enmity between Richard Steele and Jerome Wrexham.

"Dammit all, Gilbert," exclaimed the Duke, as he picked up a pheasant leg, "disagreements among players in a theatrical company are not unusual, are they!"

"Not at all, Edmund, but this one is more complex than most, and has spread throughout the company. Wrexham disrupts almost every rehearsal with some asinine remark or other against Steele, or some snide comment about Wandrous. All during the Christ Tide rehearsals, and through each of the Harlequin and Columbine Christmas pantomime shows, he carried on like a madman. Almost destroyed the performances."

"How does Steele respond?"

"With amazing patience and maturity, considering that he should be the aggrieved party."

"How aggrieved?"

Weston told Fox the story of the wager on Androgyno's Dream, which had long since spread through the entire company. Quincy and Susannah Forbish had told Richard they had seen Wrexham collecting a large sum immediately after the fifth race. Richard and Felicia had also gone to Banstead Downs to query Lancelot Higginbotham, and several trainers and jockeys. All these had laughingly greeted Richard along the same general line.

"Oh, so you're the party who bet on Wrexham's fixed race, are you?"

To add insult to the corruption, four days after the race Wrexham arrived at the theater in a handsome sedan chair, all rich leather with several hundred gold-headed nails, expensive clear glass windows and his monogram in swirling, ornate gilt on both doors. And he sported a new silver-headed walking stick as he entered the backstage door.

"A few members of the cast believe Wrexham's story that he actually bet on Androgyno's Dream," said Weston, sipping his French burgundy.

"Several others, who are rather envious of all the attention Steele has been getting of late, believe Wrexham cheated him out of the money, and are delighted about it. But most, knowing Wrexham over a period of years, are quite certain that he concocted the entire story of the fixed race from the beginning for no other purpose than to swindle Steele out of fifty pounds. I, myself, feel quite certain the latter is the case."

"And Steele has taken it well?" There was a note of doubt in Fox's voice.

Weston shrugged.

"He was most bitter the morning Wrexham told him he had lost, but it was the day of the first presentation of *Volpone,* and somehow—you'll recall; you were there—Steele pushed the matter out of his mind and gave a fine performance. The next day, before the entire company, he told Wrexham he knew he had been cheated. He warned Wrexham to keep away from him, except for whatever professional relationship was necessary."

"What did Jerry do?"

Weston grinned.

"He gave quite a performance of outraged innocence

240

. . . cried that this was the thanks he got for trying to help a completely incompetent candle snuffer. . . ."

Weston paused to finish his wine.

"I thought they would come to blows, but Steele controlled himself and walked away. And amazingly enough has controlled himself ever since . . . even under occasional strong provocation on Jerry's part. . . ."

"Tell Jerry I wish to see him," said Fox finally. "Any time next week. If he connived to swindle young Steele out of what were no doubt his life savings, I don't understand why he continues to carry on. . . ."

The person who most clearly understood the reasons behind the oddly reverse reactions of the two key participants in the Androgyno's Dream incident was Felicia Wandrous. She understood best because she herself had been, and continued to be, a major influence in bringing about those reactions.

On the way home on the night of Richard's triumphant performance as Mosca, she pulled her cloak tight around her neck against the driving wind.

"That finally explains it, love. That's why Jerry has behaved so completely unlike his true self ever since the night I asked him to drop his vendetta against you last spring. . . ."

She lowered her head and turned toward Richard, away from the blast of cold air coming from the river.

"I remember, now, that I did mention that you had saved sixty pounds. . . ." She paused to catch her breath.

"The greedy swine!" she said. "I had no idea he could be so patient, conceive such as elaborate device for getting the money. . . ."

"There must be something I can do," said Richard.

Felicia stopped, took his arm, looked up into his face. The tip of her nose was red, her eyes tear-filled from the cold.

"No, Richard, no. That's precisely what he would like . . . to see you lose your head, become so upset that it affects your work."

They walked on, arm in arm, striding quickly.

"Especially now," Felicia continued, "that you have become so fine an actor. . . . By next spring, love, you'll be able to play a benefit for yourself. If your popularity grows, as I know it will, you'll soon earn that fifty pounds and considerably more. . . ."

"But, Felicia, I must take some action!"

"Simply refuse to have anything to do with him outside the theater. Ignore him except as our work requires. I shall do the same!"

They had reached the door of Felicia's house.

"I'll tell him so in front of the entire company tomorrow," said Richard.

"That will humiliate him."

Richard smiled a stiff, frozen smile.

"Yes," he said grimly, and kissed Felicia good night.

Mary not only took the news of his loss well, but insisted that Felicia was absolutely right.

Felicia's strategy proved most effective. Richard's accusation and his strong statement the next morning shook Wrexham, and he embarrassed himself before the company with his ineffectual blustering. Then as the season progressed, and Richard performed flawlessly in a series of key roles in a variety of plays, Wrexham became increasingly irritated and frustrated. It helped not at all that three weeks after the Androgyno's Dream event, he lost eighty pounds at hazard at Lady Gertrude's, and was forced to sell his elegant sedan chair. His own performance suffered because of his internal fury and frustration.

He became more and more difficult at rehearsals, frequently and pointedly criticizing either Richard or Felicia or both. They ignored him, but Weston found it unpleasant to have to chastise Wrexham constantly for his rather stupid and unwarranted criticisms, and his attempts to interfere with Weston's direction of the plays. Weston told Wrexham that he had had dinner with the Duke, and that the Duke wished to see Wrexham. But Wrexham felt the Duke merely wished to rebuke and lecture him on the basis of Weston's report, and so did not go to the Duke's home.

He did not, that is, until the second week in January, when he believed Weston had perpetrated the final insult upon him. It was then that Weston told the cast that on the following Monday they would begin rehearsal for a new Shakespeare series, opening with *Romeo and Juliet*. Richard Steele, he told them, would play Romeo; Felicia Wandrous, Juliet; Jerome Wrexham, Mercutio.

Richard let out an uninhibited, piercing scream of joy, rushed across the stage to Felicia and threw his arms around her. He kissed her, and danced wildly around the stage with her, almost knocking over several of their colleagues. Wrexham did knock over Susannah Forbish, as he rushed toward the door and out of the theater in a blind rage. Wrexham had played Romeo for the past three seasons and it was incomprehensible to him that his changed appearance made him an unacceptable Romeo.

Although it was quite late, Richard and Felicia felt they must celebrate this most wonderful of all the nights of their lives. They supped at Pickering's Inn, and retired, with a bottle of ebullum and two goblets, to their favorite room. Giddy with wine and sheer high spirits, Felicia called Richard Romeo and he referred to her only as Juliet for the next three hours, during which they made love as Shakespeare's doomed young lovers never had.

"And no Capulets nor Montagues to mar our union," said Felicia, as for the fourth time Richard softened inside her, kissed her tenderly on the forehead, dismounted and collapsed at her side in utter contentment.

"Felicia," he said earnestly, "you must marry me."

She leaned over and kissed his shoulder.

"Next spring . . . perhaps."

She nudged his ribs and indicated the window with a nod of her head. Thick white snowflakes were falling, so thick they almost seemed a hanging cotton blanket in the moonlit night. It was almost four o'clock in the morning. They were sure both Mary and Edith would understand their need to celebrate.

They dressed quickly in the cold room, and trudged, ankle-deep in snow and slush, through the deserted streets toward Middle Temple Lane. By the time Richard reached Billingsgate, the snow was almost six inches deep and coming down heavily. In the moonlight it had a bluish cast. Before he entered his house, Richard looked back at the scene. It was hard to think that Billingsgate could be beautiful, but tonight it was. All clean, blue-white purity under a star-bright, moonlit sky. To Richard, cold as he was, the whole world, life, Felicia were beautiful!

Mary was sleeping soundly, snoring gently, with Farquhar behind her knees. Richard resisted the temptation to wake her to tell her the joyous news. As he undressed he looked out the window at the still-falling snow. It was piled in eccentric mini-hills on the sill, halfway up the casement panes. He recalled that the playhouses, Lincoln's Inn and Drury Lane and all the others had closed down for three days after a severe snowstorm the first week in January. He hoped, now, that this picturesque falling of flakes would cease before the business of the city was stopped again. He did not wish to have the rehearsals nor the performance of *Romeo and Juliet* postponed even for a day. It seemed he had waited all his life for this. To play opposite his adored Felicia in this most romantic of all Shakespeare's works.

About the same time that Richard and Felicia were undressing in their room at the Inn, Jerome Wrexham reached the Duke's elegant brick mansion near St. James Palace. Covered with the blue-white puffy snow, in the moon glow the huge house, with its dome, its columns, triangles and arched windows, looked like something which should decorate a giant party cake. The butler who answered the door informed Wrexham that the Duke was not at home, and Wrexham asked if the Duchess was still awake. After he had confirmed that the Duchess indeed wished to see Wrexham, the butler escorted him to the huge library, where Sarah Fox sat awkwardly on a deep-cushioned damask upholstered lounge, in the corner nearest the fireplace. On a table beside her stood a cut glass decanter of brandy, a silver goblet and a silver candelabrum which held four large candles.

She put down the book she was reading, and smiled as Wrexham made his way across the thick carpet of the oak paneled room, with its shelves of books and portraits of the ancestors of Edmund and Sara Fox.

"As Hawkins informed you, Jerome, Edmund is out of the country. I hoped you would not be averse to spending a few moments with a lonely old woman."

She had difficulty speaking. The pressure of the other organs against her lungs caused a shortness of breath. Her ample bosom heaved with effort beneath the night dress and blue satin robe. Wrexham knelt before her, took her hand and kissed it. He looked up into her soft blue-gray eyes. They did indeed show loneliness, a desperate loneliness. Her nose was long, her lips were too full, and her chin receded slightly. Her complexion was mottled, with pink blotches on the pale skin. She had lovely silken, brandy-colored hair. But she did look all of her thirty-three years. *Gad,* Wrexham thought, *what a plain woman!*

He rose from his knees.

"Not averse! Never averse, dear Sarah! A privilege I wish I could enjoy each day . . ." He paused as he seated himself on the lounge beside her. He leaned toward her.

"Each night . . ." he whispered boldly.

The Duchess blushed.

"Edmund has gone to Antigua," she said, flustered.

"Oh?"

"Two weeks ago, the day he had dinner with Gilbert Weston, we had a letter from Edwina, his sister. She's quite ill. Edmund felt he must go at once."

Wrexham looked pointedly at the large blue satin globe of her belly. With great concern in his tone, he said, "Will he be back before the child . . . ?"

Bitterness choked the Duchess's words.

"Very probably not. The voyage alone takes four, five, six weeks, depending on weather. How he will find Edwina, I do not know. . . ."

Wrexham reached out and took her hand, placed his arm gently around her shoulder.

"Dear Sarah," he said softly, "dear Sarah."

Tears misted the Duchess's eyes.

"Edwina's own child is but two months old. Edmund cares far more for his new niece and his dear sister than for me."

Self-pity caused the tears to overflow, run down the Duchess's cheeks. She dabbed the streaming tears with a silk handerchief.

". . . or our own child," she sobbed.

Wrexham drew her close, patted her shoulder and kissed her moist cheek, where new tears flowed.

"Oh, Jerry, I'm so wretched. So alone. So . . . miserable."

She moved her head so that Wrexham's mouth was now on hers, instead of on her cheek. He lowered his hand on her shoulder to her waist, slid it carefully and gently around, so that it rested on the crest of the mound that was her stomach. He did not press his lips hard against hers. Tenderness was the theme. He felt her arm go around his neck, pull his face tighter against her. Her mouth opened wide. Wrexham opened his mouth, and when they were both out of breath, he slowly moved his lips to her chin, kissed it lightly, brushed the length of her neck with his lips, and moved down to the cleavage of her bosom. There he nuzzled, burrowing his moist mouth, his mustache and beard gently into the warmth of her full breasts.

She put both hands on his head.

"Do you ever think of the night after the masquerade, dear Jerry?" she whispered, her voice trembling.

Wrexham raised his head several inches from her bosom. While his right hand unbuttoned her satin robe, he said hoarsely, "Often, so often, sweet Sarah. I not only think of it, I dream it over and over. . . ."

He had thought of it once or twice, remembering how unsatisfying it had been. But now he managed to lift her swollen left breast out of the night dress, and kissed, then sucked hard on the protuberant nipple. He tasted the unborn child's milk. It was sweet, and Wrexham found himself truly excited. He had made love to a pregnant thirteen-year-old girl once years before. He had impregnated her himself, and she was only one month pregnant, when he did. He had never made love to a woman as far advanced in her pregnancy as the Duchess, and, much to his surprise, it turned out to be the most exquisitely sensual experience of his life.

He had to proceed with extreme care, and the positions were frequently awkward and ungainly, but that only made the affair more exciting . . . that and the hungry, almost insane abandon with which Sarah Fox conducted herself. She seemed to be trying to condense a lifetime of wild lovemaking into this single episode. She clutched him and kissed him, and bit and scratched him, and sucked him until he felt he must scream.

When it was over, she cried quietly, lying on her back on the lounge, ignoring the fact that the ripped night dress was pushed up to her chin, and that her huge belly, her bruised breasts and all the rest of her lay exposed and glittering with sweat in the glow of the still roaring fire and the candlelight. Since Wrexham had not undressed, he merely pulled his breeches back up and put his shoes back on. He walked over to the table, and poured brandy into the large silver goblet. He drank more than half of it in one gulp. Then he went to the lounge, and sat beside Sarah Fox.

"Drink, sweet Sarah," he said softly, holding the goblet out toward her. She sat up, took the goblet and drank the rest of the brandy. He went to the table and filled the goblet again. He took it to Sarah, then drank from it himself while she adjusted her night dress and robe.

Wrexham saw by the tall clock, in its case of dazzling marquetry, that it was two-thirty. He and the Duchess finished the brandy, and when he looked at the clock again, he saw that it was five minutes past four. The Duchess yawned, struggled to her feet, and waddled across the room to pull the tassle that rang the bell in the servants' downstairs quarters. Wrexham was too drunk to realize what she was doing.

He laughed as she waddled back to the lounge.

"You walk like a duckling, dear Sarah," he said, patting her thigh. She smiled, and her head dropped to her chin. She seemed to doze, but when the door opened some ten minutes later, she raised her head, and peered at the sleepy figure of the butler, in a worn, woolen robe, holding a candle.

"Hawkinshhh," she said, attempting, unsuccessfully, to sound her regal self, "wake Fishhh . . . Fitzzz . . . Fitch . . . tell him bring 'round the coach."

She waved a hand.

"Wann 'im take my noble shentlemunnn companion home. . . ."

As the butler bowed and withdrew, Sarah Fox fell over on her side and immediately began snoring. In the coach later Wrexham half-dozed, admiring the lovely winter scene, as the grumbling coachman drove him through the hushed streets. It was not until noon the next day when he awoke that he realized the Duke would almost certainly learn of his visit. He had the feeling that Sarah Fox was eager for her neglectful husband to know. He worried about how the Duke might react, but in any event, he finally decided there was nothing he could do about it now, and it had been extraordinary.

Felicia opened the door to her apartment, singing. She was cold and weary, but happy. Then she heard Edith's anguished moan, coming from the bedroom. She knew that Edith's baby was due any day now, and she half expected the labor pains to come on at any moment. When she lighted the candles on the bedroom dresser, however, and saw Edith sitting on the edge of the bed, crouched over, moaning softly, she knew that these were not labor pains.

"Oooooh," groaned the pregnant girl, "I'm such a fool."

Holding both hands over her vast stomach, she said, "On the way home from the apothecary, I remembered the delicious plum pudding we had at the Steeles' on Christmas day, and I just had to have some. I stopped at the tavern on Ironmonger's Lane, and had two large portions of plum pudding. . . ."

Felicia grinned at her.

"And," confessed Edith, moaning again, "three tankards of ale."

Felicia quickly got out of her wet clothes, put on a warm night dress and robe, and helped Edith as she rushed to the window, tugged it open, stuck out her head and vomited. The cold blast of air from the open window whipped up new flames in the small fireplace of the bedchamber. Edith was shivering when Felicia closed the window again and got into bed. Felicia, keeping her robe on, climbed in beside her, and the two women snuggled together until the room was warm once again.

Felicia awoke first, a little past seven o'clock. She had not had a great deal of sleep, but she felt well, and was still exuberant over the prospect of playing Juliet to Richard's Romeo, still savoring the ecstasies of the previous night. She looked out the window, and saw immediately that neither she nor Edith, nor almost anyone else in London would be going to work that day. It had stopped snowing, but many of the drifts in the street were taller than a man of average height, and the lowest level of the frozen snow was close to eighteen inches.

It had turned bitter cold, a full twenty degrees lower than it had been on the previous day. Neither Felicia nor Edith knew it then, but it was so cold that the ocean had frozen over a full two miles from the shore line, and the Thames was a solid broad path of ice. The ships in the harbor were rigid in the grasp of the frozen water.

Richard was bitterly disappointed when he awoke, almost at the same time as Felicia. He went to the window and saw the frozen white and gray buildings and streets. He, too, realized he could not go to work, and he feared the inclement weather might last long enough to cause a postponement of *Romeo and Juliet*. Mary had risen before him. She sat huddled near the fireplace, a candle on a table beside her, a sewing basket at her feet, and her hands busy with a greatcoat she was mending.

Fortunately Richard had filled several large buckets with coal from the bin in the cellar, and three times during the day he poured fresh heaps on the fire. After the third time, he sat down to resume rereading his own sides as

Romeo and noticed that he had, unintentionally, put one of his woolen stockings on inside out. He smiled.

"Look, Mary. My stocking . . ."

Mary leaned forward, squinting to see the seam, and grinned happily.

"That's a certain sign of good fortune, dear."

Richard nodded.

"I hope it means that the weather will clear so that we can go into rehearsal on *Romeo and Juliet* and open as scheduled."

Then dusk came early, and a slashing rain began to fall. By dark, the rain had turned to sleet. It battered ceaselessly against the window of the small room. Richard had lit a new large candle, which he placed on the center of the table, as Mary brought over their supper of mutton stew in wooden dishes. In the middle of the meal, the flame on the candle flickered strangely, then turned almost completely blue. Wax dripped down its side in a thick torrent, wrapped itself around the candle. Mary stared at it. A horror-stricken look came into her eyes. Her right hand quivered as she pointed at the candle. She held her left hand to her mouth as she began to cough.

Richard put down his spoon and stared at her.

"What's the matter?!?"

She stopped coughing and moved her finger closer to the candle to indicate the dripping wave of wax, wrapped around the candle.

"A blue flame," she gasped. "A blue flame . . . and a winding sheet . . ."

Richard looked at the candle.

"It means," said Mary in a suddenly hoarse, trembling voice, "that someone in the family will die soon."

The candle flame sputtered. A blob of golden orange flame spurted upward from the wick, washed out much of the blue.

"Mary, you can be most irritating at times. Those ancient superstitions are ridiculous." Richard was annoyed with his mother.

He, himself, of course, was superstitious, as were most actors, but his temperament was such that he ignored the superstitions which foretold tragedy, and leaped upon every opportunity to note those which spelled good fortune. Mary made the sign of the cross, closed her eyes, lowered her head and prayed. Richard pretended to be amused, but he was not truly unconcerned.

Felicia stood by the window in the bedroom of the apartment. In the pitch black night, she could see nothing, but the ceaseless pelting of the sleet against the window pane gave the impression of some clawing beast trying to get in. She looked at the small clock over the dresser. The minute hand had reached ten, the hour hand was on eight, when Edith screamed again. It was true. The pains were coming approximately every fifteen minutes now. They had started about the time the rain had begun to fall, coming at long intervals of time, then shorter and shorter.

Felicia walked to the bed where Edith lay and took her hand. Beads of sweat covered Edith's face. Her hair was dank and pain glazed her soft brown eyes. On Felicia's face there was compassion and fear. She knew she should simply prepare to deliver Edith's baby. Willy Nillingham had brought up buckets of water. But Felicia was terrified. The nightmare horror of her own baby's death forced itself into her mind and would not fade. She squeezed Edith's hand, said, "Hold on, love. I'll be right back."

She put on two extra pairs of stockings, a pair of boots, two petticoats, two dresses. She wound a shawl tightly around her waist and put another one around her shoulders. She covered her head with the heaviest wool cap she possessed, and then struggled into a greatcoat and an old oilskin coat and hat, which she hadn't used since the days when she had gone yachting with a wealthy young shipbuilder's son some years earlier. She put on two pairs of woolen gloves, forcing one over the other.

It was difficult for her to move, and she almost fell down the flight of stairs on her way to the front door. Outside, the powerful gale struck her as though it had singled her out as its individual archenemy. Gale or no, she was determined to get Dr. Thorndike. He was an extraordinary man. In a day when most doctors would have nothing to do with childbirth, considering it indelicate, and purely the work of midwives, Thorndike insisted on delivering the children of pregnant patients. Thorndike's home was only a little more than a mile away, but it took her almost an hour to get there. The rain had melted much of the heavy snow, and the sleet had glossed the freezing slush over with brittle layers of ice. Over and over, Felicia stumbled, fell to her knees, rose again, and pushed forward against the torrents of frigid water slashing away at her.

The lashes on her eyes were frozen, and she was almost blinded by the driving rain. Her face was completely numb. The breath came in clouds of vapor from her gasping mouth. Her lungs, coated with icy air, ached. She cried, and the tears froze on her cheeks. Finally she stood before Dr. Thorndike's door. She fell to her knees, and pounded on the heavy oak. It seemed hours, though it was no more than five minutes before the door opened. A tall gaunt elderly woman, holding a heavy scarf around her neck, stood there. It was Mrs. O'Flaherty, the doctor's housekeeper.

The doctor had left more than two hours earlier in his carriage to see a patient in the West End. Mrs. O'Flaherty did not know when he would be back that night. She pulled Felicia into the warm hall as she explained.

"Come and sit by the fire, child. I'll fetch ye some hot rum."

Felicia fell to her knees, before the roaring fire in the sitting room. In less than a minute a large puddle of water had formed around her. She gloried for a moment in the heat, taking off her gloves and holding them toward the flames to dry. As Mrs. O'Flaherty came into the room with a large tankard of steaming rum, Felicia climbed to her feet.

"I must get help," she gasped. Breathlessly, she told the housekeeper of the imminence of the birth of Edith's baby.

"Drink this first, child," said Mrs. O'Flaherty, pushing the tankard into Felicia's hands. Her fingers were still so numb she dropped the tankard, and the rum became part of the puddle her wet clothes had formed. Mrs. O'Flaherty took the tankard, pushed Felicia toward the fire.

"Sit there a moment longer. I'll get you another."

She returned as Felicia shivered in front of the flames and knelt before her, holding the tankard to her mouth. Felicia tried to sip the hot rum, but she was shaking so hard, it ran back out of her mouth, and down her chin. She spoke again, desperately, hardly able to get the words out of her numbed lips, "I must get help!"

Finally Mrs. O'Flaherty told her about a midwife who lived a half-mile from Dr. Thorndike. She described the house and the location precisely, and Felicia pulled her wet gloves on, adjusted the wet layers of clothing about herself and staggered out into the vicious night. The storm had not abated, and it took her another hour to reach the house.

Mrs. Krutch, the midwife, was the largest woman Felicia had ever seen. She was a young-looking and vital thirty. She was not fat, but she was almost six feet tall, and everything about her was large: her arms, her legs, her hands and feet, her mouth and nose. She had bright and warm deep blue eyes. Her hair was an auburn crown. Felicia was colder than she had ever thought it possible to be. Her teeth chattered, as she gasped out her plight to Mrs. Krutch. She had not even finished when the large woman rushed back into the house. In an unbelievably short time, Mrs. Krutch was before her, dressed in oilskins and boots and gloves, too, but they fit her well. She swung a large leather bag in her right hand, as she rushed Felicia to a small stable in the rear of the house, and hitched up a donkey to a cart.

"Climb in," she pushed Felicia into the rear of the cart. "Cover yourself with that tarpaulin. I know where Middle Temple Lane is."

As Felicia pulled the tarp over her, Mrs. Krutch jumped up onto the seat and drove the donkey out into the bitter blackness. Felicia, knees drawn up under her, held the stiff, heavy tarp over her. The cart slipped and bounced and skidded along in the frozen slush. Felicia banged against the sides of the cart. Over the relentless hammering of the wind-lashed sleet on the tarp, she could hear Mrs. Krutch shouting, screaming, cursing, pleading with the donkey to keep staggering ahead. In less than ten minutes there were two inches of freezing water in the cart. The blood in Felicia's veins and arteries seemed to have turned to liquid ice.

She shook so violently that she thought she would surely fall from the cart. Then, once more, the terrible picture of her own baby's death flashed through her mind. She felt as if she were in a strange hell—not a hell of fire and brimstone, but of never-ceasing waves of frigid waters, and a thousand stabbing knives of ice . . . and a thousand babies dying. She got out from under the tarpaulin and stiffly managed to climb up on the seat beside Mrs. Krutch. It seemed better to have the cold sheets of rain hitting her directly, than listening to it under the tarp. Her teeth chattered in her numbed head. The incessant shivering seemed to be shaking her brain into delirium.

By the time they reached the house at Middle Temple

Lane, Felicia was burning with fever, and shaking more violently than ever. When the cart halted, she just sat there, with the rain beating down on her, moaning and staring straight ahead as though in a trance. Mrs. Krutch helped her down from the seat and led her into the house. At the closed door of the apartment a bedraggled old brown dog sat on his haunches, whimpering over and over, as he pawed feebly at the door. Felicia did not recognize Oscar, Willy Nillingham's nearly blind pet. Indeed, she did not seem to know where she was. Inside the apartment there was dead silence.

Mrs. Krutch moved Oscar aside gently with the toe of her boot, and with her arm still around Felicia's waist, pushed against the door. Just then, a piercing scream sounded from within. As Mrs. Krutch and Felicia entered, a wiry, bald-headed, ancient man stumbled forward to meet them. Felicia did not even recognize Willy Nillingham.

"Thank God ye've come," he gasped. "She's been screaming like that for the past half hour. I think the baby—"

Mrs. Krutch interrupted him, pushed Felicia toward him.

"Take care of her," she ordered. "Get her out of these wet clothes, dry her completely, wrap her in the warmest things you can find, make a bed however you can there by the fire. . . ."

As she spoke she was whipping off her soaked gloves and outer garments and making her way toward the bedroom. Nillingham nodded, said, "There're three kettles of hot water in the fireplace in there . . . and a dozen clean cloths. . . ."

As Mrs. Krutch entered the bedroom, Edith, soaked in perspiration, screamed again. Mrs. Krutch was barely in time. Twelve minutes after she positioned herself before Edith's widely spread legs, and ordered her to bear down, the baby was born. Mrs. Krutch permitted herself a brief smile, wrapped the girl-child warmly, and placed her gently in the bed beside the exhausted mother. Then she rushed out into the kitchen–living room. Nillingham had improvised a pallet of blankets before the fire, and Felicia, bundled up to her neck, lay upon it.

Her face was a deep pink and completely covered with glistening bubbles of perspiration. Sores had formed on her lips and around her mouth. A delirium of pain had

253

veneered her eyes. She stared straight ahead, still obviously unaware of where she was. She had developed a steady, hacking cough. The midwife placed a large hand on Felicia's forehead. She winced and frowned at the incredible heat. She had never felt as extreme a fever. She struggled into her storm gear, saying to Nillingham, "Keep her covered; try to get her to drink as much water, milk, any liquids you can find except alcohol; place cool wet clothes on her forehead. . . ."

At the door, she turned back.

"And pray hard that the fever breaks. I'll be back soon as I can find the doctor."

Oscar pranced feebly toward her as she went out, but she closed the door before he could get in. He positioned himself before it and began whimpering again. Mrs. Krutch considered it a good omen that it had stopped raining, but in the still freezing slush, the going was difficult. Twice, the donkey slipped, and Mrs. Krutch had to be careful to let him find his own footing, lest he break a leg. It took her forty minutes to reach Dr. Thorndike's house. She felt it was another good sign that he had come home just an hour earlier. He had retired, but when she told him about Felicia the doctor rushed to dress and reharness his horse. Felicia was a very special patient to Dr. Thorndike. He had delivered her baby, almost ten years earlier, and treated Felicia through the terrible tragedy a month after the baby's birth.

He thought about the symptoms Mrs. Krutch described now as they sped as well as they could through the dark and frigid night. He knew that it was a most severe disorder of the lungs, and if its effects were as severe as Mrs. Krutch indicated, on as basically healthy a girl as Felicia, it was deadly serious.

In Dr. Thorndike's carriage, it took less than a half-hour to reach the house in Middle Temple Lane. At that, they were ten minutes late. Felicia was dead.

❧ 24 ❧

Harvey Thorndike was more than a doctor. He was a compassionate man and a friend. In the still bitter, freezing night, before taking Mrs. Krutch back to her donkey cart in his stable, he drove the short distance to Father Whittaker's snow- and ice-covered parish house, adjoining the church on the waterfront. He awakened the priest, and told him of Felicia's death, explaining that it might be best if Father Whittaker broke the tragic news to Mary and Richard Steele. Shocked and grief-stricken, the priest agreed. When the doctor and midwife left, he poured himself a large glass of whiskey, and drank it slowly while he dressed. He had two glasses of whiskey before the cold and misty dawn broke and he departed for the Steeles'. He rationalized his delay on the grounds that the terrible news would be difficult enough for Mary and Richard to accept in broad daylight, let alone upon being awakened in the middle of the night.

He was right. Mary immediately burst into choking, uncontrollable crying, managing only to mutter, "The poor dear child . . ." over and over, between sobs. Richard's mouth fell open and his sea eyes widened. Deep in the pit of his stomach a hard, sick knot formed. His heart swelled and pounded painfully in his chest, till he thought it would burst. He shook his head in a gesture of bewildered, futile protest. His throat ached as he tried to gasp the word, "no," but he could not. Then with a terrifying suddenness, a half-cry, half-scream tore from deep within him, from his very bowels. He fell into a chair, buried his head in his arms on the table. His back and shoulders shook convulsively, while muted, strangled sounds came

255

from his crushed mouth. Farquhar rubbed against his trembling leg again and again. Father Whittaker, tears streaming down his lined cheeks, patted his shoulder gently. Mary, trying unsuccessfully to check her own crying, stood beside him, stroked his raven hair.

The Richard Steele of a half-hour earlier, the Richard Steele who was filled with the joy of love and dreams come true, also died that morning. In his place a numbed and empty Richard Steele, a breathing ghost, went through a charade of being alive.

Although Felicia Wandrous was an atheist, she was buried in the churchyard of Father Whittaker's parish at Mary Steele's insistence. On that foggy, frigid morning, Richard stood at the graveside, dry-eyed. He had long since shed every tear in his shattered heart. He heard Father Whittaker's hoarse and trembling voice, reading the burial prayers; he heard the sobbing, the profound and diverse expressions of grief all around him. Felicia was a well-loved young lady, and the gravesite was crowded.

Susannah Forbish, clutching Quincy's strong hand, wailed loudly, and Jerome Wrexham wept with melodramatic fervor as the wooden coffin was lowered into the grave. Richard took his hand out of his mother's, moved imperceptibly toward the yawning gash in the frozen earth. A strong impulse to throw himself into the grave gripped him. Romeo's words flashed through his head,

"Shall I believe that unsubstantial death is amorous and that the lean abhorred monster keeps thee here in dark to be his paramour? For fear of that, I will stay with thee and never from this pallet of dim night depart again . . . here I will remain with worms that are thy chambermaids. O, here will I set up my everlasting rest. . . ." He took a step forward, then stopped and fell to his knees. He lowered his head as the gravediggers began to cover Felicia's coffin.

Weston closed the theater for three days to honor the memory of Felicia Wandrous, and then on the following Monday rehearsals for *Romeo and Juliet* were to begin. Weston had arranged to have Nell Faversham replace Felicia as Juliet. He assumed that Richard would play Romeo as scheduled, although Farley Shannon had said he was not quite sure Richard would be up to continuing. They decided not to ask Richard about this, feeling that it would be unwise to implant in his mind even the slightest thought that he should not continue in the role. He was an actor, and it was his task to carry on.

Shannon had come in from Stratford for the first rehearsal expressly to help Richard through the ordeal, if he should require help. When time for the rehearsal came, and all the players were gathered, Richard had not yet arrived. An hour passed, and he still had not come. Weston had seen him at Pickering's Inn often in the past three days, drinking heavily, and guessed he might be there this morning. Shannon went out into the brittle winter morning to find him, while Weston rehearsed some of the scenes without Richard.

Ben Pickering, at the bar, caught Shannon's eye as the elderly actor-coach scanned the room. There was a troubled look on Pickering's face, as he nodded toward a table in the corner, where Richard sat with a bottle and a glass of brandy before him. As Shannon walked by the bar, Pickering said, "I'm mightily concerned about the lad. He's just not interested in anything."

Shannon stopped for a moment. "Has he had a great deal to drink?"

Pickering shrugged.

"Not really . . . what he's had seems not to affect him. . . . He just sits staring into his glass. I told him we had a letter from my daughter Tillie this morning—she's arrived in the Massachusetts Bay Colony—and he hardly heard me."

Shannon smiled at Pickering, touched his arm and walked to Richard's table. He pulled up a chair.

"Mind if I join you, lad?"

Richard looked blankly at the elderly actor he idolized.

"You know rehearsals began an hour ago," said Shannon kindly.

Richard lifted his glass to his lips.

"Drink?" he asked Shannon.

Shannon shook his head.

"Come to the theater with me, Richard."

"I can't, Farley. I just can't."

"Did Felicia or your mother ever tell you about Felicia's early days in the theater?"

Richard shook his head, poured more brandy into his empty glass.

"Did you know about her father and mother? Did she ever talk to you about them?"

Richard drank, and shook his head.

"Her mother was a fine pianist and singer, worked at Dorset Garden. Her father was a playwright." Shannon's voice broke. "A nobleman, a certain Duke, insulted Elinora Wandrous one night, and Alexander Wandrous challenged him to a duel."

Richard sat up straighter.

"Alex Wandrous was killed . . . unnnhhhh. . . . Elinora took poison and died. . . ."

He paused, looking piercingly into Richard's eyes.

"Felicia was twelve."

Richard lifted his glass to his lips, put it back on the table without drinking.

"She was playing the good angel in Kit Marlowe's *Doctor Faustus*," said Shannon, ". . . never missed a performance."

Pickering came over to the table.

"Richard, would you like something to eat? Bess has made some fine veal pies."

Richard shook his head. Anguish shredded the dullness in his eyes as he looked at Shannon. He shook his head again.

"I can't, Farley. The lines keep going 'round and 'round in my head. . . . They tear me to pieces. There was so much between Felicia and—we talked about *Romeo and Juliet* so long . . . so many times. . . ."

"Did she ever tell you about her baby?" Shannon continued. "She was in love with a young man, son of an earl. Fine lad, except when he was drinking . . . unnnhhhhh . . . and he did much drinking . . . turned him into Satan's own monster. . . . They were to be married. . . . She became pregnant. Her lover was furious . . . didn't want a child . . . demanded Felicia abort it . . . unnnhhhhh. . . . He said he would not marry her unless she got rid of the baby. . . . She refused. . . ."

Shannon paused, reached for Richard's half-full brandy glass.

"Mind?" he asked, lifting the glass toward his lips.

Richard waved a hand.

Shannon finished the brandy in one long drink.

"The child was two months old, a girl. The young man demanded Felicia give the child away. She refused . . . always an independent little tigress. . . ."

He poured more brandy into Richard's glass and drank.

"Felicia didn't see the man . . . Frederic . . . that was his

name . . . errhhhh . . . didn't see Frederic again for another month. . . . Then he came to her apartment. roaring . . . demented drunk—Mary . . . your mother was
there . . . unnnhhhh. . . ."

He rubbed his thin, bony right hand across his eyes.

"She had just begun sewing for the company. . . . She'd
been taking care of Felicia. . . . Didn't you know, at
all. . . ?"

Richard shook his head. "I only knew that she was
away a good deal of the time. . . . I was five. . . ."

"He struck Felicia. . . . She returned his blows . . .
fought him fiercely."

Shannon paused, struggled to catch his breath and
drank more brandy. He looked down at the floor. He
spoke so quietly that Richard had to strain to hear him.

"He snatched the child out of the crib . . . by her ankles
. . . smashed her head against the wall."

Richard felt the blood rush from his face. His stomach
turned over, and he could taste the bile in his throat.
Shannon looked up, into Richard's horrified eyes.

"Felicia was in a play I was directing at the time . . .
last play I ever directed as a matter of fact. . . ."

Again he seemed to struggle for breath.

"She was fourteen. Missed not a single performance,
Richard . . . errrrrhhhhh . . . not one. Wasn't very good
. . . performance was a little cold . . . not her usual
delicate and moving self . . . too cold for Juliet."

Richard surprised himself. He had been quite convinced that there were no more tears in him, but now he
felt the moisture form in his eyes, spill over and streak
his gaunt cheeks. He said nothing. He rose from the chair,
threw his cloak around his shoulders and walked toward
the door. Shannon donned his greatcoat and followed.
Neither of them said anything all the way to the theater.

With a single exception, every member of the company,
from Weston to the newest player from the provinces,
contributed to a greater or lesser degree to an almost unnaturally hearty air all through the rehearsals. No one
mentioned Felicia or commiserated with Richard. They
went about the business of putting together a new presentation of *Romeo and Juliet*, as though tragedies came
only from the pens of people like William Shakespeare,
and were created for the sole purpose of enabling players
like themselves to practice their art.

The sole exception to this was Jerome Wrexham, who

deserted Nell Faversham's side to come over and put his hand on Richard's shoulder.

"You should not have come, dear boy," he said. "We all know how deeply you loved Felicia. . . ."

Gilbert Weston, who had been under a brief siege by Wrexham to recast the play with Wrexham as Romeo, strode to them quickly.

"Could we try it from the opening scene, Richard?" he asked, ignoring Wrexham completely.

Richard stared coldly at Wrexham, nodded to Weston and walked toward Roland Finch, who was playing Romeo's cousin, Benvolio, and with whom Richard would work in the opening scene. Wrexham walked back to Nell Faversham.

Somewhat to his own amazement, Richard found that he fell into the spirit, the totally professional attitude of the group, in spite of Wrexham's actions. He did not notice the frowns on the faces of Gilbert Weston and Farley Shannon, who recognized that he was playing the role in a distinctly mechanical manner.

"Why such is love's transgression . . ." he explained to Benvolio. "Griefs of mine own lie heavy in my breast, which thou wilt propagate to have it pressed with more of thine. This love that thou hast shown doth add more grief to too much of mine own."

He even managed a weary grin as he continued.

"Love is a smoke made with the fume of sighs, being purged, a fire sparkling in lovers' eyes; being vexed, a sea nourished with loving tears. What is it else? A madness most discreet, a choking gall and a preserving sweet . . ."

It was almost noon, time for the dinner break, when he was required to play through his first bit with Nell Faversham as Juliet. When Weston had introduced him to Nell, he had nodded politely, hardly noticing her. He had paid no attention to her at all while he worked. He had not noticed that Jerome Wrexham was earnestly attending her all through the rehearsal, and he had not seen the irritated glances Catherine Clark directed at Wrexham.

Weston and Shannon felt Richard lacked enthusiasm and passion when he read his first lines describing his reaction to Juliet, whom he has not yet met.

"What lady's that which doth enrich the hand of yonder knight?"

And when the servant replied, "I know not, sir," Richard went on.

"O she doth teach the torches to burn bright. It seems she hangs upon the cheek of night as a rich jewel in an Ethiop's ear. Beauty too rich for use, for earth too dear. So shows a snowy dove—a snowy dove—"

He could not think of the phrase, stopped and flipped to the proper page in his folio, found it and continued.

"So shows a snowy dove trooping with crows, as yonder lady over her fellows shows. The measure done, I'll watch her place of stand, and touching hers make blessed my rude hand. Did my heart love till now. . . ."

After the brief exchange with Capulet and Tybalt, and their exit, he strode toward Nell Juliet. He took her hand.

"If I profane with my unworthiest hand this holy shrine, the gentle sin is this, my lips, two blushing pilgrims, ready stand to smooth that rough touch with a tender kiss."

Nell Juliet smiled faintly.

They were still working together when Weston announced the noontime break.

Nell touched Richard's arm.

"Richard, would you have dinner with me?"

Richard had intended to return to Pickering's and have a quiet drink by himself, but he became aware of the soft, pleading look in Nell's eyes. He nodded and started toward the stage-right wings. Nell followed. A strong, biting wind was blowing as they walked toward the Inn. Nell hurried to keep alongside Richard.

"I'd heard that Jerome Wrexham was an accomplished woman chaser," she said in an amused tone, "but I had no idea he began his pursuits so promptly, and with such aggressiveness."

"Wrexham and I are not friends," said Richard, with a curtness that surprised Nell.

They were seated opposite each other at the Inn. After a moment Nell began on a different note.

"Have you noticed I'm a rather large woman?"

Richard looked at her, baffled. He had not particularly noticed, but he recalled, standing beside her on the stage, that she was indeed as tall as he. He looked now at her oval face, her slender neck and shoulders sloping toward a full, but certainly not an overblown, bosom. The puzzlement showed on his face.

"For Juliet, I mean," Nell continued. "I've never played Juliet before, and I can't imagine why Gilbert asked

261

me to . . . except possibly that no other actresses were available on such short notice. . . ."

"You're not that large."

"Oh, I'm not denigrating myself, Richard. I believe I'm handsome enough. It's just that I never thought about playing Juliet, and I'll need your help."

Richard nodded. "Do you want to order dinner?"

Nell had the kidney pie and a large tankard of ale, both of which she consumed with great relish, while Richard had another glass of brandy. Neither Richard nor Nell noticed that Catherine Clark had come in with Jerome Wrexham, or that Catherine seemed upset with Wrexham, who in turn kept glaring at Nell Faversham and Richard. Nor was Richard aware that Shannon and Weston were reassuring themselves that Richard would get back into his acting stride.

"I like Faversham," said Weston. "I think she may help Steele over this bad time."

The cast only worked for another hour at the theater after dinner. Weston and Shannon were patient with Richard's too-frequent lapses and mechanical readings. They felt this was all that could be expected under the circumstances, and they hoped that, in the next two days of rehearsals, he would regain some of the warmth and naturalness he had displayed so often in recent roles. As Richard finished his last scene with Nell, she asked if he was free that afternoon.

Richard looked at her without answering. He had nothing to do until that evening's performance of *The Spanish Fryer*, an uninspired, politically oriented play of the kind the theater presented occasionally to please the Crown and the Tories, which was the new name for the party of the members of the court, the council and their supporters.

"I would be most grateful if you would come home with me, and work for a couple of hours," said Nell. "I need so much help in this role."

Richard shrugged.

"I should prepare you for Peter," Nell said when they were seated in the hackney on the way to her small apartment.

"Peter?"

"My husband. He's a poet, and he's been writing plays, but not too successfully. He favors works which tend to criticize the king and the court and the government. . . ."

"That's a bit dangerous. I understand they arrested a

playwright last year, and sent him to Bridewell." Richard smiled wanly.

Nell nodded.

"Yes, that was Elias Tremaine . . . and they took him to Bridewell in a turnip cart, through the streets, with a crown and a set of horns on his head."

From outside the window of the hackney came a wild bellowing. Richard and Nell looked out to see a stout constable chasing two ragged ruffians, each of whom held a dead chicken by the neck. The hackney clattered on through the dismal slush and ice-covered streets.

"Peter drinks a good deal," said Nell, "but it's because of the pain. Two years ago these severe stomach pains came upon him, and they have persisted and grown worse ever since."

"What do the doctors say?"

Nell shrugged.

"They've tried everything: that witch's brew of herbs, diascordium, purging powders. . . . He must have had a hundred glysters, if you'll excuse—"

Richard knew about the enemas, usually given by an apothecary. Nell continued, "They had him drinking plague water, brandy flavored with herbs, but at eight shillings, six pence a quart, we just could not afford it."

She paused.

"Nothing helped. Now poor Peter just drinks gin, and will have nothing to do with any of them, doctors, apothecaries, any of them."

Outside, a heavy fog had begun to drift in off the river.

"If Peter seems cantankerous, please pay him no heed. It's just the pain," Nell finished.

Peter Faversham was almost six feet tall and weighed a little less than ten stone. Richard was shocked by the skeletal appearance of this hundred-and-thirty-pound man. A few strands of thin, wispy, mouse-colored hair covered his skull and hung down to his shoulders. His dust-gray eyes were sunk deep in their sockets and burned with unceasing agony. His dry skin was lined across the high forehead and at the corners of the sharp nose and thin-lipped mouth. The cheeks were sunk tight against the upper rows of teeth. His shoulder blades protruded under his wool shirt like clipped wings.

When Richard and Nell entered the small high-ceilinged room, Peter looked up from the paper on which he had been writing with a quill pen.

"Well," he said in a dry, rasping voice. "Home is the new Juliet!"

Nell introduced Richard, explaining he was playing Romeo, and that they had come home to work. Peter lifted a glass of smoke-colored liquid to his mouth, then barked at Nell, "Go fetch another glass, so our murdering lover from Verona may join me in this potion of the lesser gods."

He waved at a chair alongside his table, and Richard sat down.

"Gin!" said Peter. "Drunk for a penny! Dead drunk for tuppence!"

Nell set the glass on the table, and Peter poured it full for Richard. Richard drank a mouthful, and his stomach turned. It was the vilest liquid he had ever tasted. Peter laughed at the expression on Richard's face as he pointed to a pile of papers at the side of his table.

"Would you like to read my current epic? I'm just completing Act One. It deals with the political intrigue between the king's whores, and . . ."

"Peter," interrupted Nell softly, "I wanted to work with Richard on the play. We haven't too much time. . . ."

"I'd like to read it another time, Peter," said Richard. "Perhaps you'd let me take home what you've finished."

Peter ignored Richard and glared at Nell.

"What the bloody hell do you do at the theater? Don't you get enough rehearsal there? How much time do you need to play this romantic donkey shit?"

He snatched up the pile of pages, shoved them at Richard.

"Here, read them. . . ."

He struggled to his feet, grasped his gin bottle by the neck and staggered toward the bedroom.

"Wherefore art thou, fucking Romeo!" he shouted. From the bedroom there came a thumping sound. Richard imagined he had flopped onto his bed.

"He'll be all right," said Nell. "Forgive me . . . he was a little worse than usual. He was so loving and gentle a man before he became ill."

Without the knowledge that her husband had a terminal cancer, which was eating away his insides, Nell nevertheless sensed he was dying. She had resigned herself to it. Now she continued to flip the pages, finally stopped, smiled faintly and said, "Well, why not? Let's begin at 'Romeo, Romeo, wherefore art thou, fucking Romeo?' "

Richard smiled, turned to the place in his own folio, as she continued, "Deny thy father and refuse thy name; or if thou wilt not, be but sworn my lover and I'll no longer be a Capulet."

It went well until moments later when Nell was in the middle of her "good night" speech.

"Sweet, good night. This bud of love by summer's ripening breath may prove a bounteous flower when next we meet. Good night, good night. As sweet repose and rest come to thy heart as that within my breast."

He spoke his line, "O, wilt thou leave me so unsatisfied?"

He realized, of a sudden, where they were heading. His heart began to beat wildly. His throat felt dry, and he was hardly able to follow the next few lines.

Then the voice of Nell Juliet crashed upon his heart.

"But to be frank, and give it thee again. And yet I wish but for the thing I have. My bounty is as boundless as the sea; my love as deep—the more I give to thee—"

Richard had been standing. Involuntarily he touched his chest.

"Please, Nell." He sank into a chair, breathing hard, his heart pounding.

"I think we need no more rehearsal in this scene."

He flipped pages.

"Perhaps we could go to Scene Five in Act Three."

Before he rose again, he began to take another drink of the gin, sipped a bit, thought better of it and replaced the glass on the table. Nell wondered why he had turned so pale. From the bedroom an agonized groan sounded.

They continued rehearsing until it was time for Richard to go back to the theater for the performance of *The Spanish Fryer*. He had no appetite, so he never even thought about supper. In the political drama, he portrayed a super-patriotic lieutenant in the Coldstream Guards. It was an unexciting and undemanding role, and he went through it without incident, and the play drew substantial applause from the Tories.

As Richard prepared to leave the theater, Gilbert Weston patted him on the shoulder.

"Well done, lad," he said. "We'll see you at rehearsal in the morning."

It was a brisk, clear night and Richard had planned to

stop at the Inn for a drink, but changed his mind and walked rapidly through the deserted streets toward home. He realized, now that he thought about it, that every moment he was on stage, playing Chauncey Harmon of the Guards, he had literally ceased to be Richard Steele. He recalled what Farley Shannon had said to him on a number of occasions.

"Possibly the greatest blessing in being an actor is that while we are portraying a role, villain or hero, noble or ignoble, we have not a single care of our own."

And thinking of Shannon, Richard's throat constricted and there was an ache in his heart as he remembered Shannon's stories of Felicia's tragic past. His eyes misted again as he realized the courage she had displayed. Obliquely, his mind skipped to thoughts of Peter Faversham.

If ever he had seen a dying man, thought Richard, Peter was that man. And he marveled at how Nell Faversham bore up under the situation. It was plain from her manner that she loved him. How, Richard wondered, was she able to watch him, edging ever closer to death, day in and day out, and proceed with her own work at the theater. He knew that she also performed and actually managed the Goodman's Fields playhouse, and that Harold Spifford, the former owner, had taken over again when Gilbert Weston called upon Nell to help out at Lincoln's Inn Fields.

Mary greeted him at the door when he came in. There were deep inverted arcs of purple beneath her brown eyes, and her face seemed a bit more lined and gaunt since Felicia had died, but miraculously her coughing had stopped, and in some strange way she seemed to Richard to be stronger than she had been in many months.

"Have you eaten today?" she asked.

Richard realized he had not.

"I thought you might not.

"I made a Grateful pudding," she said. "It will be warm in a few minutes." She placed the pudding on a metal sheet over the coal fire.

Before he settled himself at the table, the small room was filled with the delicious scent of the raisins and ginger in the pudding.

"Farley Shannon told me about Felicia's father and mother, and her baby this morning," Richard said.

Mary spooned the pudding into a wooden dish and brought it to the table. "A brave child . . . a brave and

266

lovely woman . . . so brave . . ." She seemed about to cry as she went back to the fireplace to spoon more pudding into a dish for herself. Richard stirred his pudding aimlessly.

"What ever happened to the man who killed the baby . . . Frederic. . . . What. . . ?"

Mary shrugged, again fought back the need to cry.

"We tried—I called on Father Whittaker, and we went to see Tom Culoghen—he had just become a magistrate. We wanted Frederic arrested, punished—but his father had great influence. Before we could do anything, Frederic had gone off to the colonies . . . Virginia, I think."

She took a deep breath, raised a spoonful of pudding to her mouth, replaced it in the dish. She sighed.

"Best not to dwell on it, Richard. Best to forget. . . . Did you go to rehearsal this morning?"

Richard nodded. Then he told her about Nell Faversham, and Peter.

"I brought home a play he's writing. I want to read it tonight."

"Did you drink a great deal today, Richard?" Mary asked. She was aware that he had been drinking heavily for the past four days.

"Nothing since noon."

"I'm glad, dear. It's no solution to anything."

"I know."

It was not that Richard was less overwhelmed with grief over Felicia's death than he had been. He still felt emptied of all emotion. The joy of performing Romeo no longer existed. It was merely another part in another play —or at least he would strive to approach it in that way. As they had at the Favershams', he knew the more intimate scenes between Romeo and Juliet, those he and Felicia had lived, would tend to tear him apart. But he was determined to see it through, to give the best performance he was capable of giving. He was an actor and it was his job to do that. Felicia would have wanted him to. He lay awake half the night, thinking of Felicia . . . of her unquenchable spirit, her extraordinary talent, her selfless giving, her love. The ache of missing her, of realizing she was gone forever permeated his entire body. He forced himself up from the pallet, lighted a candle and began to read Peter Faversham's play. It was called *First Whore, Last Whore.*

At first he could not concentrate on the shaky, though

readable, handwritten lines. He read the beginning over four times, five, and then the powerful, poetic phrases gripped him. He was stunned. Peter Faversham wrote as brilliantly bitter blank verse as Richard Steele had ever read. Colorful, full of vivid, frightening imagery, lustful, hateful characters, larger and more terrifying than life. *First Whore, Last Whore* was more shocking than *Macbeth*, more stunning than *Dr. Faustus*. But it was also screamingly treasonous to the King and the Council and all the Court. Were it ever presented, its author would surely be hanged, along with any player bold enough to appear in it.

25

As Gilbert Weston and Farley Shannon had often said to one another, the fascinating aspect of the theater was that one never knew what would happen next. Both men had anticipated difficulty in guiding Richard Steele through *Romeo and Juliet*. And though he was technically almost flawless it did, indeed, seem impossible to help him to bring his performance the warmth and fire of which they knew he was capable.

Jerome Wrexham had been difficult ever since Weston had announced that Richard Steele would play Romeo, but now, on the second day of rehearsal he became maniacally uncontrollable. Embittered at being cast as Mercutio, Romeo's dashing friend, instead of in the title role, Wrexham seemed determined to overwhelm all other players on the stage. His attitude seemed to be that if the audience did not see him as Romeo, they damned well would remember him as Mercutio—long after they had forgotten Richard Steele's Romeo.

Weston said nothing as Wrexham ranted through his first scene. He literally shouted his lines as though he wanted to be heard throughout London. He also employed gestures to shame a provincial amateur. He almost stuck his finger in his ear on the line "run through the ear with a love song," and he actually burst into melody rather than spoke at times. Finally he wheeled toward Weston and bellowed, "What nature of asinine tongue-twister have we here! That idiot Shakespeare had no concept of an actor's problems!"

He then spoke slowly, sarcastically, creating a travesty of the alliteration.

" '. . . the blind bow-boy's butt-shaft,' indeed! I'll simply say 'cupid's butt-shaft.' "

Patiently Weston took him aside, and so quietly the rest of the amused company could not hear, explained to Wrexham that learning the alliterative line was worth the effort for the lilting sound it gave the speech. He also tried to persuade Wrexham to be a touch less declamatory. For a brief time, Wrexham made the effort, but when Benvolio announced shortly, "Here comes Romeo, here comes Romeo," Wrexham reached new peaks of melodramatic hysteria.

"Without his roe," he boomed, "like a dried herring. O flesh, flesh, how art thou fishified! Now is he for the numbers that Petrarch flowed in. Laura to his lady, was a kitchen wench (she had a better love to berhyme her); Dido a dowdy; Cleopatra, a gypsy; Helen and Hero hildings and harlots. This be a gray eye or so, but not to the purpose. . . ."

He turned sarcastic, made a deep bow.

"*Signior* Romeo, *bon jour.* There's a French salutation to your French slop. You gave us the counterfeit fairly last night."

And in the brief exchange with Romeo which followed, he read his lines with such cutting venom that they no more represented the well-intentioned and mischievous chiding Shakespeare meant to convey, than a hurricane resembles a sigh.

But the crisis in the preparation of the play came in the afternoon, when they ran through the key scene in the third act, when Mercutio Wrexham played his denunciation of and his challenge to Tybalt with such vehemence that he almost frightened Trelawny who was playing Tybalt. And when Romeo Steele came into the scene from stage left, and tried to calm the disputants, Wrexham snarled at him with utter scorn. "O, calm, dishonorable, vile submission!" Turning to Tybalt, he threatened, "Tybalt, you ratcatcher, will you walk?"

Trelawny, sounding frightened, instead of properly defiant, said, "What wouldst thou have with me?"

Mercutio Wrexham strode forward, pushed his own face inches from Tybalt Trelawny's.

Wrexham's spittle flew into poor Trelawny's face as he delivered his speech. Mercutio stepped back and drew his rapier. Shakespeare's script called for Romeo to intercede, to try to prevent the duel, and finally to step between

Mercutio and Tybalt as they brandished their rapiers. The rapiers were tipped with round steel caps, so that no actor could be run through by accident, and Weston tried to stage the fight scene with such precision that it would appear that Mercutio had indeed been stabbed after a ferocious battle.

Wrexham shoved Richard with his left hand, as he chopped and slashed with his rapier in his right. During one attempt, as Richard pushed Wrexham away, stood firmly between him and Trelawny, shouted, "Hold, Tybalt! Good Mercutio!" Wrexham's sword slashed downward and cut through the upper part of the left sleeve of Richard's wool shirt. A thin line of blood darkened the sleeve. Then Tybalt, under Romeo's arm, stabbed Mercutio. It was done well, Tybalt's long blade sliding neatly under Mercutio's upstage armpit, so that to the audience it would appear he had been run through.

In the excitement of the action, Richard hardly noticed the torn shirt, or the scratch on his arm. Weston did, just as Wrexham Mercutio fell to the ground, clutching his breast. He wanted to stop the scene to see if Richard was all right, but Mercutio Wrexham had already launched into his death scene. Never had an actor perished so eloquently.

With brave irony, yet managing to blame Romeo for his defeat with a venom that would have horrified author Shakespeare, Mercutio Wrexham declaimed, "No, 'tis not so deep as a well nor so wide as a church door, but 'tis enough, 't will serve! Ask for me tomorrow and you shall find a grave man. I am peppered, I warrant, for this world."

And then, glaring up at his friend, Romeo, who knelt beside him, holding his hand, Wrexham Mercutio screamed fiercely,

"Why the devil came you between us! I was hurt under your arm!"

Deep into the part, Romeo said, with apologetic warmth,

"I thought all for the best."

After their interchange Mercutio finally tore his hand away from Romeo, reached up toward Benvolio, standing over them.

"Help me into some house, Benvolio, or I shall faint," he declaimed desperately. "They have made worms' meat of me!"

And then achieving the seemingly impossible feat of

doubling the decibel count of his scream, shrieked, "I have it, and soundly, too. Your houses!"

And he fell to the stage floor, dead.

Weston came to Richard, as Wrexham rose from the floor, brushing off his clothes, a self-satisfied expression on his face.

"Is your arm all right?" he asked, lifting the sleeve.

"Just a scratch," said Richard. "It's already stopped bleeding."

Weston went to Wrexham and took the rapier from his hand. The protective steel ball was missing from the sharp tip of the blade. Weston called for the property man and gave him the rapier with orders to find the steel ball, which had fallen off, or replace it before the next day's final rehearsal. He then took Wrexham aside and began to talk to him quietly. The company was preparing to leave for the afternoon, when Wrexham shouted to Weston, "God-dammit, Gilbert, you would be better advised to ask the others to play more dynamically, and bring their performances up to mine, instead of badgering me about subduing my own exciting portrayal!"

And he stalked out of the theater.

Romeo and Juliet had been performed successfully innumerable times since Shakespeare's own company played it in the provinces in 1592, when London's theaters were closed because of the plague. But there are times in the theater when plays, however well written, fail. Such an instance was the presentation of *Romeo and Juliet* at the Lincoln's Inn Fields Theatre in that February of 1717. Wrexham simply could not be brought into line. Richard managed little more than a technically adequate and mechanical performance, except in one or two scenes, which he played with great emotional impact. Nell Faversham probably gave the best performance on all three nights of the play, but it was far from the finest Juliet ever seen.

And the failure was not due to lack of trying, at least on the parts of Richard and Nell Faversham. On the afternoon of the third day of rehearsal they went to Nell's house again to work over their respective death scenes, and the latter sections of the play. Peter Faversham looked worse than he had several days earlier. He waved Richard to a chair, and ordered Nell to fetch another glass. Richard had brought back his foul papers (as first-draft pages were called in those times) on *First Whore, Last Whore*.

"Peter, in my humble opinion, this is a powerful and moving play. . . ."

Faversham poured him a glass full of the vile gin, and drank half his own glass of gin, wiped his mouth with his bony forearm, belched and grimaced in pain. He glared at Richard through the glazed agony in his eyes. Richard continued, "If you would change the setting from London, to Italy or Denmark or Spain . . . anywhere but England, and camouflage the characters, I think any company would be proud to present the play. . . ."

Faversham finished his drink and poured himself another.

Richard said firmly, "I think the play would be a tremendous success."

Faversham shoved the pages off the table onto the floor and glared at Richard.

"What the infernal, bloody hell do you know? You're nothing but a fucking romantic actor. . . ."

Nell put her arm around Peter's shoulder.

"Please, Peter . . ."

He leaned both palms on the table to push himself to his feet. He rocked as he turned toward Nell. Then he raised his right arm and, with a vicious backhand sweep, smashed her across the cheek. Richard rose to grab him, but Nell pushed Richard away. Tears formed in her eyes, as her husband staggered to the bedroom. Then they heard a terrible, choking sobbing which continued in a chilling, steady rhythm. Nell wiped the moisture from her eyes. She touched Richard's arm.

"Forgive him, Richard," she said. "He's hurting so much. Thank you for coming . . . and for the remarks about the play. I can't work anymore today. . . . He needs me. . . . I'll see you tomorrow."

Richard patted her shoulder. His upper left arm, where the rapier had scratched him, had begun to itch and ache slightly, but he ignored it. He was filled with an empathy for Nell's plight and Peter Faversham's desperate condition.

The first of the three evenings on which *Romeo and Juliet* were presented went fairly well. Where Richard had his greatest difficulty, as he knew he would from the rehearsals, was in the scene in the churchyard, near the end of the play, when he has killed Tybalt's friend, Paris, and has opened Juliet's tomb. Not realizing that the Friar has given Juliet a long-lasting sleeping potion, and believing her dead, Romeo plays a long scene over the unmoving body, before he himself takes poison. Richard worked through the first portion of the speech, but then his voice began to break.

". . . O my love, my wife! Death that had sucked the honey of thy breath hath no power yet upon thy beauty. Thou art not conquered; Beauty's ensign yet is crimson in thy lips and in thy cheeks, and death's pale flag is not advanced there. . . ." As he spoke on he fell to his knees over Juliet's still form again, and his voice began to crack.

"Ah, dear Juliet, why art thou so fair? Shall I believe that unsubstantial death is amorous. . . ."

He was weeping genuine tears. By the time he reached the last several lines of the speech the words tore painfully from his throat.

"Eyes look your last; arms take your last embrace, and lips (O you, the doors of breath), seal with a righteous kiss a dateless bargain to engrossing death!"

He reached into the pocket of his scarlet velvet waistcoat and took out a vial.

"Come bitter conduct, come unsavory guide, thou desperate pilot, now at once run on the dashing rocks thy seasick weary bark."

He put the vial to his lips, tilted back his head.

"Here's to my love!" he cried. "O true apothecary, thy drugs are quick."

He leaned forward and kissed Nell Faversham's lips.

"Thus with a kiss I die," he said, and fell forward across Nell Juliet's body.

Restrained applause sounded throughout the house, as though the audience was reluctant to defile this sacred place with vulgar noise. The Friar, Gilbert Weston, entered with his lantern and spade. Moments later, at the end of the play, as Richard stood in the wings listening to the Prince read his closing lines, Richard's upper arm began to throb. He was so absorbed in the curtain speech that he was unaware of the throbbing.

"A grooming peace this morning with it brings," said the Prince somberly. "The sun for sorrow will not show his head. Go hence to have more talk of these sad things: some shall be pardoned and some punished. For never was a story of more woe than this of Juliet and her Romeo."

On the night of the third performance, just before the curtain was due to rise, Richard's upper left arm was aching steadily. The night before, he had noticed that the area of the scratch was puffed and discolored, but again he had ignored it. Now Nell Faversham came in the stage door. When Richard saw her in the dim backstage light, once again he forgot about his arm completely. There was a large bluish bruise, speckled with tiny broken blood vessels on her left cheek, and her lips were swollen.

Richard stopped her as she tried to hasten to the makeup corner.

"Are you all right?"

She nodded and hurried on. When she came away from the makeup table, she looked presentable. That evening's performance was the poorest of the three. Nell was nervous and uncertain throughout the play. Wrexham soared to new peaks of flamboyant histrionics, and Richard struggled dolefully to complete the scene at Juliet's tomb. The pain in his left arm was so severe he felt feverish and nauseous. Yet when the play ended, he insisted on taking Nell to Dr. Thorndike, and persuading the doctor to accompany them to the Favershams' home to see if there was any way he could help Peter Faversham. Peter had beaten Nell severely, but she was not so much worried about herself as about Peter's rapidly deteriorating condition.

"Sometimes I think he is taking leave of his senses . . . carries on like a madman," she told Thorndike.

When they came into the small apartment, a foul odor assailed their nostrils and immediately they witnessed Peter Faversham hanging from the center beam in the room. His tongue protruded from his purple face; his eyes popped out of their sunken sockets. The sphincter muscles in his rectum had given way, and the stench of the excrement prevaded the room. It even dominated the odor of the gin, which puddled the floor at the fireplace, where Peter Faversham had apparently smashed a nearly full bottle before placing the noose around his neck and kicking the chair out from under himself.

Dr. Thorndike sent Richard for the nearest constable, with instructions to bring a death wagon. Hours later, when the body had been removed, and Dr. Thorndike and the police and the municipal officials left, Richard asked Nell to come home with him. She shook her head and went into the bedroom to get a fresh kerchief. Richard waited, perhaps ten minutes, but she did not come out. He heard muffled sobbing, and went into the bedroom. Nell sat on the bed, crying softly into the handkerchief. Richard went and sat beside her. He put his left arm around her shoulder, and the dull pain in the arm seemed to catch fire, reminding him that it had been hurting all through the evening.

Gently, with his right hand, he lifted Nell's chin. The infinite sadness in her eyes brought tears to Richard's. Still gently holding her chin, he leaned forward and kissed her tenderly on the mouth, put both arms around her and rocked her quietly. After a time, they made love. Neither knew how they came to get undressed or how they found themselves entwined on the bed, both crying softly.

It was the quest of two desperate souls, reaching out for love lost forever, trying to find in each other a renewed reason for living, seeking a small measure of beauty in the face of the ugliness and finality of death. Neither could say why they had done it. They knew only that it had brought them a kind of comfort . . . brief surcease from a nameless terror.

"Forgive me, Nell. . . . I don't know what happened. . . . I did not mean to take advantage. . . ." Richard looked into Nell's tormented emerald eyes.

She touched his cheek, placed a finger lightly on his lips.

"Nor I, dear friend," she said.

The burning agony in his left arm awakened Richard from a deep sleep the following morning. He groaned, and Mary, who had been up for more than an hour, rushed to see what was wrong. Richard rose from his pallet and held out his arm. She was shocked. The scratch itself had become an ugly, scab-covered path running jaggedly for eight inches along the crest of the swollen and discolored lump of flesh that was Richard's arm.

Richard staggered to a chair. "God, my head aches!" he moaned, feeling more nauseous by the moment.

"You get back in bed," Mary ordered.

She threw on her heavy clothing and went out into the cold February morning. In an hour, she returned with Dr. Thorndike. The doctor looked at Richard's wound and frowned.

"How did it happen?"

Richard told him about the accident during the dueling scene at the rehearsal a few days before.

"It was most foolish of you not to come to me long before this, Richard. The infection has spread and become quite gangrenous," Dr. Thorndike admonished him.

He opened his bag and took out several instruments, asking Mary to heat some water and give him some clean cloths.

"Ready for a bit of pain, son?" he asked. Richard nodded.

Dr. Thorndike cut open the scabrous wound, and cleaned large amounts of pus and tainted blood from it. He then sprinkled a powder into the open area. Richard gritted his teeth, and fought back the tears. The powder burned sharply. His head ached badly now, and the nauseous feeling in his stomach intensified.

"I'll be back to see you tomorrow afternoon," Thorndike told Richard. "Meantime, as little movement as possible. Stay in bed and rest."

Mary Steele walked to the door with the doctor. He patted her shoulder.

"He'll be all right, Mary. It will just take some time to clear up the infection. . . . I'm happy to see you're feeling so much stronger."

Mary Steele's remarkable, newly gained vigor was a surprise to Thorndike. He hoped for something of the same kind of miraculous change in Richard. He was greatly concerned that the infection might spread, and the gangrenous condition worsen . . . even to the point where it might be necessary to amputate Richard's arm.

For two weeks Richard's fate hung in the balance. The infection seemed to respond to the treatment for a day or two, then it would flare up again and spread. At the end of the first week, Dr. Thorndike began making two calls each day. Twice he bled Richard, but the headaches continued, and the fever came and went. Richard had many visitors in that two-week period. Everyone in the Lincoln's Inn Fields company came at least once, with the single exception of Jerome Wrexham, who did not come at all.

When Gilbert Weston learned of Richard's gangrenous condition, he conducted a quiet investigation. The company's property man was convinced the protective steel ball tip of the rapier had been removed deliberately. Weston also had a vague recollection that Jerome Wrexham had quickly wiped the blade of the rapier against his velvet trouser leg before handing it to Weston after the duel.

Pursuing his suspicions further, Weston had stopped in at Norman's Apothecary, the one nearest the theater, and learned that Wrexham had purchased a small quantity of a poisonous powder a few days before rehearsals began. Wrexham had told Norman that he wished to get rid of some rats that had invaded his apartment. Weston knew he could prove nothing against Wrexham, so he said nothing to Richard, nor to anyone else. But he did make up his mind that, one way or another, he must get Wrexham out of the company as soon as possible. He would discuss the situation with the Duke as soon as Fox returned from Antigua.

Nell Faversham did not come to see Richard until the end of the first week. Fatigue and deep grief still showed in her emerald eyes. She had told Weston she would like to go back to Goodman's Fields as soon as he could spare her, but he had told her he needed her, and would for some time. Mary was quite taken with Nell, and Nell with Mary. On Nell's first visit, Richard was surprised to find that he had no romantic notions about her at all. He felt she was a good friend but he did not feel at all toward her the way he had toward Felicia. It seemed that Nell had the same platonic feeling toward him, for she talked freely of the early days of her courtship, and her marriage when Peter had been a bright, gentle, loving man. Her heart was filled only with memories of Peter.

To his surprise, Richard found himself able to, indeed eager to, talk to Nell about Felicia. It was the first time, since her sudden death, that he had been able to talk about her to anyone. Among other episodes, he told Nell about the fight with the ruffians, and of Felicia's deadly effectiveness with the stone in her leather-thonged purse.

"She was such a glorious actress," Nell said. "I would sell my soul to be able to act with such artistry."

Nell visited Richard every day after rehearsal for the next ten days. On the first of March, considerably weakened, Richard returned to the theater. Coincidentally, it was the day of the first benefit performance of the season, a benefit Jerome Wrexham was giving for himself. In the early years of the century, the benefit practice had been greatly abused by actors. They played benefits for themselves early in the season and late in the season. Soon the playhouse proprietors and managers resented this abuse of the practice, because it was costing them much money and they prevailed upon the Lord Chamberlain's office to issue a directive on April 17, 1712, forbidding any benefits before March 1.

Thus on the first permissible date for a benefit in 1717,

Wrexham played Petruchio in *The Taming of the Shrew*. The benefit system called for the playhouse to deduct forty pounds from the total evening's receipts to cover its nightly charges. The player, for whom the benefit was performed, actively and aggressively sold tickets to all his friends, and kept all receipts over and above forty pounds. If the total receipts fell below the forty pounds, the player was responsible for making up the difference to the playhouse.

Wrexham's benefit was highly successful, netting for the actor ninety-three pounds, four shillings. All the boxes were filled with ladies and gentlemen of quality. Sarah Fox, due to have her baby any day, nevertheless busied herself and persuaded scores of her friends to buy tickets. Lancelot Higginbotham helped Wrexham sell tickets to the sporting gentry, and Mother Magruder brought her husband and all the whores of her establishment. Cleopatra Magruder was ecstatic at this first opportunity to see Wrexham perform. And he was indeed impressive as the dashing and dominating hero of the story.

Nell Faversham played the fiery Katherine, and performed excellently in every scene in the play in which she resisted Petruchio's dominance. In the final scene, she almost choked on many of the lines in her long speech of submission, and adulation of her husband, Petruchio.

When Wrexham Petruchio commanded her, "Katherine, I charge thee, tell these headstrong women what duty they owe their lords and husbands," she took a deep breath before forcing herself into the reply. She actually closed her eyes, and turned from the audience, more toward Wrexham than was necessary, as she said, "Thy husband is thy lord, thy life, thy keeper, thy head, thy sovereign; one that cares for thee, and for thy maintenance commits his body to painful labor both by sea and land, to watch the night in storms, the day in cold, whilst thou liest warm at home, secure and safe; and craves no other tribute at thy hands but love, fair looks and true obedience . . . too little payment for so great a debt."

She opened her eyes and saw Wrexham standing before her, head held high, eyes glistening, a broad self-satisfied smile on his gold-bearded face. Even with his shoulders thrown back, his paunch extended inches beyond his chest. She forced herself to go on with the speech, losing conviction toward the end.

When Petruchio Wrexham declaimed happily, "Why

there's a wench! Come on and kiss me, Kate," Nell rose from her kneeling position, and he took her in his arms and kissed her passionately. He held her tightly, and prolonged the kiss with open mouth. Nell kept her own lips compressed, though she feared to fight away from him and destroy the intent of the scene.

It was a fine play, an excellent comedy, a huge success, and Nell Faversham enjoyed it all, except for that final scene, which she considered ridiculous and degrading. Yet Nell was an actress, and she played her role, inwardly denouncing William Shakespeare for a chauvinistic boor. *And the same to that preening peacock, Jerome Wrexham!*

They took their final bows to enthusiastic applause, Nell and Wrexham, holding hands, standing at center stage and forward from the full cast flanking them. Nell had a forced smile on her lips; Wrexham's beaming smile was not forced at all. When the curtain came down, Nell tried to take her hand from Wrexham's, but he would not release her. He spun her sharply to him and embraced her.

"Now a proper kiss, dear Nellie," he said and pressed his mouth against hers, pulling her tightly against him. She struggled fiercely, trying to beat against his chest, to push him off, but she was pressed too closely against him to achieve any force. When she succeeded in moving her mouth away from his, he simply lowered his head and began to kiss her neck. The other players stopped at the sounds of the scuffle, and watched Nell's struggle with amusement. She finally broke Wrexham's grip, took one step away from him and swung her right arm in a savage round-house arc hitting him flush on the left side of his head with a tightly clenched fist. He gasped and staggered slightly.

"Dammit, woman, are you insane? Have you no sense of sport!"

But Nell strode angrily off to her dressing quarters, and Catherine Clark muttered, "How unfortunate Faversham saved that for backstage, instead of doing it in the last scene!"

The rest of the company guffawed and chuckled as Wrexham marched off angrily. Gilbert Weston had watched the incident with Richard Steele.

"A fine, fiery young lady, that Faversham!" commented Weston. When the excitement subsided, he drew Richard to a quiet corner of the backstage area, put his arm around Richard's shoulder.

"Farley Shannon and I have planned a bit of a surprise for you, lad," Weston said. "How would you like to play a benefit performance for yourself the last week of this month?"

Richard could hardly believe his ears.

"Oh . . . Gilbert . . . I'm greatly flattered, but I wouldn't dare. I . . . I . . . I don't think I could sell enough tickets. I . . . I'm hardly well enough known."

"I've already talked to the editors of *The Tatler* and *The Spectator*. Both will happily publicize the event. . . ."

Richard looked at him in disbelief.

"After all," said Weston, "you would probably be the youngest actor to play Hamlet in years."

"Hamlet!" Richard gasped.

"Farley Shannon is sure you could play it with great effectiveness. And so am I. And Farley and I, as well as Nell Faversham, other people in the company, Father Whittaker and Dr. Thorndike, will all help sell tickets."

"I'm truly not sure I'm up to it, but if you and Farley think I am, I'll try."

Weston patted him on the back.

"Good lad. We'll keep you on leave of absence until opening night of *Hamlet*. You can spend all your time regaining your strength and studying with Farley."

After Felicia's death, Richard had been firmly convinced that he would never again feel this superb thrill . . . this ecstatic amalgam of trepidation and eagerness to meet a new challenge. He worked even harder than he had on *Volpone*. He studied day and night with Farley Shannon, and spent a good deal of extra time with Nell Faversham, who was to play Ophelia.

Shannon set the tone for the entire three and a half weeks of Richard's work in their very first meeting. Seated across from Richard in his small, comfortable library, with a glass of port at his elbow, Shannon said, "Son, the greatest actors in the theater have played this role. In Shakespeare's own company, their finest actor, Richard Burbage, performed it. And so did his esteemed rival, Edward Alleyn, though Alleyn was the Wrexham of his day— unnnhhhh—much inclined toward flamboyancy."

He sipped his wine.

"Burbage died a few years after Shakespeare, and Joseph Taylor became the ranking performer to play

Hamlet at both the Globe and the Blackfriars—errr-hhhh. . . . Take some wine, Richard—unnnhhhh. Then my own colleague, Thomas Betterton, possibly the greatest actor of them all, performed it, and brought fresh and exciting nuances to the magnificent role . . . unnnn-hhhh. . . . How well do you know the play?"

"Fairly well." Richard smiled. "You may recall I made my own debut in it not too long ago."

"Oh, yes." Shannon nodded. "I'd forgotten—the nervous messenger . . . unnnhhhh. . . . Those days are long gone. You are an actor young man, an accomplished actor. I've never worked with anyone who has progressed as rapidly in as short a time."

"Thank you, Farley, I can't tell you how much your saying that means to me."

Shannon waved a hand.

"Shakespeare himself tells us, as he told the players, how to do Hamlet." And as Richard listened raptly, Shannon spoke Shakespeare's words in the most conversational of all tones.

"Speak the speech, I pray you, as I pronounced it to you, trippingly on the tongue; but if you mouth it, as many of our players do, I had as lief the town crier spoke my lines—unnnhhhh."

He sipped some wine.

"Nor do not saw the air too much with your hand, thus; but use all gently, for in the very torrent, tempest (as I may say)—errrhhhh—whirlwind of your passion, you must acquire and beget a temperance that may give it smoothness—"

Speaking the lines seemed to bring new life to Shannon's tired, pain-filled eyes. He grinned broadly before proceeding.

"O it offends me to the soul to hear a robustious periwig-pated fellow tear a passion to tatters, to very rags, to split the ears of the groundlings who for the most part are capable of nothing but inexplicable dumb shows and noise."

Richard drank some of his own wine and looked eagerly at Shannon as the elderly actor paused for breath.

"May I?" he asked, and when Shannon nodded, he continued the speech from where Shannon had left off.

"Be not too tame neither, but let your own discretion be your tutor. Suit the action to the word, the word to the action, with this special observance, that you overstep not the modesty of nature, to show virtue her own feature. . . ."

Shannon shook his head.

"No, no, lad, you've omitted an essential thought or two."

He continued the speech.

". . . with this special observance: that you overstep not the modesty of nature; for anything so overdone is from the purpose of playing, whose end, both at the first and now, was and is to hold, as 'twere, the mirror up to nature."

He paused for a long, deep breath, sipped wine and continued. Then he shook a finger at Richard and he drew another deep breath for his finale.

". . . O, there be players that I have seen play and heard others praise, and that highly (not to speak it profanely) that, neither having the accent of Christians nor the gait of Christian, pagan nor man, have so strutted and bellowed that I have thought some of nature's journeymen had made men and not made them well—errrhhhh—they imitated humanity so abominably."

He leaned back in his chair, exhausted. Then he laughed, as heartily as Richard had ever heard him laugh. "There's an entire instruction in acting in a single speech!"

Richard had never worked harder than during the rehearsals of Hamlet. The first time he read through the carnage-filled final scene with Shannon—in which Hamlet; his uncle, King Claudius; his mother, Queen Gertrude and Laertes all die—it struck him that Jerome Wrexham, having played Laertes, may actually have tipped the rapier he used in the *Romeo and Juliet* rehearsal with poison. It was how Laertes murdered Hamlet, and how Hamlet, in turn, killed Laertes and then his uncle, the King. *With a rapier with "point envenomed."* For a moment he was again filled with bitterness and hatred for Wrexham. The confounded rascal did everything so obviously, yet somehow beyond proving.

The play, and particularly his performance, was the greatest success of the season. The writer for *The Spectator*, a veteran theater-goer, dared draw a comparison with Thomas Betterton:

Young Steele, of course, does not match the legendary Thomas Betterton's portrayal of the tragic Prince of Denmark, but notwithstanding his tender

283

years, his performance demands he be ranked with the most accomplished of today's players, and possibly heralds his supremacy in the theater of tomorrow.

Thanks to provocative notices in *The Spectator* and *The Tatler* before the engagement, and the industrious efforts of all his friends, the benefit was also a financial success. Father Whittaker sold many tickets, including six to the warehouse man, Francis Bruce, and four to Horatio Busk and Timothy Tipp, who attended in the upper gallery with a couple of loud and appreciative harlots. Nell Faversham persuaded a goodly portion of her Goodman's Fields following to buy seats, and Dr. Thorndike convinced a long list of former and present patients they must attend. Mary Steele had written George Storey about the benefit, and Storey had come in from Hertfordshire with a party of five friends.

Richard netted forty-two pounds, twelve shillings after the house collected its forty pounds.

The morning after this triumphant evening, a distinguished gentleman named Theodore Hawlings of the law firm of Hawlings, Laffery and Massinger called at the home of the Steeles.

Felicia Wandrous's last will and testament had been probated, and she had left one hundred and fifty pounds of her estate to Mary Steele, and a like amount, the balance of her total wealth, to Edith Forrest. In mid-April, Richard and Mary Steele and her two-month-old baby daughter, Felicia, moved into the cottage at Waltham Cross. Mary and Edith had pooled their resources to make the purchase.

Richard's salary per acting day was increased another five shillings to twelve shillings, making him one of the highest paid actors in London. He purchased Sally O from Ben Pickering, and took a room at the Inn on a permanent basis, making the twelve-mile trip to Waltham Cross only on the days he was not acting or rehearsing.

He did not take the room in which he and Felicia had shared their love. That he simply could not bear to do. But when it was unoccupied, he occasionally entered the room and stood at the window, looking out into the spring night, recalling the sweet and treasured moments, and intensifying the painful loss he felt now, in spite of his sudden remarkable success as an actor.

26

In the spring, nature provided a continuous, varied, startlingly beautiful, sometimes amusing, sometimes exciting
dumb show in the North Atlantic below the Tropic of
Cancer. As the brig *Odyssey* left Antigua harbor on this
April morning in 1717, bound for Dover, England, the
water was a rolling liquid carpet of aquamarine, across
which a myriad of sunbeams danced. Overhead multihued,
exotic tropical birds swooped and soared. Six hours out, a
grampus, a small whale, surfaced alongside the ship and
swam lazily with it. Some of the passengers, discovering
the plump mammal, exclaimed and called their friends,
and soon many were throwing pieces of bread, carrots,
odd bits of meat and fish to the whale. As each piece was
thrown, the cavorting whale thrust forward, or twisted or
thrashed to catch whatever was thrown to it, actually
catching many of the objects in its small mouth.

In a brief time, the whale tired of the game, and finding
the menu uninteresting, dove into the depths and disappeared. Forty minutes later a school of dolphins appeared
off the starboard side of the ship, and performed graceful, arched diving routines in and out of the blue-green
sea. Their sleek bodies seemed to be tinted with the
ocean's green gloss, artfully blended with shimmering
gold.

All this was wasted on Edmund Fox, the Duke of
Cheltenham. He paced the deck restlessly, unmindful of
the passengers at the rails, ignoring the sailors who danced
hornpipes and jigs with some of the younger ladies from
steerage to the tinny music of jew's harps and penny whis-
tles. His mind was full of the events of the past week at

285

the Plantation Edwina in Antigua, and with curiosity and concern over what might have transpired in London since his departure in February.

He was troubled over the condition in which he found his sister, Edwina. She was only a year younger than Edmund, and ever since their earliest childhood, they had been the best of friends. Indeed, the Duke loved her more than any other living being. When he was ten, and she nine, they had even participated in a half-dozen fumbling sexual experiments with each other, but soon found these dull, and restricted their future activities to more orthodox games and pastimes.

One day, when he was twenty-five, Edmund had met a dashing young man, named Gabriel Marlowe, at the cockfights at the royal pit at Birdcage Walk. Marlowe was five years younger than Fox. He was a tall, athletic-looking man with a premature streak of white in the center of his sleek black shoulder-length hair. It was evident from the wrinkles at the corners of his squinting, gunmetal-gray eyes and his leathery complexion that he spent much time in the sun. Instead of an eyebrow, he had a shiny, pinkish scar over his left eye. There was a slight hump in the center of his aquiline nose, as though it might once have been broken. Beneath the nose, a full black mustache gave him the appearance of a thirty- rather than a twenty-year-old man. He had a strong, square jaw, and full, sensuous lips. Though he walked with a slight limp, he moved with grace.

Edmund Fox was impressed with the large amounts Marlowe wagered, and with the cool and cheerful manner with which he accepted victory or loss. They had supper together at Edmund Fox's club that night, and became good friends. Marlowe, it seemed, was captain of a slave ship, and had been for more than a year . . . possibly the youngest captain of such a vessel in the country. The scar, the disfigured nose, the limp were all the results of various fights he had had since taking to the sea at age ten.

The two men freely exchanged stories about their backgrounds and their interests. Fox found Marlowe's descriptions of seafaring and slave-trading absorbing, and he was surprised to learn how profitable employment as captain of a slave ship could be. Marlowe was paid fifteen pounds per month, and given ten slaves out of every hundred he landed in the West Indies. Since West Indian plantation owners paid one hundred gallons of rum for a slave, and the rum was highly negotiable in England, Marlowe earned a tidy sum from this phase of his business. Additionally, he was given five percent of the ship owner's profit on every cargo he took out, and an additional five percent on every cargo he brought back. Finally, a substantial amount of cargo space was consigned to him, for whatever purpose he chose on every voyage.

He told Edmund Fox that in another year, perhaps sooner, he expected to have enough money to purchase a fair-sized sugar plantation in Antigua. He loved the island and talked about it in ecstatic terms. A week after they met, Fox invited Marlowe to dinner at the family mansion, and introduced him to Edwina. Edwina Fox was a striking young woman who looked a great deal like her brother. She had his same bright gray eyes, straight nose and thin, well-shaped mouth. Her shining brown hair was full, rich and beautifully coiffed.

Edwina Fox had never met a man she liked or admired as much as her brother. She had never been in love, but she was fascinated by Gabriel Marlowe. She and Marlowe, sometimes alone, sometimes in the company of Edmund and Sarah Palfrey, attended many events in the next two months before Marlowe was scheduled to sail again.

Marlowe left England for seven months on his next slave-trading voyage, but when he returned he resumed his relationship with Edmund and Edwina Fox. In another year Marlowe had accumulated enough wealth to purchase the plantation in Antigua. Edmund Fox became a fifty-percent partner in the venture. One week before he was scheduled to leave for Antigua, Gabriel Marlowe and Edwina Fox were married. And Edwina left London to make a new life with her dashing husband in the tropical island.

The trade winds began to blow harder now, billowing the square sails of the foremast and mainmast of the brig. The sun was a softer butter yellow, less fiery than earlier in the day. The Duke went to the five-foot by six-foot cubicle, which was his stateroom, to put on a muslin jacket over his shirt. He came out on deck again and went to the rail, gazing at the azure water, wondering what was wrong with Edwina.

For reasons undetermined, she and Gabriel were unable to have children for years. Then, unexpectedly, last summer, Edwina had become pregnant and in mid-January gave birth to a baby daughter. They named the child Georgina. Busy with his own affairs, the Duke had not seen his sister or her husband since their wedding, though they had kept in touch, writing each other regularly. Edwina had always seemed happy and contented, and Marlowe had made a spectacular success of the sugar plantations. In the first year, he had sent Fox six hundred pounds as his share of the first fiscal twelve-month profit, and a larger amount each year until the present check for twenty-two hundred pounds, which Fox had in his leather purse this very moment.

Still Edmund Fox had no idea of how enormously successful Gabriel Marlowe had become until he visited him on this trip. Plantation Edwina was the second largest sugar plantation on the entire island, covering thousands of acres. The mansion Marlowe had built on a hill two miles from town overlooked the beautiful aquamarine bay with its bustling shipping activity, the town and its markets, and hundreds of squares and rectangles of rich sugar cane, waving like verdant wheat. In its far more colorful and exotic way, the mansion and its surroundings were as impressive as anything in London or Windsor. Two hundred and sixteen slaves lived and worked on Plantation Edwina.

"I've lost count of how many are my own bastards." Marlowe had winked at Fox one balmy evening as they drank brandies on one of the terraces.

"Serves numerous purposes, Edmund." He laughed. "Keeps the more passionate young girls happy, stocks the labor supply with the finest future bucks and child-bearers God or man can make . . . my very own!"

Marlowe's fornicating with the mulatto and black women on the plantation did not shock nor surprise Edmund Fox. Indeed, at Gabriel's invitation, he spent two most exciting and satisfying evenings with three different mulatto women, one age sixteen, and two age twelve. What did surprise the Duke was the fact that Gabriel Marlowe was so well loved and respected by all of the blacks on the plantation—at least as far as their attitudes were evident to the Duke.

Now, having observed Gabriel's behavior during an entire week, Edmund Fox guessed that Marlowe managed to maintain this relationship by his kind and considerate treatment of the slaves, and a reasonable amount of discretion in pursuing his assignations. Edmund wondered, of course, whether Gabriel's carnal activities with the slave women were responsible for what was wrong with Edwina. But after studying her actions, and reviewing the entire situation in depth with Gabriel and with Edwina's doctor, a Frenchman named Andre Gilraux, Edmund was sure that Marlowe's wholesale infidelities had little, if anything, to do with the situation.

Even in England, Edwina had grown up in a milieu in which women accepted the existence of their husbands' mistresses. Here in Antigua, Edmund observed, every woman he met was completely oblivious to the frequently open flirtations and illicit, extramarital affairs of their husbands, whether the affair was with a caucasian or a black or mulatto woman.

The doctor told Edmund that Edwina's troubled condition was not at all unusual, assuring him that many women who have children later in life experience the severe post-birth depression that Edwina was feeling.

Now Edmund Fox stood at the rail and watched a silken indigo sea slowly swallow the red wafer that was the sun. When the sun was gone, a sky streaked with apricot, violet and saffron gradually turned ashen gray, then black. The Duke watched the transition, untouched by its beauty. He was wondering, again, what had happened in England during his absence. Finally as countless brilliant stars filled the ebony tropical sky and the winds blew colder, Edmund went into his cramped cabin, lighted the candle, which had been lashed to his table, and began to read the recommendations Gabriel Marlowe had written for converting one thousand acres of cane fields into pasture for raising cattle and sheep in order to revitalize the land, where only cane had grown, and to give the island another source of revenue. He wanted Edmund Fox to review these with the steward at his country estate where they had raised cattle and sheep for several generations.

But the Duke could not keep his mind on the data. He wondered, as he had for weeks now, if Sarah had had her child. He wanted a boy, and wanted very much to be present at the birth. He hoped and prayed that she would not suffer the same kind of depression Edwina was suffering, after the birth. Worse, there were dangers as Dr. Gilraux had pointed out, for women in giving birth after thirty. After a light supper of lobcourse, a beef stew, he went out on deck again. Briefly he wondered what was taking place at the Lincoln's Inn Fields and the Goodman's Fields playhouse. He hoped the problems Wrexham was creating in his ridiculous rivalry with young Steele had been resolved.

He permitted himself some fantasy-filled thoughts concerning Felicia and Nell Faversham. He was quite convinced he could never persuade Felicia Wandrous to become his mistress. She seemed iron-willed in her resistance to noblemen. In Nell Faversham's case, he still had hopes. He did not understand how a woman as handsome as she could tolerate the kind of life she lived with her husband.

On the thirty-second day of the voyage, the *Odyssey* was far north and east of Antigua, nearing Falmouth, and even in early May the weather had been nasty for days. There had been three days of rain and storm, and almost everyone aboard had been seasick continuously. The captain was the single exception. He was a grizzled old sea horse. Periodically, he would visit the Duke in his cabin and proclaim happily, "She's blowin' fair, she is, your Grace. . . . We're makin' ten knots per hour, and will soon see landfall!"

At the peak of the storms, the Duke could hear him, in the adjoining cabin, bellowing sea chanteys:

"Oh, grog is the liquor of life
The delight of each free British tar . . ."

The Duke still felt poorly when the hackney drove him up to the front door of the mansion near St. James Palace. It was a foggy morning, dismal for May, and Edmund Fox had a sick feeling in his stomach as he opened the door to his home. He could not tell whether it was a physical residue from the journey, or a psychological forewarning that something was dreadfully wrong.

Having heard the Duke at the door, Hawkins, the bald butler, now met his master in the foyer. His visage was grim, but Hawkins had a dour face even on the cheeriest of occasions.

"Good morning, Hawkins. Is the Duchess up?"

Hawkins nodded briefly toward the right.

"In the library," he muttered.

The Duke hurried directly toward the large oak double doors of the second room along the broad, carpeted hallway to the right. He knocked, turned the bronze knob and entered. He gasped as he saw the Duchess.

290

"Sarah—my dear . . ." He hurried toward her, hands outstretched.

"You on'ry fi' week late, Edmuh . . ." the Duchess muttered.

The shock of seeing ber in the thronelike, ornate wheelchair was severe, but when Edmund stood directly before her, and saw the paralyzed condition of her face, he paled. He felt his knees weaken, and his hands began to tremble. A bubble of saliva curved from the corner of the mouth to the point of her chin. Her complexion was sallow, and the right eye was so motionless it seemed to be made of glass.

He fought to control himself, and knelt before her. She pulled her hand away sharply when he attempted to hold it, and adroitly wheeled the chair around so that her back was to him. He moved around in front of her.

"I'm so sorry, dear Sarah. So sorry I was not—could not—be here."

A tear ran down her cheek.

"Your . . . son . . ." she sobbed, taking a handkerchief from the breast pocket of her flowered satin shirtwaist to wipe her cheek.

"Your . . . son's 'n . . . nurs'y." She rang a small silver bell on a table beside the chair and almost immediately a large, middle-aged woman came in to the room.

"Cumberly," the Duchess said, her sobbing under control, "take me ou' 'n gar'n."

The nurse wheeled her toward the French doors at the east end of the large room, opened the doors and pushed the chair into a corner of the terrace beside a large urn which held golden orange chrysanthemums. Sarah Fox stared, her left eye still moist, but staring straight ahead, as unblinking as her right. Her chin quivered, and she gripped both arms of the wheelchair fiercely, but she did not cry again. Her husband watched her for a moment, considered going out to the terrace to talk with her further, then changed his mind and headed for the stairs to the second floor, and the room they had set aside as the nursery long before he left for Antigua.

Another nurse, this one a good deal younger than the woman attending the Duchess, opened the door. She was thin, with dark compassionate eyes, and an extremely gentle manner. The Duke began to introduce himself in a normal tone, then dropped his voice to a whisper as the nurse held her finger to her lips to indicate that the baby in the large, canopied, gilded crib was sleeping.

Then he received another shock. Although it was a relatively warm day, there was a fire in the fireplace at the far side of the room. The baby was wrapped in a half-dozen woolen blankets. Only his head showed. To Edmund Fox, the head seemed no larger than an apple. He could see tiny blue veins in the eyelids over the closed eyes, and the lips were so pale a pink they seemed almost white. The nose was a small dot of flesh, stuck between two sunken ivory-colored cheeks. Wisps of dark hair were slicked across the top of the incredibly small round skull.

"He weighs less than a quarter stone," said the nurse. When she saw the look of grave concern on Edmund Fox's face, she hastened to add, "but he is growing, and he will be fine. Dr. Spencer comes to see him every day."

She looked at the clock on the west wall.

"In fact, the doctor should be arriving momentarily."

Fox felt foolish in asking the question, but was most curious to know.

"Has he been christened?"

The nurse nodded.

"John," she said. "I believe the Duchess said that was both his paternal and maternal grandfather's name."

The Duke managed a feeble smile.

Just then Dr. Godfrey Spencer came into the room.

"Edmund!" he said heartily, apparently unconcerned about waking the baby. "Happy you've returned! Sarah had a difficult time. Understand you were called—emergency, rather—to visit Edwina. . . . How is she?"

Spencer had been both the Palfrey and the Fox family physician for many years.

"She has these inexplicable, recurring fits of despondency. Her doctor says it's not uncommon. . . ."

"Not uncommon at all," said Spencer. "Childbirth is difficult for all women after middle age. I know you've seen Sarah. . . . Poor woman almost died."

He studied the Duke quietly for a moment.

"Most unfortunate you had to leave when you did. She's extremely bitter. Feels you should have been here."

"I know that, Godfrey, I know. But Edwina's last letter sounded so desperate, so . . . He paused. "What did happen to Sarah? What is her disorder?"

"Entire right side is paralyzed, Edmund. She always

was a rather tense, high-strung woman. Most fortunate she lived at all. Even more fortunate, the baby lived."

"Is there a cure? Can she recover?"

Spencer shook his head.

"I'm sorry, Edmund, but I must tell you the truth. A paralysis of this kind is completely irreversible. There's no possibility at all she will even improve, let alone recover."

The Duke choked back an urge to sob, a feeling of both sorrow and frustration.

"On the other hand, Edmund," said Spencer crisply, "you may thank God the baby will live . . . and, the Lord willing, will grow up to be a healthy young man."

After the doctor checked and treated the baby, Edmund Fox went back to the Duchess on the terrace. The sun had burned away the fog, and after a time she agreed to join him for a cup of chocolate, and they talked. Edmund Fox found it difficult to conceal the pain he felt, listening to the difficulty Sarah had in speaking. The immobility of the right side of her face made her garble many of her words and phrases. She tried to speak politely in friendly tones but Edmund sensed that she had been hurt by his absence beyond the point of genuine forgiveness. Several of her remarks gave him the strong impression that she definitely blamed him for her paralysis, as well as for the frail, sickly condition of their son.

In the calmer moments of their conversation, she told Edmund that Jerome Wrexham had been kind and extremely helpful to her. He had visited her daily in the critical period right after the birth and her sudden paralysis, bringing her flowers and assuring her that the Duke would be home very soon. He had even recommended the man who had built the special wheelchair for her, had helped the man design it to Sarah's own specifications. It was the same man who had built the sedan chair for Wrexham, and he was indeed an excellent craftsman. Naturally, Wrexham said nothing about the fact that the maker of the chair had paid him a commission of twenty pounds for getting him the order.

After a little more than an hour, the Duchess tired, and Cumberly came to take her to her chambers. The Duke went into the morning room and poured himself a large glass of brandy. He drank it straight and then immediately had another. He was sad, bitter, frustrated and confused. He did not know of any way he could make up for the tragedy that had befallen Sarah. Life with a wife in her condition seemed depressing at best, unbearable at worst, but he would have to make do. He poured himself one more glass of brandy and decided to go and see Gilbert Weston before he got too drunk. Best to get back into life's normal activities as quickly as possible. Settled at a secluded corner table at Lady Gertrude's—which was quiet this early in the day—the two men exchanged amenities. They ordered wine and dinner. Gilbert Weston inquired after Sarah and the new baby—Wrexham had already brought the entire company up to date on the situation, with emphasis on his own major role—and asked about Edwina and her husband. The Duke filled him in rather curtly and gloomily. As the sommelier opened their wine bottle Weston said, "It seems to be a time of tragedy, Edmund."

Then he told the Duke of Felicia Wandrous's death, and the suicide of Peter Faversham. Edmund Fox was shocked. He was surprised at how deeply moved he was at the news of Felicia's death. It was as though they had been as close as he had hoped they might be. He pressed Weston for details, then finally and abruptly changed the direction of the conversation, as if he was suddenly eager to discuss a relatively trivial matter, one within human capacity to control, to move beyond the oppressive atmosphere of sudden and violent death and crippling illness.

"How proceeds Wrexham's feud with young Steele?" he asked.

"It's as bad or worse than ever," Weston told him, detailing the difficulties they had had with *Romeo and Juliet,* and Wrexham's cutting of Richard, accidentally or otherwise. He described Wrexham's triumphant benefit performance in *The Taming of the Shrew,* and the ludicrous backstage finale when Nell Faversham had punched Wrexham in the head.

The Duke managed to chuckle.

"Spirited young lass, that Nell," he commented.

Weston nodded, continued.

"Most unfortunate of all, Edmund, was the remarkable success young Steele achieved in playing Hamlet. Wrexham is insane with envy."

He described the overwhelming reaction of the playgoers, the extravagant critical praise, and most of all, the audiences Richard had been drawing in every presentation since *Hamlet.*

"We must find a solution, Gilbert," said the Duke, pushing aside his untouched dinner plate. "They are both valuable players."

"I think I have a solution. I've been awaiting your return to discuss it."

The Duke sipped his wine, looked at Weston quizzically.

"When Felicia died," said Weston, "I found it necessary to bring Faversham in to replace her. It was impossible to find another competent actress on such short notice. . . ."

The Duke nodded. Weston continued.

"I persuaded your friend Spifford to resume his task at Goodman's Fields until you returned and I could discuss the entire matter with you. It delayed his retirement plans a bit, but he was most cooperative."

"Henry is a gentleman," said the Duke.

"I have in mind," said Weston, "making Jerry Wrexham the leading actor-manager at Goodman's Fields, and keeping Faversham with our company."

The Duke's shrewd, but tired, brown eyes showed his interest.

"When I initially proposed the idea to Faversham she was not too keen on it, didn't want to leave her friends at Goodman's Fields, was reluctant to give up working as actor-manager . . ."

He forked a bit of trout to his mouth, swallowed.

". . . but since her husband's death, she has changed considerably. She has become very fond of our group—excepting Wrexham, of course—and since young Steele has less and less time to aid me with management details, she could help—would be happy to—in that area."

"How would Jerry feel about working in a less prestigious unlicensed theater?" asked Fox.

Weston smiled.

"Two factors would quickly overcome whatever loss of prestige he might feel. For one, he would be able to present the plays and entertainments he believes most worthy and popular. He has long disagreed with my selection of repertoire. . . ."

"I know."

"And it may work out well both for Goodman's Fields and our own playhouse. I'm sure Wrexham's repertoire, perhaps an emphasis on musical programs featuring himself, and more bawdy comedies and drama, will attract a substantial audience, while we could continue to offer the more serious works, more selective humorous plays, outstanding pantomime, and occasional concerts and recitals."

"Appealing to two different audiences." Fox nodded. "Seems perfectly logical."

"The second factor, would be the one dearest to Jerry's greedy little heart."

He sipped his wine.

"He's now earing thirteen shillings, four pence per acting day. If we added to that, perhaps, forty pounds per year for taking on all management duties, I'm sure he would be most happy."

The Duke smiled.

"I think he will be happy if we give him twenty additional pounds per annum. Let me talk to him this evening."

As it turned out, Wrexham was delighted to have the opportunity to show the Duke how a playhouse should be operated. He said that he assumed that if he did as spectacularly successful a job as he knew he would do, the Duke would consider retiring Weston, and making Wrexham manager of Lincoln's Inn Fields.

"Of course, of course!" said Edmund Fox, and then permitted Wrexham to bargain him all the way up to an annual additional manager's recompense of twenty pounds, from the Duke's original offer of fifteen. *And*, the Duke explained, he was only adding this additional five pounds because of the kind attention and assistance Wrexham had given the Duchess during her recent trying times. Wrexham studied the Duke intently, trying to determine from the gleam in his eyes, the tone of his voice, whether Sarah or one of the servants had told the Duke of Wrexham's recent erotic coupling with the Duchess. But Fox gave no sign that he meant anything other than what he was saying.

Nell Faversham was pleased with the new arrangement, as were all the members of the Lincoln's Inn Fields company. Wrexham was to be replaced by a young actor named Lawrence Talbot, who had worked extensively with a small company in the provinces and had studied with Farley Shannon. All the changes were to take place with the beginning of the new season the following September. With everyone aware that the present, frequently uncomfortable situation would prevail for lit-

tle more than a month, the rehearsals and the performances began to go smoothly. And as the end of June
drew near, they were all busy making their plans for the
summer, in addition to their daily work at Lincoln's Inn
Fields.

Wrexham had been booked for a return to the scenes
of his triumphs in Dublin, and had arranged to take
Catherine Clark with him. Richard had contracted with
Sidney Colby to play for eight weeks in midsummer at
Richmond Hill. Gilbert Weston would go back to Bath to
take over the management of the playhouse there. Nell,
however, had made no decisions. She was torn between
what she considered her need to continue to keep busy,
and the desperate urge of her physical being for rest and
relief.

The Duke tried hard to reestablish his friendly, if un-
romantic, relationship with Sarah, but she could not bring
herself to respond with more than the barest civility.
She was snappish and full of self-pity, and plagued her
husband with constant variations on the theme that Edmund cared far more for his sister than he did for her.
Which, of course, was true. As the days passed, the
Duke's solution to his domestic problem was simply to
stay away from home as much as possible, and to seek
more desirable feminine companionship elsewhere.

On the fifth day after his return from Antigua, he
persuaded Nell Faversham to join him for an after-theater
supper at Lady Gertrude's. It was the first opportunity
he had had to talk with her alone since his return.

"Though I did not know him," he said to Nell after he
had ordered their wine, "I was sorry to hear of your husband's tragic death."

"Thank you. And I, to learn of the Duchess's terrible misfortune. . . . does the child continue to be well?"

Fox nodded, and for moments they fidgeted through
an awkward silence. Then through most of the meal they
talked about the theater, and the roles Nell had played.
Finally Edmund reached across the table and placed his
hand gently over Nell's.

"Are you still living in the same house, where . . ."

Nell lowered her head.

"Yes. I know it's not wise, but I truly have not had
time to find new quarters."

He squeezed her hand.

"I have a lovely small house in Pall Mall. It's unoccupied at the moment. . . ."

Nell smiled, but made no response.

"I know you would be quite comfortable there. . . ."

He waited, looking into her emerald eyes, and when she still made no reply, he said, ". . . and I would have no objections whatsoever to your continuing your work in the theater. I—"

Nell gently withdrew her hand from his.

"I think the relationship you seem to be proposing would be a happier one for both of us if we knew a good deal more about each other."

Edmund looked at her thoughtfully.

"I have no experience at all at being a gentleman's mistress," she continued. He smiled.

"I think I would have great difficulty pretending passion," she said earnestly.

The Duke lifted his wine glass, smiled and nodded.

"To getting to know more . . . a great deal more . . . about each other, dear Nell."

Nell lifted her glass and they drank the toast.

In the next two weeks, Edmund Fox took Nell boating on the Thames, to a gala at Ranelagh, to the cockfights at the royal pit at Birdcage Walk, and on three more evenings to supper at Lady Gertrude's. He even introduced her to lanterloo and hazard. Fox was agreeably surprised to discover that his pleasure in Nell's company far exceeded anything he had experienced in any previous relationship with a mistress. This was particularly surprising, since he had not yet bedded her.

On the last three occasions on which they had met, he put his arm around her shoulder, as the carriage clattered up to her house. He drew her to him, and kissed her. He had not felt so genuinely, foolishly, happily romantic since his eighteenth year, when he had briefly courted a beautiful young French lady of sixteen, whose parents took her back to Paris before Fox, then Lord Edmund, could consummate the affair.

Nell, for her part, was even more surprised and delighted with the relationship than the Duke. For so many years, ever since Peter Faversham's disorder had altered his personality so drastically, Nell had buried herself in her work. Her life consisted of long hours in rehearsal, performances, and offstage and backstage activity, dealing with costume designers, scene painters, carpenters, printers, even plumbers—in the daily operations of the small Goodman's Fields theater. That combined with patiently trying to care for the tortured and abusive man she loved had become her life. She had literally forgotten what it meant to give herself over to the simple enjoyment of leisure time.

A wonderfully euphoric feeling came over her as they drifted on the clean, deep green Thames, beyond Hammersmith and Kew Gardens and the Old Deer Park, far south and west of humid, stinking London, and the polluted waters around the city's docks. She could not remember when she last felt so relaxed. At the Ranelagh gala she was as delighted as a child, as they strolled among the colorful tents, joined the dancers around the maypole dressed with fragrant garlands.

She had been to cockfights twice with Peter, before he became ill, but she found the drunken crowd and the bloody, savage battles repulsive. At Birdcage Walk, she was somehow drawn into the excitement, and wondered later how she could have enjoyed this barbaric sport. She did enjoy immensely the gambling at Lady Gertrude's. Refusing to accept the Duke's money, she bet modestly with her own limited funds, and won, both at loo and hazard. The Duke was a charming, attentive and bright companion. Nell had never had a more pleasant two weeks in her life.

At the theater, Richard Steele noticed the change in Nell. From day to day, she seemed to work with more enthusiasm, more vitality. He was pleased for her, even envied her a little, wishing he could somehow find the same spirit for living. Three days before the official end of the season, at a noontime dinner at Pickering's, Nell told Richard about her outings with the Duke.

"He's a most considerate man, Richard," she said finally. "I've become very fond of him."

"I'm happy for you, Nell. You richly deserve a share of life's pleasures."

"When do you leave for Richmond Hill?" she asked.

"July first," he said. "I'll have almost a month with Mary at Waltham Cross. You would hardly recognize her. She seems to have regained her youth in the country."

Nell studied Richard's tired face. There were deep, grayish circles beneath his eyes. The sea-colored irises seemed dull, and the whites were bloodshot. Through the long season, he had lost most of his copper color, and his skin was ashen. His hand trembled as he lifted his brandy glass to his lips.

Nell said, "The month at Waltham Cross will do you good, Richard. You have been working much too hard."

He shrugged. He had developed an odd pattern of life. Each night, on stage, he was gay, vivacious, ebullient, dashing, heroic, comic, even depressed or sad if necessary, as the roles he played called for a given succession of emotions. Each morning, and often into the early afternoon he worked doggedly, preparing himself for his next role. If the rehearsals were brief, he went to Gilbert Weston's office and helped Weston and Nell Faversham with the company's account books, in which were recorded salaries, rent, taxes, costs of scenes and machinery, costumes and wardrobe maintenance, printing and other activities.

Occasionally, he would play cards with some of his colleagues, and two or three evenings of the week he rode out to Stratford to visit and play chess with Farley Shannon.

One evening, Shannon said, "Richard, you have become one of the finest young actors in England, and possibly one of the most unhappy people in the universe."

"Not really, Farley. It's just that I can't seem to generate enthusiasm for anything but my work," Richard said.

"That's not good, lad. In due time, that lack of enthusiasm will take over and corrode your playing."

Always, Richard ended the evening in his bed at the Inn, through too many hours of too many long nights, remembering the beautiful moments with Felicia, and feeling a terrible desolation without her. Even at Waltham Cross on his off days, and now in the last week in June, after three weeks of rustic inactivity, he felt restless and oddly disoriented. It pleased him to see his mother, red-cheeked, bright-eyed, pulling weeds, turning soil, pinching off bugs and insects in the vegetable or the flower gardens; to watch her singing as she sewed or cooked; or as she sat reading of an evening, a contented look on her face. There were no coughs and no blood-stained kerchiefs.

Edith Forrest was as warm and pleasant as she could be. Yet Richard had a strange, unreasonable feeling of resentment, not only toward Edith, but even toward baby Felicia. Intellectually, he knew that Edith could have done nothing to prevent Felicia's death, but irrationally, unreasonably he held her responsible. He tried, but never very successfully, to be warm and friendly toward Edith, as she was toward him. He ignored the lovely baby girl altogether. It bothered him that he behaved so, but he could do nothing about it.

Nell Faversham paid an unexpected visit to the cottage on the Sunday before Richard was to leave for Richmond Hill. Lancelot Higginbotham was now presenting bullbaiting events every third Sunday on George Storey's acreage, in an arena not far from the Steele-Forrest cottage. The noise of the usually drunken crowd reached the cottage on Sundays when the events apparently were extraordinarily exciting. To Mary and Edith, this was the single, unattractive aspect of living there. Mary had talked to George Storey about it, but he had signed a five-year agreement with Higginbotham before the Steeles and Edith bought the cottage, and he had no choice but to permit the events to continue for three more years.

The Duke had asked Nell to attend the bull-baiting event with him that Sunday. She had told him she disliked bull-baiting intensely, but would come out to Waltham Cross and visit the Steeles while he watched the baiting. It would be her last chance to see Richard and Mary before the new season opened next fall. They spent a pleasurable and relaxed afternoon together. Then Richard and Nell left Mary and Edith and the baby in the cottage while they went for a walk in mid-afternoon after tea.

It was a rare summer day. The sun was bright and warm in an unblemished cerulean sky. The hills, the trees, the shrubs and growth all around them were lush, painted every shade of green from palest lime to deepest jade. Linnets, robins, larks and blue jays swooped and soared, singing in various natural harmonies. Richard and Nell sat in the shade beneath a thickly leafed oak tree. A sudden roar of crowd noise sounded from the east.

"Sounds like the torture of the bull is proceeding satisfactorily," said Richard.

Nell took Richard's hand.

"I wish I could help you, Richard."

"I'm all right." He smiled wanly. "I'll be fine. I'll be busy at Richmond Hill . . . How is the Duke?"

"He's very good to me, Richard. Very sweet, attentive . . ."

She drew a deep breath.

"I've moved into his house in Pall Mall. He has a large mansion in Windsor. He goes there almost every summer."

Richard idly tore a cluster of buttercups halfway down their stems and gazed at the small, shiny yellow buds.

"He also has a small cottage nearby, in Windsor. I'm moving into that for the summer," Nell continued.

Richard reached for her hand, leaned forward and kissed her cheek.

"Don't look so defiant, so guilty, Nell. I have never known anyone who merits a happy summer more . . . and one, I hope, that will be filled with tender loving."

As it turned out, the tender loving began that very night. Edmund Fox drove up to the cottage in his carriage, visited briefly, and then he and Nell rode off. On the way back to London, they stopped at a small country inn where they spent the night. In the past two weeks they had learned a good deal about each other. Now, on this idyllic, star bright summer night, they began to learn a great deal more. The Duke was a tender lover, and Nell Faversham, sexually starved for more than seven hundred troubled nights, was the most passionate, fiery partner Edmund Fox had ever enjoyed. And the passion was, in no sense, pretended.

Richard, once again unable to fall asleep, stared at those same brilliant twinkling stars. In the west bedroom, baby Felicia began to cry. He heard the sounds of Edith climbing from her bed, shuffling to the baby's crib. He heard the creaking of her chair as she rocked back and forth, softly singing a lullaby to the crying infant. Richard was ashamed because of the ridiculous feeling which overcame him: to have someone sing a lullaby to him. He felt lost, empty and very much alone.

302

✺ 27 ✺

The girl's name was Wilhelmina Housman, and it was one of the few times Richard had been with a woman since Felicia's death. She had cinnamon-colored hair, which hung over her gently sloping shoulders, down to her hips. On the right side, the hair had fallen over her chest, concealing all of her full, round breast except the hard, protruding sepia nipple and the areola surrounding it. The ends of the silken hair, hanging in front, touched the cinnamon triangle of pubic hair between her ample thighs. With a sweep of her right hand, and a toss of her head, she whipped the hair behind her. With her left hand, she continued to caress Richard Steele's genitals, and stroke his limp member, trying to coax it into serviceable rigidity.

Richard lay flat on his back, in the bed in the small room of the public house in Richmond Hill. His hands were clasped under his head; his eyes were closed and there was a half-tortured, half-embarrassed expression on his face.

"Goddamit, Dickie," said the naked, fifteen-year-old actress, "my arm feels like it is about to fall off. . . . What must I do to arouse you?"

She had already done all she knew, all she had learned in several years of abundant and colorful sexual activity as a member of a company of traveling comedians. All to no avail. Richard could not be stirred.

"Forgive me, Willie," he muttered wearily. "It's not you. . . ."

"Perhaps you had too much to drink," said Willie, getting on her knees to try again with her warm, moist mouth.

303

Richard knew it was not that. He *had* consumed a great deal of Irish whiskey, drinking with Fitzhugh Fitzhugh before and after supper, after the last show. But three weeks earlier, when he had found himself in this same bedchamber, his regular room at the house for the summer, with another voluptuous female member of the Colby company, an oversexed, thirtyish Italian actress named Lucia Pastorini, he had done no drinking at all and had been unable to perform.

Lucia had used every technique known to a practiced international courtesan, and just after dawn had finally aroused Richard to rigidity, when he chanced to look out the window over Lucia's lovely olive shoulder and see a squirrel run across the bough of the maple tree. A numbing feeling of *déjà vu* overwhelmed him, and he wondered foolishly if that was the same squirrel which had scampered across the bough that unforgettable night he and Felicia had spent here. He immediately became limp, and unarousable thereafter.

He had deliberately taken the same room when he arrived at Richmond Hill for this summer's work, telling himself that he must overcome these stupid psychological blocks, that somehow he must find his way back to the world of the living. But nothing seemed to work. Lucia cursed him roundly in Italian, turned on her side with her back to him and soon fell asleep. Her snoring sounded angry and frustrated.

The episodes with Wilhelmina and Lucia gave quick rise to the rumor around the Colby company that Richard preferred boys and men, and three evenings after the disappointing night with Willie, a forty-year-old actor in the company graciously invited Richard to spend the night with him. Richard declined firmly and angrily enough to convince one and all that males held no sexual appeal for him whatsoever. The company was baffled by Richard's lack of interest in their favorite offstage sport, but soon accepted the situation, and pursued their bedchamber activities in various orthodox and unorthodox combinations without this strange young man from Lincoln's Inn Fields.

The roles in the presentations at Richmond Hill were not nearly so demanding as those at Lincoln's Inn, so Richard soon found an additional new way to occupy his time and mind. He worked with Sidney Colby in editing, adapting and condensing many of the works of Shakespeare,

Marlowe and other renowned playwrights. He discovered that Fitzhugh Fitzhugh wrote short farces and comedic skits, and he began to collaborate with the magician on some of these. Fitzhugh also taught him some new magic tricks. On many nights, they sat in the pub's kitchen, talking (or less often, writing) until Richard was quite numb with fatigue and whiskey, and ready for sleep. He frequently awoke the next morning with an aching head, and a thick, evil-tasting tongue, but he was always ready for his performance in early afternoon and evening.

One night after Richard had matched Fitzhugh drink for drink through the first five goblets of Irish whiskey, he said, "Fitz. What did you see in Felicia's palm that first evening we met?"

Fitzhugh looked into Richard's eyes.

"I saw an early death," he said. "More . . . more . . ." he shook his head sadly.

"More . . . I saw her entombed in a coffin of ice."

Richard held his hand across the table, palm up.

"See me an ending soon, Fitz. Ice or flame. I do not care which . . . but see it soon!"

Fitzhugh shook his head.

"It's the whiskey talkin', lad. Ye've too much to give. . . . Ye're as foine a player as ever trod the boards. . . . The dear lass would have wanted ye to go on. . . ."

Richard pushed his hand forward.

"See, Fitz. Read and say . . ."

Fitzhugh took his hand, stared at the palm for several moments. The candle on the table flickered in a sudden draft from the open window. Fitzhugh nodded.

"I see a journey . . . a long journey."

"Dammit, Fitz. You speak like an old gypsy. Say me some truth."

"Drink yer drink, Richard, and hold yer tongue. Ye've as long a lifeline as I've seen in a thousand palms."

Richard finished his whiskey.

"Hold her mem'ry in yer heart, lad. But don't let yerself rot, like overripe fruit. The lass lived a brave life, and would'a wished ye to live likewise."

A letter from Nell Faversham just before the close of the summer season bore the same message. She described the medieval castle at Windsor, which Richard had never seen, and the picturesque town itself. The Duke's estate was not far from the castle, and the small cottage Nell occupied was less than a mile from the home of the Duke. She had seen the king and a party of courtiers riding back from a hunt one day, and she and the Duke frequently took quiet rides through the cool, shady forest.

"I am concentrating particularly," she wrote, "on the plays in which you and I will have roles, and I look forward with great pleasure to working with you again. I hope that in this new season I will begin to approximate the excellence of your playing, and be a credit to the company.

"But most of all, dear friend Richard," she said, "I hope your own summer has brought you peace of mind, and the renewed zest for life, which I know lies buried within you. I know how dearly you loved Felicia Wandrous, and I understand how her sudden departure would have seemed the end of your world. Although I did not have the privilege and joy of knowing her, I believe simply from having seen her on stage, that she was the kind of person, who would wish you to go on—not only with your excellent work in the theater, but with your life.

"Until I see you in September, I beg to remain ever, your humble and grateful friend, Nell Faversham."

Back at Waltham Cross, with a full week before he was to report at Lincoln's Inn Fields, Mary expressed concern over the fact that he looked gaunt and haggard, and he cut down drastically on his drinking. Edith Forrest's schoolmaster, Josiah Olney, came to visit one day, and Richard, Mary, Josiah and Edith had an interesting afternoon playing cribbage and walking through Epping Forest. Watching Josiah and Edith feeding and playing with the cherubic-looking seven-month-old Felicia, Richard for the first time felt a warm tenderness in his heart. This, and his mother's own increasingly glowing health, made him realize that he did indeed have a good deal for which to be thankful.

But on the following day Father Whittaker rode out to Waltham Cross with more disheartening news. Richard could not imagine how he had been able to complete the journey without tumbling from his horse. Richard and Mary met him as he staggered up the road to the door. Edith had taken the baby for a stroll in her carriage.

Father Whittaker put an arm around Mary, kissed her on the cheek, then embraced Richard with the other arm, as they guided him to a chair at the kitchen table.

He pounded the table with his right fist.

Indignant, excited, incoherent, the priest nevertheless finally managed to convey that Monsignor Walsh was going to bring him up on charges for having buried Felicia Wandrous, a non-Catholic, indeed an atheist, without administering last rites, in consecrated ground. Mary and Richard became as furious as Father Whittaker. Richard had brought a half-dozen bottles of Irish whiskey back from Richmond Hill, and he now opened one. They talked heatedly about Christianity, and religious bigotry. Mary Steele became drunk for the first time in her life. When she passed out, Edith and Richard put her to bed. Father Whittaker continued to drink until he fell asleep, his head resting in his arms on the table, and Richard lifted, heaved and tugged him to his own bed.

Richard sat up drinking long after Edith retired. Twice during the night the baby cried. Richard cried, too, and presently fell asleep, slumped in the chair in which he sat. It later developed that Father Whittaker was not excommunicated, but he was put through a long, difficult hearing, and sternly warned never to commit such a deed again. For the next six days, Richard resumed his heavy drinking.

On the seventh day, even though he felt poorly, Richard found himself eager to get to the theater for the first meetings of the new season. He was particularly anxious to see Nell Faversham again. Nell was already on stage with a cluster of other players when Richard arrived. She rushed to him, threw her arms around him and kissed him enthusiastically. Then she held him at arm's length, and an expression of concern showed in her emerald eyes.

"You look not at all rested, Richard! Was the summer difficult?"

Richard shrugged.

"Not really," he said. "What happened to your lip?"

The left side of Nell's mouth was slightly swollen. It marred, slightly, the healthy, vital look of her. Her cheeks glowed with a warm peach color; her eyes sparkled; there was a sheen to her red hair.

"I spent yesterday at Goodman's Fields, helping Jerome Wrexham become familiar with his new duties as manager. He has not changed."

"Did he strike you?"

She laughed again, shook her head.

"No. He was standing over my shoulder as I was going through the account books for scenery painting and carpentry. He slipped his hand down into my bodice. I bit his arm, and when he pulled his hand away, he hit my mouth rather sharply. . . .

Richard had noticed that Catherine Clark had not yet arrived at the theater.

"Was Clark with him?" he asked.

"No. She stayed in Dublin. Jerry brought back a beautiful young man named Brendan Geoghan. He's seventeen and has already had two plays produced in Ireland. He's writing a new play with Jerry and living with Jerry. He has the most soulful doe eyes I've ever seen."

"I didn't know Wrexham wrote plays."

Nell smiled.

"Perhaps he's writing with Geoghan in the broader sense: counsel, advice, loving encouragement. . . . At any rate, if the play's produced, I'm sure you will find Jerry's name on it as coauthor."

She paused, then said, "He's also developed another talent. He's learned to play the lute."

Gilbert Weston joined Nell and Richard then. He had had a touch of the gout during the season at Bath, but it had passed quickly, and for the most part he had enjoyed a busy and prosperous summer. Susannah Forbish was not returning to the company. She had married Quincy, and would travel with him and the circus. Weston had already replaced her with Kitty DuPree, a seasoned actress, who left the Drury Lane company to join the Lincoln's Inn Fields group. He had just learned that Catherine Clark was not returning, so he had initiated a search for a replacement for her.

As was his annual custom, Weston had visited Farley Shannon on his return from Bath. He told Richard and Nell that the distinguished actor and coach had had a difficult summer.

"His strange disorder seems to be worsening," he told them. "Dr. Thorndike is at a complete loss to help him."

Richard rode out to see his elderly friend that very afternoon. Richard was shocked at Shannon's appearance. The old man's long, lean body seemed to have shrunk. His curved spine had his upper body into a permanent stoop. The unrelenting agony of his ailment had carved new lines in his ashen face and glazed over the keen eyes. Still, he extended a bony hand, and greeted Richard cheerfully.

"It is a great pleasure to see you once again, lad," he said. "How was the Richmond Hill season?"

"Quite good. Colby sends his deepest respect and fondest wishes."

Over several glasses of port, they sat and talked for some time. Shannon suddenly leaned forward and peered closely at Richard.

"Unless my eyes deceive me, Richard," he said, "you appear rather haggard. Have you been drinking?"

Richard nodded.

"A bit . . . possibly a bit too much."

Shannon shook his head.

"Cease, Richard. I beg you. Too many fine actors seek comfort in alcohol. Fight the temptation. Keep control. . . ."

Richard looked into his pain-filled gray eyes and suddenly felt vaguely ashamed of himself. .

"I will," he said. "Are you well enough to work with me occasionally this season?"

Shannon smiled a weary smile.

"Of course, lad. You hardly need my help any longer, but it will give me the greatest pleasure—as it always has —to work with you."

In the next few weeks, Richard did bring his drinking under control. He visited Shannon three or four times each week. Many days, they did not work at all, but merely talked about the theater, or played chess or cribbage. When they did work, it was for very brief periods. Richard got immense satisfaction out of the obvious pleasure Shannon derived from his company, and Richard himself enjoyed every moment with the old man. Though they worked infrequently, Richard recognized that Shannon's coaching often enabled him to put an extra fine edge on a performance to create subtle but vital nuances in a role.

The season went extremely well—the best the company had ever experienced. More and more, Richard was discovering that the most fulfilling hours of his life were those he spent onstage. For the duration of each play, he left Richard Steele and his empty heart in some dark corner of the deepest backstage recesses, while he entered the body and mind, the heart and soul of the person he was playing. For hours he reveled in the joys, suffered the sorrows, gloried in the triumphs, withstood the defeats of numerous and various human beings who were not Richard Steele. He gradually discovered that this utter absorption with each of the characters he portrayed enabled him to understand himself and his own problems better.

By midseason, he was enjoying the weekends at Waltham Cross with his mother and Edith Forrest and the child, Felicia. He fished in a nearby stream, took long walks with Edith in Epping Forest, helped Mary with the garden and once even permitted himself to be talked into attending the nearby bull-baiting with George Storey. On several weekends, when the Duke was otherwise occupied, Nell Faversham came out to Waltham Cross to visit. The transformation in Nell continued to amaze Richard.

Onstage, there was a chemistry between her and Richard, which made them favorites of London's theater goers. For a time, Weston, and even Richard, feared that the fact that Nell was the Duke's mistress might create morale problems in the company. But she was so careful never to use her relationship with the Duke in any way (indeed, she never made any reference to it), and she worked so diligently that she won the respect and friendship of every member of the group.

Wrexham created no problems. He managed the Goodman's Fields playhouse shrewdly. Since the nonpatent theaters were not permitted to present dramas except in the guise of rehearsals, Wrexham concentrated on starring himself in musical concerts. On his last trip to Dublin, he had lost weight, had shaved off his beard and mustache, and now he looked almost as young and as handsome as his new roommate, Brendan Geoghan.

His musical repertoire was ingeniously selected and paced. He presented two different programs of some twenty-five minutes each, in which he skillfully intermixed a wide variety of songs. There were favorite songs from earlier plays. Such as *Britons, Strike Home* from *Bonduca* and *I Burn, I Burn* from *Don Quixote*.

There were patriotic songs, such as *The Roast Beef of Old England,* or *Oh, London Is a Fine Town,* or *The Hyde Park Grenadier,* along with compositions appealing to various trades and occupations, including *The Sailor's Song, Song in the Character of a Butcher's Wife,* or *Ballad on My Lady's Twitcher.* These appealed greatly to the galleries, where many of the patrons had sailed the seas, dealt in meats or twitched the corsets of ladies of fashion.

The programs also included love songs, and naughty ballads to win the approval of the pit and particularly the beaux and their ladies in the boxes. One of the favorite songs of the older ladies of quality was *The Misses Lamentation for Want of Their Vizard Masks in the Playhouse*. This humorous ditty bemoaned the law banning the flirtatious masks, which was passed in 1704.

It was a mark of Wrexham's superb talent that he could perform all of these widely varied types of songs with great success. To further ensure his popularity, and the appeal of the musical programs, he imported a new master of music from Brandenburg, Germany, and persuaded the Duke to permit him to add three more musicians to the nine-piece orchestra. The new German master of music brought in an extraordinarily talented flageolet player from his own town. There were precious few competent English musicians in these times. On several of the more romantic numbers, Wrexham accompanied himself on lute.

In the dramatic "rehearsals," he featured himself as the dashing lover, or the mischievous beau, who cuckolds the dull husband, in the bawdiest comedies and dramas he could find.

On two occasions, at Pickering's Inn, he attempted to interest Nell Faversham in a rendezvous, but she made it clear that she was as faithful to the Duke as if she were married to him. Wrexham was bitter about these rejections, and resented Nell only because her actions cast doubts about his irresistibility. So far as his sexual needs were concerned, they appeared to be served well by his new Irish male lover, augmented by fairly regular visits to Cleopatra Magruder.

As Gilbert Weston frequently did, he wound up the season with a Shakespearean series. The last of the dramas, to be presented in the final week, was *Julius Caesar*, and Richard was to play Brutus; Nell, his wife, Portia. This was one of Shannon's favorite Shakespearean tragedies. On the Monday before the Thursday night on which the play was to be presented, Richard went out to Shannon's after the initial reading at the theater. The old man seemed to Richard so feeble that Richard said he had not come to work, but just for a brief visit, and to let Shannon know they were doing *Caesar*. Shannon nevertheless directed Richard to a place in his bookshelf, where he found a rare quarto edition of the play, published in 1690. The edition listed the cast in which Shannon and Thomas Betterton had played. It had originally been printed as a playgoers' guide. Now Shannon insisted on reading through the key scenes of the drama with Richard.

But soon after they began to read, Shannon clutched both his knees and grimaced in pain. He tried to arch his bent back. He groaned.

"The pain now often becomes quite severe, lad. It seems to leap from one joint in my ancient body to another—unnnhhhh—pour us a drink, please."

Richard did, and he drank with Shannon, and gave him a medicine that Dr. Thorndike had prescribed. The medicine obviously contained a potent drug, because less than fifteen minutes after Shannon had swallowed it, he began to slur his words. His eyes closed, his head fell to his bony chest and he was asleep. Richard picked him up carefully. Despite his height, the old man weighed surprisingly little. Richard carried him into his bedchamber and placed him carefully on the bed. Quietly he left the house.

The following day, just before noon, a young man, who was a fencing instructor in the school adjoining Shannon's home, came to the theater and gave Richard a package carefully wrapped in scarlet velvet, tied with a golden cord. Richard recognized the young man, to whom he had been introduced on a visit to Shannon's some time ago.

"Mr. Shannon asked me to bring this to you this morning, sir," the young man said. Richard thanked him and, when the rehearsal ended, went to his dressing table and opened the package. It contained the Roman sword Richard had seen on the wall of Shannon's theater room. He stared at the glistening jewels encrusting the hilt and ran his fingers over the rich, brown leather sheath. The placard, in its gilded wooden frame, lay under the sword. Richard moved the sword and read the beautifully lettered message again.

Under the placard was a folded sheet of foolscap. Richard sat and read the letter Shannon had written:

My dear Richard,

I hope you will not have too much difficulty reading the scribbling of this palsied hand. Despite the potency of Dr. Thorndike's vile-tasting medicines, I was awakened by the pain in the middle of the night, and I remembered that I had wished to make you a gift of my most treasured possession, the sword given me by my good friend, Betterton. I send it along now, because I realize you may not have the opportunity to visit me again before you open *Julius Caesar* on Thursday.

Richard frowned. He wondered what could have given Shannon the idea he would not come out before then to work on the Brutus role. He read on.

It was not so long ago, my dear young friend, that we worked together to prepare you for the role of Brutus's faithful servant. I smile now as I recall how earnestly you strove to perfect your portrayal of the devoted Strato. No role too small, no lines too few for you to approach with anything less than the determination to play with perfection.

And now, so soon, you play Brutus. We will not work nearly so hard to prepare you for the portrayal of this heroic and noble character, simply because there is little—indeed, virtually nothing—more I can teach you. By sheer hard effort, by instinct, by a talent the good Lord bestowed upon you—even by the cruel accident of fate, which robbed you of a great love, thus forcing you to lavish all your own passion on your second love, the stage—by all these, you have become as fine a young actor as the theater has ever known.

Richard's eyes misted. Nell Faversham came to stand beside him, and he looked up at her briefly, but returned to Shannon's letter.

I am exceedingly proud of you and grateful to have played a small part in your development. For my humble services, I would now like to submit my final bill. It is the earnest request that you remember always that the theater is one of man's nobler arts, and that acting is a profession of which you may be justly proud. In a long life, I have found it to be so, and have spent a good part of that life attempting to inculcate this truth in others by my actions and my teachings. I love and admire you deeply, young Richard Steele, and I know you will carry on the work of

Your humble servant,
Farley Shannon

Tears rolled down Richard's cheeks. Quietly, he handed the letter to Nell Faversham. With one arm on his shoulder, she read Shannon's obviously painfully written, shaky words. Gilbert Weston chanced to walk by Richard's table, and sensed the deeply emotional atmosphere. He looked questioningly at Richard and Nell. Richard wiped the moisture from his cheeks, waved a hand to indicate the letter which Nell handed to Weston. The manager's and the actress's eyes glistened with tears, too, as Weston handed the letter back to Richard.

"I would like to ride out to Farley's now, to thank him," said Richard, realizing they had not yet finished the morning's rehearsal.

"By all means, lad," said Weston.

Neither Weston nor Nell had said anything to suggest that they even remotely suspected that Farley Shannon's letter was a farewell message. Even though Richard had the eerie feeling that it might well be, he doggedly refused to permit the possibility to enter his mind. He spurred Sally O to her greatest speed to get to Stratford.

Less than a quarter-mile from Shannon's home, a sudden storm broke. There was unusual daytime thunder, and lightning slashed the darkening skies in brilliant, angry spasms. Richard was soaking wet when he reached Shannon's home. He ran up the short path to the door, lifted and dropped the brass knocker sharply, again and again. When there was no response, he pushed open the unlocked door. There was no one in the kitchen, the main room of the house. The silence seemed to Richard to have the quality of an invisible wall, through which he had to push his way.

He moved into the bedchamber. The bed was unmade and empty. Richard heard hard breathing as he walked toward the door to the theater room, and realized the breathing he was hearing was his own. There was only one window in the theater room, on the north side. The light which entered the room through the window was soft. Richard saw Farley Shannon, seated in his favorite Queen Anne chair on the small stage, at stage left, a few feet in from the wings. This was the position from which he had worked with Richard a hundred times and more.

Richard ran up to the stage. Shannon had obviously died in pain. It showed in his staring eyes, in the frozen gaping mouth, in the death grip of the long fingers of the bony right hand, clutching the arm of the chair. Crushed in his left fist was the quarto edition of Julius Caesar.

A sustained rumble of thunder sounded, and ended abruptly in a booming crash, which seemed to shake the thatch-roofed house. Three quick flashes of lightning filled the room with a sudden alternating succession of almost blinding iridescence and then darkness. Richard threw his arms around the already stiff and discolored corpse of Farley Shannon and pressed his face to Shannon's cold cheek. Inexplicably, the words of Calpurnia, wife of Julius Caesar, ran through his head.

"When beggars die there are no comets seen. The heavens themselves blaze forth the death of princes."

As he sobbed, and tears streamed down his cheeks, he heard Caesar's reply.

"Cowards die many times before their deaths; the valiant never taste death but once. Of all the wonders that I yet have heard, it seems to me most strange that men should fear—seeing that death, a necessary end, will come when it will come."

Richard sank to the floor beside Shannon's chair. He did not know how long he sat there. Finally he went over to the adjoining fencing school, and he and the fencing master fetched the village constable.

Shannon was buried the morning of the day on which *Julius Caesar* opened. It seemed all London turned out for the services at St. Paul's Cathedral. Onstage that night, Richard found himself performing with the most supreme confidence he had ever experienced. In his earliest entrance, Shannon's sword, hanging from the heavy leather belt around his waist, gave him a mystic sense of power he had never before felt on stage or off. He *was* Brutus.

With the sword in his hand, as he and his fellow conspirators slew Caesar, he was a zealous patriot ridding his country of a despotic, power-crazed tyrant. At the tragedy's end, when he ran upon the sword, now held firmly in the hand of his devoted servant, Strato, he died Brutus's noble death. The sword seemed to have power which truly transformed Richard into Brutus, and transported him to Rome. He did not seem to be acting at all. The same uncanny transformation took place on all three nights of the presentation.

The veteran theater-goer, who wrote for *The Spectator*, and who had earlier ventured to compare Richard's performance of Hamlet to that of the great Thomas Betterton, wrote of Richard's Brutus:

> Through the years we have seen several performances of extraordinary excellence, displays of the thespian art so exquisite as to make one tremble with terror, weep in deepest grief, sing for joy. But this spectator maintains—nay, insists—that he has never seen a more inspired performance than that of young Richard Steele in the role of Brutus in *The Tragedy of Julius Caesar* at the Lincoln's Fields Inn playhouse last week.

At the last performance of the play, not only the audience, but the entire cast on stage, after the final curtain, applauded Richard's work. He was enormously moved as he bowed again and again in deepest thanks.

It was a fitting end to the season. In Richard's heart it was also a pathetically inadequate expression of gratitude, and a tribute, however insignificant, to the noble life of Farley Shannon.

28

One of the ladies of quality at the last performance of *The Tragedy of Julius Caesar* was the Marchioness of Clanisham. She sat in the nearest box at stage left. She applauded delicately along with the rest of the far less restrained audience at the play's end. With her was the Marquess, who had dozed through most of the performance, but had been awakened by the outburst of applause.

"I must have that young man!" said Lady Clanisham. The Marquess could not hear her for the noise.

"Eh?" he asked, leaning toward her.

"I must have that young man," she repeated, nodding toward the stage where Richard was taking a final bow.

"Of course, my dear," said the Marquess.

He knew she would have him, and she did. Few of the Marchioness's wishes went unfulfilled. She had been born Elizabeth Finley, thirty-six years earlier, the only child of an earl, and had been catered to since the day of her birth. At nineteen, she had married Rupert Seymour, the Marquess of Clanisham, who was then forty-one. He went to new extremes in pampering his regally beautiful bride. Seven months after their marriage, the Marchioness gave birth to twin girls, whom they named Daphne and Diana.

A few years after their marriage, the Marquess learned that a gambler and entrepreneur named Richard Nash had promoted some twenty thousand pounds, which he was planning to invest in improving the roads from London to Bath, and in modernizing and beautifying the already popular resort. The Marquess bought several large tracts of land, and built an elegant mansion in Bath. Al-

317

most immediately, the young Marchioness assumed leadership of the elite social set at the resort. Nash was highly successful in his development plans for Bath, and by 1718 it was the favorite watering place of the English nobility, virtually all the Kingdom's gentry, and was frequently visited by royalty from friendly foreign countries. The Marchioness gave elaborate galas and supper parties at the mansion, and presented plays and entertainments in her huge, elegantly decorated assembly rooms all through the summer.

Now, on the closing night of *Julius Caesar* at Lincoln's Inn Fields (with the Marquess wearily bringing up the rear), she made her way backstage. Actors, beaux and their ladies alike, made way for her as she strode by, leaving an aromatic trail of powder and perfume in her wake. Lady Clanisham was a striking-looking woman. While current fashions found almost all women of quality wearing their hair in simple styles, close to the head, the Marchioness wore her rich amber hair in a swirling, towering crown, a coiffure which would not come into fashion for several years. Her gown was a shimmering Persian silk, silver in color. A recent act of Parliament prohibited importation of materials from Persia, India and China, and many ladies of fashion had given up wearing such materials, but not the Marchioness. Above the bodice of her gown, her full, rounded bosom swelled. A brilliant ruby hung from a gold chain around her graceful neck, and a glistening lip salve gave her full red mouth a softer radiance than the ruby.

In the crowded backstage area, people moved aside to let her pass. She quickly made her way to Gilbert Weston.

Weston greeted her effusively and respectfully. For the past three summer seasons, she had been trying to persuade him to give up managing and acting in the New Theatre, the small twenty-five by fifty foot playhouse in Kingsmead Street at Bath. She wanted him to present the plays in the elegant and spacious assembly rooms in her home. It took her less than twenty minutes of negotiation to convince Weston that, this summer, he must make the change. Her forceful charm, plus doubling the fee the New Theatre could pay him left Weston no choice.

"You understand, of course, Gilbert," she said, after they had agreed upon his remuneration and perquisites, "that I expect you to bring along young Richard Steele."

Weston hesitated.

"I'm not sure, my dear Lady," he said, "I believe young Steele may be committed to Richmond Hill."

"Uncommit him," commanded the Duchess. "I'll pay him fifty pounds for the summer . . ."

"But . . ."

". . . and as I've arranged for you, I'll also provide him with his own suite of rooms in my home at no charge."

"But, Lady . . ."

"But me no further buts, Gilbert. I also wish you to purchase for him at my expense an entire wardrobe from silver-buckled shoes to periwig. On the evening of your arrival, I will have a gala supper for you and young Mr. Steele, and I want him to be appropriately attired."

Richard had not made a final commitment to Sidney Colby, and when Weston told him about Lady Clanisham's offer, he was stunned, and readily accepted it.

Bath was some hundred and twenty miles west of London, just south of the Cotswold Hills. Even traveling over the improved roads, it still took three days to make the trip. Richard had never even gone to any of the wells in London itself. On one occasion, Mary had tried to persuade him to accompany her to one in Clerkenwell, named Bagnigge Wells, after Bagnigge House, where Nell Gwyn, the actress/mistress of Charles II had lived. Another time, he had had supper with Father Whittaker at Sadler's Wells, the most popular of the spas in the city. But Bath was a revelation to him. Weston directed the driver of the carriage to a shopping center in the village. Here were clustered as smart an array of small retail establishments as Richard had ever seen on his few visits to the fashionable West End in London. It was early afternoon of a sun-drenched June day, and the clean, tree-lined streets were crowded with shoppers. All were expensively dressed, but they seemed an odd mix of bright young pleasure seekers, and elderly ladies and gentlemen with various afflictions.

Weston led Richard into the shop of a peruker. Richard assumed Weston wished to purchase a wig for himself, which indeed he did. But when he insisted Richard try on some of the periwigs, Richard protested. He had never worn a wig offstage in his life, and had no wish to spend money on one now. Weston had held back the information that Lady Clanisham desired to finance a complete wardrobe for Richard. Now, he explained that she wanted Richard to be sure to live up to the image of him she had created for her friends, sartorially, as well as in every other way, befitting one of London's leading young actors.

Richard felt uncomfortable, but at Weston's insistence, tried on various tye wigs, long bobs, bag wigs, spencers, and tuck-up wigs, and even an ornate, high-fashion, full-bottomed wig, divided into three masses of curls. He finally selected a simple wig, precisely the same color as his own raven hair. It was of equal length all around, but divided in two in the back, and tied with small, black silk bows.

Weston bought himself one of the full-bottomed, curled wigs. It looked well on his florid, round face. From the perruquier's, they went to an exclusive men's apparel shop, and thence to a cobbler's, and by four o'clock Richard had acquired a wardrobe he had never dreamed of owning. He had a pearl-gray velvet coat with large, heavily embroidered cuffs, tight-fitting breeches to match, a new turquoise shirt of wool with a ruffled collar, and stockings of the same material and shade. His new shoes were gray leather, with high turquoise heels and silver buckles. He felt awkward walking in them.

Still, when he appraised himself early that evening, in the long looking glass in the bedchamber of his suite, a prideful vanity possessed him. Unconsciously, for the first time in his life, he drew in his stomach, expanded his chest, lifted his chin, smiled—almost a smirk—with utter satisfaction at the handsome figure of the elegantly attired man in the mirror, smiling back at him. Had he been able to muster even a trace of his earlier objectivity, he would have realized his posture was quite like Wrexham's and just shy of a peacock's preening.

This sudden self-confidence and indulgence in vanity was strange, for only hours earlier, when a butler opened the door of the huge brick mansion, Richard was literally moist with nervousness. His stomach churned. His lips and throat were dry.

The sight of Lady Clanisham did nothing to alleviate his distress. She was gracious enough as she rose from the ornate Queen Anne chair and smiled at her guests. There was certainly nothing intimidating in the fluid, graceful manner in which she walked to them, delicate hand extended in greeting.

"Welcome, dear Gilbert," she said softly, then turned to Richard, again extending her hand. Richard knelt awkwardly, took her hand, and touched its back with his lips.

320

As he looked into her gold-flecked, brown eyes, he had the uneasy feeling that she was appraising him, the way she might a new racing stallion she had just purchased. Still, her deep, rich voice was warm as she said, "And most welcome, Mr. Steele. We are honored to have the finest young actor in London in our home."

With her were her sixteen-year-old twin daughters, Daphne and Diana. They knew Gilbert Weston from earlier seasons, and after they had greeted him, Lady Clanisham introduced them to Richard. They seemed like younger and slighter replicas of Lady Clanisham herself. Physically, they were identical. Both had the same glowing amber hair as their mother, the same full, sensuous mouth, straight regal nose and high cheekbones. Their waists were slightly slimmer than the Marchioness's, and their bosoms not as full, though quite well-developed. They even had the same gold-flecked brown eyes, but it was in the expression in their eyes that the twins were different. He was not quite sure what the difference was. Both gazed up at him worshipfully. But later, as he recaptured the moment in his mind, he realized that in Daphne's eyes mischief danced, and Diana's expression was shy and serious. Their openly idolatrous attitude enabled Richard to overcome his own awe of their mother and the overwhelming, ornate surroundings. He literally felt his nervousness evaporating and self-confidence returning.

It was the first time in Richard's career that he became fully aware of the adulation of his audience. The first flush of awareness came, of course, onstage after the final performance of *Julius Caesar*, with the ovation he received from both colleagues and playgoers. Lady Clanisham's fantastically generous insistence that he play the season in Bath had fanned the fire of his growing self-esteem. Her praise in welcoming him bellowed the flame once more. The obvious adoration in the postures and expressions of Daphne and Diana was an added fuel, which created a potentially dangerous inferno of self-worship. For this evening, as he went down to meet the guests who were to honor him and Gilbert Weston at supper, Richard was not thinking of what Farley Shannon had done for him, or how Felicia Wandrous had guided him through the frightful earliest days. He was full of the feeling that he was probably the finest actor in the English theater, and that people, young and old—particularly these noble people who summered at Bath—idolized him. *What a feeling! What a glorious, indescribable feeling!*

On the journey from London, Gilbert Weston had explained to Richard that the repertoire at Bath would be quite different from that of Lincoln's Inn Fields. Lady Clanisham and her friends preferred lighter fare. They liked obscure one-act plays such as *The Petticoat Plotter* and *The Hypochondriack,* and outright farces and musical pieces as *entr'acte* entertainment.

Among the works of the better known playwrights, they preferred William Wycherly's *The Country Wife* and, particularly, William Congreve's *Love for Love.* An infrequently performed play they favored was Francis Beaumont's satire on the popular theater, the mock heroic comedy called, *The Knight of the Burning Pestle.* The Shakespearean favorites were *The Merry Wives of Windsor, The Two Gentlemen of Verona, Much Ado About Nothing* and *The Tempest.*

"They will frequently have entire programs of music and dance and many novelty attractions," said Weston, "and on such occasions, we will not be involved at all. Lady Clanisham brings in a superior master of music and a choreographer each season."

Richard found the schedules far less demanding than even the light workload at Richmond Hill. In the first week he worked three evenings, and each of his appearances was received with great applause. In the second week, he played Ferdinand, son to Alonso, the King of Naples, in a version of *The Tempest* such as he had never seen or heard of before. It was a musical version, with much singing and dancing, and Heinrich Bauer, a German master of music, and Wilson Taylor, a choreographer, had as much to do with adapting the play and staging it as did Gilbert Weston. Richard was particularly fascinated by the atmosphere dances, which Taylor created. One was called *The Four Winds,* another *The Six Watermen,* and a third, the most spectacular of all, *The Grand Dance of the Spirits.* He enjoyed performing the two numbers he sang, although Herr Bauer was not too pleased with his musicality, since the best Richard could manage was to talk-sing the songs.

It seemed that no matter what he played, the elite audiences loved him. They not only applauded his onstage work, but vied with each other for his company and attendance at the social events they sponsored. Richard's seduction by the Bath regulars was complete. Early each morning, he rushed down to the dungeonlike dressing room of the baths, donned his full-length bathing suit and stumbled his way through the steamy passage into the shallow bubbling waters, open to the warm sun and air.

On most mornings, Lady Clanisham and the Marquess, as well as Gilbert Weston and several other ladies and gentlemen Richard had met at previous assemblies would visit the baths. All were dressed in full-length bathing suits. The ladies doused themselves daintily, careful not to splash too much water into the small floating trays attached to their waists. The trays contained handkerchiefs to daub away perspiration, as well as snuff boxes and puff boxes. Many of the ladies would converge on Richard, and he would do his best to appear modest in the face of the lavish compliments they paid him and his acting.

After the bathing, Richard would join a convivial group in the pump room, where a small orchestra supplied soothing music, while the guests drank their prescribed quotas of the unpleasant tasting mineral waters. From the pump room, Richard walked the short distance back to the mansion of the Marquess and Marchioness of Clanisham for breakfast. Richard had never seen, let alone eaten, breakfasts of this kind before. Everyone present, including Daphne and Diana, had at least one glass of ale or beer; the Marquess had three or four, as did most of the other male guests; Lady Clanisham herself had one. Weston usually had two glasses of ale, and soon Richard found himself drinking an equal amount. With the beer or ale, they ate large slices of wheat breads, thickly covered with butter, and platters full of anchovies, pickled oysters or other savories.

Then, no matter how wicked or illicit the behavior of the evening previous—and a good deal of naughty activity went on—all adjoined to the abbey for morning services. Richard did not attend the services. He took the occasion to return to his chambers to study a part, or if his own rendezvous of the night before—and he had an increasing number—had tired him, he undressed and slumbered for an hour or two. Many early afternoons, he took fencing lessons with Wilson Taylor or spent time riding, strolling around the attractive countryside or shopping with one companion or another. He bought an expensive damask table cloth, a lovely wool shawl for Mary and a box of embroidered linen handkerchiefs for Nell.

In Bath, the dinner hour was three o'clock. Dinner at Lady Clanisham's reminded Richard of the extravagant spread of edibles at Lady Gertrude's establishment. The long table in the rich, oak-paneled dining room was laden with roasts of mutton and beef, several kinds of meat pie, two or three fish entrees, chicken, goose and duck, as well as a variety of cheeses, vegetables and fruits in season, breads and various puddings, sweets and tarts. Beer, ale, wine, coffee, cocoa were all available in limitless quantities. Richard ate and drank heartily at every meal. At most dinners, Daphne sat at his right, and Diana at his left. Daphne carried on a flirtatious conversation, sprinkled with sophomoric double entendres. Diana talked to him seriously about the theater, music and the dance. She was a great admirer of William Shakespeare, and discussed his works quite intelligently.

During one meal, Daphne said softly, "You know, Richard, I often walk in my sleep."

Richard looked up from the slice of mutton he was cutting, smiled.

"And," said Daphne, "I sometimes wander into the wrong chamber . . . in the middle of the night."

Richard, mildly embarrassed, laughed.

At his left, Diana said sarcastically, "Pay her no heed, Richard. She pretends to be a *femme fatale,* but if you so much as kissed her cheek, she would scream."

Coquettishly, Daphne tilted her head, cheek close to Richard.

"Try me, Richard. Kiss me. . . ."

Richard looked around the table, laughed nervously.

Lady Clanisham glared at Daphne.

"If you young ladies cannot stop annoying Mr. Steele," she said coldly, "we will devise new seating arrangements."

At the other end of the table, the Marquess swallowed a large mouthful of roast beef, chuckled and turned back to resume his conversation with Gilbert Weston.

Between dinner and tea time most of the gentry strolled the quiet, tree-lined streets in their best finery. At tea time, a small orchestra played, and the ladies and gentlemen danced. The dancing began with the minuet. Each gentleman took two ladies to the center of the dance floor, danced a series of short minuet steps to the triple meter of the bank with one of the ladies, then released her and repeated the series with the second lady. When one threesome finished, the next gentleman with two ladies stepped forward. Only one couple occupied the dance floor at a time. When all who wished had enjoyed a turn at the minuet, the band played tunes in a livelier tempo, and numerous couples took the floor and whirled and pranced in the more abandoned country dances.

Richard frequently took Daphne and Diana out to the dance floor for the minuets. Diana was by far the better of the twins in this dance, and Richard imagined that he felt a tremor in her fingers as he took her hand. He felt sure that the light in her eyes, in the glow of the huge candelabra, was a light of love. Indeed, the intensity of the adoration in her gaze often made him quite nervous. Daphne, on the other hand, was flirtatious during the minuets and almost shockingly suggestive in the country dances. In spite of the long hours he spent with the twins during mealtimes, and at formal assemblies, Richard had not made romantic overtures to either of them.

He felt it more politic to choose as partners for his romantic and sexual affairs older women who made it plain that they were not seriously interested in a permanent attachment, but merely wished to enjoy the excitement of the moment and the summer. His sex life was frantic and full, and, surprisingly enough, dull and unsatisfying.

On a number of occasions, particularly when he had had too much wine at supper, he still found himself unable to perform sexually, but most of the time he managed to carry out the business of intercourse or variations thereon. He frequently pondered upon the strange fact that the same basic physical acts, which had given him such ecstatic pleasure and such a total sense of fulfillment with Felicia, left him so discontented and untouched (sometimes even disgusted) with the succession of attractive and willing ladies at Bath.

Between his social activities, his drinking and eating habits and romantic carousings, he soon found that he was feeling sluggish and ill-tempered a good part of the time. The irony that this condition should befall him in a health resort never occurred to him. By the sixth week of the summer, he had gained a full stone in weight. He was finding his assignations less and less interesting, and he was even beginning to lose his enthusiasm for his work.

One week Lady Clanisham decided not to present any plays at all, but to restrict the entertainments to musical concerts and dances, interspersed with several novelty acts, which the Marquess had discovered with a traveling company on one of his frequent business visits to London. Wilson Taylor, the choreographer, devised a program of dances of various nationalities including terpsichorean presentations called *The Bonny Highlander, The Dutch Skipper, The Turkish Dance,* and *The Folie d'Espaigne.* On another evening, Wilson staged two elaborate dances on *Commedia Dell' Arte* themes.

Herr Bauer almost resigned his post when Lady Clanisham insisted he permit two Frenchmen to do their vocal imitations of a flute, a double cortell, a French horn and a trumpet between the acts of a condensed version of his favorite opera. On another evening, a contortionist supplied the *entr'acte* entertainment. In this nondramatic week, both Richard and Gilbert Weston indulged themselves in every activity, overindulged in the elaborate meals, and drank heavily. Richard felt drained and weary, and Weston's gout began to act up.

It was then, in the next to the last week of the season, that Lady Clanisham decided that the entertainment programs should return to drama, and with a vengeance. She had heard that Queen Elizabeth had been so enchanted with the character of Sir John Falstaff in the two parts of *Henry the Fourth* that she commanded William Shakespeare to write a play in which the knight would be featured. Thus Shakespeare had created *The Merry Wives of Windsor.* Now Lady Clanisham told Weston that she would like him to adapt the play and present it with Richard Steele in the role of Sir John Falstaff.

"But my dear Elizabeth," protested Weston, "Richard would be ludicrous as Falstaff. He's a paunchy, bearded old rascal, a . . ."

"Precisely, Gilbert! Precisely why my friends will be astonished and delighted to see young Richard in the role."

"But dearest Elizabeth, Richard may rebel. . . ."

"He is being paid well not to rebel. And even if you, and he himself, lack faith, I believe he is a fine enough actor to play any role. I know. . . ."

"But, my dear Lady . . ."

"Your profusion of buts distresses me, Gilbert. You are the most butful man I know. Please do as I request!"

That, of course, closed the matter.

Richard was intrigued by the idea, but when Weston gave him the folio, he was horrified to discover that he was having great trouble learning his sides. He found it even more difficult to prepare himself psychologically to play the part of a knight who woos two women simultaneously. In his befuddled head, there was some kind of conflict between a vague fidelity he believed he still owed Felicia, and the meaningless indulgences with the ladies of Bath. What it all had to do with Falstaff and the merry wives he did not know. After the third afternoon of rehearsal, Weston drew him aside.

"What is wrong, lad?" he asked, an expression of great concern on his face.

Richard shrugged.

"I wish I knew, Gilbert. I suddenly find it so difficult to accomplish the simple task of learning my lines that I can hardly play them with proper meaning."

Weston sighed, and winced as the pain that signaled an onslaught of gout stabbed his left instep. He patted Richard's shoulder.

"I understand perfectly, lad. I feel much the same about my own work. I should have continued with the New Theatre. The management there is professional. . . ."

He uttered a sharp cry of pain and hobbled to a nearby chair.

"Are you all right, sir?" Richard asked, alarmed.

Weston nodded.

"Just the gout acting up again. . . . Lady Clanisham is a lovely woman, but most unpredictable and eccentric. I had no idea she would impose her theatrical and dramatic concepts on us with such force. . . . I should never have persuaded you to come to Bath. In spite of the money, and . . ."

"It's not your fault at all, Gilbert. I have been behaving like an idiot."

He paused.

"But we've got two more days before the performance. I'll work all day, into the night. . . ."

Weston nodded.

"And I, Richard."

They worked together that evening after supper, all the next morning and afternoon, and again through the evening. On the night before the performance, Richard tumbled into his soft bed, so physically and mentally weary that his back and his head ached. Scenes from the play spun through his head.

Lying in bed, folio in hand, Richard turned to a particularly difficult scene, and by the bright light of the three candles in the silver sconce on his bedside table began to read.

The words blurred before his eyes. He tried to read on, but his eyelids seemed heavier and heavier. Finally the pages fell from his hand to the floor, and he was asleep. He did not even extinguish the candles.

Then he felt the silken sheet slide from his body, felt his night dress being lifted, a hot, moist mouth pressed to his lips, smooth fingers touching his genitals. He thought he was dreaming. He thought it was Felicia, and he became rigidly erect and groaned as he turned. Only when the arms pulled him tight against the soft, naked body, and the fingernails tore thin tracks of blood in his back, did he awaken. There was less than an inch left of the candles, but they still cast a soft glow across the lovely young body beside him.

She pressed against him fiercely, her mouth tight against his, her hands frantically clutching his broad back. The candles made highlights of her amber hair, her high cheekbone, her closed eyelid, the side of her regal nose. He held her tightly and entered her. When she moved her lips away from his for a moment, he gasped, "Daphne . . . Daphne . . ."

The girl pulled away from him, sat up abruptly, her bosom heaving with passion, and now with fury.

"I knew you would say that! *Diana! Diana! Diana! Not Daphne!*" she screamed.

"Forgive me, dear Diana," Richard stuttered. "I . . . I . . ."

The door to the bedchamber opened, and a female voice whispered angrily.

"I thought so. I heard you open your door. I thought you might . . ."

Young Lady Daphne rushed to the bed and grabbed two hands full of her sister's long, silken hair. Diana screamed, and scratched at Daphne's face with both hands. Richard tried to separate them, but Daphne pulled Diana from the bed, and Diana, in turn, ripped Daphne's silk night dress from her. Striking, biting, scratching, tugging at each other's hair, crying and screaming, the two naked young ladies rolled around the thick Oriental carpet of the bedchamber. Richard danced ineffectually around them, reaching down, trying to separate them, only to be cuffed with a misplaced swing now and then.

The fighting had reached such a furious pitch that neither the combatants nor Richard heard the door swing open again. But suddenly, the Marchioness, Lady Clanisham herself, loomed above the disheveled nude young women still locked in vicious struggle and the hapless young actor in his night dress, kneeling on the floor beside them, awkwardly trying to pull them apart.

"Cease!" she commanded.

Richard rose to his feet, and the girls released their grasps on each other. They lay on their backs for a brief moment, gasping, tears running down their cheeks, their bosoms and bellies heaving. Lady Clanisham stood over them. In her gold velvet robe, and night cap to match, she looked like an informally attired Goddess of Wrath. Her twin daughters sat up. The Goddess extended a stiff arm, pointed to the door.

"Go to your chambers! Immediately! Go!"

Diana minced to the bed, sobbing, and retrieved the pink silk night dress she had left there. She quickly slipped it over her head. Daphne picked up the tattered shreds of her own pink night dress and held one substantial piece over her breasts as she backed toward the door, following her sister. Richard, red-faced and perspiring, stood before Lady Clanisham. He spread his arms, said, "I don't know what to say, my lady. I was sleeping, and . . ."

Lady Clanisham glared at him. She advanced upon him. He backed toward the bed, felt it hit the back of his thighs. He sat down. Lady Clanisham stood over him. Arms folded over her bosom, she stared down at him.

"I did not bring you here as a plaything for the children, Richard."

"I know. I didn't . . . that is, I wasn't . . . I mean I was asleep and Daphne . . . no, Diana . . . Diana came . . . and Daphne . . . I called her Daphne and . . ."

The candles had almost burned out. They flickered and sputtered. Richard was startled to see a sudden broad smile break out on Lady Clanisham's handsome face. With a flourish, she whipped the embroidered golden cap from her head. She shook her head once, left to right. The amber hair tumbled in silken profusion to her shoulders. Richard was stunned as she unbuttoned the robe and slipped out of it. She was naked, and she had a far more voluptuous body than either of her children. For a fleeting moment, Richard was terrified at the thought that the

329

Marquess might miss her and come into the room. There had certainly been enough other unexpected visitors that night.

As though she were reading his thoughts, Lady Clanisham said, "The Marquess is in London." She pushed him over on his back, reached down and helped him remove his own night dress.

Just as she lay back on the bed and pulled Richard's head down to the curly amber triangle of hair where her lush thighs met, the candles went out. She smelled just like the ginger and raisins in Bessie Pickering's Grateful pudding. The late August moon, beaming through the wide, arched window made soft bluish highlights on the backs of Richard's thighs, his buttocks, back, neck and bobbing raven head. The light shone on Lady Clanisham's wide-spread legs and thighs, her full, heaving breasts and hard, protruding nipples, her beautiful face with its high cheekbones and regal nose, all now moist with perspiration. She smiled a broad, self-satisfied smile, and the moonlight heightened the happy expression in her wide-open, gold-flecked eyes.

During his stay with the Marquess and Marchioness, Richard had occasionally wondered why the Marquess seemed so perpetually weary. On that night he found the answer. The Lady proved insatiable in bed. Dawn chased the blue moon from the skies, and the newborn sun flooded the bedchamber with warm light. Lady Clanisham was still fondling Richard's limp member to no avail. After the fourth long, sustained coupling, with the Lady astride him, swiveling and bouncing with merry abandon, Richard had exploded for the final time. He flung his arms out at his sides, closed his eyes and fought to catch his breath. Between each of the four couplings there had been erotic games, several of which seemed to Richard Oriental in their unorthodox ingeniousness. He was utterly exhausted. Lady Clanisham climbed from the bed, slipped into her robe, dexterously piled her hair and stuffed it beneath the gold-colored cap.

"You are not quite as excellent a lover as you are an actor, Mr. Steele," she said, and waved at him as she left the room. Richard was unconscious before the door closed. Gilbert Weston tried to wake him about nine o'clock, but could not. Finally, at dinner time, a little after three, Richard came into the ornate dining room. Lady

330

Clanisham was in her usual place at one end of the table, radiant and regal as ever.

Daphne and Diana were extremely subdued. There were scratches on their faces, that powders and creams could not quite conceal. But what surprised Richard was to see the Marquess himself at his regular place at the head of the table. He was in deep conversation with Gilbert Weston when Richard entered. Richard learned later that he had returned from London early that morning. Daphne and Diana had concocted a tale about their horses running under the low-hanging branches of a tree. Richard never did find out whether the Marquess believed their story, or whether he had any idea that Lady Clanisham had spent most of the night in Richard's bed.

The only comment the Marquess made to Richard was his greeting as Richard entered that afternoon.

"Ah, young Steele," he shouted heartily across the long room, "Gilbert tells me you are doing *The Merry Wives*."

As he took his seat between the quiet twins, Richard hoped no one noticed him wince or wondered why his face was pink. *I am, indeed, doing The Merry Wives,* he thought wearily, *but not very well,* he stole a furtive look at Lady Clanisham at the end of the table. She smiled graciously and said, "Please try the mutton today, Richard. It is extraordinarily tender."

In the middle of the rehearsal that afternoon, Richard and Gilbert Weston had a surprise. Nell Faversham came into the assembly room as Richard was playing his part ... poorly.

29

Richard leaped nimbly from the stage and walked quickly toward Nell, arms outstretched, a broad smile on his face. He would not have described his feeling upon seeing her as that of a drowning man to whom a rope has been thrown, but the sensation was akin to that. He took her hands in both of his, looked into her sparkling emerald eyes, then drew her to him and kissed her on the cheek and mouth.

"Nell! How wonderful you're here!"

She hugged him warmly, kissed him again on the cheek.

"I've missed you, Richard. We all have. Mary and . . ."

Then she saw Gilbert Weston sitting in a chair at stage left with his leg outstretched, his foot heavily bandaged and resting on a second chair. Richard took her to Gilbert and they exchanged warm greetings.

Nell stayed at a small inn near the New Theatre on Kingsmead Street for the eight remaining days of Richard's commitment. Weston agreed to cancel the rest of the rehearsal on the day Nell arrived. Richard rented two fine horses, and they rode north, out of Bath, up into the Cotswold Hills. On the way, they dismounted once, tied the horses to a tree beside a rippling brook and sat beside the brook.

"Mary was a mite upset that you hadn't written at all," said Nell. "That was one reason I decided to come to visit you."

"I'm sorry, Nell. I haven't done all sorts of things I should have. . . ." He lay back in the thick grass, hands clasped behind his head, and gazed at a huge gray-white cloud moving through the sky.

"And I've done all kinds of things I shouldn't have. . . . But you said Mary is all right. No relapse. No cough . . ."

Nell laughed.

"She's more than all right. You would have enjoyed so much being at Waltham Cross in the past week. Father Whittaker managed to get the first sabbatical he's had in twenty years—an entire week—and he came to spend it at Waltham Cross."

"I'm happy to hear that. The Father is so intense; he works so hard, Mary and I often worry about him."

Nell smiled.

"I'm not too sure his one-week holiday relieved all his anxieties. You know that George Storey and your mother have become quite good friends—often play cards together, stroll in the woods. . . ."

"I know; it's been very good for Mary."

"Well, Mr. Storey was about quite a bit during Father Whittaker's visit, and the Father didn't seem to approve."

She laughed lightly.

"I know Catholic priests are pledged to forego earthly romantic relationships, but I would swear Father Whittaker was actually jealous of Mr. Storey."

A bold blue jay hopped to within two feet of them.

"Mary and the Father have been the closest of friends as far back as I have any memory." Richard smiled.

"Well, it was most amusing, and rather heartwarming, to see Father Whittaker and Mr. Storey vying for your mother's attention. They were like a pair of awkward schoolboys."

"I know Mary would enjoy that."

"Enjoy it! She took altogether shameless advantage of it. I don't know whether you appreciate it, Richard, but your mother is quite a coquette."

"It's nice to know she's that lively again. It's how I remember her, when I was a small boy."

"Lively and effective. Did you know that she persuaded Mr. Storey to pay a Mr. Higginbotham, the man who presents the bull-baiting, some sort of penalty to discontinue the events."

"Good for her," beamed Richard. "They were a noisy nuisance."

"Your little cottage has been a beehive of romance all summer. . . . Do you know Felicia's father?"

Richard looked puzzled. For a moment he was confused.

"Edith's schoolteacher, Josiah," Nell said.

"Oh, yes, of course."

"Well, his wife died early this summer. I think just several days after you left for Bath. Josiah has been spending every weekend at the cottage. I think he's just waiting for what he and Edith feel would be a respectable time after the death, before they marry."

They rose, and brushed the grass and dry dirt from their clothes, and strolled for a time.

"That will be nice for all of them," said Richard. "How is the baby?"

"Adorable. The loveliest, liveliest three-year-old I've ever seen."

A cloud passed before the sun and diffused the day's brightness. Almost simultaneously, the bright expression in Nell's eyes seemed to fade. A note of sadness came into her voice.

"It's strange about children," she mused. "Little Felicia is so healthy, so bubbly, and Edmund's son, John, is cranky and miserable most of the time."

"What is his disorder?"

Nell shrugged.

"The doctors cannot say. He has the brightest, most intelligent dark eyes imaginable. They almost seem the eyes of an adult. But there is a strange glint in them; perhaps he has pain. He is frail, and small, but the doctors insist there is nothing wrong with him at all. Edmund's family doctor is certain he will outgrow his complaining nature."

Nell had told Richard that Edmund Fox had left for Antigua two weeks earlier. He was transporting two prize bulls and six cows in excellent health to his brother-in-law, Gilbert Marlowe. He was taking Angus Britt, the most knowledgeable cattleman in England, with him. The Duke and his brother-in-law were determined to bring cattle-raising to Antigua.

"How is the Duke?" Richard asked now. The sun brightened the scene again, and Nell's eyes shone.

"I love him, Richard," she said simply. "I would do anything to alleviate any situation which troubles him. I wish there were some way I could help with little John."

She lowered her head, grimaced, spread her arms.

"But of course I cannot. The Duchess, naturally enough, despises me. Just before last season ended, Edmund requested me to come to his home one day with some Lincoln's Inn Fields papers which required his signature. I was in his study with him when the nurse brought in young John. I asked Edmund and the nurse if I might pick him up, and they said yes. But I held him for no more than a few minutes—I was saying the silly, loving things one says to a baby—when the door burst open and the Duchess wheeled herself in, in her chair."

Richard turned on his side, reached out and took Nell's hand. Her voice quavered.

"Do you know the Duchess, Richard?"

"I've never met her."

"Her entire right side is paralyzed, from head to foot."

"I know. Gilbert told me."

"She gets about in a wheelchair, very ornate. . . . It looks somewhat like a miniature throne. When she speaks, her words are often hard to understand . . . twisted, sort of . . ."

She took Richard's hand.

"But what she screamed at me that day was very clear. She said, 'put down that child, you filthy whore . . . put him down at once.' Her face was flushed. Spit ran down her right jaw. I don't think I've ever seen such hatred as burned in her good eye!"

"I've been told she hates all players, everyone in the theater."

"Particularly her husband's whores," Nell said sadly.

"I don't think there's anything whorish about your relationship with the Duke, Nell. Don't let yourself think so."

Nell shrugged.

"The Duchess is so strong. Even while she was cursing me, she wheeled the chair toward little John as I put him down. She swooped him up into her lap with her left arm and wheeled out. The poor little tyke hung onto her neck, terrified. Edmund was embarrassed. He apologized, began to make explanations . . ."

"Is there any possibility he may divorce her?"

Nell shook her head.

"None. None whatsoever. I would not want him to. The poor, crippled woman loves him in her own way. And Edmund would never forsake her in her condition."

Richard changed the subject. "Windsor was pleasurable?"

Nell smiled.

"Most pleasurable. I never dreamed any place on earth

could be so idyllic. You and Mary must come visit me there next summer."

They had a delightful cold supper of thin slices of Westphalian ham and an assortment of cheeses with some wine at a public house in the Cotswold Hills, and then rode leisurely in the soft twilight back to Bath. In the next two days Richard concentrated frantically on trying to master the Falstaff role. Between rehearsals he showed Nell the sights and sounds, the people and places of the health resort. She chose not to join the bathers on the first morning, but in the pump room, she agreed to try the mineral water. When she took her first sip, she pursed her lips and wrinkled her nose.

"Ugh, how unpleasant!"

Richard sipped his own water and laughed.

"I don't understand it," Nell said. "How can anything as unpalatable as this improve your digestion . . . or do whatever it is supposed to do to increase your measure of good health?"

Richard chuckled again.

"Have you taken the baths?" Nell asked.

"Quite a few times, early in the summer. Then I tired of rising so early. I—"

"Did it improve your disposition?"

"Not noticeably."

"Did you contract any strange ailments?"

Richard raised his eyebrows.

"Ailments?"

"I saw one old gentleman taking the waters this morning, Richard, with sores on his arms and shoulders and face, which could well have been marks of the pox."

"Oh, yes. I do remember seeing him. That was Sir Wesley Fenster."

"And there was a very thin, middle-aged woman with two large boils on her face."

"Yes. Lady Alice Morton."

Richard sipped his water.

"That's why they're here, Nell. Seeking a cure."

"Did it ever occur to you, Richard, that they could be polluting the waters. Waters of high temperature are particularly potent germ breeders."

Nell never did take the waters. She enjoyed the stroll through the warm, clean, tree-shaded streets. She browsed in the smart shops. She danced daintily, or vigorously as the occasion demanded, with a number of noble gentlemen at the teatime gatherings and ate and drank heartily at the gala suppers. She indulged only lightly in the heavy breakfasts and expansive dinners. She attended every performance at Lady Clanisham's assembly, except for three evenings when she went to see the presentation at the New Theatre, the program in the large room at the George and the drama at the Globe. She felt it her professional duty to review these offerings.

Then the festivities were over. Gilbert Weston, whose gout had grown increasingly painful during the last week —so painful that he had to get an understudy to play his role in *The Merry Wives*—decided to stay in Bath to see if the waters would effect a cure before he had to return to London. Nell was invited to join Richard and Weston, the Marquess and Marchioness and their daughters for breakfast on the morning of their departure. They had almost finished when Lady Clanisham turned to Richard.

"As I mentioned on the evening of the first performance, dear Richard, I think your Falstaff was distinctive and memorable. Yet in all candor . . ."

She paused and looked around the table, as though daring anyone to challenge her next remark.

". . . in all candor—and I think our relationship of this long summer has earned me the privilege to be frank—in all candor, some of your performances were not quite as memorable."

Richard felt himself blushing.

The Marquess said, "Now, my dear, this is no time for criticism. This . . ."

The Marchioness ignored him. She looked directly into Richard's eyes.

"Not quite," she repeated. "However, you are a young man, full of promise. I hope you will return next summer to fulfill some of that promise."

At the door, the Marquess shook Richard's hand vigorously. Lady Clanisham held out hers to be kissed, which Richard dutifully did. Daphne and Diana, each in turn, placed a decorous cheek to Richard's lips. All bade Nell a fond farewell, and Weston hobbled forward to kiss her goodbye.

They were a mile and a half beyond the eastern edge of Bath, clattering through the woods on their way back to London. It was an extraordinarily lovely Indian summer day. The air was crisp, the sun bright. The autumn leaves on the trees flanking both sides of the road made walls of riotous color. They were alone in the carriage, bouncing, rocking from side to side. Richard leaned back in the leather seat, brooding. Nell placed her hand over his.

"Richard, am I your friend?"

"Of course."

"May I speak the truth?"

He stared at her with mild irritation.

"Naught else, Nell. Speak."

"I have been reluctant to say it . . ."

"Say, Nell. Say whatever needs to be said."

"I think your performance in *The Merry Wives* was a most forgettable hodgepodge."

"The wig felt insecure. The beard itched. The damned pillow pressing against my stomach interfered with my breathing. . . ."

Nell took his hand, said kindly, "It wasn't the wardrobe or the props, Richard."

He withdrew his hand, sat up straight.

"The audience seemed to like it. The applause was enthusiastic and sustained."

"Led by Lady Clanisham!" Nell added.

Richard frowned.

"Have you not noticed our audience in the boxes at Lincoln's Inn Fields, Richard? There is no applause, no sign of commendation from the ladies, or their beaux for that matter, for any play, until a high-placed leader indicates approval. Then all react as though they were witnessing Betterton doing Hamlet."

"The part was wrong. I was miscast. Neither Gilbert nor I felt I should do Falstaff."

Nell shook her head.

"You are too fine an actor to say that, Richard."

He hung his head, nodded.

"You're quite right, Nell. I was inexcusably inept. Not only in *The Merry* Wives . . ."

"What's wrong, Richard? What happened?"

"I don't know. Bath, I suppose. And my own stupidity. I was so busy bowing and scraping, and wallowing in the praise and adulation, I never seemed to have time to work."

"You're not the first actor to succumb to excessive flattery, Richard."

"I didn't honestly work on a single role. There always

seemed to be something else to do. I overindulged—in everything . . . food, ales, wines." He paused and sighed. "Women."

"Perhaps you needed that. An interlude of sorts. Are you ready to go back to work now?"

Richard smiled.

"I think I will be after a couple of weeks at Waltham Cross."

On the next two evenings at sunset they stopped at public houses for supper and to spend the night. On the second night, they stayed at a quaint inn in Willesden called The Goose and Gander. The proprietor was a short, bald-headed man, with white tufts of hair at the sides of his head over his ears, and twinkling, intelligent blue eyes. As they took their places at the polished table in the kitchen, he came to them, bowed and said, "Begging your pardon, sir. Are you not Richard Steele?"

Richard nodded, pleased. He waved toward Nell, said, "And this is . . ."

The proprietor held up his hand. His eyes danced.

"No need to tell me, young sirrah. The beautiful lass is none other than Miss Nell Faversham."

He bowed to Nell, beamed.

"I saw you in *The Taming of the Shrew*. You were most delightful. And that Jerome Wrexham! So masterful!"

The proprietor was an avid theater-goer who made the trip to London at least one day each week of the season to see the plays.

They took separate but adjoining rooms in the Inn, and in the middle of that night Richard awoke with a terrible feeling of loneliness.

He longed to knock on Nell's door, to lie with her. But then he realized he was not sure whether he simply sought comfort in what he felt was his aloneness, or whether he was deceiving himself, and subconsciously planning to talk Nell into a sexual encounter out of pity for him. A vivid picture of their desperate lovemaking the night of Peter Faversham's death flashed in his mind. He concentrated his attention on the black branches of a tree in the moonlight outside his window till the lovemaking vision vanished. He realized he would be home at Waltham Cross the following afternoon and certainly had no valid reason to be lonely, so he lay awake till morning, thinking of the foolish things he had done at Bath and trying hard not to let Felicia come back into his thoughts, vowing to work hard this season to redeem himself as an actor.

The next day he was truly startled when he saw Mary. He had dropped Nell off at her house in Pall Mall and gone on to Waltham Cross. It was late in the afternoon, and a blazing tangerine sun, low in the west, was shooting off gold and silver streaks into the pale blue sky. Mary came running down the path from the cottage as the carriage drew up. Perhaps it was the glowing light of the near-sunset, but as she came toward him, she seemed to have become ten years younger than when he had left her in June. Inside the cottage, he saw that the lines at the corners of her eyes and across her forehead were still there, but her tan complexion was so radiant, her brown eyes gleaming with such good health, that he kissed her again and again and repeated over and over, "You're positively aglow, Mary. Aglow!"

"You have gained more weight than you should, Richard, but I adore every ounce of you!" She looked at him sternly, and then hugged him again.

A beautiful, chubby child with long blond hair, wearing a blue- and yellow-striped dress, toddled into the room. Precariously, she made her way toward Richard.

"Gweetings, unca Whica'," she piped. "We happy you home."

Edith, who with Mary's help had spent hours coaching little Felicia to make this speech, came up shyly behind her daughter. With her, holding her hand, was Josiah Rawlings, Felicia's father, a tall, lean, sad-looking man, with large dark eyes, that were like a basset hound's.

Richard picked up little Felicia as she reached her plump arms for his knee, and kissed her soundly on each cheek.

"My, what a big and beautiful young lady you've become," he enthused.

It was altogether a joyous homecoming. Farquhar honored him by sleeping wih him instead of with Mary. Sally O whinnied with pleasure when he went out to the stable early the next morning before anyone else had risen. He hitched her to a rickety cart and rode out to Epping Forest. There he spent the entire morning felling several trees and chopping them up into log lengths for the fireplaces. By the time he finished loading the cart his

340

entire body ached. He was reminded of the early days of several summers past when he suffered much the same agonies on the docks. But he grunted contentedly as he climbed back onto the cart's seat, glorying in the revival of his long-neglected muscles.

As the days passed the aches and pains vanished. Josiah had taken over all the work on the vegetable garden, and it was in superb condition, weedless, with loose, rich soil surrounding the thriving plants. Mary had concentrated her efforts on the flower garden, and Richard caught his breath when he first viewed it. It was surely one of the most colorful and lush small gardens in the kingdom. Mary was almost incoherent, she spoke so rapidly and enthusiastically, as she strolled with Richard down the rows, identifying each plant, telling stories about some, as though they were people. But Mary's true pride was her rose garden. She had concentrated on just three species: a rich scarlet, a velvet, pure white, and a tea rose, blending burned orange with delicate beige.

"You know that book of philosophers we have, Richard?"

He nodded, smiling at her breathless enthusiasm.

"One of them was a rose gardener, it seems. If you remember Theophrastus, he said, 'if a rose bush be cut or burned over, it bears better flowers, for if left to itself it grows luxuriantly and makes too much wood.' "

"So you keep them well-cut and burned over."

"Pruned, yes. Do you know the story of these red and white ones?"

Richard shook his head.

"They are the Tudor Rose. After the War of the Roses, York and Lancaster united, and there was a little poem: 'Henry VII did the roses unite; his own were red, and his wife's the white.' "

Richard took a deep breath, inhaling the sun-kissed fragrance surrounding them.

"Doesn't smell quite like Billingsgate, does it?" he said happily, and kissed his mother's cheek as she carefully scissored a short, thorny branch of beautiful tea roses to add to the collection in the basket on her arm. It was a tranquil and enchanting week. He and Mary took long walks through the dazzling autumn countryside, all the way to George Storey's bull-baiting arena and beyond. As they passed the arena one day, a huge white and brownish-red bull, securely tethered with a heavy chain, snorted at them and pawed the dirt with his right hoof.

"George paid Mr. Higginbotham, the promoter of the baitings, twenty-five pounds to relinquish his rights to the arena for the last two years of their agreement," Mary informed Richard as they went by.

"So, it's George now, is it!" Richard said in mock seriousness.

"Now, Richard, don't tease. He's a very nice man. . . . After the end of the month there'll be no more baiting."

"Greater love hath no man than to give up his income from bull-baiting for the woman he . . ."

Mary slapped him sharply on the shoulder.

"You stop that teasing, Richard!"

He occasionally walked with Edith while Mary stayed with Felicia. Mary pampered and played with the child so much it would have been difficult for a stranger to say whether Mary or Edith was the mother. Edith and Josiah were indeed planning to be married in the near future.

"Are you looking forward to the new theater season, Richard?" Edith asked Richard one afternoon.

"Most eagerly. I have an entire misspent summer to atone for."

He described briefly the frantic and dilettantish life in Bath, and how foolishly he had succumbed to the inane flattery.

"Well, you are a very fine actor, Richard. And a most handsome one at that."

"Fine actors work at their craft. And handsome is as handsome does," said Richard.

As much as he enjoyed every aspect of the brief time at Waltham Cross, before he would have to report to the theater at Lincoln's Inn Fields, the pastime which had the most beneficial and recuperative effect on him was the fishing. Daily he walked to the deep, clear stream about a quarter-mile from the cottage, almost halfway to the bull-baiting arena, and sat on the bank, propped against a large convenient rock, fishing pole in hand, line dangling down into the gurgling water.

He thought a thousand thoughts. He reflected on the past. He took quick, tentative glances into the future. *Felicia at Richmond Hill.* How heart-stirringly beautiful! *Farley Shannon doing Julius Caesar.* In his mind he saw the sword now hanging over his bed back at the cottage and recalled Shannon's words. *"Remember always that the theater is one of man's nobler arts, and that acting is a profession of which you may be justly proud. . . . I know you will carry on the work. . . ."* He had read the letter so many times, the words were indelibly stamped on his brain, transformed into a spoken speech by Shannon, which Richard would remember always.

A fish pulled timidly at his line. He tugged hard, and whipped in the line. A small trout wriggled on the hook. Carefully, with the fish slipping in his fingers, he unhooked it and tossed it back into the stream. Putting another worm on his hook, he denounced himself once more for the asinine way in which he had wasted the summer, and determined to make up for it with hard work in this new season. The warm autumn sun soon made him drowsy. He thought about Felicia in the carriage on the way to Richmond Hill, giving him the medallion. He held the pole with his left hand and reached into his shirt to finger the gold trinket lying against his chest. Then, unaccountably, Fitzhugh Fitzhugh's words seemed to sound in his ears: *"Hold her mem'ry in yer heart, lad. . . . Don't let yerself rot like overripe fruit. . . . She lived a brave life, and would'a wished ye to live likewise."*

A strong tug came on the line. This fish bent the pole, forced Richard to his knees, then to his feet. When he finally pulled it in, he beamed. It was twice as large as any trout he had ever caught. It would make a fine supper.

All of the days of his stay had been beautiful, alternatingly warm and crisp, but always bright with sunshine. White, puffy clouds had added intriguing forms to the robin's-egg blue skies. The weather seemed a gift of the gods, and the last day before he was to report to Lincoln's Inn Fields, a Sunday, was the most brilliantly beautiful of all. In midafternoon Richard left the house with Mary and little Felicia. Josiah and Edith remained behind. It was an unspoken arrangement, the purpose of which was to give the couple an opportunity to make love.

Richard would go down to the stream to fish. Mary, pulling Felicia in the bright red wagon her father had built for her, or walking with the child, would happily idle away enough time to permit the lovers a rare opportunity to enjoy each other. Mary and Felicia walked with Richard to a small knoll above the stream at which he fished. There he lifted the child and sat her in the wagon. He kissed her on the cheek and patted her gold head. She pulled him back by his shirt, put her arms around his neck and kissed him wetly on the mouth.

"Ca'sh a big fish, uca Wicha'," she said.

"Have a nice ride." Richard smiled and put his arm around Mary's waist and kissed her. He watched as Mary pushed the wagon down the gentle slope of the knoll and ran lightly after it, waving back to Richard. He continued to gaze fondly as they reached the low point of the small hill, and the wagon rolled to a halt. Mary was wearing a yellow linen dress, embroidered with small green forget-me-nots. It was tied with a bright green silk ribbon at her waist, and had a wide-bottomed skirt. Her gray-streaked brown hair shone in the sun. Richard thought she looked like a young girl as she turned back one final time to wave and blow him a kiss. Richard trotted down the knoll to his favorite spot on the bank of the stream. He put a fat, wriggling worm on his hook, tossed the line into the clear, babbling water and sat back, completely relaxed.

Some ten minutes passed before he heard the noise for the first time, a sound like distant thunder. It did not disturb him. He knew it was the crowd at the bull-baiting arena, and he expected to hear it intermittently for the next hour or two as the more spectacular and bloody episodes of the baiting occurred. He had caught three trout, two of which he threw back into the stream, before the warm sun and the soft, autumn breeze lulled him to sleep. Some time later—he had no idea how long—he was shocked awake by the roar of the crowd.

At first, he thought it was merely his drowsy, half-asleep state that caused him to imagine that the noise was louder, that it was coming closer. Then he shook his head and leaped to his feet. It was plainly louder. And it had changed from a solid, rumbling mélange of discordant sound to an assortment of fragmented, individually recognizable noises clashing and reverberating into a lunatic hullabaloo.

As he raced up the slope toward the terrifying din, Richard's ears and mind registered the thudding of a wild bull's hooves, its mad snorting, the hoarse, desperate bellowing of the half-dozen bullocks, shrieks and screams, and more distant roaring panic from the crowd further away. The tumultuous cacophony exploded into a deafening crescendo as Richard reached the crest of the knoll.

344

The blood froze in his veins. He paled. His heart threatened to tear out of his chest. Down the slope of the knoll, where it flattened out, not more than twenty meters from the crest, three-year-old Felicia sat in her red wagon, tiny fists to her wailing mouth, eyes round with horror.

The torn and bleeding bull charged straight toward the wagon. A hundred or more darts hung on the bull's back and flanks. His left ear hung loose, ripped away from his head. His eyes were red with blood. Mucus and blood dripped from his snorting nostrils and gasping mouth. The huge body was slashed in numerous places.

Not more than a dozen paces behind him, running almost neck and neck, six muscular, leather-booted bullocks in short-sleeved open shirts cursed and bellowed, waving their heavy oak cudgels over their heads, ready to strike as soon as they could catch the tortured animal. Some distance behind the bullocks, gasping, screaming, laughing and shrieking baiting-fanciers, a dozen men and two young women rushed to keep up with the excitement. The rest of the crowd were far behind, and many had given up the chase.

Mary Steele was pulling the wagon by a stout rope with all her strength. As Richard raced down the slope toward her, he realized that he could not possibly reach her before the bull. Mary knew, in the same instant, that she could not pull the wagon out of the bull's path before the bullocks caught up with the crazed beast. It was plain that the charging bull, heading straight for the red wagon, would crash into the wagon and the child.

Mary dropped the rope, and raced around to position herself squarely between the oncoming animal and Felicia. Her timing was dreadfully precise. In a pathetic, futile gesture, she extended her arms, held up her hands, palms out, to ward off the charge. Richard was less than five meters away, still racing headlong at full speed, when the bull's huge lowered head crashed into Mary just above the waist. His left horn plunged deep into her body, and as he raised his bloodied head in a vicious upward thrust, he lifted Mary off the ground.

The bull swung his head from side to side, reared up on his hind legs, trying to throw Mary aside and race away from his torturers. But the horn was too deeply imbedded in Mary's body. Beyond pain, mercifully unconscious and more dead than alive, Mary hung from the bloody head like a grotesque rag doll, arms and legs flailing, head bobbing and jerking with each desperate move of the beast. Scarlet streaks intermixed with the green forget-me-nots on the doll's yellow dress. The autumn air was filled with shrieking and wailing, the roaring curses of the bullocks and the thunderous sounds of the bull, himself not too far from dying.

Desperate, insane with shock and grief, Richard hurled himself against the stampeding bull, grabbed the right horn, and tried to drag the raging animal to the ground. The effort was totally futile. The new attack simply enraged the desperate animal to give him sufficiently renewed strength to hurl Mary's bleeding and torn body away to his left, directly into the running feet of the nearest bullock, and rip the flesh in the under part of Richard's right upper arm as it threw him across the grass into a bush to its right.

The exhausted beast stumbled to his knees, rose again and was about to charge at the red wagon when two of the bullocks landed smashing blows on his head. One crushed his skull on the right side; the other opened a three-inch-wide gash from his eye to his nostril. All six bullocks clubbed at the beast until he fell over on his side, writhed in final agony and lay still. The brawniest of the bullocks, gasping painfully, clubbed him once more in the center of his skull and spat upon him.

Richard crawled across the grass, got to his feet, stumbled and pushed his way through the small, excited crowd surrounding his mother. She lay still and white. The pupils of her eyes had rolled back, and her mouth was wide-open, frozen in mid-scream. Crimson froth rolled slowly down the side of her jaw. Most of the skirt of the yellow dress was now reddish-brown, and the forget-me-nots had turned black with blood.

Richard knelt beside her, fighting off the need to vomit. He took her hand. Blood dripped from the wound in his arm and made dark spots on the green silk sash. Her hand was already cold. Richard pressed it to his mouth and shook with the sobs, which came from deep within his chest and choked him. In her red wagon, Felicia wailed and trembled, tears streaking her terror-stricken face. One of the two young women who had run all the way from the arena, a young prostitute, knelt beside the wagon, took Felicia in her arms and cried along with her.

The sun was still high in the bright blue sky. Suddenly,

a strong, chill wind began to blow in from the north. The trees in a nearby maple grove whispered like a coven of gossiping old hags. From each tree, myriad leaves—once living green, now withered tan and brown—cascaded to the earth.

❧ 30 ❧

Father Whittaker looked like a dim ghost shrouded in black. Richard was oblivious to the throbbing of his bandaged arm as he stared fixedly at the back of the priest's tall, bulky form in its full-length cassock. Father Whittaker seemed to be trembling in the cold, thick fog. He *was* trembling. He had begun to quiver when he read the first Latin words of the service at Mary Steele's grave. The trembling had become increasingly severe as he read on. His deep voice quavered, broke and leaped intermittently to a high pitch. He seemed on the edge of hysteria.

The fog was so palpable Richard could taste it as he nervously licked his lips. Nell Faversham squeezed his hand, keenly aware of Richard's desperate effort to maintain control of himself. Flanking them and behind them were more than two score of Mary's friends. Behind him, he could hear Edith Forrest sobbing, and the steady whimpering of Felicia, and her father's soft murmuring, trying to calm her. Next to them were Ben and Bessie Pickering, and George Storey, pale and consumed with guilt at not having halted the bull-baiting sooner.

Uncontrolled sobs began to punctuate Father Whittaker's reading. Every so often, Richard glanced away from the priest's back off to his left. The mist was so heavy he could not see the tombstone, but he knew it was there. Not twenty-five meters from where Mary Steele was being buried lay the ashes and dust of Felicia Wandrous. Over her grave was the headstone of white marble, on which was engraved:

348

FELICIA WANDROUS
Born May 10, 1694 Died February 5, 1718
HER LOVE WAS
DEEP AND BOUNDLESS AS THE SEA

Richard had had the stone placed there immediately after his performance in *Hamlet*. He had purchased it with the first substantial money he had earned. Grief over his mother and the refreshed memory of Felicia's death overwhelmed him. He felt as though he were suffocating. He closed his eyes tightly and clenched his fists so tightly that Nell uttered a sharp exclamation of pain as his fingers dug into her hand. Then an unearthly sound, half-shriek, half-shout, exploded in the air. Richard opened his eyes to see Father Whittaker, still screaming madly, turn and rush toward him. When he was a step away, Richard could see the wild look in the sea-green eyes, in the strained, gaunt, tear-streaked face. But the priest did not go to Richard. He pushed the prayer book at Tom Culoghen, at Richard's left.

"Can't do it, Tom, . . ." he gasped. "Can't . . . can't . . . finish the service. . . . Go on . . . take it!"

He shoved the book into Culoghen's hands, pushed between the Scots police magistrate and Richard, and through several people behind them, and ran, staggering and stumbling, off into the dense fog. Culoghen hesitated for a moment, as though he would run after his old friend, but then turned, strode forward and took Father Whittaker's place, standing over the grave in front of the mourners. It took him several moments to find the place in the prayer book where Father Whittaker had broken off, but he did, and continued the reading.

Immediately after the service, however, Richard and Tom Culoghen rushed to the priest's parish house. Nell, Mrs. Culoghen and Lily wanted to come along, but the magistrate sent them off in a carriage to Pickering's Inn, where he told them he and Richard would join them. The fog was even heavier on the waterfront than out in the graveyard. Richard and Culoghen saw smoke coming out of the chimney of the tumble-down parish house as they approached. The smoke was darker than the moist grayness of the mist. Culoghen banged loudly and persistently on the wooden door. There was no response. He lifted the latch and pushed, and the door opened. An unpleasant odor of burning cloth assailed their nostrils as they rushed into the kitchen. Tufts of thick, acrid smoke wafted back into the room from the fireplace. The heavy, black wool cassock was smothering some of the coals of the fire.

Father Whittaker sat at a scarred wooden table to the left of the fireplace. There was a large bottle of Scotch, a half-filled glass, a crucifix, a leather-covered Bible and several paper-covered prayer books on the table. At his feet lay a scarlet and white, gold-frogged vestment. He stared dumbly at the smoldering fire. As Richard and Culoghen advanced toward the table, the last of the cassock burned away, the coals brightened and in places flared into blue-orange. The resurgent blaze seemed to rouse the priest. He gulped down his whiskey, scooped up the wooden crucifix, the Bible and the prayer book, and staggered toward the fire.

"Arnold! What on God's earth are ye doin'," shouted Culoghen.

But Father Whittaker, having dropped one of the prayer books on his faltering way to the fireplace, tossed the cross with the impaled figure of Christ, the Bible and the other book onto the burning coals. As he turned, Culoghen threw his arms around him and half wrestled him back to his chair at the table. Father Whittaker stared up at Culoghen dumbly, moved his head slowly and saw Richard. He waved an arm.

"Ahhhh, my ol' frien' an' my shon . . . my dear son. Sit an' join cel'brasion. . . ."

He struggled to his feet, stumbled toward a cupboard, returned to the table with two glasses. He poured each glass full of whiskey, spilling some, and refilled his own glass. Richard and Culoghen pulled scarred wooden chairs up to the table.

"Drink . . . drink, . . ." the priest urged drunkenly, lifting his own glass high, spilling a bit.

"To the burning of the artifacts of the hypocritical holy man," he roared, and drank more than half the Scotch in his glass without drawing a breath. The whiskey ran down the corners of his mouth, along his black-stubbled jaw. When neither Culoghen nor Richard touched their glasses, Father Whittaker glared at them.

"Drink, damn you! Drink, Tom Culoghen! Drink, Richard!" He rose shakily to his feet, leaning on the table with one hand, lifting his glass in the other.

"Drink to a hypocric'l idiot who ded'cated hish uselesh

350

life to *nothing*. . . ." He finished the whiskey in his glass, hurled the glass savagely against the far wall.

"Nothing . . . ab'slutely nothing!" he shouted, raising both arms overhead. ". . . to a God, who never existed . . ."

His hands dropped to his sides and a mad look came into his eyes as he staggered a step backward. He laughed maniacally.

"Or worse . . . worse yet . . . mayhap in the service of a bloody God, who glories in the ag—agon—agonies of the innocent . . ."

He leaned a wavering arm on the mantel over the fireplace, knocked over a brass candle holder. The glowing coals intensified the lunatic gleam in his stormy sea eyes.

". . . a fucking God, who revels in the mangled dying of the pure of heart . . ."

He stared down at the fire. Small flames flickered around the edges of the thick wood cross on which the brass figure of Jesus was impaled. He nodded repeatedly with maniacal vigor.

"Yes . . . yes . . . yes . . . a blind madman God, meting out . . . eternal vengeance . . . because they nailed his shun—his son to the cross!"

Richard and Tom Culoghen stared at the priest, spellbound by the fervor of his sacrilegious denunciation. To approach him or interrupt him somehow seemed out of the question. Now he pushed himself away from the fireplace, staggered toward the table, stopped abruptly. He raised his arms and his eyes to the boarded and thatched ceiling of the room. He screamed, "No! No! There cannot be so cruel a God! There is *no* God!"

He drew a deep, tortured breath. Then, with the words tearing from his throat, he challenged, "If there is a God . . . let him strike me dead . . . now . . . here . . . on this spot!"

His arms dropped wearily to his sides; he staggered forward, collapsed into his chair. He flopped his arms on the table, and his head fell forward, banging hard on the scarred wood. He groaned, sighed and was still. Then he made a rumbling sound and settled into a steady, rhythmic snoring. Tom Culoghen touched the priest's shoulder with sympathetic affection. He drank his whiskey.

"He loved your mother, Richard," he said.

Richard nodded and took a long draft of his own Scotch. He had not slept in the two days since Mary's death. His physical and mental weariness had made him numb. His heart and soul were so swamped in sorrow that he felt no special isolated pity for Father Whittaker's plight. His grief was so monumental, his exhaustion so extreme, that his every thought and word were purely mechanical. Now he finished his drink and poured himself another.

"Why don't you go back to your family, sir," he suggested to Culoghen. "You have a long trip home."

"What will you do, Richard?"

He shrugged.

"I'll stay here with Father Whittaker awhile."

It was not that he felt the priest needed his care. He was simply too exhausted to even think of moving. His bandaged right arm ached. He took another drink.

"Perhaps we should put him to bed," suggested Culoghen.

The thought of trying to lift Father Whittaker's large hulk and carrying it to the bedroom seemed unworthy of consideration.

"I think he'll be all right. You go ahead, sir. Say my farewell to Mrs. Culoghen and Lily."

The magistrate patted him on the shoulder and left. Richard finished his second drink and poured another. He sat staring at the glowing coals in the fireplace, his mind a gloomy blank. Before he finished his third drink, he placed his arms on the table, lay his head upon them and fell asleep. The priest and the young actor, raven head to raven head on the hard table, escaped their bondage of grief for a few hours in drunken slumber.

Richard was awakened by a heavy hand clumsily stroking his cheek over and over. Out of the corner of his eye, his head still resting on his folded arms, he saw that Father Whittaker had moved his chair around so that he was at Richard's side. He also saw the half-empty glass of whiskey in the priest's right hand. Richard's neck was stiff, and the weight of his head had restricted the circulation in both arms so that they were numb. He felt nothing, even in the wounded right arm. Father Whittaker stopped stroking his cheek. Richard groaned as he sat up. He stared at Father Whittaker and saw that the priest's eyes were half-closed and dulled with drink. It was early evening, and in the dim twilight Father Whittaker's dark stubble seemed to have turned coal black. He slumped in his chair.

He reached out and touched Richard's hand. Tears

filled his eyes and rolled down his cheeks. He nodded again and again. His voice was thick; he slurred his words and paused frequently between phrases.

"I *am* your father, Richa . . ."

He finished his drink, wiped his hand across his mouth. He shook his head.

"Not your . . . stinkin' father who . . . art in heaven, hallowed . . . be . . . thy name. . . ."

He squeezed Richard's hand.

"Your real, flesh 'n blood . . . despic'ble . . . righ' here on bloody earth . . . hypocrite father. . . ."

He nodded again, tears still pouring down his face, mucus dripping from his nose. He had trouble catching his breath. In maudlin, broken tones, he said, "I planted a seed 'n the sweet'est girl in'a Kingdom. . . . Were I a true . . . man . . . I'd 'a married 'er . . . cared for 'er, like a true husban' . . . 'n been a true father to you, son."

Richard's mind and heart were in a turmoil. Part of him found this drunken, slobbering priest repulsive. Another part of him pitied this confused man who was telling him he was his father. Mary had always told him his father had died at sea in the second year of Queen Anne's war in 1704. In his exhausted, grieving state he could not understand why his mother had lied to him. He also could not understand why it mattered.

Father Whittaker crushed Richard's hand in both of his.

"I love you, son," he sobbed. "I have always loved you."

Richard struggled up from his chair, leaned over and put his arms around the priest. He kissed him on the cheek, then patted his shoulder affectionately and turned and walked toward the door. At the door, he turned back and said wearily, but with feeling, "I love you, too, father."

Even as he walked out into the stench of Billingsgate at low tide, he was not sure whether he meant Father, in religious terms, or father, as in the man who had planted the seed.

BOOK TWO

* * *

**Nell, Nancy Lucia,
Shannon and Evangeline**

* * *

BATH, THE PROVINCES
AND GOODMAN'S FIELDS

* * * *

Every natural man is born full of sin, as full as a toad is
of poison, as full as ever his skin can hold.
Mind, will, eyes, mouth, every limb of his body, and every
piece of his soul, is full of sin. . . .

Thy heart is a foul sink of atheism, sodomy, blasphemy,
murder, whoredom, adultery, witchcraft, buggery; so that if
thou hast any good thing in thee, it is but as a drop of rose
water in a bowl of poison.

Thou feelest not all these things stirring within thee at one
time, but they are in thee, like a nest of snakes in an old
hedge.

From a sermon by an 18th century English Reverend

31

Richard Steele's behavior in the ten days following his mother's death and Father Whittaker's drunken revelations baffled everyone who knew him. Most of all himself. He did not appear to be grieving, although, of course, he was. He arrived punctually for all rehearsals, worked earnestly and played Orlando flawlessly in *As You Like It*, the season's opening presentation. He was able to bear in mind his disappointment with himself over the wasteful summer at Bath, and his determination to rededicate himself to his profession, despite the shattering tragedy. His work was the one phase of his life he pursued with grim concentration. Yet the applause from the boxes, the pit and the gallery gave him no pleasure or satisfaction. Inexplicably, the approval of the audience suddenly meant nothing whatsoever to him. He acknowledged it with gracious, professional bows and strode off into the wings unmoved.

Offstage, he spoke when he was addressed, but never initiated a conversation. During the rehearsals he sat by himself, concentrating on learning his part, occasionally discussing a scene with Gilbert Weston, who had recovered from his latest attack of gout. He was not rude or unresponsive. He merely seemed to have lost all capacity, indeed all desire, to communicate unless it was essential.

He slept very little. When he tried to, he frequently awoke in a cold sweat, in the grip of a nightmare. In one such horrendous dream, he saw Mary, a panic-stricken, terrified look on her face, pitifully extending her arms as she had the day the bull gored her. But in the nightmare, Richard saw himself rushing toward her and plunging his head into her already torn abdomen. In another dream, she made the same pathetic gesture and this time it was Father Whittaker. Screaming curses, he smashed Mary's hands aside and slapped her repeatedly, forehand and back, viciously, over and over again, until her face was swollen and bleeding.

One night, in the dream, the same raging bull gored Felicia instead of Mary, and Father Whittaker stood by, laughing madly.

Early each morning Richard would come down to the kitchen from his room at Pickering's even before Ben and Bessie were awake and prepare strong coffee for himself. He would drink perhaps a half-cup and go out into the chill streets of the fall dawn. He walked without purpose or direction. Yet he always managed to arrive at the theater ten or fifteen minutes before the scheduled time for the rehearsal, completely prepared for the morning's work. When the rehearsal concluded, he left the theater quietly and walked the city again without any fixed destination.

He wondered every now and then what he was doing. Was he searching for something? Was he running away? From what? From whom? He did not know. He simply walked. On the third day, as he started out of the theater after rehearsal, Nell stopped him.

"Richard, are you all right?"

"Of course." He smiled a lifeless smile, gently pulling his arm away from her hand, and walked out.

The next day she stopped him again and asked him to have dinner with her at the Inn.

"I'm not hungry, Nell. Please forgive me."

On the fourth day Gilbert Weston took him aside when he arrived for rehearsal.

"Richard, I'm deeply worried about you."

"Why?"

"You seem so removed from—from—all of us."

"Is my work satisfactory?"

"More . . . more than satisfactory, lad, but . . ."

"Please, Gilbert, I appreciate your concern, but I am perfectly all right. Believe me."

After each evening's performance, he left the theater the same way he left after rehearsals. Quietly, without a word to anyone. On several occasions Nell and other members of the company asked him to join them in a card game, a party at someone's rooms, a late supper. Always he politely rejected their invitations.

One night, at the end of the first week after Mary's burial, Ben and Bessie Pickering waited up for him until well past midnight. When he came in, they were truly puzzled. His coat was torn at the seam of the left arm. It was dirty, and both knees of his blue breeches were soiled. His face was smudged with dirt, and his left cheek seemed swollen. Yet his expression, when he came in, was almost placid, less neurotic and tense than they had seen him at any time since the funeral.

Ben Pickering pushed aside the copy of *The Spectator* he had been reading.

"What happened, lad?" he asked.

Richard smiled.

"Nothing, really."

They insisted he have a kidney pie Bessie had warmed for him, and a glass of ale. He went through the motions of eating and drinking only because it seemed less troublesome than to try to convince them that he was not hungry. They told him about a letter they had just received from Tillie. She had had a baby boy. Her husband and she had named the baby Ben. Tillie had inquired about Richard and sent her love. Richard congratulated the Pickerings on becoming grandparents, listened politely to the rest of their report on Tillie, then excused himself and went up to his room to bed. He lay in the darkness, trying to understand and evaluate his emotions. After the episode of this evening, he thought he was beginning to understand one aspect of what was going on within him. He was filled with a bitterness, an absolute rage over life's gross injustices. *Yes! But what of it!* Each day as he walked about busy, stinking London city, he saw signs of wretchedness, misery and worse.

That very evening, on the way back to the Inn, he had been walking along Fleet Street. He came to the Fleet Ditch. It seemed more cluttered each day with vile, evil-smelling mud, refuse, horse manure, bullock dung and occasional corpses of rats, cats and dogs. At St. Paul's there was a white-haired old man, whose sick, rheumatic eyes blinked sadly. His head was held fast between the two planks of the pillory. He had twisted his head so that the nail, which had been driven through his right ear, had torn through the lobe, and the flesh of that ear hung loosely. Saliva drooled out of his mouth on that side.

Beyond St. Paul's, as he passed a narrow alley, he heard sounds of scuffling, grunting and an occasional, quick, stifled scream. He did not have his cudgel or any weapon with him. He had decided, when he left the Inn the first morning after Mary's burial, that he would carry the cudgel no more. Now, as he heard the noises of conflict, he felt suddenly and ridiculously elated. He charged into the dark alley. As he drew near enough to distinguish the parties, he saw that four young ruffians, all approximately in their early teens, were punching and kicking away at a heavily cloaked figure. The victim seemed to be trying to protect some possession from the boys, as well as to fend off their attack.

Richard grabbed the back of the greasy leather collar of the first man he reached, and pulled with all his might. He was stunned at his own strength as he spun the assailant against a stone wall four feet away. A square-faced, stocky man, who smelled strongly of gin, released his hold on the cloaked figure, turned toward Richard and threw a wild blow at Richard's head. Richard blocked the blow and kicked the man viciously in the groin. With an agonized scream, the man sank to his knees, clutching his crotch. Richard kicked him squarely in the face, and he fell forward into the hard dirt, moaning.

A third man leaped upon Richard's back, wrapped his arms tightly around Richard's neck. He was very light. Richard reached up and grabbed his arms, and discovered they were extremely thin, simply grimy skin covering bones. He released the arms, and suddenly reached back over his own head, toward the head of the youth on his back. He grabbed thick, matted hair in both his fists and tugged savagely as he bent forward. Shrieking in pain, the boy released his hold on Richard's neck. By his hair, Richard flung him against the stocky lad a few feet away, who was still on his knees, hands holding his bloody face, and moaning. The last of the foursome raced out of the alley, turned left at the Fleet Ditch and kept running.

Richard put his arm around the gray-haired old woman in the cloak. She clutched a shabby leather purse in her bony hands. As they came out of the alley into the slightly brighter light of the moon at the Fleet Ditch, the old woman was just beginning to catch her breath.

"Thank ye, an' God belss ye, luv," she gasped. "They were tryin' ta rob me, the bloody barstards."

Richard saw that the thin lips and the puckered skin

360

surrounding them in her haggard face were painted a bright red. The effect was clownlike. As he leaned toward her to make certain she was not hurt, he could smell, above the rank odor of the air all around them, the nauseating aroma of a long unwashed body, an overabundance of cheap powder and perfume, all blended with sweat.

"What say ye ta a leetle fuck, lad," she suggested coquettishly, smiling to exhibit rotting yellowish teeth.

Richard patted her shoulder and started to move away.

"Hold on, now," she called after him. "There'll be no charge, an' I'll do ye real special!"

He kept walking, faster. He felt good. He wished the fourth assailant had not run away. Before he reached the Inn he passed a grog shop, one which remained open all night. In the dim light of the window of the shop, Richard saw the amateurishly printed sign: DRUNK FOR A PENNY —DEAD DRUNK FOR TUPPENCE. A young girl, of about ten years of age, emerged. She was gaunt-looking, with dirty blond hair, and she held a bottle of gin in her hand. By her side walked a fat, middle-aged man with beady eyes and a bald head. The girl paused in the littered street just outside the shop. She lifted the bottle to her lips, tilted her head and drank. She had hardly swallowed once when the fat man snatched the bottle, cuffed her on the side of the head and drank a long draft himself. She took his hand, started to sing a bawdy song as they walked off. Richard had an impulse to run after the fat man and hit him, but he fought it off and continued on his way to the Inn. He wondered how much of an inconvenience it would be to the Pickerings if he were to hang himself in his room that night. But he dismissed the thought quickly.

On the following Saturday afternoon he found himself at Temple Bar in the course of his walk from the theater. He made his aimless way north and east through various twisting lanes and alleys, and soon he heard a distant rumbling noise. It had a familiar sound. A knot formed in his stomach, and his mouth went dry. It was the sound of a crowd, a large boisterous mob. He was about to turn back and walk away from the roaring cacophony, when he realized it was coming from the vicinity of Newgate Gaol. Morbid curiosity drew him on.

Soon he stood on a rise at the very edge of the huge gathering of people. There were close to three thousand in the vast open area surrounding the notorious prison, and they had assembled to witness the hangings. Even as Richard gazed ahead to the high prison wall, the body of a man, rope securely fastened around his neck, was hurled over the wall. The other end of the rope was tied to a broad wooden beam extending out from the wall. The man's body snapped to a sudden, jarring halt in its descent. His feet hung no more than a meter from the ground. Just once, in a futile last desperate try, his hands reached for the rope, then his arms whipped out, away from his body, and flapped wildly, like a grotesque, severely wounded bird. His legs kicked furiously for a moment, as though he were running in space. Then his face darkened and gradually turned black. His eyes bulged. His tongue hung obscenely from the gaping hole of his mouth. He still twisted and writhed.

In front of Richard, and all around him, the orgiastic, ecstatic bellow of the crowd swelled and soared like a discordant Satanic concert.

Richard did not stay to see any more hangings. Less than two hours later he was on the Lincoln's Inn Fields stage leaving romantic messages in verse on the prop trees of Arden Forest. Nell, on this particular evening, gave an unusually appealing performance as the witty and paradoxical Rosalind, and Richard's Orlando complemented her beautifully. The applause was extraordinarily enthusiastic and prolonged. Joining Nell at center stage after she finished her teasing epilogue, Richard still felt none of the elation that had meant more to him than payment in pounds in seasons past. It seemed that the moment Orlando's last line was spoken, Richard Steele became, once more, the mindless seeker after an elusive dream that always escapes, leaving him face to face with his own bleak despair.

Nell held onto his hand as he headed for the wings.

"Richard, please come home to Pall Mall with me," she pleaded. "The Duke is still in Antigua, and I have been very lonely."

"I'm sorry, Nell, but I could not assuage your loneliness. I must be alone . . . at least for a time."

"You should not be alone, Richard. It's not good." She took his hand, looked pleadingly into his eyes.

"Do you not remember how you stayed with me when Peter died? I needed you . . . most desperately. I think you need me now. . . ."

He shook his head, pulled his hand away from hers

and stalked toward his dressing table. Gilbert Weston watched, spread his arms in hopeless resignation as he saw the pained look on Nell Faversham's face.

Not far from the theater in Lincoln's Inn Fields was a footpath that led northward to one of the most unsavory and dangerous sections of the city, Shire's Lane, known to many as Rogue's Lane. Criminals of every description lived here. From Shire's Lane underground passages ran to various sections of the Strand, and the thieves, footpads, pickpockets and highwaymen used this honeycomb of tunnels as escape routes when constables were on their trail. For no explicable reason Richard headed up the footpath toward Shire Lane this night.

It was a night when heavy banks of fog filled the sky and drifted past the half-moon, keeping the narrow, unlit, dirt alleys and lanes alternately in total or half-darkness. The streets in Shire Lane were deserted. At this hour even the residents of the area feared to wander. As suddeny as though she were a spirit, a young girl appeared out of the fog and stood before Richard. As a large patch of fog wafted past the moon, he could see in the pale, bluish light that she was attractive in a brittle way. She had long, dark hair and flashing dark eyes, a pert nose and a full sensuous mouth, painted boldly scarlet. She wore a dark, wool dress that clung tightly to her upper body. The dress was cut so low that almost her entire full bosom, cream white in the moonlight, was exposed.

She was a head shorter than Richard, and she looked tauntingly up into his face.

"Ye're lookin' at the most passionate puss in the lane, luv," she informed Richard, with a hand on her hip. "Think ye're up to 'avin a 'elpin."

Richard smiled at her. He had no real desire for sex, but he was curious about where she might take him. Before he could reply, his head exploded. There was a quick, sharp pain. Brilliant, miniature objects of light like diamonds and jagged, irregular forms of varied design splashed and whirled before his eyes for the fraction of a second. Then impenetrable blackness came, as though he were floating underwater, eyes open, in a pool of thick, ebony ink.

He regained consciousness gradually, not sure whether the fact that he was shivering with cold or the ache in his head had awakened him. He reached up and felt a lump the size of an egg above his right ear. It was almost dawn, and the fog had lifted. He discovered that whoever had hit him on the head had dragged him into a littered alley in Shire Lane. He had had three pounds, and a few shillings and pence in the pocket of his breeches when he left the theater. The money was gone. Also gone were his black wool coat, his gray waistcoat, his linen shirt, his silver-buckled shoes and his gray silk socks. Out of some strange sense of modesty, they had left him in his breeches.

He groaned, still shivering, as he got to his feet. He brushed off some of the slimy debris in which he had lain. The streets were completely deserted. He began to trot, as much in an effort to warm up as to hurry out of the area. His head throbbing with each stride, he trotted all the way to Pickering's Inn. He let himself in with the key Pickering had given him 'way back when he first took the room, while Felicia was still alive. Panting, he went to the bar and poured himself a goblet of brandy, trying to catch his breath before he sipped the drink.

The run from Shire Lane had warmed him, and his first long drink of the strong brandy burned in his stomach and warmed him even more. He went across the kitchen to the fireplace, stirred the dying embers and poured fresh coal atop the newly aroused flames. His head still throbbed as he sat back in his chair, sipping more of the brandy. Frowning, he pondered his actions of the last several days and nights. Why had he gone to Shire Lane? He was fully aware how dangerous it was! Why, earlier, had he rushed into the dark alley off the Fleet Ditch? Any idiot would know it was a reckless and stupid thing to do! What had drawn him to the hangings at Newgate Gaol? It came to him as a sudden shock that he might have been considering ending his life . . . or having someone end it for him.

He rested his elbow on the table, leaned his head into his hand, rubbed his eyes with thumb and forefinger. It was quite ridiculous! He did not want to die! He looked up, glanced around at the dimly lit, familiar kitchen of the Inn. It was full of memories. He decided what he needed was to get away from all people, things and places familiar, to build a new life. He looked down and realized for the first time that his hand had been resting on the open pages of a copy of *The Daily Courant*, which someone had left on the table. The bottom of his brandy goblet had made a moist ring around a news report of the sentencing at the previous week's sessions at Old Bailey.

Richard scanned the item absently, as he took another drink.

Immediately below the Old Bailey report was a paid notice. Richard read it through once, then read it again slowly.

A THEATRICAL OPPORTUNITY

The present Proprietor and Manager of a most reputable traveling Company of Comedians would have no objection to entering into a partnership with any Gentleman Actor, possessed of a good figure and talents for the stage, and who is able to command an equal capital with said Proprietor and Manager. Whoever has such talents and is inclined to treat on that head must have 100 to 200 pounds at his own disposal. The Company will be at White Swan Inn near Gunnersbury Park for the entire fortnight from 15 September to 30 September. Theophilus Canaday, present Proprietor and Manager will greet interested parties there.

An hour later he had washed and dressed and saddled Sally O. It was Sunday, and there was no rehearsal or performances. He had made up his mind to join Theophilus Canaday's Company of Comedians. He had never head of them. He knew, too, that many an actor in a traveling company would sell his soul to work in a company in one of the two patent theaters in London, but that did not bother him. It did not seem at all ridiculous to him that he was giving up his coveted and hard-won spot at Lincoln's Inn Fields to join a wandering troupe. He had a vaguely formed, but positive, notion that the responsibilities, which would go with the partnership, plus his acting roles, would fill out his days and bring him peaceful nights. It never occurred to him that Canaday might make arrangements with some other actor.

Most of all, it seemed overridingly important that he get *out* of London, away from the stench and the violence, the misery and death. That he might simply be trying to run away from himself and his memories never crossed his mind. He envisioned a succession of leisurely wagon journeys in the clean, green summer. He pictured vivid autumns, brisk, snow-white winters and budding, rainbow springs. He saw himself playing before simple, unsophisticated, loudly appreciative audiences—no snuff-addicted beaux onstage—audiences much like those at the fairs.

His head still ached dully, but the cold air of the September morning was so bracing he did not mind it. Josiah Olney was spreading mulch with a strong odor of manure around the plants in the vegetable garden when Richard rode up. He was surprised when Richard told him that he was planning to leave London to join a traveling company, and that he wanted to sell his half of the cottage to Josiah and Edith.

"But I couldn't pay you much more than a hundred pounds," Olney said.

"A hundred pounds would be fine," said Richard. He himself had saved more than sixty pounds, and he felt that with Olney's hundred he would be able to buy the partnership in the Canaday company. Edith and baby Felicia were in the Olneys' bedroom. Felicia had been ill with a fever ever since the horrifying experience with the bull. She constantly woke up in the night, screaming and crying, suffering all sorts of terror-filled dreams.

Edith was sitting in a rocking chair beside the fine, wooden crib Josiah had built for the child. She held Felicia in her arms, rocking her back and forth, singing softly to her. The mother's round face was pale, and her eyes were dull with lack of sleep. Felicia's cherubic face was a deep pink, and there was a feverish gleam in her eyes. She whimpered as she looked up at Richard.

Richard knelt before her and took her pudgy hand in his. He kissed her hand, then her hot cheek.

"There's no more bad bull, baby. The bad bull is gone. . . . No more."

He rose, and as he did he looked down into the child's crib. A shudder went through him. He went into his own bedroom and collected the few possessions he wished to take with him: the Brutus sword and plaque from Farley Shannon, some dozen books and folios and quartos of plays, his odd assortment of clothing and a small collecion of letters, Felicia's, and Farley Shannon's. He packed everything carefully in two large saddlebags.

As he came out of the room carrying the bags, Josiah asked, "Can you stay for the wedding next Sunday, Richard?"

"If I'm still here, I'll certainly come, Josiah. But I'll likely be gone before then."

He held out his hand, and Josiah took it.

"Good luck and happiness, Josiah."

"And to you, Richard."

Then Richard suddenly realized that he had not seen Mary's cat.

"Where's Farquhar?" he asked.

Olney shrugged.

"We haven't seen him since Mary's funeral. Hasn't been around at all."

Richard adjusted the saddlebags along Sally O's flanks and walked down to Mary's flower garden. A fair number of the red and white Tudor roses were still in bloom. With his knife Richard cut enough of the large, beautiful flowers to make two substantial bouquets. Ignoring the pricking of his fingers by the stems' thorns, he tied the bouquets and placed them carefully, stems down, into the saddlebags. He rode slowly. Even then, many petals fell from a number of the roses before he reached the waterfront graveyard.

Felicia's grave was closest to the post, outside the graveyard, to which he tied Sally O, so Richard walked there first. Solemnly, he knelt and placed one of the bouquets on the ground before the headstone. He closed his eyes and told Felicia, without words, how much he loved and missed her. Then he walked the short distance to his mother's gravesite. He was pleased to see that the stone he had purchased for her had been engraved and put in place. It read:

MARY STEELE
SWEET MOTHER TO MANY
Born April 14, 1686   Died September 3, 1718

Richard placed the second bouquet against the stone, and knelt again, now with tears spilling from his eyes. As he knelt beside the stone, a sudden gust of wind swept across the graveyard and a chill ran through him. He realized, of a sudden, why he had shuddered when he looked down into Felicia's crib. The "doke," the impression in the crib where the child had lain, had not been smoothed out. One of Mary's superstitions held that if the doke were not smoothed out when a person arose in the morning, an evil spirit might lie in it, and would then have power over the person who had slept there forever after.

Richard rose and shook his head, trying to push the

foolish, superstitious thought from his mind. He was startled by a small orange- and tan-striped creature that darted at him from a clump of bushes just outside the cemetery gate. Farquhar trotted eagerly to Richard, rubbed against his leg, turned, rubbed again and repeated the motion over and over. Richard reached down and picked up the sturdy yellow-eyed cat. He stroked him for several moments, and Farquhar purred loudly.

Richard put him down, said, "Goodbye, Farky," and walked toward Sally O. As he mounted, he looked back. Farquhar was sniffing the roses against the headstone. He pulled his head back abruptly, as one of the thorns stuck his nose. He swept the roses away with two strokes of his paw and lay with his back against the stone as Richard rode off to Father Whittaker's parish house. He wanted to bid him a proper filial farewell.

At the waterfront parish house, Richard got no response to his knocking. He grasped the latch and pushed the door open. The kitchen appeared to be in precisely the state in which Richard had last seen it. The three glasses and the whiskey bottle were still on the table, although all were empty now. The scarlet and white vestment still lay on the floor, beside one chair. Richard walked across to the fireplace. The coals had long since burned to ashes, but in the grayish pile a metallic gleam caught his eye. He knelt and saw that the brass figure of Christ on the cross had melted into a formless blob. The wood of the cross was dust, indistinguishable from the coal dust.

Richard called, "Father! Father!" He had a sudden feeling that he might find the priest in bed, ill or worse. He ran to the bedroom, but it too was empty and had an air of total desertion. He remembered that it was Sunday, and realized that his father could be at the church. Although it was long past time of the last Mass, he trotted over to the rickety church. On a raised wooden step before the battered door sat two bronzed, leathery old sailors with pigtails.

One was reading aloud to the other from a dog-eared prayer book. He moved a stubby finger along the lines, tracing and mumbling each word of the prayer slowly to his friend.

"Is Father Whittaker inside?" asked Richard.

The reader looked up and shook his head.

" 'E 'asn't been 'ere in a week, mate. Was no Mass today. We 'ave no idea where 'e's gone to."

Richard walked the short distance to The Billowing Sail. Among the half-dozen seamen at the bar was Horace Busk.

"Have any of you men seen Father Whittaker?" asked Richard.

Busk scowled at him.

"Yer in the wrong place, actor," he growled. "Ye'll find no fuckin' Christ lovers in 'ere."

The owner of the pub, an old, tall, beefy man behind the bar, bellowed, "Shut yer blasphemin' bloody mouth, Busk!" In a quieter tone, he said to Richard, "No one knows where the father's gone to, son. Disappeared more 'n a week ago. Friend o' his died, and 'e 'as'nt been seen since. . . . Good man, the father! Good man!"

Richard thought his father may have gone to visit his old friend, Tom Culoghen, but when he checked the police magistrate two days later, just before riding off to Gunnersbury Park, he learned that Culoghen had not seen nor heard from his father either. On this Sunday, however, Richard rode out to Pall Mall. He wanted to tell Nell of his decision, even before he told Gilbert Weston on Monday.

The small house the Duke had supplied Nell was at the western end of Pall Mall. The street contrasted vividly to the foul-smelling docks from which Richard had just come. It was wide and quiet and lined by stately elms, their leaves turning warm autumn colors. Although Nell's house was small, it was of brick. In the rear, it had a lovely terrace, from which one had a view of the Royal Gardens. Nell had occasionally seen the King and his courtiers strolling there. From the terrace, through the crisp-leaved trees, the towers and gables of Whitehall, a half-mile away, could be seen.

Richard had never visited Nell here before. As they sat in the richly appointed drawing room, he looked around at the brocaded walls, the paintings of stern-visaged noblemen, the veined Italian marble fireplace with its gold andirons, the polished rosewood clock. Soft evening twilight, slanting through the arched windows, made a path across the deep, Oriental carpet.

"Very elegant," commented Richard.

Nell blushed.

"I'm still a bit ill-at-ease here, Richard. But I must

say, it's a charming place to live. . . . I'm so grateful to Edmund."

When Richard told her about his plans, a shocked expression came over her face.

"No! no! Richard, you can't. You just can't throw away your career. You're a brilliant actor. . . . The Company needs you. You just cannot leave!" She paused. "I need you!"

But after an hour of discussion, Richard convinced her that it was essential to his well-being that he leave London. His reasons were not quite clear and his logic seemed flawed, but she could sense that his instincts were dictating the move, that he was certain that leaving the city would relieve some powerful self-destructive tensions within him.

Nell sat with him as he presented his proposal to Weston at the theater the next day, at which time Richard added a new rationalization for his resignation. This furthur reason for his leaving had occurred to him during the night, and it had now assumed considerable imporance in his mind.

"Do you remember the letter Farley Shannon wrote me just before he died, Gilbert?"

"I do. Quite well. It was most touching. He would not have wanted you to leave Lincoln's Inn."

"He would, Gilbert. Here in London, theater is well-established, recognized by the Crown. In the provinces, throughout the kingdom, players have no such sanction. If I can help spread appreciation for the theater, recognition, acceptance . . ."

"Gad, my dear boy! You sound as though you were embarking on a new career as a missionary."

Weston continued to raise objections, but Richard was adamant. Finally, the manager said, "Well, Richard, you certainly cannot leave until I find an adequate replacement. And that may take some time, since the season has already started."

Nell, who had remained silent through the long exchange between Richard and the manager, now said, "I think we may be fortunate in that respect, Gilbert. I saw Francis Caryll last week. He's quite unhappy at Drury Lane, and has not yet signed his contract for the new season."

Caryll was an outstanding young actor who was almost as popular as Richard.

"Do you think he would sign with us?" asked Weston.

"I'm quite certain of it. And probably at less than we are paying Richard."

Richard smiled. Nell was ever the business woman, a true rarity.

"Can he secure a written discharge from Drury Lane?" Weston inquired.

"I have no doubt about it at all. Indeed, they may be rather relieved to have an end to dealing with his tempermental outbursts. . . . He's not the lovable, agreeable lamb Richard is, you know."

Weston was obviously not concerned with the problem of Caryll's temperament, having worked with Jerome Wrexham and other difficult acors. Now he put his arm around Richard's shoulder.

"Go then, lad, with my blessings. And know that you can come back to Lincoln's Inn whenever you wish."

So it was that Richard rode off early the next morning, which happened to be September 15, from the home of Police Magistrate Tom Culoghen in Stepney, on his way to Gunnersbury Park. Culoghen had assured him that he would exert every influence to have a search made to find his old friend, Father Whittaker.

At Shepard's Bush, less than two miles from Gunnersbury Park, the open fields on both sides of the road were still green, dotted with occasional patches of yellow and white daisies, lavender and burned orange ice plants, and other wild flowers. He reined Sally O into the field at his left, rode her to a nearby oak and tied her up. He unstrapped the saddlebags from her back.

It had occurred to him that the Canaday company would no doubt have far fewer players than the twenty men and eleven women who comprised the Lincoln's Inn group, and he wondered how they adapted plays calling for large casts, if indeed they presented such plays. He was quite certain that in addition to making condensations of the plays, the Canaday players each performed several roles in a given work. It would be interesting.

He took his folio of *The Tragedy of Julius Caesar* from a saddlebag, sat in the shade of the oak and began to read it, speculating on ways he would adapt it for a smaller cast.

He was quite absorbed in the reading when he heard a series of yelps and the sound of thumping hooves in the distance off to his right. He happened to be looking right ino the path of the sun, and he shaded his eyes with his hand. Perhaps fifty meters from where he sat a magnificent black stallion, with a small rider on his back, was bucking and dancing. To Richard it seemed the rider must surely be thrown by this wild animal.

He cast aside his folio, frantically untied Sally O and leaped upon her back. He whipped her to her greatest speed, charging straight toward the stallion. He did not know whether the stallion had seen him, or merely sensed his onrushing advance, but it streaked away across the broad field. He urged Sally O to greater speed, and they gained slowly on the stallion, whose rider was now bent low over the horse's extended neck. Richard shouted a warning, as he saw the black steed was streaking straight toward a thick, high hedge of stiff barberry. Without breaking stride, it leaped over the hedge so gracefully it seemed to be flying. Sally O charged up to the barrier and almost threw Richard over her head as she skidded to a halt. Breathing hard, Richard watched in awe as the stallion landed on the other side of the hedge and, without breaking stride, continued racing across the field.

Richard felt foolish and unreasonably annoyed. Obviously the stallion was not a runaway horse, but a magnificently trained animal, handled by an expert rider. As he watched, the black horse reared on his hind legs, perhaps two hundred meters across the field, and whipped around to take the hedge again, gracefully, almost effortlessly. The rider trotted the horse back to where Richard sat on Sally O. He was indeed small enough to be a professional jockey, and very young. A dark wool cap was pulled tight on his head. He wore a loose, white denim shirt, the armpits stained with sweat, tight, white breeches and shiny, calf-length black boots. He was breathing hard, trying to smile and catch his breath at the same time. He had straight, white teeth, a nose slightly large for the oval face, and startlingly lavender eyes. His cheeks glowed cherry red.

As soon as the reckless rider spoke, Richard knew the rider was a girl.

"Hope I . . . didn't . . . alarm you, sir . . ." the girl gasped. "I didn't realize . . . anyone was watching me."

"As long as you're all right," Richard said. "You ride very well."

"I should. I've been riding since I was three."

She patted the stallion's sleek black neck.

372

"And Harlequin is a beautiful horse. Responsive. Loves to jump."

Richard looked at the white diamond on the front of the magnificent stallion's head. It was obvious why he was named Harlequin.

"Would you know where the White Swan Inn is?" Richard asked.

"Yes. We're staying there. I'll be glad to direct you. I'm going back myself."

They trotted back to the oak tree, and Richard adjusted the saddlebags on Sally O once more. The girl waited patiently.

"I'm Richard Steele," he said as he mounted Sally O.

The girl reached out a small hand.

"I'm Nancy Lucia Canaday," she said, then gasped and placed a hand to her mouth.

"Gadzooks! Are you *the* Richard Steele?"

Richard, still mildly stunned by the realization that this marvelous equestrienne was a girl, and a Canaday as well, smiled.

"If you mean the actor . . . I am."

"Weeee!" she squealed, and pulled the rein so that Harlequin stood on his hind legs, front hooves high in the air.

As he landed again, she yelled, "Let's go!" and raced to the road, heading westward to Gunnersbury Park. Richard followed, hard pressed to keep the stallion in sight.

⚜ 32 ⚜

"Well, then, if ye haven't murthered somebody," said Theophilus Canaday, "could it be that ye're fleein' the fury of a cuckolded husband?"

He was a broad-shouldered, handsome man in his late thirties, with long blond hair, a trim mustache, a large nose and strong chin. His right foot tapped rapidly. He sucked at his clay pipe and let the smoke drift out of his nostrils as he grinned at Richard Steele. There was a twinkle in his lavender eyes, which were a shade darker than his daughter's.

Richard shook his head, smiled.

"And ye're truly, cross yer heart, Richard Steele!"

Richard nodded.

"And ye want to leave the Theatre Royal at Lincoln's Inn Fields to join the humble Canaday banditti troupe for personal reasons ye do not care to state!"

Richard nodded again. The Canaday Company of Comedians was hardly a banditti group. They did not perform in barns. That was quite plain. No banditti troupe ever owned a wagon such as the one in which Richard, Canaday and Nancy Lucia now sat. It was longer and wider than any show wagon Richard had ever seen. The outside was painted a royal blue. Against the brilliant blue, handsome gilded lettering announced the company's business:

THE CANADAY COMPANY OF COMEDIANS
Concerts of Vocal and Instrumental Music

****

Stage Dances and Pantomime
National, Stunt, Game & Grotesque Dances
Acrobatics and Specialties

****

Gratis: Rehearsals of Meritorious Drama

****

Our Great Bills Delineating Current Programs
May Be Inspected At Your Friendly Tavern,
Coffee House or Other Fine Local Establishments

The wagon had six wheels; the spokes were painted royal blue and the hubs gold. Inside, where Richard seemed to be having such difficulty convincing the show's proprietor that he was Richard Steele, the wagon was, in effect, a three-chamber suite. The center section contained a small but sturdy walnut desk, behind which sat Theophilus Canaday. Richard faced him in a comfortable chair alongside the desk, and Nancy Lucia sat in another across from her father. There were shelves against one wall of this section, on which were stacked dozens of books, folios and quartos. The shelves also held two large stacks of the company's Great Bills, as the playbills of the day were called. In every way, this central section of the wagon was as completely equipped a theatrical office as Gilbert Weston's.

A movable wall separated this office section of the interior from the wagon's rear section, which held scenic flats and a large number of properties: from a cobbler's bench and a collapsible sedan chair to swords and rapiers in their scabbards and a tea table with an assortment of silvered and gilded glassware. Alongside these props was a tall cabinet with drawers, each containing nails of many kinds. Various sizes of hammers, axes, saws and other tools hung from the cabinet's side. Atop the cabinet stood a dozen cans of paints, and one can with an assortment of brushes.

Richard had been led through this prop and maintenance room when he had been ushered into the wagon by Canaday. Flanking the central office section, on the other side and separated by a permanent wall, was the Canaday's bedchamber and breakfast room. Canaday had also showed Richard the hinge and hook arrangement by which the central office section could be converted into an open stage. Canaday had designed the multipurpose theatrical wagon, and he and the other male members of the company had built it themselves.

Richard had noted that this was only one of four of the company's wagons. The other three were smaller, having only four wheels, but all were painted in the same rich, bright royal blue, and lettered with the same gilded message detailing the company's entertainment offerings. The Canaday Company was indeed far from being a banditti troupe.

Richard smiled at the still doubtful expression on Canaday's lean, handsome face, the thoughtful look in young Nancy Lucia's eyes as she studied him. She had removed the wool cap when she came into the office, and her silken, raven hair, black as Richard's own, softly framed her oval face. The lavender eyes took on a startlingly beautiful quality as did her rose-tinted olive complexion and the full, generous mouth. The nose, though slightly large in proportion to her other features, seemed to lend a measure of character to the delicate loveliness. Richard guessed her age to be twelve or thirteen.

Instinctively, he liked everything he had seen and sensed in the brief time since the girl had breathlessly introduced him to her father. Canaday had been painting a scenic flat depicting a Roman forum when Richard and Nancy Lucia rode up. From another wagon, a short distance away, Richard heard a woman's voice, singing a lilting Italian song in a clear, bell-like soprano.

Nancy Lucia had introduced Richard to her father with unquestioning, girlish enthusiasm, and was initially surprised at her father's interrogation. But she was a bright miss and her father's daughter, and Canaday's suspicious attitude raised some doubt in her own mind. Yet she felt certain Richard was no fraud, and wanted to prove it.

"Did you ever do *Volpone*, Mister Steele?" she asked suddenly.

"Yes, last season."

"What part?" asked Nancy with a reluctant note of challenge in her voice.

Richard leaped to his feet and launched into Mosca's soliloquy in the opening of the third act. He used the same intense, flighty gestures as he had onstage at the Lincoln's Inn Fields performance.

"I fear I shall begin to grow in love with my dear self, and my most prosperous parts . . ."

He got just that far, when Canaday slapped the desk top sharply.

"Gadzook's!" he exclaimed. "It *is* Richard Steele!"

Nancy Lucia giggled happily.

"We were not working that week, and we were only ten miles from London, so we came to see you."

She looked at him with undisguised admiration.

"You were so vile! So sly! So beautiful!"

Canaday raced through the office into the prop room and to the rear door of the wagon.

"Niccolini! Niccolini, my love! Come see a surprise!"

Canaday returned to the office, beaming happily at Richard. In a few moments, Richard heard light steps clatter up the steps of the wagon. A strikingly beautiful woman in her early thirties rushed into the office.

"Today is a day for surprises," she said. "I have just discovered that the peruker sent us a woman's wig instead of the man's we ordered. What's your surprise, Theo?"

She had a rich voice, and spoke perfect English with a faint and peculiar combination of accents: traces of Italian and even fainter traces of Theophilus Canaday's lingering Irish accent. She had gleaming sable hair, which had been coiffed recently, but had collapsed into a rakish pile on her perfect, oval head. Her skin was a darker olive than her daughter's; her nose and mouth were smaller, her eyes bright hazel. She was a classic Latin beauty. Her black cotton dress had a white collar and a white apron that failed to conceal the lushness of her well-rounded figure.

"This is my wife, Margherita Niccolini," said Canaday with obvious pride and pleasure. He turned toward Richard.

"This, my love, is the surprise! Master Richard Steele, who wishes to leave the Theatre Royal in Lincoln's Inn Fields to join our little family."

She stared at Richard, then looked at her husband in disbelief. She made dismissing gestures with both hands.

"The exciting young Richard Steele, who played the most heartrending Romeo I have yet seen! . . . The young man *The Spectator* dares compare with Betterton! . . . I don't believe it!"

She strode toward Richard and looked up into his eyes.

"Why, in heaven's name, would you wish to leave the Theatre Royal?!"

Canaday laughed heartily.

"We've been through that, dear Niccolini. Personal reasons. Perhaps someday he'll tell us. . . ."

They took Richard on a tour then. The wagon in which Margherita Niccolini Canaday had been singing was the wardrobe and costume wagon. Here were racks of gowns and cloaks and greatcoats and waistcoats and petticoats of various designs, materials and colors. A shelf held more than a dozen wigs, some men's, some women's, again in many styles and shades of human hair. There were boots and feathers and dancing slippers. On a table were bolts and fragments of damask, satins, silks, cotton and other fabrics, and several pairs of shears, and a box full of spools of thread of many colors. Richard felt a pang as he thought of his mother.

More of the area of the wagon was occupied by a double bed and a small table and two chairs. As they were about to leave, a short plump woman no taller than Nancy Lucia climbed the steps into the wagon. She had graying blond hair, a small nose and merry gray eyes.

Canaday put his arm fondly around her shoulder.

"This is Cecilia Hogsdon." He introduced the woman to Richard. "She is my cousin Cecil's wife and the hard-working genius who puts together the outrageous outfits Niccolini designs."

"Ah, but most of all, she's a fine actress," said Mrs. Canaday, leaning down and kissing the plump woman on the cheek.

Mrs. Hogsdon was impressed when Canaday told her Richard was joining the company.

"Most welcome, sir," she said. "We'll all try hard to make you happy."

Richard walked with the Canadays across the green field toward the wagon where the two young men were now washing down its bright blue sides.

"Cecil is in the village setting bills," said Canaday on the way. "We only arrived yesterday, and it will take my friendly cousin most of this fine day to visit every tavern, inn, coffee house or other place of business where we may be able to post and distribute our Great Bills. . . ."

"Uncle Cecil is a most humorous Falstaff," interrupted Nancy Lucia.

"That he is," said Canaday, "and a most excellent bill setter. He stops to chat and have a wee drink, and on occasion exercises an extra measure of charm to win over the kind of misguided proprietor who believes our presentations are devices of the devil."

The two young men halted their washing as the Canadays and Richard approached.

"Lads," said Canaday, "I have the great privilege of introducing to ye Richard Steele, late of the Theatre Royal in Lincoln's Inn Fields . . ."

He put his arm around Richard's shoulder.

"And about to join our humble family. . . . This is Cecil and Cecilia's son, Henry."

He nodded toward the shorter of the two men, a slender, wiry-looking youth, approximately Richard's age. Henry Hogsdon had shoulder-length, rust-colored hair, delicate features, and an odd eager, yet vulnerable, expression in his gray eyes.

He curtsied, said softly, "Most honored indeed, Master Steele."

"And this," said Canaday, "is Frank Hogsdon, our heroic strong man, and a player of noble roles."

Frank Hogsdon appeared several years older than his brother, perhaps twenty-two or -three, and was approximately six inches taller, Richard's height. He had the same rust-colored hair, but it seemed coarser than Henry's, and was cut short. His eyes were the same shade of gray as his brother's, but they had a strange, suspicious and, at the same time, arrogant quality. Hard muscles bulged under his cotton shirt and tight cotton breeches. He squeezed Richard's hand with great force.

"Pleasure, Steele," he said curtly.

The wagon the brothers shared contained additional stage properties, two beds, and some personal apparel of the two men, hanging from hooks on the wall. The fourth wagon, to which the Canadays led Richard, smelled faintly of horses and some sort of strong medication. One wall was hung with saddles, harness, saddlebags and reins. On a table against the wall were piles of coarse, heavy blankets, and four bottles of liniment. There was a small bed, and alongside it a table. On the table were a candelabrum with four half-burned candles, a hautboy (the flute-like musical instrument) and a small

379

pile of papers with musical notations. In a corner stood two pairs of leather riding boots.

"And here," said Canaday, "resides the equestrian princess herself, Miss Nancy Lucia Canaday."

"I take care of the horses," said Nancy Lucia, "and I love them all."

At the moment, the horses were in the Inn's stables. Before her ride that morning, Nancy Lucia had brushed, watered and fed them.

"We have four Clydesdales, two Percherons, and Harlequin, who's an Arabian stallion," she told Richard proudly.

"Horses!" said Mrs. Canaday with mock irritation. "One would think your father was a centaur, Nancy Lucia. Tell Mister Steele, rather, of your music, your singing, your dancing."

Canaday laughed.

"She even dances on the rope. But we all perform several functions."

Richard was startled to discover, in the hours and days that passed, how many functions each of the members of the company did perform. The following evening at six o'clock, he witnessed their first performance in the new theater, which had been built in the cockpit of the White Swan Inn.

He told Canaday that he wished to acquire a partnership in the company, as per the offer in the notice in *The Daily Courant,* but Theo puffed his pipe, tapped his nervous right foot and said, "I would like nothing better, Richard, but Niccolini and I think it best that ye live with the company for a week or so, to be certain it's truly what ye want. Ye'll find it quite different from theater patented by the Crown."

Richard took a room at the Inn, and the day after he witnessed the first show, Nancy Lucia knocked at his door and asked him if he would like to take a morning ride with her. In the same field where Richard had first seen the girl on her lively Harlequin, they stopped and sat under a tree for a time.

"Have you and father completed arrangements for you to stay with us?" asked the girl anxiously.

"No, Nancy, but I hope we will. . . . I'm almost certain we will."

"It will mean so much to all of us. . . . Please call me Nancy *Lucia*."

"I noticed that everyone calls you by both names. Why?"

"It's a sad and lovely story," she said. "Mama and father met when the Queens Theatre in Haymarket opened. I think it was 1705, or thereabouts. Father had just come down from Dublin to join the company. The management had decided to offer Italian opera along with the plays. Mama came in with a company owned by her parents. The first opera they did was *The Loves of Ergasto*. Mama and father fell madly in love. They went off and married secretly."

Sally O whinnied, and Richard and Nancy Lucia looked over to see the horses nuzzling each other. Nancy Lucia continued.

"When the opera company was ready to return to Italy, Mama refused to go along. She and Father told Mama's parents they were married, and Mama was pregnant. Her mother understood, but her father was furious. It seems he had been grooming her to marry a nobleman of some kind, not an actor. Father's mother had died just before he'd left Dublin, and he wanted to name the baby Nancy after her—if it was a girl, of course. Mama was convinced she would never see her mother again, and she wanted to name the baby Lucia, after her mother. . . ." She paused. "Well, they made a compromise. They agreed that they would name the first baby Lucia Nancy Canaday, and the second, if it was a girl, Nancy Lucia." Her lavender eyes misted. "The first baby died of a fever a month after she was born . . . I was the second baby. From the earliest times I can remember, any time anyone called me Nancy in Mama or Father's presence, they would correct them. . . . *Nancy Lucia, please*, they'd say. . . . They still do. By now, that's how I think of myself . . . Nancylucia, as though it were a single name."

"One word or two, it's a lovely, lilting name, Nancy Lucia. I haven't had a chance to tell you. I enjoyed the performance last night immensely. You play the hautboy beautifully, and you dance so well. Particularly with Henry."

"Hank is magnificent. Maybe the best dancer in the kingdom. And so sweet!"

"He's an incredibly effective pantomimist, too."

"Yes . . . Isn't Mama a beautiful singer? I wish I had inherited her voice."

"You have talents enough." Richard smiled with admiration.

Nancy leaped to her feet. "We'd better get back. Hank and Frank and I have to rehearse some of the things we do in the outdoor show. We're giving one Saturday, you know."

As they mounted the horses, she said, "Please, Mister Steele, decide you will stay with us."

"Why don't you begin calling me Richard, just in case I do."

She grinned.

"Shall we race back, Richard?"

Richard nodded and spurred Sally O. It was no contest. Harlequin won by six lengths. As Richard watched the girl leap from her stallion, almost before he came to a stop, he thought how warm and fresh and genuine she was. If ever he had had a sister, Nancy Lucia was precisely what Richard guessed he would have liked her to be.

On the following Saturday afternoon, an extraordinarily sunny Indian summer day, he rode into the village with the family in the large show wagon. He watched in awe at how efficiently Theo Canaday, Cecil Hogsdon and his sons, and Nancy Lucia opened up the wagon, created an outdoor stage, and gave another performance, totally different in every respect from that which they had given at the theater.

By the end of the first week, Richard convinced Theo and Niccolini that he had seen enough, that he was certain beyond doubt, that he wished to acquire the offered partnership in the show and travel with it. Before they settled on a price, the Canadays insisted that Richard go through the account books with them. Theo and Niccolini flanked Richard at the walnut desk in the office, as he turned the pages of the books.

They were kept meticulously in a neat, flourishing Old World hand by Niccolini. The accounts were perfectly detailed. One page was headed: CHARITABLE CONTRIBUTIONS. Niccolini waved a hand as Richard studied the page.

"Benefits we play for worthy causes," she explained. "Children's orphanages; homes for older, indigent people. . . . Unhappily, the list also includes more personal benefits . . . bribes, really, to certain venal justices, mayors, other officials from whom we must secure our licenses to play."

The greatest single cost item—Richard recalled it had also been the largest expense at Lincoln's Inn Fields—was that covering salaries and wages for each of the members of the company. The compensation covered both their work as performers and as costume designer, menders, cleaners, cooks, handymen or any of the many other functions they individually performed.

When they were satisfied that Richard had absorbed and understood all the figures, Theo Canaday said, "It's a healthy enterprise, lad, and with yer participation, and a little help from the good Lord and the weatherman, it can become even more profitable. . . . There's one thing I must add!"

Richard looked at him expectantly.

"We've all worked hard for more than ten years, Richard, to earn the Canaday company the reputation it enjoys."

He looked toward his wife.

"We've dismissed seven excellent actors and two actresses over those ten years for reasons I'll term 'behavior to the detriment of the company's good name.'"

"Too much drinking, and too much fornication," inserted Niccolini.

Theo smiled at Richard.

"Ye strike me as a decent lad, Richard, but we read the reports about yer fights with Jerome Wrexham. Seemed a woman was concerned. . . . We'll not tolerate such activity here."

"I understand."

"There'll be a clause in our agreement, which will state that if ye misbehave in any way to hurt the company—*in Niccolini's judgment and mine; no one else's*—we may return your money, and dismiss you from the company."

"I accept that. Your notice mentioned a hundred to two hundred pounds as the . . ."

"Niccolini and I discussed that, Richard. Frankly, ye'll be such an asset to this company, that even a hundred pounds seems exorbitant to . . ."

"A hundred will be fine, Theo," said Richard, and extended his hand. As they shook hands, Niccolini reached across and put both her hands over theirs. She smiled at Richard. There was a twinkle in her bright hazel eyes.

"We do understand that a handsome and healthy young man requires occasional sexual release, Mister Steele. We merely ask that you be discreet, most discreet. Preferably with, er—ah, shall we say, courtesans. Rather than with the young ladies of the towns and villages we play."

Richard grinned at her.

"Don't worry about that, Mrs. Canaday. And please call your new partner Richard."

"Indeed, Richard," she said eagerly, and kissed him enthusiastically on the cheek. "Please call me Niccolini. Everyone does, and I've almost forgotten I have a given name."

It was a Sunday, and they had done the outdoor show in the afternoon, and had the rest of the day free. After supper with the entire company in the Inn's kitchen, Richard excused himself, borrowed paper, a quill pen and ink from the innkeeper, and went to his room to write Nell Faversham. He wrote with such enthusiasm that he frequently penned a word he did not intend, crossed it out, and wrote another word after it.

Dear Nell,

I have just become the one-half proprietor of the Canaday Company of Comedians. It is a remarkable troupe. What they do is theater, yet is not theater. It may sound daft to you, but it is less than theater as presented at Lincoln's Inn and yet more. The two Great Bills I send herewith will give you some idea. It begins with a brief prologue:

Our company could not strive harder to please
Were it comprised of twenty more performers
    than these;
We sing and we dance and we mime for your
    pleasure,
And gratis, pray note, do great plays for good
    measure.
We hope when our divertissement comes to an
    end
You'll applaud and commend us to all of your
    friends.

Then Theophilus announces, "And now we begin with a bow to the crown, *The Dance of the Court Cards.*" Niccolini, who is Canaday's wife, plays a

384

spinet, and the other five members of the company dance out of the wings, each wearing two boards representing playing cards.

After the dance, Niccolini, which is her maiden name, by which she is called by all, sings "De Mi Cara," a beautiful operatic piece. She was with an Italian opera company before she met Canaday, and she is a beautiful woman. After Niccolini's song comes another dance, this one performed by Henry Hogsdon, a young cousin of the Canadays, my age, and Nancy Lucia, who is the Canadays' daughter. Henry, whom all call Hank, is probably the best performer in the entire company, and an exquisite dancer, as graceful a dancer, dear Nell, as ever have I seen.

Following this romantic dance comes the first "gratis rehearsal" performance—you remember that it is illegal for any companies excepting our patent houses to present drama. Frank Hogsdon, Hank's older brother, and Theo Canaday do the scene wherein the ghost of Hamlet's father comes before him. Frank Hogsdon is a loud and poor actor. He shouts and waves his arms in a terrible manner. He even makes Theo's acting, which itself is of the flamboyant James Quin school, seem subdued.

Right after the Hamlet scene, Niccolini plays the spinet and Nancy Lucia the hautboy in an instrumental interlude. This is to enable Theo to change costume and reappear as a red-cheeked, knobby-kneed Irishman. In this apparel, he does a humorous Irish piece called THE WHIP OF DUNBOYN.

The point of the quill pen had deteriorated, and the writing began to become smudged and erratic. Richard went down to secure a new pen from the innkeeper. When he read what he had written, he frowned at the letter's messy appearance, but he went on.

While I am writing of Niccolini I must say that she also cooks for the company, and is an extraordinary cook. She concocts dishes I have never before tasted, full of flavorful spices. She is a marvelous woman. But I must continue with the show.

He did indeed continue to describe the show in detail until he reached the finale.

Just before the last dance is finished, Theo steps out of the group and speaks an excellent epilogue, somewhat out of breath, but loudly, while the dancing goes on. He says,

"Our epilogue has been hailed as a brief delight:
Clap your hands, excuse me, and good night."

With these words, and clapping his own hands, he bows off and the rest of the company dances off, and there is great applause. The whole show runs a little over three hours, and the audience leaves in a most happy state, as they indicate by long applause.

Richard realized suddenly that this was his last sheet of paper. He went downstairs again, and persuaded the innkeeper to give him another half-dozen sheets. He also took a large tumbler of brandy up with him. He sat back and thought for a time about their other presentation, the outdoor show, which he wished to describe for Nell. He sipped his brandy, then dipped the quill pen in the inkpot and wrote again.

On Saturday and Sunday afternoons, this remarkable company presents an entirely different entertainment out of doors, weather permitting. This show is presented on the company's own stage, which is quickly contrived from a large show wagon.

He frowned in deep concentration as he struggled to describe the triple-sectioned wagon, and the manner in which it was converted into an outdoor stage. When he completed the description to his satisfaction, he took a long sip of the brandy and continued.

On this excellent stage, Theo, dressed quite nattily as a gentleman, complete with wig and plumed hat, simply announces the first act as "Frank, Hank and the Little Lass," and the Hogsdon boys and Nancy Lucia run up the steps onto the stage and indulge in a frantic acrobatic and tumbling act. As poor an actor as is Frank Hogsdon, he is an excellent acrobat and tumbler. He is strong and muscular, and many of the ladies in the audience exclaim over his physique which he parades proudly. Theo follows this exciting opening with a brief and simple magic act—Fitzhugh Fitzhugh taught me most of the tricks some time ago—and Niccolini assists him. Her voluptuous appearance in a flaming red, form-fitting satin costume adds greatly to the appeal of this act. The seemingly innocent but seductive poses she strikes at appropriate moments takes the audience's eyes away from Theo just when he is doing the slyest sleight of hand.

Cecil and Cecilia Hogsdon then do a hilarious dance called "The Burgomaster and His Frau." And then Niccolini sings a medley of Italian and English love songs with Nancy Lucia accompanying her on the hautboy. Frank then does imitations of all the sounds of a Hunt. He makes noises like the huntmaster, shouting, the hounds baying, even the fox snarling when he is treed.

And, you will find it difficult to believe this last presentation! The thirteen-year-old girl, Nancy Lucia, does a rope dance. Her agility is amazing. She turns on the rope, and seems about to fall once or twice, but does not. It is a fine finish and wins much applause.

For the show in the theater at the Cockpit, the charge is three shillings for the first ten benches and two shillings for the last ten. A little more than a hundred people attended each of the three performances. For the outdoor show, there is no charge, but all during the show, and particularly at its conclusion, members of the company pass a hat, or hold out an apron, and solicit donations. The company's people are so appealing, especially the females, that the collections are quite good.

Theo and Niccolini insisted I investigate the account books for the past season, and the company grossed a little over twenty-three hundred pounds in approximately forty weeks of playing. The salaries for the members of the company total three hundred and sixty-five pounds per year, and the other expenses are not excessively high, since almost all the work and services, which at Lincoln's Inn we paid for, are done by members of the company. I will draw one hundred pounds per year as my salary, the same as Theo, and at year's end we will divide whatever net profits there are.

Much more than the earnings involved, dear Nell,

what appeals so strongly to me is the prospect of working with this remarkable group of show people. I will not only act, but I will try to help Theo with the booking, and the writing and adapting and condensing of the plays. Niccolini insists she will make a singer out of me. And Hank is eager to instruct me in the dances. I, in turn, will do all I can to pass on to Nancy Lucia, Hank, Theo, Niccolini, Cecil and Cecilia all that I have learned from my years of study with our saintly friend, Farley Shannon, whose work is well-known to, and most highly regarded by, all the members of the company.

You may have noted that I omitted the name of Frank Hogsdon in the company list above. The omission is deliberate. Frank is an egotistical and arrogant fellow, and is quite convinced that he is not only the handsomest, strongest, most intelligent creature in the universe, but also the finest actor. Theo and Niccolini have already cautioned me that I will have to proceed with great care in improving the thespian quality of the company. For some time, I will surely not take over any of the roles Frank is doing. But I am certain all will work out.

On a separate sheet I am listing our itinerary for the next six months. You will note that we will be in Leeds, Stamford, Chester, Manchester, Preston, Lancaster, Nottingham, Derby and Worcester on one date or another, as well as in numerous smaller towns for briefer periods along the way. If you will discuss with your postman the approximate delivery time from London to these various points, you will be able to write me how you fare, and how proceeds your relationship with our friend, the Duke, our dear director, Gilbert, and all the other members of the company, to whom I beg to remain always,

Your grateful and humble servant,
Richard Steele

He thought for a moment, then wrote again.

P.S. I think, often, of Father Whittaker. Please let me know if he has returned, or if there is any word of him.

Richard read the letter over. Satisfied that he had

covered all matters quite creditably, he went to bed and slept better than he had in a long time. He looked forward to the morning ride he had promised to take with Nancy Lucia, and his first meetings with Theo to set the program for becoming a working part of The Canaday Company of Comedians.

It was a new life for Richard. He had little idea of the surprises it held.

"Frank?" Richard asked in disbelief. "You want me to share a wagon with Frank?"

It was just after noon. All the members of the company had finished their final light dinner at the White Swan Inn, and were on the way out of the kitchen to hitch up the horses to the wagons for the first leg of their journey to the towns in the north. Canaday, walking beside Richard, took a last long pull at his pipe, tapped out the remaining ash in his palm, blew out the bowl and stuffed the pipe in the pocket of his wool coat. As the smoke trailed out of his nostrils, he grinned at Richard.

"He's not a monster, lad. It's the only possible arrangement. I meant to tell ye last night, but ye disappeared right after supper."

"I believe Hank and I would be much more compatible," protested Richard.

"Ah, but there's Nancy Lucia, and only the three wagons, other than the show wagon."

Richard looked puzzled.

"Someone has to move into Nancy Lucia's wagon," said Canaday patiently. "She and Hank have been the best of friends, almost from the time they learned to walk. And gentle Hank is not interested in girls the way most young men are." He paused, stared at Richard, said softly with no leer at all in the tone, ". . . if ye gather my meaning?"

Richard nodded, still seemed baffled.

"I couldn't very well ask ye to share a bedchamber with our Nancy Lucia, now could I? None of us feel the

390

lass would be altogether safe with Frank, fine a lad as he is. . . . With Hank a curtain between the beds will be all that's required."

Richard's face brightened suddenly.

"How about Niccolini? Couldn't she move in with Nancy Lucia?" He paused. "And you and I could share the show wagon chamber."

Canaday shoved Richard playfully.

"Now, lad, ye wouldn't be wantin' to separate a man from his lovin' wife, would ye! Even if I would be willin' to make the sacrifice—and I surely would *not*—Niccolini would never stand for it."

He took Richard by the arm, and stopped him a short distance from where the rest of the troupe were already hitching up the horses.

"They're several good reasons for the arrangement, lad, havin' nothin' to do with the nocturnal comforts of Theo and Niccolini. And havin' much to do with the responsibilities of the new operating partner in the Canaday company."

The puzzled look returned to Richard's face.

"I don't know whether ye've sensed it in the short time ye've been with us, Richard, but Frank and Hank are not too fond of each other. Oh, they get along well enough; they're both fine young men, in their own ways, but Frank is contemptuous of Hank's sweet and gentle ways, doesn't understand young men inclined that way at all, at all."

Niccolini called from the show wagon, "Theo, we are having a bit of trouble with this harness. Can you hurry it up a bit!"

She and Nancy Lucia were harnessing the Clydesdales.

"Be right there, my love," said Canaday, but turned back to Richard. "And dear Hank considers his brother coarse and vulgar, and sometimes doesn't conceal his feelings too well. Between their mother and father, and Niccolini and Nancy Lucia and my own schemin' self, we've managed to keep them both under control."

He beamed, slapped Richard on the back, "And now, lad, I'm happy to be able to separate them, and turn a full partner's share of the problem over to you."

Richard nodded, beginning to understand, even flattered a bit by Canaday's assignment. But Canaday had not finished.

"I'm sure ye've also noted, lad, that Frank is by far

the finest acrobat, and the worst actor, in the company. I've been workin' with him for many years, and I've tried to teach him what I know, but I have my own limitations."

Richard began a protest.

"No, I think you're quite . . ."

Canaday waved away his words.

"Never ye mind, lad. I know I'm passably competent. But I'm an unusual actor, the rare breed who knows what he can do and cannot do. I'm far more accomplished a showman and a businessman than an actor, and I never had too much competent training."

Niccolini yelled for him again, and he took Richard's arm and walked slowly toward the wagon.

"Now you, me lad, have studied with the great Farley Shannon, and I've seen ye play two difficult roles extremely well with a fine Theatre Royal company. I'm countin' on ye to impart some of what Shannon taught ye to all of us"—he nodded—"yes, lad, includin' me. And most of all to our muscular young colleague, Frank Hogsdon."

Richard tried to help with the last of the harnessing of the four Clydesdales, but he was awkward and there was little left to do.

"I know ye'll proceed with great caution and patience in that respect, lad," Canaday called across the broad brown back of one of the two lead horses. Nancy Lucia pulled a buckle a couple of notches tighter on the mottled gray rear horse on Richard's side.

"And maybe," said Canaday, chuckling, "Nancy can teach you a thing or two about hitching a team of horses to a wagon."

By the time the company left the Gunnersbury Park area, everyone in the company had come to call Richard by his first name. Everyone except Frank Hogsdon. He addressed Richard always, curtly, as "Steele." But Richard was patient and friendly and totally unaggressive with his new wagon mate. By the end of the first week, Frank began to call him Richard, and began to relax with the new coproprietor. After that, the relationship began to go well. Living with the muscular, acrobatic actor, working with him day after night after day, Richard began to suspect, then gradually realize, that Frank Hogsdon's macho bluster, his arrogant posture were a cover-up for a deep insecurity. He discovered that, deep down, Frank did not believe he performed his work well, and that he did not like acting or traveling.

One morning, some three months after Richard had joined the company, they were headed toward Manchester, where they would play during most of the worst of the winter period. It was a December day, and there was a feeling of snow in the air. Richard and Frank sat together on the hard seat of the trailing wagon of the show train, bundled up in heavy sweaters with greatcoats over them. Frank held the reins of the Percheron as the wagon rocked slowly along. They passed a farmhouse, sitting high on a rolling hill. It was surrounded by neat squares of cultivated fields, stubbly and denuded by the last harvesting. The farmhouse was of freshly painted, white clapboard. It gleamed in the wintry sun and smoke curled lazily from the chimney.

Frank nudged Richard with an elbow, nodded toward the house. Small vaporous clouds popped from his mouth as he spoke.

"That's what I want, Richard, a farm where I can work, and grow my own food, and raise cattle and chickens. I'm sick to death of this gypsy life!"

"I thought you liked this life, Frank. You surely have always seemed to enjoy your work."

Frank shook his head vehemently.

"Not anymore. Not for the last couple of years. It was all right when I was a snotty-nosed child, but I'm grown, and I'm tired of doing tricks like some trained monkey for a motley bunch of oafs in one dull town after another."

It was the longest speech Richard had ever heard him make, and still he was not through. He took a breath of the cold air, then mumbled, "And you *know* I'll never amount to anything as an actor."

"You're improving all the time." The big man shook his head again. "No. I'm just a little quieter. I can *feel* I'm no good. Acting is for people like you and Hank. . . ." He paused suddenly. "No offense!" he added quickly. Richard knew he was right about his acting. He simply was not an actor. Now Frank made it plain that he would much rather put his muscle to work doing something practical and useful like farming.

"Don't say anything of this to Theo or anyone," Frank pleaded. "I don't want them fretting about it. It will be at least another couple of years, and I'll give them plenty of notice."

Richard could see what Frank meant about the gypsy life. It was hard in many ways. But that was one of the reasons Richard relished it, that and the novelty of it, and most of all the pleasure he found in the people with whom he was working. He had grown extraordinarily fond of all of them. This new life kept him mentally and physically occupied from early morning till late night, seven days each week. It gave him a sense of fulfillment in the help he was giving the others, while at the same time, giving him the satisfaction of learning and growing as an entertainer and manager.

One of the company's problems was that they had an insufficient repertoire of dramatic presentations, as well as song and dance material. The result was that attendance invariably tapered off before they were quite ready to leave the larger cities where their stays were longer. This was simply because all of the citizens of the community who were interested in the theater and general entertainments had already seen them at least once, and many several times. This problem of repertoire was compounded by the fact that, in many instances, the company returned to play the same cities, towns and villages year in and year out, and it was essential that a fair amount of new repertoire be added, and older material dropped, each year.

Canaday had found himself unable to keep up with this repertoire demand. What it required, with a company of personnel as limited as the Canaday group, was the creation of original one-act plays and farces, and, more important, the adaptation and condensation of the popular plays of the day, or specially prepared single scenes or medleys of scenes from these plays as written.

It was also essential that a reasonable number of new vocal and instrumental selections, and amusing and exciting dance routines, be created each season.

Canaday had help, of course. Cecil Hogsdon, who had been a schoolteacher for years before going into the traveling show business with his cousin, was quite capable of assisting Theo in condensing and adapting plays, but he had a poor sense of drama, and was not too effective in any work but that which he did on the comedies.

Niccolini and Nancy Lucia between them kept the

musical repertoire fresh and sparkling. Both wrote original compositions and arranged the work of other composers. Hank Hogsdon did even better, choreographing new dance and mime routines. Frank devised variations on the acrobatic stunts, so they seemed new. Cecilia contributed not at all to the repertoire situation, because her work in sewing new costumes, keeping all the wardrobe mended, washed and cleaned, left her little time beyond her performing onstage. Richard threw himself wholeheartedly into doing everything in his power to help alleviate this problem, as he did into every facet of his new life.

Two days after Frank Hogsdon's revelation of his secret ambition to become a farmer, the company arrived in Manchester, cold and weary. Theo Canaday had a regular arrangement wih Manchester House, one of the most spacious of the public houses in the city. At very special rates, he and Niccolini, and Cecil and Cecilia Hogsdon had large rooms, and each of the people in the company had a smaller private room. The following afternoon, at the end of a long rehearsal that Richard conducted, Frank Hogsdon took him aside.

"I've never talked with you about this, Richard," he whispered, "but . . . would you like to have a woman? I mean . . ."

Richard was startled. He looked around quickly to see if any of the other members of the company were close enough to hear them. He was taken aback at Frank's invitation because of its timeliness. For the past two weeks, on a number of nights, sometimes two nights in succession, he had been having erotic dreams. In the last of these dreams, just three nights earlier, his partner in the lurid fantasy had been Niccolini. Awakened by the spasms which shook him, he was shocked. He had never consciously thought of Mrs. Canaday in that manner, although he had admired her lush figure. Now he put his hand on Frank Hogsdon's shoulder.

"Why do you ask?"

"Well, you're young and manly. You're not like Hank, and there's a house here on King Street with exceptional girls . . . Ye House of All Nations."

Frank snickered wickedly.

"And indeed it is. There are white women and black and Chinese and Indian. Some are very young. . . . All

395

of them are very attractive. I go often when we're in Manchester."

After supper that evening, a Wednesday (they were not to give their first performance until Friday), Richard walked with Frank through the chill, dimly lit Manchester streets a short distance to Ye House of All Nations. It was a plain stone and mortar building of a fair size. The bawd was a thin, horse-faced Englishwoman with hard eyes, the blue-gray color of ice in winter moonlight. She knew Frank, and she greeted him as cordially as she could, but at her best she achieved little warmth.

"Ah! Our fine stud, young Hogsdon is back. Ming Toy for you?"

Frank nodded enthusiastically.

"Mother Higgins, this is my good friend, Richard Steele. Choose a very special lady for him," he said seriously.

"Delighted, sir." She bowed stiffly to Richard. "Any special preference?"

Though he was older, and certainly more mature, Richard felt more ill-at-ease here with Mother Higgins than he had on the night he met Cleopatra at Mother Magruder's.

"I—I—would just as leave—leave it entirely—I mean whichever lady you feel . . ."

The corners of her thin lips turned imperceptibly upward, her version of a sympathetic smile. She took Richard's arm and led him down a long hall to a small room.

"Please make yourself comfortable, sir. Your lady will be along in a moment. You'll find her most exciting, a true Old World courtesan." She smiled.

He looked around the ornate, maroon-and-cream-wallpapered room and at the elaborate silver-plate chandelier with a dozen candles glowing warmly. There was a table with gracefully curved rosewood legs and a veined marble top. On the table there was a large basin of clean water and many freshly laundered, neatly folded towels. Richard looked at the large bed against the far wall. It had a rosewood headboard, with carvings of plump cupids embracing each other. The spread was deep maroon, embroidered in white silk with the same cupids in the same embraces. Richard felt a stirring in his groin as he removed his coat, his broad tie, and began to unbutton his shirt. The door opened slowly, and Richard almost fainted.

The woman who entered wore a robe of sleek white satin, tied with a black satin belt at her incredibly slender waist. She smiled wantonly as she strode slowly toward Richard. Her hair was black, raven as Richard's own, and though it had been carefully coiffed, it lay collapsed in a rakish pile on her head, and in places fell to her shoulders. Her hazel eyes gleamed in the candlelight. He was certain it was Niccolini. His heart pounded in his chest, and his head spun with confusion.

He backed toward the bed, and the woman moved a little more quickly toward him. She whipped off the black satin belt with one graceful sweep of her hand. As the robe fell open, she wriggled her shoulders, and it fell away to the thickly carpeted floor. Her body was exactly as Richard had dreamed it three nights ago. The breasts were full and firm, with large, deep brown, almost black nipples, and brown aureoles the size of guineas around the nipples. From her unbelievably small waist her hips swept out into magnificent curves. Her olive skin glistened in the warm candlelight.

Only when she placed both her hands on his cheeks and looked up into his eyes did he realize she was not Niccolini. The eyes were hazel, and they were bright, but they were predatory, and they had a stupid, mindless quality, lacking the sparkling intelligence in Niccolini's. And her face was round, not oval like Mrs. Canaday's.

"Bocce mi, cara mia," said the whore, and moved her moist, open mouth to Richard's lips. She was everything Richard had ever heard about Old World courtesans. She was so artful that he erupted shamefully quickly the first two times he entered her. She performed many of the same rites of amour upon him which the Marchioness had performed in Bath, but with a tantalizing Latin languor. Then she introduced Richard to another technique that was madly, distinctively Italian and probably the kind of thing Lucretia Borgia had done before she poisoned a lover.

Her name was Francesca, and she spoke almost no English. But she had no need to. The repeated, muted *"bueno, buenos"* and *"cara mias,"* and the passionate moans and groans were language enough. After two hours, Richard thanked her, dressed and walked down the hall, where Mother Higgins greeted him.

"Through so soon, sir?" she remarked with poorly concealed scorn. "Would you like tea?"

"Brandy, if I may, please. Is Frank about?"

The corners of the lips did their poor best to achieve another smile. "Hardly, sir. He'll be at least another hour or two. Was Francesca satisfactory?"

Richard said quickly, "Indeed. Very."

Mother Higgins ordered a black manservant to bring a decanter of brandy. Making Richard comfortable in an elegantly furnished sitting room, she asked whether he would like to pay her five guineas. When he did, she bowed stiffly, asked him to please come again soon, and strode off as a loud knock sounded at the front door.

Richard felt sated. As he sipped his brandy, a depression settled over him. He was irritated with himself. He did not know why he should be depressed. He had enjoyed the carnal interlude, yet the depression continued and deepened. He finished one glass full of brandy and poured himself another. He began to think about the show they were to do Friday, and how much work it still needed, particularly Frank's part. Then finally, after almost two more hours, Frank appeared. He paid Mother Higgins, joined Richard in a final brandy, and they walked back to the Manchester House.

"Did you enjoy it?" asked Frank.

Richard nodded. "Yes, yes," he said gloomily.

"You're an odd one, Richard," said Frank, shaking his head.

A persistent knocking at his door awoke Richard early the next morning.

"Enter, enter," he grumbled.

Nancy Lucia came in, dressed in a heavy, knitted yellow wool sweater. Her raven hair was piled under a matching yellow wool cap. She flicked her riding crop impatiently against her brown leather boot. The beige breeches fitted her lithe figure snugly. She strode aggressively to the bed.

"I thought we were going riding this morning. It's a lovely crisp day."

The morning ride with Nancy Lucia had become somewhat of a ritual. Occasionally Theo joined them, but most days they rode alone. They usually talked as they cantered along. Richard told her some of his experiences at Lincoln's Inn Fields, and she recounted many amusing, and a few harrowing, stories of the troupe's experiences in their travels. She also taught him riding and jumping techniques. In a modest way, Sally O was becoming a jumper and enjoying it as much as Richard.

But this morning Richard twisted in the bed, pulled the blankets tighter around himself, groaned as he stared up into Nancy Lucia's clear, lavender eyes.

"Not today, not today. I'm not feeling too well."

"Will you make the rehearsal?"

It was scheduled for noon.

"Oh, yes, I'll be fine by then. . . . See you then, Nancy Lucia." He turned away from the accusing look in her eyes.

"You went to that place last night, didn't you!" There was disappointment as well as anger in her voice.

"What place?" muttered Richard foolishly. He felt guilty, and he was irritated with himself for feeling that way.

"You know very well what place, Richard. That bawdy house where Frank always goes."

She flicked his blanketed rump angrily with the tip of the crop.

"Owww," exclaimed Richard, but she was striding toward the door, and out, slamming it behind her.

Richard grinned. He thought she was behaving exactly like a younger sister who is proud of her big brother but has discovered for the first time that there is some clay in his feet. He grunted, turned over again and in a few moments was asleep. He awoke just in time to wash and get dressed and go down into the assembly hall for the rehearsal. He did not have time to eat but didn't mind, since he was not hungry in the least.

He and Theo and Cecil Hogsdon had worked out a condensation and adaptation of *As You Like It*. They had been cutting, rewriting and editing it for four weeks, and had been rehearsing it for the past three. Richard felt it was almost ready for presentation Friday. The players enjoyed the challenging doubling. Richard played both Duke Senior, who had been banished and was living in Arden Forest, and the Duke's son, the dashing Orlando. Theo performed the roles of the evil Duke Frederick, and Orlando's wicked brother, Oliver.

Nancy Lucia played the princess Rosalind, who masquerades for most of the play as Gannymede, the shepherd lad. Niccolini was her cousin, Celia, who disguised herself as Aliena, the shepherdess.

It had required a good deal of artful butchery to twist

some plot situations so that there was time for wardrobe changes for those doubling, and to eliminate the several instances where a player doing two parts was called upon to make appearances in the same scene. Richard was not particularly happy with the presentation, but he thought it would be well-received. The rehearsal went smoothly enough considering the circumstances. Every time Richard signaled Niccolini a cue to play the spinet, she responded with an eager nod of the head and what Richard interpreted as a sly, knowing smile. How she could have known about last night, let alone his erotic dreams, he did not know, but he felt, strangely, that somehow she did know. Nancy Lucia was cool, but responded to Richard's direction with professional efficiency. They were all up in their parts, and Frank was surprisingly good. The visit to the international bordello seemed to have invigorated him.

The next two mornings Nancy Lucia made it a point to be off on her ride before Richard came down from his room. He was amused by her attitude, and assumed she would get over it soon enough. On Friday, the entire company went to Draper's Hall, the theater where they performed in Manchester, and ran through the entire show once more. Ninety percent of it was new, but it all worked quite well, including Richard's participation in the dance numbers, and the ensemble singing routines. After a break of some two hours, which they spent in a nearby coffee house, they returned to Draper's Hall. Every last seat in the theater was filled. The show played as though they had been doing the new material for a year. Everyone, without exception, was excellent.

In a jubilant mood, they rushed back to the Manchester House, planning a celebratory supper. But off stage Nancy Lucia continued to ignore Richard. In the large, comfortable kitchen of the house, with a warm fire burning in the fire place, she sat at a table with her mother and father and Hank, talking animatedly to her young cousin. As he slit open a thin package that had come for him in the afternoon post, however, Richard caught Nancy Lucia stealing glances in his direction several times. The package was from Nell Faversham. It contained a thin paperback book and a dozen sheets of foolscap neatly folded in half.

"Do you mind if I read this?" Richard asked the Hogsdons. "I've been anxious to hear."

They nodded and Frank ordered drinks. Richard glanced at the title of the book.

THE NIGHT OF THE KNIGHT
or
THE TRIBULATIONS OF SIR LAUNCELOT
THRICE BLESSED
A Romantic Comedy by
BRENDAN GEOGHAN AND JEROME WREXHAM

"Seems one of my ex-colleagues has written a play." Richard put the book on the table and began to read Nell's letter.

Dearest friend Richard,

I was most pleased to receive your interesting letter. My congratulations on becoming proprietor of so distinguished and talented a company. You surely must be the youngest such proprietor in our profession. I am extremely proud of you.

There is so much to tell of the happenings here that I hardly know where to begin. But begin I must with the matter which is of most pressing concern to you, the whereabouts of Father Whittaker. Immediately upon the morning of the receipt of your letter, I went down to the waterfront to the parish house and the church. Both were deserted and seemed to have been in disuse for some time. In a disreputable pub, a nasty man told me that Father Whittaker had jumped into the river and drowned himself because he realized he could not save the souls of any of the "fucking denizens of the docks." That was his mean description. The man semed drunk, so I would not take his story to be the fact. The simple truth, I regret to say, is that no one has seen Father Whittaker since the funeral of your dear mother. I myself believe that he has just gone off to another place to get away from the scene of his deep sorrow. Perhaps, even as you yourself have done, dear Richard.

The serving girl came with the drinks. Cecil asked if he might look at the printed play.

"Of course," said Richard, and looked over to catch Nancy Lucia stealing another look in his direction. He sipped his port wine and saw Theo Canaday rise to his feet.

"Friends," shouted Theo in his rich voice, "permit me to propose a toast to the finest young theatrical manager, director and actor I have ever encountered . . . our dear colleague, Richard Steele."

All the members of the company lifted their glasses and shouted, "Hear, hear!" Several groups at other tables in the kitchen applauded. Richard blushed, rose, bowed briefly in all directions, then lifted his own glass.

"Thank you," he said. "And permit me to ask you, my dear friends in the Canaday Company, to drink to yourselves, the most gracious, gentle and talented group of players a man could hope to encounter in a thousand lifetimes."

Again there were calls of "Hear, hear," and applause from surrounding tables. They all drank.

"That includes you, too, Nancy Lucia," said Richard to the young girl. She blushed and raised her wine glass to her lips. Richard sat down and resumed reading Nell's letter.

You inquire of my relationship with Edmund. It pleasures me to say that it is as warm and enriching (and I do not mean monetarily) as I could ask. He is a dear man, and I wish I could be more of a comfort to him than I am. His situation with the Duchess, and particularly with young Lord John, who is three, is a baffling and troublesome one. The Duchess's condition gets no worse, nor better either. She will no doubt go through her entire life in her present paralyzed condition. But her bitterness increases as the years pass, and even in these, his earliest, years she seems to have implanted a dislike of the Duke in the mind of his child.

John is extraordinarily advanced for his age in many ways. At three, he seems to hold some promise of becoming a musical prodigy. Jerome Wrexham, who has added some skill at the harpsichord to his talents, has taught the child to play several simple melodies. Wrexham is the baffling element in Edmund's domestic quandary. As you know, he has been a favorite of the Duchess's for some years, even though she holds most people in the theater in contempt. He has taken to visiting the Duke and

Duchess quite regularly, and often visits in the Duke's absence. Edmund has said to me that he sometimes feels that Wrexham is more a father to the child than he is. Yet there is little he can do. Wrexham's work at Goodman's Fields is producing substantial revenues, and gives him an obvious professional reason for seeking out the Duke's company fairly often. Beyond that, Edmund says, Wrexham seems to be the only person from whose presence the Duchess derives any pleasure at all.

In Edmund's situation, I am happy to tell you that matters in Antigua, at least, seem to be in hand. Edmund's sister, Edwina, seems thoroughly recovered from the sieges of deep depression from which she suffered for some time. Their young daughter prospers. The cattle-raising project has developed to the great satisfaction of both Edmund and his brother-in-law, Gilbert Marlowe. But speaking of Wrexham, I must now tell you about his activities this season. I do not recall whether you were aware that when he came back from Dublin at the beginning of this season he not only brought along Brendan Geoghan—you did know that—but also brought back Catherine Clark. The three of them are living together in what must be one of the most hilarious and hectic *ménage a trois* arrangements in London. Cat and Brendan despise each other and are at each other's throats constantly, and Wrexham takes great pleasure in behaving in such a way as to make first the one, and then the other, jealous.

You will find along with this letter a copy of Wrexham's and Geoghan's play, *The Night of the Knight*. I am quite certain that Brendan is actually its sole author—I have had occasion to discover that Wrexham can hardly write two intelligent sentences in succession—but Wrexham no doubt earned his coauthorship by his effectiveness in having the play presented and printed. I must say that it was very well-received, so well that we will undoubtedly present it again before the season is over, and possibly for two or three days or a full week. I think you will find that in a pixilated Irish way, it is quite a humorous play. It is about a knight who has three wives, none of whom knows of the existence of the other two—but you will read it for yourself.

403

Cecil Hogsdon had returned to reading the play, and just at that moment he chuckled and tapped Richard's arm.

"This is quite funny, lad, quite!"

"So my friend tells me." Richard nodded and continued reading.

But much funnier than the play itself was the party at Pickering's following its premiere. The Duchess was giving the party, and she actually attended for an hour. It was one of the few occasions on which she has ever left her home. After she left, Wrexham concentrated on setting Brendan and Cat against each other. They began to argue, raising their voices louder and louder, until they were both screaming. Then Brendan threw a glass of port into Cat's face, and Cat threw her stein of ale into Brendan's face, and hit him over the head with the stein. They got into a most savage scratching and hair-pulling battle. They tore half the clothes off each other, and scratched each other's faces and upper bodies. And all the while, Wrexham stood on the table, swinging a huge tumbler of brandy, and cheering them on. Of course, he was quite drunk by that time. Ben Pickering and his nephew, Jamie, finally were able to pull Cat and Brendan apart, and the party ended.

Gilbert was not at the party. His gout keeps recurring, and the poor man is in agony a good part of the time. He asked me to be sure to convey his fondest good wishes, and asks that you write him if you ever find the time. He has also been having a great deal of trouble with Francis Caryll. Caryll is an excellent actor, but even more temperamental, obnoxious, egotistical and troublesome than Wrexham. Yet he is very popular, so Gilbert cannot do much else but work with him.

I have one other pleasant and happy bit of news, which I think will surprise you. Susannah Forbish had a baby! Yes, Susannah! Susannah and Quincy. You know that Forbish is in her late thirties or early forties, but whatever her age, she had a healthy, nine-pound baby boy. She herself almost died in giving birth, but after a long recuperative period, looks absolutely marvelous. She has lost a great deal of weight, and is actually more beautiful and sensuous than when she was so heavy.

The doctor says the baby will grow up to be a man of normal, average height, not a dwarf at all. Forbish and Quincy brought him to the theater last week. He is seven months old. He looks like Forbish, but when we all remarked to this effect, Forbish said no, no, no. The baby was lying in his basket on the large table in the wardrobe room, and Forbish unbundled him, whipped off his diaper, and said, "No, he takes after his father! See!"

I did not know that Quincy was noted for the large size of his organ, but I will certainly concede that young Quincy, at seven months of age, has the largest penis I could imagine any infant having. Forbish is indeed a proud and happy mother, and Quincy, an adoring and loving father and husband. Both asked me to be sure to send you their love.

This was where this page of the letter ended. When Richard slipped the page to the rear, he was surprised at the change in the handwriting on the newly revealed page. Nell's penmanship normally was gracious, curling, easy flowing, the lines straight and unwavering. The writing on this page showed signs of a trembling hand. The lines dipped slightly and climbed perceptibly. Richard read.

I pondered long, dear friend Richard, over whether I should write you this last unhappy news. Even now as I try to write it, I am not certain it is wise of me to do so. Yet I feel you would want to know. There was a terrible tragedy out at Waltham Cross a fortnight ago. The cottage burned down and Edith and Felicia and Josiah all perished. No one knows how the fire started. It seems as though they were all asphyxiated by smoke, before their bodies were burned. But they are all gone.

Richard stared at the sheet of paper, read the shocking words again. The serving girl placed dishes before the Hogsdons, put Richard's kidney pie down before him. Clutching the letter in his hand, he pushed himself away from the table. He said nothing. He walked blindly out of the kitchen, up the stairs to his room where he flopped into a chair, elbows on his knees, head in his cupped hands. Tears began to wet his palms. *God!* he thought, *can it be that some people are doomed, and doom those who love them . . . even before they are born.*

His door opened, and he heard soft footsteps hurry across the room toward him. He did not look up. The girl stood before him and gently stroked his head. He looked up into Nancy Lucia's lavender eyes, round with concern and compassion. She pulled his head against her young breast, continuing to stroke his head.

"Is there anything we can do, Richard . . . anything?"

He shook his head.

Heavier footsteps sounded in the hall. His door opened again, and Niccolini and Theo Canaday came in.

"He'll be all right," said Nancy Lucia, continuing to stroke his head gently. He reached to the table beside the chair, where he had placed the letter, found the page with the words about the Olneys, and handed it to Niccolini. As she finished reading the passage aloud, Nancy Lucia pulled Richard's head close to her breast, tried to choke off his sobbing.

She wanted to stay the night with him, but Richard refused to permit her to do so. Her parents said nothing. They stayed with Richard for a brief time, and when he seemed to have regained control of himself, they all said again how sorry they were and left. Richard did not sleep that night. He lay wide awake, all the old wounds, the memories of Felicia and Mary, torn open again.

In the morning, when he rose, he stood over the bed, staring down at the doke, the impression of his body. Painstakingly, he brushed across the impression over and over again, until it disappeared entirely and looked as though no one had ever lain there. It was an eccentricity he pursued the rest of his days.

❦ 34 ❧

He tried to shake off an edgy restlessness that made his hand tremble as he inserted the key in the lock of his door. He heard another door, farther down the hall, open. He looked over his shoulder and saw that it was Nancy Lucia. She was dressed in riding clothes, as he was. It was a little after dawn, possibly a half hour before either of them would normally rise. They met at the head of the stairs.

"I thought I would wait downstairs for you," said Nancy Lucia. Her lavender eyes were bright and clear. Her olive cheeks were touched with pink. The yellow wool cap hid her raven hair.

"I had the same idea," said Richard.

"Are you all right?"

"Yes. I didn't sleep too well, but—"

"Your eyes are all red."

He nodded. They went down the stairs and through the deserted kitchen of the house, and out to the stables.

"They must have been good friends. I'm sorry . . ."

"They were." He took a deep breath.

Sally O and Harlequin nuzzled each other as they were led out of their stalls.

"I'm sorry I was so stupid about . . . about Frank's place. I know it's none of my business. You can go anywhere you wish."

He smiled wanly. "Yes. I can."

He shrugged, mounted Sally O. She spurred Harlequin and rode off a little ahead of him. When he caught up, he cantered beside her.

"You were very good in the show yesterday," he said. "Everybody was."

"Thanks to you. You've been very good for all of us."

"And you for me."

Richard had been overwhelmed last night by Nancy Lucia's compassion, the depth of her concern. He was happy that she was prepared to forgive, however reluctantly, "big brother's" transgressions. Now as they cantered along, with a feeble winter sun slowly climbing into a pewter sky, they continued to talk about the show. By the time they returned to the house, Richard was eager to throw himself into the day's work schedule. The Manchester engagement was highly successful. Frank Hogsdon had gone to his favorite bawdy house three more times while they were in town. Each time, he asked Richard to join him, but Richard declined. During a break in the rehearsal, the morning following Frank's last visit, Frank took Richard aside.

"Why didn't you tell me?" he asked.

"Tell you what?"

"About Francesca. I decided to try her for a change last night. She's amazing. I can hardly move this morning."

"I've noticed," Richard laughed.

"Didn't you think she looks a great deal like Niccolini?"

"No," Richard lied, "I hadn't noticed."

That same week, Richard wrote magistrate Tom Culoghen to inquire whether the police investigation had discovered what had happened to Father Whittaker. His answer came within a fortnight. There was no word, no clue. He simply seemed to have disappeared.

It was almost spring when the Canaday company took the road northwest to Preston and Lancaster. These were smaller towns, and the company played shorter engagements there, but the performances went just as well as they had in Manchester. Richard still enjoyed the intervals of travel, even over the hard, uneven winter roads. The constant change of scene fascinated him, and he continued to find great pleasure in his work.

In Leeds, however, they ran into an unexpected difficulty. The magistrate with whom Theo Canaday had made his arrangements to permit the company to perform had died early in the fall, and Theo and Richard had to see the new magistrate before they could open.

"And you will perform no dramatic works." The magistrate's pudgy fingers were interlocked, resting on his enormous paunch. His voice was surprisingly thin, coming out of the thick lips in the fat, florid face.

"Only rehearsals, yer honor. And purely at no charge, gratis you understand, completely gratis. Our patrons pay only for the excellent musical concert and the dance program."

The magistrate grunted, cleared his throat.

"And you will do benefit shows for the Leeds Orphanage and Saint Swithin's Church."

"Oh, indeed. The same two benefits."

The magistrate held up a pudgy hand.

"Three!" he corrected. "I must request that you perform a special benefit for the Leeds branch of the Fraternity of the Sailors of Acadia."

Richard and Theo knew that Acadia was the Canadian port, which the English navy had captured to end Queen Anne's war against the French three or four years ago.

Theo said, "A pleasure, yer honor. And who is the responsible head of the Leeds branch of the Order?"

The magistrate grunted again, ran a tongue over his thick lips.

"I happen to have the distinction of being the organization's executive director. You may present the proceeds of the benefit directly to me."

"The same fifty percent of the gross receipts?"

"I think sixty would be more appropriate," said the magistrate, "considering one thing and another."

Theo nodded.

"Thank ye, yer honor."

As he and Richard reached the door on their way out, the magistrate wheezed, grunted and called, "Mister Canaday!"

Theo and Richard turned back.

"One more thing! I think you should be aware that I have appointed a constable to make a head by head count of all persons attending all three benefit performances."

"Good! Good!" said Theo. "Helps us make certain of the accuracy of our own accountings."

Outside, Richard said, "These corrupt justices infuriate me. Acadia, indeed! The thieving pig will pocket every penny of that money."

"Of course," grinned Canaday.

"And appointing a constable! That adds insult to the thievery."

"That's not a problem, lad. I'm sure the constable is one I know well. We'll give him a pound or two, and his count will somehow be not quite accurate. Our friend, the justice, will get a full thirty percent of our receipts. We can do no less."

This was one of the phases of life with the company which Richard despised. The problem of renewing the repertoire was endless and difficult, but he continued to prepare and polish and rehearse the cast in new material, month in and month out. He also worked hard to become proficient enough in the musical and dance numbers to make a contribution. Niccolini gradually got him to the point where he could carry a tune. He sweated for hours on end to master the two movements of what the grand dance master, Weaver, called Serious Dancing: the Brisk, and the Grave.

It was almost two years before he could dance the Grave movements passably well. Hank performed the movements over and over for him, saying lovingly, "Easy bendings, easy risings, easy bendings, and easy risings, easy one-and, easy two-and."

Richard tried, but the bendings and risings were never easy enough.

"Please, dear Richard," said Hank patiently, "not so quick, less force, please. It must be essentially soft, soft and easy."

The Grotesque and Scenical Dancing, at which Hank was a true artist, Richard could never master. Both styles were essentially pantomime, and Richard had worked too long, utilizing words and his tongue as major instruments, to convey his meanings without them. He knew he could never become an effective mime. But he tried, and tried and tried. He reveled in the hard work, the creative side of life with the company. But he could not abide the graft and the groveling. He had all he could do on occasion to hold himself back from assaulting some of the more flagrant leeches.

Some of these were quite ludicrous, but nevertheless effective. One day, Richard and Niccolini and Theo Canaday were going over the accounts in the office of the show wagon, when a gaunt, wild-eyed man with long graying hair rushed through the prop room into the office, screaming.

"Where is 'e? Where is the confounded caitiff? I'll jail 'im for a year. It's flagran' malpractice, is what it is! Operator of teeth! Ha! More like butcher is what 'e is!"

Richard knew the man—the honorable Montague Blodgett, justice of the peace of the small village in which the company was presenting its shows—but he could not quite follow Blodgett's hysterical complaint. To Theo and Niccolini it was plain. They had gone through this type of situation many times. Richard found out later that Blodgett perpetrated something like this on them about every second year.

Frequently, especially in the smaller towns, individual members of the company offered special services gratis to public officials and other influential citizens of the community. This was done not only to secure performing licenses and avoid prosecution for presenting drama, but to build good will for the company and improve the popular image of entertainers and theatrical people. Theo frequently painted a new sign for an innkeeper; Niccolini gave music lessons and occasionally presented a politician's wife with some attractive item out of the company wardrobe; Nancy Lucia gave riding lessons and instructions in horsemanship; Cecilia Hogsdon did mending; Hank taught dance; Frank did an occasional job requiring muscle; and Cecil Hogsdon extracted decayed teeth.

In this town, one of the smaller communities on the company's route, the justice's slovenly wife was a woman who kept her blubbery cheeks stuffed with marzipan or hard sugar candies a good deal of the time. Consequently her teeth were in an even more advanced state of decay than those of most of the older women in the village. She complained to the justice that two of the teeth were giving her excruciating pain, so Blodgett prevailed upon Theo Canaday to have Cecil Hogsdon pull the offending molars.

Now, in the office, Theo leaped from his chair to confront the raging justice.

"Cecil's gone ahead to the next village to set some bills, yer honor. What's happened? What may we do for ye?"

" 'E pulled the wrong teeth, the blunderin' calf's head,"

411

shouted Blodgett. "The two that were givin' my Elsie such pain are still killin' 'er!"

"Oh, how unfortunate," said Niccolini, a most sympathetic expression in her tone and in her hazel eyes. "But sometimes it is difficult to judge which are the troublesome teeth."

"A capable operator of teeth should be able to judge," screamed Blodgett. "I demand satisfaction, or this company shall never set foot in my jurisdiction again!"

"I have something which will help," said Niccolini. "Just one moment, please." She hurried out of the wagon and returned in a few moments with a small bottle in one hand, and a bright orange and brown shawl over the other arm.

"Please ask your lovely wife to rinse her mouth with a glass of this medication and swallow it slowly. Two or three treatments will relieve her greatly."

She handed the shawl to Blodgett.

"We made this for your Elsa, and planned to give it to her before we left, as a farewell gift. Now, if you will oblige us, you may take it to her with our fondest wishes."

The justice took the shawl and the bottle of medication, muttered an unenthusiastic goodbye and left.

"That wasn't our good whiskey, was it?" asked Theo.

"Of course not, dear Theo. It was that inexpensive but potent sugared alcohol we keep for the Blodgetts in our lives."

"Sorry we had to part with the shawl, love. I know it was one of your favorites."

Niccolini shrugged.

"I was tiring of it anyway. And our four shows here earned more than sixty pounds."

"Good, good," beamed Theo.

"Is Cecil so incompetent an operator?" asked Richard finally. "I don't recall any other such complaints."

"Of course not, lad," said Theo. "Every tooth in Elsie Blodgett's head is rotted. It would have made no difference which two he extracted. Shall we get on with these accounts?"

Niccolini and Theo were undisturbed by the incident, but Richard was disgusted. Still, as time went on, there were other incidents that outraged him even more. Some six months after the Blodgett episode, the company was playing its route of garrison and seaport towns. In one particular town the official preferred an outright payment to him of ten pounds, rather than waiting upon the proceeds of a pseudo-benefit performance.

"A bribe is a bribe in any case," he told Richard and Theo cheerily, "and I would much rather collect it honestly."

They expected no problems, but when they arrived at the town's New Concert Room in the Half Moon Yard, a fiery-eyed man, with long dark hair and a full beard, was standing on a box a few feet from the Concert Room's entrance, making a loud, dramatic speech.

"The players you will see in yonder Concert Room," he bellowed in a deep, rich voice, "are all whores and vagabonds. Down through the years, the Christian church has found them to be extremely prejudicial to morality and religion."

He raved on and on.

"Quite an orator," grinned Theo, as he and Richard hastened to the backstage entrance. Halfway through the company's first dramatic presentation, with Theo, Richard, Niccolini and Nancy Lucia performing, three constables raced up to the stage and arrested them. As they walked to the office of the magistrate to whom they had paid the ten pounds, Theo winked at Richard, and his wife and daughter. The bearded orator, who was a reverend, testified eloquently that the company had been presenting a dramatic performance dealing with lewdness and murders and profane actions. He further declared that the dances and musical numbers were at least frivolous, if not licentious.

Three other leading citizens of the town, devout churchgoers, denounced the appearance of the company, although they admitted they had not attended a performance. Theo made the defense. He was as eloquent as the reverend.

"My Theo has the silver tongue," whispered Niccolini to Richard. But it availed them little on this occasion. The magistrate found them guilty of violating the law against dramatic presentations and fined them five pounds each. Theo and Richard insisted on a private audience with the magistrate after the fine had been paid, and the office was cleared.

"I had no choice," the justice explained regretfully, "the religious element in the town has grown very strong."

"But we paid ye, yer honor," protested Theo.

413

"I did not then fully realize the power of the clerics and their followers."

"But that was only yesterday!"

The magistrate shook his head sadly.

Outside, Richard fumed. "The hypocritical bastards! How dare they?"

Canaday shrugged.

"We'll just write this one off, lad. Never ye mind, we'll make it up in the next town. Winchester is always good."

Of course there were those in the populace of every community, who found the players fascinating, and some of these caused even bigger problems than the anti-theater people. One such young lady almost caused the Canadays to invoke the morals clause in their agreement with Richard. It was during his fourth summer with the company. They were encamped near the theater in Salisbury, where they were to play. After the first of the evening performances at the theater, a plump, apple-cheeked, blue-eyed girl, with hair the color of golden wheat, made her way backstage and rushed up to Richard.

"Oh, Mr. Steele," she gushed. "Ye are quite magnificent. Could I speak with ye in private for just a moment?"

There was such a pleading look in her round eyes that Richard walked off to a quiet, isolated section of the backstage area with her.

"I wish to join yer company and be an actress," said the young girl earnestly, almost desperately.

"I'm afraid we have no opening, Miss." Richard tried to move away from her, but she clutched his sleeve.

Then out of a more brightly lit section of the backstage area, Nancy Lucia strode toward them.

"Begging your pardon, Miss," she nodded toward the girl. "Richard, we're leaving. Are you coming along?"

Richard nodded eagerly, tore his arm away from the girl's grasp.

"Sorry, Miss," he said, and rushed off, with his arm around Nancy Lucia's shoulder.

"Who was that?" she asked.

Suddenly, a big, burly man pushed past them and rushed to the girl.

"*There* you are!" they heard him shout angrily as he reached her. And as they walked out of the backstage entrance, they heard the girl say sharply, "Leave me alone, Samuel. Just leave me alone!"

"Who was it?" Nancy Lucia asked again.

Richard shrugged.

"I don't know. She wants to be an actress."

"Pretty enough," said Nancy Lucia as they unhitched Sally O and Harlequin from the posts in the yard behind the theater. "You didn't encourage her, did you?"

"Now why would I do that?" Richard grinned. "We really don't need another ingenue. You do nicely!"

They played Salisbury on the Wednesday and Friday night of the week, but the girl did not return, and both Richard and Nancy Lucia forgot about her completely. On Saturday, as was their custom whenever the weather permitted, the company did their outdoor show. Theo and Richard had agreed some time ago that Richard should not work in the outdoor shows, but should utilize his time to concentrate on condensations and adaptations of popular plays and other dramatic material. On this Saturday, a particularly bright and cheery June day, while the show was still on, he finished a medley of scenes on which he was working. Thusly, he decided to walk the half-mile to a clear stream near the encampment, and bathe and swim. He had not had an opportunity to bathe so thoroughly or to frisk in such refreshing water for some time.

His back was turned to the bank, and he did not notice when the blond, blue-eyed would-be actress ran gaily down an embankment, undressed behind another tree, and raced toward the stream. Richard turned just in time to see her at the water's edge. He was standing in the stream, waist deep, shaking water out of his eyes. The sudden sight of the long-limbed girl with her full, firm bosom, golden hair streaming behind her, was like a vision from one of his erotic dreams.

He had been celibate ever since his visit to the bordello in Manchester, almost four years. He had been able to endure this monastic existence only by burying himself totally in his work, going to bed exhausted each night, waking with a full program of work the next day. Occasionally he awoke in the middle of the night, tortured by uncontrollable animal desire, forcefully reminded of his natural urges by the hot rigidity of his erection. When this happened, he would suffer quietly, trying to think of some matter of business concerning the show, and if the rigidity did not subside he would fondle himself until he exploded into limpness, and was relieved. It was necessary to do this quietly, so that he would not waken Frank, and he always felt uncomfortable and uneasy.

The erotic dreams also overtook him intermittently. Niccolini was still frequently the partner, although in the most recent dreams, he had cavorted with Nancy Lucia. In the past year or two, she had developed much the same lush figure as her mother. On such occasions he usually awoke, feeling somewhat ashamed and guilty. He firmly believed that incest was sinful, and he still felt like a big brother to Nancy Lucia.

Now the sight of this blond nymph splashing toward him, arms outstretched, pink-scarlet nipples on cream-colored breasts, excited him and made him slightly dizzy. She almost knocked him over as she crashed against him. She squealed with delight and crushed him in her arms, her mouth warm and wet on his. He put his arms around her and kissed her passionately. Sliding one hand down her smooth back to an amply rounded buttock, he tugged her more tightly to him. Under the water, he felt himself growing larger and increasingly rigid. There was a wild stirring in his groin, and he felt hot blood rushing to his head.

She dug her fingers into his muscled back. He bent his knees. His erect rod slid between her soft, silken thighs, warm even in the cool water, and entered her. She put her arms around his neck and wrapped her legs around his waist. They clung together, searingly coupled. Richard exploded, but he did not stop. He kept kissing her, tongue darting, lips nibbling in liquid fire kisses. He clutched her buttocks fiercely in both hands. Her tongue was as artful as his, and she swiveled her bottom in his passionate grasp, so that soon he was hard again, inside her. When he exploded the second time, he opened his eyes. He was facing the bank of the stream.

On the bank stood Nancy Lucia. He unhanded the still swiveling buttocks, tried to pull his mouth away from the still-hungry lips, which nibbled at him. Before he could release himself from the girl's embrace, Nancy Lucia ran over the embankment and was gone. He tried to walk to the bank. The blond girl was hysterical. She threw her arms around him from behind, held on as he struggled toward the tree beneath which he had laid his clothes.

"Do not go, Mister Steele! Do not leave me," she pleaded. "I must go with ye."

Richard struggled loose.

"You can't . . ." he gasped. He stared at her. "Gad! I don't even know your name!"

"Anne. Anne Burney. Take me with you!"

She threw her arms around him again as he was trying to dry himself with a cloth he had brought along. She almost knocked him to the ground.

"Get dressed, Anne. We'll talk," he gasped.

She grasped his head in both hands and tried to kiss him on the mouth again, but as he twisted to step into his breeches, she missed the mouth and kissed him loudly on the ear. Then she raced off to a nearby tree, and dried and dressed herself. Richard walked grimly to her as she was brushing her hair.

"Ah, dear Mister Steele, ye will take me to the company, now, won't ye?"

"I can't, Anne. We simply have no opening. We cannot afford another player."

"Ye need not pay me. Just my food and board . . ." She paused, said coquettishly, "And I can sleep with you!"

Richard shook his head. It took him most of the rest of the afternoon to convince her she could not join the company at once. Then he was able to leave her only after he promised that he would come back to Salisbury for her as soon as the first opening in the company occurred.

She threw her arms around him, pressed her mouth to his.

"Make love to me once more," she pleaded. "Just once more . . . please!"

He would not have even if he could. He did not sleep well that Saturday night, and he was nervous all day Sunday. He more than half expected Anne Burney to show up and announce that she was going to travel with the company in the morning. He was greatly relieved when they finally had the wagons packed and rode out of the Salisbury encampment. Nancy Lucia had treated Richard frigidly. So aggressively cool was her attitude, that both Theo and Niccolini on separate occasions asked what was wrong. When she shrugged off their questions, they insisted she be more civil toward Richard.

The company was approximately three miles from the

417

encampment, headed southeastward to Winchester, when the wagon train came to a sudden stop.

"What can this be?" asked Frank, sitting beside Richard on the seat of the last wagon in the train. Then they heard Cecil Hogsdon's excited voice, two wagons ahead, shouting, "Come out of there! Come down out of there this instant!"

As Richard and Frank leaped down from the seat of their wagon, they saw Nancy Lucia and Hank jump to the ground from the wagon in front of them. They all raced to the wardrobe wagon. Cecil was pulling a young blond girl out of the rear of the wagon by her wrist. In the lead show wagon, Theo and Niccolini had driven some twenty meters ahead before they realized the smaller wagons behind them had stopped. Now they rushed back to join the rest of the company.

"Who are you, Miss? And what on earth are you doing hiding in those clothes racks?" demanded Cecil. His paunch was rising and falling with the exertion of jumping from the wagon and wrestling the girl out of it. His gray eyes were more puzzled than angry.

"It's Richard Steele's whore," Nancy Lucia said scornfully.

"I'm not a whore," whimpered Anne Burney. "I want to be an actress."

The girl tore out of Cecil's light grasp and ran toward Richard, throwing her arms around him. From the direction of Salisbury came the sound of horses' hooves, running at great speed. In a moment, the horses came charging around a bend in the road, roaring toward the company's wagons and the group standing in the field at the side of the road. Three men, two in their midtwenties, one fortyish, but all large and muscular, leaped from the horses and ran toward the knot of actors. Richard recognized the largest of the three. He was the brawny man who had come to get Anne Burney backstage at the theater. This one now charged directly toward Richard and tore Anne Burney's arms from around Richard's neck.

"I knew we'd find ye here!" he bellowed. He spun the girl into a nearby bush. He swung a swooping roundhouse right and hit Richard a crushing blow on the side of the head. Richard fell to his knees, shaking his head groggily. Frank leaped on the back of Richard's attacker. The second of the younger men, only slightly less bulky and powerful-looking than the one who had hit Richard, grabbed Frank by the back of his collar and tore him off the back of his companion. Cecil waddled in to aid Frank, but the older of the threesome of attackers, moving with surprising agility, stepped in and drove a hard fist into Cecil's ample stomach.

Cecil said, "Ooooofff!" and turned a greenish color. He sat on the ground, a tortured look on his chubby face as he struggled to breathe. Richard struggled back to his feet. He and the muscular young giant who had hit him stood toe to toe, slugging at each other. Richard's blows seemed to be having no effect at all. The large young man had a gleeful look on his face as he pummeled Richard. Nancy Lucia leaped on the man's back, her arms tight around his neck, as she tried to strangle him. He reached up to tear Nancy Lucia's arms away, but Richard drove a hard right, then a powerful left into the man's stomach. Richard's fists hurt. Pain shot up his right arm. He felt as though he had broken the thumb on that hand. As each of the blows landed, the man grunted, but he tore Nancy Lucia's arms away from his head and flung her off to the side. She landed a foot away from Anne Burney, who was kneeling beside a bush, biting her fist, a frightened look in her round blue eyes. In a blind fury, Nancy Lucia crawled toward her and punched her on the jaw. Anne Burney began to cry.

"I'm sorry," said Nancy Lucia and put her arm around the girl. She looked back to where Richard was fighting, in time to see his opponent land a huge right fist on the side of Richard's face. Richard staggered to his right, fell to his knees, then rolled onto his back. He lay there unconscious, bloodied and breathing hard. Niccolini had come to the assistance of Theo, but to no avail. The older of the three men had knocked Theo unconscious, and Niccolini now knelt beside him, cradling his head in her arms, wiping blood away from his swollen mouth with a kerchief. Some distance away, Hank was sitting on the ground beside his father. His left eye was bruised and swollen. His lip was bleeding, and he was holding his right ankle, which he had twisted badly.

"Damn, damn, damn," he kept muttering.

Frank and the second of the younger bruisers continued to wrestle each other all over the ground. The giant who had knocked out Richard trotted toward them, dancing nimbly alongside as they rolled over and over.

At one point, when they had rolled so that Frank was on top, sitting astride his man, the fellow's burly companion pulled Frank off with both hands by the shoulders of the coat. Frank knelt on the ground, head momentarily down, puffing and panting. The man, standing over him, clubbed him on the top of the head with an enormous hard-boned fist, and Frank fell forward on his face. He lay quietly. The older man had already dragged Anne Burney to his horse. Throwing her across the saddle, he climbed up behind her. The two younger men now mounted their horses and, with a contemptuous glance back at the wounded Canaday Company of Comedians, rode off.

When the nursing was completed—Nancy Lucia had put aside her anger with Richard to minister to him personally—and the bruised vanquished were back in their individual wagons, Richard sat in the office section of the show wagon with Theo and Niccolini.

"All I can say," said Richard through swollen lips, a hand to his aching jaw, "is I'm sorry it happened. I'm sorry you were all hurt."

Theo winced as he tried to put the stem of his pipe through his puffed lips. His right eye was half-closed, the flesh around it an ugly purple. His right foot tapped more nervously than ever.

"Ye remember the clause in our agreement about bringing discredit on the company . . . the morals clause, lad," he said sadly. His bruised mouth did not distort his speech quite as badly as Richard's. Richard nodded. Niccolini spoke softly, with deep regret in her tone.

"If you had only remembered my advice. You remember, Richard? Courtesans, I suggested. Discretion, discretion!"

"I know, I know," Richard nodded again. "But you mus' b'lieve I didn't plan it. I don' even know how she foun' me. . . ."

Richard had explained the entire episode in great detail. He truly didn't see how he could have stopped Anne Burney from hiding herself in the costume rack of the wardrobe wagon. He hadn't seen her, nor had anyone else in the company.

Finally Theo said, "Well, let's forget it this time, lad. But don't let it happen again. If ye do, for God's sake, don't get involved with the daughter of the village blacksmith."

Richard grinned and muttered his thanks.

"Especially," said Theo, "if she has two older brothers."

The next day Richard wrote Nell Faversham, with whom he corresponded regularly. He told her all about the episode of the blacksmith's daughter who wanted to be an actress, except for the interlude in the stream. As usual, he found a responding letter from Nell some four weeks later, in Dover. Everything was moving along well with the Lincoln's Inn Fields company except that the Duke had broken his leg, and there was an alarming incident involving the Duke's son, young Lord John, now eight years old.

35

. . . Edmund was thrown from his horse during the last hunt and suffered a fracture of a bone in his lower left leg, Nell wrote. Since he could not leave his home, Gilbert Weston and I had to meet him there last Saturday to discuss a new problem which had arisen in connnection with Francis Caryll. It was nothing serious. We were sitting in the library, when I heard a mournful sort of melody being played on the harpsichord. It came from the music room, which is further down the hall from the library.

Suddenly, the music stopped with a crashing chord. All three of us were startled, and Edmund looked a bit nervous. But we went on with our discussion. Then, after several moments, a wild, desperate yelping and howling came from the direction of the music room. I rushed out and ran down the hall to the room. Young Lord John was beating a small Yorkshire terrier bloody with the knobby silver head of a walking stick. The poor dog was leashed to the leg of the harpischord bench, and could not escape. He was madly dashing from side to side, sometime managing to get under the bench, but when he did John would poke him viciously with the stick to force him out, and beat him savagely. I ran in and tore the stick out of the boy's hand. He kept shouting, "The stupid dog won't sit up! He won't sit up!" John is amazingly strong for his size, and I had all I could do to take the stick from him. He screamed and cursed all the while I was wrestling with him. Gilbert had lumbered into the room, and was helping me subdue the boy, when the duchess wheeled in from the terrace. She came up to the door of the music room and began screaming.

"Leave that child alone, you scum!" she shouted. Edmund finally came hobbling down the hall on his crutches, and the duchess screamed at him. "I'll thank you to keep this filthy whore out of my house, Edmund!" John had run to her and was kneeling beside her chair, crying. I picked up the poor, bleeding dog and took him out to the stables, where one of the stableboys helped me clean him up and bandage him. I took him home with me, and I think he will live, although he may be lame in one leg. It was a terrible experience. I told Edmund that I would not come to his home again. He understood completely, of course.

Richard was sorry to hear of Nell's difficulties, but his own problems soon drove all thoughts of the duke, the duchess and their vicious child from his mind. The longest lasting and most distressful result of the brief battle with the brawny Burneys was the damage to Hank's ankle. He had twisted it severely while trying to kick one of the Burney brothers during the scuffle. Richard's and Theo's bruises and contusions healed quickly and well, and with the artful application of creams and powders they did not lose a day's work. But Hank could hardly walk, let alone dance on the sprained and swollen ankle. And it was six weeks in the healing. In the interim, Richard had to substitute in the dance numbers. This effort, along with all his other duties, would have been burden enough, but during this time, when he worked closely with Hank for protracted periods, Hank developed a demonstratively adoring attitude toward him, which made him feel uneasy.

Three days after Hank resumed his own dancing assignments, Frank sat beside Richard at supper.

"You recall my telling you about that farm just outside Manchester, the one on which I made the offer?" he asked Richard.

Richard took a mouthful of Niccolini's special spicy stew and nodded.

"I had word from the attorney in Manchester that Griffin, the farmer, has agreed to sell. I'll be wanting to leave early next spring."

This was substantial notice, but Theo and Richard found that replacing Frank Hogsdon was not easy. There were acrobats aplenty available, and more than a sufficiency of actors, but actors who were passable acrobats, and acrobats who could read a dramatic or comedy line effectively were hard to find. Finally Nell (who via correspondence had been trying to help, in the search) informed Richard that Quincy's Circus would be playing near Folkestone about the time the Canaday company was there. Richard and Theo rode over, and Quincy and Susannah Forbish introduced them to Virgil Hoope. Hoope was an acrobat with Quincy's circus, who had ambitions to become an actor, and Quincy never believed in standing in the way of any of his performers.

Theo and Richard discovered that Hoope was not as good an acrobat or an actor as Frank had been. Yet he was strong and willing and eager, if apparently a bit dull-witted. Theo and Richard spent a pleasant day visiting with Quincy and Susannah and other members of the circus troupe. The baby was a bubbly, cheerful child, so lively and robust that Richard felt he might well grow up to be one of the show's strong men.

Back in Folkestone, Frank and Richard worked with Virgil every spare moment for the next two weeks, and at the end of that time Frank left to go to his farm. By mid-spring, Virgil seemed to have reached the limits of his capabilities, both as actor and acrobat. Theo and Richard continued to work with him, but by mid-May they were ready to give up and settle for what they had. They put word out with Quincy, Nell and other friends that they might still be interested in another dual-purpose entertainer if one could be found, but in the meantime they made do with Virgil.

Hoope was taller than Richard, three years older, with close-cropped, bristly yellow hair and faded green eyes, which gave the impression he was about to fall asleep. He was a bore to live with, and for a time matters became even more difficult, when he fell in love with Nancy Lucia. At the end of May, after one of the outdoor shows on a Sunday, he startled her by proposing marriage, and she rejected him in a much more abrupt and nasty way than she had intended. Later, back at the encampment outside Hastings, she took Hoope aside after supper.

"Virgil," she said gently, "I didn't mean to act as though I find you repulsive. I just don't happen to be in love with you. Do you understand?"

"Oh, certainly," said the acrobat, seemingly not troubled at all by her rejection. "I just thought I'd ask."

Nancy Lucia seemed to have gotten over the jolt of coming upon Richard's tryst with Anne Burney. Her concern over the beating he had taken from the Burney brothers had pushed her anger out of her head. She and Richard had resumed their rides, and spent much time together. Virgil bored Richard through a number of long nights, seeking his advice on what Virgil might do to win Nancy Lucia's heart. Richard gave him no encouragement at all.

It was just outside Hastings, two weeks later, that a catastrophe befell the company. They left the encampment early in the morning of a bright day in early June. They were due in Eastbourne to begin a series of performances there the following evening. The sun was a bright golden ball in the clear blue sky, but by early afternoon a thick mist began to blow in from the east, across the English Channel, and by late afternoon the heavens had turned an oppressive smoky gray, and angry black clouds obscured the sun. They stopped briefly for supper, then climbed back on the wagons and headed for Bexhill, halfway to Eastbourne. About ten o'clock it began to rain, moderately at first, then heavier and heavier. Finally the waters poured down in a veritable deluge. The night was black, with the feeble crescent moon almost continuously obscured by ominous cloud banks, and few stars were able to pierce the ebony sky.

The wagons rolled on. Everyone had donned black rubber rain gear, and the wagon mates alternated on the driver's seat, the men taking longer shifts than the women. For an hour or more, the rains beat relentlessly down on the hard roofs of the wagons, making a maddening, drumming sound. Then a hard wind gusted from the northeast, and the rain slashed savagely against the sides of the wagons, drenching the drivers.

"This can't keep up," Theo muttered to himself.

But it did. The hard dirt roads, baked into firm pathways by a month of almost continuous sunny weather, became avenues of slimy mud. Soaked to the skin and chilled, Theo, driving the lead show wagon, urged the Clydesdales on. The broad-backed Scottish horses slipped and stumbled, but slogged ahead, the long hair plastered muddily to the backs of their powerful legs. Finally, the fury of the storm diminished. The velocity of the wind decreased, then the blowing seemed to cease altogether, and the rain to come down much more lightly. Richard, in the trailing wagon, breathed a deep sigh of relief.

But the surcease proved unhappily temporary. The storm had only paused to catch its breath. Within the hour, the northeast wind began to blast at the wagons with such fury that they leaned and rocked and threatened to topple onto their sides. The rains whipped against them in savage partnership with the wind. Theo wiped a hand across his eyes, barked through the tumult of the water and wind at the Clydesdales. Suddenly the wagon toppled crazily to the right. Theo had seen the dark forms of the two Clydesdales on that side stumble and stagger as they apparently ploughed through some kind of muddy ditch in the road. They pulled their way through and dragged both the right front and rear wheels into the ditch.

The wagon did not move forward, but the wheels dug themselves individual and ever-deepening prisons of mud. Theo quickly realized what was happening. He leaped down from the wagon seat, raced to the rear prop area and emerged in brief minutes with two heavy oil lanterns. Swinging one in each hand, he slogged his way toward the back wheel, studied it for a moment, then slogged forward to inspect the front wheel in the feeble light of the lamps. By the time he reached the front wheel, the company had all slipped and slithered their way toward him in the wet, whipping darkness.

"Only thing to do is try to jam some heavy planks under those wheels," gasped Theo, wiping water out of his eyes.

Virgil carried two planks, each a foot wide and four or five feet long, one under each arm. Richard, Hank and Cecil brought out sledgehammers. Nancy Lucia, garbed as the rest in the heavy black rubber gear, went forward to pacify the nervous, miserable Clydesdales, while the men worked. In the flickering, wan light of the lanterns, with the rains slashing at them, they jammed a plank under each of the two deeply sunken wheels.

"All right, Nancy Lucia," shouted Theo. "See if you can get them to move ahead. . . . Slowly now . . . very slowly."

Instead of climbing up onto the seat and driving the Clydesdales, Nancy Lucia took the lead horse on the right side by the shoulder harness and, speaking into his ear, led him forward.

"Come on, now, Sandy. That's a good lad . . . easy, Sandy, easy . . ."

Sandy moved wearily ahead. His companions obediently followed. Inch by torturous inch, the wheels slid rather than rolled up the slanted planks as the men stood watching, eyes eager and desperate in their wet faces.

"That's it, Nancy Lucia," shouted Theo, breathing hard. "Easy, girl, that's it. . . . Good . . . good . . . easy—"

Suddenly the front wheel skidded sideways off the plank. As the horses continued to tug, the plank stabbed into the wheel. Two spokes snapped with a loud succession of cracking sounds, sharp against the whistling, pounding of the storm. The wheel began to slide itself a new channel in the thick mud.

"Whoa! Hold it, Nancy Lucia! Hold it!" shouted Theo. But before the Clydesdales stopped, the rear wheel skidded off its plank. Theo crawled under the wagon on his stomach, and tried to dislodge the plank from the spokes of the front wheel. Richard crawled in to help him. Virgil was trying to lift the wheel, an effort a brighter man would have recognized as futile.

"Damn!" grunted Theo. "I can't budge the—aghhh . . . aghhhhh . . ."

Richard heard the tortured gasp, and watched as Theo clutched his left arm, just above the elbow, with a muddy right hand. In the wavering lantern light, he caught a fleeting glimpse of the pain and panic in Theo's eyes, before Theo fell to the ground, face down in the mud under the wagon. Both Theo's hands were now clutching at his chest. He raised his head out of the mud with a desperate effort, gasping hungrily for air. Choking sounds escaped the wide-open mouth, shadowed and lighted by the fitful flame of the lanterns.

Richard remembered the stifling summer day the old dockworker in Horatio Busk's gang had suffered what a doctor later had termed a failure of the heart. He recognized the symptoms now in Theo's hungry, open-mouthed gulping for air, the frantic fingers clawing at the slippery rubber coat.

"Easy, Theo," he said and, putting his arm around Canaday's shoulder, tried to slide him out from under the wagon. He got him out and held him in both arms. Niccolini, apparently sensing that something had happened,

427

had left her work with the books and now came running toward them. Nancy Lucia rushed back to Theo and Richard.

"Virgil!" shouted Richard, "take him back to our wagon. Put him in my bed. Quickly!"

Virgil lumbered forward and picked Theo Canaday up in his arms. The rest of the troupe made way for him, and he strode toward the last wagon in the train. Once he almost slipped in the mud, but he recovered without dropping Theo.

"What is it, Richard?" screamed Niccolini.

"I don't know. Seems to be his chest, his arms. We must get him to a doctor."

He turned to Nancy Lucia.

"Nancy Lucia, Cecil, Hank! Hitch two of the Clydesdales up to my wagon. It's got less weight in it than any of the others."

Nancy Lucia, Cecil and his son staggered forward clumsily to the Clydesdales. Frantically, with the rain beating down on them, they unhitched the two lead horses.

"Where's the nearest doctor, Niccolini?" asked Richard. "Is there one in Bexhill?"

"No. Eastbourne. There's a good doctor there. He tended Cecil last season when Cecil had a stomach disorder!"

In the mud and the stormy darkness it was difficult to get the Percheron pulling Richard's and Virgil's wagon unhitched, and the Clydesdales secured in the double harness that Nancy Lucia and Hank dragged out of her wagon. While they were working with desperate speed, Richard and Niccolini had climbed into the wagon, stripped the heavy rubber gear from Theo, dried him completely, and laid him on Richard's bed, covered with warm blankets. All the while, he struggled for breath and fought against the pain in his chest and arms. Now, with Niccolini by his side, holding his hand, murmuring comforting words to him, he lay with his eyes closed, fists clenched against the sharp torture. His mouth remained open, stretching wider in recurring spasms, trying to draw in precious air.

On the seat of the wagon, with Richard beside her, Nancy Lucia held the reins, and shouted and whipped the weary Clydesdales through the black night toward Eastbourne.

"Will he be all right, Richard?"

"I'm sure he will." Richard spoke with more conviction than he truly felt. "You may be driving the horses a bit too hard, Nancy Lucia. The road is treacherous."

"I can't hear you!" Nancy shouted, leaning toward him, frantically flicking the long whip over the backs of the Clydesdales. Richard raised his voice over the sound of the blasting rain, repeating his warning. Nancy Lucia nodded grimly, but seemed unable to control herself. He said no more, until another fifteen minutes had passed. Then he leaned toward Nancy Lucia and took the reins and the whip from her hands.

"Let me take it for a while, Nancy Lucia. You need a little rest."

The Clydesdales slowed to a more tolerable pace, but if Nancy Lucia noticed, she said nothing. Ironically, five minutes after Richard had taken the reins, Nancy screamed as they saw the dark form of Sandy, the lead horse on the right, stumble, fall, try to rise and stumble again. Macduff, Sandy's companion, ran along several meters, dragging his crippled mate. Richard pulled hard on the reins, halted the team and leaped from the wagon. Nancy Lucia was right beside him. In the mud, they sloshed their way to the fallen horse. He hung by the harness, lying half on his left side, his front right leg dangling. The lower part of the leg, from the knee cap down, flapped sickeningly back and forth, as the horse made a frantic effort to right himself.

Even in the darkness, Richard could see the look of agony in Sandy's right eye. He turned toward Nancy Lucia. Horror showed on her dripping face.

"My god! His leg is broken!" she gasped.

Richard ran back to the wagon. Three years ago, the company had been held up and robbed by highwaymen, and Theo had purchased sets of two flintlock pistols for each of the four company wagons. Richard took one of the pistols out of the cabinet in which they were kept, checked to see that it was loaded. Theo still lay with his eyes closed, but he now held Niccolini's hand in both of his. Pain still showed on his face, but he seemed to be drawing breaths with little less desperate effort than earlier.

"What is wrong, Richard?" whispered Niccolini.

He shook his head and rushed out of the wagon.

Nancy Lucia was kneeling in the mud beside Sandy.

Tears ran down her cheeks with the rain. She had un-hitched him, and led him off to the side of the road. He lay on his left side, panting, a mournful, pain-filled look in his bright brown right eye, the broken leg wobbling pitifully. Nancy Lucia put her face to the Clydesdale's head for a moment, then rose to her feet and turned her back. Richard shot the horse through the head. Together he and Nancy Lucia readjusted the harness so that Macduff could pull the wagon without his mate. Nancy Lucia sat beside Richard, head down, sobbing uncontrollably. Richard held her to him with one arm, urging the horse on. He prayed that Macduff would not have a similar accident on the dark, treacherous road. Every time the horse stumbled, Richard's heart skipped a beat. He was not certain Theo would last until they reached Eastbourne under any circumstances. But if anything happened to Macduff, it would surely mean the end. Grimly, they rode on.

By the time they got to the doctor's small house, the rain stopped altogether. The doctor came out to treat Theo in the wagon. With Niccolini, Nancy Lucia and Richard anxiously standing by, he questioned Theo about the severity and location of the pain in his arms and chest. He listened hard, head against Theo's breast, to the labored breathing. Dr. Christopher Wilks had a more extensive knowledge of anatomy and medicine than most practitioners of his day. He urged Niccolini to keep Theo quiet, and rushed back into his house. There he prepared a powder from a few leaves of a foxglove plant. He put this aside, and with quiet efficiency mixed a potion of syrup of maidenhair, horehound, balsam of sulphur made with oil of turpentine, black cherry water and several other ingredients. This was a prescription he had found useful in relieving persons who had difficulty in breathing.

Fortunately for Theo, the foxglove plant was later discovered to contain the base for digitalis, and came to be used extensively in cardiac cases. A half hour after Theo had swallowed Dr. Wilks' powder and drank the medicine he fell asleep, breathing heavily, but regularly. Dr. Wilks prescribed the dosages of the foxglove powder and the lung medicine Niccolini was to give her husband.

He took her hand, said gently, "Niccolini, I think your husband has come to the end of his career as a traveling showman. I'm afraid he will have to retire into a far more sedentary occupation."

"But he will be all right?" asked Niccolini.

"If he exercises care and good judgment. I'll prescribe a diet, and medication, and a program of mild activity for him. But you must make certain he's careful. Another attack of this kind could be fatal."

The rest of the company had already set up camp in the rain-soaked field outside Eastbourne, where they always quartered on their visits to the seacoast town. When Theo awoke from a long sleep, he felt weak, but glad to be alive. He could not leave his bed, but he insisted the company fulfill the Eastbourne engagement, making whatever adjustments they could in both the indoor and outdoor shows.

The following morning, after sleeping a few hours, Richard, Nancy Lucia and Virgil went back to the place where Sandy had died. All three worked more than an hour digging a deep grave in the still soggy earth by the side of the road. Finally, thanks to Virgil's great strength, and with the aid of ropes, they were able to get the horse into the grave and cover it. Nancy Lucia cried all the way back to the encampment. The rest of that afternoon, Richard worked with the entire company and rearranged the program for that evening's performance. It was ragged and certainly lacked enthusiasm, but the Eastbourne audience, composed largely of sailors, enjoyed it.

Theo stayed in bed, fidgeting and fussing all the time, for the first three days after his attack. The fourth day was a Saturday, and he got up out of bed, and insisted that he would do the first of the outdoor shows that afternoon. Niccolini was furious with him, and Richard, Nancy Lucia, the Hogsdons all tried to dissuade him, but he insisted.

In the middle of his opening speech, he collapsed on stage, clutching his upper right arm with his left hand. Niccolini had brought along a small packet of the foxglove powder, and she now took it from the pocket of her gown, giving him a half-spoonful and a tumbler of water. Then she gave him a spoonful of the lung medicine. The audience was in a turmoil, pushing toward the stage. Nancy Lucia ran to the foot of the stage and pleaded with them to stand back. Richard raced to Sally O and rode to fetch Dr. Wilks. Virgil carried Theo off to the side of the stage, where he lay with his head against Niccolini's breast. Nancy Lucia held his hand. Virgil recaptured the small crowd's attention by launching into a rowdy tumbling routine. Then Hank danced on to do a pantomime number.

Richard arrived shortly with Dr. Wilks and they finally cut the show short. Virgil carried Theo to the bed in the show wagon, where the doctor gave him a tumbler full of a brandy and herb tonic.

"Theo," he said severely, "unless you are determined to end your life, you must have complete rest while you are here in Eastbourne. Before you leave, Niccolini will find a little house somewhere. No more traveling. None —whatsoever! Do you hear me?"

Theo, breathing hard, sheepishly nodded agreement. The doctor visited him every day for the remainder of the engagement. Several times, it seemed certain he would die. Niccolini never left his side. He asked her at least to do her segments of the shows, but she would not hear of it. Her musical contributions were missed, but the company managed to put together acceptable patchwork performances. Nancy Lucia and Richard, between shows, searched for a place in the area where the Canadays could live. At the end of the first week, they found a small cottage in Bexhill. Theo and Niccolini moved in there when the company left Eastbourne. Hitched alongside Macduff was a Clydesdale they named Sandy the Second, which they purchased from a wagonmaker in Eastbourne.

Nancy Lucia was devastated at having to leave her mother and father behind. It was the first time in her life that she had been without them. But she was now almost seventeen years of age, and both Theo and Niccolini insisted she go with the company. Richard tried to give her as much comfort as any brother could. The wagon arrangements were changed. Cecil and Cecilia Hogsdon took over the bedchamber in the large show wagon, and Hank moved into their wagon. Nancy Lucia had her own wagon to herself once more, and Richard continued to share his quarters with Virgil Hoope. But that was simply the nighttime sleeping arrangement. Most of the time, as they traveled, Richard and Nancy Lucia sat side by side, guiding the team of four Clydesdales pulling the lead show wagon.

A week after they left Theo and Niccolini at Bexhill, they were riding north once again. It was a warm day, with a high orange sun in the sky. Richard was holding the reins, when Nancy Lucia put her arm through his and squeezed his arm against her.

"Richard, I don't know what I would do without you. I miss Father and Mama so much."

"I know. I miss them, too."

"What's going to happen to the company, Richard?"

"We'll go on." He patted her knee. "Everything will work out."

She kissed his cheek.

They became closer than ever, working on the vast number of new problems the show faced with the elder Canadays suddenly gone. The first priority, of course, was to find replacements for Theo and Niccolini. Richard placed notices in *The Daily Courant, The Spectator* and *The Tattler*. He wrote Nell, pleading for her help. He had Quincy's itinerary, and he wrote Quincy and Susannah Forbish, asking them to help in the search. Only when he actually set forth his needs in the notices and in the letters to his friends did he fully realize what he was seeking: a capable actor and actress; a person familiar with scheduling a show and making "special arrangements" with public officials; a musician and singer; a person who could keep the books; and to add a laughably ludicrous qualification, preferably also a woman, who could cook! He omitted this last requirement from the notices.

In the next three months he had nineteen letters from applicants. Sixteen of the letters were obviously written by young people with no experience whatsoever. A dozen seemed to come from semiliterate, romantic, stage-struck Anne Burneys. As Nancy Lucia and Richard went through the letters, Nancy Lucia disposed of these with short expressions of contempt and disgust, and a toss of the sheets into the large trash receptacle in the office wagon. The other three were strangely similar. They were both shrewdly written. Each described the talents and capabilities of the applicants as being precisely what Richard's notice called for. Each listed long experience with theatrical companies. Each requested that Richard send five pounds to enable them to close out their present affairs and as coach fare to enable them to come to join the show. Richard could recoup the money, they said, out of their salaries. Richard showed these letters to Cecil with great enthusiasm. Cecil soon disenchanted him.

"We ran a notice for players seven years ago, lad," he said, "and we got a dozen letters much like these. We were young and innocent then, and Theo sent the money to two of the applicants. Last we ever heard of them."

At the crestfallen look on Richard's face, Cecil slapped him on the back.

"Don't be discouraged, lad. Someone will turn up one of these days. But the kingdom is full of rascals like those, who make a practice of swindling hard-working comedians like us."

For what seemed like months that would never end, Richard worked as many as twenty hours out of the twenty-four each day trying to keep the company going at something approximating its usual standards. The members of the troupe helped in every way they could. Cecil tried to assist Richard in the bookings and the relations with authorities, but he was an easy-going, unambitious kind of man who looked forward to retiring himself, in another year or two. He laughed and joked and got along well with the proprietors of the theaters and assembly halls and other venues they played, but he was totally inept as a bargainer. With corrupt magistrates and justices, he was even worse. They took unconscionable advantage of him. Richard was not very much better. He tried to stand firm, and refused to be overcharged for exhibit quarters. He fought bitterly with the more unreasonable and greedy grafters, but he hated this phase of the business, and it depressed him and tended to damage the creative side of his work.

Nancy Lucia filled in extremely well in the musical aspects of the show, and took on the task of keeping the accounts. She did this with great difficulty and made many mistakes, but by sheer perseverance she improved and managed to keep the books in good order.

But it was a losing battle, and Richard did not know how much longer he could go on. Then, once again, Nell Faversham came to the rescue. In her work for the Duke, assisting Gilbert Weston at Lincoln's Inn Fields, as well as Jerome Wrexham at Goodman's Fields, she spent a great deal of time offstage traveling in search of new talent. Late in November, she was in Norwich, one of the

434

leading inland towns of the kingdom. An excellent permanent company of comedians had developed there. She spent a week with the managers and the players in the company, and learned that two of the outstanding players, a husband and wife team, David and Portia Sutherland, were anxious to organize a company of their own, preferably a traveling unit.

She had witnessed their performances in three plays, one a romantic comedy, and the other two, Shakespearean tragedies, and found them excellent. She had also learned that Sutherland had written three plays which had been performed by the Norwich players. She had asked the Sutherlands to have supper with her, and told them about Richard's search to replace Theo and Niccolini in the Canaday company.

"Dear girl," said David, in his deep, cultivated voice, "we could quite conceivably be interested. Have you any idea whether Steele and Canaday would consider selling an interest in the company?"

Sutherland was an unrelenting Thespian, a man who was onstage at all times. He was always meticulously dressed and groomed. He wore silver-white wigs, in the full-bottom style affected by most dignified men of all the higher professions, notably attorneys He carried a sterling silver snuff box, which he used frequently. He was in his late thirties, and had a strong, handsome face with a square jaw, thin well-shaped mouth, piercing black eyes, and a sharp, aquiline nose.

"I'm quite certain they would," said Nell.

"Does the notion appeal to you, Madam?"

Sutherland always referred to his beautiful, brittle wife, Portia, as "Madam." She was a year or two older than he, and as much a twenty-four-hour Thespian as he. She, too, dressed well, and spent many hours grooming herself. Her eyes were as dark as her husband's, but had a softer, less piercing quality.

"Indeed it does, sirrah," said Portia Sutherland.

Nell wrote Richard about the Sutherlands. He communicated with them and arranged to meet them in Leicester right after Michaelmas. The Canaday company was playing in Nottingham, and Leicester was roughly a halfway point between Nottingham and Norwich. Nancy Lucia joined him on the trip, since she was authorized to speak and act for Theo and Niccolini.

The meeting went extremely well. Richard was impressed with Sutherland's cool, dignified manner, and felt certain that he would not only do to replace Theo Canaday as an actor, but that his rather commanding presence would serve him well in booking and bargaining with public officials. Portia Sutherland, it turned out, played the harpsichord quite well, and although her smoky, low voice with its limited range could not handle the operatic and concert repertoire Niccolini's had, she assured Richard she had a small repertoire of songs requiring ranges of an octave and less, and could develop other material of this nature. She would not keep the account books, but would oversee Nancy Lucia's work in this area, and she could not cook.

They settled on an agreement whereby the Sutherlands purchased Theophilus's and Niccolini's fifty-pecent share in the company for an immediate payment of fifty pounds, and the stipulation that they would pay an additional ten pounds per month for the next fifteen months. David Sutherland would draw the same salary as Theo had collected; and Portia, the same as Niccolini. Richard was reluctant to bring up the business of the company's reputation, as Theo had with him, but he felt he must. Sutherland laughed his deep, theatrical laugh.

"Fear not, dear boy." He slapped Richard's back. "Portia and I are firm believers in keeping all peccadilloes strictly in the family."

Portia Sutherland nodded affirmation and winked at Richard. Sutherland proposed that the company name be changed to The Sutherland and Steele Company of Comedians. Richard rejected the proposal firmly.

"The Canaday company has built its reputation over a ten-year period, David. It would be foolish of us to give that up for the empty egotistical satisfaction of seeing our names on the wagons."

Richard stood firm, and the name was not changed. Over the next six months, Richard was disappointed to discover that David Sutherland was not nearly the help he had hoped he would be in handling the bookings and special arrangements with public officials. Sutherland was indeed impressive, and too conscious of his own impressiveness. With the venue owners and public officials, he was often overbearing and difficult. Especially in the smaller villages, he seemed unable to veil his contempt and scorn for owners and public officials he considered peasants and calves' heads.

The entertainment quality of the show, particularly in the dramatic portions, improved a good deal. The Sutherlands were far more accomplished actors than the Canadays. Musically the appeal of the show was not quite as great, but the dance and mime presentations improved, since both the Sutherlands turned out to be capable dancers and mimes. Portia Sutherland was also able to lead slow-witted Virgil Hoope into developing some difficult new acrobatic routines by carrying on a casual, intermittent affair with him, and ooohing and aaahing over his musculature.

Portia Sutherland's dalliances with Virgil Hoope were only one element of what had become a most distressing change in the atmosphere around the company. Distressing, at any rate, to Richard, Nancy Lucia, and Cecil and Cecilia Hogsdon. *Not* distressing to the Sutherlands, Hank and Virgil! As the months passed, it became obvious that Richard had not caught the meaning of David Sutherland's remark about the Sutherlands' belief in keeping peccadilloes in the family, or the significance of Portia Sutherland's wink. It was plain from the noises of revelry which could be heard on many nights, and even occasionally during the day, from the bedchamber of the main show wagon, that the Sutherlands enjoyed a good deal of cunnubial lovemaking.

Yet David and Portia each attempted in a most casual and unpredictably intermittent fashion to carry on affairs with any willing members of the company, male or female. David made occasional advances to Richard, Hank, Virgil and Nancy Lucia. Cecilia Hogsdon and Cecil apparently did not appeal to him. Portia attempted to seduce all. When they were rejected, they accepted the rejection lightly. When they were accepted, they enjoyed the liaison while it lasted, and seemed to forget what had happened within an hour of its conclusion.

The relationships were established within the first three months. David had discovered that Richard and Nancy Lucia could not be persuaded to participate in their revelries under any circumstances. Cecil, he had not even attempted. But he found Hank and Virgil willing not only to spend an occasional romantic hour with him, but also learned that Virgil was more than happy

437

to join him and Portia in tripartite hanky panky. Similarly, Portia soon discovered that Richard kept himself so occupied with his duties that he had neither interest in, nor time for, random affairs, and that Nancy Lucia was not only not interested in dallying with her, but was shocked by the suggestion. Portia at least tried Cecil and Cecilia before accepting the fact that they could not be persuaded to participate. She had her occasional flings with Virgil, discovering that Hank preferred David.

So the atmosphere around the Canaday company became drastically different from what it had been before the Sutherlands joined. The company split into two factions: the bacchanalian group consisting of the Sutherlands, Hank Hogsdon and Virgil Hoope; and the conservatives comprised of Richard, Nancy Lucia and the elder Hogsdons. When the company put up at various public houses along the route, footsteps sounded in the hallways, and doors opened and closed at all hours. When the troupe set up camp during the spring and summer engagements, there was much extraordinary traffic between wagons.

One evening when Richard was working with David and Portia Sutherland on an adaptation of a scene from *The Merchant of Venice*, Richard brought up the subject of the amoral activity the Sutherlands had engendered in the company.

Sutherland stared at Richard in utter astonishment. He opened his sterling silver snuff box, placed a pinch of snuff in a nostril and sniffed elegantly.

"My dear boy, are you seriously objecting to the innocent amusements in which Madam and I have been indulging?"

"It's not just you and Portia—"

"Of course not, dear boy! We have brought pleasure and excitement into the difficult and dull lives of some of our colleagues. We would be delighted to do the same for you, if you but showed the mildest interest."

"But, David—"

"We restrict our amusements most diligently to members of our own family. We consort not at all with the calves' heads and frumpy fraus who constitute our audiences. Outside our intimate little troupe, we comport ourselves with the utmost reserve and dignity at all times."

It was true. Richard sighed, and returned to the discussion of the courtroom scene in which Shakespeare's Portia foils Shylock, the Jew. The Sutherland Portia reached out, placed her hand over Richard's, smiled seductively and winked.

❧ 36 ❧

The man who looked like the ghost of Theophilus Canaday chuckled feebly.

"Reminds me of the early days with the Dublin company," he said. The words came slowly, haltingly from his pale lips. He sat hunched in the cushioned chair in the kitchen of the cottage in Bexhill. There was a blanket around his shoulders, in spite of the warm temperature in the room. Richard tried to carry on the conversation nonchalantly and animatedly as though he was completely unaware of any change in Theo at all. But it was impossible. Just a little over a year ago, he and Nancy Lucia had left Theo and Niccolini here in the cottage. In that year Canaday seemed to have withered into a feeble caricature of himself.

His once glittering brown hair had thinned to graying strands, covering the back and sides of his head, leaving all of the top of his skull exposed. His lavender eyes were now sunk deep in their sockets. They bulged, and seemed to be smeared with a dull, translucent paste. His skin was sallow. His mustache drooped lifelessly over lips that were more purple than pink. The veins in the thin hands stood out like dark purple strings, and the knuckles threatened to break through the skin.

When Nancy Lucia and Richard had come into the house, Canaday had been sleeping. Niccolini had come forth quietly to greet them, with tears in her eyes. Speaking softly, so that she would not awaken her husband in the adjoining room, she told Richard and Nancy Lucia how sick Theo had been. Two months ago, Dr. Wilks had administered a potent glyster, an enema, which seemed over the next six days to empty him of everything he had ever consumed in his entire life. When that seemed to have no beneficial effect, the doctor and an apothecary had bled Theo of almost thirty ounces. He was now back on the foxglove powder and brandy and herb tonics, and he seemed to be regaining his strength slowly. Like virtually all physicians of his day, Dr. Wilks knew little about the heart or its ailments. But he was desperately trying to find some way to help Theo.

Now Niccolini said to Richard and her daughter, "When he awakens and comes out, please don't act too alarmed over his appearance. Be as natural as you can. Just seeing you two again will improve his condition."

Within the hour they heard a stirring in the bedroom, and Niccolini went in and soon came out with Theo at her side. He impatiently pushed aside the hand she tried to keep on his arm. Nancy Lucia fought back the shock she felt at first sight of him. She rushed to him and put her arms around him as naturally as she could.

"Father, it's so good to see you again." She kissed him warmly on each cheek, then on his lips. Richard stepped forward, and took Theo's hand, but he was afraid to squeeze it in greeting. The limp, bony feel of it was frightening. Theo took his chair, adjusted his blanket around his shoulders.

"The confounded doctor has been trying to kill me as ye can see, but I'm a hardy old soul, and will be ready to join ye again very soon."

He drew a deep breath.

"Niccolini, get the children some wine. Now, tell me, how goes it with the company."

Richard and Nancy Lucia alternated in describing the Sutherlands, and, with all the humor they could bring to bear, told about the merry mix of liaisons, which had become the way of life for half the members of the company. At this point, Theo remarked that it reminded him of his old Dublin company. As Niccolini put a glass of the ruby port wine on the table beside Theo, he reached out and slapped her playfully on her ample behind. Niccolini seemed to have gained all the weight Theo had lost. Eating constantly, devouring the richest of foods, was apparently one of the ways in which she coped with the unending concern, the physical and emotional wear and tear of the around-the-clock caring for her ill husband.

"If truth be told," said Theo, managing a sip from the half-filled wine glass in a trembling hand, "the Niccolini Opera Company of Venice was far more lascivious than the Dublin troupe, or any of the English companies for that matter. It was yer humble servant, Theophilus Canaday, who rescued fair Niccolini from that lustful band of coloraturas and bassos."

"Come now, Theo my love," said Niccolini, "our most industrious seducers were no match for you and your friend, Gilhooley. No wench was safe in the same county with you."

Theo grinned at her.

"Till ye came along, and showed me the error of me ways, dear Niccolini."

He managed another sip of wine and became moderately serious.

"Does the libertine climate disturb ye? Has it damaged the company's reputation at all, at all?"

They assured him it had not. His dulled eyes seemed to grow increasingly bright as Richard and Nancy Lucia took turns in bringing him up to date on the activities of the company.

"Our musical presentations are not nearly as exciting and entertaining as they used to be. Portia is no Niccolini," said Richard.

"She sings like a frog," said Nancy Lucia.

"A seductive frog," laughed Richard. "She has little voice, but a tantalizing way with a song. But we miss you sorely, Niccolini." He turned back to Theo. "And you most of all, Theo. Not only your versatility as an entertainer, but your expert handling of the people we must deal with. You know how inept I always was at that end of the business."

"You are not inept," protested Nancy Lucia. "If Sutherland would lower the tilt of his nose, and behave less as though he believed he were Thomas Betterton, your task would be much easier."

Theo Canaday would have kept them talking about the company until he keeled over in his chair, but Niccolini noticed that he was turning ashen and his eyelids were drooping.

"I've got to prepare supper," she said, "and Theo, my dear, you must rest for a while."

He protested, but Niccolini, Nancy Lucia and Richard

all insisted, and he finally gave in, permitting Niccolini and his daughter to escort him back to the bedchamber.

It was early August, and since the company had had an exceptionally good year, they had decided to take a holiday through the entire month. The Sutherlands and Virgil had taken the wagons back to Norwich to be repainted and prepared for the new fall tour. Hank had decided to vacation in London. The elder Hogsdons had gone to stay with friends in Dover. Richard had accepted Nancy Lucia's invitation to spend two weeks in Bexhill, visiting with Niccolini and Theo. He was then planning to spend the final fortnight of the holiday with Nell at Windsor, since the Duke was leaving in mid-August for another trip to Antigua. Now, as Niccolini prepared supper, Richard and Nancy Lucia went for a walk. The cottage sat up on a hill, overlooking a rock-strewn, sandy stretch of Channel beach. Nancy Lucia took Richard's hand as they strolled along the shore.

"I'm frightened, Richard. Father seems so ill."

"I think it was the bleeding." Richard searched his mind, seeking some positive, comforting thought. "Didn't you notice how his spirits seemed to lift while we were talking about the company."

"He did seem to brighten, didn't he?"

"I think he suffers as much from missing the adventure and activity of show life, as from his physical disorders. I think Niccolini and your father both miss traveling with the company."

"Apart from touches of gray in her hair, Mama seems to be thriving, though she's gotten a bit plump."

"She's as beautiful as ever," said Richard.

Purely out of instinct and compassion, Richard had diagnosed Theo Canaday's condition quite accurately. The following morning he rose from his pallet in the kitchen of the cottage (Nancy Lucia occupied the second bedchamber) before any of the Canadays awoke, and rode over to Eastbourne to see Dr. Wilks.

"It's a true dilemma, lad," the doctor told him. "I discovered, unfortunately, that the bleeding and the glysters did not help his condition at all. It's not a matter of impurities in the blood. I'm certain that if he were strong enough to resume his vagabonding, he would be much happier, and even regain some measure of good health. But he is simply not constitutionally up to it. The strenuous road life would kill him."

Back in Bexhill, the Canadays and Richard sat for most of the day in the small, sweet-scented, colorful garden overlooking the sea. Again, Richard and Nancy Lucia regaled Theo and Niccolini with stories about the show. They described the hilarious confusion and arguments that had ensued, the night David had arranged an assignation with Hank, and Portia a rendezvous with Virgil, both in the show wagon at the same time. Nancy Lucia performed some devastating imitations of Portia Sutherland, singing some of her naughtier songs.

As the days passed, Theo Canaday gradually began to resemble his former self. Color returned to his cheeks. He cast aside the blanket. At the end of the first week of Richard's and Nancy Lucia's visit, he insisted on joining Niccolini, Richard and Nancy Lucia for walks along the beach. The walks exhausted him, but after a brief sleep, he awoke bright-eyed and exhilarated. On the Monday of the second week of Richard's visit, Dr. Wilks came to see Theo. He was surprised at the improvement in his patient.

"I feel I can go back to the company in the fall," said Theo. "What do you think?"

"Only at the risk of your life, Theo," said Wilks firmly.

Two days before Richard was scheduled to leave, he sat in the kitchen after supper with Niccolini and Nancy Lucia. Theo had retired.

"Mama, I think I'll stay here and help you take care of father. I can find some kind of work in the village, Nancy Lucia said.

"No, dear child! That would be the worst thing you could do. The company was his life, but he knows there is little hope that he can ever go back to it. The best he can do is to continue to live it through you."

She sighed.

"In truth, sweet Nancy Lucia, I feel much the same way about it." She placed her hand on her daughter's arm.

"If you could write us from time to time, as often as you can, to tell us about yourself and Richard, and what is happening with the company, it would . . . well, it would almost give us the feeling we were with you."

Nancy Lucia went to Niccolini and put her arms around her.

"Of course. Of course, I will write. It was most selfish

and thoughtless of me not to have written to you all season."

On the morning Richard was scheduled to leave for Windsor, he and Nancy Lucia took a stroll along the beach.

"Must you go to Windsor, Richard?" Nancy Lucia looked into his eyes. "I'll miss you so much."

He smiled at her and put his arm around her shoulder.

"I haven't seen Nell in a long time. It will just be for a couple of weeks, and I'll see you in Norwich."

They climbed some rocks along the path leading back up to the dirt road that led to the cottage. Before they reached the summit, Nancy Lucia stepped in front of him and looked up into his eyes.

"Richard," she said shyly. "Please kiss me goodbye."

He laughed, placed his hands on her shoulders and kissed her lightly on the lips. But she reached up and pulled his head down hard against her mouth. She kissed him with a strange ferocity that almost bruised his lips. Then she turned and raced to the cottage. Richard looked after her, baffled. Later that morning, when he stood alongside Sally O, loaded down with saddle bags, Theo, Niccolini and Nancy Lucia all said their goodbyes.

Theo put his arms around him, hugged him tightly and kissed him on the cheek.

"God be with you, lad," he said.

Niccolini held him tightly in her plump arms, and kissed him over and over with short, ardent kisses. She began weeping.

"Come back soon, Richard," she sniffed. "Soon."

Nancy Lucia kissed him again, long and fiercely. She wiped a tear from her eye as he mounted Sally O.

"See you in Norwich." She waved as he rode off. Richard felt as though he were leaving his own family. But he was anxious to see Nell Faversham again.

Nell greeted him warmly. They had a fine supper of roast duck, vegetables, a rich trifle with heavy whipped cream and berries, all prepared and served by Mrs. Korn, a cheerful middle-aged woman. Afterward they sat on the terrace at the rear of the elegant house in Pall Mall, sipping brandy. A brilliant, full, silver moon hung high in the ebony sky. Stars were thick and bright all around it.

Richard stared at Nell Faversham in the moon's bright

glow. He had found himself staring at her intermittently all through dinner.

"There's something quite different about you, Nell," he said now. She smiled.

"How different, dear Richard? Have I gained weight?"

He looked into her bright emerald eyes.

"Just enough, possibly, to make your figure more striking than ever," he laughed. "But it's not that. It's the glint in your eye, the tilt of your head. It's a look almost regal . . . no, not so much regal as businesslike, a nononsense look that is quite becoming."

"Thank you, Richard. Since I wrote you last I have given up acting, singing and dancing almost entirely. I am the directress of operations for all of the Duke's theatrical enterprises. I supervise the activities at both Lincoln's Inn Fields and Goodman's Fields."

"My congratulations, Nell. A most remarkable post for a woman. I do not believe any other woman in the kingdom has ever held a position of such responsibility."

He sipped his brandy.

"Do you find it difficult? Is there not a good deal of jealousy, some resistance?"

"Of course, but not nearly as much as either Edmund or I anticipated. You may well be able to guess where I am encountering the greatest resistance."

"Wrexham!" said Richard promptly.

"Jerome Wrexham! It infuriates him to have to be accountable to a woman, particularly a woman who takes her responsibilities most seriously and is totally impervious to what Jerry still considers to be his irresistible charm."

"Is Goodman's Fields still doing well?"

Nell sipped brandy, looked thoughtful.

"Extremely so, but receipts for the last two weeks of the season did not seem to be what I think they should have been. Jerry is in Dublin for the summer again, and I'm taking the opportunity to make a complete review of his books for the entire past season."

"How is his frantic romantic life?"

Nell shrugged.

"I think Brendan Geoghan has moved out and left him. And I think Jerry has been drinking and gambling quite heavily again. He's found a new companion in these past times in the Goodman's Fields company, a nice young man named Robbie Grigsby. We brought Robbie and his

446

wife, Emily, and their four-year-old daughter, Evangeline, into the company last year."

"Are they actors?"

"Emily and Robbie are, and young Evangeline plays the kit—you've seen that tiny, toylike violin—and sings and dances in a most captivating manner."

"How is Gilbert?" asked Richard.

"Except for the gout, he is as wonderful as ever. He not only accepts me in my new role, but is genuinely delighted that Edmund dared defy tradition to give me the opportunity. How are the Canadays? And how are the Sutherlands?"

Richard told her of Theo's attack during the storm, and his forced retirement. Then he talked about the Sutherlands. He smiled ruefully as Nell filled his glass.

"As you know, David and Portia are excellent actors . . . but their intracompany philandering has become rather awesome." He chuckled. "They make our friend Wrexham seem like a monk."

Nell smiled.

"We've been aware for some time, dear Richard, that few members of our profession take vows of celibacy."

"Oh, I'm not too troubled by it. It has settled into somewhat of a pattern within the company. To our dear public we are still a wholesome, moral troupe of players who bring them jolly and enlightening entertainment." He paused. "I do wish David could relieve me of much more of the booking and business phases of the operation than he has thus far."

Two nightingales began to sing to each other in a nearby maple. Richard drank his brandy and gazed off toward the towers of Whitehall.

"I feel more and more that my own acting skills have deteriorated considerably in the past several seasons."

"You must not let that happen, Richard."

As always, exchanging ideas and discussing problems with Nell was satisfying and helpful. In the next ten days, he relaxed as he had not in a number of years. He and Nell went riding and walking in the deep forest, green and cool even on the hottest summer days. They fished, and in the evenings had long discussions about their respective plans for the upcoming season. Yet at the end of the first week and a half, Richard found himself becoming restless. He lay awake most of the tenth night wondering how Theo and Niccolini were faring, and he could hardly wait to see Nancy Lucia again to find out whether Theo's health continued to improve.

With her usual perception where Richard was concerned, Nell sensed his restlessness, and when he told her he thought he had better leave a couple of days earlier than he had planned, she saw him off with an enthusiastic and friendly kiss.

The Canaday company wagons were encamped in a lush field about a half-mile out of Norwich. With Sally O trotting easily down the hard dirt road toward the town, Richard caught sight of the wagons in the distance, while he was still more than a quarter-mile away. He thought the glaring golden sun and the brilliant azure skies were playing tricks with his vision. The wagons seemed to be red. As he drew closer he saw that they were indeed red, vivid, screaming scarlet! He spurred Sally O, and in a moment they drew up before the large show wagon.

Richard stared, open-mouthed at the sight. Against the gaudy scarlet, in each of the four corners of the side of the wagon, were two figures of large-bosomed dancing girls, painted in sunshine yellow. In the center, near the top, and dominating the upper quarter of the side of the wagon, were the letters S, C, S. The C was twice the size of the other letters, but all three letters were painted in a style filled with flourishes. Underneath this wild yellow whorl were the words:

The
SUTHERLAND-CANADAY-STEELE
Company of Comedians
Presents
the Kingdom's Premier
Concerts of Music and Dance

****

Between the Acts of the Concerts—
Gratis Presentations of Rehearsals
of Works by England's
Outstanding Poets and Dramatists

****

Outdoor Amusement When Weather Permits—
Featuring Spectacular Acrobatics and Specialties
Concerts of Music and Mime

As Richard continued to stare, stunned by the spectacular change from the previous dignified royal blue and gold, a deep voice beside him boomed, "Striking, what, dear boy?"

David Sutherland stood at his elbow, beaming. Richard looked slowly around, and saw that the three other wagons, standing nearby, had also been painted red.

"It is loud and vulgar, David. What ever possessed you to do it?"

Sutherland looked hurt, then angry.

"This is an amusement company, dear boy, not a traveling monastery."

"How dared you change the name without consulting Theo or me or . . ."

"Canaday has nothing whatsoever to do with the company's policy, dear boy. And you should be pleased to declare your proprietorship, even as I am. I've left the Canaday name most prominent."

"The least you could have done was consult me!"

"That was hardly necessary, dear boy. The new name is obviously not only a fair compromise, but a most ingenious method—if I say so myself—of continuing to trade on the Canaday reputation, while at the same time introducing the new proprietors and the leading player of the company."

Richard was aware of Sutherland's use of the singular in referring to "the leading player." Richard considered himself a finer actor than Sutherland, and the leading player. He also was shocked at Sutherland's audacity in putting his name first in the threesome. He was speechless with fury as he led Sally O to his own wagon. Virgil was practicing some tumbling routines. Richard greeted him absently in passing, and unloaded his saddlebags and possessions into the wagon.

He was still fuming when he went into the show wagon after supper that evening to talk with Sutherland again. He had decided to drop the entire matter of the change of name and the scarlet wagons. There was nothing he could do about either. Sutherland noticed his cool manner as he entered the wagon.

"Relax, dear boy," he said cheerily. "In time you'll become accustomed to the changes and recognize the true value of the new name, and the arresting quality of the scarlet fronts."

"I've come to discuss the initial presentations," said

449

Richard coldly. "I believe we open in ten days in Ipswich."

"Precisely. And I have a delightful surprise for you, dear boy. I've written a new one-act play. An excellent romantic comedy." From a carton at the side of the desk, he took a sheaf of bound pages, and handed them to Richard.

"Love, Honor and Betray," he said. "I'll play Reginald, and you have the interesting role of Paolo. Read it tonight, dear boy. I'd like to put it into rehearsal as soon as the Hogsdons and Nancy Lucia arrive. I believe they're all due in tomorrow."

Richard took the play.

"I'm not too sure we should try to prepare an entirely new play for the first presentation of the season. The time seems rather short."

"Nonsense, dear boy. With a little cramming, everyone can be ready for Ipswich ... quite comfortably."

Hours later, Richard lay in his bed, across from Virgil, reading *Love, Honor and Betray* by candlelight. Suddenly, he hurled the bound pages against the wall. Startled, Virgil sat up.

"What! What's wrong, Richard?"

"Sutherland is an absolute egomaniac!" screamed Richard, jumping out of bed, donning his breeches and slipping into his boots. He retrieved the play, stalked out of the room and strode across the field in the moonlight to the show wagon. Once inside, he came upon David and Portia Sutherland in a complex embrace on their bed. They unraveled themselves in the moonlight, and the naked Sutherland leaped to his feet. He made a move to his small broadsword hanging on the wall, then recognized Richard.

"Gadzooks, dear boy!" he said agitatedly. "Don't ever do that again. I thought you were a bandit!"

Richard threw the bound play across the short space of the wagon width. It struck Sutherland on the chest.

"Never!" shouted Richard. "Never! Fourteen lines in the entire play! Who do you think I am!" Portia sat up in the bed, her small breasts highlighted in the moon glow.

"Why don't you undress, Richard, and come to bed where all three of us can talk it over?" she laughed throatily.

But Richard was already storming out of the wagon.

The next day Sutherland agreed to rewrite the part of Paolo. Shortly after noon, a carriage drawn by Harlequin and another horse drove up to the company encampment. Richard saw them arrive and rushed to meet them. Niccolini and Nancy Lucia flanked Theo Canaday, as all three walked slowly toward the show wagon. They stared, as though hypnotized by the garish scarlet fronts and the loud yellow letters proclaiming the "sCs" company. Nancy Lucia was most bitter about the change, but Theo insisted it was more than fair, since he certainly had no further claims on the company. Niccolini said nothing, but it was plain that she was shocked and displeased.

"It's abominable," said Richard shortly, "but too late to do anything about it, so let's forget it."

In spite of the shock of seeing the company in its new flamboyant dress, Theo and Niccolini spent a pleasant three days visiting with their old colleagues. Hank returned from London, where he had made the acquaintance of Brendan Geoghan. The two were working on a musical play. The Hogsdons had had a restful month with their old friends in Dover.

After supper on the first evening that the entire company was assembled, Cecil told Theo Canaday, "I envy you, Theo. I look forward to the day I can retire. Perhaps in another season or two."

Theo said nothing. It would be futile to try to explain to Cecil how much he missed traveling with the show. Theo was an adventurer, a born showman, and Cecil was not. Deep in his heart, Theo still fervently hoped to regain his health, so that he could once again resume a theatrical career. And Niccolini prayed that such a miracle might yet happen. Nancy Lucia wept quietly as she bade her parents goodbye on the last day of their visit, but she was glad to be staying on with Richard and the company.

After the elder Canadays left, the company stepped up its rehearsal schedules. Sutherland had rewritten *Love, Honor and Betray*, but Richard still felt it was unsatisfactory and refused to begin rehearsals of it. Sutherland pushed and pleaded, coaxed and cajoled and even threatened, but Richard was firm. He did not like the play in the first place, and he considered the Paolo part inadequate, if not altogether insipid. When he simply refused to do it, the company began to feel the strain of the relationship between David Sutherland and Richard Steele.

Nevertheless, they opened in Ipswich, and the shows went smoothly, drawing excellent crowds. On a Tuesday of the third week in Ipswich, Richard wrote a letter to Nell Faversham, and in checking the itinerary for the new season he noticed that Stamford had been booked for November. He went into the office, where Sutherland was working on *Love, Honor and Betray* once again.

"David, don't you remember when I told you that we do not play in Stamford?"

"Oh, yes. I remember your mentioning it, but a committee from the town came to see me in Norwich. It's a fine engagement, covers the period of the annual bull-running celebration. Huge crowds . . ."

"We know about the annual bull-running. That's why we won't play it."

"It's a major event. As important as the races in Darby, Michaelmas in Leeds or Quarter Sessions in Birmingham. People come from miles around to celebrate the running of the bulls."

Richard breathed deeply. "Understand this, David! We play no towns where they celebrate the running of the bull!" he said in chopped, flat tones.

Sutherland pushed his chair back, rose angrily. He slammed his fist on the desk.

"Goddamit, Steele!" he spat. "The bull-running in Stamford goes back to the thirteenth century . . . more than six hundred years. We play it! Do you understand? We play Stamford on November thirteenth this year!" His face was purple with anger.

"Now get out!" he commanded.

Richard advanced toward him, tearing the itinerary in half. Sutherland backed to the wall, reached up and took his small broadsword out of its scabbard. Richard strode to within inches of him, trembling with rage. The sea eyes blazed with fury, glaring directly into Sutherland's piercing black ones which glistened with fear. He could not know what had driven Richard to this near-madness.

It was an accumulation of reactions. Richard was too soul-deep an actor not to have resented Sutherland's placing his own name first in the new company title. It was not thought of, nor referred to, as "top billing" in that day, but a true actor took as much pride in being listed first in the bills then as now. Richard was also far more angered than he indicated by the blatant insult to his craftsmanship as an actor when Sutherland seriously proposed he play the insignificant Paolo role. But Richard was fundamentally too peace-loving and gentle a man to be driven to violence by these professional denigrations.

It was only when he discovered that Sutherland had booked Stamford during its bull-running celebration that the volcano erupted inside Richard. The earlier insults became contributing internal lakes of hot lava. Years earlier, when he had first joined the company, Theo Canaday had mentioned that he planned to book the company into Stamford during the annual bull-running celebration. Richard told him then he could not join them on that occasion, and finally told him, as briefly as he could, about Mary's death. Canaday understood, and did not book Stamford that year, and rejected all invitations from the town's committee to play there in the years that followed.

Richard tore the itinerary papers in halves once again and hurled the papers into Sutherland's face. He knew that contemptuous gesture would trigger Sutherland into striking with the sword. But as Sutherland began to raise his right arm Richard executed a succession of three movements with such rapidity that they seemed a single motion. The fingers of his left hand closed on Sutherland's right wrist before Sutherland had raised the sword. He held Sutherland's arm in an iron grip. At the same instant his right fist drove forward into Sutherland's stomach.

Even as Sutherland bent forward sharply at the waist and the breath screeched from his gasping mouth, Richard's left fist swung upward in a vicious arc, which began just above his own ankle and ended with the hard cracking sound of bone smashing bone. Richard stood back, breathing hard. He looked at the bleeding knuckles of his left hand, and down at Sutherland's face on the floor, lying on its side, two teeth showing through the smashed, bloodied flesh of the mouth.

The sword lay three inches from Sutherland's outstretched right hand. Richard stepped forward quickly, and picked it up. Standing over Sutherland, he raised the sword over his head. A noise like the crowd at a bull-baiting kept roaring around inside his head.

Over the roaring noise, a voice screamed.

"No, Richard, no!"

He turned toward the door and saw Nancy Lucia standing there, the back of her hand over her mouth. He dropped the sword beside Sutherland, and went to the door to walk out with Nancy Lucia. They walked, and talked, and walked some more till dawn. It was the first time Nancy Lucia heard what had happened to Mary.

⚔ 37 ⚔

Like a jungle struggle between two lions, the confrontation between Richard and David Sutherland over the Stamford booking seemed to determine leadership of the "sCs" company. For Richard it was a Pyrrhic victory. The brief argument and physical encounter brought back a searing vision of that horrible day at Waltham Cross, one he had not suffered in many years, awake or in nightmares. It took him a month before he managed to forget once more. The effort left him depressed, and confused about the direction of his life, all over again. He felt increasingly certain that he was losing his touch as an actor.

Sutherland's changed attitude toward him ultimately made it necessary for him to assume greater responsibility in the areas he disliked, the booking and the dealing with public officials. The evening after the encounter, Sutherland approached Richard at the end of a rehearsal. Portia had patched his swollen mouth quite expertly. He held a hand out to Richard.

"I'm sorry about last night, Richard. I will book no engagements in the future without your approval. I wrote the Stamford committee this morning that we would be unable to fulfill our commitment there."

"Thanks. I appreciate it."

Sutherland turned away, and then went back to stand face to face with Richard.

"One other thing, Richard. I read over *Love, Honor and Betray* again. I think it needs a good deal more work. I may even discard it."

Richard wondered when Sutherland would begin to

address him as "dear boy" again. For the next two weeks Sutherland's new subdued demeanor also seemed to affect the libidinous activity around the company. David appeared not to have the heart for it, and his swollen mouth and two chipped teeth were additional deterrents. Portia tried to keep David and Virgil interested, but experienced only marginal success. Hank had apparently developed a serious relationship with Brendan Geoghan in London. He spent a good deal of time writing Geoghan, and politely rejected David's and Virgil's occasional advances. He talked about Geoghan's charms and talents to Richard and Nancy Lucia frequently.

But by late November, when the company was back in the Gunnersbury Park area, matters seemed to gradually return to the pre-Stamford status. Richard had requested that David talk to the justice of the peace, who was expressing dissatisfaction with the benefit arrangements.

"I'll be most happy to, dear boy," said David. "I think you've been carrying altogether too much of the burden of dealing with these calves' heads lately."

On the Monday which marked the beginning of the last week of their stay at the White Swan Inn, Richard and Nancy Lucia were having supper in the kitchen of the Inn after the evening show. Nancy Lucia was feeling particularly happy. Her musical numbers had won exceptional applause, and she had just received a letter from Niccolini, saying that Theo's condition was much improved. Nancy Lucia had been writing home at least twice, and often three or four times, a week, and Niccolini had written that her letters were like a sweet, effective medicine.

"I'm glad your father is feeling better," Richard said. There was an odd lack of enthusiasm in his voice.

"What's wrong, Richard?"

"Have you been aware of my work this season?"

"Of course. How do you mean?"

"My acting. I have an uncomfortable, insecure feeling onstage that I've never had before. I have this dread of overacting, and then I find myself underplaying to the point of lethargy."

"It hasn't been that bad, Richard."

He grinned wryly.

"Not that bad, but bad."

Nancy Lucia was too honest to contradict him.

"What's the reason, Richard? What has happened?"

He shrugged. He hesitated to say that he believed it was probably because he had been playing so long with a group who were not themselves quite first-rate actors. He had not had the guidance of a Farley Shannon, nor the astute, caring direction of a Gilbert Weston. His energies had been dissipated; his concentration on shaping his roles, on acting techniques shattered by the many other problems involved in the day-to-day operation of the company.

"I don't know," he told Nancy Lucia. "I'll just have to work a little harder."

"There's a woman at the door smiling at you," said Nancy Lucia.

Richard looked up and saw Nell Faversham. She hurried toward the table, hands outstretched. She wore a small hat with a green plume, which matched her wide-skirted green satin gown. Richard stood up and took her hand. She leaned forward and kissed him on the cheek.

"This is my dear friend, Nell Faversham—Nancy Lucia Canaday, Nell."

Nancy Lucia looked up into Nell's bright, emerald eyes. She was captivated instantly by Nell's friendliness as Nell reached forward and took Nancy Lucia's extended hand in both hers.

"I'm so happy to meet you, Nancy Lucia. Richard has talked to me so often about you and your father and mother. I feel as if we were old friends. . . . How is your father?"

She paused as she saw Richard pulling another chair to the table.

"May I join you? I don't mean to intrude."

"Please do," said Nancy Lucia. As Nell sat, Nancy Lucia said, "My father is much improved, thank you. . . . Richard has told me much about you. And about your important position."

"What brings you to Gunnersbury Park, Nell?" asked Richard. A plump, red-cheeked serving girl came, and Richard ordered wine and the roast beef Nell said she would like for supper.

"You're both certain I'm not intruding on a private conversation?"

Richard and Nancy Lucia urged her to continue.

"Well, I have a nasty problem," she said, "and as I have done often in the past, I come again to dear Richard for help." She turned to Richard. "To come directly to the point: as manager, Wrexham has been plundering the company like a pirate. Last season he persuaded us to give Will Lambert, the carpenter, and Luigi Camarata, the scene designer at Goodman's Fields, each an increase of fifteen pounds for the season." The serving girl brought Nell's wine and refilled Richard's and Nancy Lucia's glasses. Then Nell continued. "I discovered that Wrexham forced each of them to give him ten of the fifteen pounds."

"That is not an uncommon practice," said Nancy Lucia. "Father told me of a manager of his Dublin company who forced each of the actors in the company to give him a part of their pay regularly."

"How did you find out about Wrexham?" asked Richard.

"I got into a dispute with Luigi over a careless piece of painting he had done on a rustic flat. It was very poor. I told him that in view of the generous increase we had given him, we expected a more earnest effort from him. He became angry and one word led to another, and he finally blurted out that the increase meant little, since he was forced to give most of it to Wrexham. He then also told me of Wrexham's arrangements with Lambert."

"Did you confront Wrexham?"

Nell paused as the serving girl placed her supper before her.

"Not immediately. There were other problems. I think I told you about Wrexham's new drinking and gambling companion, Robbie Grigsby. Well, Jerry and Robbie have been half drunk during one, often two, performances each week since the season started."

She paused, then said with some heat, "And we have discovered that Jerry has been keeping some portion of the week's receipts for himself for some time. I had a very careful count of the attendance made each week for the past four weeks, and the receipts Jerry deposited in the bank have been at least fifteen percent less than the total taken in."

"He's a common thief," said Nancy Lucia. "Why do you not have him arrested, or at the very least, dismiss him."

Nell smiled.

"It's not that simple."

"Our friend Wrexham has influence with persons,

who have influence with the noble proprietor. It's a long, complex story," Richard explained.

Nell ate some roast beef, and sipped the red wine.

"What Edmund and Gilbert Weston and I have finally worked out is that we will bring Jerry back to Lincoln's Inn Fields as a leading actor and singer. Gilbert dislikes the idea intensely, but he realizes that, in light of the Duchess's support of Jerry, there is little else we can do. At least at this point. Jerry, of course, was reluctant to come back, but Edmund gave him a substantial increase over what he was earning at Goodman's Fields, even with Lambert's and Camarata's contributions, and Gilbert has promised him the choicest of parts. He's going to do King Lear next week, and Othello after that."

Nancy Lucia was a bit confused by Nell's usage of the given names, but Richard explained the group of characters.

"Doesn't this create new problems with Francis Caryll?" asked Richard.

"No. Caryll is leaving to join Drury Lane. Gilbert will be happy to be rid of him."

Richard finished his wine.

"Well, then, your problem seems happily resolved. Temptation has been successfully removed from greedy Jerry's reach, and you have an adequate replacement for the temperamental Caryll. . . ."

". . . And?" Nell looked directly into Richard's puzzled eyes.

Then she glanced at Nancy Lucia, and thought she saw an expression of concern cloud the younger woman's lavender eyes. Richard finally said, "Oh, yes, of course. You need a new manager for Goodman's Fields. Is that a position difficult to fill?"

"Possibly not," said Nell, and smiling first at Richard, then at Nancy Lucia, she noted definite alarm in Nancy Lucia's eyes. She turned back to Richard.

"I think you would make an excellent actor/manager for the theater, Richard. Absolutely ideal! And we could pay you a good deal more than your earnings with your own company."

As Nell's words sank in, Richard felt an enormous elation surge through his entire body. At the moment in his life when he was most discontented with the daily problems of operating the traveling company and the quality of his own acting, when his relationship with

Sutherland had reached its nadir and when the adventure of vagabonding seeemed to be losing its appeal—at this very moment, Nell was offering him an opportunity to get back to the professionalism of London. Goodman's Fields was virtually on the metropolis's doorstep, only a little more than a mile out of town, and the acting standards were considerably higher than any traveling company's.

As though she were reading his mind, Nell said, "The management duties are not nearly so demanding as with a traveling company, Richard, and you will have an opportunity to concentrate on playing major roles in well-produced presentations once again."

Richard reached across the table and took Nell's hand. With intense enthusiasm, he said, "I'll need time to find a replacement for myself with the company, to set things in order. . . ."

Nancy Lucia stood up suddenly.

"Excuse me, please." Her voice was low and tense. "I've got to write home."

"See you in the morning, Nancy Lucia." Richard waved cheerfully. Nell looked after her. She did not turn back to Richard until Nancy Lucia had walked across the long kitchen, and up the flight of stairs leading to the players' rooms. Nell thought that Nancy Lucia had made the walk with a peculiar stiffness. Nell had also detected moisture in Nancy Lucia's lavender eyes, and a trembling quality in her last words as she rose abruptly from the table. Beside himself with the good news, Richard had noticed none of this.

He said excitedly, "I should be able to work everything out by the end of the week!"

He lifted his wine glass.

"To Richard Steele's return to the stage!"

"To your return!"

Richard was so joyously overwhelmed by this sudden turn of events that he did not even notice a certain reserve in Nell's toast. While Nell finished her supper, he discussed with her the steps necessary to effectuate the change.

He was certain Sutherland would be able to find a replacement for him from among his former colleagues at Norwich quite promptly. That very evening, he told Sutherland about his intention to leave. Sutherland made a theatrical speech about how impossible it would be to

460

get along without Richard, and how sorely they would miss him. He promised to try to find a replacement as soon as possible.

"You have left an indelible mark on the Sutherland company," he said, with an emotional tear in his eye. Richard smiled as he looked at the small scar at the lower left corner of Sutherland's mouth. Two days later, a handsome, young experienced actor from Norwich arrived at the White Swan Inn. Sutherland had dispatched a special messenger to bring him to the show immediately.

When Richard told Nancy Lucia how he planned to handle his fifty percent interest in the company, she said quietly, "That's very generous of you, Richard, and I'll do my best to work with David as much in the manner you yourself might work with him as possible."

"I know you'll do fine, and I'll be in communication with you—and Nell and Theo and Niccolini. . . . We'll all be ready to help with any problems that may arise."

They were sitting at breakfast, and Nancy Lucia pushed aside her buttered bread and coffee and rose from the table.

"If you'll pardon me," she said, "Harlequin was limping this morning. I must see to him."

Nell watched her walk off, nervously flicking her riding crop against the side of her boot, her back straight and rigid. Richard began to speak eagerly, but Nell was puzzling over Nancy Lucia's tepid reaction to Richard's arrangement.

There was a performance at the cockpit theater on Wednesday evening, another on Friday, and on the outdoor stage on Saturday. Richard worked in all of these with more zest than he had since the first day he joined the company. On Saturday evening, the company gave a farewell party for him in the kitchen of the White Swan Inn. There was much drinking and feasting, and many tears were shed, as each member of the company bade Richard Godspeed, and told him how much they would miss him.

Portia Sutherland had kissed him passionately early in the evening, pressing herself against him.

"I do regret that we never got to know each other intimately, Richard," she sighed.

David Sutherland made another elegant speech extolling Richard. Nancy Lucia missed all of this. Very early in the proceedings, she excused herself from the table where she was sitting with Richard and Nell, saying she had a severe headache and must retire.

Richard kissed her warmly on the cheek, and told her he was sorry she was feeling poorly.

"We'll have breakfast in the morning before Nell and I leave," he said.

But the following morning, she was not present for breakfast. Richard went up to her room and knocked. There was no response. Then he went out to the stables and discovered that Harlequin was gone. Nell had come out to Gunnersbury Park in a carriage drawn by two fine dappled gray horses, driven by a coachman. She was waiting at the carriage when Richard came back from the stables.

"She's gone off for a morning ride," said Richard in a puzzled tone. "I'm quite surprised she would not have a final breakfast with us."

Knowing that there were times when a woman needed to be alone, Nell suspected that this was such a time for Nancy Lucia.

"Would you like to wait for her?" she asked.

"No, no. I'll write her from Goodman's Fields as soon as I get settled."

The carriage headed eastward in the sunny, brisk morning toward London. As it rolled past the open field where Richard had first met Nancy Lucia, Nell pointed out the carriage window on Richard's side.

"Isn't that Nancy Lucia? Under that tree?"

Richard looked. Harlequin grazed near the tree. Nancy Lucia stood in its shade, gazing toward the carriage. From that distance, in her breeches, yellow wool sweater and cap, she still looked like a young boy. Richard did not remember that this was the tree under which he and Nancy Lucia had sat the morning after he joined the company. Too much time had passed, and he had traveled to too many places. Nancy Lucia waved as the carriage rolled by. Richard shouted up to the driver to stop. He waved for Nancy Lucia to come across the field to the carriage.

"Come kiss me goodbye, Nancy Lucia!" he shouted. But Nancy Lucia just continued to wave for another moment, then dropped her arm and stared at the ground.

He blew Nancy Lucia a wild kiss, and waved again, as the wagon rolled off. Nell's womanly intuition told her quite clearly that there were tears in Nancy Lucia's vulnerable lavender eyes.

There were nine men, four women and a child in the Goodman's Fields company. As soon as Nell had Richard moved into the small cottage near the theater, where he would live, she assembled the company onstage, and introduced each member to the new actor/manager. To Richard, the most captivating member of the company was Evangeline Grigsby. She was not quite five years old, the smallest child of that age Richard had ever seen. She could easily have been mistaken for three. At least until she moved and spoke. She acknowledged Nell's introduction by stepping forward and making a graceful curtsy. With no traces of baby talk or lisp at all, she said cheerily, "Most pleased and honored, sir."

She seemed to Richard most appealing, totally unaware of her precocity. She had silken, light blond hair, cornflower blue eyes and a small straight nose. Her cherry lips turned up slightly at the corners, so that she appeared always to be smiling an innocent smile. Her father, Robbie Grigsby, was a short, stocky man with a loud and hearty manner. Even though he was only in his early thirties, five or six years older than Richard, the small, broken blood vessels of excessive drinking showed in his puffy cheeks and bulbous nose. He had blond hair, not as light as Evangeline's, and a jutting jaw. Evangeline's mother, Emily, was even shorter than her stocky husband. She was slim, and had the same cornflower blue eyes, and light blond hair as Evangeline, but six years of being married to Robbie had left her with a subdued and long-suffering look.

Nell had almost completed the introductions when a door at the side of the small theater banged open, and heavy footsteps marched toward the stage. In the semidarkness, Richard did not realize it was Jerome Wrexham until Wrexham had climbed the steps up to the stage, and rushed up to Richard. He looked trim, if a bit heavy and florid-faced, and had grown his beard and mustache again.

"Steele!" he exclaimed. "My old friend, Richard Steele!" He tried to embrace Richard, but Richard held him off.

"You seem not to have changed at all, Jerry," he said coldly. "Nor have I."

Wrexham was embarrassed, though he recovered quickly.

"I merely stopped by to assure you that I stand ready to render whatever assistance you may need in your new duties, lad." He looked around at the assembled cast.

"The members of the company will testify that during my tenure, Goodman's Fields has enjoyed the greatest prosperity in its history."

Most of the men and women remained silent, but several snickered audibly.

"I'm sure Richard will call upon you if he feels you can help, Jerry. Thank you for your kind offer," Nell Faversham said.

In the years since Richard had seen him, Jerome Wrexham had not improved his ability to detect sarcasm in the spoken word. He accepted Nell's remark with a deep bow and a pompous, "I stand ever ready to be of service."

Richard threw himself into his new duties with characteristic fervor. The first play the company presented under Richard's management was *Julius Caesar,* in which Richard played Brutus. Using the Thomas Betterton sword, which Farley Shannon had given him, Richard felt greater elation during the performance than he had experienced since the last time he played this same role on the stage of Lincoln's Inn Fields.

An older member of the company, an excellent actor named Emmett Nicholson, played Caesar. Robbie Grigsby performed the role of Cassius. He was quite good, but he had the same tendency toward excessive declamation and flamboyancy as Wrexham, and other actors of the Quin school. Emily Grigsby surprised Richard with the sensitivity of her performance as Brutus's wife, Portia. And the actor who played Mark Antony, a thirty-year-old man named Arthur Reinhart, was excellent.

Another remarkable surprise of the evening was Evangeline Grigsby's performance in the musical and dance numbers between the acts of the play. Dressed in a long yellow silk taffeta gown, with a cornflower-blue silk belt around her waist, and two ribbons of the same silk in her hair, the little girl was enchanting. The sparkle in her eyes, the natural beaming smile, the authority in her every movement added up to an electric stage presence, which completely captured the hearts of the audience.

She played several merry airs on the kit, while Robbie and Emily danced. Then she sang a wistful song about a little girl in love with a soldier, and a charming ditty about elves. She danced a solo dance called *The Highland Lilt,* and then did a sprightly minuet with her father. The applause, when she finished between the second and third acts of the play, was so prolonged it took the actors more than another five minutes to bring the audience back to the mood of the Shakespearean tragedy.

When the curtain came down on *Julius Caesar,* the patrons stood and clapped and cheered. The actors took a half-dozen curtain calls, and the audience was still applauding. As Richard finally came into the wings, Nell Faversham threw her arms around him.

"Oh, you were magnificent, Richard. It is so wonderful to have you back."

It was wonderful to be back. Nell quickly familiarized him with the company accounts. Everyone in the company was friendly and cooperative. Lambert, the carpenter, and Camarata, the scene designer, liked Richard, and brought new enthusiasm and creative skills to their tasks. Richard was busy doing precisely what he wanted to do, and he was happy. *For two entire days.*

The second performance of the week went just as well as the first, and Richard was enjoying the plaudits of the audience. But when he went to bed in the pleasant room in the cottage a strange melancholy enveloped him. He lay awake trying to fathom an explanation for his mood. He got up and decided to write Nancy Lucia. He also wrote to Theo and Niccolini. While he was writing, he felt better, but when he finished, the feeling of discontent came over him again. It could not be that he was lonely! Since his arrival in Goodman's Fields, he had hardly been alone for fifteen minutes except to sleep. He finally fell asleep that night, but the next morning he awoke in the same melancholy mood.

That evening Nell noticed. Sitting across from him in The Black Boar, the small tavern near the Goodman's

Fields theater, she asked, "What's troubling you, Richard? Is something wrong?"

"I don't know." He shook his head. "Everything is proceeding just as I hoped it would, but I feel strangely sad, and alone . . . for no reason at all."

"Have you heard from Nancy Lucia?" Nell asked, surprising Richard with the question.

"No. I did not expect that she would be writing so soon . . . but I wrote her last night."

A week later, the postman delivered a letter to Richard at the cottage. He accepted it without enthusiasm. He was beginning to think that melancholia was to be his natural state. But when he looked at the handwriting on the envelope, his spirits bounced. The letter was from Nancy Lucia.

He read avidly as he walked back into the cottage. Most of the letter contained news of the company and how they were faring. Suddenly Richard stopped and went back and reread the last paragraph.

> Frank asked me to marry him, and I said I would! He could not believe it. *Nancy Lucia and Frank Hogsdon! Frank with his whores of all nations! Nancy Lucia a farm wife! Nancy Lucia, a girl virtually born on a stage!*

His immediate impulse was to race out to the stable, mount Sally O and ride off to Colchester. But he continued reading.

> I have notified David of my intentions to leave the show at the end of the Colchester engagement, and he says he will have no trouble bringing in an actress from Norwich, although she will not be able to do the rope dancing. David thinks the rope dancing is becoming passé at any rate. I suppose one of these days Hank will go to London, and Aunt Cecilia and Uncle Cecil will retire, and the show will be The Sutherland Company of Comedians from Norwich. But I don't know why I should care.
>
> Frank left for Manchester yesterday, and I will meet him there. Since we are not too far from London and Goodman's Fields, I thought I would

come and say goodbye to you in person on Saturday before I go up to Manchester. I hope you will be glad to see me. Also hoping you have been well and happy in Goodman's Fields, and with fondest good wishes to Miss Faversham, I am

Your humble and devoted friend,
Nancy Lucia

The following morning, while they breakfasted at the Black Boar, Richard showed the letter to Nell.

"Did you ever hear of anything more insane??" he demanded as she returned the letter to him.

Nell smiled.

"Why is it insane? Many people are happy living on farms. It's a very wholesome life."

"It's ridiculous!" said Richard angrily.

He was gruff and impatient with the company the next two days. On Saturday, Nancy Lucia rode up to the cottage just before noon. Richard had been waiting since dawn. He rushed to the door to meet her, and they kissed briefly. When they were seated in the small, sun-filled kitchen, Richard demanded angrily, "Have you lost your senses, Nancy Lucia? You can't marry Frank!"

"Oh! Can I not? Why not?"

"He's your cousin."

"No, he isn't." Her lavender eyes danced. "He's my cousin once removed. And it would not make any difference anyway. The nobility are always marrying blood relations."

He got up and stood over her.

"Well, you just can't marry him. That's all!"

"He's a very nice man. Strong and handsome. Why can't I marry him?"

Richard lifted her up out of the chair by her upper arms. Embracing her fiercely, he pressed his mouth hard against hers. He held her tightly to him and kept kissing her until both could hardly breathe. He continued to kiss her, but softly now, with an open mouth, so they could draw breath as they kissed. She reached her arms around his back, and they clung to each other, kissing ever more passionately, until they were both so weak they could hardly stand.

Nancy Lucia flopped into the chair, her lavender eyes

gleaming with happiness, her soft mouth bruised and wet.

Richard stood over her. He took her hands.

"You . . . can't marry . . . him," he gasped, "because . . . you must . . . marry me!"

"Well," said Nancy Lucia, also gasping, ". . . that . . . is a . . . sensible reason."

38

The Soaring Gull was a small, weatherbeaten but sturdy inn about a half-mile from the Canadays' cottage in Bexhill. Richard's and Nancy Lucia's room was on the second floor, with a large salt-encrusted window looking down on a stretch of beach and a rocky cove. Even with the window shut against the chill fall air, they could hear the muted roar of the surf. Its persistent crashing against the rocks was a repeating rhythmic chord. Through the window a three-quarter moon poured a soft silver glow across their uncovered naked bodies in the bed. The flickering flame from the fireplace cast ever changing highlights on their glowing flesh.

"You are such a gentle lover, Richard," whispered Nancy Lucia. "I knew you would be."

Leaning on one elbow beside her, Richard ran his hand from her cheek, down her slender neck and from her silken side to the slim waist and the gently swelling hip. He clutched her buttock and pulled her toward him.

"A little less gentle each time," he said with mock savagery. She turned on her side to face him, threw her arms around him, pulling his upper body tight against the hard nipples of her breasts. He caressed her buttocks in both hands, and leaned forward to kiss and suck her left breast. She felt his burning erection against her upper right thigh. She moved in the bed so that he could kiss her left breast, more easily, shifting so that he was suddenly between her thighs. In a moment, seemingly without effort on his part or hers, he was inside her. It was the fourth ex-static coupling of the long, incomparably beautiful night.

This time, they moved tenderly against one another, side by side. The feverish smell of their bodies was a maddening perfume. Richard turned slowly on his back, and with his strong hands on her hips, moved her along with him, so that in a moment she was sitting astride him.

He was large inside her. She leaned forward, with her hands on the side of his head, and put her open mouth to his, as she made continuous rising and falling motions with her pelvic area. He clutched her buttocks and pulled her fiercely down upon him. After a time, he exploded again, but Nancy Lucia remained astride him. She lay quietly forward, her full breasts pressing against his chest, her head alongside his shoulder, stroking his hair and his cheek. He caressed her smooth, moist back languidly, his eyes closed, his breath coming in an even, contented rhythm. Her silken hair hung against the side of his face. Her moist open mouth found his again, and her tongue played with his. The heated, passionate woman aroma of her stiffened him inside her once more. As he filled her, and surged deeper into her, he gently turned her on her side. With their arms around each other, they moved slowly back and forth. And the thrusting became more and more and more rapid, and deeper and deeper and deeper until they both wanted to sing or scream with ecstasy.

For Richard it was like it had been with Felicia, but even more fulfilling, perhaps because they were married, and he felt secure in their devotion to each other. For Nancy Lucia it was more thrilling than she had dreamed in the most intense and lurid of all her girlish fantasies about Richard. There was a giving and taking of pure love and passion between them, and their child was most certainly conceived on that never-to-be-forgotten nuptial night. Spent finally, and lying quietly side by side as dawn's roseate light poured into the room, they still held hands.

"Have you quite rid yourself of that brotherly feeling toward me?" chided Nancy Lucia. Richard managed a sleepy grin.

"Not really," he teased. "I've just been discovering how pleasurable incest can be."

She turned and kissed him lightly on the lips.

"Richard, I must tell you something," she said softly. He was almost asleep.

"Unnhhh?"

"Frank never visited the show. And he's been married for over a year."

Richard sat up.

"He has? Then that letter . . ."

"He married one of the ladies in that house he used to go to. A lady named Francesca. Aunt Cecilia was ashamed to tell anyone, but she told Mama, and Mama told me."

"Then that letter. . . . You just made it up? You just made up the whole business of getting ready to marry Frank. . . . I never dreamed you could be so deceitful, Nancy Lucia."

"I think not deceitful. Clever! And I'm not nearly so clever."

Richard leaned on an elbow and stared at her lovingly in the soft dawn light.

"It was Nell's idea," Nancy Lucia said. "She came to see me in Colchester. She told me you were miserable, and she was sure it was because you missed me."

Richard continued to stare.

"She said you loved me, but were just too foolish to realize it. You had trapped yourself into thinking of me as a sister. She said some nice men are often like that!"

"It appears she was quite right. . . . But *Frank*! I don't think Nell ever met Frank or knew anything about him."

"Oh, she didn't. Frank was my idea. Nell just suggested I write you that I was marrying someone . . . anyone . . . to make you realize you loved me."

She paused.

"I thought Frank was a happy invention."

Richard smiled wryly.

"A very nice contrivance." He took her in his arms again.

"You women are a deceitful lot." He kissed her lightly, added, "and I'm glad! Good night, my love!"

As he lay down and turned over on his side, she snuggled up to him, sighed and said, "Good night," though morning was almost upon them.

They had decided to be married in Bexhill because they knew it would mean a great deal to Niccolini and Theo. The Canadays could hardly contain themselves for joy. Niccolini wept uncontrollably with happiness as she kissed her son-in-law and blessed him. And Theo choked with emotion.

471

"Lad, ye have made me the happiest man in the kingdom," he said again and again.

Seated beside Edmund Fox, the Duke of Cheltenham, in the small village church, listening to the vicar read the marriage vows, Nell Faversham had beamed at the results of her handiwork. The wedding party afterward at the Canadays was a gala affair. Gilbert Weston come down from London with several members of the Lincoln's Inn Fields company. Ben and Bessie Pickering brought a huge wedding cake, and trays of puddings. Quincy and Susannah Forbish had left the circus in Bedford, and David Sutherland canceled three days of the engagement of The Sutherland Company of Comedians of Norwich in Cambridge so that he and Portia, the Hogsdons (except Frank, who was too far off in Manchester) and Virgil could attend.

Niccolini played the spinet, and there was singing and dancing, and feasting and drinking all through the long afternoon, into the early evening. Just before sunset, Susannah Forbish and Portia Sutherland, both having had too much wine, got into a hair-pulling brouhaha because Susannah objected to Portia's blatant advances toward Quincy. The combatants were soon separated, however, and persuaded by Quincy to kiss and make peace. During this interlude, Richard and Nancy Lucia slipped away to the Soaring Gull.

In the fifteen or sixteen ecstasy-filled hours that followed, they were convinced that they were blessed above all humans, that never had two people been so supremely happy and contented or so fortunate. But when they awoke at noon Nancy Lucia thought it strange when Richard carefully and energetically wiped his hand across the area of the sheets where he had slept. Rubbing her eyes sleepily, she asked, "What are you doing, love?"

"It's an old superstition I have," he said, in what struck his new bride as an oddly subdued tone. He came around and sat on the edge of the bed on her side. He took her hand, and said, "I would like you to promise me that you'll wipe away your doke, when you arise each day, too."

Nancy Lucia laughed hesitantly.

"Are you serious?"

"Yes, very," he said in the same quiet, subdued tone. She was neither more nor less superstitious than Richard, and she had never heard of this particular odd be-

472

lief, but she loved Richard with all her heart and would agree to anything he asked. She leaped out of bed, laughing, and aggressively stroked away the impression where her body had lain. Richard did not explain the superstition, nor how he had come to believe in it until a time much later. And long before they had reached the Canaday's cottage, walking hand in hand, they had both forgotten about dokes and superstitions. They were drunk with love and the joy of living.

Back at Goodman's Fields, it seemed their euphoria would continue forever. Nell had no trouble persuading the Duke to permit her to increase the budget at Goodman's Fields to allow for a modest salary for Nancy Lucia.

One night, at the end of the second month of these happy, busy times at Goodman's Fields, after she and Richard had made love, she said softly, "Richard, I think I am with child."

Richard sat up in bed.

"How wonderful!" he shouted. He took her in his arms and kissed her tenderly and exclaimed over and over, "How absolutely wonderful . . . how wonderful . . ."

And soon they were making love again. Dr. Thorndike confirmed the pregnancy. He warned Nancy Lucia to be careful while riding, and insisted she give up jumping. Professionally, matters progressed well.

Richard worked hard, and all the members of the company were cooperative. Robbie Grigsby continued to drink rather heavily, and occasionally spent late nights in London with Jerome Wrexham, but he made certain he was sober enough to perform well, even if, now and then, he worked with a throbbing head.

Early in the season, there was some concern that there might be changes in the Lord Chamberlain's office, and that the new administrators might become stricter about permitting the nonpatent theaters, such as Goodman's Fields, to perform drama—even in the guise of gratis rehearsals. King George had died, and his son, George II, ascended to the throne. Edmund Fox told Gilbert Weston, Nell and Richard that the new king and his late father had been at dagger's drawn for years, and that George II was not kindly disposed to the deceased king's ministers. But the Duke was friendly with the new king's queen, Caroline of Anspach, and had a good relationship with Robert Walpole, who controlled the council, and was thus able to handle the political situation. Richard had no problems continuing his dramatic presentations as he wished.

Lincoln's Inn Fields had one of its greatest successes that season. Weston presented a new ballad musical, *The Beggar's Opera*, written by a talented young man named John Gay. It was so popular that it ran for sixty-three nights. Jerome Wrexham had a secondary role in the production, but carried on as though he were its leading player, and the main reason for its success. The extraordinary acceptance of this musical presentation actually turned out to be a help to Goodman's Fields, since that portion of the theater-going citizenry which preferred drama to musical presentations had one less patent house at which they could see dramatic works.

The unparalled attendance at Lincoln's Inn Fields in this period led directly to the building of a large and elegant new theater at Covent Garden. The Duke and more than forty other affluent members of the gentry subscribed to shares costing three hundred pounds each to build the new theater. Edmund Fox purchased three hundred pound shares in his own name, and additional three hundred pound shares each in the names of members of his family and of Nell Faversham. He was one of the most influential directors of the new theater. One of his privileges was that he was entitled to two boxes at each performance.

The premier at the elegant playhouse was a major social and theatrical event. A newly organized company of excellent players was to present one of the best known and liked plays of the day, William Congreve's *The Way of the World*. On the opening night, Nell Faversham had supper with Nancy Lucia and Richard in the cottage at Goodman's Fields. Ever since they had come to Goodman's Fields, the Steeles had made it a practice to go into London one evening each week to see one of the presentations at Lincoln's Inn Fields or Drury Lane, and dine with Nell or one or more of their other friends.

When Nancy reached the beginning of the seventh month of her pregnancy, however, her midsection had become so round and huge that she could not ride a horse at all, and it was even awkward for her to ride in a carriage. So when the much-discussed Covent Garden Theater was to open, the Steeles had not been to London in more than eight weeks. Nell could not go to the premiere performance, herself, because the Duke was taking a large party from the Court, and the Duchess was to accompany him on one of her rare visits to the theater.

While they were supping on the aromatic and spicy veal pie, which Nancy Lucia had prepared, Nell explained this situation.

"So," she said, laughing, "I am relegated to a box tomorrow night. I will be escorted by a good friend of Edmund's, a Lieutenant Roland Tighe, on leave from the Virginia militia, and I would be most happy if you two would join me."

"I don't think Nancy should chance it," said Richard, glancing lovingly at Nancy's stomach, which kept her an uncomfortable distance from the table. "It seems to me our son is due at any hour."

"Dr. Thorndike says I have at least another week or two," protested Nancy Lucia. "Please, Richard, let us go."

Reluctantly, unable to hold out against the two women, Richard finally agreed, and late the following afternoon Nell's carriage drove up to the cottage at Goodman's Fields. Nancy Lucia, with Richard's nervous assistance, managed to climb into the carriage. She was wearing a low cut, off the shoulder, bright yellow satin *contouche*, tied with a lavender velvet ribbon between her swollen bosom, and the immense globe of her abdomen. The gown was tight over her creamy breasts and the upper circumference of her stomach, and from there hung loosely straight down to her lavender slippers. A black velvet cape was thrown over her shoulders. She wore a yellow lace cap over her short cut, glistening hair. As comic as her figure might seem, her face had the special glow that imminent motherhood bestows upon healthy young women. Her lavender eyes glistened, and there was a natural rose color in her cheeks. She survived the jouncing, bouncing ride into London extremely well, and Richard had not seen her so excited in some time.

Nell was already seated in the box with Lieutenant Tighe. He was a handsome, hard-jawed young man, with a dark, waxed mustache and wavy black hair. His scarlet uniform coat and beige breeches seemed to have come directly from the tailor's. Lieutenant Tighe, in addition to his military duties, wrote and produced plays in his army company in Williamsburg. He had been an actor before emigrating to the colonies. The lieutenant, Richard and Nell were soon embroiled in a conversation about the theater. Tighe was stressing how fortunate they were to have the kind of theater they had here in London.

"Apart from our own company, and a few other army stage groups, there is yet almost no theater in the colonies. A dancing master named Stagg and his wife opened a wooden barn of a theater in Williamsburg years ago, but there are virtually no professional companies."

Richard was intrigued with Tighe's lamentations about the lack of theater in the colonies. He wondered fleetingly whether taking a company there might not prove an exciting and profitable enterprise. Apparently, his years of traveling with the Canaday company had instilled in him an appetite for adventure, of which he was hardly conscious.

Nancy Lucia was not participating in the conversation at all. In utter fascination, she looked around the crowded auditorium, cooling herself with a fashionable fan made of thin white chicken skin and decorated with a lovely pastoral scene, which Nell had given her as a wedding present. The new theater was even larger than Drury Lane, which seated twelve hundred people. But it was not the size of the theater which excited her. It was a combination of elements: the smell of newness and the heated bodies of thirteen hundred people, most of them crammed together on the backless benches in the pit, or squeezed tight in the first and upper galleries; the mélange of color; the freshly gilded figures and curlicues in the rococo proscenium arch; the rich, maroon velvet curtain; the dazzling colors, seemingly every shade in the spectrum, of the gowns of the ladies in the boxes flanking both sides of the theater. Nancy Lucia thought they looked like blossoms in flower boxes. These colorful costumes contrasted vividly with the relatively drab garb of the patrons in the pit and the galleries.

But what the citizens in those sections lacked in color they made up for in sound. In the galleries, particularly the upper gallery, loud and ribald action was taking place. There was much quaffing of gin and ale and beer, munching of apples, oranges and walnuts. Sailors and craftsmen's apprentices and merchants' clerks and cooks and footmen and parlor maids and pimps and prostitutes gossiped noisily, sang merrily or argued vehemently. In a far corner of the gallery, Nancy Lucia saw one disreputable-looking couple—his breeches at his knees, her black skirt held high—standing with their arms tight around each other. No one paid them any attention.

Possibly the most interesting sight in the buzzing auditorium was on the stage, even though the evening's play had not yet begun. The apron of the stage extended further out into the pit than any stage apron Nancy Lucia had ever seen. The entire apron was peopled with beaux and fops. Some sat, some stood, some paraded back and forth with their gold- or silver-headed walking sticks, waving to ladies and gentlemen in nearby boxes. Some paused, far downstage, and ostentatiously took from their pockets jeweled or gold or silver snuff boxes, and administered a pinch to their nostrils. They were like peacocks prancing, showing their elaborate curled wigs, their expensive, frilled and gem-decorated clothing.

One of the fops shouted up to Nancy Lucia. She smiled at him, and nodded a greeting, although she could not hear what he said. Richard looked annoyed. All this cacophony was cushioned by the orchestra which played on the pit level just beneath the fore portion of the apron. It was the first time the orchestra had been set in this location. At Drury Lane and Lincoln's Inn Fields, the musicians played in a tiered section above the proscenium arch.

"Do you think we will ever see the day when they will not sell seats on the stage?" asked Richard irritably. "I find it most distracting as an actor. I've had evenings when their behavior has actually ruined my performance."

Nell said sympathetically, "I surely understand, Richard, but those gentlemen paid half a guinea each for their seats. More than the gentry in the boxes."

Lieutenant Tighe said, "I agree, Richard. We've eliminated the practice at our performances."

From an adjoining box, a loud, sonorous voice said, "Thank you, Hawkins. You may leave now."

It was Jerome Wrexham. Nell had noticed that the Duke's dour-faced butler, along with the parlor maid, had been occupying the box. She assumed they had been sent along to hold the box, as was the custom of the day, since no seats were reserved, even for the theater's shareholders. She had idly wondered who might arrive to take the seats, since she did not expect that the Duke, himself, would return for the second night, and she was not surprised to see Wrexham. Over the years he had continued industriously and artfully to nurture his relationship with

477

the Duchess and, in his own fashion, with the Duke. But most of all he had worked to ingratiate himself with the young man who now followed him into the box from the small drawing room behind it. The young man was Lord John Fox, eleven-year-old son of Edmund and Sarah.

Young Lord John's arrival with Wrexham was another distressing example of the unhappy relationship which had developed between the boy and his father. Nell knew that the Duke would have done everything in his power to persuade John to attend the opening-night performance with him and the Duchess, but John had obviously rejected his father once again and chosen to attend the second night with Jerome Wrexham. The Duke had told Nell, not too long ago, that John had spent his birthday with Wrexham, had left the mansion shortly after noon, and had not returned until mid-afternoon of the following day. The Duchess's persistent denunciations of her husband had poisoned the youth's mind quite effectively. John consistently and openly showed his dislike for his father.

Lieutenant Tighe, Richard, Nancy Lucia all stared, along with Nell, now at Lord John Fox. He was an arresting sight, exceptionally tall for his age, almost as tall as Wrexham or Richard, but startlingly thin. He held himself self-consciously erect, with his bony chest out and his sharp chin high. His complexion was pale. The left corner of his mouth lifted in a permanent sneer. The pallid skin of his cheeks was stretched tight across the bone structure. The eyes were the most startling feature of the face. They were a gleaming mahogany, so dark they were almost black, and a fire seemed to burn behind them. They were sunk deep in their sockets, under thin eyebrows and an extraordinarily high forehead.

He wore a black silk tricornered hat, edged with gold trim, and garnished with royal purple plumes, bent inward on the upper rim. His black silk coat fitted him perfectly, snug at his narrow waist, flaring dramatically at his thin thighs. The coat had lapels of the royal purple velvet, and turned back cuffs of the same material. Beneath the coat, he wore a waistcoat of the royal purple velvet, elaborately embroidered with gold flowers and set with half a dozen small diamonds. The top two buttons of the waistcoat were unbuttoned to display the intricately frilled white silk shirt. He wore two neckcloths, in the style of the day's military men: a royal purple silk neckcloth covering an under one of white muslin. The neck-cloths were kept in place by a brilliantly sparkling diamond pin. His black silk breeches were tight on his stemlike thighs and ended just below his knees, where his thin legs were covered with white silk stockings. He wore black silk shoes with royal purple high heels.

Hanging from his waist was a rich leather scabbard, embossed with serpentlike gold figures. The hilt of the sword was of gold with jeweled insets. It was a magnificent weapon. In the past month, on two occasions, young John Fox had happily used the sword, defending himself against two different bands of the predators which roamed London's more disreputable late-night streets. The ruffians, attracted by the ostentatious display of his gems, quickly learned that this youth's slight appearance was deceiving. He wielded the sword like a fencing master, with ruthless and deadly quickness. Word seemed to have spread in London's predatory circles that the dazzlingly bejeweled youth had best be left alone.

Now, in the new Covent Garden theater, as Wrexham took his seat, John Fox stood and for a moment surveyed the auditorium. The look on his face was contemptuous. When his eyes rested on the beaux on the stage, he waved both hands delicately toward them, saying crisply in a reedy, preteen voice, "Strutting imbeciles!"

The candle glow from the chandeliers struck highlights on the jeweled rings he wore on eight of his fingers. As he took his seat, he caught Nancy Lucia's eye. He stared directly into her eyes for a long moment, then shifted his gaze to her bosom. Finally, he smirked as he stared boldly at the large round ball of her stomach, resting on her lap. Nancy Lucia nervously stopped fanning herself and held the fan protectively over her bulging stomach. She felt as though this garish, strangely mature youth was undressing her with his dark eyes.

A tall, distinguished-looking actor strode downstage to the very front of the apron. Raising his voice so that he might be heard over the still noisy crowd, he began the play's prologue:

"Of those few fools who with ill stars are curst,
Sure scribbling fools, called poets fare the worst;
For they're the sort of fools which fortune makes,
And after she has made 'em fools, forsakes.
With Nature's oafs . . ."

479

Nancy Lucia did not know whether she was simply upset by John Fox's rude, lascivious stare, or whether it was the closeness of the theater, but as the prologue continued she began to feel faint and a sharp pain in her abdomen made her gasp. She fought back the dizzy feeling and the pain, and forced herself to smile as the audience quieted and the actor continued with Congreve's amusing prologue. She was determined not to spoil this evening for Richard and Nell. But the pains continued. She could not tell with what frequency they were coming, or whether there was any regularity about them, for she was forcing herself to concentrate on the action on the stage. By sheer will, she made herself laugh heartily each time her companions in the box and the audience laughed, although she felt much more like screaming.

She felt that she was turning pale, and hoped no one would notice. She fanned herself and stared fixedly at the stage, not understanding a word of the play, but still simulating the reactions of the people around her. The pains were now coming quite frequently and regularly, and they were increasingly severe. Once, she could not help gasping loudly. Richard turned to her and said anxiously, "Are you all right?"

Nell looked at her and took her hand. "You're having pains!"

Suddenly the pain was excruciating. Nancy Lucia bit her lower lip so hard it began to bleed. She kept her teeth pressed against the lip. The pain screamed out of her glazed eyes. She stumbled to her feet, with Nell still holding her hand. Richard leaped to her side and put an arm about her waist.

The audience was roaring with laughter and the laughter drowned out Nancy Lucia's piercing scream as Nell and Richard, with Lieutenant Tighe following, led her in to the drawing room behind the box where Nancy Lucia collapsed on the Queen Anne lounge. She lay back, her eyes rolling, beads of perspiration thick on her face. She continued to bite her bleeding lip, trying to fight back the need to scream. The pain was now an unceasing succession of dagger thrusts, and she clutched her stomach, finally unable to stand it any longer. She screamed and gasped with each stab. Richard knelt beside her, stroking her moist cheek and whispering loving words. He was trying to fight off the panic building inside him. In his mind, a wild confusion whirled. He was hearing again the halting, tear-cracked words of Father Whittaker, telling him and Mary that Felicia had died, trying to bring help in time to deliver Edith's baby. Horrific visions flashed in his head: Mary, the baby and the maddened bull; the Olneys burning to death in the thatch-roofed cottage at Waltham Cross.

Nell rushed back out to the box. Nancy Lucia screamed again. Richard took her hand and squeezed it. He heard Nell's voice, loud and clear, over the sound of the actors on the stage, and the now confused audience sound, a strange mix of baffled concern and impatient complaint.

"If there's a doctor or midwife here, come at once, please!" shouted Nell. "A doctor! A doctor! Or a midwife! Hurry please! Hurry! A lady is giving birth!"

She ran back in to the drawing room.

"Lieutenant," she said to Tighe, "please stand at that entrance and don't permit anyone in, unless a doctor or midwife." The lieutenant rushed to the drawing room entrance just in time. He had hardly reached it when thumping footsteps sounded on the stairway leading up from the pit, and down from the gallery.

Nell knelt beside Richard at the lounge, took Nancy Lucia's hand, said urgently, "Richard, fetch Dr. Thorndike. Please hurry. We'll care for Nancy Lucia."

Richard did not want to leave his wife, but he retained enough control of his reasoning powers to realize that they would need the caring and expert services of Dr. Thorndike, whether he should arrive before Nancy Lucia had the baby or after. He kissed Nancy Lucia's hot, sweat-beaded cheek, and rushed past Lieutenant Tighe to fight his way through the crowd of people, which was now trying to get into the drawing room to see what was happening. Tighe had drawn his sword, and was holding the crowd back successfully.

"Doctor? Midwife?" he questioned repeatedly, as one man or woman pushed forward to the front of the mob. On the stage, the actors carried on with Congreve's witty play. In the pit, a fat-cheeked woman turned to her husband who was a doctor.

"Go on, Conrad. Go on up."

"Don't be ridiculous, Flora," said the doctor. "You know I don't practice births. It's indelicate!"

But moments after Richard left, a stout, gray-haired woman fought her way out of the crush on the second bench in the upper gallery and pounded down the stairs, pushing her way through the crowd at the drawing room entrance.

"Make way, ye louts," she bellowed. "I'm a midwife, and the finest in London city."

A man in a leather cap did not move out of her way quickly enough. She clouted him on the side of the head and soon stood before Lieutenant Tighe.

"I'm a midwife," she announced. Tighe smelled the gin on her breath, and wondered for a split second whether he should permit her to enter.

"I've twelve of me own," she shouted, "and delivered five score more. Out'a me way."

Nancy Lucia screamed again as the midwife reached her.

"'Ere, 'ere!" She whipped away Nell's scarlet cape, which Nell had used to cover Nancy Lucia, and spread it on the carpeted floor.

"Get 'er down 'ere!" she ordered Nell. "It'll be a lot 'andier fer me to take out the wee one."

Nell helped Nancy Lucia to the floor. She lay with her feet toward the box, so that the gaping crowd could not stare at Nancy Lucia's spread legs and swollen stomach. Under the *contouche,* Nancy Lucia wore nothing but a chemise, as was the style of the day. The midwife yanked the chemise and *contouche* from her ankles, up over the huge mound of her stomach, and bunched it on her bosom, under her chin. She moved around and knelt between Nancy Lucia's thighs.

"All right now, dearie," she said. "Let's 'ave a bit o' serious bearin' down. . . . Ah, that's it . . . harder . . . more . . . that's it, me girl. . . ."

In a remarkably short while, she took the baby out. She leaned forward and chewed away at the umbilical cord until she bit it through. Deftly, she tied it and then handed the baby to Nell.

Nell had ripped away a section of the petticoat beneath her farthingale, and had sent a man to fetch water. Now she wiped the squalling infant clean, oblivious to the slimy stains over the sleeves, bosom and waist of her pale green silken gown. Her eyes misted as she gazed at the small, wrinkled face of the babe in her arms, the toothless little mouth, wide open and yowling. She looked down at Nancy Lucia, who was now lying quietly, breathing deeply and evenly, a beatific smile on her pale, moist face.

"He's beautiful!" Nell said reverently. Then she saw

the look of horror and shock come into Nancy Lucia's eyes, as Nancy Lucia raised her hand to her mouth. Nancy Lucia was looking beyond Nell, in the direction of the box. Nell turned, with the baby in her arms, and saw young Lord John standing before the maroon velvet drape, which separated the drawing room from the box.

His dark mahogany eyes burned with excitement. His tongue flicked nervously from side to side across his thin lips. His right hand was against the crotch of his tight silk breeches. The long, slender fingers of his left hand trembled at his side. Nell had never seen a look of such undisguised lust on any face. Behind John, and a little to his left, stood Jerome Wrexham, who appeared slightly embarrassed. Obviously, they had both climbed over into Nell's box from their own. Nell was quite certain they had watched the entire delivery.

"Get out!" said Nell with cold fury. "Get out of here immediately!"

The contemptuous sneer replaced the evil look of lust on John Fox's pale face. He bowed gallantly, making a sweeping gesture with his right hand.

"As you wish, madam," he said in his piping voice. "We were merely standing by, in the event we might be of service."

"Get out!" Nell snapped again. She heard Nancy Lucia sobbing quietly. As they left, a wild burst of laughter sounded from the auditorium. William Congreve wrote very humorous plays, and *The Way of the World* was his wittiest.

Nell knelt beside Nancy Lucia, holding the infant, who began crying again.

"Richard! Where's Richard?" Nancy Lucia called feebly.

"He will be here in a moment, dear, in just a moment." She held the squalling baby cradled in her right arm, and took Nancy Lucia's hot hand in her left hand, praying that Richard would return soon—and with the doctor.

e❧ 39 ❧

Nell had been aware, of course, that John Fox was a strange child. She knew that he had a vicious streak and an uncontrollable temper. But she also knew from periodic conversations with the Duke that he was brilliant. In the way of fathers, perpetually seeking to emphasize the commendable traits in their offspring, Edmund had told Nell how impressed Reverend Montague, the Fox house chaplain, was with the boy's progress in reading and writing. His only weak subject was Latin. John's fencing master insisted to the Duke that he had never had a more apt and enthusiastic pupil than young John. The musical compositions John wrote and played on the spinet, beginning at age nine, attested to the truth of his music master's statement that the boy was exceptionally talented.

Indeed, ever since the age of six, when John, like the son of all noblemen, began his studies, the Duke had dwelled on these accomplishments to such an extent that Nell was stunned by John's behavior at the theater. Had she been aware of his activities since his eleventh birthday this past winter, she would not have been so amazed. On that day, Jerome Wrexham had come to the Fox mansion slightly after noon. John and the Duchess were just finishing dinner in the ornate, oak-paneled dining room, when Hawkins announced Wrexham.

"What are your plans for John today?" Sarah Fox had asked.

"We begin with the hangings at Tyburn, and then I have a series of surprises. Please do not wait up for us, dear Sarah. John and I may be a little late. Indeed, if you have no objections, John may stay with me tonight."

484

The Duchess moved her wheelchair away from the damask-covered table.

"I have no objections at all, dear Jerry. I know my young man is in loving hands."

John went to his mother and kissed her tenderly on both cheeks.

"Happy birthday, sweet Johnny," she said. "May your pleasures be many today."

She had given him a hundred pounds to splurge as he wished. And she had also bought him a complete new wardrobe, including a star-shaped ruby pin for his neck-clothes.

"Come to the hangings with us, Mother!" John urged. "Jerry says they promise to be quite special."

The Duchess waved her unparalyzed hand.

"No, dear Johnny. I enjoyed them immensely at your age, but I can no longer tolerate the screaming and shouting of the rabble."

It was an overcast, but warm, humid day. They took one of the smaller Fox coaches, so that John could drive it himself. The afternoon began with fine promise, with John flicking the frisky English mare with the long whip to speed her through the crowded streets. He laughed heartily, as he almost ran down an occasional slow-moving pedestrian, and twice he lashed out with the whip at a clumsy, absentminded dolt or doxy.

The Tyburn hangings were a major entertainment event for the poverty-stricken populace of the area. Virtually all the paupers who lived on Oxford Street, men, women and their ragged children, jostled each other for favorable positions near the gallows platform. Thousands of other tattered citizens of the kingdom trudged their way to Tyburn from Paddington, and from the smaller hamlets as far away as Edgeware. A substantial number of the gentry also attended. They arrived in coaches and carriages, and arrogantly drove their way through the mobs of the poor to the best positions before the hanging trees. Here many of the fops and beaux, and other ladies and gentlemen of quality climbed to the tops of their conveyances for a better view of the proceedings. The elegant dress of the noblemen and ladies was a colorful contrast to the dull gray rags of the masses.

Wrexham and young John climbed to the roof of their coach. They were among the most spectacularly caparisoned of all the gentry. Wrexham, an experienced hand at these events, had made it a point to learn the names and crimes of the four condemned.

As the burly, black-bearded hangman and his obese, pig-eyed assistant made their final preparations at the gallows built to take all four victims at once, Wrexham told John, "First to be turned off, lad, is an old butcher, Otto Filch. Gave wrong change to a customer, and when the biddy complained, he attacked her with a knife."

John pointed to a huge cauldron with a fire beneath it on the platform.

"What's the purpose of the cauldron?"

Wrexham laughed.

"You'll find out in good time, Johnny boy. In good time."

The hanging of the butcher was not particularly exciting. He was an old man, and he merely trembled and muttered, as though praying, while the hangman put the noose around his neck, marched him up to the gallows and opened the trapdoor beneath his feet. As the hangman and his assistant pulled the body higher so all could have a better view, the butcher's twitching corpse quieted and hung still. The *oohs* and *ahhhs* and general exclamations from the crowd lacked enthusiasm.

"Ah, but now. This will be a most amusing turn off," said Wrexham. A cart, pulled by a donkey, made its way through the crowd to the foot of the hanging platform. In the cart was a young girl in her mid-twenties and a boy no more than seven. The girl lay on her back, tied securely to a wide board. She was quite pretty, though her face was smudged with dirt, and her blond hair was dry and matted. She squirmed and writhed on the board. Defiance, rather than fear, blazed in her dark eyes. The boy was bound securely hand and foot. He sat in the cart beside the lashed, angry girl, weeping steadily. Tears and the snot from his running nose were smeared across his dirty, terrified face.

"That's a whore named Kitty Kean," said Wrexham. "She worked in a house on Fleet Street years ago. I could have predicted she would come to no good end. She constantly insulted and cursed the patrons. One night when I was there—Kitty must have been about your age—she actually struck a gentleman. . . ."

Wrexham interrupted himself with a laugh.

"She said he was abusing her. The bawd threw her out."

"Why is she being hanged?" asked John.

"She stole a man's purse. She'd gone into whoring on her own and wasn't prospering at all. No decent house would have her. Getting too old and nastier than ever. Pretty Kitty Kean she used to be." Wrexham laughed again. "She's not so pretty now."

The boy in the cart wailed loudly as the cart came to a halt before the platform.

"Who is the filthy child?" asked John.

"It's Kitty's bastard son. He's been arrested four times for begging."

John looked down, fascinated by the struggling girl on the board. A flaccid pale breast had escaped her dirty black cotton dress.

"She's a bold one," he said.

"They'll only half-hang the boy," said Wrexham. "Cut him down before he dies. Just to teach him to give up his wicked ways."

The tall, muscle-bound hangman and the fat assistant trotted down the stairs from the platform. The assistant picked up the boy and threw him over his shoulder like a sack of potatoes. The boy struggled helplessly, as the assistant carried him up on the platform, and managed to bite the assistant's bulging, sweaty neck. The fat man hurled him to the floor and kicked him.

"Be quiet, ye worthless bastard," he yelled. The crowd roared, some cheering the boy for showing a bit of fight, some jeering the assistant.

"They'll hang Kitty first," shouted Wrexham over the noise of the crowd. "Seeing his mother turned off will serve as a lesson twice taught for the stupid lad."

The powerful hangman was about to lift the board, girl and all, onto his shoulder, when Kitty Kean shouted, "Untie me, ye stinkin' ox. I'll walk up to the bleedin' tree like a lady!"

Those in the crowd close enough to hear shouted, "Untie the doxy. Untie her! Untie her!"

The big, black-bearded hangman made a courtly bow and released Kitty Kean from the board. She tried to leap to her feet, but her stiff limbs betrayed her, and she fell to her knees. The hangman reached out to take her by the arm. She slapped his hand away.

"I don't need yer bleedin' 'elp!" she shouted, and leaped from the tail of the wagon, grimaced in pain as her bare feet hit the hard earth. She forced a rigid smile as she walked, head held high, to the stairs and up onto the platform.

The crowd cheered.

"Ho, what a proud little whore 'ave we 'ere," shouted the hangman. He took her arm, led her to a tall, up-ended bucket beneath a gallows alongside the one from which the butcher's body dangled. The boy, his hands and feet still bound, slithered serpentlike across the rough wooden boards toward her.

She looked down at him and her blazing dark eyes misted.

"Don't cry, Willie love," she said. "It'll all be over and done with in a blink."

The hangman put the thick noose around her slender, dirty neck.

"A loverly necklace fer ye, dearie, to be wearin' when ye lay with the devil."

He lifted her by the waist, standing her on the tall, up-ended bucket. She spat down upon him.

"I'd sooner lay with the devil than with you, ye murderin' scum!"

The crowd whistled and applauded and screamed their approval of the doxy's defiance. The boy cried. John Fox stared at the girl on the bucket, enthralled. The hangman and his assistant shoved the bucket quickly out from under Kitty Kean. The body dropped sharply. The tongue sprung rigidly from the gaping mouth. The dark eyes popped. The face turned a glistening mauve. Kitty Kean did a ghastly, macabre dance in the air, arms and legs flailing. Then the slender, grimy corpse went limp and dangled beside the elderly butcher.

The crowd cheered and roared. Men, women and children threw their arms around each other and laughed and danced in orgiastic delight. Kitty Kean's bastard son tried to bury his head in the hard boards of the gallows platform. His narrow back heaved with his sobbing. The hangman untied him and, holding him by the collar of his tattered shirt, led him toward the gallows alongside his mother's. The boy swung both aching arms at the hangman's grip, twisted, kicked, tried to bite. The hangman laughed and pushed him ahead. The shirt tore and the boy broke away. The fat assistant stepped in his way as the child raced toward the stairs, screaming, "No! no! I don't want to die! No!"

488

"The foolish beggar thinks they're really going to hang him, too," said Wrexham.

John Fox was still staring at the dangling body of Kitty Kean. The boy charged head first into the bloated paunch of the hangman's assistant, knocking the breath out of him. Before he reached the steps, the hangman grasped a handful of his hair, and dragged him toward the gallows again. The boy fought and kicked, and cried over and over, "No! No! Don't hang me! I don't want to die!"

The crowd began to shout.

"Coward! Coward! Shame! For shame! Shame! Coward!"

The hangman threw a rope around the boy's scrawny neck, knocked him to the ground, knelt on his chest, and pulled the rope tighter and tighter. The boy's face turned a bluish purple, darkened. He tore desperately, hopelessly against the muscular arms of the hangman. When his struggles became feeble, the hangman suddenly loosened the rope, whipped it away from the boy's neck, got off his chest, and stood beside him. The boy gasped. Slowly the dark empurpled face lightened. The hangman nodded at the fat assistant. The obese man threw a bucketful of water over the gasping lad. Then the hangman pulled him to his feet by the hair of his head and led him down the stairs to the cart. The assistant tied him to the tail of the cart by the wrists.

"Back to the jail," shouted the hangman, and as the driver whipped the donkey, and the animal moved away through the crowd, the fat assistant trotted after the stumbling, falling boy and lashed him several more times with a rope. People in the crowd cursed the tortured boy, and spat at him, denouncing him for his cowardice, as the cart moved past them.

The hangman and his assistant went back onto the platform and began to work around the cauldron standing at one side of the platform. The assistant stoked the fire. The hangman used a large metal object to stir a thick glossy black substance in the cauldron.

"Is that tar?" asked John.

"Tar, indeed!" said Wrexham.

"What use is made of it?"

"You'll soon see, lad."

Ten minutes passed, and the crowd was growing restless. Two beaux on a nearby carriage roof, who had apparently had too much to drink, began an awkward, futile duel. Both fell off the roof to the ground, where they put aside their swords and threw their arms around each other in a warm embrace. As they climbed back up to their carriage roof, another cart came through the crowd. In the cart stood a tall, handsome man, with glistening black hair combed back and tied neatly in a small pigtail. He had a luxuriant, curled, black mustache, and he was dressed in a scarlet velvet coat frogged with silver, and tight-fitting scarlet breeches. The shirt under the coat was of white silk and was elaborately frilled. He wore white silk stockings and shining black leather boots. He steadied himself on the side of the rocking cart with his left hand, while he waved at the crowd, like a conquering hero, with his right. As he drew nearer, John could see that he was holding onto the side of the cart because his feet were tightly chained.

The crowd cheered wildly. Those flanking the path of the wagon reached out and tried to touch him. From the coach and carriage tops, a number of fashionably clad ladies threw him kisses.

"Do you know who that is?" yelled Wrexham in John's ear over the roar of the mob. John shook his head, staring in fascination at the dashing figure in red.

"It's Gallant Jack Kallem, the highwayman."

"I might have guessed."

John remembered now, reading of the exploits of Kallem. For more than a year, the bold robber had terrified travelers coming into and leaving London. Week after week, he suddenly appeared on his gleaming bronze thoroughbred, brandishing pistols in both leather-gloved hands. One week he chased down a coach at Blackheath, the next at Hounslow Hill, then a hackney at Finchley Common or Hampstead Heath. The constables, watches and police officers never knew where he would strike next. He worked quickly and ruthlessly. On one occasion, a coachman tried to whip him off, and Kallem shot the man dead. Only two weeks earlier, he had held up the carriage of the Prince of Wales in Berkely Square, and made off with a small fortune in jewels and money. On numerous occasions, ladies in the parties he robbed pleaded that a ring or brooch or pin held great sentimental value, and in each such case Kallem bowed graciously as he sat his horse and returned the valued item to the lady.

"Do you know how he was captured?" asked Wrexham.

"I read that a marchioness he had robbed became his mistress," said John, "but then, when she discovered that he was unfaithful to her, she told the police they would find him in her bed on a certain night. . . ."

"And so they did!" said Wrexham.

The hangman unchained Kallem, and together they strode to the stairs and up to the gallows platform. The highwayman waved enthusiastically to the crowd all the time. The cheering was loud and constant. When the hangman tried to put the noose over Kallem's head, the highwayman took it from him.

"Permit me, friend hangman!" he said in a loud voice. He made a deep bow to the audience, first to the right, then to those directly in front of him, then to the left. Then he placed the noose around his own neck, pulled it snug, and blew kisses to the crowd with both hands. The mob roared its approval. Ladies of quality and ragged women in the multitude threw kisses back to him. Many wept and wailed when the trap snapped open, and Gallant Jack Kallem did his own version of a strangulation minuet, and finally hung still. The hangman and his assistant knelt and, in turn, cast a pair of dice.

"What are they doing?" asked John.

Wrexham laughed.

"The scoundrels are casting the dice to see who will get Kallem's fine clothes and boots."

The hangman apparently won, for he leaped to his feet and threw his arms in the air in triumph. They cut the highwayman down and undressed him, and took his boots from his feet. Although their own bulky bodies hid him from view to a certain extent, many women in the audience turned their heads away, feeling it indiscreet to view the dead man's naked body. The hangman folded the scarlet velvet coat, breeches, shirt and stockings, and lay them in a neat pile at the side of the gallows. Then he took a large knife from his belt and disemboweled Gallant Jack Kallem. While the hangman was performing this surgery, the fat assistant shaved the highwayman's head. The crowd had quieted as they patiently waited through these gruesome proceedings. They were still muttering and droning on in a subdued manner, when the hangman and his assistant lifted Kallem's corpse and put it into the cauldron of melted tar.

They left it there, while they cut down the corpses of the elderly butcher and the young whore. Several men

491

from Surgeon's Hall climbed up to the platform to claim these cadavers. They took the bodies away in their Surgeon's Hall cart. The hangman and his assistant donned heavy leather gloves and lifted Kallem's maimed and glistening black corpse from the cauldron of tar. They placed the slimy black figure on the platform and fixed irons around it. Then they tied the gallows rope to the iron-bound, tarred cadaver, and hoisted it high on the tree. The crowd cheered again in an exhausted and feeble manner. Most of them realized that this was the end of the festivities. The hangman collected Kallem's clothes and boots, and the assistant gathered their various instruments. Then the mob began to disperse.

As John urged his horse through the stragglers, he looked back. The tar on Kallem's corpse had already stopped dripping. By nightfall it would harden, and for an indeterminate period, the corpse would hang there on Tyburn as a warning to all malefactors.

"Do you know where Lady Gertrude's is?" asked Wrexham, as they raced up Oxford Street.

"I've heard my father mention it, but I've never been there."

Wrexham directed John to the mansion in Pall Mall. Its elegant appointments and elaborate menus did not impress young John because he was accustomed to such luxuries. But the gaming room fascinated him. Wrexham had already taught him to play lanterloo and hazard in private games at his home, but the brilliantly lit, busy card and dice tables in the vast gambling hall excited the youthful nobleman. He could hardly wait to begin playing. Wrexham was extremely hungry—the hangings always gave him an appetite—and he wanted to indulge in a long, leisurely supper of many courses, with much fine wine, but John was impatient. He picked idly at a salmon dish, and had one glass of Lady Gertrude's Rhenish wine.

"If you're going to spend the rest of the night stuffing yourself, Jerry," he grumbled, "I'll go ahead and play by myself."

Reluctantly, Wrexham finished the roast pheasant on his plate and drank off a large glass of Burgundy and rosé. They went directly to the hazard table. Even the buxom, saucy barmaids walking among the players with drinks did not distract John. The first time he cast the dice, he threw the main, a seven, and won ten pounds. His next cast was a four. As he shook the dice for his next throw, Wrexham began to place a five-pound wager that John would make his chance, throw a four before a seven. John stopped him.

"No, Jerry. There are only three possible combinations for casting a four, and six for a seven. It's a poor chance."

The crowpee, covering the wagers for the house, paying or collecting, looked at John strangely. Not too many players understood the odds and percentages of hazard; even fewer talked about it as they played. Wrexham withdrew his bet before John made his next cast. It came up as even, and Wrexham smiled at having saved the five pounds he had not wagered. John had explained the hazard percentages to him several times. But all this mathematical wracking of the brain vexed Wrexham. He preferred to play by sheer gambler's instinct, as ready to wager on a four chance as an eight chance, if he had the feeling he would win.

As the evening progressed, he played his own style more and more. John continued to calculate and play the odds on his bets. After two hours, Wrexham had lost a hundred and forty pounds, and John had won over two hundred. He was excited and jubilant. Wrexham insisted they play lanterloo for a time. For the first hour, they both won rather steadily. Then John's luck turned, and he lost hand after hand. By eleven o'clock he had lost the two hundred pounds he had won at hazard, and an additional fifty. Wrexham, however, had won a hundred and twenty pounds. Finally, John slammed a losing hand down on the table and rose angrily.

"I'm tired of this stupid game, Jerry. I want to leave!"

Wrexham was reluctant to leave while his luck was running so well, but after all it was John's birthday, and Wrexham did have a *pièce de résistance* planned for this night. Outside in the carriage, he said, "Now, just follow my directions, Johnny boy. I am going to take you to a paradise you have never known."

When Wrexham introduced Lord John to Mother Magruder, the youth was not so sure he was going to enjoy this climax to his birthday celebration. The old bawd's teeth had all rotted in the years since Wrexham first patronized the establishment. She had become so heavy that she could hardly rise from the large armchair in which she sat. Her curled orange hair was more outlandish than ever, and her arms and body were grotesque.

She nevertheless greeted Wrexham heartily in her thin voice, and carried on about how honored she was to have Lord John become a patron of the house. His height and the oddly mature look in his burning dark eyes gave her the impression that he was sixteen rather than eleven. Her expert judgment was that this would, by no means, be the young man's first sexual experience. In any event, the earlier young noblemen started whoring and developing a taste for mulatto or dark women, the better.

"I'm sure our ladies will please you, your Lordship," she piped. John did not like the smell of her. But fifteen minutes after he had been led into Cleopatra's room, he forgot all about the gross bawd.

Somehow, despite the use and abuse she had undergone in the decade or more since Wrexham had spent his first night with her, the Jamaican girl had managed to retain her sultry beauty. She had become a bit heavier in the hips, and her breasts sagged slightly, but she was still exotic and lovely. Her skin was as finely textured as ever, and she exuded sensuality. The fact that there was a certain hardness in her eyes made her seem even more exciting to John. She was already a highly accomplished practitioner of the sexual arts, when Wrexham first enjoyed her, but over the years she had added and perfected numerous additional erotic techniques. Mother Magruder was proud of saying that Cleopatra could arouse a marble statue, and satisfy the lust of all the Gods. The Jamaican whore had no trouble arousing John. Satisfying him was another matter.

Two years earlier, he had been seduced by a dimwitted, but voluptuous and oversexed upstairs maid in the Fox mansion. Her name was Rosa Bottomley. Rosa's approach to fornication was primitive and basic. She hardly bothered with kissing and caressing. But young John found her exciting, and their frequent, secret couplings developed an extraordinary sexual maturity in the youth.

On this night of his eleventh birthday, his lustful appetite and his stamina stunned Cleopatra. It was dawn, and John was still insisting on a repeat performance of the initial perversion she had practiced on him hours earlier.

"King Rex," Cleopatra whispered to Wrexham, as John waited sleepily for him at the door as they were leaving, "where you find this young animal? Please don' bring him again for a week, maybe two."

Wrexham drove the carriage through the deserted early morning streets to his own house. John dozed all the way. About noon the next day, Wrexham was having breakfast when John staggered out of the bedchamber. Wrexham's elegant green satin robe looked ludicrously large on him. He had it wrapped around himself twice and had belted it.

"Jerry," he said, joining Wrexham at the breakfast table, "I must thank you for a most exciting and enlightening birthday. I never dreamed there were women like Cleopatra."

"Oh, there are many. Possibly not all as accomplished. But many, Johnny boy, many!"

He handed John a flat package lying beside his plate on the table. John poured himself coffee and tore open the package. It was a thin paperbound booklet. On the cover in bold red letters the title was printed.

MAN OF PLEASURE'S
KALANDER FOR THE YEAR

"It's the current edition of an annual catalog of the city's better whores, Johnny. Names, addresses and specific talents. I think you'll find it interesting."

John read the first listing.

MICHELLE ARMAND—17 years of age; nine stone; five feet, two inches tall; buxom; narrow-waist; full-hips; satin skin; clear complexion; silken black hair; dark brown eyes. An appreciative daughter of Sodom; specialist in Parisian techniques of amour. Number 6 Leadenhall Street.

John grinned and read through four more listings.

"These sound enticing, Jerry. I shall surely sample several."

In the months that followed, he sampled more than several, including some who practiced the more extreme forms of perversions. Devotees of the Marquis de Sade were among those who appealed to him most. He pursued a strange ritual after most of these nights of debauchery. Returning home to the mansion, no matter the hour, he climbed the stairs and proceeded to his mother's bedchamber. There he undressed quietly and got into bed with her. He had slept with her until he was almost eight years old, but in the past three years he had not come into her bed. The first time he did, after his eleventh birthday, Sarah Fox was startled.

"It's all right, Mother," he whispered in the dark. "Just put your arm around me, please." She held him to her thin body with her unparalyzed left arm.

"What is wrong, dear Johnny?" she asked anxiously.

"Nothing, Mother. Nothing at all. I'm just tired."

She stroked his hair, and in a few moments he was asleep. And after hours of lying awake, wondering what was troubling her strange son, the Duchess fell asleep too. Bright sunlight was coming through the richly draped window, when she was awakened. John stood beside the canopied bed, completely dressed. In his right hand he held a lovely bouquet of flowers, which he had picked in the garden.

"Cumberly will be up with breakfast in a few minutes," he said. When the nurse left the breakfast with them, he joined his mother, speaking enthusiastically about a new musical composition he had written.

"It's just for you, Mother," he said.

After breakfast, in the music room, he played it for her on the spinet. It was a lilting melody but in a minor key, with a quality of infinite sadness. A tear formed in the Duchess's left eye, and rolled down her cheek.

"It's lovely, Johnny, very moving."

"I call it 'Lost Lad's Haven.' "

She rolled her chair to the spinet bench, reached forward, took his left hand from the keys and kissed it.

Beginning a few days after his eleventh birthday, John made these late-night or early-morning visits to his mother frequently, sometimes once a week, sometimes once in ten days or a fortnight. He went whoring once or twice a week—occasionally returning to Cleopatra, but more often trying one or another of the ladies listed in the *Kalander*. On nights when he went with Wrexham, he usually stayed at Jerome's house. When he went alone, he spent the rest of the night sleeping at his puzzled and troubled mother's side.

Had Nell Faversham known of these activities, she surely would not have been as surprised or shocked as she was by John's behavior at the Covent Garden Theatre during the birth of Nancy Lucia's baby. And she would have been better prepared for his even more bizarre actions when he came to call at her house in Pall Mall two weeks later.

৫ 40 ৯৯

In the fortnight between the birth and the young nobleman's unexpected visit neither Nell nor Nancy Lucia nor
Richard thought of John Fox at all. From day to day
there was grave uncertainty as to whether Nancy Lucia or
the baby would survive. Richard and Dr. Thorndike had
arrived at the theater no more than fifteen minutes after
Nell assured Nancy Lucia that Richard would be there
soon. By that time, Nancy Lucia was afire with fever, and
the baby continued to wail loudly and without surcease.

"Let us take her to my house," said Nell urgently. Dr.
Thorndike knelt beside Nancy Lucia, made a quick inspection and nodded in somber agreement. Richard lifted
Nancy Lucia in his arms, and Nell carried the squalling
baby, wrapped warmly in Nancy Lucia's cape. Lieutenant
Tighe led the way through the noisy, curious crowd, with
the doctor and midwife following, and the group struggled
its way out of the theater. In the guest bedchamber of
Nell's house, Dr. Thorndike treated Nancy Lucia and gave
her a medicine which enabled her to sleep. The baby slept
fitfully for several hours. Richard did not go to bed at all.
He moved anxiously from Nancy Lucia in the large bed
to the improvised crib Nell constructed with cushions and
an arrangement of odd pieces of furniture. Dr. Thorndike had instructed them not to permit the baby to sleep
with Nancy Lucia until she overcame her fever and
stopped her restless twisting and turning. Many infants of
the day died of what was called "overlaying," instances
where the mother rolled over and smothered the baby
sleeping at her side—inadvertently in some cases, quite

deliberately in all too many desperate, poverty-cursed births.

For a week, Dr. Thorndike visited Nancy Lucia and the baby every day. In the first two days at Nell's, Nancy Lucia's fever mounted dangerously. Dr. Thorndike could hardly conceal his deep concern. But he continued to treat her with a diaphoretic of salt of wormwood, volatile salt, armoniack, ginger powder, sugar candy and oil of cloves, and on the third day the fever broke. Richard's prayers had been answered. As Nancy Lucia recovered, Shannon seemed to improve, too. Though the infant had not yet been christened, they all referred to him as Shannon. Richard and Nancy Lucia had long ago decided to name him after Richard's revered coach.

By the end of the first week, Richard was sleeping with Nancy Lucia and Shannon in the large bed in the guest room. The doctor advised Nancy Lucia to remain inactive for at least another fortnight. Richard went back to work at Goodman's Fields, leaving Nell's house early each morning, and returning late in the evening on days when no shows were scheduled, and well after midnight on the three days the shows were presented. He was tired, but happy and grateful that Nancy Lucia and Shannon were becoming healthier each day. By the middle of the second week after Shannon was born, Nancy Lucia was permitted to sit up in a comfortable chair by a window overlooking the gardens. Here she nursed Shannon several times each day, and during the night. It was late in the evening on a Friday at the end of this second week that young John Fox appeared at the house.

Mrs. Korn, Nell's only servant, answered his knock. John was dressed elegantly, as usual, with his sword hanging at his side. In each hand, he held a small bouquet of mixed flowers. He rudely pushed past Mrs. Korn and strode directly toward the sitting room, whence came the voices of his father and Nell Faversham. The Duke and Nell were seated on a blue and green satin lounge. Before them, on a gracefully carved rosewood table, were a bottle of brandy and two glasses. At the Duke's side rested the gold-headed walking stick he had been forced to use ever since his fractured leg had left him with a limp. John grinned at their obvious surprise and discomfort as he walked across the room to stand before them.

"Don't be embarrassed, Father." His reedy voice seemed to give the sarcasm an exceptionally sharp edge.

"I understand that it is necessary for you to visit the directress of your theatrical enterprises quite frequently."

"What are you doing here?" demanded the Duke, beginning to push himself to his feet. Nell had said nothing to the Duke of John's behavior at the theater. Now she put a restraining hand on the Duke's arm, as she looked up at the tall youth.

"Please be seated, John," she said politely.

John handed her one of the bouquets as he took a chair.

"Since I'm leaving for Eton on Monday, I thought I would. come and say goodbye—to you and to Mrs. Steele. . . . I brought these for her."

He held out the second bouquet of flowers.

Nell placed her own bouquet on the table before her.

"Thank you, John," she said haltingly.

"May I see her?"

"Oh . . . of course. She's upstairs. It's the first room. . . ."

Before she could finish, John rose, bowed, strode quickly to the stairs and climbed them two at a time. The first door he opened was Nell's unoccupied bedchamber. The second was the guest room. Nancy Lucia was in the chair by the window, nursing Shannon, staring lovingly at his small face. Shannon's eyes were closed blissfully. His pink mouth and pale cheeks worked energetically, as he sucked hungrily at his mother's full breast.

John's sudden entrance startled Nancy Lucia. She looked up in alarm. He had been holding the bouquet before him, but now he dropped the hand with the flowers at his side. A mad glow shone in his dark eyes, as he stared at the suckling baby. The flowers fell from his hand. Nancy Lucia screamed as he charged toward her and grabbed Shannon viciously out of her arms. Shannon wailed with anger at being torn away from his supper and at the sudden pain of the ungentle hands, which now rolled him aside on the carpeted floor.

John, in a half-crouching position, plunged forward, pinned Nancy Lucia to the chair and pressed his open mouth hard against the naked breast. Nancy Lucia screamed again, struck at his head with both fists, trying to get out from under his weight. The harder she fought, the more ferociously he held her and sucked. When she screamed again, he began to bite her. The pain was excruciating. She gasped, caught her breath, and screamed

500

once more, so loudly and piercingly that she felt as though the sound would shatter her own eardrums. She grabbed John's hair in both hands, and tried to pull his head away from her breast. But he only bit harder. Nausea blended with the agonizing pain. She had the feeling he was biting through the flesh around her nipple. Shannon wailed and wailed.

Nell burst into the room. She rushed to the baby, picked him up and placed him on the bed, where he continued to cry. John pushed away from Nancy Lucia and turned to face Nell. Nancy Lucia, blood trickling down her torn breast, leaped out of the chair and charged at John. She began beating at his head with both fists, shouting curses as she struck him over and over. The attack took John totally by surprise. Females of his acquaintance, either in noble circles or among the whores he had more recently come to know, were not aggressive. He had had no experience with ladies of the show and theatrical world, many of whom had independent and often revolutionary attitudes quite at variance with the beliefs of the vast majority of women in the kingdom.

He tried to duck and twist away from Nancy Lucia's blows. He finally pushed her off, but as he did, Nell landed upon his back. She tore at his hair and pulled him to the floor. Nancy Lucia hurled herself to her knees beside him and again began punching him with both fists. Desperately, he swung his arm in a long backhand sweep and slammed Nancy Lucia across the side of the head. She fell away from him. Nell grabbed him around the neck, but the besieged boy tore away from her too. He sprang to his feet, and as Nell tried to close in on him again, he slapped her viciously across the face and placed his strong hands around her throat. His back was to the door, and he did not see his father hobble in. The Duke limped quickly up behind John, raised his walking stick, and clubbed him across the shoulder with its heavy gold head. Nell and Nancy Lucia had backed away from the struggling son and father, and now John, defending himself against the repeated blows from the stick with his left arm, managed to reach down and whip his sword out of its scabbard. He stepped back, just as the Duke raised the stick once more. John sidestepped nimbly, made a lightning sweep with the sword, and somehow flicked the stick right out of his father's hand. It pinwheeled through the air toward the bed. No one saw where the stick landed.

Nancy Lucia and Nell stared in petrified fascination as John held the point of the sword against his father's throat. The tall, sweating, disheveled boy, trembling with rage and excitement, moved his right hand imperceptibly forward, and the pressure of the sword's point forced the Duke to stumble backward until his shoulders touched the gold- and blue-flowered wall. John's quivering right hand held the point against the left side of his father's throat. Nancy Lucia and Nell, hands to their open mouths, hardly dared breathe. They stared, wide-eyed, at the Duke's face. Neither had ever seen such an expression. Fear, yes. But more than fear. Fear, giving place to a despairing sorrow. Then the expression changed. He squared his shoulders and stared defiantly into his son's blood-smeared face.

John's right hand trembled ever so slightly. His left was clenched in a hard fist at his side, and shook more violently. His breath came in short, harsh gasps. His dark eyes burned with an unholy fire.

"Father," he spat out finally, "this is my last . . . warning. . . ." The high-pitched tone of his voice made the threat sound extraordinarily malevolent. "Do not ever— under any circumstances—do not ever strike me again!"

He moved his right wrist almost imperceptibly, the merest twist, before he slid the sword back into its scabbard. A thin line of blood appeared on the Duke's throat, running horizontally from the left side, where John's sword had rested, to just beyond the Adam's apple. John stepped away from his father, backed toward the door, still clutching the sword. At the door, he made a low bow toward Nancy Lucia and Nell.

"Till we meet again, dear ladies," he said. The words had an ominous quality, despite the reedy tone of his voice. Both women rushed to the bed, where Shannon was still wailing. The Duke hobbled over to retrieve his stick, which had landed on the bed, the gold head inches from Shannon's left ear. Nancy Lucia took Shannon back to the chair by the window, covered her severely bitten breast, and lowered the nightgown to expose her untouched right breast. As soon as Shannon's hungry mouth found the protruding nipple, he began to drink. While Nancy Lucia, still trembling and breathing heavily, nursed the baby, Nell washed and bandaged the bitten, bruised breast.

Head bowed, sobbing quietly, the Duke hobbled from

the room. He was sick over what his son had done to Nancy Lucia and terrified at the thought that John could well have cut his throat. Perhaps most of all, he despaired over the bitter fact that he knew no way to halt his son's increasingly demented behavior. When Nell came downstairs, she found Edmund sitting on the lounge, his head in his hands. Nell sat down beside him, putting her hand on his shoulder. He shook his head. There was a choking sound in his voice, as he said, "I do not know what to do, Nell. I just do not know!"

Nell's voice quivered with emotion.

"He should be imprisoned, Edmund. I know you cannot do it, but he should be imprisoned!"

He raised his head and looked into Nell's eyes. There was desperation and pleading in his gaze.

"He's going away, Nell. For four years. Perhaps, at Eton . . ."

He could see that Nell understood his agony and empathized with him. But he also could see that she felt Eton would not prove an answer to the fearsome dilemma.

Richard did not arrive at Nell's house until almost two o'clock in the morning. The Goodman's Fields' doorkeeper had gotten drunk, had gotten into a fight with one of the patrons and had been arrested. Richard spent more than an hour at the conclusion of the evening's performance, persuading the justice of the peace to release the man. Nancy Lucia and Nell had decided they would say nothing to Richard about John's attack. They were certain he would seek vengeance against the youth, and they wanted no further trouble. They thought it unlikely they would see John Fox again for many years, if ever. Nancy Lucia had little trouble concealing the damage to her wounded breast, since Richard made no effort to make love to her during this convalescing period. And Shannon showed no signs of the rough handling.

In fact, back at Goodman's Fields, the baby flourished. And it was no wonder. He was the adored darling of the entire company. Without exception, and including Robbie Grigsby, everyone showered Shannon with warm affection. The show people loved babies and were uninhibitedly demonstrative in displaying their adoration. The women insisted on being allowed to hold him during rehearsals; the men pinched his cheeks in passing and remarked on what a strong, handsome babe he was.

The *child* in the company loved Shannon most of all.

Evangeline Grigsby behaved like a miniature, surrogate mother to him. All the while the company rehearsed, or during the course of the performances when she herself was not onstage, she sat in the wings on a stool beside the crib Richard had built for the baby, and rocked him while singing softly to him. When Nancy Lucia fed or diapered him, Evangeline stood by, wide-eyed, playing with his pudgy fingers. Soon Nancy Lucia permitted her to do the diapering. And when Shannon was weaned, Nancy Lucia happily allowed Evangeline to feed him the milk and mush and squashed fruits and vegetables he ate. The little girl loved to wipe the pulverized foods, slithering down his plump chin, back into the hungry baby mouth. And to clean him up after a feeding, and kiss him resoundingly on each cheek and his beautifully formed mouth.

One evening when Shannon was eighteen months old, Richard came offstage during a performance of *Twelfth Night*. He stopped beside Evangeline and Shannon in the crib.

"You're due onstage in fifteen minutes, little mother," he said, stroking Evangeline's blond head. She looked up at him. In the dim backstage light, she stared into his eyes.

"Shannon has the same eyes as you, Richard," she said. The baby was attractive and appealing, but even apart from his physical features Shannon Steele was indeed a child blessed. He had three families who loved him dearly. First, of course, his natural mother and father; secondly, the Goodman's Fields company, led by Nell and Evangeline Grigsby; and lastly his grandparents, the Canadays. Goodman's Fields did not close during the summer. Since both the patent theaters, Lincoln's Inn Fields and Drury Lane, shut down, July and August were profitable months for the smaller unlicensed theater.

Shannon spent summers with Theo and Niccolini. Richard and Nancy Lucia made the trip to Bexhill immediately after the Friday performance, and had understudies play their roles in the Monday shows, so that it was not necessary for them to return to Goodman's Fields until Wednesday each summer week. Theo's health had improved. He still had occasional chest pains, but his appetite was good and he had regained some weight. Niccolini had become a decidedly plump matron.

Dr. Wicks had prescribed a carefully controlled program of exercise, consisting of walking and riding, for

Theo, and had even persuaded him to purchase a Chamber Horse for winters and days when the weather was inclement. This was a sixteen-foot-long board, on which was mounted a cushioned chair with hooped arms, and a footstool on another, sliding board. By sitting in the cushioned chair, placing the feet on the stool and pulling on the arms of the chair, one simulated the motion of riding a horse.

During a late summer day in Shannon's fifth year, when it had rained for ten consecutive hours, Theo sat the boy beside him on the Chamber Horse and began to slide vigorously back and forth.

" 'Ere we go now, Shannon lad, a-ridin' o'er the rollin' hills o' Kildare, on the way to Tullomare and the Grand Canal."

Shannon beamed. He loved his grandfather's highly colored tales of his youthful adventures in Ireland, his early days with the Dublin company, the comedic misadventures of the fledgling Canaday company. Theo was a talented storyteller, not averse to exaggerating where necessary to lend a tale an extra touch of spice or humor. Shannon's grandmother also told him stories of her childhood in Venice, and the travels of her parents' opera company, when she was a child as young as Shannon, to Naples and Rome and other Italian cities. Her own mother (with whom she still communicated) was ill at this time, so Niccolini tended to stress the heroic role of Shannon's Italian great-grandmother in these tales. Her stories leaned more toward romance than the derring-do of Theo's wild yarns.

Theo also taught him to draw, and Niccolini taught him to play the spinet. From the age of five, Richard and Nancy Lucia read him the plays and sonnets of Will Shakespeare and other playwrights and poets and began to teach him to read and write.

When Shannon was almost six, one Antoine DePeyroney, a young Frenchman who had become a British subject, opened a fencing and dancing school near the theater in Goodman's Fields. Richard and Nancy Lucia arranged for Shannon to have lessons in these pursuits, in exchange for helping DePeyroney to read and write English. And all through these years, Evangeline Grigsby continued to lavish her care and affection on Shannon.

When he was six, and she was ten, they appeared to be almost the same age. In addition to the remarkable eyes,

Shannon had inherited most of his father's other physical characteristics. He was unusually tall and broad of shoulder for his years. His extreme youth showed mainly in the innocent quality in his eyes, and the still little-boy cheeks. Evangeline, on the other hand, was destined to grow to adulthood as short as both her parents. Four years his senior, she was only inches taller, but emotionally she was a good deal more than four years older than Shannon.

She attended dancing class with him. He was very fond of DePeyroney, and enjoyed his fencing lessons, but he was less fond of the dancing. At the end of one lesson, during most of which he danced a minuet with Evangeline, she threw her arms around him and kissed him enthusiastically on the lips. There were four other preteen boys and four other girls in the class, and they tittered at Evangeline's boldness, and teased the blushing Shannon. Shannon broke Evangeline's grip, stepped back and slapped her sharply. Tears sprang to her cornflower-blue eyes, as she put a hand to her stinging cheek. DePeyroney rushed forward and grasped Shannon's arm.

"Zat is not nice, Monsieur Shannon," he scolded. Shannon tore loose from his grip and ran angrily out of the room as DePeyroney knelt beside Evangeline.

"Do not cry, *cherie*," he said gently, wiping her tears with a kerchief he took from his cuff. "In a veree short time, Monsieur Shannon will be mos' happee to receive from the so beautiful Miss Evangeleen a kiss!" It would be four years before DePeyroney's prediction came true.

At seven, Shannon began to do walk-ons and play minor parts in some of the Goodman's Fields productions. Of all his interests, he enjoyed acting most, and paid close attention to Richard's zealous coaching. Unfortunately, Shannon had inherited his father's limited vocal equipment, and he was not very good at dancing, so he was used sparingly in the concert numbers between the acts of the plays. But Richard believed he had genuine possibilities as an actor. Evangeline took the acting lessons along with Shannon and she, too, was an earnest pupil.

Shannon was almost ten, when the company was rehearsing a production of *A Midsummer Night's Dream* one crisp fall morning. Evangeline was playing the difficult role of Puck. Shannon was merely playing Mustard-Seed and (in several different costumes) various other fairies in Titania's fold. When the rehearsal ended in the

506

early afternoon, he and Evangeline walked to their favorite place, a stream about a quarter mile from the theater. He sulked as they sat on the bank, holding their fishing poles, envious of her advanced role in the performance. It seemed suddenly important to him to demonstrate to Evangeline that he could do some things better than she. He put down his pole and rushed to a nearby apple tree, tall and heavy with rich green leaves and red fruit.

"See if you can climb as high as I," challenged Shannon, leaping to grasp the lowest branch with two hands and pull himself up on it. Evangeline ran to the tree and stood beneath it, smiling, as Shannon, sitting comfortably on the branch, looked down at her. She jumped several times, trying to reach the branch, but each time she missed it by inches. Shannon, pleased by her failure, climbed higher and higher. He was twelve feet from the hard earth, when he yelled down. "Would you like me to get you that beautiful apple out there?"

The apple to which he pointed was obviously the prize of the crop. It was large and round, deep red and glistening in the afternoon sun. It hung near the slim end of the high branch.

"I do not think you should try," shouted Evangeline, but Shannon was already squirming, inch by inch along the length of the limb, breaking away small twigs and sending a shower of leaves down upon Evangeline. He was sure he could reach the apple. The limb began to bend. He stretched his right arm as far as it would go, and lunged. There was a sharp cracking sound as the limb snapped. Shannon tumbled from the tree, the broken branch between his thighs. He did a somersault in midair and landed on the side of his head. The ground was suddenly above him, and the fruit-laden, green-leaved branches of the tree were below him, and the ground and the tree spun and spun and spun until there was total blackness. The last sound he heard was Evangeline calling his name.

He awoke with his head in Evangeline's lap, and before he opened his eyes, he heard her sobbing.

"Oh, Shannon, Shannon, please be all right. I love you. Please do not die."

He felt her hand stroking his cheek. His head ached, and his neck felt painfully stiff, but her smooth fingers felt soft on his cheek. He kept his eyes closed.

"Please, Shannon," Evangeline kept saying softly, with tears in her quavering voice. "Please!"

507

He felt her budding bosom against his ear, and suddenly her soft, warm lips were on his as she bent forward and kissed him. She alternated between kissing him tenderly and whispering his name, over and over. He almost did not mind the sharp ache in his head and the stiffness in his neck. Finally, he opened his eyes. A look of sheer gratitude and joy flashed in Evangeline's blue eyes. Her whole face seemed to brighten in the sunlight. Even the tears on her cheeks seemed to glisten happily.

"Oh, Shannon. You're all right. Thank God. . . . You are all right, aren't you?"

Shannon lifted his face toward her mouth, even though the movement hurt both his head and his neck. Their lips did not quite meet. He reached up, and pulled her head down toward him with a hand on the silken hair at the back of her neck. Her lips touched his, and followed his mouth as his aching head fell back into her lap. The pain in his head miraculously converted into a dizzy feeling of ecstasy. They kissed and caressed each other for a while, tentatively, awkwardly. Evangeline finally said, "I think we'd best go home, Shannon. Are you all right?"

"I think . . . I think . . ." Shannon stuttered. "I think I love you Evangeline. Is that all right?"

Finally DePeyroney had been proved a prophet. Shannon *was* most happy to receive from Evangeline a kiss.

৶ 41 ৶

John Fox's life during these same years was far from
blessed. At Eton he proved a brilliant student, but one
whose antisocial behavior made him the scourge of the
university. He gambled and drank heavily, and only a
constant flow of large sums from his mother kept him
from going to debtors' prison. He was involved in a succession of scandalous escapades. One involved another
young man, the son of an Earl, who, for a while, was
his lover. When they had a falling out one night, John
wounded him in a duel. Fortunately, the boy lived, and
refused to prosecute any case against John.

There were two heterosexual scandals that involved a
barmaid and a waitress. John had lived with each of them,
in turn, for a brief time. He had beaten the barmaid half
to death, and, later, had savagely damaged the waitress
during a perverted sexual orgy. In the middle of his third
year at the university, the dean informed Edmund Fox
that they would have to expel his son. Bribes to the barmaid and the waitress, as well as several witnesses, and
instructors at the school, kept John out of prison during
those three years.

It took another considerable monetary outlay to gain
his admittance to the university at Winchester, where the
Duke and Duchess hoped he would be able to complete
his studies. This was one of the most trying periods of Edmund Fox's life. They had hardly settled John at Winchester, when a letter arrived from the Duke's sister,
Edwina, in Antigua, telling Edmund that her daughter,
Georgina, not quite fourteen years old, was to be married.

On his return from Antigua and the wedding festivities, he told Nell about the wedding one night.

"I simply do not understand it, Nellie," he said. "Georgina is a beautiful young lady. I'm certain there are any number of aristocratic and wealthy young men from among whom she could choose a husband. Yet she has settled for this doltish nineteen-year-old Herbert Grooves, the son of an insignificant plantation owner. And her whole attitude toward him before and during and after the ceremonies seemed to me almost contemptuous."

Nell was lying beside him in the bed in the house at Pall Mall. She took his hand. It had occurred to her that Georgina might be pregnant, but she did not mention this.

"I'm also gravely concerned about Edwina," Edmund continued wearily. "She seemed distraught all the time I was there. It seems to me she is suffering a severe nervous disorder . . . but Gabriel laughs it off. He, at least, seemed his usual exuberant, vital self."

Nell was the one person in the world to whom he could tell his troubles, and she was unfailingly empathetic. Now she put an arm across his bare chest and kissed his cheek again. He turned on his side and took her in his arms.

"Nellie, my dear. You are truly a port of serenity in the endlessly raging storm which has become my life. I do not know what I should do without you."

"That's quite poetic, dear my Duke," said Nell. "I would be most pleased to be a port of love and romance, as well as serenity."

In the candle glow, the Duke looked at Nell's long red hair, lying on the white silk pillow, at her sparkling emerald green eyes.

"You are, dear Nellie. You are."

He kissed her on the mouth and the throat and each full breast in turn. And for a brief interlude there was only warm, loving, responsive Nellie, and nothing else in the world mattered.

Nell's guess about Georgina proved correct. Seven months after the marriage, she gave birth to a baby girl. Edwina wrote, and told Edmund they had named her Gabriella. About the same time, John Fox was beginning to misbehave at Winchester. At the end of the second year, he was again expelled. He had brought four street prostitutes into the university dormitories and organized a student orgy, which had led to the death of one of the young women, and the wounding by knife of one of the students. His parents, in desperation, decided to send him to Paris to continue his education. They put him under the supervision of Henri Lafoche, a strict and highly respected disciplinarian, who ran a school which specialized in training headstrong and difficult scions of the nobility.

John proved to be the French disciplinarian's most notable and shocking failure. At the end of the second year, Lafoche wrote Edmund Fox, urgently requesting that he come to Paris to discuss his son.

Lafoche was a short man, with a glistening bald head, a thin black mustache and goatee and steel-gray eyes in a gaunt face.

"I regret to have found it necessary to request you to make this voyage, your Grace, but circumstances permit me no choice. I could not commit to paper what I must tell you." He spoke with a heavy French accent.

The Duke waited while Lafoche tugged at his beard.

"In the past four months, three prostitutes were murdered in Montparnasse. Each in a similar, extraordinarily brutal manner . . . each marked by a unique and revolting mutilation."

Edmund Fox felt as though his heart was going to stop beating. It swelled in his chest and choked off his breath. A hard, sick knot formed in his stomach. He intertwined his fingers tightly over the gold head of his walking stick, fighting to control himself. Lafoche rose, and walked to a cabinet against the wall on the right side of the small room. He opened the cabinet door, took out a package and came back to the desk. He pushed aside his ink pot and pens, cleared enough space on the desk to open the package before the Duke.

A fawn beige waistcoat with two large dry brownish stains, and a splatter of smaller stains of the same color, lay before them. Four silver death's-head buttons gleamed dully. A fifth button, the second from the top, was missing.

"Do you recognize this garment?"

"I believe it is similar to one my son owns," said the Duke, struggling to control his voice.

"It *is* your son's." Lafoche's voice was cold, unemotional. "Observe, please, that one button is missing!"

The Duke stared at the gap between the first and third buttons and nodded.

"The missing button was found in the hand of one of the murdered women." He paused. As he rewrapped the waistcoat, he said, "It is in the possession of the police."

The Duke's jaw muscles tightened. He began to perspire. Lafoche walked back to the cabinet.

"Where did you find the waistcoat?" the Duke asked, his voice hoarse.

Lafoche came back toward the desk with another package, this a long, narrow one, wrapped in heavy cloth.

"In your son's room, your Grace. He made no great effort to conceal it. Why he did not, I do not know. I found it stuffed in the rear of his closet."

He unwrapped the slender package. Before Lafoche completed the unwrapping, Edmund Fox knew what he would see. It was John's favorite sword. The same cold steel he had felt against his own throat. Lafoche indicated a stained cavity among the jewels in the gold basket hilt.

"There was a small ruby in that place," he said in the same icy, flat tone. "It, too, is in the possession of the police."

The Duke closed his eyes, rubbing them hard with the fingers of his right hand.

"The gem was found in the shabby bedroom of the last woman who was killed," said Lafoche. "John is a most careless murderer."

"When was the last woman killed?" Edmund Fox asked, his voice quavering.

"Just before I wrote you, two weeks ago."

"When did you find the sword and the waistcoat?"

Lafoche looked mildly irritated at the question.

"Just before I wrote you. I lost no time communicating with you, once I knew."

Lafoche rewrapped the sword, took it back to the cabinet and returned to his desk.

"You did not notify the police?" asked the Duke.

Lafoche stared at him in puzzlement, as though he could not believe the Duke would ask such a question.

"Of course not."

"Why not?"

"You cannot be serious, your Grace. Why not? Why not?"

Edmund Fox continued to stare at him.

"The women were mere whores!" Lafoche said angrily. "It would be ridiculous for us to bring disgrace upon the Academy." He paused and narrowed his eyes as he looked at the ashen-faced Duke. He rose and walked to the cabinet, returning with the two packages. He placed them on the desk before the Duke.

"You may give these to the police if you wish, your Grace," he said, standing over the Duke.

The Duke stared at the packages. His knees began to tremble, then his shoulders shook. He closed his eyes, resting his forehead on his interlocked hands which held the head of his walking stick.

By God. I should, he told himself. *I should go to the police. I should let justice take its course, and rid the world of this monster I have spawned.* He felt hot tears wetting the backs of his hands. Finally, he looked up.

"I'll take the packages with me, Monsieur Lafoche," he said with a sudden, unnatural calmness. He reached into his pocket.

"You are going to the police?" Lafoche asked, surprise and alarm in his tone.

The Duke placed his check book on the desk and took the headmaster's pen. Then he handed the check for one thousand pounds to Lafoche.

"This should cover the cost of the coat and the sword . . . and your trouble in keeping them for me," he said wearily. Lafoche looked at the check and bowed.

"It is much appreciated, your Grace. John may be more tractable when he leaves the school."

Edmund Fox hated himself at that moment. But he knew that he would hate himself even more if he turned his son over to the police. There was the effect it would have on Sarah; the disgrace it would bring to the family name. But he also believed his possession of the coat and sword might prove his one feeble opportunity to halt John's insane behavior. Later that morning, in John's small, sparsely furnished room at the school, the Duke told his son he now had the waistcoat and the sword.

"I intend to keep them, John," he said coldly, "in a very secure place. They will be brought forth only in the event of my death, along with an exposition of their significance in the deaths of these women."

John stared at him in contemptuous silence.

"Or," said the Duke, "if you ever again commit a violent crime against anyone."

"You haven't yet asked me if I killed those whores," said John, coldly.

The Duke was stunned by the remark.

"The coat and the sword are yours, John. The police found the missing button and gem at the sites of the murders."

"Someone stole the sword and the coat!" John said blandly.

"Stole them? Who?"

"I do not know who."

"Someone stole the coat and the sword? Wore the waistcoat to a rendezvous with a woman, killed her with the sword . . . and then returned the sword and coat to your closet. . . . Is that what you expect anyone to believe?"

"That is what happened!" John stared at his father.

The Duke shook his head. "You are obviously lying, John."

"Thank you, Father. You always did have great faith in me."

The Duke knew his son was lying, but he had the strange feeling that John himself believed he was telling the truth. The boy had actually convinced himself that someone had stolen the coat and sword, committed the murders and put the weapon and waistcoat back in his room. Edmund Fox realized there was no point in debating the matter further. They returned to England. On his first night back in the mansion of his parents, John Fox slept with his mother. She held him to her flabby, unparalyzed side as she spoke to him.

"Can you not tell me what drives you to these foolish actions, dear John?" she whispered in the darkness.

She knew nothing of the murders, of course. Between them the Duke and John merely concocted various fanciful, relatively innocuous tales of disobedience, boyish rebellion and such, to explain John's expulsions. Now John shook his head, pressed against her flaccid, withered bosom. She felt the wetness of his tears on her throat.

"I do not know, Mother. I do not know," he said, a note of desperation in his muffled voice. "I cannot tolerate the domineering instructors. Monsieur Lafoche was a martinet. He reminded me of Father."

The Duchess stroked his thick hair and wiped away the tears on his cheek.

"Your father has always been a selfish, thoughtless man, Johnny, but you must learn to control yourself. You are a brilliant and sensitive young man, and you must find an outlet for your talents."

They were merely words, and Sarah Fox knew, by this time, they were nothing more, but she knew no other way to respond to this lost man-child lying beside her. And John Fox, too, knew they were merely words. But he liked to hear them. For a few brief hours in the dark night, they enabled him to delude himself into believing that he would somehow escape the devils which possessed him.

"Sarah, I have no idea what we can do to save John from himself, but I do know one thing that may prove helpful." The Duke was breakfasting with his wife the following morning.

She wheeled her chair to face her husband more directly across the damask-covered breakfast table.

"What may that be?"

"Do not give him the outrageous sums of money you have been lavishing upon him. If you make it clear to him that you will no longer buy him out of untenable situations, he could conceivably learn to control himself!"

"I will never forsake him!"

"Forsaking him is one thing!" The Duke pounded the table. "Paying his way into hell is quite another!"

He reached for his walking stick and hobbled angrily out of the room. At the time, he did not realize that he had made some impact on his wife's thinking. The next day, John Fox moved in to Jerome Wrexham's apartment. The past several years had found Wrexham on the brink of personal disaster several times. He was drinking heavily, gambling at the racetrack, the bull-baiting events and the cockfights, and spending two or three evenings each week at Lady Gertrude's, and he welcomed John as he would a new life.

When John then went to his mother and told her he was moving in with Wrexham, she was very pleased with the news.

"Mother," he said casually, as they sat in the morning room, "I'll need a thousand pounds. I left Paris penniless, and Jerry wishes to borrow a modest sum from me." In the three weeks before John's arrival at his home, Wrexham had once again gambled his way into a desperate situation. He had run up a new score of two hundred pounds at Lady Gertrude's and had told John of his situation.

"Now, John," the Duchess frowned, and tried to speak firmly, "you must stop squandering money. Our resources are not bottomless, you know."

She wrote him a remittance, but when she handed it to him, she said snappishly, "See that this lasts you for a time."

"Thank you, Mother."

He kissed her forehead.

Wrexham and John spent the day in Wrexham's comfortable apartment, eating, drinking and bringing each other up to date on their respective activities in the years since they had seen each other. With the specter of enormous debt removed from his life, Wrexham was a much relieved man.

"Did you know that your father had the royal patent of Lincoln's Inn Field transferred to Covent Garden?" Wrexham asked.

"No. Does it matter?"

"Indeed it does. We do little drama at Lincoln's Inn now. The concentration is largely on musical programs and a great deal of pantomime and dance."

"That should suit you, Jerry. You sing beautifully."

"It does, to a degree, but it limits my roles."

The fact was that Wrexham's debaucheries had taken their toll. He was considerably heavier than he had ever been, with a pronounced paunch, puffy, veined cheeks and an empurpled nose. The full, rich beard and mustache did little to camouflage this. He still did sing well, but he was completely unacceptable in romantic roles. He was no longer the popular favorite he had been seven or eight years earlier. Gilbert Weston, who in spite of his gout continued to manage the theater, kept him on simply to avoid creating problems for the Duke with his wife. The Duchess still considered herself Wrexham's patron.

John told Wrexham how painfully dull life had been at Eton and Winchester, and even in Paris. He glossed over and made light humor of the violent incidents of his recent past. When mentioning the prostitutes in Montparnasse, he merely described with some relish the sadistic exercises he had practiced upon them and nothing more.

Actually, the middle-aged actor and the incorrigible young nobleman were good for each other. Believing he could borrow money from John in any emergency gave Wrexham an easy confidence in his gambling, and John paid gladly. The Duchess became increasingly difficult about giving him money, the Duke's admonition having registered upon her. And her health was failing, making her more irritable in all situations, including the unpleasant scenes that developed out of John's constant requests for money. In the end, however, he was always able to cajole her into giving him what he needed.

From John's standpoint, the fact that he now had a companion (whenever he desired one) in his wild escapades tended to make him pursue his pleasures in a more rational manner. Wrexham had no intention of going to prison for some ridiculous sex crime, and he constantly cautioned John against going too far in his sadistic practices. In addition to their activities as frequent gambling, drinking and whoring companions, John and Wrexham also became lovers.

For almost four years their lives were a thrilling blur of sybaritic, dissolute days and nights. The gambling went well; they handled their beer and wine and liquors commendably; only one prostitute threatened to go to the police, but an extra ten pounds silenced her.

And then in a compressed, incredible three months it all came to an end.

❧ 42 ❦

It was a peculiar unrelated combination of persons and events which planted and nurtured in Richard Steele's mind the seed of the idea of taking a theatrical company to America. The brief discussion with Lieutenant Tighe in the box at Covent Garden the evening Shannon was born was probably the genesis. Tighe's comments about the great hunger and need for entertainment in Virginia had impressed Richard. Possibly Nancy Lucia's restlessness as the years passed at Goodman's Fields was another factor. Nancy Lucia was happy. But she had been born in a show wagon, and had spent the first nineteen years of her life traveling, and the wanderlust was in her blood. She did not complain, but the urge to travel revealed itself on a number of occasions. One summer day, as they sat on the beach at Bexhill, watching Shannon and his grandfather splashing about at the shoreline, a ship appeared on the far horizon.

"I wonder where that brig is going?" Nancy Lucia said wistfully.

"Probably France," said Richard, squinting in the glare of the bright sun on the water.

"Perhaps out into the ocean and on up to Ireland," said Nancy Lucia with a dreamy look in her lavender eyes. "Or even across the sea to America. Have you ever thought about going there?"

Richard looked toward the shallow water where Theo and Shannon stood. Theo was pointing at the ship, saying something to Shannon. Richard leaned over and kissed Nancy Lucia's cheek.

"Don't say anything to your father, my little gypsy, or he'll be wanting to leave in the morning."

But Richard realized, even as he spoke, that he himself was growing restless once again. The consistent success of the company at Goodman's Fields was almost becoming monotonous. He was in need of a new challenge. A playwright, Henry Fielding, who later was to write some of the most successful novels of the day, was another who unwittingly helped nurture the idea of the American theatrical company in Richard's head. Fielding had written several clever plays satirizing the government. They were extremely popular, and one fall, Richard presented Fielding's most recent work at Goodman's Fields. It was possibly the most biting satire on the King's Council ever performed. Though the play was well-received, the day after the initial performance Nell told Richard that the Duke wished him to attend a meeting the following day.

In Gilbert Weston's office, Edmund Fox addressed Richard, as Weston and Nell listened attentively.

"I'm sure you were not aware, Richard, of how extremely displeased Robert Walpole, the head of the King's Council, has been with Fielding's plays. But I cannot describe to you his ire. He is determined to put an end to plays which so blatantly hold the government up to ridicule."

"But Edmund," interrupted Nell, "the Fielding comedies are so good-humored and clever. Has Walpole no sense of humor. . . ?"

The Duke cut her short.

"Walpole's sense of humor or lack of it is not our concern, Nell. We operate by the grant of patent at Covent Garden, and by the leave of the King and Council, and it is incumbent upon us to avoid incurring the displeasure of Walpole or any other members of the government."

How seriously Walpole objected to the presentation of Fielding's kind of plays was demonstrated by the passage, as the 1737 season ended, of the new Licensing Act. Nell read it to Richard and Nancy Lucia at supper in the cottage at Goodman's Fields one evening.

Richard frowned. The new laws seemed to outline a set of restrictions similar to those of the present Licensing Act.

"Hasn't that always been the case? Plays may be legally performed only by the patent theaters?" Richard asked.

"No, dear Richard. The restrictions have been greatly broadened, and the law will be enforced far more rigidly and severely than before. We will have to present only the most innocuous kinds of light music and pantomime programs at Goodman's Fields for a time."

The new restrictions took a good deal of the pleasure and challenge out of working at Goodman's Fields. That summer, at supper with the entire family on a Saturday evening at Bexhill, Richard asked, "Theo, do you know anything about the colonies in America?"

"Only what my old friend, Gilhooley, wrote me several years ago. He emigrated to Maryland originally, then moved on to Virginia. The last I heard, the old reprobate was an overseer on a tobacco plantation."

"Would you think a theatrical company might fare well there?"

A broad grin broke out on Theo's lined face. His lavender eyes sparkled.

"Lad, a theatrical company would fare well in any place on God's green earth where there are people. Man needs to have his hour of entertainment and amusement."

"It would be difficult, and probably dangerous, of course," said Niccolini. "We read that in many places there are savages and wild beasts."

"Can we go, Father?" asked Shannon, who was now eleven years old. "Can we?"

Nancy Lucia laughed.

"Not this very day, love." She sighed. "But perhaps one day."

"I have been thinking," said Richard seriously, "that if one assembled an entire company right here in England and took along wardrobe and basic flats and scenery to do perhaps a dozen of the most popular plays, the company might be well-received in the more advanced colonies."

"It would indeed, lad," enthused Theo, "and I'll design and construct the flats and scenery for you. I have been working on some interesting new ideas."

"We could rehearse on the ship going across!" said Shannon.

"It would be a most expensive undertaking," said Niccolini. "How large a company had you thought of taking?"

"We could possibly do it with seven, as you did with the Canaday company, but I would much prefer to take thirteen or fourteen, as we have at Goodman's Fields."

"I'm not too certain you could find a dozen competent actors who would venture it," said Niccolini. "Many believe that only convicts, indentured servants and religious fanatics go to the colonies."

"Nonsense, my dear," protested Theo. "Any man with a bit o' the adventurer in 'is heart would leap at the opportunity. Indeed. if my own health continues to improve we may well join the company ourselves. A change of scene would do us both good."

Niccolini shook her head.

"Yes, just what you need, Theo dear. A three-month voyage across the stormy Atlantic."

They discussed no concrete plans on that occasion. But when they discussed the project with Nell, she was enthusiastic about the idea. The Duke, however, was in bad spirits when she told him about Richard's proposal, and he rejected it out of hand. With the restrictions on performing drama drastically enforced through that entire season and next, business at Goodman's Fields fell off considerably. Richard, Nancy Lucia and the entire company worked through these days in a desultory fashion. The idea for the American expedition was temporarily lost in the general gloom. But as the 1740 season began, the three-year-old Licensing Act was less strictly enforced. Henry Fielding gave up writing plays and devoted himself entirely to writing novels. No other playwrights or producers chose to prick the government's pride with their work. Soon, due to the Duke's influence, Richard was able to ignore the Act entirely at Goodman's Fields. He resumed presentation of the more popular plays with renewed vigor.

It was during the initial performance of one of these that the idea of organizing an American company was once again pushed to the forefront of Richard's mind. The direct instruments of the rebirth of this notion were two fops seated on stage left. Richard did not even know their names. The company was doing *Julius Caesar* once again. Richard was playing Brutus with the magical Farley Shannon–Thomas Betterton sword. The production was an exceptionally important one to Richard and Nancy Lucia because in it, Shannon Steele, almost fourteen, was undertaking the most difficult role of his young career. He was playing Cassius. To a greater degree than ever before, he experienced all the signs of nervousness. But unlike his father in an earlier day, he did not forget his lines. As the performance began, he was doing beautifully.

Richard had the feeling that his own performance as Brutus was surpassing anything he had done in years. He felt that glorious surge and indefinable glow an actor knows when he has an audience enraptured. Then the fops began to chat. They had apparently lingered too long over whiskeys at their club. They talked and giggled as though they were still enjoying their drinks. The other beaux on the stage, and many in the pit and the galleries, began to shush them, and irritably demanded they be silent. For a time, Richard and the other members of the cast ignored them, and proceeded with their playing. It was still early in the first act. Cassius and Brutus were onstage. Even at the risk of confusing Shannon, Richard finally turned away from his son, strode toward the fops, and said in a loud voice, "You gentlemen would find it much quieter in the Black Boar, a comfortable tavern just down the road!"

One of the bewigged dandies waved a hand at him, said in slurred tones, "Oh, that's perfectly all right, sir. You are not disturbing us."

The audience laughed. Richard, agitated, nevertheless turned back to Shannon.

"What means this shouting? I do fear the people choose Caesar for their king," he said in ringing tones.

Cassius Shannon, his voice quavering and obviously distracted by the incident and the continued chattering of the fops, replied, "Ay, do you fear it? Then must I think you would not have it so."

Brutus Richard said, "I would not, Cassius; yet I love him well. But wherefore do you hold me here so long? What is it that you would impart to me? If it be aught toward the general good, set honor in one eye and death in the other, and I will look on both indifferently; for let the gods speed me as I love the name of honor more than I fear death."

"I love the name of honor, and Florinda and Bessie and Jane. . . ." said one of the fops loudly. Richard could stand no more. As Shannon started to speak his next lines, Richard rushed to stage left, and grasped each of the two fops on the shoulders of their elegant coats. He yanked them from their chairs and shoved them toward the wings.

One broke his grip, and Richard pulled the Betterton–Shannon sword from its scabbard and swung it viciously, slapping the fop who had broken loose across his tight-breeched bottom with the sword's broadside. The fop yowled and raced for the wings. The second fop had turned, and had begun to dash across the stage in the opposite direction. Shannon stood in his path and slowed him just enough for Richard to catch up to him. Richard slammed the flat side of the sword across his fat behind twice before he escaped into the wings.

The house was in an uproar. The merriest comedy ever played there never elicited such sustained screaming, laughter and applause. As Richard tried to quiet the audience so that the tragedy could proceed, he wondered whether Farley Shannon's and Thomas Betterton's sword had ever been put to more ignoble use. The company was well into the second act before the audience settled down enough to enable Richard, Shannon and their fellow players to recapture the mood of the tragedy. Shannon performed well. Backstage, while he was being congratulated, Richard grumbled to Nancy Lucia,

"I would give anything to eliminate having those calves' heads sitting on stage."

He knew that he would never be able to persuade Nell, Gilbert Weston, the Duke or any other manager or proprietor in England to give up the substantial income from the sale of the on-stage seats, and so establishing his own company in America became a goal he had to achieve at any cost. If Gilbert Weston could have read his mind, he would have accused Richard of behaving like a theatrical missionary once again.

"We must find a way to take a company to America, Nancy Lucia," Richard said that night at the cottage. "If the Duke will not finance us, we will have to secure funds elsewhere."

"Why do we not discuss it with Nell again?" suggested Nancy Lucia.

On the following day, they rode into London to see *The Fickle Fair One,* a masque presented at Covent Garden. Jerome Wrexham, now employed by the Covent Garden company, was in good form. Apart from an excellent performance in the musical play, he sang a specialty number, written and popularized by a leading composer of the day,

Richard Leveridge. It was called *In Praise of Love and Wine,* and could have been written expressly for Wrexham. Nell seemed unusually animated and excited from the moment she met them in the box at the theater.

"I have a surprise for you, but I will not disclose it until we get home to Pall Mall," she said, before the performance began.

"Oh, Nell, please do not be a tease," said Nancy Lucia.

"We would like to discuss the American company again, Nell." Richard's tone was serious.

Nell looked startled.

"Indeed, Richard? On this very evening? What prompted you to raise the matter again at this particular time?"

"It has not been out of my thoughts, Nell, but last night, during *Caesar,* we had an experience which fired my feelings anew."

He told her about the episode with the fops, and she laughed merrily.

"We will discuss the American company. But after supper, if you can manage to be so patient."

"And the surprise?" asked Nancy Lucia.

"And the surprise!" agreed Nell, with a mischievous twinkle in her emerald eyes.

After the performance, Ben Pickering greeted them enthusiastically at the Inn of the King's Men. Neither the Inn's stocky, muscular proprietor, nor his wife Bessie had changed a great deal over the years. They had each added a quarter stone or two, and their faces were a bit more lined, but they were as ebullient and full of vitality as ever.

"Bessie," yelled Pickering, "d'you have the letter?"

Bessie came out from behind the serving counter and reached into the pocket of her apron. "All manner of happy news, Richard. From Tillie," she said.

"And a particular note of glad tidings for you, Richard!" said Ben.

Bessie handed Richard the letter. On a number of previous occasions over the years, the Pickerings had permitted Richard to read Tillie's long letters. Her handwriting was like that of a child, graceless and uncertain. But the letters were always full of detailed news of what was happening to her and her family. The last time the

524

Pickerings had heard from her, more than six months earlier, she had four children and was pregnant with a fifth.

Richard looked at the first page of the letter, and up at the Pickerings, a startled expression on his face. The handwriting was firm, graceful and masculine. Richard could see at a glance there were no misspellings. The letter was obviously written by a person whose grammar and penmanship were excellent. Pickering chuckled at Richard's astonished look.

"Our Tillie has an amanuensis. Her Jason no longer sails the seas. He is a customs officer in York, now, and so has time to write Tillie's letters for her."

Jason Roughead was the "super cargo" Tillie had married more than ten years ago. As Richard read the letter, written by Jason, but dictated by Tillie, they learned that Jason had had enough of life on the oceans, and had decided he wanted to settle down and spend time with his family. They had sold their house in Salem, and had moved to York, a seaport town in Virginia. Tillie had had her fifth child, her second daughter. The letter sounded uninhibitedly joyous. The children were all glowingly healthy; Jason liked his new work; York was an attractive and interesting community.

Then Richard read about the Roughead family's visit to the inland county-town of Williamsburg, during the public times there. They had attended the fairs and several musical concerts. They had not had such a pleasurable time in all their days in America, since Salem in the Massachusetts Bay Colony frowned on amusements of this kind. The children were so excited they could hardly get to sleep at night.

"What a lovely little family," commented Nancy Lucia. Richard saw the affectionate diminutive name by which Tillie had always called him. He read on.

"I know that you still see Dickie Steele every so often." He winced, but continued reading, ". . . and I have the most wonderful news for him. You remember that nice Catholic priest who came in with Dickie perhaps every fortnight or so? The one who drank such large quantities of Madeira, especially for a man of the cloth? We saw him in Williamsburg! We were walking by the new William and Mary College, and he came out the front gate, holding a young

Indian boy by the hand. As soon as I saw him, I knew that I recognized him.

"I did not know who he was right off, but I had to find out. The three oldest children were with me, and they began to talk to the Indian boy, who just smiled at them because he did not understand a word they said.

"Bold as you please, I said to this strong-looking, white-haired man, "I'm Tillie Roughead—I mean Tillie Pickering. I'm sure I know you, sir." He tipped his hat and smiled. "You do indeed, child," he said. "I am Arnold Whittaker. I was *Father* Whittaker when last I saw you."

"Yes! Yes!" I shouted. "You were Dickie Steele's priest. I knew I knew you!" I introduced him to Jason, and we invited him to join us for a beer or two. He was happy to come along with us to a crowded little tavern—gadzooks, all the taverns were so crowded you could hardly squeeze your way in— *Tillie insists I write this precisely as she says it— J.R.*—but Father Whittaker, or rather Mr. Whittaker, would only drink coffee. He said he had not had a drink of whiskey or wine or beer in many years.

"He immediately asked about Dickie—" Richard said the name rapidly, and winced again—"and I was happy to tell him all the good news you had written me about Dickie and his beautiful wife and son, Shannon."

Richard exhanged pleased smiles with Nancy Lucia and Nell, and read on.

"There were tears in Mr. Whittaker's eyes, he was so overjoyed. He said he had written Dickie years ago, when he first gave up drinking, but he supposed Dickie never received the letter, since he never heard from him. He told us they are starting an Indian department at the college, and Mr. Whittaker will work with the young Indians. He seemed shy about talking too much about his work, but I would guess that he has been working with the Indians for some time. The young Indian boy with him—his name was Attakullakulla; neither Jason nor I know if that is the correct spelling, but it means Little Car-

526

penter—at any rate it was plain to see that he worshipped Mr. Whittaker. I am sure Dickie will be happy to learn this news. If he wishes to write Mr. Whittaker, he can send a letter to him at the William and Mary College.

"Please give Dickie my fondest wishes. Jason is frowning at me as he writes this. I like to arouse his jealousy by telling him that Dickie was my first love, and I kissed him in the stables."

Richard faltered as he read this portion, but he struggled through it. Nancy Lucia reached across the table and grasped his hand. She smiled at him. He had told her about Father Whittaker, and his fruitless search over the years. Nell also knew the story, of course. She beamed as Richard read the news. Tillie had enclosed a poem by a a Mr. Drayton. Richard passed this around, and they read it while they ate their supper, happily discussing Tillie's letter and speculating on life in York and Williamsburg. The poem, entitled *Virginia*, began

> "Earth's only paradise.
> Where nature hath in store
> Fowl, venison and fish
> And the fruitfullest soil . . ."

Nell was still beaming and looking mischievous, as she and Richard and Nancy Lucia arrived at Pall Mall. Mrs. Kroll brought brandy and glasses to the rosewood table in the sitting room, and Nell placed a sheaf of papers on the table.

"Nancy Lucia," she said, "I know you will not take it amiss if I tell you that over the years Richard and I have often seemed to experience a most unusual phenomenon. We seem to think of, and act upon, a given matter at precisely the same time, without either of us aware the other is doing so. Does that sound confusing?"

Nancy Lucia smiled. "Only slightly so, Nellie. But I do know what you mean. The same phenomenon occurs between Richard and myself. Perhaps it is because we each, in our own way, love him." She paused to smile at her husband. "I am not certain I can stand another surprise tonight, Nellie, but I am still curious," Nancy Lucia continued.

Nell lifted several blue sheets of paper from the pile on the table. The pages she left were white, and a larger size. She handed the blue pages to Richard.

"It is your evening for reading letters, Richard. The Duke received this yesterday. He wanted me to discuss it with you as soon as possible."

This letter was written in a heavy sharply angled masculine hand.

"My dear Edmund," it said. "I have just returned to the plantation from an extended stay of two full weeks in Williamsburg, where I attended to much personal business and several matters for the Governor during the Public Times. I had not been to Williamsburg since the Public Times last April, a year ago. You know that, for the most part, I greatly prefer the serenity and well ordered gaiety of life here on the Estate, where one's comforts and pleasures are looked to promptly and efficiently. I was utterly astonished by the enormous crowds of people which thronged the county town."

Richard smiled, looked from Nancy Lucia to Nell, and sipped his brandy. The next portion of the letter, which was filled with news of the colonies and seemed of small significance until he reached the last paragraphs of the lengthy correspondence.

"At the races I happened upon an old friend, Lieutenant Roland Tighe, and the subject of his last visit to England came up. . . ."

Richard paused, and looked at Nell again. The connection between the letter and their occasional discussions about the American company were becoming clearer.

"Read on, read on," urged Nell, grinning impishly.

"Do, Richard!" added Nancy Lucia impatiently, and Richard did.

". . . I had no idea you and Roland were acquainted. He told me he had attended the plays and concerts at Covent Garden, Lincoln's Inn, Drury Lane, and Goodman's Fields. He said you were more active than ever in the theater, in your own discreet but influential manner. He mentioned a young lady in your employ, whom he admired greatly. I take it for granted you admire her as well, you old *roué!* But my conversation with Tighe reminded me of how much I do miss the decent and pleasurable theater, which is unavailable here. So I come to the main point of this lengthy missive. I suggest it may be well worth your while to come to Virginia, to explore the possibility of organizing a company, and establishing a professional theater here. Or, if you are unable to come yourself, perhaps you could dispatch the young lady as your envoy. I would be honored and mightily pleased to render her every assistance. Very seriously, old chap, I would enthusiastically make any reasonable subscription to such an endeavor. I urge and plead with you to give the suggestion every consideration."

Richard looked up at the women again, smiled broadly and sipped his brandy before reading the last of the letter.

"Via this same packet, I am sending you a supply of a new tobacco called Aranoacke. We have been exporting a good deal of it to Holland and Denmark, and I thought you might wish to try it. Do let me know whether you will undertake to bring the joys of the theater to the entertainment-starved gentry of Virginia, including

Your devoted friend,
George Rakestraw."

"Mr. Rakestraw is an old friend of Edmund's," Nell explained. "They attended Eton together, and were partners in business before Mr. Rakestraw returned to America."

She took another sip of brandy.

"Edmund was quite impressed with the letter," she said.

"It surely is an interesting and persuasive commentary on the need for theater in America, or at least in the colony of Virginia," said Richard.

"Between Tillie's letter, and this one from Mr. Rakestraw, the fates seem to be pushing us toward the colonial shores," said Nancy Lucia happily. "This is our surprise then, Nellie?"

"Only the first part," said Nell. "Edmund asked me to work with you two to determine the approximate cost of organizing and transporting a company."

She picked up the sheaf of papers on the table. "This is the second part of the surprise," she said. "I spent last night, and a good part of today, making a start on the estimate."

She handed the papers to Richard, and he and Nancy Lucia read them slowly and carefully together. Nell had prepared her study on the basis of a company of fourteen people. She had allocated an average of 100 pounds for each of the fourteen players for their salaries the first year, thus arriving at a total cost for this item of 1400 pounds.

"You'll note that I have not listed the names of any players. Aside from the Steele family, I'm not sure anyone else in the Goodman's Fields company—or for that matter the Covent Garden or Lincoln's Inn people— would give up their careers here for this adventure."

"Oh, I know the Grigsbys will go," said Nancy Lucia. "I have talked to Emily and Evangeline about it, and they are quite eager to go."

"I mentioned it casually to Emmett Nicholson some time ago," said Nell, "and he was horrified at the thought. He believes America is full of Indian savages, criminals and indentured servants from England."

Richard laughed. "That's because he spends all his spare hours at Old Bailey. I'm certain I will be able to persuade Emmett that there are more people like Mr. Rakestraw and the Rougheads in America, than the motley mob he envisions."

Richard turned to the next page, and noted that under the heading, *Transport*, Nell had simply made a large question mark.

"I did not know what to estimate to transport the company," she explained. "I know that convicts and indentured servants are shipped at a cost to the contractors and merchants of approximately five or six pounds each, and . . ."

"This company is not going to cross the ocean below decks, on meager rations. . . ." Richard began.

"My, we are belligerent!" said Nell, laughing. "Please don't snap my head off, Richard. I had no intention of suggesting the company be shipped off like convicts and servants. I was just explaining why I haven't yet written in the transport estimate."

"I'm sorry, Nell," said Richard contritely. "I'm so excited about the whole idea, I feel as though the company already exists. . . ."

"I went through all our account books for the past two seasons," said Nell, "and made a list of the nineteen plays which drew the largest attendance in that period."

They sat up until four o'clock in the morning, discussing the repertoire and other items in Nell's carefully prepared preliminary study. She had made lists of wardrobe items and scenery she felt she could appropriate from the stock of the Covent Garden, Lincoln's Inn Fields and Goodman's Fields companies.

"My father would like to contribute some ingenious special scenery on which he is working," said Nancy Lucia.

Richard nodded. "Yes, and Niccolini has designed several interesting and very clever new multi-purpose costumes," he said. "Perhaps we may be able to persuade Cecilia Hogsdon to sew them for us."

At last, weary but still filled with excitement, they decided to retire. As she and Richard walked hand in hand behind Nell, up the stairs on the way to the bedchambers, Nancy Lucia said, "Nellie, do you think the Duke will really finance the company?"

Nell smiled. "I am almost certain he will. No matter what the cost. He seemed more excited by Mr. Rakestraw's letter than I."

In the guest room bed, Richard took Nancy Lucia in his arms.

"I have never felt so enthusiastic about anything in my life," he whispered, and kissed her neck. "I think we should be ready to sail by the end of the season," mumbled Richard kissing her breasts.

"That is only three months," said Nancy Lucia, stroking his hair. "Do you really think we can be ready in so brief a time?"

Richard had her left nipple in his mouth, and was moving his tongue around it. He made a sound, which Nancy Lucia took to mean yes. He was caressing her buttocks, and she felt his hot hardness against her thigh. She leaned forward, nibbled his ear and threw a leg over his hip. Richard really had no idea how difficult a task it would be to organize the American company. He had even less idea of what its ultimate strange composition was destined to be.

At this particular moment, on this particular night, as he entered his loving wife, neither he nor she thought about America at all.

❧ 43 ❧

"I am very fond of you, Richard. I beg you to give up this foolhardy project!" said Emmett Nicholson.

The distinguished old actor and Richard were seated at a table in the Black Boar tavern, three days after Richard and Nancy Lucia had spent the night at Nell's.

"If it was so foolhardy, Emmett, the Duke would hardly have agreed to finance it. You will be earning the same amount as you are at present, and you will own shares in the company as well."

The Duke had not only agreed to finance the venture; he also said he would make all the arrangements for the transportation of the company himself. A couple of card-playing companions of his, Shanley and Ackers, the shipbuilders, were just completing refurbishing an East Indiaman. The Duke believed the ship would be ideal for the purpose.

"Do you know how many miscreants stood trial at Old Bailey last year?" asked Emmett.

"That has no bearing on . . ."

"More than five hundred, Richard! And of those, three hundred and fifty or more were convicted."

"But Emmett . . ."

"Only sixty of those convicted were sentenced to be hanged. The rest were transported. And do you know to where?"

He did not wait for an answer.

"To America! Almost three hundred were transported to America, and most of those either to Maryland or Virginia!"

"For every ten convicts, Emmett, there are thousands

533

of decent people who live orderly lives in the colonies—people who are hungry for amusement, for professional theater!"

Nicholson waved away these immaterial thousands.

"Furthermore, Richard, of those sixty condemned to the gallows, about thirty were later spared the rope on condition of transportation. Add thirty more to that three hundred!"

"The Duke is no fool, Emmett. He is investing several thousand pounds to give us this opportunity. . . ."

"Nor am I a fool, Richard. I have had a fine career here at Goodman's Fields. There is nothing you can say to convince me I should cast it aside for a most uncomfortable journey across treacherous seas to a land infested with murderers, robbers, rapists and blackguards of every description. Rather, Richard, let me persuade you to remain here. You are an extraordinarily talented young man with a beautiful wife, a handsome son, your future assured. What could you possibly gain . . ."

This time Richard interrupted.

"The unmatchable joy, Emmett," he said earnestly, "of facing a new challenge, of taking theater to a land which knows it not. The right to present such plays as we wish to present, in the manner we choose; the possibility of rewards beyond our wildest dreams!"

Nicholson stared at him. "Do Nancy Lucia and Shannon share this mad enthusiasm?"

"Share it and more!"

"God go with you, then, my young friend. We will miss you sorely."

He lifted his tankard of ale. "To a safe journey. And much success!"

"Thank you, Emmett," Richard said in weary resignation.

Richard was depressed by his failure to recruit Emmett Nicholson, but he consoled himself with the rationalization that Emmett had simply lost his sense of adventure because, at forty-two, he was too old. But Richard was both depressed and stunned when every member of the Goodman's Fields company and the other major companies, with the exception of Arthur Reinhart and the Grigsbys, refused to join the expedition.

After Nell and Richard had been turned down by almost all the players at the three theaters, Nell even asked

Jerome Wrexham to join the proposed company. Nell knew Wrexham hated her, and their relationship was an odd one. He had never forgiven her for rejecting his advances, and her disclosure of his chicanery as manager of Goodman's Fields further alienated him from her. But because of her relationship with the Duke, Wrexham maintained an outwardly friendly attitude toward her. Nell realized that Richard might not be happy having Wrexham in the American company, but Jerome was an excellent entertainer. Nell felt Richard could handle him, and most of all, she was becoming convinced that they had to take players where they could find them; that beggars simply could not be choosers. Subconsciously, she may even have looked forward to being able to remove Wrexham from her own areas of activity. For she always had the feeling that he would do her damage, if he could.

His response to her proposal that he join the American company surprised her. He looked at himself admiringly in the glass on his dressing table, brushed his thick mahogany hair one more stroke. Then he turned to Nell and said, "I do agree with you and the Duke, Nell, that America is fertile and virgin territory for talented actors. Especially virgin," he laughed. "All kinds of interesting virgins."

Nell managed a feeble chuckle at this typically sophomoric jocularity. He continued, more seriously, "I have considered the possibility of going there myself. And I may still go at the opportune time. But you cannot honestly believe I would go with a company headed by Richard Steele."

"He's a very capable manager, Jerry. And a fine actor!" Wrexham snorted.

"That is your opinion, dear Nell. You are blind to his shortcomings. For several years, under his management, business at Goodman's Fields was so poor the Duke considered closing it."

He was referring to the recent period immediately following the passage of the 1737 Licensing Act, knowing well enough that the restrictive law was responsible for the decline in business at the theater. Nell realized it was hopeless to argue with him. It was obvious that he hated Richard Steele, even more than he hated her.

Wrexham had told Nell the truth. In the past four years, he had twice considered going to America. For he thought it the perfect ultimate refuge from his creditors. He and John Fox had done extremely well with their gambling for the most part. Yet twice they had suffered drastic losing streaks, simultaneously. Several gamblers with whom they wagered regularly threatened them with dire physical harm.

The Duchess had put John on a fixed allowance of a thousand pounds per year, an extravagant sum by normal standards, but not adequate to cover John's expenses during periods when he lost heavily and consistently for a time at the race track, the bull-baiting arena, the cockpit and Lady Gertrude's. Neither John nor Wrexham could fathom what had suddenly frozen the Duchess's earlier unlimited generosity. They guessed it might be her continuing failing health, which made her increasingly irritable and disagreeable. They did not know that in the course of another bitter argument over their son, the Duke had revealed to Sarah that her son, John, was a murderer. She refused to permit herself to believe him capable of such horrors, but she finally became convinced that the excessive funds she had been lavishing upon her son were indeed helping to destroy him.

What made John's and Wrexham's present financial situation more precarious than it would normally be was their purchase of a magnificent two-year-old thoroughbred horse. They bought the horse at the peak of one of their heaviest winning periods. The horse's name was Lucifer. Lucifer won the first three races in which he was entered. But the money John and Wrexham earned from the winning purses and wagers was quickly absorbed by the cost of caring for the animal, and the salary of his trainer, Jamie Macleash, who was one of the finest trainers in the kingdom.

At that moment, Lucifer was a financial burden, yet Wrexham considered the horse the best investment he had ever made. He knew that, in time, they would win large amounts of money, but beyond that, ownership of Lucifer fulfilled one of Wrexham's boyhood dreams. He had always wanted to own a race horse, and his ownership gave him a new status around the track, which pleased his vanity mightily. Their joint ownership of the horse also proved to be a surprisingly strong stabilizing force on John Fox.

John's reaction to the young horse at the auction the day they brought Lucifer amazed Wrexham. He had never seen his companion display such gentle, warm affection to any living being, except his mother, the Duchess. John spent time almost every day at the stables, visiting Lucifer, taking part in his feeding and grooming and riding him around the track. He discussed the horse's development with Macleash the way a doting parent might discuss a child's progress with a schoolmaster. Wrexham did not understand the cause-and-effect relationship, but John's love for the horse seemed to reduce his need to drink excessively, and to hurt the women with whom they consorted. In some strange way, being Lucifer's master seemed to humanize the young nobleman.

When Nell Faversham discussed the American company with Wrexham, he and John had not thought of escaping to the new world in some time. Everything was progressing beautifully for them. Wrexham had just scored a rare triumph at Covent Garden in a leading role in a masque, *Neptune and Amphitrite*. Both *The Spectator* and *The Prompter* had remarked on his stellar performance. Lucifer had just won another race, his fourth in succession, and for the moment, neither John nor Wrexham owed a penny to anyone. And they had an orgy planned for that very evening at their rooms, with two of the singers from the Covent Garden company and two of London's more artful courtesans.

A less bacchanalian gathering took place that same evening in the Steeles' cottage at Goodman's Fields. Nell was having supper with Richard, Nancy Lucia and Shannon and telling them of her unsuccessful effort to recruit Jerome Wrexham.

"It is probably just as well," said Richard. "I would have accepted him. He is a more than capable actor, and a superb singer, but I am certain we would have had problems with him."

"We do not seem to be progressing too well," said Nancy Lucia, as she placed a steaming platter of roast veal on the table. "Perhaps we should give up, or at least postpone the plan."

Shannon spoke up quickly.

"No, Mother! We have seven already, between the Grigsbys and Arthur and ourselves. We need but seven more!" They planned, that night, to travel to the provinces, when their schedules allowed, in their search for actors.

When the Duke agreed to finance the company, Richard had vowed to present at Goodman's Fields, in the final three months of his stewardship, the most impressive programs the theater had ever known. He believed he owed it to Nell and the Duke to leave them with a theater operating at its peak. Happily, the decision of most of the company to stay on at Goodman's Fields made it easier for Richard to keep that vow. He and Nancy Lucia and Nell had worked on the repertoire and plotted out a substantial part of it.

Now they resumed their planning, with Shannon quietly sitting by, but paying close attention to the discussion.

"In the last fortnight in May," said Richard, "I would like to do *Macbeth*, *Richard III*, and in the final days of the season, *Romeo and Juliet*."

Nell and Nancy Lucia looked at Richard, surprised, but pleased. Both knew how much he loved the tragic Shakespearean romance. And both knew what an extraordinary effort he must make to play or present it. Nell's eyes became misty now, as she recalled Richard's struggle to overcome the shattering grief and disappointment at having been robbed of the chance to play Romeo to the Juliet of his beloved Felicia.

Nancy Lucia, too, was aware of the emotional effect involvement with *Romeo and Juliet* had upon Richard. He had told her of Felicia, had showed her the gold medallion, which he had worn until their wedding night at the Soaring Gull. He kept the medallion in a small gold box, and every now and then, Nancy Lucia came upon him, with the open box in his hand, staring at the medallion. She could not help a fleeting pang of jealousy, though she understood completely. She placed her hand over Richard's at the table. He cleared his throat and looked down at his plate to avoid the eyes of the two women.

"You know that in April and early May we will be doing comedies by Congreve, Jonson and Farquhar. I think the Shakespeare works will enable us to close the season quite strongly."

Nell dabbed at her eyes with a kerchief and said softly, "I think it would be a lovely ending, Richard." Then she swallowed, and said in a more businesslike tone, "Most of the repertoire for the next three months, then, will also serve as a rehearsal for the presentations in America."

"Precisely," said Richard. He turned to Shannon. "And what do you think, young man?"

"It's excellent, Father."

"Are you prepared to play Romeo?" asked Richard

538

without warning. Shannon was just past his sixteenth birthday. He stared at Richard. Finally he said, "You seemed pleased with my Cassius. I know I'll do as well with Romeo."

Nancy Lucia put her arm around him and kissed him on the cheek.

"Romeo was a youth just like you," she said.

"And Juliet was a lovely child, just like Evangeline Grigsby," said Richard.

Shannon's jaw dropped.

"Father! How wonderful! Evangeline will be overjoyed! May I go and tell her?"

"By all means," said Richard.

Shannon raced from the cottage and ran down the road to the public house where the Grigsbys and the other members of the Goodman's Fields company had their rooms. Nancy Lucia put her arms around Richard. She and Richard, as well as Nell, were aware of the romance which had developed between Shannon and Evangeline over the past several years. The two were inseparable. Shannon was still too young, but he and Evangeline and their parents all simply assumed they would be married in another couple of years.

As Richard watched the love between the two young people blossom, he was poignantly reminded of his own courtship of Felicia. The intense delight with which he had looked forward to playing Romeo to Felicia's Juliet was something he would never forget. He knew that young Shannon was now feeling much that same joy.

"You are an adorable man, and a most thoughtful father," said Nancy Lucia, kissing his cheek once more. Nell's eyes became misty again.

"What will we do about finding players for America?" asked Richard gruffly. "Let us make some plans!"

"Have either of you heard from Henry Hogsdon recently?" asked Nell.

"Not in some time," said Nancy Lucia, "but Hank would be ideal."

"Yes," agreed Richard. "Perhaps you could write Cecil and Cecilia. They may know his whereabouts. . . ." He paused. "Do you think they might be interested in joining us?"

"No," said Nancy Lucia firmly. "They are content in their retirement. Nothing could move them. But I will write about Hank."

They agreed that Nell would ask Gilbert Weston to take over rehearsals, and Arthur Reinhart would play Richard's roles, while an understudy played his own, so that Richard could visit several provincial companies in a quest for venturesome actors. But to his dismay, he found that provincial actors were as reluctant to chance their futures in America as were the players in London.

One besotted leading man with a company in North Hampton agreed to join, but Richard discovered that he was deeply in debt, and was merely looking for a means of escaping his creditors. Richard felt certain that constables would run him down before he boarded ship. In Coventry, Richard learned that Quincy's circus was playing in Birmingham, so early one morning he rode north to see if the dwarf or Susannah Forbish might be able to help. They greeted him heartily with wide open arms and kisses. Since Richard had last seen or heard from them, their family had increased to five. They had two sons, one nine, and one fifteen, both of normal growth, and both healthy and happy to be working with the circus as tumblers and acrobats. Their oldest son, now twenty, was pursuing an acting career, and was with a traveling company.

Susannah checked the company's itinerary and found they were due in Nottingham the following day. Quincy and Susannah both felt that the boy would be most eager to join Richard's American company. If the circus were not flourishing, they themselves would be happy to leave it and join Richard. They were venturesome souls, and their eldest son was an even greater advocate of high adventure. For the first time, Richard learned Quincy's full name. Quincy was his last name, and Socrates his given name. He had never used it, and had thus come to be known simply as Quincy. Susannah, however, had insisted they name their first born after Quincy, and she proudly called him Socrates. And so he grew up, as proud of the Greek given name as his mother.

Richard left early the next day for Nottingham, and arrived there before noon. The traveling company was a small one, consisting of two wagons. It was encamped just outside the town. Richard found Socrates Quincy without difficulty. He was a tall young man, just an inch or two shorter than Richard. He had wavy, blond hair and intelligent dark eyes like his father. He was rehearsing a scene from *Much Ado About Nothing* with an attractive woman,

540

perhaps a year or two younger than he. She had rich, auburn hair, green-flecked brown eyes, a delicately shaped mouth and small nose.

Richard introduced himself to Socrates, and explained his long friendship with Quincy and Susannah. The young man presented his companion.

"This is Genevieve Little. The love of my life, and a fine actress!"

Richard told them about the plans to organize the American company. They expressed great interest. Eagerly they played several scenes for him and invited him to their performance that evening at Ironmonger's Hall.

Richard went. They were quite good. The girl was still rather stiff and self-conscious at times, but Socrates had all the flamboyant showmanship of his mother, and the intelligent control of his father. The young couple joined Richard at a nearby tavern after the show, and they finalized arrangements to join the American company. The couple, who planned to be married, decided to consider the trip to the colonies as their honeymoon.

Richard went back to the public house, where he was staying the night, full of renewed optimism about the American company. Socrates and Genevieve made nine. If he could find four or five more players, they would be ready to go. As he climbed into bed, a thought struck him. He was not very far from Manchester. In the morning, he would go to see Frank Hogsdon. Frank had been quite positive about his preference for life on the farm, but it was worth a try. They could use a strong man like Frank.

Frank's farm was on the southern outskirts of the city. As Richard rode up the hard dirt road toward the weather-beaten wood frame house, he could understand why some people might be enchanted with the rustic life. It was a perfect spring day. A platinum sun shone in the clear cerullean sky. All about him were the open green meadows, dotted with colorful patches of wild flowers. Birds sang in the trees. A flock of chickens ran across the road, as he approached a cowshed. From the shed, he heard a plaintive "moo," and when he looked in that direction, he saw Frank Hogsdon. Frank was actually milking a cow. He turned just as Richard entered the shed.

"Good morning, Farmer Hogsdon," said Richard cheerily.

Frank leaped to his feet, wiped his hands on his soiled cotton trousers, rushed to Richard and threw his arms around him.

"Richard Steele!" he shouted. "I cannot believe it! Do you know that I was thinking about you just last night?"

Richard hugged him heartily.

"It must have been at the same time I began thinking about you. I was in Nottingham."

With his powerful arm around Richard's shoulder, he marched him into the house. In the small kitchen, he put a pot on the coals in a fireplace.

"I'll heat up this coffee," he said. "Sit down, Richard. Tell me about yourself."

Richard looked around the ill-kept room. Unwashed wooden bowls and tin cups sat on a cupboard near the stove. A soiled shirt hung over the back of a chair in the corner. Mud and dirt littered the wooden floor. A tattered curtain hung askew at the single kitchen window. It struck Richard that the room lacked a woman's touch.

"I heard you married, Frank," he said.

Frank wiped out two mugs with a soiled cloth, poured black coffee, and sat opposite Richard at the wooden table.

"I did." He sighed. "You remember Francesca?"

Richard nodded.

"It was good, Richard, but she was a lazy wench. Hated to get 'er ass out'a bed."

Richard waited, sipped the bitter coffee.

"She ran off about a month ago. With an Italian glovemaker from town. Goddam caitiff was making a pair of leather work gloves for me. I'd already paid him ten shillings. Made off with the gloves and Francesca. I think they went to Italy."

"I am truly sorry, Frank, but . . ." Richard said.

Frank waved a hand.

"It's all right, Richard. A man gets tired of all that fancy fucking in time. She never stopped. Fuck, and eat, and sleep. And sing a little. Italian songs. Nice, but no work. Ever."

Richard made a sympathetic sound.

"How have you prospered with the farm?"

Frank got the pot and poured more coffee. Richard

542

pushed his aside. It was the most bitter, evil-tasting coffee he had ever drank.

"Poorly, Richard, poorly! Last winter everything froze. Past summer too much heat. I wish I was back with the show."

It was then that Richard told him about the plans to take a company to America. And that was how he recruited the tenth member of the company. Frank took a slight loss on the sale of the farm, but he did not mind that at all, so excited was he to be entering the world of the theater again.

In the next four weeks, Richard and Nell alternated in traveling to various provincial towns, interviewing and auditioning actors. Out of more than fifty, only six were willing to join the American group. Unfortunately, all six, four men and two women, were virtually rank amateurs, with no apparent talent. And then Nancy Lucia had a response from Cecilia Hogsdon about Hank. He was teaching in a dancing school at Stratford on Avon, near Farley Shannon's old home. Richard went out to see him, and found him concluding his work with a class of six young men and three women. Richard was shocked at Hank's appearance. He had lost weight. His skin was sallow, and his cheeks were sunken. There were dark, purplish half moons under his gray eyes. The eyes were bloodshot, as though he had not been sleeping enough, or had been drinking too much, or both.

"What is wrong, Hank?" asked Richard as they sat at The Bird in Hand, a nearby tavern. "You appear ill."

Hank shook his head.

"Have you heard what happened to Brendan?"

"No. I did not know him."

"You knew we were living together?"

"I had heard that."

"Last month we went to Dublin. Brendan and an older playwright, Dion O'Neil, and I were in a tavern one evening. All three of us were drinking more than we should. Dion and Brendan got into an argument over whether Shakespeare was a better playwright than Jonson. They began to insult each other in that wild, Irish manner. And then they began a duel. I could hardly believe it. I was sure they were jesting. But O'Neil killed Brendan, stabbed him right through the heart!"

He shook his head.

"I still cannot believe it happened," he said. He lowered his head and rubbed his eyes. Trying to hold back the tears, he began to sob. He shook his head again.

"He was such a beautiful man, Richard. So gentle. So talented. What a ridiculous, pointless way to die!"

Richard pulled his chair alongside Hank, put his arm around Hank's slender shoulders.

"Forgive me, Richard." He looked around at the other patrons of the tavern, who were staring at them, some with curiosity, some with contempt.

"Why did you not come to stay with Nancy Lucia and me?" Richard asked.

"I did not want to see anyone. I wanted to die alone."

"Well, now you will come and stay with us. Indeed, we are about to embark on a journey . . . a journey which may be of interest to you."

Richard then told Hank about the plans for the American company, and thus Hank became the eleventh member of the company, which would go to the new world. And four in the group were veterans of the Canaday company. Richard was in a jubilant mood, as he and Hank arrived at Goodman's Fields that evening.

The following morning, Nell came to the cottage, equally excited. She was delighted to see Hank again, and to learn that he was going to join the company, but she also had good news of her own. "I've just returned from Ipswich, Richard," she said breathlessly. "A young man there is giving the most chilling and powerful performance of *Richard III* I have ever seen."

"Who is he?"

"You would not know him. His name is David Garrick. He has been working at various theaters in the provinces under several names. I tried to persuade him to join our American company, but he is not sure he wishes to leave England. I think you should go to Ipswich and talk to him. He will be there one more week."

"I will go Tuesday," said Richard.

⚔ 44 ⚔

On the same day that Richard Steele visited Frank Hogsdon at the farm in Manchester, Jerome Wrexham and John Fox sat in their special box in the stands at Epsom Downs, surrounded by other elegantly-clad gentlemen and their ladies. Wrexham and his younger companion were confident that the day would be one of unprecedented triumph and profit. It was March 15. Although Wrexham had played *Julius Caesar* a number of times in his career, it never entered his mind that this was the Ides of March. He had been far too busy making arrangements to assure Lucifer's victory in his fifth race. Lucifer was favored in any event, but Wrexham wanted to make certain he would win. A handsome bay named Dark Knight was the only other horse considered to have a chance against the swift Lucifer. His jockey, Archie Whipple, was an old friend of Jerome Wrexham's. And a corrupt one. Wrexham had bribed him to be certain that, under any circumstances, he would hold back Dark Knight just enough to enable Lucifer to win.

With this double assurance of victory, Wrexham and John wagered more on this race than on any single race ever before. John had wheedled his failing mother into giving him a thousand pounds. He had wagered that, plus an extra thousand pounds in credit the gamblers allowed him. Wrexham's wagers totaled eighteen hundred pounds. Whipple also bet a substantial sum on Lucifer.

The Epsom course, sometimes called Banstead Downs, was within driving distance of London. The sun was brilliant as the carriages and post chaises of the nobility continued to arrive, along with the donkey carts and wagons of craftsmen and tradespeople of the middle classes. A substantial number of the lower classes trudged their way to the track on foot. There was something about Epsom Downs which fostered a remarkable congeniality among the throng. Noblemen and ladies chatted with tradespeople and grooms and jockeys as though they were equals. Under other circumstances the aristocrats would hardly deign to recognize the existence of these lesser mortals.

"Now our race, Johnny boy! Our race!" Wrexham slapped John Fox on the back, as the horses in Lucifer's race pranced and skittered their way to the post, guided by their colorfully clad jockeys. Lucifer was a magnificent animal. His sire was an Arabian steed named Desert Devil; his mother a swift, light English mare called Jezebel. Lucifer had his father's powerful chest, his mother's slender legs with the broad hoofs of an Arabian. He was gleaming white, except for his legs from hoofs to knee joints, his chest and his ears. The black lower legs looked like boots; the black chest, a warrior's shield; and the ears, a devil's horns. It was the ears and the fierce luster in the fine animal's dark eyes which prompted the breeder to name him Lucifer.

"In less than ten minutes we should be down in the winner's circle, Johnny," said Wrexham, clutching John's arm excitedly. John Fox was staring fixedly at Lucifer. Several times, the horse wheeled sharply and kicked his front legs high in the air, almost unseating his jockey, Timmy Rockwell. But Rockwell sat him confidently, bringing him back to earth, holding the reins loosely, patting his silken gleaming white side. The little jockey looked proud and cocky in his gold and black silk blouse, black breeches and glistening black boots.

"That horse is the most beautiful creature I have ever seen," said John in a hushed, almost reverent tone, as the horses finally settled. In a moment they were off. Lucifer made a poor start and was trapped behind three horses, one of them Dark Knight, riding along the rail.

"Damn!" cursed Wrexham.

"Break through Lucifer!" screamed John. "Break through! Break through!"

The air was filled with the screams and shouts and cheers of the crowd. At the first turn, Rockwell tried to take Lucifer to the outside, but again one of the front running horses blocked him off. Rockwell drifted back to the inside, only to be trapped again.

"Take him through, Timmy!" shrieked John. Wrexham pounded his right fist into his left palm, over and over, standing, breathing hard, his eyes riveted on the pack of beautiful, streaking animals on the track. On the far turn, with Rockwell still desperately trying to find an opening between the horses in front of him, Archie Whipple earned his money. He whipped Dark Knight frantically, to take a lead of a full length on the horse at his left. He widened the gap another length, then moved in to the rail. Timmy Rockwell hardly had to tug his reins to direct Lucifer into the opening. The magnificent, muscular steed instinctively charged for the space left by Dark Knight between the two horses flanking him. Lucifer rocketed ahead, lengthening his stride.

In seconds, he was neck and neck with Dark Knight. And then he passed the bay. He was no more than twenty meters from the finish line when he stumbled, staggered three more strides and plunged, proud head first, on to the hard dirt of the track. He rolled over twice, and lay on his side, his black-booted legs kicking spastically. Timmy Rockwell went flying off his back, hit the ground a horse's length ahead of and to the left of Lucifer. He tumbled awkwardly three times, like a shattered gold and black ball, before he lay still, flat on his back, unconscious. Archie Whipple could not swing Dark Knight to either side of Rockwell's prostrate form in time. Instinctively, the horse tried to leap over Timmy's still form, but it had all happened too quickly. Dark Knight could not adjust his stride for the leap. His left rear hoof cracked Rockwell's head open, and Dark Knight stumbled and crashed to the track. Whipple flew from his back. Dazed, he crawled on hands and knees to the infield. Here he collapsed, face forward on the grass.

A third horse, Charming Bess, slashed into the fallen Lucifer, still lying on his side, desperately pawing the air. Two of his legs were broken. Through the clouds of dust, amid the hysterical screaming and roaring of the crowd, a horse named Apple Eater, who had been running six lengths behind the pack, went by the carnage to the finish line and won the race.

Wrexham stood in the box, stunned, trembling with fury and frustration, staring at the havoc before him. John Fox dashed from the box and savagely beat his way through the frantic crowd toward the rail. He pushed people, hit them, tore at their clothes to get them out of his way. He was oblivious to the curses, the blows that struck him, the angry hands which ripped at his own elegant apparel as he made his way, closer and closer to the rail. When he reached it, he blindly pushed aside a large, fat woman to give himself enough room to leap over the rail.

He ran down the track like a madman, past the broken-headed corpse of Timmy Rockwell, to Lucifer. He reached the horse before anyone else. He knelt beside Lucifer's head, looked into the dark, desperate eyes filled with pain. Tears ran down John's gaunt cheeks as two men pulled him to his feet and away from the horse. He fought frantically to get out of their grasp, but they were too strong. They dragged him, kicking and struggling all the way, to the jockeys' quarters. They held him down on a cot in the long, narrow room, reeking of sweat and medication. After a long time, he became calm enough so they could leave him alone. He lay there, crying quietly, his arms hanging limply at his sides. When he looked up, he saw Wrexham standing over him.

Wrexham had watched them shoot Lucifer in the head, and remove the bodies of the wounded and dead horses and men from the track. It was the first accident at Epsom Downs in two years, and by far the worst since the big stakes races began there in 1730.

"They had to destroy him, John," said Wrexham. A shrieking sob tore itself from John's chest. He reached out from the cot, and threw his arms around Wrexham's knees, crying with his head against Wrexham's thigh. Wrexham stroked John's damp, disheveled hair absently, staring straight ahead, ignoring the hushed jockeys, trainers and grooms around them. John was inconsolable. Wrexham got him back to their rooms, and poured brandy for both of them. His mind, ever alert to any threat to his survival, was already struggling with the question of how he would raise the money to pay off the enormous debt to the gamblers.

"How did it happen, Jerry?" wailed John. "How could it have happened?"

"I do not know, Johnny. It all happened so quickly."

John finished his brandy in a gulp.

"Was it Timmy's doing? Perhaps he should not have whipped Lucifer into that opening!"

But the dead jockey had not whipped Lucifer at all.

548

The horse had charged into the opening as soon as it appeared.

"I do not think Timmy was at fault," said Wrexham.

"Whipple should have moved away sooner," said John, filling his glass again, and drinking it half empty.

"It is done, John. It is done, and we are deeply in debt once again."

John looked at Wrexham blankly. He finished his brandy, and poured another.

"He was such a beautiful animal," he said, his voice quivering. He began to cry quietly again. In less than two hours, after finishing a decanter of brandy, with little help from Wrexham, John staggered into the bedchamber and threw himself, face down, on the bed. In a moment, he was snoring heavily. Wrexham sat in his favorite chair in the handsomely appointed drawing room, and continued to sip brandy slowly.

At seven o'clock, John was still sleeping soundly and noisily. Wrexham went to Lady Gertrude's. It was the first time he visited the elegant establishment without indulging in a meal. Tonight, as he took his marker to the counter's window for a hundred pounds worth of chips, Kingsley, Lady Gertrude's manager, now rheumy-eyed and gray, come over to him.

"Terribly sorry about the accident, Jerry," he said. "Lord Twombley told us about it when he came from Epsom this afternoon."

Wrexham nodded his thanks and strode to the hazard table. The modishly gowned and jeweled ladies and their strikingly dressed escorts around the table, and all about the room looked at him with curiosity and sympathy. They whispered to each other about the tragic accident. Wrexham ignored them and played grimly. In the first hour, he won a hundred and sixty pounds, but in the next hour, he lost that, and the hundred with which he had started. He signed for another hundred and lost that in less than twenty minutes. He realized he was playing recklessly, which was his fatal inclination when under pressure. But tonight, he decided to stop.

"This is simply not your day, Jerome Wrexham," he told himself. "Not your day at all!"

John was moaning between snores, but still asleep when Wrexham returned to their rooms.

549

The following morning, Wrexham found him at the breakfast table in a heavily embroidered purple silk robe. He was unshaven; his eyes were bloodshot; his hand trembled as he lifted the coffee cup to his lips. Wrexham patted his shoulder.

"Are you all right, Johnny?"

"Hardly." Elbows on the table, John rested his uncombed head in his hands. Wrexham sat opposite him, and poured himself coffee.

"Considering that the tragedy was not of our making, Johnny, do you think the Duchess will advance you three thousand pounds?"

John looked up, wincing in pain as he shook his head.

"I did not expect to get the last thousand. She vowed that would be all I would get for the rest of this year."

Wrexham laughed mirthlessly.

"She has said that before, has she not?"

"Many times, but each time more forcefully." Coffee spilled as he lifted the cup to his lips with a trembling hand. "I doubt that she will give me anything. Certainly not three thousand."

"Even if you tell her you are in danger of being physically harmed? Severely harmed?"

John looked up, frowned at Wrexham, then smiled feebly.

"You are, Johnny boy," said Wrexham grimly. "We both are. Not right at this moment. Not for another week, perhaps not for another month. But sooner or later. The gentlemen to whom we are indebted pursue most aggressive collection methods!"

John nodded quietly.

"I suggest you make yourself presentable, and visit her this afternoon," said Wrexham.

Wrexham waited most of the afternoon for John's return. It was almost six o'clock when he arrived. He walked to the serving table and poured himself a glass full of brandy. He sipped at it as he walked to the flowered damask lounge. Wrexham poured himself a drink, too.

"She refused you!" he said, standing at the serving table. John nodded.

"No three thousand," said Wrexham quietly. "Did she give you anything?"

John shook his head.

"She could not talk with me too long. She is feeling

very poorly. Dr. Spencer has attended her every day this week." He paused, and took a long drink.

"I went to Epsom to see Lucifer. They have taken him away," he said, tears filling his eyes once again.

"How old *is* she, John?" asked Wrexham. A gleam, which was not reflected candlelight, came into his mahogany eyes.

"Old?" asked John.

"The Duchess. How old *is* she?"

John shrugged. "Sixty-one . . . or -two."

"She has lived an extraordinarily long life for a woman with so serious an affliction. The doctor thought she would die right after you were born."

John finished the brandy and held the glass out to Wrexham. Wrexham filled it, and returned it to him.

"I imagine you will be quite a wealthy young man, when her suffering ends," said Wrexham. He sat down beside John on the lounge. He put his arm around him. John drank his brandy slowly, tilting the glass until it was empty. He shrugged Wrexham's arm from around his shoulder, and walked to the door. There, he turned back and stared levelly at Wrexham out of moist, bloodshot eyes. Wrexham had no idea what the stare meant. He smiled uncertainly at John. John turned and went out.

Wrexham was working that night, and he was not too concerned when John did not return at all. John frequently stayed out two or three nights in succession, sometimes a week or more. Occasionally he went back to the family mansion. And now and then he stayed with a favored prostitute, who pleased him. When John did not return for that full week, Wrexham began to worry. He was concerned, in part because he was genuinely fond of John, but even more because he knew that John was his single best chance of extricating himself from his current financial dilemma. He was also becoming edgy because he was torn between the grim hope that John had understood his broad hint about how beneficial the Duchess's death would be—and the alarming conviction that if John tried to hasten her demise, he would bungle the job and perhaps even involve Wrexham in some way.

By the following Tuesday, when John had still not returned, Wrexham decided to try his luck again at Lady Gertrude's. He was in the middle of a lonesome, but sumptuous meal when Frederick Kingsley joined him.

"How is John?" asked the slender, gray-haired manager.

Wrexham looked puzzled.

"I assume he is in good health. I have not seen him in some time."

"Are you no longer sharing quarters?"

"Yes, indeed. But John has his own life, his own interests. He stays away occasionally. . . . These are strange questions, Frederick."

"Forgive me, Jerry. I do not mean to offend you, or alarm you, but he behaved strangely when he came in last Friday. He lost quite heavily again."

Kingsley paused, waving a bony, long-fingered hand at a waiter to refill Wrexham's wine glass.

"We learned how much he lost at Epsom Downs, Jerry. And he owed us thirty-four hundred pounds until yesterday."

Wrexham chewed a large piece of roast veal, staring evenly at Kingsley.

"Yesterday," the gambling house manager continued, "the Duke came in and we told him how deeply indebted John was. He paid the thirty-four hundred pounds in full, and told us that, henceforth, neither he nor the Duchess would be responsible for John's debts. He is serving us with legal notice to that effect. Naturally we cannot permit Lord John to play unless he has the funds."

Wrexham sliced another bite of veal. Looking down at his plate, he asked quietly, "And I, Frederick? Are you considering cutting off my credit as well?"

Kingsley smiled, but there was no humor in his rheumy green eyes.

"You are a highly paid actor, Jerry. You have resources. You have been a valued patron and friend for many years. Lady Gertrude always considered you one of her favorite gentlemen. You have always found the means to meet your obligations. We have no intention of cutting you off."

He rose, and placed his bony hand on Wrexham's shoulder.

"You only owe a few hundred pounds at the moment. We would not begin to become concerned until you approached five hundred."

Kingsley had a gentle and oblique way of stating credit limits. Wrexham took another hundred pounds that night, and after a long, tense, erratic four hours at lanterloo, he managed to win eighty-five pounds. Wearily, he made his way home. John had not yet returned. Three days later, after a nervous performance, during which

Wrexham forgot his lines twice, he decided he needed some sexual release. He went to Mother Magruder's.

"Help me up! Help me up!" the gross, orange-haired bawd squeaked at her black manservant, as she saw Wrexham enter.

"I'm glad you've come, Jerry," she wheezed, waddling painfully toward him. "Come! Come with me!"

She led him down a short hall to a small room, dimly lit by candles in a glass chandelier. Propped up against two white silk pillows in a large bed was a black woman. She had long, raven hair. Her sad, dark eyes were almost closed by the puffy, glistening greenish-purple flesh beneath them. Her lips were also swollen, and caked with dried blood. Her black hands trembled as she reached up to Wrexham. Baffled, he stared at her. He did not know her.

"It's Cleopatra, Jerry," piped Mother Magruder in a thin, angry voice. "That son of a noble, crippled bitch did it."

Wrexham reluctantly took one of the extended, quivering hands.

"Show him!" screeched Mother. "Show him your breasts!"

Cleopatra lowered the white silk sheet from her shoulders to her waist. Brownish red blood stains showed on the white cotton bandage tied around her ebony chest, like a halter. Gingerly she lifted it away, and Wrexham saw the purplish gashes on the gleaming ebony breasts; the lacerated aureoles around the savaged nipples.

Tears ran down Cleopatra's damaged face.

"Bad mon, king rex," she shook her head. Wrexham could hardly make out her words through the swollen mouth. He dropped her hand, patted her shoulder and walked toward the door. Mother Magruder waddled after, panting with the effort to keep up with him.

"I warn you Jerry. If that bloody bastard ever comes in here again, I'll have him arrested! Do you know how long it will be before that girl can work again? I did not show you what he did to her below! Insane! That's what he is! A bloody madman!"

She collapsed in her huge chair, huffing and puffing, trying to regain her breath after the long walk, and the vehement speech. Wrexham took a mulatto whore named Minerva, and after two uninspired and mechanical couplings, he left. John had still not returned.

The following morning, Wrexham decided he had better go to the Duke's mansion. He did not know what he expected to find there.

Hawkins answered the door, and when Wrexham said he wished to see either the Duke or the Duchess, or Lord John if he was there, Hawkins stepped aside to permit him to enter the ornate foyer. He left Wrexham there and returned in a moment. Wrexham followed him into the morning room.

The Duchess sat in her wheelchair in the sunlight by the large, velvet-draped window. The Duke, hands clasped behind his back, paced nearby.

"Come in, Jerry, come in," he said coldly. Wrexham bowed, and strode toward the Duchess.

"Is John with you?" asked the Duke.

Wrexham did not answer. He continued toward the Duchess till he stood directly before her. He had not seen her in some six months, but she seemed to have aged six years in that time. Her face had become swollen and yellow with age. It was severely lined on the unparalyzed side, and smooth and flaccid on the numbed right side. Saliva glistened on the sallow jaw. A light mustache showed above her upper lip. Wrexham took her left hand, lifted it to his lips, and kissed it.

"Dear Sarah," he murmured.

"Where is John?!" she demanded, snatching her hand away. Her eyes were mean and beady. Wrexham shook his head.

"I do not know. I thought he might be here."

"We have not seen him since the day after the accident at Epsom Downs," said the Duke. Wrexham surprised himself by deciding to make an open, honest, direct plea.

"You know that he is in deep financial trouble, Edmund," he said.

"We are aware of that. We have already paid his indebtedness at Lady Gertrude's."

"He owes a great deal more than that. He wagered extremely heavily on Lucifer. Five thousand pounds!"

Wrexham's mind had automatically seized upon the opportunity to acquire two thousand more than they owed, if possible. To his surprise, Sarah Fox, rather than the Duke, made the final devastating statement.

"We will give him no more money, Jerry. I realize Edmund has been right. I should have listened to him long before this. The more money we give John, the easier we make it for him to buy his way to his doom."

"But he owes the money to some ruthless and dangerous people, dear Sarah. Professional gamblers and usurers . . ."

"We understand that," said the Duke.

"They may kill him!"

The Duchess glared at her husband, then at Wrexham with her good eye. For a moment, Wrexham thought he had won his point. The Duke looked at Sarah, then turned back to Wrexham.

"You know they will not do that, Jerry. If they are professionals, they will beat him. Perhaps severely. But they will not kill him. They would be defeating their own purpose. I know people who have dealt with these rascals."

Wrexham turned toward the Duchess.

"Sarah," he said, his voice deep with compassion. "I cannot tolerate the idea of having John hurt. Please . . ."

She wheeled her chair around so she faced the window, away from Wrexham.

"Get out, Jerry!" she said hoarsely, between clenched teeth. "Edmund! Show him out!"

When Wrexham got back to their rooms, John Fox was lying on the large bed he and Wrexham shared. The sight of him shocked Wrexham. His elegant clothes were soiled and spotted with dried blood. His brown hair was dry and dirty; his face smeared and filthy. He stank. He lay on his back, snoring loudly and whimpering and moaning between snores. Wrexham accidentally knocked an oil lamp from a bedside table as he rushed forward to inspect John more closely. The crash awakened John and he sat up in the bed, screaming. He stared at Wrexham, drew back with his arm as though he feared Wrexham were going to strike him. He screamed again, and kept on screaming, louder and louder. Wrexham pushed him over on his back, clamped his hand over John's mouth to choke off the screams.

"It's all right, Johnny boy," he said soothingly. "It is all right. It's I. Jerry. It is all right . . . all right . . ." Trembling, John finally put his arms around Wrexham's neck, buried his face against Wrexham's chest.

"How did you ever get through the streets like that without being stopped?" Wrexham asked finally. "You must have scared people out of their wits."

John had so high a fever, Wrexham could feel the heat of his forehead through the thick velvet waistcoat Wrexham wore. Holding John's shaking body, a long ago vision of the night he buried Lady Fingers flashed through Wrexham's mind. John was as filthy as Lady Fingers had ever been; and as scrawny.

"Where have you been?" Wrexham asked softly.

"I do not know, Jerry. Many places. Antoinette kept me. Did I hurt her?" He stared at Wrexham. His dark eyes blazed with fever. "I do not know. I cannot remember."

It was true. Ever since Lucifer had been put away, John's mind had been in as real a bedlam as that which existed in the notorious insane asylum at St. Mary's of Bethlehem in London. Unbalanced with grief, drinking incessantly, dazed with lack of sleep and food, John had reached a state where he could not distinguish which incidents in the past several weeks were reality and which were dreams.

He knew he had been to see his father and mother. He thought he had killed them both.

No, Wrexham assured him. That had only been a dream. John breathed a long sigh of relief.

He had gone to Lady Gertrude's. Three or four times, he thought. He believed he had won more than ten thousand pounds, but that must have been a dream, for he had no money. Either it had been a dream, or he had been robbed.

No, Wrexham told him sadly, it had been true enough. He had lost, not won, at Lady Gertrude's.

He remembered dreaming that magnificent Lucifer had fallen and been shot, after a horrific accident at Epsom Downs, but he knew that had been a nightmare, because he remembered very clearly standing in the winner's circle at Epsom with Jerry, placing a huge garland around Lucifer's silken white neck, and receiving an excellently wrought and engraved sterling silver cup.

No, Wrexham explained to him, slowly, carefully. No, the winner's circle was the dream. Lucifer was dead.

John cried again, clutching Wrexham desperately. After a time, he sobbed quietly, and finally asked, "Did I kill Cleopatra? I think I did. Or was it Antoinette?"

"Not Cleopatra," said Wrexham, "but you hurt her."

John nodded.

"Why would Mother not give me any more money,

Jerry? She and Father have more money than they can use. Why would they not give me some?"

"Perhaps they will, Johnny boy," said Wrexham. "You had better clean yourself up, and get back to sleep. You are feverish, and trembling."

"Are you sure I did not kill them?"

"Very sure," said Wrexham. "I have just come from a visit with them."

Wrexham helped John undress, and bathed him. Finally John fell asleep. Wrexham burned the soiled, bloody clothes in the marble fireplace, one item at a time. He stood there watching the once elegant apparel smolder, burst into fitful flame, subside, flame again and burn to ashes. He wondered what he would do with John. He wondered how he could persuade the Duke and Duchess that John must have at least three thousand pounds.

In the next few days, John improved considerably, responding to Wrexham's gentle nursing. On the fifth day, Wrexham read a small item in *The London Chronicle*. The mutilated body of a prostitute had been found in her room in a decrepit old building in Shire Lane. Her name was Antoinette Dupre. John was still in bed, but now he was resting comfortably. Wrexham took the paper in to him and showed him the item. John read it silently and nodded grimly. It was no dream. Tears formed in his eyes again.

Two days later, on the first day that John was really up and about, he and Wrexham had an unpleasant pair of visitors. The cold-eyed, tastelessly dressed men informed Wrexham and John that their employer wanted a firm commitment as to when he could expect the money they had wagered with him on Lucifer at Epsom Downs. Wrexham, an old hand at situations of this kind, handled the collection agents diplomatically. He was nervous during the entire exchange because he could see that John was on the verge, several times, of insulting the men, and arrogantly demanding they leave the house. Only the fact that John had not fully regained his strength prevented him from doing so.

When the men left, Wrexham said, "Johnny boy, please say nothing when these people call on us. Permit me to handle the situation. They can be quite impatient with displays of arrogance, and are easily insulted."

"Thugs of their ilk are the dregs of the kingdom!" said John. And Wrexham could see John was feeling better.

The following night they went to Lady Gertrude's where John made quite a scene when told he could not be advanced any money. Wrexham managed to quiet him by taking a hundred pounds worth of chips, and giving fifty to John. They played Hazard, and won four hundred pounds between them. It was a beginning. But when they returned home, John began drinking again.

Wrexham drank with him, observing John quietly. Wrexham had always prided himself on his own fortunate lack of conscience, his ability to force out of his mind and heart any qualms he suffered over having done injury to or defrauded another person. But as he watched John refill his brandy glass, he felt a grudging admiration and an uneasy sense of awe over John's capacity for wiping out of his consciousness the most violent and vicious acts of the recent past.

John said, "I think our luck has changed, Jerry."

"I pray you are correct, Johnny boy."

45

Richard Steele watched the deformed man on the stage of the small theater in Ipswich. Apart from the rich, ringing, yet horror-haunted voice coming from the stage, there was utter silence in the crowded house. Richard recalled what Farley Shannon had told him about true applause. There are many ways an actor may persuade an audience to loud applause, but to keep them hushed, hanging on every word, hardly daring to breathe—that is a kind of applause, which only truth and genuine merit can earn.

Richard felt conflicting emotions. Undeniable admiration for the superb demonstration of the actor's art he was witnessing, and yet the natural, momentarily disturbing actor's feeling of jealousy. Confident though he was of his own hard-earned thespian skills, he knew he could not quite equal what the man on stage was accomplishing. It was the mixed feeling Farley Shannon had experienced and described to him, when Shannon had worked with Betterton.

On the stage, the succession of ghosts of those whom King Richard the Third had murdered, had made their speeches and vanished, and the hunchbacked monarch was alone in his tent on the battlefield at Bosworth.

The actor delivered his lines with such monumental power that the rapt silence of the audience held until King Richard was slain. Then, like the bursting of a dam, the applause came in a deluge. Derby and Richmond were hard-pressed to read their closing lines. Richard Steele rushed backstage to keep his prearranged appointment with David Garrick. A half hour later they were seated opposite each other at a table in a nearby coffee house.

"How old are you, Mr. Garrick?"

"Twenty-four. Please call me David, Mr. Steele."

"If you will call me Richard. . . . You are a remarkable young man. How long have you been acting?"

"Several years. Mainly with amateur companies. But of late, I have worked with a number of professional provincial groups."

"You show every mark of expert coaching."

Young Garrick nodded. "I have been fortunate. To begin with I studied at Dr. Johnson's private school. I believe a decent general education is a decided asset to an actor. But most importantly, I have been coached at length by the great Charles Macklin."

Richard had seen Macklin a number of times. His performance of Shylock in *The Merchant of Venice* struck Richard as the most exceptional, naturalistic portrayal of the part he had ever seen.

"Why have you not come to London?" he asked.

"I have not felt quite ready. I have not even worked under my own name in most places. My brother would never forgive me if I should appear publicly, and be criticized in any way."

Richard smiled. "Criticism is one of our occupational hazards, David. Is your brother in the theater?"

"No. We were wine merchants. He still conducts our wine business, and was quite upset when I told him I must leave to become an actor."

"Nell Faversham told me you and she had discussed our plans to take a company to America."

"Yes. I appreciate your interest, but I could not consider that, Richard. I require the security our established theater represents. I do not feel I could contribute adequately to a pioneering venture."

Richard stared at Garrick for a moment. The young man had the most expressive face, the shrewdest dark eyes he had ever seen.

"Would you consider doing *Richard III* at Goodman's Fields? It is close enough to London to attract the attention of the leading theater people, and . . ."

"I would like that, Richard. But only if my name is not

used. Should I not be received well, I would not wish to embarrass my brother and friends in London."

"I assure you you will be well-received. You are an extraordinarily fine actor!"

Garrick's face lit up with pleasure.

Nell and Richard worked out the great bill for Garrick's *Richard III* with the young actor. It read:

GOODMAN'S FIELDS
At the Late Theatre in Goodman's Fields
Will Be Presented
A CONCERT OF VOCAL
AND INSTRUMENTAL MUSIC
DIVIDED INTO TWO PARTS
Tickets at Three, Two and One Shilling
Places for the Boxes
to Be Taken at the Inn of the King's Men
Near the Theatre.
N. B. Between the Two Parts of the Concert
Will be Presented an HISTORICAL PLAY Called
LIFE AND DEATH OF
KING RICHARD THE THIRD
Containing the Distresses of R. Henry VI,
The Artful Acquisition of the Crown
by King Richard,
The Murder of Young King Edward V
and His Brother in the Tower,
THE LANDING OF THE EARL OF RICHMOND,
And the Death of King Richard
In the Memorable Battle of Bosworth Field,
Being the Last That Was Fought Between the
House of York and Lancaster.
With Many Other True Historical Passages
The Part of King Richard by A GENTLEMAN
(Who Never Appeared on Any Stage)

Then the bill listed the balance of the cast and their roles. Richard was to play Buckingham; Nancy Lucia, Lady Anne; Evangeline, Prince Edward (it was not unusual for a young lady to play male roles).

After the listing of the cast, and description of a dance interval, the bill concluded:

561

To Which Will Be Added
a Ballad Opera of One Act, Called
THE VIRGIN UNMASKED
The Part of Lucy by Miss Grigsby
Both of Which Will Be Performed Gratis, by Persons
For their Diversion
THE CONCERT WILL BEGIN EXACTLY AT
SIX O'CLOCK

There was a carnival atmosphere around Goodman's Fields those last two weeks in May. Richard, Nancy Lucia, Nell and Shannon and all the players were busy from early morning until late at night. They were performing their current presentations and rehearsing the productions to follow. The actors and actresses who were to audition to replace the Grigsbys and Arthur Reinhart arrived. It was decided that Emmett Nicholson would succeed Richard as actor/manager. Nicholson and Richard conducted lengthy, careful auditions of twenty-seven entertainers to select the players who would replace those who would soon depart for America.

At the same time, frantic preparations continued for the journey to America. Then Niccolini and Theo Canaday came up from Bexhill to spend the last two weeks with Nancy Lucia, Richard and Shannon. Niccolini had continued to gain weight, and was now even more plump than ever. Theo's condition had been erratic. For a time he seemed to improve and appeared quite robust. Then, if he over-exerted himself in any way, he experienced the chest pains again, and became gaunt and sallow. He seemed more feeble than he should now, because he had been pressing himself to complete several surprises for the American company.

Hank Hogsdon had moved out of the cottage, and joined his brother, Frank, Socrates Quincy, his new bride, Genevieve, and the other players at the public house near the theater. Niccolini and Theo stayed at the cottage. It was a joyous time. No one mentioned that in a brief fortnight they would part; that Niccolini and Theo might never see their daughter, son-in-law and grandson again.

Niccolini had designed a multi-purpose costume, which Cecilia had sewed. Its upper half was a blouse, which could be worn inside out. On one side it was white and green striped dimity with dark bright green buttons. The other side was a silk gold cloth, with deep red glass buttons, which shone like rubies. The lower half of the costume was a full length skirt. On one side, the skirt was the same green dimity as the green stripes in the blouse, and on the other, the same silk gold cloth as the blouse. If a player wore the white and green striped blouse with the green dimity skirt, the effect was of a lovely summery gown. If the gold blouse and gold skirt were worn, the effect was regal, fit for a royal assembly.

Theo made a similarly interesting contribution. He had designed and constructed a four-way flat, made of shutters. On one side of the flat, Theo had painted a scene depicting a Roman or Grecian forum. When the shutters were raised on that side, there was a rustic country scene. On the opposite side of the flat, with the shutters down, one saw a raging, wind-lashed green-gray sea beneath a sky full of dark, angry clouds. With the shutters raised, one saw a grim battlefield, strewn with corpses of noble warriors, and a darkling sky splashed with brilliant orange and yellow cannon bursts.

The entire company was assembled at the theater for a rehearsal when the wagon arrived from Bexhill. Nancy Lucia and Evangeline took turns modeling the multi-purpose blouse and skirt. The combination fit both of them beautifully. Then Theo demonstrated the functions of the four-way shuttered flat. All the players, the scenic designer, the carpenter and the wardrobe lady cheered and applauded each successive revelation of costume and scene.

Nancy Lucia threw her arms around her mother.

"It is so lovely, Niccolini! Every time I wear it, in a thousand plays, I will think of you!"

Happy tears shone in Niccolini's eyes. She wiped her puffy olive cheeks. Shannon put his arm around her and hugged her close. Richard pounded Theo's back, when Canaday finished demonstrating the ingenious flat.

"Masterful, Theo!" he exclaimed. "How did you ever do it?"

"If I can't be with ye, lad. At least, a bit o' me handiwork will be! We've also got a little shingle we would like ye to take along!"

When the carpenter had uncrated the flat, he also found a length of board, six feet by two feet.

It was painted a deep, rich navy blue. And against the shining blue, gold letters read:

"THE STEELE CANADAY
COMPANY OF COMEDIANS
Direct from London, England"

The last E in STEELE and the C in CANADAY were linked by the gold outline of a heart.

"Niccolini and I hope ye'll nail that on yer first wagon," said Theo.

Richard hugged him fiercely. Then Shannon ran into the small knot of his parents and grandparents and there was general hugging and kissing. All the assembled company members applauded and cheered.

Word of the vitality, the creativity, the jubilation that was erupting at Goodman's Fields spread around the countryside, and quickly reached London's busy streets. Night after night the small theater was filled. And each presentation seemed to glow and sparkle more than the one before.

Garrick's *Richard III* lifted them to new peaks of excellence. By the night of the third performance of the play, everyone in London with any interest in the theater at all was talking about the spectacular drama at Goodman's Fields. By the fourth night, business at Covent Garden, Lincoln's Inn Fields and Drury Lane had fallen off alarmingly, while the doorkeeper and ticket taker at Goodman's Fields were hard-pressed to placate those who could not get in because the theater was filled.

On the fifth night, which was an off night at Covent Garden, Wrexham persuaded John Fox that they must go to see the play. John had completely recovered, and to Wrexham's astonishment, seemed to have forgotten all the distressing and violent incidents of recent weeks. It was as though he had convinced himself they had all been nothing more than bad dreams. He and Wrexham had been to Lady Gertrude's twice more, and had won on one occasion, and lost on another, showing a net combined gain in their assets of twenty-six pounds. The Duke was away from the city for a few days, and Wrexham had been trying to persuade John that he must visit his mother, and somehow convince her she must give them the money to pay off the increasingly impatient gamblers.

During the week, each of the gamblers to whom they owed money, excepting the famed Higginbotham, had sent ugly representatives to warn them they must pay their obligation, or suffer dire physical consequences. The last of these dunners had come that afternoon, and one had nearly lost his temper and struck John, when John arrogantly demanded he leave the house and desist from hounding them over such a niggardly debt. Only Wrexham's acquaintanceship with the collector, and his persuasive powers saved John from being assaulted. Now at the theater, John was irritated by the pushing, noisy throngs, and Wrexham's failure to secure a box. All the seats in the auditorium, including the boxes, had long since been occupied. Wrexham took John backstage, and there in the last minute hustle and bustle before curtain, they found Richard Steele.

"Richard, this is Lord John Fox, the Duke's son. I do not know if you remember him."

Richard did not recognize the tall, thin young man. It was more than fifteen years since he had seen him, and then under circumstances during which his introduction to the boy had been an insignificant event. He had long since forgotten the episode of the disobedient dog, and Nell had told him nothing of Lord John. He extended his hand to John.

"It was a long time ago, but I have worked with your father for many years."

John ignored the proffered hand.

"I believe Jerry means for us to be seated on the stage, though I despise being thrown in with those insipid fops."

Richard stared at John curiously. He was dressed as elegantly as any of the beaux. Wrexham said quickly, "John prefers a box, Richard, but I realize there are none available. Perhaps you could arrange for two more chairs on the stage." Richard did, although the stage was already crowded.

John Fox had never seen Shakespeare's play about the misshapen, ruthless Duke who became King Richard III. And David Garrick captured his attention from the first moment he shuffled to center stage, crouched over, the hump on his back a vile burden, his dark, expressive eyes blazing bitterness. In the opening scene when Garrick, as the malformed Duke of Gloucester, spat out his envy of his brother, the Duke of York, John moved forward on his chair, rudely pushed a gentleman at his left, and ordered him to sit back a bit.

". . . and now," Garrick Richard was saying contemptuously, "—instead of mounting barbed steeds to fright the souls of adversaries, he capers nimbly in a lady's chamber to the lascivious pleasing of a lute."

Garrick turned slowly to his left. It seemed to John that the actor was staring directly at him, as Garrick continued. "But I, that am not shaped for sportive tricks, nor made to court an amorous looking glass; I, that I am rudely stamped, and want love's majesty to strut before a wanton ambling nymph; I, that am curtailed of this fair proportion, cheated of feature by dissembling nature, deformed, unfinished, sent before my time into this breathing world, scarce half made up, and that so lamely and unfashionable that dogs bark at me as I halt by them!"

He glared around the stage at his feet, as though he expected a pack of vicious mongrels to attack him. He looked up again, scanned the audience slowly from left to right, but gave the impression he was squinting into a brilliant sun.

Continuing on he seemed to stare again, directly at John Fox. "And therefore, since I cannot prove a lover, I am determined to prove a villain!" He turned away, and strode toward stage right two steps, sweeping the hushed audience from left to right once again as he moved, awkwardly yet grimly strong. John lost track of the bitter words which continued to explode from the actor's lips. John, himself, was not deformed at all. Indeed in an emaciated, dramatically sinister way he was quite handsome. Yet he felt rudely stamped spiritually. He had always felt thus. Why, he did not know.

In the crowded, unnaturally quiet theater, he was suddenly alone, and the thought struck him that he had long since determined to prove a villain. Suddenly the strange moment of reflection passed, and he turned back to the action on the stage before him.

In scene two of the first act a beautiful woman appeared on the stage. It was Lady Anne, striding sadly alongside the bearers of the coffin of her father-in-law, King Henry, the Sixth. Blood dripped from the coffin onto the stage. John Fox stared at the lovely woman in the candle glow of the overhead chandeliers. Her lavender eyes were sad. He stared at the eyes as if transfixed. He believed he had seen those eyes before, but he could not remember where or when. Somehow he related them to a stirring episode in his life, but he could not remember what it was. His eyes followed Nancy Lucia, playing

566

Lady Anne, clad in flowing funeral black silks, her raven hair hanging softly to her shoulders, as she walked slowly across the stage, until she came upon Duke Garrick.

John rudely pushed the fop beside him back again, whispered irritably, "Sit back, sit back!"

He leaned forward and listened raptly as Lady Anne accused the Duke of having murdered the King.

John watched the blood drip from the coffin, as he listened to Lady Anne's words. "O God! which this blood made'st, revenge his death! O earth! which this blood drink'st, revenge his death."

She raised her arms skyward and her voice broke, as she begged, "Either heaven with lightning strike the murtherer dead, or earth, gape open wide and eat him quick, as thou dost swallow up this good king's blood, which his hell-governed arm hath butchered!"

John followed the exchange between the Lady and the Duke tensely. Finally Nancy Lucia Anne demanded a confession.

John kept trying to remember where he had seen this beautiful woman with the lavender eyes. He paraded a long line of prostitutes he had used and abused through his mind, one by one, but the lady with the lavender eyes was not among them. He turned his attention back to the action before him. Perhaps it was the unrelenting violence, the succession of dastardly murders, the twisted character of King Richard himself—whatever it was, John Fox had never witnessed a play with which he identified so thoroughly.

He was startled when, in the fourth scene of the fourth act, old Queen Margaret, Queen Elizabeth and the Duchess of York held forth before the Palace. Margaret was played by Emily Grigsby. Her face was made up with chalk powder, white and sickly, with heavily penciled wrinkles and lines. She was bent over, and her voice had the uncontrolled, cackling quaver of the aged. Emily Grigsby did not know John Fox. She merely happened to be positioned during the scene so that she seemed to be looking toward him. As she began her remarks to the Duchess of York, mother of the murderous, malformed Richard, John Fox's paranoia convinced him she was talking about him. He broke out into a cold sweat, as the old lady spoke.

". . . from forth the kennel of thy womb hath crept a

hell hound that doth hunt us all to death. That dog that had his teeth before his eyes, to worry lambs, and lap their gentle blood; that foul defacer of God's handiwork, that reigns in galled eyes of weeping souls, that excellent grand tyrant of the earth, thy womb let loose, to chase us to our graves!"

The beaux at John's left had edged out to block his view again, and John shoved him back angrily, almost knocking him out of his chair. The fop was about to say something, when he noted the wild gleam in John's eye.

He moved his chair away. Emily Grigsby as Queen Margaret raised her voice.

"O upright, just, and true-disposing God! How do I thank thee that this carnal cur preys on the issue of his mother's body, and makes her pew-fellow with others' moan!"

When the play ended, John sat with his elbows on his knees, his head resting in his hands, while the aristocrats on the stage, the audience in the pit and galleries applauded, whistled and cheered. Wrexham stood over him, and placed his hand on John's shoulder.

"Are you all right?"

John nodded, but did not raise his head. He was emotionally spent. The dance interval followed the grim history of *Richard III*. It served to calm John, and the one act ballad opera, *The Virgin Unmasked*, altered his mood completely. The mercurial changes in John's moods were not only an everlasting surprise to Wrexham, but were beyond John's own understanding. As disturbed as he had been by much of the Shakespeare history, just so delighted was he with Evangeline Grigsby in *The Virgin Unmasked*. He was enchanted with her diminutive, yet full-blown figure, the naughty sparkle in her cornflower eyes, and the sheen of her golden hair.

As Evangeline took her last bow and started for the wings, John jumped up from his seat and rushed toward her. He caught her arm and pulled her toward him.

"I must tell you, my dear. You were completely captivating."

Evangeline had had problems with over-enthusiastic and appreciative stage-seated fops before. She smiled mechanically, said, "Thank you, sir," and tried to move on. But John now had an arm around her shoulder, and was forcing her, with him, to a relatively isolated corner of the backstage area. Her back was suddenly against a

568

dusty wall. Annoyance showed in her eyes. She put her hands on his chest and tried to push him away. He grasped her wrists.

"Do not be alarmed, my sweet. I mean you no harm. I simply want you to have supper with me."

Wrexham stood a short distance away, smiling.

"Please, sir." Evangeline spoke firmly, struggling harder now to tear away from John. "I have a previous engagement." She smiled, with all the charm she could muster.

John tightened his hold.

"What is your name, my dear?" He had never bothered to look at the play bills.

"Evangeline Grigsby," said Evangeline, still trying to break John's grip on her wrists. Actors, their friends and many beaux and ladies milled all about John and Evangeline. No one paid them the slightest attention. The heaviest concentration was around David Garrick, the new man of the hour.

"Ah! Evangeline!" said John. "Perhaps you will sup with me tomorrow evening."

"Please let go. You are hurting me." Evangeline was becoming angrier by the moment. Shannon was standing with Richard and Nancy Lucia and a small group of friends six feet from where John held Evangeline. Now, for the first time, he noticed that Evangeline was apparently struggling to break the grasp of this tall, thin man.

Just then, John leaned his face down toward Evangeline's. "Permit me to kiss you just once, my lovely. Just to sustain me till I see you on the morrow."

He released her wrists, but immediately threw his arms around her, pulled her tightly to him, crushing his mouth against hers. She tried to kick and break his hold, but he had her arms pinned to her sides. Shannon pushed past several people, grabbed John by the shoulder, and tore him away from Evangeline. John was several inches taller than Shannon, but not nearly as broad nor as strong. His eyes blazed angrily as he glared at Shannon. He reached for the sword at his side, but before he had it more than six inches out of its scabbard, Shannon held him by the wrist. He ripped John's hand away from the sword. Then he let go of John's wrist, but in the same motion, he swung his clasped fists in a slashing downward action fiercely against the side of John's head.

John fell to the ground, shook his head, scrambled to one knee, and quickly this time, got the sword out of the scabbard. Before John could rise, Shannon kicked viciously at the forearm of John's sword hand, and John shrieked with pain. The sword fell from his numbed fingers. Shannon pounced on him, both fists swinging. Wrexham rushed in to grab Shannon's shoulders. He tried to wrest him away from John. Richard charged up behind Wrexham, and with a strong arm around Wrexham's neck, pulled him away from Shannon. Richard spun Wrexham against a wall.

"I was merely trying to separate them," spouted Wrexham indignantly.

"Let him up, Shannon," said Richard, grasping Shannon's shoulder. Shannon rose, backed away, still panting and furious. Evangeline ran over to him, and put her arms around him. John got to his feet slowly. Richard picked up the sword and gave it to Wrexham.

"Get him out of here, Jerry," he said.

"You have not heard the last of me, you stupid brute!" John screamed at Shannon, as Wrexham pushed him through the crowd and out the backstage door.

In the carriage on the way home, still trembling with rage, rubbing a bruise on his cheek, John asked, "Who was that lout?"

Wrexham could not help smiling.

"You were present at the birth of that lout, Johnny boy, one night at the Covent Garden theatre. His name is Shannon Steele."

A shocked look came into John's dark, burning eyes. "You mean then, Lady Anne, the one with the lavender eyes, was Mrs. Steele!"

Wrexham nodded with a smile.

The night was not over. When they entered their drawing room, John and Wrexham were startled to see two men lounging in their favorite chairs.

"Good evenin', Jerry, old fella," greeted Banger Shaw, sitting in Wrexham's chair, a large glass of brandy in his hand. Banger was almost fifty, but he was still a powerful-looking man. He was now bald, and his eyebrows were a fuzzy white, over his chilled steel eyes. Polly Heffelfinger was not with him. The large-beaked dunner had been killed in a fight three years earlier, when he and

Banger had attempted a forceful collection from a burly dockworker.

Banger's companion, seated in John's favorite grained leather chair, his feet resting on a small table, was a young man, no more than twenty-five. He wore a leather cap on a dark, scraggly-haired head. He was rather handsome, though his eyes bulged somewhat and were the pastel green color of those of certain fish. They were also completely expressionless. He was tall and muscular.

"This is Ignatius Shipley, Jerry," said Banger, in a friendly tone. "New lad. Very good at 'is work. A little eager, but very good!"

Wrexham smiled feebly, and nodded toward Shipley. Shipley stared at him without expression.

"Old 'igginbotham wants ter know when 'e kin get 'is money, Jerry," said Banger. "Says it's been almost three months. Too long, don't ye know!"

John advanced toward Shipley.

"Get out of my chair," he spat.

Shipley stared up at him. He did not move, nor change expression.

"Now, John—" Wrexham walked toward him.

But John was already reaching for his sword. Shipley gave a mighty grunt, and shot out of his chair as though he were on springs. John got the sword out of its scabbard this time, but before he could raise it, Shipley's right fist crashed against the left side of his head. He dropped the sword and staggered four feet to his right. His knees hit the lounge, and he fell over onto it. He lay there, holding the side of his head.

Shipley took the sword, and walked to the lounge. He raised the sword high over his head, stabbed it downward hard, inches from John's head. It went right through the lounge cushions and webbing, and stuck into the wood floor. The jeweled hilt, and six inches of the gleaming blade, showed above the cushion of the lounge.

"Next time, I'll shove it up yer arse and cut out yer tongue from the inside," he said calmly, looking down at John. His fish-eyed face was still without expression. Banger came over, and gently pulled him away from the lounge.

"All right, Iggie lad, that's fine. 'Is Lordship is a little headstrong."

Wrexham put one arm around Banger's shoulder, the

571

other around Shipley's. He had to stand on the toes of his right foot, Shipley was so tall.

"I appreciate your call, gentlemen," he said, placatingly. "Lord John is about to inherit a great deal of money. Please tell Lancelot I shall call on him very soon —to pay both his Lordship's debt and my own."

John just lay there, pale and trembling, glaring at all three of them. After the dunners left, Wrexham said, "John, I believe you had better visit your mother tomorrow. Time is getting quite short!"

46

John Fox sat up most of the night after the visit of Higginbotham's dunners, brooding and drinking brandy. He dozed fitfully, but each time he did, he began to dream. They were lurid, disturbing dreams. *Nancy Lucia Steele, lying on the scarlet cape on the floor of the drawing room behind the box in the Covent Garden theatre.*

Evangeline Grigsby in her bedchamber, kissing a hunchbacked, regally dressed man. "Do not be a voyeur, John Fox," the hunchback admonishes. "Go away and visit your mother!"

Mobs of leather-capped, mean-eyed muscular men, converging on John, as he scrambles to hide under the bed.

"What are you doing down there, Johnny?" demanded Wrexham, as John tried to crawl under the bed. Wrexham had retired hours earlier. John woke with a start, looked up at Wrexham.

"I was dreaming," he mumbled. He rose from hands and knees, walked back out to the drawing room and poured himself another drink. He brooded some more. At ten o'clock in the morning, he washed and shaved. Desperate, dark bloodshot eyes stared at him from the looking glass. His hand trembled as he held the blade to his throat, slid it upward to remove the soapy lather. He dressed in a handsome blue velvet suit and bejeweled waistcoat his mother had selected for him in a happier day.

At the Fox mansion, he went around the side of the huge, stone house to the gardens. The formally designed, well-tended area was ablaze with late May blooms. Roses

573

of every color, buds and full-blown unfurled velvety blossoms and chrysanthemums, white, vermillion, green, gold, competed with a dozen other species in a contest of riotous color. Breathing the heady scent of the near summer profusion of flowers, neatly edged green hedges, verdant grass, John felt slightly dizzy as he gathered a bouquet.

He went into the morning room through the terrace overlooking the gardens. His mother sat there in her wheelchair, her head on her chest, fast asleep. Across from her sat Cumberly, her aging nurse.

"Good morning, your Lordship," whispered Cumberly.

John walked quietly to his mother's chair.

"Is she all right?"

Cumberly shook her gray head. "She hardly slept at all last night. Dr. Spencer was here again this morning. He seems quite discouraged."

"Is my father at home?"

"I believe he is expected to return from Scotland tonight."

"Will it be all right if I wake her?"

"Oh, yes. I'll leave you with her."

Cumberly left the room, quietly closing the door behind her. John stood over his mother. For almost three minutes, he simply stared down at the ugly, pallid and worn face. The position of her head on her chest pushed several layers of fatty skin out under her chin. The flaccid skin rose and fell rhythmically with her breathing. She reminded John of a frog. He touched her shoulder gently. She woke, wide-eyed and frightened, and uttered a sharp scream. Then she looked up and saw her son.

"Oh, it is you! I was having a bad dream."

He held the fragrant bouquet out to her, and she took it. She wiped the back of a hand across the spittle on her chin.

"Thank you, John," she said coldly. She wheeled herself to a nearby marquetted table, and dropped the flowers on it. She wheeled around to face John.

"I suppose you want money!" she said.

Then she noticed his bruised face, the deep circles under his burning dark eyes. She wheeled herself to him, and peered up into his face.

"You have been hurt!" she said, trying to conceal the note of concern.

"It is nothing, Mother. Those debts. Some ruffians decided to threaten Jerry and myself."

"Sit down," she said coldly.

He touched his bruised cheek, winced, and said, "I wrote a new composition for you, Mother. May I play it?"

She stared at him, and said nothing. He went behind her chair and wheeled her down the hall, into the music room. She made no objection. He settled the wheelchair beside the spinet bench, sat down on the cushioned seat and began to play. He played some of the melodies which had pleased her in the past.

"Remember this?" His long fingers picked skillfully at the keys. She nodded.

Lost Lad's Haven. You are shameless, John."

He smiled wanly and continued to play. She suddenly began to groan. He looked across his shoulder, and saw that she was clutching her chest.

"Are you all right? Shall I call Cumberly?"

She shook her head, breathing hard. She waved a hand.

"No, no. Go on playing."

He did, and her spasm of pain passed.

"Lovely, Johnny," she said. "Lovely. But you cannot have any money."

He smiled again, and changed key.

"This is new. I just wrote it yesterday."

He spoke over the delicate rippling sound of the spinet.

"It has no title, Mother. You name it . . . please."

He kept playing. It was a moving, sorrowful song in a moody, minor key. Sarah Fox thought it the loveliest, if the saddest, of all the compositions he had written. Sadder even than *Lost Lad's Haven.* John looked across his shoulder at her again, continued playing the doleful melody.

"What would you call it, Mother?"

"The Last Days," she said quietly. She took a kerchief from the cuff of her black silk blouse, wiped her moist cheek and dabbed her eye. She sniffed and sat up straighter in the chair. He finished the song, with a fading, down scale glissando, then an abrupt strong minor chord.

"You cannot have any money, John. Those bruises on your face are a result of my ridiculous indulgence of you,

575

throughout your life. You will find a way out of your present financial morass, and be the stronger for it!"

He rose from the bench, stood beside her.

"I must have the money, Mother. I simply must!"

She shook her head. Her good eye seemed as empty of feeling, as lifeless as the eye on the paralyzed side of her face. John read there the final rejection! He reached down and snatched up the cushion of the spinet bench, and with one quick step, slammed into his mother's chair. She began to cry, but before a sound escaped her lips, the cushion was over her face. He held it tightly there with his left hand, while his right pressed hard against the back of her head. The flaccid, weak body in the chair twisted futilely, briefly, then sagged into limp stillness. John held the cushion against the purpling face for another five minutes. He thought he saw vile denunciation in the popping, rheumy, dead brown eyes staring up at him over the top edge of the cushion. Even in the paralyzed one, which had expressed nothing as far back as he could remember.

His hands trembled as he removed the cushion from his mother's face. He placed the cushion back on the bench. He sat there for ten minutes, breathing deeply, fighting to control his shaking hands, waiting for the weak feeling in his knees to pass. Finally, he ran to the door, flung it open and shouted, "Cumberly, Cumberly! Come at once."

When the nurse came running, haltingly, down the short hall from the drawing room, he said frantically, "Have someone fetch Dr. Spencer. My mother has fainted. I cannot revive her. Hurry!"

Dr. Spencer was not at his residence, and it was three hours before Hawkins was able to reach him. The Duchess had long since turned cold and blue. Dr. Spencer indicated on the Certificate of Death that the cause was a failure of the heart. In truth, he did not know the specific cause. In Sarah Fox's condition, it could have been any one or a combination of a number of deficiencies and disorders.

Back at the rooms he shared with Wrexham, John said wearily, "My mother died this morning, Jerry."

Wrexham put his arm around John's shoulder, walked him to the lounge in the drawing room, and poured a glass of brandy for him.

"I am sure it is for the best, Johnny. All for the best. She has come to an end of her suffering."

Wrexham did not ask how she died. He did not want to know. John sipped his drink, stared at the richly carpeted floor.

"She named it 'The Last Days,' " he said.

"Eh?"

"My song. I played her a new composition. She named it 'The Last Days.' "

"Appropriate, Johnny. Very appropriate."

Four days later, Sarah Fox's last will and testament was read. John, his father, Cumberly, Hawkins, fifteen other members of the Fox household staff, and Jerome Wrexham were summoned to the offices of Snowden, Twink and Featherton, attorneys at law. Ephram Twink read the testament. Modest bequeaths were made to all the servants. Then Twink intoned in his sepulchral voice, "To my old friend, Jerome Wrexham, I bequeath a thousand pounds. Although Jerome's relationship with my son, John, has not proved an entirely beneficial one, I do believe he endeavored in his own fashion to give my son attention, love and counsel."

Wrexham winked briefly at John, as Twink read on.

"To my son, John, I bequeath fifty thousand pounds—" Twink cleared his throat, coughed and cleared his throat again and repeated ". . . fifty thousand pounds, with the provision, however, that he shall be given these funds only in such sums and on such occasions as my husband, Edmund Fox, Duke of Cheltenham, approves and considers proper. Upon the death of my husband, should it occur before the demise of my son, John, the fifty thousand pounds I bequeath him, or whatever portion of it remains intact, shall be placed in a trust in the Bank of England, and a competent official of said bank shall assume the trusteeship exercised until that time by my husband, Edmund Fox."

John listened to the silver-haired barrister's words in utter disbelief. Wrexham paled, and stared at John. Edmund Fox looked straight ahead, stony-faced and expressionless. John sprang abruptly out of his chair, raced to the door, and out of the somber, rosewood-paneled office. No one ran after him. There was an awkward moment of silence. Then the Duke nodded to Twink to continue. Wrexham rose slowly, waved a hand toward Twink.

"I beg to be excused," he said, and walked to the door in a daze. Little remained to be read, in any event. The remainder of the Duchess's considerable estate was left to the Duke.

Wrexham did not see John for three days. And no one in any of the places they frequented saw him, or heard anything of him. It began to rain early on the fourth day after the reading of the will, and it rained all day. Wrexham came home from the theater, weary and depressed. He was expecting visits momentarily from one or more of the dunners. He had a light supper, several brandies, and then decided to retire. He lay in bed for a long time, listening to the rain pounding on the roof, slashing against the windows. Finally he fell into an uneasy and restless sleep.

He dreamed that he was on stage at Covent Garden, playing a scene in *The Beggar's Opera*. Three other cast members were on stage with him. Suddenly, and without explanation, they went berserk. One picked up a bench and hurled it against the downstage entrance door on stage left. Another picked up a chair, and began to smash a table cluttered with goblets and dishes. The third did a mad dance, stomping in circles around Wrexham. The noise was deafening, but in the dream, Wrexham kept on singing. There was a sudden crashing sound, louder than any of the previous noises, and Wrexham woke with a start. He was conscious of the continued sound of the beating rain, but the banging and crashing came from the drawing room. He lit a candle in a brass holder on the table beside his bed, and in his nightshirt and night cap, stumbled out to the drawing room.

A bedraggled apparition stood before him. John Fox had knocked over a heavy table with an oil lamp on it; had staggered into the rolling serving table, shattering a decanter of brandy, a bottle of whiskey and a half dozen glasses. A strong alcoholic smell permeated the room. As Wrexham stumbled toward John, John fell over backward onto the flowered damask lounge. A small puff of down stuffing spurted out of the cushion into which Ignatius Shipley had plunged the sword. Wrexham stood before the unconscious figure on the couch, holding the candle close to him.

He remembered clearly that for the reading of the will,

John had dressed elegantly in his finest black silk coat and breeches. He wore his embroidered and jeweled gray waistcoat and two neckcloths, the black silk over the white muslin. In special memory of his mother, he wore the solid gold pin for the neckcloths, which the Duchess had given him when he went off to Eton. The pin was formed of the gracefully wrought initials of his names. The J and F made an unusual and intricate design. He wore gray silk stockings, clocked in black, and shining black leather shoes with high silver heels.

To Wrexham, he appeared now to have been fished out of the Thames, and he smelled as though he had been. Wrexham guessed that he must have walked a considerable distance in the rain. His brownish hair was plastered to his head. There were deep scratches on his face, but they had stopped bleeding. The neckcloths and the gold initial pin were gone, and half the front of his shirt had been ripped away. The black silk coat and the gray waistcoat, as well as the breeches, were pasted tight to his body by the rain. The high heels had broken off the black leather shoes, and the heel-less shoes and the gray silk stockings were thick with slimy brown mud up to the knees.

Wrexham undressed John and put him to bed. As he removed the wet coat, waistcoat and breeches, he noted darker, thicker splatters on all three. He suspected these were blood stains. He started to build a fire in the fireplace, then changed his mind, and decided to keep the clothes and shoes. He folded them carefully, wrapped them in a pillow case, and hid them at the rear of a high shelf in a closet. His suspicion of what had happened proved correct. This time the murdered prostitute's body was found immediately.

On the second day after John's watery return, *The London Chronicle* published the story. Again a brief item. Her name was Becky Bliss. She was fourteen, and had been murdered and mutilated in the same manner as Antoinette Dupre. The police had found several items of material evidence, which they believed would lead them to the murderer. The items were not described, but Wrexham guessed they would probably include the JF gold neckcloth pin, possibly even one or both of the silver heels. Wrexham did not bother to show the item to John, who never read newspapers.

Once more, John did not recall where he had been.

He did remember spending the night with a prostitute, and exciting himself in his usual fashion, but he did not remember the girl's name. It was over in the Newgate area. Now, he sat brooding, occasionally insisting Wrexham play cards with him, playing his sad songs on the spinet and drinking himself into fitful sleep. He dreaded the return of the dunners. The morning the story appeared in *The Chronicle*, Wrexham told John he had an idea about how they might raise the money. He asked John to try to relax, stay home and do nothing rash, particularly if any of the dunners appeared.

"Just tell them—politely, please—that I have made arrangements to get the money, and we will pay them in the next several days," he told John.

He went to see Lancelot Higginbotham in the office of the gambler-entrepreneur near the Epsom Downs race track.

"I hope ye've brought me my money, Jerry. It's been a long time," said Higginbotham.

"I have not, Lance, but with your help I should be able to pay you in full very shortly—and with a fine bonus!"

Higginbotham looked at him suspiciously.

"What kind of help?"

"I'm certain you know more than one constable in the Newgate district who may be interested in earning an extra bob or two."

"Depends on how much and for what."

"I want him to arrest a man for murder."

"Who? For what murder?"

"Lord John Fox. For the murder of a little whore in Newgate."

"I thought you and Lord John was friends," said Higginbotham.

"We are. After John is arrested, but before he is brought to face a magistrate for indictment, I want this same constable—and whatever accomplices he requires —to help him escape from jail. I presume it would be Newgate prison."

Higginbotham rubbed a pudgy hand over his bald head. The rings on his finger sparkled in the candlelight from the overhead chandelier. He brought the hand down, interlaced its fingers with his other hand, and rested both on the checkered waistcoat covering his paunch.

"Yer confusin' me, Jerry. Ya want 'is lordship arrested,

and put in jail, and then ya want 'im to escape? All in the same day?"

"Precisely! How are your connections on the dock?" Wrexham smiled. "If I recall properly, you have engaged in a transaction or two involving transported convicts, an occasional slave, and now and then a spirited indentured servant."

Higginbotham tugged at his brushlike black mustache, smiled mirthlessly at Wrexham.

"Sometimes I think ya know more about my business than you should, Jerry Wrexham!"

Wrexham slapped him on a beefy thigh.

"Anything I know will go to the grave with me, Lancelot. I am certain I need not tell you that."

Higginbotham nodded.

"I'm confused, Jerry. What have my maritime connections to do with this mad game?"

"I want the constable, or whoever handles the escape, to take John directly to the docks . . . to a ship ready to leave for America."

"This will take more than the lone constable yer talkin' about, Jerry. Spell it out fer me, step by step, as ye would fer a backward six-year-old, and I'll tell ye how many people we'll 'ave to involve. . . ." He paused, took a cigar from a box on his desk, lit it, and said, ". . . and 'ow much it'll cost!"

Wrexham carefully explained his plan, in minute detail.

"Do ye really believe that will work?" asked Higginbotham, wide-eyed with astonishment as Wrexham finished.

"If there is a proper ship sailing at the time we've discussed. And if the people you recruit are at all capable."

"Don't worry about that," said Higginbotham.

"Then I know it will work, Lance. And whatever you tell me your little helpers will have to receive is fine. And for you . . ." Wrexham paused now. He leaned forward and punched a straight index finger into Higginbotham's flabby bosom. ". . . for you, my friend, one thousand pounds over and above the money Lord John and I owe you!"

Higginbotham looked at Wrexham with sheer admiration in his small pale blue eyes.

"Let's work out the timin'," he said, blowing an enthusiastic puff of smoke into the air. It took Wrexham and Higginbotham two days to work out the details of the plan, and recruit the participants. Wrexham told John Fox what he believed John needed to know. John was mystified, but had little choice other than to take Wrexham's word that the plan would enable them to pay off their debts. On the third day after Wrexham's meeting with Higginbotham, a burly, red-faced constable came to the Wrexham–Fox rooms, and arrested John Fox. An hour later, John was in Newgate jail, horrified by the stench and the dirt, the animal sounds, the filthy appearance and stupid and wild actions of his cellmate, and other inmates of the prison.

Wrexham arrived at the Fox mansion about the same time John was thrown into his cell. The Duke was working on some papers in the library when Hawkins showed Wrexham in.

"I fear I have some bad news for you, Edmund," said Wrexham, taking a chair alongside the Duke's richly carved rosewood desk. The Duke looked mildly alarmed, waited.

"John has been arrested. For murder."

"Who—who did he murder?"

For an instant, the thought flashed in Edmund Fox's mind that John had been arrested for the murder of his mother.

"A prostitute in Newgate," said Wrexham. "I think her name was Bessy Blitz, something of the sort."

Edmund Fox rubbed his forehead and shook his head.

"I suppose it had to happen sooner or later," he said, half to himself. "How much do you know about it? Have they enough evidence to try him? Will he be indicted?"

Wrexham nodded somberly.

"More than enough evidence, I'm afraid, Edmund. Do you remember the gold pin, made of his initials?"

The Duke nodded.

"They found it in the girl's room. That and other items belonging to John."

"Then there *will* be a trial!" He clenched a fist, pounded the desk. "I dread it! The disgrace! It will ruin my standing at court. . . ."

Wrexham merely nodded agreement to the Duke's statements.

"And I suppose John will be hanged!" said the Duke,

running his fingers agitatedly through his thick, graying hair.

"More likely he will be transported," said Wrexham quietly.

Confused thoughts exploded in Edmund Fox's mind. He tried to analyze them, even as they appeared and vanished like random bursts of light. He recalled his quandary during the time in Paris when he could have had John arrested, and probably convicted. What now? He did dread the notoriety, the disgrace a trial would bring. He was sickened at the thought of a Fox, a member of a proud family, dying at the end of a rope this late in the eighteenth century.

But *transport!* That went directly to several other important considerations. He had long feared John's violent inclinations. He had never forgotten the night his son held the sword's point to his throat. Since the reading of Sarah's will, his fear had become vastly magnified in his mind. He lived with it every day. He knew how bitter John was over not being given his inheritance outright.

"What did you say?" he asked suddenly, as he realized Wrexham had spoken.

"I said, that is why I am here. I can arrange to have John transported. *Without a trial!* Before he makes an appearance in a magistrate's court!"

Disbelief struggled with desperate hope in Edmund Fox's eyes.

"I do not understand, Jerry."

"You know I have long had connections with a large number of interesting people," Wrexham said, playing the situation for its full worth. "Persons in various pursuits and of several talents."

Edmund Fox still waited, disbelieving, yet hopeful.

"Today is Tuesday," said Wrexham slowly. "I can have John out of Newgate jail by four or five o'clock this morning—that is, Wednesday morning." He paused again for dramatic effect. "I can take him to a ship, a perfectly sound merchantman, which will leave for America with the tide, at approximately nine o'clock this same morning!"

He leaned back in his chair, folded his arms, waited for the Duke's reaction. It was slow in forming. Hope grew as each second ticked by, that the cunning mind of Jerry Wrexham might actually have concocted a scheme to accomplish all this. Wrexham read the Duke's eyes.

When he saw the eager gleam of high hope, he said, "I will go with John . . . to America!"

Again the Duke was startled.

"I do not understand, Jerry! You will go with John? Why? You refused to go to America with my Steele company. . . ."

"You know how I feel about Richard Steele! I have long thought about going to America. Now I am ready. John and I are both ready."

The Duke rose from his chair, stared down at Wrexham, trying to fathom these strange statements.

"John's inheritance was fifty thousand pounds, was it not?" asked Wrexham, looking directly into Edmund Fox's eyes.

"You want me to give John . . . you want me to give you and John fifty thousand pounds?"

"It is his. It rightfully belongs to him," said Wrexham quietly. The Duke shook his head and sat down behind his desk again.

"Fifty thousand pounds?" he repeated, looking at Wrexham, anguish in his eyes. "I cannot . . . at least give me time to think about it."

"John is scheduled to appear before a magistrate at ten o'clock tomorrow morning. Once he is indicted, I will be unable to carry out these plans."

Edmund Fox buried his head in his hands. A large clock on the east wall struck the hour.

"I will need time to execute these plans, Edmund. There is precious little left!"

The Duke looked up.

"In the past year, Jerry, I have encountered serious financial setbacks. I cannot give you fifty thousand pounds. I'll give you twenty-five."

Wrexham felt that if he pressed the matter, he could raise it to at least thirty-five, but in truth, he had been prepared to settle for ten.

"Thirty-five," he said firmly.

The Duke shook his head.

"I will have difficulty getting together twenty-five at this hour."

"I have always liked you, Edmund. You have always been fair with me. Twenty-five it is!"

Wrexham pulled his chair up to the desk.

"This is what we must do," he said, and outlined the plan, step by step. Edmund made notes regarding specific times, the location of the ship on the docks and the name of the ship, the *Bonnie Matilda*.

"John and I will be waiting," Wrexham said finally.

John Fox was pacing the narrow cell at Newgate prison like a caged jackal at twenty minutes past four Wednesday morning. He was nauseous and had a severe headache. His dirty unshaven cellmate snored heavily as he slept on the filthy straw mat on one side of the cell. A large rat scampered across the floor, darted past John, and into a crevice at the base of the wall. John heard footsteps coming down the stone floor of the narrow corridor. The constable who had arrested him stood at the cell door with a jailer. The jailer turned the heavy key in the lock and swung the door open. The constable grabbed John roughly by the arm, pulled him out of the cell, rasped, "Walk quickly, mate. Quickly and quietly!"

The jailer stood aside, and remained at the cell door. The filthy, ragged figure on the straw mat snored on. John and the constable rushed quietly out a side door of the corridor. A hackney waited in the foggy, moonless darkness. In a half hour, John smelled the stench of the Thames, distinct from that of the odoriferous city streets through which they had just clattered. The constable again took him by the arm, and directed him to a gangplank. In the dense fog, John could barely make out the ghostly form of the ship. The lazy flapping of the sodden sails sounded somehow sinister. The constable rushed John up the gangplank. Then a pair of strong arms embraced him, and he felt a familiar beard against his cheek.

"Johnny boy," said Wrexham cheerily, a note of relief in his voice. "Welcome aboard!"

There was a small knot of men. John recognized Lancelot Higginbotham. Then he made out the features of his father. He gasped in surprise, but said nothing. There was a third man in the group, Peter Halbert, the ship's captain. John stood by quietly, shivering in the clammy mist.

In the hum of muted conversation, the Duke handed out packets, one to the dark-coated, bearded captain, one to Higginbotham, one to the constable who had brought him aboard. John watched, as the men opened the packets and counted the paper notes. At Wrexham's side stood a large leather suitcase. The constable grunted a brief remark, left the group and trotted down the gangplank to the hackney. The Duke moved away from the captain, Higginbotham and Wrexham and hobbled toward John, leaning heavily on his walking stick. He looked into John's haggard, haunted face.

"Goodbye, John," he said.

John sneered at him.

"Thank you for everything, Father. I hope you rot in hell!"

Head bent low, the Duke made his way to the gangplank, moving carefully and slowly on the slippery boards. Higginbotham clapped Wrexham on the back.

"Jerry, yer a bleedin' genius," he said. "Wot a stinkin' shame ye decided to waste yer talents on the stage!"

He turned toward the bearded man in the dark coat.

"Cap'n. Always a pleasure to do business with you. Take good care of my friends. I'll see ye when ye return!"

He looked at John, shivering at Wrexham's side.

"Yer lordship," he said, "I 'ope ye'll find the Indian wenches to yer liking."

He waddled down the plank, whistling a merry tune. The merchantman sailed a few minutes past nine o'clock. The hundred pounds the Duke had given Captain Halbert bought John and Wrexham a small, but clean, five by six foot cabin, which Halbert chose to call a stateroom. With the door of the cubicle securely bolted, Wrexham transferred the twenty-two thousand pounds in the suitcase to a strongbox he had brought aboard.

"Old Lancelot is truly a magician," he exulted, as John watched him stacking the hundred-pound notes into the strongbox. "Not only did he find us a ship, but a sturdy merchantman with a reliable captain and a well-disciplined crew. I would hate to be making this passage on one of those filthy convict or slave ships!"

Wrexham was feeling pleased with himself. It had cost three thousand of the twenty-five thousand pounds to pay Higginbotham's bonus, the bribes to the constable, the Newgate prison guard, the hackney driver, and their transport aboard the *Bonnie Matilda*. But between them, Wrexham and John owed more than that amount to the other gamblers, and to Lady Gertrude's. And they would never have to pay those debts.

John was so relieved to be out of the stinking madness of a rat-infested Newgate prison that he uttered not a word of complaint during the first three days of the voyage. The sea was calm, and the journey most pleasant. On the fourth day, strong winds began to blow. The *Bonnie Matilda* was making ten knots an hour, rising and falling, rocking and groaning in the sea's slashing swells. Then the rains came down. John and Wrexham sat at the small, scarred wooden table, bolted to the floor in the small cabin. A flickering candle, lashed to the table top, cast a fluttering melancholy glow about them.

"I cannot eat this slop!" John pushed his bowl away irritably. "What the devil is it?"

The bowl slid toward Wrexham. He caught it with one hand, pushed it across to John.

"Hold onto it, Johnny," he said angrily. "You are not at your club. This is perfectly good lobcourse."

John spooned the mixture in the bowl.

"What are these soggy, stringy lumps?"

"That is salt beef, Johnny. It has been tenderized by hanging overboard in the sea for several days. If you do not care for it, eat the onions and potatoes. You cannot survive on rum alone."

Complaining all the while, John nevertheless finished the lobcourse, and drank two more full cups of rum. Then they played whist for a while. Each time he drew a poor hand and lost, John grumbled, even though they were not playing for money. As they played, Wrexham pondered on what a miserable companion John Fox had become. Miserable, thought Wrexham, and dangerous.

After several hours the rain ceased. The winds died down. The *Bonnie Matilda* sailed along smoothly at an even six knots. They decided to retire. John climbed into the sailcloth cot, hanging by chains from the ceiling. The cot hung above the narrow wooden bed on which Wrexham slept. John groaned as he struggled into the hanging cot.

"Jerry, I do not understand why I must sleep in this confounded cloth cradle, while you have the comfort of a bed."

Wrexham slid into the bed and sighed resignedly.

"You are much lighter and nimbler than I, Johnny boy. Not to mention several years younger. Were I to sleep in the cot, I would likely tumble down upon you in the middle of the night."

An hour passed, and John began snoring in the darkness, but Wrexham could not sleep. He lay in the hard bed, speculating on what they would do when they

587

reached America. With twenty-two thousand pounds, they had many alternatives. He could probably purchase a tobacco plantation of modest dimensions. But that did not appeal to him. And he could think of nothing John could do on a plantation, except possibly molest the slave women. John's snoring became increasingly loud, uneven and irritating. He reached up and poked John's bottom with his fist until John stopped.

Perhaps he could organize a theatrical company. There had to be some competent actors in the colonies. He remembered that a capable English actor named Anthony Aston had gone to America a few years earlier. But then, what would John do in a theatrical company. He hated the theater almost as much as his mother had. He could write music, of course, but most of what he wrote was more suitable for funerals than amusement.

Finally Wrexham fell asleep.

He was awakened by a strong, sour odor which seemed to be suffocating him. His right arm had been hanging down along the side of the bed. It felt moist and sticky under the thin cotton shirt he was wearing. He reached over and felt his right arm with his left hand. The fingers touched a cold, slimy substance, which seemed to cover the entire right arm. He staggered to the table, and lit the lashed candle. He looked at the soiled cotton sleeve on his right arm, and at the wooden floor beside his bed. Yes, John had vomited upon him, and he was now lying on his back, snoring loudly. Wrexham reached up and shook him angrily by the shoulder.

"Get up and clean yourself!" said Wrexham angrily, as he removed his cotton shirt and wiped himself with a cloth. John groaned, but swung down out of the hanging cot. He cleaned himself and the mess on the bed and the wood floor. Wrexham sat at the table, glaring at him as he worked. When he finished, John said, "I'm going up on deck for a while. I cannot sleep in this stinking room."

After he left, Wrexham sat quietly and drank a large glass of rum. Presently, he too clambered up to the deck. The sea was calm. A brilliantly glowing silver full moon played hide and seek with the clouds, now shining brightly on the dark waters; now sliding behind a thick black cloudbank; then peeking forth again to light the merchantman in the sea below. At the top of the steps leading from the cabin, alongside a coil of rope, Wrexham found a marline spike. He slid it into the waist of his heavy cotton breeches. He looked around the deck, but saw no one. He walked the length of the ship, and sighted John at the aft rail, watching the foaming wake.

As he came up behind John, John heard him and turned.

"Sorry I did that, Jerry," he said contritely. Wrexham put his left arm around John's shoulder.

"You are forgiven, Johnny boy. You cannot help it if you are sick. You never could help it, could you?"

His hand was on the marline spike at his waist. With a quick motion, he withdrew it, raised it, and struck John viciously on the side of the head. John dropped to the deck, unconscious. Wrexham put the spike back in his breeches and looked around in all directions. There was only the sound of the soft breeze, the lapping water sliding away from the port and starboard sides of the ship.

Only the bright moon looked down as Wrexham lifted his thin, emaciated friend and dumped him over the rail into the foaming wake. As the body hit the water, the full moon went behind a heavy cloud again.

❧ 47 ❧

Never had so many people gathered in the Pickerings'
Inn of the King's Men on a single occasion. Extra tables,
chairs and benches had been moved in. There was hardly
room for the serving wenches to make their way among
the celebrants with the platters of cold meats, cheeses
and freshly baked bread; the trays laden with bottles of
whiskey and wine, ale and beer.

Now the eating was over. The drinking continued. The
room was filled with a constant buzz, frequent outbursts
of laughter, non-stop chatter, and the clatter of platters, the
clinking of glasses and goblets. The room was warm and
smelled of the pungent, lingering aroma of the long day's
roasting and baking; and of tobacco and sweating bodies.
The entire companies of the Lincoln's Inn Fields, Covent
Garden, Drury Lane and Goodman's Fields theaters
were assembled. Three knights from the Lord Chamberlain's office, and editors and writers from *The Prompter,
The Spectator* and *The London Chronicle* were special
guests.

Edmund Fox rose from his seat on the bench at a long
table, which had been set up in front of the bar. Flanking him, on either side, were the players who were to
embark for America at ten o'clock on the following morning. He tapped a tankard on the table before him with
a spoon, trying to get the attention of the reveling players.
Gradually, the noise in the room subsided.

"My friends," said the Duke. "As you know, we are
gathered tonight to say prayerful and heartfelt *bon voyage* to our venturesome colleagues, who leave on the
morrow for our colonies in America. But before we pro-

590

ceed to that exceedingly pleasant business, I must take up two extraneous matters."

He moistened his lips with a sip of wine.

"The first," he continued, "deals with what some of you have referred to as 'the mysterious disappearance of Jerome Wrexham.' Nell Faversham and I have already explained to Jerry's Covent Garden colleagues that Jerry left more than a week ago for America."

Buzzing began in the room again. The Duke held up a hand.

"Please," he said, "I know some of you will jump to the conclusion that Jerry's departure for America a week before our Steele-Canaday company leaves signifies an obvious connection between the two events. I want to assure you there is none. Jerry left for the colonies for purely personal reasons. My own son, John, accompanied him for similar personal reasons."

Again the buzzing. The Duke paused, wondering fleetingly if any of the players had heard anything about the murdered prostitute or the strange events which followed. Again, he lifted his glass, sipped wine, and continued.

"The second matter I wish to mention deals with a highly talented, relatively recent arrival upon our London theatrical scene. I am sure many, if not all of you, have seen David Garrick's remarkable performance as Richard the Third at our Goodman's Fields playhouse. I learned just this afternoon that young Mr. Garrick has signed a contract with our friendly competitors at Drury Lane for next season. I wish to extend congratulations to Mr. Garrick, and compliment our Drury Lane colleagues on acquiring his services. Mr. Garrick, please stand!"

The handsome, stocky actor rose from the table where he was seated with the Drury Lane manager and two of the leading actresses. His piercing dark eyes gleamed, and a broad smile broke out on his face as he waved both hands at the applauding players around him, bowed and resumed his seat.

"And now," said the Duke, "we come to the pleasurable business of the evening. As you know, I have been associated with the London theatre for many years, and I have participated in many theatrical ventures. No undertaking has given me as much pleasure as my humble participation in the bold enterprise, which begins tomorrow morning, when the Steele-Canaday Company of

Comedians, Direct from London, boards the good ship, the *Elusive Pam*."

There was an outburst of applause, and again the Duke raised his hand and continued.

"This newly refurbished East Indiaman, after a notable career carrying precious cargo between our beloved kingdom and the East Indies and the Far East, begins a new life, plying the Atlantic sea lanes to the American colonies.

"She has carried many a valuable cargo in her day, but never a cargo so priceless as this group of players, who board her on the morrow!"

Again applause. Again, the Duke quieted his audience.

"A priceless cargo, these players in the first theatrical company, organized, equipped, trained and rehearsed here to bring the culture, enlightenment and amusement of England's theatre to our cousins in the New World. In a moment, I want you to meet each of them individually, but before you do, I wish to say a few words about their leader, Richard Steele."

Now there was the wildest, most spontaneous clapping, stomping and whistling yet. The Duke smiled, and held up both hands. He looked down at a sheet of foolscap beside his plate on the table.

"Years ago," he sad, "that distinguished actor, Thomas Betterton, wrote this concerning the Art of Playing, and the Duty and Qualifications of Actors."

He read slowly and clearly.

". . . I have not found in all the clamors against the stage, anyone that denies the usefulness of the drama, if justly managed. The wit of man cannot invent any more efficacious means of encouraging virtue and depressing of vice. The moral lessons, which the stage presents, may make the greatest impressions on the minds of the audience because the instruction is conveyed with pleasure and by ministrations of passion, which have always a stronger remembrance than the calmer precepts of reason.

"But then I think there is no manner of doubt that the lives and characters of actors must contribute very much to the impression the fable and moral will make."

He looked around at the multitude of players, and back to his foolscap.

> "For to hear virtue, religion, honor recommended by a prostitute, an atheist, or a rake makes them a jest to many people, who would hear the same done with awe by persons of known reputation in those particulars."

Now there was an uneasy muttering here and there in the room. Too many of the ladies present were little more than prostitutes; any number of the men, rakes; not a few atheists. These were taking the Duke's words as a reprimand. The Duke read on over the grumbling.

> "For this reason, I first recommend to our players, both male and female, the greatest and most nice care of their reputation imaginable."

He pushed the foolscap aside, looked fondly down at Richard Steele, seated at his right.

"No player of my acquaintance," he finished, "has ever lived by Betterton's words more faithfully than this young man."

Richard wiped his forehead nervously. A quick rememberance of his foolish behavior at Bath flashed through his mind. But the Duke was continuing.

"No player has ever dedicated himself more to constantly studying and refining his God-given skills. No player has done more to help his colleagues in every way possible."

He paused again, placed his hand on Richard's shoulder and said dramatically, "I give you the leader of the Steele-Canaday Company of Comedians, Richard Steele!"

First Emmett Nicholson and the players in the Goodman's Fields company, who were remaining in London, rose from their seats, applauding, shouting Richard's name. Soon all the players, at all the tables, were standing, pounding their hands and cheering. At favorably located tables in front of Richard, the knights from the Lord Chamberlain's office, and the theatrical writers and editors stood and clapped their hands. And all those flanking Richard at the long table rose and joined the applause.

The applause continued for two minutes. Richard stood

there, holding up his hands, his eyes misting. For nine minutes the room reverberated with the sound. Overwhelmed, Richard spoke into the applause, gradually quieting the room.

"Friends," he said, his voice cracking, struggling to control his emotions. "Friends, you make it difficult for me to speak. You fill my heart with indescribable joy. I can only say I am grateful and proud to be one of you. Whatever success I have achieved in the theater, I owe to a man you all knew, as noble a man as ever lived, Farley Shannon."

Again, the applause sounded.

"And," Richard continued, "to the unfailing support of our distinguished patron, the Duke of Cheltenham."

The applause continued.

"Without the financial backing of noble men such as the Duke, the theater could not grow and prosper."

Richard waited while the Duke rose, bowed to the din of applause and sat again.

"There is a lady here with us, known to most of you, to whom I also owe a great deal . . . Miss Eleanor Faversham!"

Nell, seated to the Duke's left, rose and acknowledged the applause. Richard waved a hand toward a table at which Gilbert Weston sat with a group of Lincoln's Inn Fields players.

"Gilbert Weston," he said, "guided me through many difficult days, and taught me much."

Weston beamed and bowed to his applause.

"In all our lives," Richard continued, "there are those dear people who shape our early years. My mother and father instilled in me a love of the theater and the works of its noble playwrights. And there was a young lady, whom some of you must remember—and whom I shall never forget."

His voice cracked, and for a moment he almost lost control. He swallowed, took a deep breath, and then continued.

"Her name was Felicia Wandrous, and she was an inspiration to me in every sense."

There was scattered, strong applause.

Richard leaned his hands on the table to check their trembling. Nancy Lucia reached over and placed her left hand on his right. He took another deep breath.

"Now," he said finally, "I have the privilege to present

594

to you my brave and skilled colleagues." He successively introduced the players to Nell's left and made brief, light, complimentary remarks about each one. Each stood, and bowed to their colleagues' enthusiastic applause. Then Richard introduced the players to his right. He started with the man at the far end of the table, Robbie Grigsby, and he did this advisedly. Robbie had been drinking steadily since the evening began, and was now bleary-eyed and wobbly. He could barely stand long enough to acknowledge the applause.

After Robbie, working inward from the table's end to himself, Richard introduced Emily Grigsby at Robbie's left. The long-suffering little woman rose, and shyly acknowledged the plaudits. At Emily's left sat Evangeline, and at Evangeline's left, Shannon Steele.

"Good friends," said Richard, "I would like to introduce together a young couple, whom many of you saw just hours ago in our last performance at Goodman's Fields. Romeo and Juliet, who frequently assume the names of Shannon Steele and Evangeline Grigsby!"

Shannon and Evangeline rose together. Shannon reached down and took Evangeline's left hand in his right, squeezing it emotionally. Evangeline reached across with her right hand, pulled Shannon's face down toward her, and kissed him on the lips. There was loud clapping, stomping and whistling. Shannon blushed. Evangeline blew kisses to the applauding players with both hands.

"Thank you, thank you, thank you!" she shouted between kisses. Shannon continued to blush, nodding and mumbling his thanks. Richard looked down at Nancy Lucia, beaming in the chair at his right, between Shannon and himself.

"Dear friends," he said, "I should like to tell you a secret about this lovely young lady here at my right."

Nancy Lucia reached over and took his hand. Richard smiled down at her. He looked back at the audience.

"She tricked me into marrying her," he said, his sea eyes twinkling. Nancy Lucia let go his hand, and slapped him on the arm.

He reached for Nancy Lucia's hand.

"She and Nellie Faversham contrived a means of calling my love for her to my attention. . . ." He paused, looked down at Nancy Lucia. ". . . but I assure you I have needed no reminder since the day we married. . . .

Friends," he exulted, "this is Nancy Lucia Canaday Steele, my wife, a woman for all seasons!"

The applause exploded, like a thousand drummers playing paradiddles and riffs. Nancy Lucia stood. The tears streamed down her cheeks. She reached down and took Richard's hand in her left, Shannon's in her right. Then she had to release Richard's hand to take a kerchief from her bosom. She wiped her eyes and held up her hand to still the ovation. It quieted finally, and she took a deep breath.

"Thank you. Thank you all, dear friends. I can only say that never has there lived a woman as fortunate as I. I am so proud of Richard and Shannon, and I love them more than life itself."

She paused to catch a breath, and the applause started again. She held up both hands.

"And I love you all. We will miss you . . . and England!"

She looked out at a table directly in front of the long table at which she stood. Theo and Niccolini were holding hands at the table, tears streaming down their cheeks. Cecil and Cecilia Hogsdon beamed at her.

Outside, a full, silver moon lighted London town, except when dark and heavy clouds drifted between it and the earth. A squall had blown in from the sea earlier that day, and it had rained. But then the rains had ceased and the full moon had burst forth and spent the night trying to elude the obstructing clouds. Then at dawn, a glowing sun climbed over the eastern horizon, and soon it hung gloriously high and golden in a warm hyacinth sky. On the dock at which the *Elusive Pam* awaited its passengers, there was much weeping, hugging and kissing.

It was not yet noon when the converted East Indiaman, with its cargo of players, its fresh, clean canvas sails billowing in the summer wind, slipped slowly away from London harbor. Overhead, gulls swooped, gracefully flapping their white, black-tipped wings and squawking jubilantly. At the *Elusive Pam*'s rail, the departing players stood. With tremulous smiles, they returned the kisses and the farewell waves of their colleagues and kin on the dock. The workman who had repainted the buxom figurehead at the stern of the ship, either deliberately or by a slip of the brush, had given the blue-eyed lady a scarlet and cryptic Mona Lisa smile, not quite following the sculptor's line of the wooden lips.

In this high spirited, bitter sweet moment, none of the players gave a thought to the surprises, the triumphs and tragedies they would experience during the long voyage across the ocean, and in a strange, unfamiliar land. A spray of water splashed up against the Pam's stern, and droplets rolled down the figurehead's cheeks like tears. Yet her mysterious smile held a promise of the fulfillment of their dreams.